CALIFORNIA

"An absorbing, action-packed, fast-moving novel." —*San Jose Mercury News*

"If you like dynastic history skillfully blended with fact and fiction, you'll find this a satisfying volume." —*(Palo Alto, CA) Times Tribune*

"A sweeping story." —*Macon Beacon Book World*

CALIFORNIA

*For Gail Summars—
Affectionately,
Lee Cooley 1/25/97*

Leland F. Cooley

Leland F. Cooley

5D
STEIN AND DAY / Publishers / New York

FIRST STEIN AND DAY PAPERBACK EDITION 1985
This edition of *California* was originally published
in hardcover by Stein and Day/*Publishers* in 1984.
Copyright © 1973, 1984 by Leland Frederick Cooley
All rights reserved, Stein and Day, Incorporated
Printed in the United States of America
STEIN AND DAY/*Publishers*
Scarborough House
Briarcliff Manor, New York 10510
ISBN 0-8128-8172-9

"We *californios* never knew what riches we possessed until some outsider with clearer vision landed on our hospitable shores or scaled our icy sierras or staggered across our burning deserts to take them from us—"

Anita Maria Dolores Chard Lewis
on her eightieth birthday,
El Rancho de las Flores, Proberta,
California, December 25, 1918.

CONTENTS

RELATIONSHIP OF PRINCIPALS

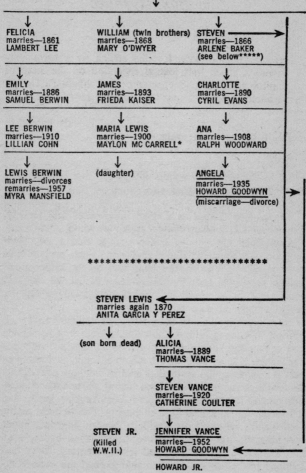

JOHN LEWIS
marries—1842
MARIA ROBLES

↓

FELICIA
marries—1861
LAMBERT LEE

WILLIAM (twin brothers)
marries—1868
MARY O'DWYER

STEVEN →
marries—1866
ARLENE BAKER
(see below*****)

↓

EMILY
marries—1886
SAMUEL BERWIN

JAMES
marries—1893
FRIEDA KAISER

CHARLOTTE
marries—1890
CYRIL EVANS

↓

LEE BERWIN
marries—1910
LILLIAN COHN

MARIA LEWIS
marries—1900
MAYLON MC CARRELL*

ANA
marries—1908
RALPH WOODWARD

↓

LEWIS BERWIN
marries—divorces
remarries—1957
MYRA MANSFIELD

(daughter)

ANGELA
marries—1935
HOWARD GOODWYN
(miscarriage—divorce) →

****

STEVEN LEWIS ←
marries again 1870
ANITA GARCIA Y PEREZ

↓

(son born dead)

ALICIA
marries—1889
THOMAS VANCE

↓

STEVEN VANCE
marries—1920
CATHERINE COULTER

↓

STEVEN JR.
(Killed
W.W.II.)

JENNIFER VANCE
marries—1952
HOWARD GOODWYN ←

HOWARD JR.

Pro Bono Publico

Howard D. Goodwyn, forcibly struck by a forty-year-old memory, stood half lost in reflection on the steps of the capitol building in Sacramento as California's Governor, Ronald Reagan, began to introduce him to the audience.

The day was a "valley scorcher" and Howdy longed to get back to his huge southern California ranch and the cooling southwest ocean breeze.

Both Howdy and the governor were outsiders who had come to California as young men. Both had left indelible imprints on their adopted state. Neither had done it the easy way.

Reagan had started as a sports announcer and Howdy, a half-starved cowboy singer from Guymon, Oklahoma, had bummed his way to Hollywood to find a job. Now they were standing on the capitol steps, each preparing in his own way to take another long step up the achievement ladder. Howdy Goodwyn smiled inwardly at the unlikely bedfellowships arranged by the political machine and by single-minded self-interest.

He couldn't speak for Reagan, but he could honestly tell himself that his ambition, the driving force that had made him one of the richest men in the West, was not now entirely selfish. He would give back something, in some way best for him, to the state that had given him everything. As tough as the going had been during those early depression years, California, incredibly Los Angeles itself, had sensitized him to a new kind of beauty. The twilight nights spent on the porch of the Franklin Avenue boarding house watching the ugly urban sprawl transformed by nightfall into a jeweled sea were etched in his memory. They had touched something in him and reawakened the same soaring elation he had felt back home sprawled beneath a tree to stare up and beyond the stars to a world of unreal aspirations. They had seemed unreal in Guymon but not in

Hollywood. That was thirty-odd years ago. Today Ronald Reagan and Howard Goodwyn were one shallow granite step apart and the governor was saying:

"At the risk of implying that there's no business like show business if you want to succeed in California politics, I want to say that *because* of, not in spite of, this man's intimate knowledge of people and his responsiveness to their needs, I know of no other man in the state who is better qualified to occupy the office I hope soon to vacate, *if* he can be persuaded, than Howard D. Goodwyn. Ladies and gentlemen, I'll resist the obvious and urge you, instead, to say, 'Hi' to Howdy."

The enthusiastic rattle of applause from the modest gathering of press representatives, party faithful, and curious passersby brought Howdy back to the present. Ducking his head in a subtle imitation of the late Will Rogers, a deliberate mannerism that over the years had served him well, Howdy smiled and waited. When it was quiet, he spoke.

"Governor Reagan, friends, I think it was President Truman who said, 'If you can't stand the heat, stay out of the kitchen.' I'd like to change that a bit and say, 'If you can't stand the heat, stay out of —'" When the expected ripple of laughter started, Howdy broke off in apparent consternation and shook his head. "I was about to say, 'If you can't stand the heat, stay out of Sacramento,' but—"

The laughter he had deliberately triggered broke over him and the governor's was loudest of all. After a moment, he signaled for silence. "That would sure be misunderstood, wouldn't it. What I really wanted to say was, 'Come on down to my end of the state and I'll show you some real heat.' I mean the heat that comes from hot issues, the heat that a lot of us generate under our collars when we see what's happening to California because a lot of other people still seem to feel that it's the best place in the world to live."

An older woman in the audience turned to her husband and said in a stage whisper, "He hasn't changed all that much. He still gives you confidence, just like he did on the radio when he sold all those things."

The man snorted derisively. "What he sold was snake oil and that's what he's still selling, only in a fancier wrapper. He's a typical native con man. They come natural to this state."

16

The woman caught the quick gleam of amusement in Howdy's eyes and lowered her own in embarrassment as he began to speak again.

"I'm real glad for this chance to tell you about some of the things the governor and I have been discussing this afternoon because they are things that affect us all."

Holding up his left hand, Howdy prepared to tick off some points, starting with his strong, stubborn thumb. "The new people who come to California have to find a place to live. So we build suburbs for them and new towns. The trouble is that in the past few years we've been building housing on our best agricultural land because that's where developers find it cheapest to build. Every year subdividers, most of them from out of state, take up to a hundred thousand acres of prime growing land out of production and bury it under slabs, driveways, and streets.

"Then we build more freeways to serve the new communities and new shopping centers and every mile of concrete and asphalt kills enough fertile soil to feed five thousand people one or more basic staples."

In the growing crowd an elderly man turned to a stranger next to him. "He's dead right. Ever since the Mexicans, California's best land has been fair game for outsiders. Damned state never has learned to protect itself."

A reporter for a Northern California newspaper chain nodded in agreement and added sotto voce: "But let us not forget while he's preaching the native gospel that Goodwyn's as much an outsider as the rest."

"Forty years ago, maybe. But he married into an old Mexican family that came up to Monterey in the late seventeen hundreds. Some of that rubbed off on him. He's got an honest feel for land."

The newsman laughed dryly. "And he's got one hell of a feel for the money land makes him, too."

Howdy's last statement had caused a murmur in the crowd and a number of people had begun taking notes as he continued.

"If I were to spell it all out, we'd melt in our own juice. But I would like to add another fact or so that will point up our need to do some very careful planning real soon."

"For instance, we have about one hundred million acres in the state of California. About one half of our land is in

17

national parks, state parks, and national and state forest preserves. A little more than one fifth of our state is given over to deserts and high mountains. But because twenty million people, about one out of every ten persons in the United States, lives in California now, ten percent of the remaining land on which we must live and work and grow our food is polluted."

He paused for effect. "I said, 'polluted.' One way or another we've polluted it."

The charge, nobody doubted that it was a fact, caused a new outburst of exclamations. Howdy went on.

"And if we don't do something constructive, starting right now, in thirty years there won't be any usable prime land left in California. And that's not only a critical prospect for us, but for the rest of the U.S.A. too, because we grow one fourth of all this country's table food and forty-three percent of its fruits and nuts—"

A wag on the fringe of the crowd called out, "Wrong! We got one hundred percent of the country's nuts here." Howdy grinned at the governor and joined in the laughter.

"The point is," he continued, "I'll run out of fingers before I've listed a tenth of the dangerous problems that face our state. I don't pretend to know the answers to all of them. But I know a good place to start. Because we believe people can live in communities built on productive land without spoiling it, we've set aside five thousand acres of our Los Nidos Ranch for a new, ecologically sound living concept that we call Micropolis Two Thousand. We believe that if we don't learn to do that, and *muy pronto,* your grandchildren and mine will be part of a new bunch of Forty-Niners who'll be digging up this state, turning over asphalt and concrete looking for the most precious resource California has ever had: good, rich land that will raise food twelve months of the year."

Governor Reagan nodded approval and led a round of applause. The reporter nudged the elderly man. "While he's helping California, let us also not forget that he'll be making a profit that would turn the old Comstock and Railroad robbers green with envy."

His companion regarded him tolerantly. "One thing about being young, son—you can get over it. Meantime, don't be so sanctimonious. The founder of your paper made his and so did young Bill Hearst. Ever been to San

Simeon?" The reporter did not respond and the old man's seamed face rearranged itself into a dry smile. "Profit's the name of the game, son. If you get your money by giving folks a fair shake, there's nothing wrong with it. And Goodwyn's always given this state a fair shake so far as I can see."

The response was cut off as Howdy began his concluding remarks and the band from Sacramento's John A. Sutter High School buttoned up loosened uniform collars preparatory to unlimbering their instruments.

Except for the inevitable scattering of obvious skeptics, Howdy saw friendly, or at least interested, faces. Reassured that he still retained his "edge," he started his concluding remarks.

"In the two hours I've spent with the governor this afternoon I was impressed again by the extent and the depth of his knowledge of California's problems. He did me the honor of thinking that I understand those problems well enough to be useful in public office."

Howdy lowered his head slightly and succeeded in looking a trifle more humble. "I'm not sure about that. But one thing I am sure of is that I'm just as concerned about our problems as Governor Reagan and I will pledge the very best I can do to help get our state back on the track. At this point in time that's not a political promise because I haven't said I would be a candidate for any office. But if I should come to believe, and the people believe along with me, that I can best serve the state in office then I'll make that an honest political promise, too." Raising a hand, Howdy smiled sincerely at his audience. "Thank you for standing and listening."

Governor Reagan, concealing the disappointment he felt that Howard Goodwyn had not committed himself more directly, nodded to the band leader as he urged the crowd to prologed applause. A moment later the strident brass strains of *California, Here I Come* drowned out the ovation.

Well back in the crowd, an affluent-looking man in his middle years addressed his younger companion.

"California, here we go. If that smooth-talking, humble-pie shit kicker runs for governor and gets in, he'll drain the rest of our northern water into his southern California swimming pools and the only cash left in the state will be the millions the son-of-a-bitch is stashing in his pockets. He's got to be stopped."

The outburst produced a smile. "That, my friend, is going to be about as easy as bottling a fart in a whirlwind."

Book I

The John Lewis Story

1 SOAKED THROUGH and struggling to control a chill, John Lewis watched from his hiding place in the dense madrone grove as the woodcutters' ox-drawn *carreta* lumbered by. The loosely lashed load of gnarled oak limbs tilted dangerously as the primitive wooden wheels slithered in and out of the soggy ruts that angled down the slope.

John had negotiated the icy half-mile swim to shore with nothing more alarming than a brush with an impertinent Pacific sea lion and an unexpected encounter with an otter that had surfaced to poke an inquisitive nose into his face, let out a startled squeak, and submerge again in the pre-dawn darkness.

Still ahead were a host of uncertainties. As hazardous as any was the prospect of having to spend a night in the densely forested mountains ringing Monterey Bay with no weapon but his sheath knife. From tales told aboard ship by older hands who had sailed in the California hide trade, John knew of the giant grizzlies that hunted there and of the packs of timber wolves whose slashing teeth, it was said, could reduce a man to a quivering mass of gory ribbon in minutes. Willingly, he would risk these beasts to reach his destination, the renegade camp at Branciforte, even though he knew well that he could not count on asylum.

Isaac Graham and Will Chard usually welcomed able-bodied men to their private militia of trappers, deserters, and adventurers, but from what he had heard, John wondered if they would welcome one as young as he.

If it turned out that Graham or Chard did not like the cut of his jib, there was a strong likelihood that they would turn him over to the Mexican governor, Juan Alvarado, or to Monterey's military commandant, Colonel José Castro, in return for the sizeable cash bounty the

23

master of the *Reliant* was certain to post in the custom-house and in the waterfront *cantinas*.

So the decision was simple. There was no alternative but to find Graham and his men and make a place for himself, for, once accepted, there was security of a sort among the feared *renegados*.

"Decent women leave the streets when Graham and his companions ride down the calle principal," they said. "And only the strongest men dare to stand downwind of them, so dreadful is the stink of their greasy buckskins and their aguardiente-laden breaths."

When the *carreta* disappeared into the timber again, John Lewis appraised his own condition and smiled grimly. "I may not be old enough or rough enough for them," he told himself, "but by heaven I'll be high enough by the time I get there!"

Shouldering his pack of spare clothing, John eased out of the thicket and made his way to the summit of the ridge. Dawn was breaking as he stopped to catch his breath. Below him the settlement of Monterey, capital and sole port of entry to Alta California, lay snugged darkly in the curving embrace of the low hills that enclosed the lower end of the bay. To the northwest, John could see a party of fast-moving horsemen crossing the barren sand dunes, heading toward the Pájaro River road leading inland to San Jose. Beyond, he could make out—lying at anchor in the bay—the familiar silhouette of his own vessel, the brig *Reliant*.

The sight of the ship's masts and spars, dead black against the lightening sky, produced a curious turmoil in him. Suddenly he found himself thinking of the letter to his sister in Brooklyn that he had entrusted to Ned. He wondered if the third mate had believed the story they had cooked up, or whether Captain Nathaniel Burke, a hard master to deceive, had put Ned in irons while he devised yet another of his cruel punishments for complicity in a shipmate's desertion.

Alice would be eighteen now. The thought of her started a quick flood of memories. Four years earlier his mother had died of consumption. A year later an undiagnosed illness had taken his father. Within a week, creditors had swarmed over the family's small general store in Middletown, Connecticut, and picked it clean.

Distant relatives in New York had taken Alice; but he

had been allowed to keep a tiny back room in the family house until he had finished his schooling on condition that he work for his keep. The tight-fisted new owners, determined to make the utmost of their bargain, had set him to doing the most menial work. When the flinty-faced mistress added the revolting task of emptying the family night jars, he stayed on just long enough to secure his diploma from the Middlesex Academy. Then, with his poor belongings and a book or two gathered into a makeshift bundle, he confronted the woman, charged her with her shortcomings as a "Christian lady," and set out for Boston. There he had met Ned James, then a stranger also in dire circumstances, and the two signed aboard the *Reliant* as apprentice seamen.

Annoyed at himself for wasting precious minutes in useless reverie, John reshouldered his oilskin pack and began the steep descent down the back side of the first range. If he could manage the unrealistic pace of four miles an hour through the rough country he had chosen as the best route to elude possible pursuers, it would still take another ten hours to reach his doubtful haven.

The lower limb of the sun had just begun to flatten against the Pacific horizon off to his left as he reached the high ground overlooking the south side of the small Pájaro River. Concealing himself, he studied the far bank. There was little traffic on the river road; but upstream to his right he could see tell-tale clouds of dust and he knew that each one concealed a party of riders.

Certain that it would be foolhardy to attempt the crossing and the half-mile run to cover on the far side, he settled down to wait for nightfall. When the last crimson thread of sunset had narrowed to nothingness, he gathered himself and moved stealthily down to the water's edge. There, poised on the tip of a gravel bar that jutted nearly across the narrow waters, he swung his pack pendulum-like several times and let it go. It arced across the open water and landed heavily in the moist sand at the foot of the opposite bank. A moment later he cleared the current, retrieved the pack, and began the cautious climb out of the stream bed.

Halfway up the bank a sound startled him. Straining to hear, he crouched beneath some overhanging brush, scarcely breathing. After a time he relaxed. The valley was full of wandering long-horned Mexican range cattle.

One of them probably had dislodged a small cobble while coming down to water. Taking a firm new grip on the pack, he scrambled to the top of the bank, peered along the road once more, then forced himself upright and set off at a dead run for the cover of a distant brush-lined draw.

Where the horsemen came from John Lewis would never know. All at once they came bearing down on him from four directions—two from the rear flanks and two from the front. He never saw the hissing rawhide *reatas* that snared his feet and arms and jerked him viciously to the ground.

Not until he was bound hand and foot and the toe of a soft Spanish boot pushed him roughly face-up did he see his captors. The one who stood over him was the only man he could really see. He was young and slender and he was smiling.

"*Buenas tardes, Señor Lewis! Créamos mucho gusto en verle!* We are sorry to detain you but it is dangerous for sailors to make a *pasada* in these mountains. Since we have a tradition of hospitality in Alta California we have come to escort you back to your ship."

Still gasping from the exertion of the run and the shock of the ambush, John struggled wildly. The men watched, laughing, and allowed him to continue, knowing that the rawhide bonds were biting deeper with each convulsion. No more than a minute elapsed before the strands across his throat left John croaking for help. Finally, when he was half suffocated, the leader knelt down. While two companions pinned his legs, the *reata* around John's neck was loosened. Once more he was rolled over, this time on his face, while the bonds were rearranged to pinion his hands behind him.

On a signal, one of the men released the rawhide looped around his ankles and he was jerked to his feet and boosted up behind the saddle of the leader's horse. His captor mounted as did the other three, and the party set off downriver toward the bay. They had ridden in silence until the man in the saddle turned to John. "*Dispensame, Señor Lewis. Estoy remiso! Me llamo Gregorio Robles—a sus ordenes.* Not always do we make such extreme precautions for the safety of our guest." He chuckled and said something in the rapid musical California dialect. The remark amused his companions.

The horses started across a shallow ford. In midstream Goyo Robles leaned forward and spurred his mount. The animal responded with a leap that sent John tumbling backward over its rump into the water. When he came to the surface, gasping, he was hauled to the opposite bank by the laughing men and remounted. Helpless to do more than try to balance with his hands tied behind him, John clenched his teeth and prepared himself for the next indignity. But none came.

Goyo led them down a steep bank to the bottom of a dry wash. The pace quickened then and an hour later the first lights of Monterey were visible. John had spent less time in Monterey than in the other trading ports along the Alta California coast. It was Mexico's most northern department and reputedly the most picturesque of the pueblos. Situated at the southerly end of the great curving crescent of the bay, it had no more than two score buildings. These were built along three broad packed-earth streets that ran from the base of the foothills down to the narrow, kelp-strewn strip of sandy beach. Behind the pueblo, dwarfing its adobe buildings, were the grass-carpeted hills with their scattered stands of oak and evergreens.

Finally, in darkness, the horsemen halted before a one-story, whitewashed adobe building whose sides and back were enclosed by a high mud-block wall. Goyo and two of his companions helped John down and half dragged him inside.

Doña Gertrudis Robles and her sixteen-year-old daughter, Maria, scurried from their chairs in alarm as Goyo and his men pulled John over to a crudely made rawhide chair and bound him to it.

In response to his mother's demanding "Que pasa?," Goyo straightened and turned to her. "My dear mother, my dear sister, we have an unexpected guest who will stay with us until morning. And because we value his presence so highly, we will make certain he does not leave us for fear of imposing on our well known *californio* hospitality. Permit me to present an exceptional yanqui *marinero*, Señor Juan Lewis." Goyo indicated his captive with an elaborately ceremonious bow.

John's sullen glare moved from the kindly-faced, patrician older woman, in whose eyes he thought he detected a look of sympathy, and fixed on the girl. Despite the chill that had begun to make him shake and the cruel bite of

27

the rawhide lashings, he found himself held by her beauty. Even though her head was lowered, he could tell from the curving sweep of the long black lashes that her eyes were uptilted and enormous, widely set in a delicate heart-shaped face. Like her mother, she was small-boned and finely made.

Goyo watched his prisoner with malevolent amusement. "So, my beautiful sister makes you forget your discomfort?"

Without warning he stepped forward and slashed John across the face with the backs of his fingers. His hand drew back for a second blow as Maria cried out in word-less protest and Doña Gertrudis called her son's name sharply.

Goyo stayed the blow and resorted to soft, mocking laughter. "Perhaps I do you an injustice, Señor Lewis. Perhaps in your present state of discomfort you do not have the evil thoughts of most yanqui pigs who look at my very desirable sister."

Then he brightened. "Well, it is nothing, this small slap in the face, or so it will seem to you when you are returned to your ship for punishment."

Doña Gertrudis moved to her son's side. "Why is this necessary? What has this man done?"

"This is necessary if we wish to collect the very rich reward that is offered for our captive. He is worth twice as much as any other yanqui sailor who has deserted. He is as strong as a bull. And he is smart, this one. He does not yet have twenty years and he is permitted to bargain for hides for his company. Impressive. No?"

Spreading his arms dramatically, Goyo sighed. "And because we *californios* are compassionate we shall see him safely back to his ship and collect not one but *two hundred dollars* as a reward that will be used to drive other yanqui pigs from Alta California." He turned menacingly toward John. "We have been fools. We have trusted you here as our brothers did in Texas. We will not make that mistake even if our governor does not agree and Mexico City does not care."

For a long moment, Goyo Robles stood poised over his captive, a hated yanqui: Then he addressed the women, "Mama, Maria, go prepare some food for our guest. He hoped to partake of Señor Graham's hospitality tonight, but we have spared him that cruel fate." A final check of

28

the bonds satisfied Goyo and after a short, whispered conversation, he left with both men and the women.

John looked around the room. To his left was a crudely made fireplace. On the rough-hewn mantel two home-made candles burned on either side of an ornate painting of the Virgin Mary holding the infant Jesus. The floor was hard-packed earth, the walls whitewashed mud plaster, and the only furniture in the room was the table and half a dozen crudely made straight-back chairs.

Now that he was alone, John thought about his decision to desert. Once again he told himself it had been the only endurable course open to him. Even though his return to the ship now would put his survival in doubt. The *Reliant* was at the mercy of a violent young master. If a sailor survived the floggings Captain Nathaniel Burke administered with near-insane relish, he would forfeit all pay, all liberty, and all but one meal a day until the ship returned to home port in Boston. There the offender would face charges of criminal violation of the Ship's Articles.

John's shipmate, Ned James, had, up to the last, tried to stop him. As John's hour to escape neared, he had whispered, his voice tight with apprehension, "Are you sure you want to go ahead with this folly, John? You know what will happen if they catch you."

"I know what will happen if I stay aboard. Maggoty meals. Porridge for another year. Walking barefoot over stony beaches balancing a hundred pounds of hides on my head. No. I've got nothing to go back to now except my sister, who is well taken care of by relatives. There may be nothing on this coast either but I have to see for myself. Scottish and English merchants are doing well here. Why not a Yankee?"

Deep in thought, John did not see Maria as she timidly reentered the room. She had been sent back by Goyo and told to watch the prisoner. When John looked up, startled, she cast her eyes down and seated herself at the table. She hoped she was concealing the excitement that had persisted from the moment she had seen the young yanqui. She had seen many foreign sailors while she and her mother pursued errands along the calle principal but none had disturbed her the way this strapping American had. Even at first glance there had been a quality of *gentileza* in his face and in the intelligent dark blue eyes that seemed to conceal little of what he was feeling. Maria was certain she had seen admiration in his eyes when he first caught sight of her. But there had been a flash of something else there, too, and it had started a strange restlessness in her.

John, watching the play of candlelight on the girl's face, thought again that in all his wanderings he had never seen one so lovely. Suddenly he became aware of a smarting sensation on his cheek. Inclining his head, he tried to raise his shoulder high enough to brush the flesh against his shirt. Instantly, Maria was at his side, bending close.

"Your cheek is scraped, señor." Using the tips of her fingers, she brushed gently at the grains of sand clinging to the flesh. Maria's manner was carefully impersonal but John could not rid himself of the feeling that the girl's light touch was also a subtle caress. The idea excited him momentarily, then the impossibility of it all moved him to wry amusement. "You've lost touch with reality, mate," he told himself. "Here you are trussed up like a hog for slaughter and you are entertaining romantic fantasies about the sister of a man who would cheerfully slit your throat if it were not for the bounty on your bloody, stupid head."

Maria was using a lace-bordered linen handkerchief to complete her ministrations. From the handkerchief, in fact from all of her clothing, emanated the clean scent of lavender and as she hovered over John, a new emotion was added to his turmoil. Like an aura, the scent of lavender had always seemed to surround his mother and his sister. Now, the haunting odor triggered a sudden and particularly poignant new onset of homesickness.

Maria straightened to inspect her work. "There, señor, you are fortunate. The skin is not badly broken."

As she moved to return the handkerchief to its place in the low-scooped neckline of her cotton blouse, her eye found another area that needed attention. Leaning so close that John's innards knotted with unfulfilled need, she pursed her lips in concentration and brushed away more sand particles trapped in the tangle of deep brown curls near his jawline.

Maria was so engrossed that she did not see her mother's knowing smile as she paused in the doorway bearing a large earthenware platter of beans, tortillas, and a cup of wine.

"It will be necessary for us to feed . . . our guest, Maria," she said as she handed her daughter the wine cup.

It took all of John Lewis' will power to keep from wolfing down the beans in their white flour tortillas. Laced with fiery jalapena sauce, they could make a man forget his hunger quickly and beg for more to drink.

When Maria placed the wine cup to his lips, he grimaced involuntarily at the sour taste of the Champlain trade wine from New York. He could not understand why the *californios* did not make their own from the grapes brought to the territory by the padres almost a half century earlier.

Goyo returned before the feeding was finished. Leaning against the table, he watched the scene and made no attempt to conceal his amusement. From time to time he addressed mocking remarks to the women in the soft, rapid *californio* dialect that John found almost unintelligible despite his diligent study of Spanish grammar aboard ship.

At the meal's end John's tremors had not subsided. He needed something hot, preferably tea, and decided to ask for it. Instantly, Goyo was all grave concern. "But, my dear friend, the fire in the *cocina* has been dead for hours. We had no idea we should be asked to entertain so late." He reached out and felt the blanket. "We shall give you another blanket, immediately."

"Why don't you let me get into dry clothes? I have some in my oilskins."

Goyo studied the bundle that had been tossed in the corner beside the front door. For an instant John thought he would agree, but Goyo turned back, smiling warily. "I think another blanket is better. If you will forgive me, I do not trust you with your hands free."

"Then untie my feet and let me get into dry drawers and trousers. I won't try anything. You can cut off my shirt if you wish. Then I shall be glad to have a second blanket."

The slender *californio* laughed. "If I free your legs you will make like an angry mule. No?"

John struggled to hold his temper. "No! Would I be fool enough to try to run to Branciforte with your chair lashed to my back like a turtle in a shell? I will not try to escape. You have my word."

Goyo's smile turned to a thin smirk. "The word of a gentleman, no doubt?"

"The word of an honest sailor!"

Instantly Goyo's expression turned to delight. "How fortunate! Not only have we saved a life but we have spared that rarest of all men, an honest sailor."

John turned appealing eyes to the women, but it was obvious that they lacked the courage to intercede. For a time he sat silently, glowering at the *californio*. Deliberately then he allowed the tremors to increase, using caution so they did not exaggerate. A bead of moisture from his nostril formed on the end of his nose. Lowering his head, he tried to wipe it against his shirt front. Before Goyo could stop her, Maria darted forward and touched it away with a cloth. Her brother's quick annoyance turned as quickly to amusement. *"Madre de Dios!* This is a big baby! First his nose, and then what next I wonder?"

Humiliated and angry, John jerked suddenly and nearly upset the chair. Goyo's hand shot to the haft of the vicious-looking knife stuck in the side of his right legging.

John sneered at him. "You would use that on a trussed-up man, wouldn't you?"

"I would welcome the excuse, Señor Lewis!"

"I'll give it to you, the first chance I get, Robles. Meantime, if you think the captain is going to pay you two hundred dollars for a sailor with the chills and fever, think again. Since there are no honest sailors, what makes you think you'll find an honest master? You've been to the customhouse. You should know better."

When Robles made no immediate response, John knew that his words had struck home.

"Bueno!" He moved to the table and shoved the lamp aside. "Maria. Bring the bundle here." Both mother and daughter went for it and hoisted it to the tabletop. Goyo worked the clove hitch free and the oilskins sagged open revealing the meager necessities John had been able to take with him. Robles snorted contemptuously and turned his face away: it was not the clothing he found offensive, but the odor of whale oil that had begun to emanate from the impregnated wet weather gear.

The girl pulled out a pair of woolen underdrawers, and his white dress ducks. Goyo took them from her and dismissed both women from the room.

When they were alone, he walked around to the back of the chair to examine the bonds. Satisfied, he began loosening the raw-hide loops around John's ankles. "If you had known how to sit on a horse this would not be necessary.

32

Now, because you are so clumsy, I must be not only your benefactor but your *camerero.*" He glanced up, smirking. "And also I must kneel at your feet."

The wet straps on the heavy leather shoes troubled him. He worked at them impatiently. "No wonder yanqui feet stink!" Then he unfastened the broad leather belt that secured the tar-smeared work trousers. *"Levántese sus asentaderas!"*

John strained to keep his backside off the chair long enough for his captor to slip both trousers and underdrawers free. Then he sat again while the wet cloth was worked from his legs. Extremely uneasy, he waited naked from the waist down as Goyo, on his feet again, stood back and studied him with wonder. "Incredible! On such a big yanqui one would expect more." He indicated the genitals trapped in a tangle of damp curls.

"Well, no matter." The *californio* extended his arms in a gesture of resignation. "But our Spanish women have much more to be grateful for than they know."

Angry enough to kill, John endured the mockery and swore that one day he would even the score. Robles reached for the dry clothing, then reconsidered. "I have a better idea. Without them you will be just as warm and less willing to leave us. *Como no?*" He walked to the door and paused to say, "I hope you are sincerely grateful for our hospitality, señor."

The smile that widened John Lewis' mouth made Goyo Robles all the more anxious to rid himself of his prisoner and collect the reward at the earliest moment. "I shall never forget it, Robles. And I shall see that you are properly thanked—if it takes me the rest of my life."

Goyo left and returned shortly carrying a second blanket. Contemptuously, he flung it around Lewis' shoulders. "If it is any satisfaction to you, señor, neither of us will sleep tonight."

With his boot, he pushed a chair away from the table and settled himself on it. "I am going to sit with you, my friend. At first light we will dress you and deliver you to the longboat at the customhouse. If you are uncomfortable now I suggest you think of the discomfort that awaits you at the captain's hands. It will help you to appreciate your stay with us."

While Robles was removing his spurs and preparing to

rest his feet on the table, John surreptitiously tested the painful braided rawhide bonds.

In the dimly lit room, listening to the night sounds that reached him through the two small unglazed windows, John suffered some remorse. He did not regret his attempt to escape—only his poor timing. Had he waited until the night before the *Reliant* was due to sail for San Pedro again he doubted that Nathaniel Burke would have lingered more than an hour or two before hoisting anchor to slip out on the tail of the ebbing tide. He had been too eager for his freedom. Now there would be no second chance.

On the bay the ship's bell tolled twice, marking one o'clock in the morning. From the hills came the eerie yelping of coyotes and overhead the stillness was disturbed from time to time by the raucous cry of a night bird.

Tipped back in his chair, Goyo Robles struggled against fatigue and watched his prisoner through eyes grown heavy-lidded. John was grateful when the *californio* chose to fight sleep with conversation.

"Juan Lewis."

"Yes?"

"Have you not wondered in what manner we found you?"

"I have."

"It was not difficult, my friend."

"How so?"

"At first you did not make mistakes. We knew you would come ashore below the old fort."

John was surprised. "How would you know that? The only man who knew I was leaving the ship and where I was going would die before he would tell."

Robles laughed easily. "When we heard you were missing we knew you would swim to the creek. They all do. It is the only safe way. So we started the dogs there but you stayed in the water so you left no scent."

"And then?"

"And then you made a mistake, up near the top. You stepped into fresh ox dung. We followed you for two or three leagues until we were certain of your destination, then we took a shorter route and waited."

"How did you know I would go to Branciforte?"

"Because every sailor on the California coast knows

34

that Isaac Graham and Will Chard will take them in. Nobody else would dare."

Goyo leaned forward. "But I must compliment you, Señor Lewis. You were much faster than we reckoned. For a sailor you move well on land. You did not keep us waiting too long at the river. For that we thank you."

John smiled bitterly in the near darkness. Half aloud, he recited the sailors' maxim.

> "A man's a fool and more o' the same
> To bet his gold on another's game."

Goyo glanced over curiously. "What have you said?"

"Nothing. I was remembering a short sermon—too late."

The *californio* made a show of being pleased. "Ah! You are a religious man."

John laughed mirthlessly. "Only when I'm in trouble."

The retort amused Goyo. "*Verdad, amigo!* Except for the padres and the women the same may be said of us all."

They fell silent then, listening to the night sounds. Faintly, they heard the *Reliant's* bell sound one-thirty. First light would not begin to gray the sky behind the Monterey hills until past five. There would be four more hours to endure.

John pondered his possibilities. He weighed the chances of surviving Captain Nathaniel Burke's punishment against those of convincing Robles that he had no personal ambitions beyond visiting the northern valley before seeking another ship to Yerba Buena. He knew Burke would flog him. He had seen the ship's master at work with the cat o' nine tails. No seaman had died from the floggings but neither had any been completely whole again.

It would do little good to protest to Robles that any other ship would be preferable to the *Reliant*. As unrelenting a disciplinarian as Nathaniel Burke was known to be, he was still considered more humane than many masters.

Somehow John managed to doze. The muffled stomping of horses in the adobe-walled compound in back of the house roused him just as the *Reliant's* bell struck the couplets that marked three o'clock.

A sharp sound nearby made him start. Goyo Robles stood in the doorway, silhouetted against the rectangle of lightening sky. He was listening intently. Some yards away a party of horsemen, apparently riding down the calle principal toward the customhouse, clattered by noisily. When the sound diminished, Goyo turned and took his spurs from the table.

"Another half hour and we go, yes?"

John shrugged. "Do I have any choice?"

Robles sat down and began to secure the ornate spurs to his boots. "Señor Lewis, you have none." He strapped the second spur in place and rose. "Maria will watch you while I awaken my friends. Then we will dress you and escort you safely back to your ship. That prospect may please me more than it pleases you, my friend. But that is how it will be." He stepped into the adjoining room and a few minutes later John heard voices.

The blanket that had been draped across his upper legs had begun to slip. In vain he tried to maneuver it back into place. The best he could do was catch it between his knees to keep it from slipping off completely. By twisting his shoulder and working the upper blanket with his chin he was able to divert a corner to his lap. He had barely managed to cover himself when Goyo came back followed by Maria. Goyo indicated John with a nod. "For an uncivilized yanqui he is very docile, but you watch him until I get the others."

The girl took one of the chairs at the table and sat with eyes lowered and hands folded in her lap.

"Maria?"

Startled, she looked up, then lowered her head again. "Si, señor?"

"Do you speak any English, Maria?"

"Poquito, señor. Pero, prefiero hablar español."

John laughed ruefully. "I would prefer to speak Spanish, too. But I do not know many words. Will you speak in English with me?"

Maria Robles lifted her head slowly and looked at him for a moment. "I will try if you wish, señor."

"I do wish. Indeed I do. I have not spoken with a lady for three months. May I ask how many years you have?"

"I have sixteen years, señor."

John shifted and winced as the bonds dug deeper into his wrists. "I have a sister. She has seventeen years and I think she is as beautiful as you."

36

The girl's luminous dark eyes brightened with interest. "Where does she live, señor?"

"In the United States of America, in a city called New York."

Maria Robles' lips formed a silent "Oh." Briefly, they were without words. Then she looked up again. "New York is a place very distant, is it not?"

Suddenly it seemed to John that New York and home and family and old friends were all on another planet. He nodded wearily. "It is very distant, *muy distante. Muy lejos, si.*"

The words surprised the girl. *"Señor! Usted habla muy bien!"*

He bowed awkwardly. *"Gracias, señorita.* I do not speak well. But I try. I must speak more but I have no opportunity. And now I will have none at all because," he nodded toward the harbor, "your brother is going to see to it that I am returned to the ship in irons."

Maria Robles lowered her head unhappily. "My brother would have all foreigners deported. He is afraid of yanquis, especially because of Texas. So is Castro. They try to make Governor Alvarado think in the same manner."

John alerted. "Doesn't he agree?"

Maria Robles shook her head. "Once he did. But no longer, I think."

In his eagerness to grasp at straws John forced the chair forward. The motion caused the blanket to slip from his shoulders. Frantically, he managed to clamp a fold between his knees. When he leaned over in a futile attempt to secure a corner in his teeth the girl jumped up. Her face averted, she caught the displaced edges and redraped them over his legs and shoulders. In other circumstances John would have been embarrassed, but between the lines of her aimless conversation he had detected a faint note of hope.

"Miss Maria."

"Yes, señor?"

"If Governor Alvarado knew that I want nothing more than to become a good citizen here," he indicated the town with a nod, "like Mr. Larkin—do you think he might let me stay?"

"He knows you are here, señor. My brother told him yesterday. He said nothing. He would be sympathetic but he does not want to go against his friends until all Alta

37

California is a sovereign Mexican state. If you were an important man and your government might be offended, that would be different."

John finished the thought. "But a common sailor is another thing. True?"

"Si, señor. For my brother, that is true."

He was considering how best to ask her to plead his case with the governor when Goyo returned with his three companions. "So, my friend, we go now."

He dismissed Maria, who retreated to the adjoining room. Some minutes later, flanked by two men on either side, John was led to the door. Out of the corner of his eye he saw Maria Robles reappear and half turned to thank her. Instantly, Goyo spun him away roughly. "I said we go—in the direction of the harbor—not my sister!" They forced him through the door then and Goyo, carrying a loaded pistol with a second one stuck beneath his sash, walked behind as they made their way down the calle principal toward the customhouse.

In Middletown or in Boston the distance would have measured no more than several long blocks. To his right were the walled gardens at the rear of a row of dwellings that faced on the next street. He knew that one of them was Governor Alvarado's private residence and that others belonged to leading native families and to trading agents. On his left was the imposing unfinished residence being constructed for Thomas Larkin. Several of the buildings had long pole lean-tos set from the eaves to the ground on their weather sides to keep the driving rain from eroding the soft adobe bricks.

Off to the southeast, just growing visible in the graying dawn, he could make out the tower and belfry of the presidio chapel, the most impressive structure in Monterey.

Some yards from the customhouse John heard loud voices speaking in English. The sounds were coming from one of the several cantinas, the miserable adobes that housed the bars patronized by sailors and by the "young women of good family" who would devote themselves to the itinerant customers "for a price."

When they were opposite the hitching posts, Goyo raised a hand. "*Espérame aqui!*" Quietly, he moved closer to the horses tethered there and examined their brands. A moment later, visibly upset, he returned and began speaking rapidly to his companions. John caught enough to learn that the animals belonged to Isaac Graham and Will Chard and their men. For an instant he thought of shouting for help but reason told him that even if he were heard the commotion would probably only compound his trouble.

Robles and his men conferred briefly and John found himself being half dragged toward the customhouse.

A pre-dawn visit from Isaac Graham had prevented the clerk, Ignacio Torres, from dispatching an oarsman to summon the *Reliant*'s longboat. A former trapper turned distiller, Graham was in the midst of making his usual sub rosa arrangements to ship casks of illegal whiskey up the coast when Goyo Robles and his men burst into the room, forcing John ahead of them. Graham whirled, his hand on the long knife stuck in his belt. "Hyar now, Goyo. You're a mite early throwing white boys off the shore, ain't you?"

Robles, taken by surprise, pretended to ignore the question. He steered John to a heavy chair against the opposite wall. Curious, Graham sauntered over for a look at the captive. After a brief inspection he turned back to Robles. "I axed you, Goyo, but I didn't hear you do me no courtesy by answering."

The *californio* completed an unnecessary testing of the rawhide bonds, then he looked defiantly at the one-time Tennessee trapper, whose eyes gleamed with malevolent humor.

"If we had been wise, Señor Graham, we would have begun these deportations much sooner!"

Isaac Graham's large nose seemed to thrust like a threatening weapon from the bramble of his dirty red beard, but he said mildly, "The p'int's took and noted, amigo. I'm storing it against the day you and Bautista'll be calling on our rifles again." He brushed past Goyo and walked to John. "What be your name, son?"

"Lewis. John Lewis, sir."

"How old be you?"

"Nineteen, sir. Coming on twenty."

"What did you ship as?"

"Common seaman, sir. And apprentice supercargo."

Graham's overhanging brow lifted. "I take that to mean you're book smart then?" Before John could respond, the trapper turned with amazing speed. "Goyo! You and your boys stay put!" He glanced over at the unhappy clerk who had half risen from his desk. "You too, Ignacio. I'll take it unfriendly if you're in such a sweat to get your bounty ye cain't let a friend among ye get caught up on news from his homeland."

Unmistakably reluctant to challenge the mountain man, Goyo and his men stood as they were. Graham turned back to John. "Why are ye making tracks? Steal? Let blood?"

"No sir. I've been a year and a half on this coast buying and droghing hides. Mostly south. Now they want to keep me against the articles. I see no prospect of getting back to Boston for another year. I thought I'd like to see the country. I was trying to get to your place when they caught me."

An expression of great delight transformed Isaac Graham's face. His high-pitched nasal voice soared. "Ye was coming visiting? How nice! I sure am touched. It ain't every day we get friendly callers." He moved closer and laid a heavy hand on John's shoulder. "Burn my britches! My eyes might get to tearing from happiness," he turned slowly toward Goyo Robles, "if it wasn't for the dishospitable nature of some."

He squeezed John's shoulder reassuringly. "Goyo, you and your friends wouldn't do me and mine out of a chance to visit with a blood brother from the United States, now would ye?"

Goyo's dark eyes shifted from the sailor to his companions and to Torres, from whom he knew he would get no help. His reply was caught in a throat strictured by rage. Robles knew he must act or lose his prisoner. His pistol might take care of Graham but the trapper's lightning-quick throwing knife would take care of him. In either event the shot would bring Will Chard and the others from the cantina in seconds. Because of Goyo's open antagonism toward *extranjeros* neither Castro nor Alvarado would be likely to take his word that Graham had precipitated the trouble. He forced the words out. "This man is a fugitive. We have an obligation to return him to his captain."

Isaac Graham's eyes widened innocently. "Well, now. On whose law are ye standing?"

No formal extradition agreement existed and Goyo Robles knew it. Had such a law been adopted Graham himself would have been expelled from Alta California. A foreigner caught entering Alta California by land or sea might be expelled on any improvised pretext and by any means, at the option of the local authorities. Goyo answered stiffly, "It is in the interests of our commerce to see that ships trading with us are not deserted by their best hands. Masters will pass us for other ports if they know we give asylum to their deserters. You should know, Señor Graham, that more sailors desert here in Monterey than in all other ports."

"That be the truth, Goyo. That be the truth." Graham turned away casually, and before they realized what he was up to he had unsheathed his big knife and slashed the bonds that secured John Lewis' hands.

Smiling amiably, he replaced the knife. "How much is on his head, Goyo? Fifty? Hundred dollars?"

Without waiting for an answer Graham stepped between John and the *californio*, who had moved toward him. "You stand stock where you are Goyo, because you're too pretty to spill your juice." Over his shoulder he addressed John. "Son, you hightail to the cantina and fetch a man named Will Chard."

Massaging his wrists, John bolted for the door. Less than a minute later he flung aside the cantina's beaded entrance drape and called Chard's name. A tall, clean-shaven, neatly dressed young man with long copper-brown hair rose from the table. "I'm Chard, sailor. What do you want?"

"Mr. Graham wants you at the customhouse right away. He's got trouble."

The words were scarcely out before Will Chard barked an order and John found himself being swept through the door by a dozen charging men. Seconds later their horses passed him at a dead run. John was only halfway down the path when he saw the men pull up their mounts, leap off, and disappear into the building. John ran up out of breath and Chard and another man met him in the customhouse doorway. Chard barked, "This is Bill Dockey. You go with him."

A grimy frontiersman dressed in fringed buckskins grasped John's arm and pushed him to one of the mounts grazing quietly between its trailing reins. "Get on, boy!"

John pulled his arm free of the shorter man's strong fingers. "My gear's in there. Everything I own."

Bill Dockey retrieved the reins and bunched them on

41

the animal's neck. "Don't fret. You'll get them. Now get on, boy. Get on!"

Awkwardly John mounted the animal. By the time he was up and had maneuvered his square-toed seaman's boots into the stirrups, Dockey was beside him. "Can you ride a horse—fast?"

John nodded uncertainly. So far as he knew, he had done nothing to encourage the animal, but an instant later the tough little mount was following Dockey's larger horse in a flat run along the low sandy embankment that bordered the edge of the bay.

Ten miles north, around the gentle arc of coastline and not far from the mouth of the Pájaro River, Bill Dockey turned inland to the bank of a narrow brush-lined creek. Hidden from view, they rested and watered their mounts. Soon they were on their way again.

They crossed the Camino Real well west of the point where Goyo Robles and his men had set up their successful ambush late the night before. Another two hours brought them to the outskirts of the pueblo of Branciforte.

A well-worn trail led up the north slope of a small canyon. They followed it until they came to a grove of redwood trees, and finally emerged at a high meadow rounded by taller redwoods. Scattered around its periphery were a dozen or more log houses. When they rode into view, men began to gather. Dockey turned to John. "You're new. They'll be asking for news. If you want to fit cozy here, you tell it to them."

"But I've been away from the states for over a year. I don't have any news."

Dockey grinned. "Then make up some." He started to ride on ahead but checked his mount and looked back. "If you do make it up, boy, make it interesting so I can enjoy it too!"

Dockey rode to the largest of the cabins and dismounted as Isaac Graham's men encircled them curiously. Not a word was spoken until John had come down stiffly from his animal. Then his guide addressed the crowd. "This here's a sailor name of—" He frowned and turned, questioning. "Name of what?"

"My name is John Lewis—out of Boston."

Dockey nodded. "Name of John Lewis, out of Boston. Mr. Lewis is arranging to miss his ship and Isaac'd like us to help him in that noble work."

Several men guffawed. John identified them easily as sailors who had "gone over the side." At least he would start with that in common.

Dockey, a short, wiry, hollow-cheeked man whose plains dialect betrayed a trace of cockney, indicated the doorway. "This is Cap'n Graham's headquarters and meeting place. He wants you to wait here until he gets back. We'll boil up some coffee. Go on in."

The cabin consisted of one room made of small, straight redwood boles. The peaked roof was supported by hand-hewn rafters. The furniture was crude and sparse, a table and a scattering of chairs and stools. Most small articles were suspended from pegs driven into the log walls. An area about eight by twenty feet at the far end of the cabin was partitioned off by canvas draped over a line. A wooden bunk was visible through the half-opened hanging. A makeshift rack above the bunk held a collection of long rifles. There were no proper windows and what light there was entered through a series of high slit-ports. Obviously, this cabin was intended to serve as the defense center in case of attack, since the ports commanded four sides of the structure.

Dockey pointed to a covered container and said to John, "If you want a chaw of dried beef, it's in that crock."

John smiled gratefully. "I could use something. Thanks." He helped himself to a foot-long strip of mahogany-hued dried beef and worried an end off between his teeth.

Dockey watched him struggling. "It ain't very filling but it'll keep you so busy you won't notice being hungry."

Lewis maneuvered a stubborn wad to one cheek and nodded. "It beats the salt horse aboard ship."

"Salt horse?"

The man turned from the stove to give him an incredulous look. "That ain't even human. What were you on—a Frenchman?"

Lewis shook his head. "I was on the *Reliant*, a Yankee brig. I don't know what the salt meat was. We didn't dare ask."

Dockey turned away, shaking his head. "I don't reckon you did."

They were silent for a time until John broached the
43

matter that was much on his mind. "Do you think Mister Graham will let me stay here until the *Reliant* sails?"

Dockey shrugged. "That's up to him. We elected him cap'n. If he likes you, that'll be right with us—unless you got some quirk that don't fit in."

"I'm peaceable. I do my work and mind my own business. I got on with my mates aboard ship."

The statement earned him a skeptical look. "Is that why you jumped?"

"No, I jumped because I found out the master was going to leave me on the coast again, curing and droghing hides. I spent six months sleeping in a hide shed in San Diego. I'm not of a mind to do that any more."

"What are you of a mind to do, boy?"

John answered honestly. "Don't know. But if they take me back aboard ship it'll be dead, in canvas."

Dockey chuckled. "It ain't the first time we heard that talk."

John decided that his best chance to persuade Graham that he could fit would lie in finding out as much as he could about this strange little isolated community of men with no apparent means of support. "I don't mean I don't like work. I'll be glad to work at anything you men do if Mr. Graham will let me stay here for a while—at least until the *Reliant* is on her way to San Diego again."

Dockey continued fussing at the stove. John decided to press a little more. "I could fit in, if you men do any of the usual kinds of work."

Dockey indicated the wooden water bucket. "Fetch me a dipper."

John complied and Dockey held it poised over the big coffee pot. "If we did the usual kind of work, boy, we wouldn't be here."

Will Chard and his men rode up an hour before sunset. Isaac Graham saw John Lewis standing in the doorway and called to a man named Joe Majors. "Give the lad his duds."

Majors released the rawhide saddle ties and let the tarpaulin drop to the ground. John recovered it and started to carry it inside.

Graham watched, amused. "Hyar now! Leave it outside. I don't aim to take no sailor boys under my robe."

Majors started to guffaw but a sharp look from Chard

44

sobered him. Graham fumbled beneath his beard to loosen the laces at the neck of his deerskin shirt. "I think I need a hair of the dawg."

Chard followed Graham inside but John, embarrassed, waited outside the door. A moment later, Graham called to him. "Come on in, lad. If you're a jug-sucker at such a tender age, you're welcome to a little fortify-cashun of the liver."

Graham smeared his bewhiskered mouth with the back of his hand while Chard took his pull at the demijohn. The powerful *aquardiente de trigo* seemed to have no more effect than plain water on either men.

Chard gave the neck a token swipe with his palm and offered the jug to John. Raw liquor was not what he wanted but he took the jug, tipped it expertly over the crook of his arm, and deliberately metered out and swallowed a large draught. As the rough spirits seared his gullet, he thanked God he'd learned to hold his own in the cantinas in San Diego and San Pedro. Almost nonchalantly he returned the jug to the table.

Graham eyed him as he reached for the jug. "Ye look like a man, ye talk up like one—and ye drink like one. What else can ye do like a man, son?"

"Pretty much whatever's needed." The statement was made with no trace of boastfulness.

"From your looks I've a mind to believe you. How about ye, Will?"

Chard finished his leisurely appraisal of the young six-footer. "I'm inclined to accept that without further proof."

Graham laughed. "I expect Henry Mueller will be asking him to prove up though."

John understood the implication immediately. He would have his measure taken and the leader would make no decision about allowing him to stay until he proved himself. He didn't have to wait long.

Later that evening when the men were gathered around the fire there was a clamor for late news from the States. John had been trying to remember everything he had heard during the past year. As he sifted through the rumors and gossip he labeled each account for what he believed it to be:

"We spoke the barkentine, *Jessie Dawkins,* out of Charleston. Her master came aboard and told Captain Burke that a fire was burning the whole city down. He said that by the time he cleared the roads over a thousand buildings had burned to the ground and only God Almighty knew the end to it. He told us it was no use putting in for anything. Not biscuits or water.

"There was a copy of the *New Orleans Picayune*, a new journal, that the *Dawkins'* master traded for our Boston journals. It had an account of a steamer named the *Moselle*. She was a stern-wheeler on the Ohio River near Cincinnati. She blew her boiler and steamed alive over a hundred souls."

A voice from the fringe spoke up. "What's happening in Washington?"

John Lewis shook his head. "We didn't hear of any late happenings. The first thing President Van Buren did was to sign the bill making the Michigan territory into a state. There are twenty-six regular states now."

Henry Mueller, an oaken barrel of a man in his late thirties, spoke up for the first time. John was surprised at the incongruity of the high-pitched voice issuing from the solid body. "I don't know about you so'jers, but I want this here smart-ass sailor boy to tell us more lies. A thousand buildings burning to the ground in Charleston and a hundred bodies boiled in Cincinnati. Them's lies. But I think I'd rather hear made-up news than the true happenings anyway—especially if they're made up by an artistic liar."

Will Chard started to rise but Isaac Graham rested a hand lightly on his knee. The man named Majors was the first to respond. His manner was facetious. "Why, Henry, ye ain't a bit choosy about your words, are ye?"

Mueller bowed with mock humility. "I admit I'm short of learning, Joe." Suddenly his manner changed. "But I reckon I got me enough words to fix the proper name to a liar when I see one."

A nervous stir ran through the group. John understood that any attempt to defend the truth of his statements would be taken as a sign of weakness. Besides, the truth was not at issue. He rose slowly from his place and forced himself to speak in an amiable tone. "I expect you'll own that I have a few words too?"

Mueller edged forward on the stump. "I grant ye that. In fact, no honest man would have need for so many words as ye been spewing tonight."

Still pretending amiability, John said, "And so in your

46

ox-dumb head you think that any man who can outtalk you is a liar! Any schoolboy reciting his lesson would be marked a liar by you too because you don't have enough light to understand even that."

Nervous laughter broke out among the men.

Henry Mueller had come to his feet upon hearing the words, "ox-dumb." The young sailor was not behaving as he had predicted. Instead of offering a defense, part apology and part outrage, Lewis was giving as well as he was taking. Isaac Graham, beaming behind the snarled brush of beard, rapped Chard's thigh with the back of his hand. "Might be we fotched up with a good one."

The second-in-command nodded without taking his eyes off the adversaries who were moving closer. "You'll know soon enough. But I want Mueller's knife."

Mueller usually enjoyed these encounters. But the word "dumb" had triggered hurt and anger whose roots went deep into the past. "No boy or man never called me 'dumb' and lived to do it twice . . . and if such there ever be . . . it won't be a scurvy bugger boy!"

"MUELLER!"

Will Chard was on his feet. "Throw that knife over here!"

Mueller glanced down at the buckhorn haft showing above his deerskin legging and seemed to hesitate. Chard's voice rang out again. "Right now, Mister!"

The move was so fast John scarcely saw it. The heavy blade grazed him and buried itself two inches in the log behind Chard, who ignored the quivering weapon as he addressed Mueller again. "I think it would be well to remember two things, Henry: you started this—and the captain and I intend to see it done fair."

Mueller's charge came before Chard had finished his warning. It was the man's favorite opening maneuver with those who did not know him. The flying, battering ram head-butt in the solar plexus usually ended the fight before it started. John was spared the full impact by instinctively angling away but Mueller's hooked left arm snagged his body and they both went down. Mueller's thick fingers caught at John's neckband and ripped it away. Immediately he was on his feet again, charging. John had only seconds to ward off the attack with a chopping blow that caught the older man on the side of the head. It did no damage but it bought John time. He began circling to get the fire at his back. Mueller watched for a moment then winked at the others. "Now here's a smart bugger-boy. Going to get the fire behind him so I can't see clear and I'll jump in it, like as not." He laughed and deliberately turned his back on Lewis to address the men. "Gentlemen. It's natural to the working of a liar's head to be figgering all the time. And its natural to a coward, to boot. You seen him weaseling around? I say he's no part of a man. I say he's a yellow fancy dancer—no sailor boy. What say ye?"

Mueller knew his men. He knew they would not reply but he also knew that if John attempted a surprise attack from behind it would instantly be mirrored in their eyes though none would call out a warning. At this game they were impartial spectators. Long since, they had judged Mueller as a good fighting man. But the sailor was a new sort. Like Chard, he was articulate and smart. Mueller was trying to goad Lewis into a fight on Mueller's own terms.

As the trapper continued addressing his audience, John Lewis moved several steps closer. "Mueller.'

The man whirled with mock surprise and indignation written on his beefy face. "Mueller? Mueller, did ye call me? *Mister* Mueller. That's what you call me. And lucky you are that I don't ask ye to kneel and kiss my hand!"

John managed a convincing show of equanimity. He knew it would be fatal to allow the older man's obvious tactics to stampede him. "Very well then, *Mister* Mueller. I want to say that if you can fight as well as you can jaw then I admit I'm whipped. And if it's all the same to you, I'd just as soon kiss your hand. It's a sight cleaner than your ugly face."

The mock surprise changed to disbelief as a loud guffaw rose from the tensed audience. For an instant Henry Mueller's mouth hung slack. Then it ovaled and a wordless bellow trumpeted from it as he charged. A step from closing he feinted to his left. When John counter-moved to avoid the charge, Mueller, as agile as a cat now, reversed his angle and the two collided and fell, John on the bottom.

A shout rang out that neither man heard. John, struggling beneath two hundred pounds of hard muscle and bone, fought frantically to keep the clawing fingers from tearing out his eyes. Suddenly he found one of his legs free. He drove it with all of his strength into his assailant's crotch. The blow produced an agonized bellow of rage but Mueller did not falter. Twice more John drove his knee into the older man's scrotum until he forced him to twist to one side for protection. The move freed his other leg. He lifted it high and crashed the heel of his heavy sailor's boot down into the small of Mueller's back. The kidney blow brought little more than a grunt. More blows followed until Mueller squirmed still farther away to avoid the hammering boot. Instantly, John twisted free. Mueller tried to grasp his thick hair but missed as John lurched backward in a half-somersault, rolled up on his knees, and shot to his feet.

There was no waiting now and John knew it. The first sledge-fisted blow struck and split Mueller's cheekbone while he was still scrambling to his feet. A second blow caught him on his Adam's apple and a squared boot-toe sank deep into his solar plexus. John attacked now with the intent to kill. If a fair fight in this company meant nothing barred short of clubs, knives, and guns, then he intended to use every advantage he possessed. He aimed another kick and somehow Mueller managed to grab his leg and they both went down again. He freed himself with a piston-like drive of his other boot, ripping a broad strip of skin from the back of Mueller's hand. Both men scrambled to their feet again, sucking for air in long, hollow gulps. For a moment they stood eyeing one another and John was aware for the first time of the strange silence that had fallen over the men around him.

He heard Mueller taunting him again in the high, raspy, nasal twang. "If you aim to play smart bear to my *dumb ox*, bugger boy, then before you do I'd call to mind that a sight more bears then bulls get killed in the pens—and ye ain't even a weaned cub yet!" He spat blood. "Killing you will be easy!"

Smiling, Will Chard turned to Graham. "Henry's not building his argument on the facts."

The captain nodded. "He ain't fighting his usual fight either."

What was obvious to Graham was also obvious to Mueller's companions. The man was behaving strangely. It had something to do with Lewis' first words—something to do with being called a "dumb ox," for those were the

49

words that Mueller had just repeated and there had been unmistakable hatred in his voice as he said them.

Mueller was moving again, circling, advancing in a slow-closing spiral. John stood his ground, turning with him, until he found himself being crowded into close quarters again. He felt certain, after assessing the damaging impact of the two blows to Mueller's head, that he could knock the man senseless if he could get within range without being trapped in the crushing embrace. Another charge would come at any moment now. Unless he could change his own strategy the result could be indecisive. As he continued to maneuver to keep Mueller in front of him, John was remembering the frequent fights aboard the *Reliant*. One stood out. It had been a grudge fight between a Swede and a Basque. It had ended when the Basque resorted to a tactic common to his people. The surprise attack had sent the big Swede crashing head first into a hatch coaming. Three days later he was dead of a skull fracture. At the time John had thought the tactic unfair but his shipmates had laughed at him.

Mueller was circling faster now, maneuvering to get his own back to the fire, to position himself so that his charge would carry his opponent backward into the circle of spectators where a close friend or two might give him some covert help in the confusion.

Snarling vile epithets, goading, attempting to confuse, he circled closer and closer. Realizing that time was running out, John made his decision. Apparently confused, he stopped and glanced around almost as though he were seeking an avenue of escape. Mueller charged. When he was a short step away John sprang upward, gathered his knees close, then rammed both legs outward like two great uncoiled springs. The boots, held close together, struck Mueller's breast bone. The blow expelled the wind from his deep-barreled chest in an explosive, asthmatic whoosh, and his thickset body catapulted backward, seemed to leave the ground, and crashed into Isaac Graham and Will Chard. John heard neither the shout of protest that went up from the men nor Graham's surprised outcry. Before Mueller's body had come to rest John leaped at him again and brought his one hundred eighty-four pounds down, feet first, onto the man's belly. A stream of sour puke geysered from the gaping mouth. All caution gone now, John had only one purpose, to kill the man who would kill him if he did not. He threw himself on the sprawled body and began driving mauled fists into Mueller's jaws with a fury that brought more cries of protest from the onlookers. Swinging madly, John scarcely felt the hands pulling. When they began to haul him away he shook them off and continued the murderous punishment. They seized him again and finally, exhausted and struggling for air, he allowed himself to be pulled free and pinioned.

Henry Mueller strangled on the clotted, half-chewed beef he had wolfed down little more than an hour before the fight. They tried to save him by forcing fingers down his throat—and smooth twigs—but his face mottled and turned blue, and his eyes, bulged wide with terror and appeal, glazed and after a minute or so the battered hulk of a body ceased its convulsing and lay still.

Fifty men, inured to violence and death, stood looking down in shocked disbelief. None was more stunned than Isaac Graham, for it was not the way death should come to a man such as Mueller.

Ever since the late twenties Graham had watched Henry Mueller drink and fight, always with roaring good humor. Once he had seen him douse a slumbering drunk's long hair with raw whiskey and set it afire. The man had been marked for life but that was no more than the usual prank played on the unwary. Graham had agreed with the others:

"It was a thing to even up someday, but it wasn't something to hold a grudge over." But this was different. This lad was different.

Chard, sensing the uneven temper of Graham and the men as they stood silently looking down at the still warm corpse, moved unobtrusively beside Bill Dockey. "Take the lad to my cabin and be sly about it. Stay there with him." As Dockey started to move away he stopped him. "And better load up a couple of my pistols and see he knows how to use them."

Unnoticed, the little mountain man eased John Lewis back into the darkness. An hour passed before Will Chard returned to the cabin. "You didn't kill him, lad. Graham knows that and so do the men. But they don't like the way you fight."

Swollen, torn, and dirty, and still struggling with his smoldering rage, John sat on the edge of the bunk pressing a wad of rag soaked in *aquardiente* against the abrasions

51

on his cheek where Mueller's fingers had clawed the flesh. "I would have killed him. He was trying to kill me."

Chard nodded. "I believe that. For some reason I don't fathom, your words unsettled him mightily."

John removed the compress and examined the dark red stains. "He's properly settled now."

Chard laughed full out. "You're not much for remorse, are you?"

"I feel none for men who are animals."

Chard looked surprised. "How about that. You're a right high-minded young man, if you mean what you say." He studied Lewis for a while. "How old are you?"

"I'll be twenty in a month." Turning to Dockey, Chard indicated the door. "Bill—fetch Lewis' things from Isaac's cabin as fast as you can without making a show of it." He turned back to John. "This may not be the best place for you for a while. When is the *Reliant* posted to sail?"

"On the morning tide, unless Captain Burke lays over hoping to get me returned."

"He might. For a good hand. No master's ever in a hurry on this coast unless he's outrunning weather. And he knows you're here and who you're with. Robles will see to that."

Chard walked to the cabin door and appraised the sky. "You'd better ride tonight. I'll send Dockey with you to Natividad. You stay there at the distillery."

John glanced at the compress and set it aside. "What if he's no happier about me than the others?"

"Dockey's my man, and he's fair. Also, he's felt Henry Mueller's weight on him a time or two. He won't be doing much mourning, believe me!" He smiled cryptically. "And, my friend, neither will I."

John was plainly surprised. "What about Graham? I mean if you aren't—uh—"

Chard cut him off. "If we don't see eye to eye, then why am I cahooting with him?"

John nodded and Chard looked off, reflectively. "We are useful to each other, for the time being. Our men guarantee us a certain security. I find it useful to take advantage of same—until I'm in a position to go into the lawful trade. He eyed John narrowly. "If you are wondering about my concern for you, lad, it is simply this—all things being equal, I may find you useful also. Does that interest you?"

The answer was immediate and direct. "That depends on what you have in mind and whether it suits my purpose."

Chard regarded John with amusement. "Tell me, lad. Aboard ship were you ever trussed up and flogged?"

"No. I did my work and minded my business."

"And I take it you weren't as quick to retort with Captain Burke as you are with me."

John grew wary. "I can't see that crawling is going to get me where I want to go."

Still amused, Chard moved closer to inspect the wounds. "We'll find out where you want to go later. Do you speak Spanish?"

"Some."

"Good. Then you'll understand the Californio saying, 'Por el canto se conoce el pájaro.' If it's true that a bird is known by its song, then I'd say I may have caught myself a young eagle!"

Dockey came in with the bundled tarpaulin. Chard issued instructions about horses and the three moved quietly to the corrals at the edge of the woods. When John and Dockey were mounted, Chard indicated a low pass through the hills. "Go to Alviso's and stay there until I can ride in. I want to judge the temper here before we add any replacements to our company."

John glanced at Dockey. "Just set me a course. I can ride alone. I don't want to bring trouble down on anybody. The men will blame him for helping me."

Secretly pleased, Chard dismissed the idea. "They'll blame me. Bill's my man. They'll not fault him for following orders. Alviso and his partner, Butron, are friendly. They leased us the land for our distillery. They like our money and our whiskey better than Alvarado's home rule. Now make tracks, lad. Pronto!"

Goyo Robles was outraged. Tokoya, an Indian and a former menial with Will Chard's band who had been banished because of his affinity for the powerful *aguardiente*, had spread the rumor that Graham and Chard were plotting to take over all of Alta California.

Goyo was determined to get to the bottom of the rumor. He told Maria, "The Indian's rumor must be taken seriously. He hasn't enough intelligence to invent tales. Perhaps, at last, I can persuade Alvarado to send Castro and his soldiers against Graham. They must be driven out of Alta California."

Maria pulled at her brother's sleeve. "You dream, Goyo. If Juan's own uncle, Mariano Vallejo, dares to say publicly that he believes the foreigners are necessary to insure our independence from Mexico, then you are stupid to believe you can force Juan Alvarado to act. All you wish to do is avenge your honor. You are angry because Lewis was taken from you. Why were you not angry when other American sailors, who were not half so agreeable, strutted like arrogant cocks on our streets, accosted the women, and rode off with Graham?"

Goyo glared at her. "So you found this one agreeable? As agreeable as he found you, without a doubt!" He turned away. "All the more reason to rid this land of foreigners, and with the help of God I am going to do that before it is too late!"

Crude by established standards, the distillery at Natividad was a master work of improvisation. Copper sheeting salvaged from wrecked vessels had been worked into large pots, set over brick fireboxes. The condensing coils spiraled down into the pots from large domed covers and were cooled by an ingenious system of wooden drip troughs. The alcohol dripped from the condensing coils into holding casks.

At peak production the distillery could produce three hundred gallons every seven days. Harry Morrison ran the still. He was a compact bandy-legged Scotsman in his mid-thirties. He had been a British Navy pharmacist who had deserted after a fatal fight in the Vieux Carré in New Orleans. After he had shown John Lewis the workings of the still, he beamed at the sailor's compliments.

"Aye! But the great problem is, Lewis, that good whiskey wants its color from ageing in char and not from the tincturing and tampering wi' nature we do here. Graham calls this 'bourbon' for sentimental reasons. But a mon that knows good whiskey would never call it more than fuel for a spirit lamp. Personally, the sweetening wi' molasses suits it more for pouring on Johnny cakes than for serious drinking. I wouldna downrate our liquor to foreigners but I miss the smoky tang of peat in it."

After the meal, John, Bill Dockey, and Morrison sat talking over a jug of *aguardiente*. John was forced to conclude that Graham's own private stock was no improvement over the run-of-the-still spirit that Morrison was serving. The Scotsman watched closely as his guest downed the first swallow with no visible reaction. "Aye, laddie, ye drink well! Either you've got a martyr's self-possession or a leather gullet!"

Still hurting from the fight, John Lewis drank so well that he had no trouble sleeping on the hard floor. Neither was he bothered by the ubiquitous fleas that infested most of the California coast. Resigned to their constant attacks, the tolerant *californios* had even composed several serenades to them. One of the songs listed the searching out and killing of the vermin as one of the services a bride and groom perform for each other.

Will Chard arrived at Natividad late the following afternoon and watched John help Morrison and Dockey set new batches of mash. Lewis handled the *quintales* of wheat as though they weighed half their hundredweight. When Morrison indicated the newcomer and nodded covert approval, Chard called John aside. "The *Reliant* cleared for San Pedro yesterday, so you are safe enough on that score unless Nathaniel Burke has made some arrangement to have you caught and sent south aboard another vessel."

Relieved, John sought further reassurance. "What about your men?"

Chard pursed his lips. "I may not sense their temper as well as Graham but I think you'll be all right, though it would be well to stay away from the camp for a time."

John nodded. "Then I'll be on my way up the valley. I'll stop at Yerba Buena for a while and look around."

"Why? Doesn't this place suit you?"

"It may be I don't suit this place."

"You suit Harry," Chard said emphatically. "Why don't you stay here and learn? I told you two days ago that I had plans that you might fit into."

John shrugged. "I have no plans. But if yours are to my liking then I'll be glad to learn the ropes, though I won't promise to make whiskey a life work."

Will Chard laughed. "If you'd settle for that, lad, I'd not settle for you! Now go about your work and I'll see that you're snugged in here and left alone—but for Harry's nagging. You'll find he is under the delusion that we should be making ambrosia for the gods."

55

From then on, John saw no one but Morrison and the Indians who did menial labor around the Natividad distillery. The Scotsman found his new hand a willing worker and a quick learner, who became so adept that the delicate malting process was entrusted to him.

Three weeks later, on a morning in mid-May, Isaac Graham and Will Chard arrived at the distillery. Their arrival made John uneasy. They greeted John curtly but they were not unfriendly; both seemed preoccupied. He found out that Graham and Chard were under pressure to increase the output of the stills. They didn't spell it out but it was apparent that the customs officials in Monterey were demanding a larger "under the table" share for not enforcing the law prohibiting the distillation of hard liquors.

Morrison responded quickly. "I've got enough copper here for another pot but we'll be needing more for the condenser. Aye! But the bonniest sight that could greet my eyes would be a brick kiln so we could fire our own and make a decent high temperature charcoal oven." The Scotsman's burr thickened with the urgency of his appeal. "Thot's what we're needing for the filtering, mon. Give me that and I'll make ye a whiskey so good they'll change the law and make it legal!"

Graham wouldn't promise the material for the kiln. "We be needing a sawmill first, one driven by water power. I've great plans for making lumber. It be profitable too—with no silent partners at the customhouse."

It was obvious to John that Isaac Graham was purposely ignoring him. He tried to fathom the reason, and concluded that he was at Natividad under Will Chard's protection and that Graham had probably agreed to the arrangement, with some reluctance.

He was surprised when Graham called to him as he was about to go to his bed. "Hyar, boy!" Graham sauntered over with thumbs hooked in his belt. "Harry tells me your brain be as strong as your back. That's what we want—men that work fair, eat fair—and fight fair."

He cocked his head speculatively while his tongue probed a segment of upper gum almost barren of molars. Dislodged particles of food spattered on the dry earth. The stench of rotting teeth made Lewis wince. "Ye'll pass muster on the first two points, but the boys be a mite uncertain on the other." The lice in his beard occupied him briefly as, with folded arms, he studied John. "I be uncertain myself. But I don't suppose leaping like a flying mule's worse than gouging or hair lifting—in the sight of the Lord. Killing one good man for another just ain't sensible. But I'd rather seen ye stomp a savage than my old friend Henry. But it wasn't a savage testing ye, was it? So, stay on hyar and Will will tell ye when the cool spell sets in over the hill. Harry's measure of ye weighs mighty on your side—a point to remember if ye get itchy."

Graham turned away abruptly and went to fix his bed in the private quarters in back of the distillery. The fetid aura surrounding him lingered.

Wakeful in his bedroll, John pondered the strange monologue. What Graham appeared to be saying was simple; he and the men did not approve of his fighting tactics but the practical need to replace a good man now dead with a good live one guaranteed a sort of uneasy amnesty. Meanwhile Harry Morrison was to be his custodian if not quite his jailor. Now that the threat of return to the *Reliant* had been removed, Lewis wondered what Isaac Graham's reaction would be if he deserted from his present company.

"He'd probably see it as an excuse to hunt me down and 'lift my hair,' as he calls scalping," John expressed the thought half aloud, recalling the grisly souvenirs that hung from Graham's belt. Not all of the scalps were Indian.

Harry Morrison was pleased to have an intelligent companion who was a good listener. Morrison spoke freely of his youth, his service in the Royal Navy, the fatal fight in the Vieux Carré that had been forced on him and his subsequent flight. He often mentioned frustration at not being able to make a good product at the distillery and of his desire to see the production of whiskey legalized.

After several more weeks of working together, Morrison surprised him. "Ye'll be havin' to make some decisions soon, won't ye, laddie?"

Wary, John tried to parry the first question of a personal nature that the man had made. "Such as?"

"Whether or not ye'll be wanting to return to the camp or stay on here wi' me?" The little Scotsman's transparent attempt to disguise his secret hope pleased John.

He smiled humorlessly. "Not much of a decision to make. Not in my circumstances."

"How so, laddie?"

"As I see it, I'm little better off now than I was aboard ship. If the air doesn't clear at the camp I'll be trading flogging for fighting."

Morrison's eyes narrowed shrewdly. "You'd do a lot worse than to stay on here wi' me."

John looked dubious. "I'm not cut out to be a whiskey baron. I think I lean toward trade."

"Trade's a profitable venture, laddie, if ye can get your boot in the door in Monterey and the proper connection with a Boston mercantile house. But I wud'na think those who monopolize it will look wi' favor on more competition."

"Who are the men who control the trade in Monterey?"

"Captain Cooper, David Spence, and lately, Tom Larkin—for the most part. And the Mexican officials who meet wi' them in the lee of the longboat to collect their 'tithe,' so to speak."

The revelation did not surprise John. He knew that Larkin had come to Monterey seven years earlier as a clerk and accountant for Cooper. Now the dour, thirty-seven-year-old Yankee from Charlestown, Massachusetts, had become rich enough to outdo his benefactor. He was building the most pretentious residence on the Calle Principal, a two-story house of adobe brick, redwood, and oak with a spacious veranda, upper balcony, and wrought-iron-barred windows. The *Reliant* had delivered much of Larkin's elegant furniture from New England's best craftsmen, along with fine glassware and silver. Larkin had checked each bill of lading and quibbled over the slightest irregularity. Captain Burke had cursed all the way from the landing to the anchorage.

In reply to questioning about Larkin, Morrison said to ask Chard. "He's been trying for years to get his boot in the door. He knows them all—and all that's worth knowing about them."

"How much do you know about Chard—and Graham?"

The question caught Harry Morrison by surprise. "More than I'm likely to tell ye, laddie."

John smiled at the rebuff and did not press. However, several minutes later Morrison surprised him in turn by reopening the subject. "What do ye know of Chard and Graham yourself?"

"Nothing—except what I can see."

58

"And what do ye think ye see, laddie?"

John pondered for a moment. "A mountain man who stinks like a backwater slough—who pretends to be a captain and leader—and a possible leader who's too clean and smart to be the mountain man he pretends to be."

A burst of laughter exploded from Morrison. "By God, Lewis, ye've a pair of sharp eyes in that head of yours." For a moment he seemed to be debating with himself. Finally, he said reflectively, "Well, laddie, what I do know can't hurt me, if ye'll use a little discretion."

John nodded.

"I'll tell ye aboot Chard first. I met him in Los Angeles, a place only a desperate sailor would find himself. He had come from New York in thirty-two and set out a vineyard. He had a very poor and very small brandy still which I was able to improve. But between the pressure from the Yankee merchants and the squeeze demanded by the officials, we were soon out of business. In early thirty-six I caught a bark to Monterey and Chard went to Santa Barbara, where he met Graham. Graham had been a hunter and trapper in Kentucky and drifted to New Mexico and then Santa Barbara. Chard was near starving, so when Graham told him some tall tales about Monterey, he threw in wi' the roughest crew this side of Botony Bay and came to Monterey. That's where we met again. I couldn't find an ear among the merchants, so Chard spoke wi' Graham." He swept the room with an arm. "And the result is to be seen hereaboot."

An obvious paradox troubled John. Will Chard was well-mannered, educated, impressive looking, strongly built, and had all the attributes of a leader. Why then, he asked Morrison, had he not been able to make a place for himself among lesser men.

"I'd say perhaps it's a lack in him. A lack of self-esteem. He's ten times the mon Graham is—but Graham believes himself to be ten times the mon he is. Will's capable of running things if he's given the chance." Morrison raised a finger. "I think 'given' is the key word. If Chard learns to take his opportunities, then he'll come into his own." He shook his head sadly. "And meantime, laddie, who knows what's behind the faults in any of us who hide out here on the California coast?"

Will Chard did not return to the distillery until the last

week in June. A replacement for John Lewis rode in with him. Chard evaded John's questions about plans. "You'll have to trust me, lad. But I give you my word as a—" He interrupted himself to laugh softly. "I give you my word that I'll lead you into no danger. If it reassures you at all, let me tell you that I have a deep selfish interest in seeing you safe."

Harry Morrison watched them pack up and mount. John had never seen him so crestfallen. The little Scotsman ignored the awkward attempt at thanks and a farewell and addressed Chard instead. "I dinna ken the reasoning that deprives me of the best apprentice I've had—not to mention intelligent company. Also, it's a rare thing to find a sailor thot drinks well. I'll be missing the lad."

Will Chard chuckled. "It's a rarer thing to see you sentimental!"

Morrison bristled. "Aye! So rare it is ye'll never see it. It's for practical reasons I'll be missing the laddie." He sniffed disdainfully. "I'm as sentimental as a hangman!" Without further comment he turned away abruptly and reentered the still house.

For the first few miles Will Chard seemed to be leading them in the general direction of the Pájaro River valley. But when he turned southwestward toward the Salinas River, Lewis grew puzzled, then concerned. That course would take them to Monterey, a place he still deemed unsafe.

Chard, sensing his anxiety, sought to reassure him. "Do not worry about Monterey, lad. The mission we are about to undertake is worth a great deal more to those in power there than the price on your head. And it could put a great deal more money than that in your pocket, and eventually in mine."

John reined up. "I don't mean to head into any trouble, not with my eyes closed," he said.

Chard laughed. "You are a hard-mouthed young mustang, aren't you, lad? I thought by now you'd come to trust me."

"I'm grateful to you for getting me out of a mess. And I'm disposed to trust you more than most."

"Thank you." Chard pursed his lips thoughtfully. "I did not want to let Morrison or that rabble at the distillery know we were heading for Monterey. Morrison's more than dependable. He'd fight for you, lad—that much impression you've made on him. But if nobody knows what we're up to, then nobody can slip. So let's ride on and I'll tell you what I have in mind. If you don't want to go along with it, you're free to go back to the distillery, or to the camp . . ." He waved a hand. "Or to wherever you wish to go. Agreed?"

Lewis hesitated, then nodded. "Agreed."

They rode in silence side by side, reining their animals to a slow canter through rippling, satiny green seas of native oats and stretches of shimmering yellow wild mustard. The clustered blossoms reached to the swinging skirts of their saddles. In front of them clouds of blackbirds whirled upward and wheeled away, darkly iridescent in the sun. Shoulder deep and scarcely visible in the cover on all sides, deer and herds of valley antelope were feeding. Overhead, the sky's clear, azure dome arced away to the horizon. It must be, John thought, one of the most bountiful and beauty-blessed lands on earth. More than anything else he wanted to be free to stay on and explore it.

Watching his companion covertly, Chard smiled to himself. He could guess that the young New Englander was coming under the same spell that Alta California had cast on him when he had ridden north from arid southern California to Santa Barbara and Monterey with Isaac Graham's party. He had been entranced by the oak-shaded open land, by shadowy canyons, and the crystal streamlets cascading from the redwood-clad slopes.

Lewis broke the silence. "I don't think I would go back to Graham's camp."

Secretly relieved, Chard responded cautiously. "I think you'd find, as I have, that the future there is limited." He stood in the stirrups to point off to the northeast. "This valley is rich. But there are others that more than match it. The Sacramento, the San Joaquin, the Sonoma, the Napa."

John looked at him with new interest. "Have you seen them?"

"Only the Sonoma and the Napa. But I have talked with Colonel Vallejo at his Rancho Petaluma. He has ridden up the Sacramento as far as some old Indian villages. I would trust his judgment. The colonel has an eye for beauty as well as for money!" It was time now, Chard judged, to set the hook. "The plan I have in mind could take you to the Sacramento valley and to the others too, if it interests you."

John grew wary again.

Chard, sensing his unasked question, said, "I am not at liberty to tell you the exact plan we have in mind but I can tell you about the men who will underwrite it."

"What would I be asked to do—beside go sightseeing?"

"Do what smart travelers do—ask intelligent questions and keep a sharp eye out for important detail."

Unaccountably a passage from Numbers came to John's mind: ". . . and Moses sent them to spy out the land of Canaan and see the land, what it is, and the people that dwelleth therein, whether they be strong or weak, few or many . . ."

He said to Chard, "I don't know that I am suited by nature to be a spy."

Chard tried to conceal his surprise. "If you don't like that word, lad, I'm sure we can find another. They call mass murderers 'generals' and mortal gods 'sea captains' and 'masters.' Would 'seeker after the truth' be more to your liking?"

John's response was swift. "Perhaps, if it's bestowed with full knowledge of the futility of the task."

If you speak such profundities in the presence of Captain Cooper and Tom Larkin, you may give them reason to be wary of you, lad. Except for Spence, they are self-learned and suspect glibness in men."

So it was out, Lewis thought. It was something that would serve the principal merchants in Monterey. Under their protection he would probably be safe. But whatever the mission, it would also serve Chard's ends. If he couldn't learn the purpose behind the job he was being offered, he could at least try to find out about the men he would serve. His first question produced a cautious response.

"Taking bad things first—against Larkin is his lack of humor and his penuriousness. In favor is his quick mind, his orderliness, and what some would call his scrupulous honesty—although I cannot always tell precisely where sharp trading and larceny overlap. He is ambitious." Chard nearly added "and ruthless." He wondered again how much of Larkin's apparent restraint was due to the man's unusual obligation to Captain J. B. R. Cooper. That was important. Lewis would learn of it in due time, but not now.

"Tom Larkin is a family man, originally from Massachusetts. He puts little store in frivolity. Most of his time is spent improving his business and his house." Chard pondered briefly. "There isn't a great deal more I can tell you about him." He would have preferred to say, "that I am at liberty to tell you."

"Cooper is from Alderney Island—a former English sea captain—naturalized Mexican now, and baptized Catholic, as is Spence. Both are married to Mexican ladies. Cooper was master of the *Rover*. A brig, I believe she was. He traded in the Pacific islands and along the coast of South America. To quote him, he tired of the "inhuman demands of the sea" and became a trader, merchant, retailer, and rancher instead. He's prospered by being all things at once. He has a son they call "John the Baptist" because he was christened John Baptist Henry. John Cooper—a scholarly sort—is away in the Sandwich Islands much of the time. William Hartnell tutored him earlier— some years before he founded his College of San Jose. John Cooper is the elder statesman among the Anglo-Californians, I'd say. Though he and David Spence arrived only a year apart, Spence coming after, from Scotland."

Lewis knew that Spence was a trader, too. Chard supplied some detail. "I'm less sure about Spence's background, lad. But I've been told that he was the California agent for Begg and Company in Glasgow. I believe he supervised the salting down of beef for ship's stores in Monterey and Santa Barbara before he decided to go into trading for himself so he could stay on the coast." Chard glanced at John meaningfully. "This land seems to lay a hand on men, doesn't it, lad?"

It was dusk when Will Chard and John Lewis picked their way out of the canyon and rode onto the upper edge of the sloping, brush-dotted mesa overlooking Monterey and the bay. Chard guided them past outlying adobes to Captain Cooper's residence.

Cooper, a ruddy-faced man with iron-gray hair, greeted them cordially. John saw that his left hand had been crippled.

He introduced them to his wife, Doña Encarnacion, who showed them to adjoining bedrooms.

The house, one of the largest in Monterey, was invitingly furnished with excellent pieces that had been brought to California around the Horn a decade earlier. In many ways the furnishings resembled those in John's boyhood home in Middletown and awakened painful nostalgia in him.

During the evening meal the conversation touched on many topics, none of which related to the purpose of the visit. At the meal's end Doña Encarnacion excused herself and Captain Cooper got a bottle of Chilean brandy from the sideboard. He was about to serve it when Thomas Larkin and David Spence arrived. They acknowledged the introduction with friendly reserve and some minutes later, around the fireplace, with brandies, John had an opportunity to study the merchant princes of Monterey.

Larkin, tall, prim, and in his late thirties, had wispy receding hair that framed a broad, high forehead and merged untidily into scruffy sideburns. His blue eyes were bland and watery as the result of a head cold. His mouth was compressed into a permanent expression of mild disapproval.

The Scotsman, David Spence, seemed kindlier and more open. His blue-gray eyes were caught at the outer corners in fine webs of wrinkles that could be harbingers of a ready smile, and his mouth was pleasant above a determined chin. The squared face and well-shaped head created the impression of a mature and capable man.

Absorbed by his observations, John Lewis was caught off guard when Cooper addressed him. "Mister, if knowing you're in the presence of a former ship's master makes you a bit stiff, perhaps you'll slack up when I tell you that technically you and I are in the same boat. We're both deserters, you know."

Larkin smiled thinly and David Spence laughed and reached over to rest a hand on the knee of Lewis' worn wool winter blues. "That should reassure you, lad. It means that under the correct circumstances, and with the proper opportunity, a criminal can redeem himself and become a useful citizen in Alta California."

Captain Cooper chuckled at John's consternation. "Port captains are blunter than judges, Lewis. What are your plans?"

John glanced from Will Chard to Thomas Larkin, whose face remained impassive. "I have no plans, sir, except not to get put back aboard a Burgess ship in violation of the articles."

Cooper nodded reassuringly. "We know about that.

You've no need to worry. It could be that you'll find an opportunity to go inland for a time. Would that appeal to you?"

"That depends, sir. All things considered, I'm a bit puzzled by the kindness I'm being shown."

"That may be less than altruism, son. You're a presentable young man and, judging from what Will tells us, capable. It may not be kindness we're offering you. It may simply be the lesser of two evils."

Thomas Larkin dabbed at his nose with a pocket cloth and leaned forward. He did not feel well and his voice was raspy and without humor. "Your presence here, Mr. Lewis, means that you are capable of independent action. Life here is filled with uncertainties. If you should take it into your head to act upon your own, it would be fair to say that these uncertainties would become far more certain."

David Spence glanced at Larkin, frowning, then turned to John. "By now, lad, you've had ample time to figure that out for yourself. Mr. Larkin simply means that if you move outside the protection of friendly associates who wish you well, your future state could not be guaranteed. This is an open land. A very rich land. It attracts men of varied character and if you are curious about why we are talking to you, I'll be plain about it. We made our proposal to Will Chard. He feels, and on second thought we agree, that he is too well known to do the job. So it is not that we have singled you out of many for our favors, it is simply that you seem to possess the qualifications and you are here, now, when we have a need for someone."

Cooper removed his pipe and pointed the glistening stem at John. "Every man-jack who has ever managed to make something of himself, did so because he was the right man in the right place at the right time. What Mr. Spence is suggesting is that—due to no particular perception of your own—you may be such a man."

Cooper reached for a sheaf of papers on the table beside him. "You'll be easier if we get to the point, lad. The charter brig *Clementine* anchored here three days ago. She's out of Honolulu for Yerba Buena and other coastal ports with general merchandise. But she's got some suspicious passengers aboard. Her master was my guest two nights ago, so my information is reliable. He's carrying an odd young fellow who calls himself Captain Johann Augustus Sutter. He is a German-born Swiss who claims to have been an officer in Charles the Tenth's personal guard in Paris. He's lugging an uncommon packet of introduction letters from leading merchants and politicians in the United States, from the commander of the North American department of Russian Alaska, at Sitka, and from James Douglas of the Hudson Bay Company." He indicated David Spence. "We have seen these credentials. They are a fact. Already he's presented them to Governor Alvarado. The governor was impressed. He asked Sutter to dine with him. Sutter was refused permission to land in Yerba Buena with a company of five white men and eight *kanakas*. He claims he wants to explore the headwaters of the Bay of San Francisco and the rivers flowing to it. His purpose is to set up an outpost at the head of the navigable waters."

Recognizing the threat such an establishment might pose for these men who had created their own secure monopoly on the California coast, John blurted the obvious question. "An outpost? Who for?"

All but Larkin smiled. Cooper leaned forward, pipestem jabbing again. "That's what you could be finding out for us."

John looked from one to the other, still questioning. "What about Governor Alvarado? Would he give permission to Sutter?"

Spence nodded emphatically. "Aye! That he will."

Open disbelief shone in John's dark blue eyes. "That could be like the master inviting the crew to start the seacocks!"

Cooper nodded emphatically. "Precisely."

"But why in the name of common sense would the governor do that?"

"Alvarado could have two reasons," Cooper said. "First, he's much influenced by Castro and Robles, who fear Isaac Graham and his—uh—men." He indicated Will Chard. "Castro has seen the power of Graham's army and as military commander of the Department of the North, that's not calculated to make Castro rest easy. There's a saying that one Yankee musket is worth ten Mexican cannon. Secondly, the governor may well want someone he can trust to watch the back door. Mexico City wants no more outsiders here but they won't give Alvarado enough troops to man the necessary garrisons. A man like Sutter could be a useful pair of eyes. Alvarado will bribe him to be loyal—probably with promises of land, promises he may not keep any better than he kept his promises to Isaac Graham."

"But Sutter himself is an 'outsider.' The letters would not change that."

David Spence replied, "Citizenship would be part of Alvarado's price for permission to set up the post. I met Sutter yesterday. He was adroit in avoiding direct answers to questions. The man is fluent in French. We are not unmindful that France is very much interested in California. And so are others.

"Sutter could be useful to Alvarado. If he's the agent of a foreign power, those of us who seek to protect this country's best interests should know about it as soon as possible." A suggestion of a twinkle shone in his eyes. "We need to have the most accurate possible appraisal of this Sutter. That is best done by someone he does not suspect of an ulterior motive." He paused for emphasis. "Now, that about states our position. I hope it also suggests the importance of the mission."

John sensed the merchants' anxiety. After a silence, Thomas Larkin addressed him. "Mr. Lewis, we are not unmindful of the uses of incentive. We do not wish to put a price on your freedom and while you are in our employ we will see that you are properly outfitted, given pocket money, and we will deposit to your credit, in Captain Cooper's firm, two dollars per day." He looked at John questioningly.

John held back no longer. "Sir, if you gentlemen feel you can trust me, I would find the arrangement quite acceptable."

Their relief was almost audible. Cooper lumbered out of his chair, offering more brandy, speaking as he refilled John's glass first. "You'll stay close by here now, John. As soon as we know for certain that Sutter has prevailed, we'll make arrangements to get you to Yerba Buena ahead of the *Clementine*." He nodded in the direction of the bay where the bark lay at anchor. "She'll make slow headway beating to windward. A good horse will get you there well ahead of her."

David Spence spoke next. "It will not be wise for Sutter to see you in our company." He removed several silver coins from his waistcoat pocket and handed them to John.

"Two leagues north, off the San Jose road, I have an empty house. Will knows it. You stay there until we send for you. I recommend that you and Will ride out tonight."

Within twenty-four hours John Augustus Sutter was informing all who would listen that he was now recruiting loyal California citizens to man a frontier colony for the governor. In poor Spanish, broken English, and in fluent French and German, he boasted that he would found a settlement to rival Monterey and that after he had received his own citizenship, he would be given a huge land grant generous portions of which would be transferred to all *californio* citizens who would come north to settle and work.

Sutter lingered only four days in Monterey after attempting without much success to arrange credit and to sign on men. Disappointed, he boarded the *Clementine* and sailed for Yerba Buena on the morning tide.

Just two hours later, in his home, Cooper was giving instructions to John Lewis. "Yerba Buena's a very small place, John. You'll be conspicuous. This letter identifies you as an agent-at-large for J. B. R. Cooper Company. Use it only if the Mexican authorities question you. As far as Sutter is concerned, you're just another merchant seamen who's jumped ship. Sutter needs men, and should leap at the chance to get you. But don't seem too eager. Stay backed off a bit. Keep your advantage."

Will Chard chuckled, "Tell him you're an expert distiller, that you were apprenticed to one of the best whiskey distillers from Scotland. You'll be indispensable."

Cooper pointed to the clothing and supplies piled on a table. "We've got you rigged out proper, John. How soon can you be on your way?"

"If you set me a course, I'm ready now."

"We've done that—with notes on the friendly places to stop for food and a fresh mount and a bed, too." He handed Lewis a map. "Will is going to ride part way with you."

In less than an hour John and Will Chard were riding north. Chard indicated the low hills ahead of them. "From San Juan keep to the flat country east of the mountains until you get to the south end of the bay and to the old Spanish Trail he's marked on the map. The streams are low now. You'll have no trouble."

Chard reined up. "I'll leave you here. Remember—keep Cooper posted. Send your messages aboard a coaster as he directed. It's customary for them to carry letters. If you're questioned too much, use the letter of authorization, but remember, the connection must be kept a secret unless you are taken by authorities. If they ask you about citizenship, say you are waiting out your year's probation."

In just sixteen hours of riding, with only the briefest stops for food and less than four hours of sleep, John rode to the hills overlooking Yerba Buena on the Bay of San Francisco. There he hobbled his mount and made a temporary camp.

From the top of a rise he could see the anchorage. No vessel as large as the brig was swinging on its cable. If the *Clementine* had worked her way north as far as the Farallones, she would wait until morning before attempting the dangerous passage through the narrows. Resisting the temptation to go into the settlement, John returned to the little camp and did what he could to make himself comfortable. Wearily, he gathered a load of fallen oak limbs, arranged them as the *vaqueros* did to make a "long fire" that would last the night, and settled into his covers.

For twelve hours he slept, scarcely stirring. When he finally awakened, the sun was a half hour above the green-splashed, yellow ochre hills on the east side of the bay. From the leather *talego*—the large saddlebag filled with provisions—he took the makings of a meager breakfast. Then he caught his mount and began a cautious exploration, taking care to keep away from El Camino Real, the old trail bearing the extravagant title, the King's Highway. To the north and west of it he recognized the twin peaks called Los Pechos because of their marked resemblance to a pair of young, upthrust breasts. Setting himself a course to the south of them he began a long probe through the wooded ravines in the direction of the ocean. It was past midday by the time he had penetrated the densely grown canyons and gained the summit of the protective ridge. He waited, hoping to catch sight of the *Clementine*'s sail. After several hours he remounted and rode back to his camp. Sometime during the third day, while he was exploring the countryside south and west of Yerba Buena, the *Clementine* made her way into port. In the late afternoon Lewis saw her, riding at anchor. Relieved that his wait was over and excited in the spite of his continued admonitions to himself to be calm, he broke camp the following morning and rode into Yerba Buena.

2 "BUT, MY DEAR JOHANN, I insist you can accomplish the same things much closer to Yerba Buena—and do them faster and better."

Jean Vioget, fellow Swiss, addressed John Augustus Sutter as the two picked their way down the grassy trail leading to the waterfront.

Sutter, reflecting, shaped his drooping handlebar mustache and smiled benignly. "True. And I will also be under constant surveillance of everybody including your *Oberbefehlshaber* Vallejo! What I wish to accomplish must be done without interference."

Vioget studied Sutter's short, wide back. If Sutter had been German instead of Swiss, he would have chosen "arrogant" to describe him. As it was, stubborn Teutonic determination was softened a bit by inborn Swiss diplomacy. "Johann, for whom do you undertake this outpost?"

Sutter stopped in his tracks. "For *me*. Only for me. I have seen what is wrong with these frontier communities. They lack organization, discipline. I shall establish the model for all such trading posts. It will exceed even Russia's Fort Ross."

"But that's bound to awaken anxiety in General Vallejo. He is already concerned about the *schabig armeekorps* of Graham and Chard at Branciforte. He fears all military forces except his own."

"Vallejo will not fear that which he will not see," Sutter said and turned abruptly toward the shed that housed the trading activities of Spear, Hinckley and Leese.

Immediately on landing, Sutter had begun negotiations with Nathan Spear and William Hinckley for two charter schooners to carry himself and the crew he hoped to hire to the location of his outpost. With characteristic impatience Sutter wished his plans to spring into being, full-blown. "Jean, do you know why God created the universe in only six days? Because he had no one to obstruct him!"

71

The pair descended the path to a point just above the muddy high tide line then turned north to the crude but serviceable warehouse.

Spear and Hinckley and their young bay captain Bill Davis were waiting for Sutter at the warehouse. The two small schooners Sutter wanted to buy were some yards offshore. An hour or so later, with negotiations completed, largely on Sutter's promises and good faith, they were rowed to the moored craft for inspection. Sutter was delighted. His limited English and Spanish almost failed him. Standing in the bow of the *Isabella* like a conquering admiral, he lapsed into such an excited torrent of German that even poor Vioget had trouble following. Struggling to control his impatience, Sutter turned to the two merchant partners. "I will need many things! Many things. Both these vessels will be filled to the gunwales when I sail this coming week."

Hinckley and Spear exchanged startled glances, then looked to Davis. Spear voiced their concern. "Even if we can fill your complete list, Captain Sutter, it will take until the end of next week before Mr. Davis can have these vessels ready for such a long voyage."

Sutter closed his eyes. "The end of the week is out of the question! It is already midsummer. Every day is precious. The stupidity of your local authorities that required me to waste weeks and travel to the governor himself has already cost me dearly." He shook his head with finality. "Impossible! I must sail on the morning of the fourth day or make other arrangements!"

Spear, Hinckley and Leese had a virtual monopoly on bay schooners that made other arrangements patently impossible. But they were not inclined to argue with Sutter's ridiculous request, since he offered the possibility of an expanding volume of business.

Sutter and Vioget left the warehouse together and walked to the rickety structure of embedded poles that was the embarcadero's only wharf. They stopped abruptly at the sight of a young man, obviously not a native, seated on an upturned rowboat. The stranger was staring dejectedly out across the bay. Sutter's questioning look brought a quick shrug from Vioget. Frowning, Sutter walked to within a yard before the young man noticed him and roused from his reverie. Sutter bowed and smiled warmly. "Good day! Good day!"

"Good day, sir." The tone was flat.

Sutter extended his hand. "Allow me to introduce myself, Captain John Augustus Sutter." He turned. "And this is my good friend and countryman, Jean Jacques Vioget, a native of Yerba Buena."

John rose slowly, steadying the bundle of belongings on the upturned keel with his left hand. "Pleased to know you gentlemen. My name is Lewis. John Lewis."

The men shook hands, Sutter with great vigor. With his usual lack of inhibition, he flung an arm in the direction of the two schooners and announced grandly, "I am admiring my new merchant fleet. Only this morning I have acquired these two splendid vessels. In four days, God willing, my company and I will set out to explore the great unknown river wilderness," he drew himself up proudly, "under a special commission from Governor Alvarado at Monterey."

The young man's obvious lack of interest puzzled and annoyed him. "You have a touch of fever, perhaps?"

As anxious as he was about this first encounter with Sutter, John was barely able to conceal his amusement. He shook his head. "I'm in round good health." Casually, he reseated himself on the upturned boat.

Somewhat b⌐ ⌐ntly, Jean Vioget said, "I do not recall seeing you ⌐⌐⌐ ⌐re, M'sieur Lewis. Have you come with the C⌐ ⌐⌐e?"

Sutter e⌐⌐loded. "Of course he has not! I came on the *Clementine*. I know every man, rat, and roach aboard her!"

Vioget tried again. "You are from where then, M'sieur Lewis?"

John allowed a second of silence to go by before he said slowly, "Originally, I came from New England."

Sutter's hands fluttered impatiently. "So? Where? What city?"

"Lately, Boston."

Sutter was growing plainly annoyed. "Lately? How did you arrive?"

"I arrived in a Boston merchantman, sir, and on this coast lately could mean a year, even two, as you perhaps know."

Sutter's china blue eyes widened. "You are a fugitive,

then? Is it not foolish to sit here and risk capture? Or are you so desperate for food that you don't care?"

John rose wearily. "I am full up with food and injustice. And I hold that no man is a fool who escapes unjust persecution."

Sutter looked nervously from Lewis to Vioget and back. "Yes, yes." Catching himself, he cleared his throat. "I mean, no indeed!"

Jean Vioget broke in. "You must excuse our curiosity, M'sieur Lewis. A stranger in this far off land is occasion enough for questions. We hope for news. Forgive us, but do you know anybody in Yerba Buena?"

"No. I arrived this morning—overland."

"From Monterey?"

"From San Juan Bautista."

Lewis nodded and Vioget was encouraged to press more questions. "But you've been in Monterey, San Pedro, and Los Angeles?"

"Not Los Angeles. San Pedro and San Diego."

Sutter interrupted. "Ah, yes. I was correct. You are a merchant sailor who is—shall we say—at liberty. Am I correct?"

John's tanned face turned grim. "You are correct. I'd rather carry a price on my head than more California hides."

Sutter's shrewd little eyes darted from one to the other. He was remembering his own bankruptcy and the threat of a debtors' prison in Switzerland. "By God, Lewis, someday I shall tell you why we are brothers!" Radiating sympathy, he sat down. "Do you know anything about these people, Lewis?"

"The *californios*?"

"Yes."

"Some are good and some are bad."

"Have any of them offered to help you?"

John's answer was a dejected shrug.

Indignant, Sutter shot to his feet. "God in Heaven! I should have known better than to ask. Barbarians! *Verdammt* barbarians! But what can you expect from a people who invented the Inquisition?" He braced his palms on his bulging hips and declared, "*I* offer you help, my friend. And I will pay you to accept." Leaning close, he scrutinized John's face. "Personally, I will pay. So you hear? Personally, from my own purse. Tell me, are you a good seaman, my friend?"

"Able-bodied, sir. At ease aloft, below, or on the quarter deck."

Sutter pointed to the smaller of the two schooners at anchor. "Could you be a reliable master of such a vessel as that one?"

John was astonished at the man's impulsiveness but when he looked at the open-decked schooner, he could barely keep a straight face. The craft was scarcely larger than the *Reliant's* longboat. "A fore and aft rig is no problem, sir, if it has better than a rag of sail, a straight keel, and a stout tiller."

"By God, Jean, in this country, I cannot make mistakes. Everything favors my plans." Sutter turned to John. "Lewis, do I interest you?"

There was no need to worry now. John knew that the more reluctant he seemed the more information he would get. He left the question unanswered until the Swiss nudged his leg. "Do I?"

"Sir, you're going off exploring rivers. I'm a deep-water man, not an oysterman. I appreciate your interest but—"

Sutter popped up again, fairly bouncing on the balls of his feet. "Do you know what I offer you, Lewis? Immunity from the law! A position as captain of the *Nicholas. Captain* Lewis. Captain John Lewis. Very distinguished. You will command your own ship, under me, of course. With Vioget here." Turning, he pointed to the larger schooner on whose transom was painted the name *Isabella.* "Captain Davis will command her and together, Lewis, we will be the first party to explore the great inland rivers. And when we find and claim our place, we will build our settlement—and my great fort."

In spite of himself Lewis' eyes reflected surprise. "Your fort?"

Sutter hastened to cover himself. "An outpost. Only an outpost. In English these distinctions confuse me. I use the word loosely. Our mission is peaceful. We will keep the great unexplored inland from falling into foreign hands. In a year I will be a Mexican citizen and in another year land will be granted to me by the Governor. As a loyal Mexican it will be my duty to see that the flag of my adopted country flies over this domain."

Sutter puffed with importance. "And those with me will

also be made citizens and I will have the power to grant land."

"How long would I be asked to sign?" John asked.

It was not a question Sutter had anticipated. He sputtered. "You do not sign. No! With Johann Augustus Sutter your *word* is good. And remember, Mr. Lewis, you will be paid in *dollars*. Twenty each month and food and quarters. That is because you are an officer, a captain."

John put a hand on his belongings, rather uncertainly, and said, "Well, I thank you for your proposal, Captain Sutter. It's interesting, but I'm not sure." He nodded toward the hillside. "I think I'd better find me a place to sleep and think on it."

Vioget, as eager now as Sutter, sprang to his feet. "You have no place to sleep? Only the woods?"

"I've slept very well in the woods for weeks now."

Resolutely, Vioget reached for John's duffle. "Tonight you sleep in my house. And you eat there, too. It is not Versailles but it has a good roof. You will not sleep on the ground like an animal."

John allowed the duffle to be taken from him. Then, flanked by the two men, he walked up the path to Vioget's cabin.

Early in November the Russian schooner *Constantine* put into Monterey for water and some emergency supplies. The master delivered to Captain John Cooper a packet of letters. Within the hour, David Spence, Thomas Larkin, and Will Chard were listening as he read aloud:

New Helvetia,
October 3, 1839

Captain J. B. R. Cooper
Monterey, Alta California.

Sir:

Finding the wherewithal to write this was almost as difficult as finding a means to send it. First, I want to advise you that Captain Sutter is writing to your firm asking for credit to acquire provisions to sustain our small company here at New Helvetia.

Captain Sutter is a man not easily fathomed. He is

76

given to much talk that might seem boasting, but he may be one of those *rara avis* whose deeds match his own accounts of same. Except for a confrontation here with over one hundred savages in full regalia and armed with spears and bows and arrows, an emergency which the Captain brought us through peacefully by reason of his courage and diplomacy (he lays claim to a special relationship with all native savages as a consequence of his experiences on the Great Plains) we have suffered no untoward hardship, beyond discomfort from the heat and from stinging insects and a certain poisonous oak-like bush that resembles the infectious ivy of the East.

The Mexican flag has flown at full staff from the moment we stepped ashore here on the banks of the Rio de Los Americanos. It is raised at sun-up each day with full military ceremony, including drum and bugle, and is lowered in like manner each evening. Even though we arrived here with two fully loaded trade schooners and a pinnace, we are woefully short of supplies. On the voyage up the Bay of San Francisco we put in at the embarcadero of Don Ignacio Martinez at Carquinez where Captain Sutter arranged with that gentleman to supply us with some livestock, seed, and certain equipment not available at Yerba Buena. Two savages were sent from here to show Don Ignacio's *vaqueros* the road but they have not been heard from. As a consequence we have all but exhausted our supplies from Hinckley and Spear and rely more and more on wild game. Fortunately the area abounds in fish, waterfowl, elk, deer, antelope, and bear.

The savages hunt for themselves; their women, a filthy lot, gather acorns, roots, and certain insects including maggots which they prize as food. They also thrive on a cooked swill made of grains which they slop into their mouths with their hands from a long hog trough.

The captain, by rewarding them with various trinkets and by generous gifts to their chief, has induced these natives to make the mud bricks for the construction of a fort, which will be the first proper building in New Helvetia.

Captain Sutter has two small brass cannon. He has

made a demand upon Hinckley and Spear for a half dozen more of larger bore for the defense of the fort. (You will also find a requisition for same in his message to you.) I believe I enjoy the captain's confidence now, but am wary of questioning his intended use of the ordinance. He seems eager to reassure all that the cannon are only to discourage an uprising of savages. To my mind the argument does not brace square when I remember that he is incredibly proud of his power of persuasion with the savages. I believe the cannon are intended more to impress Governor Alvarado of his intention of keeping his bargain. Still, it is too early to fathom Sutter's ulterior purpose. My first resistance to him has lessened somewhat and I am persuaded to judge him sincere and just in his dealings with us.

We are now four whites, ten Kanakas, and three-score savages. The Indians have come from as far north as Rio de Las Plumas and the Rio Jesu Maria to join this settlement. It was at Rio de Las Plumas that the crews of the charter schooners threatened mutiny unless we turned back. Otherwise, we might well have established this fort deeper in the wilderness for the waters of the Buena Ventura or Rio Sacramento promise to remain navigable for some leagues.

The valley is one of great beauty. Even in autumn the ground is covered with tall green graze beneath great, spreading oak trees. Their groves extend from the distant coastal mountains in the west to the first evergreens in the Sierra foothills in the east. The Indian chief, Narcisco, tells me that stands of oak and other trees line the rivers for many days journeying to the north.

Captain Sutter believes the black loam along the rivers and the redlands higher up will produce prodigious amounts of any crop suited to the climate. Hereabouts, the cottonwood trees along the river are garlanded to fifty feet with arm-thick vines festooned with great purple clusters of delicious wild grapes. I do not doubt this land's fecundity. Proof of it may be seen on every hand. Not only is the valley literally infested with wild game for the table, but also with those of value for their furs. Lately, the skies are filled at dawn and at dusk with myriad migrating waterfowl. Wedges of geese and duck move across the sky during most of the day. Every foray, for whatever purpose, is certain to set off a feathered explosion of crested quail and raise clouds of wild pigeons and dove. The streams and upper tidewaters teem with a dozen varieties of fish. To this New Englander, accustomed to hard scratch, this is a veritable land of Goshen.

Given the opportunity, I would explore this region far more thoroughly than the captain is now likely to.

If this report does not illuminate as much as you had hoped, I ask your indulgence. Rest assured that I shall enter in my journal all events of possible significance and convey same to you, Sir, at reasonable intervals.

Your obedient servant,
John Lewis

Captain Cooper laid the letter aside. The men appeared to be occupied with their own thoughts. Cooper said slowly, "I incline to think we've chosen our man well. Sutter's argument for cannon 'doesn't brace square' the lad says here. I'll wager Lewis stays on until he finds out which way the wind blows."

Will Chard said, "A settlement means new settlers and fort means new soldiers. In the end I wonder if Alvarac will find this bargain to his liking?"

Cooper grunted and rose stiffly. "He will not! Jed Smith and Joe Walker opened the back door over the Sierra six years ago. Something tells me Sutter is going to make sure the latchstring is out." He knocked the soggy heel from his pipe into the fireplace.

There was some desultory speculation about the wisdom of extending credit to Sutter.

Thomas Larkin argued for caution. "Sufficient credit to my mind means enough for food, livestock, seed, and some building material. It does not include cannon, powder, and metal for grape shot and balls. Lewis' point is well taken. Why cannon to defend Sutter against natives he boasts will peaceably do his bidding? Against whom, then? Industrious men who wish to settle there?" He regarded them sourly. "As unlikely as the possibility that

79

he'd have occasion to defend himself against an invading army." He clasped one hand in the other as though to deter it from the temptation of dispensing money unwisely. "I will agree only to the minimum risk until he shows whose colors he flies."

Chard was the last to leave Cooper's house. As he left, Cooper said, "You've done us a service, Will. I do not think I speak too hastily in the lad's favor. He has a good fist for a quill too! Come to think about it, after reading the lad's view of the valley, I may have been hasty in trading my grant on the American River for the Bodega holdings."

Chard was surprised. "I didn't know there were grants so far north."

"There are. Mine was called El Rancho del Rio Ojotska. Governor Echeandía had a notion it would be useful to have citizens holding land there. When I married my good missus, the land was gifted to us. I've never set foot on it. But now I think this fellow, Sutter, has."

The reference to Doña Encarnacion Vallejo Cooper gave Will Chard the opportunity to inquire about something that had been puzzling him. "I have respected your wishes in this matter, but may I ask why you did not want Lewis to know that General Mariano Vallejo is your brother-in-law and that Governor Alvarado is Señora Cooper's nephew?"

Cooper returned the questioning smile. "And also that Tom Larkin is my half-brother? We could not reasonably expect the lad to understand such an apparent conflict of interest. If I had tried explaining he might have got wary. I doubt if his ironbound New England schoolboy mind could understand that in doing the opposite of what the *californio* officials want, we are actually preserving their long-term interests. He'll find out in time. But by then he'll know enough about California to understand."

Chard mounted without responding and Cooper moved to drop the gate poles. "How will you be occupying your time until spring?"

The seemingly innocent question made Will Chard smile inwardly. "For want of a choice, I'll be at my present pursuits—in the hope that Lewis' findings will benefit us all."

Blandly, Cooper returned Chard's probing gaze. "Aye. A sound course, I'd think."

On the long ride back to Graham's camp in the woods near Branciforte, Will Chard struggled to chart a clear path into the future. He was disappointed that the merchants had not really expressed their gratitude for his own part in providing them with good eyes and ears.

He wondered about the possibility of joining Sutter. If his settlement was successful, it could mean excellent trading possibilities along the river. A chance to grow. Then he remembered that Spear, Hinckley and Leese would monopolize any new bay and river trade—and with Vallejo's blessings. Jacob Leese had also married one of Mariano Vallejo's sisters. That made him Cooper's brother-in-law and, like Cooper, he was also Governor Alvarado's uncle by marriage.

He laughed bitterly. His plans to become a merchant trader by worming his way into the chosen group were both foolish and hopeless. Their flunky, really. Damn the groups and their stranglehold monopoly. It had to be broken and there was only one way to do it. California must be opened up to new settlers.

Chard considered the elements he must deal with. Their complicity was overwhelming. First there was Alvarado, subject to Castro's and Robles' influence and subject to the government in Mexico City—all determined not to let any more foreigners in. He smiled, however, as he thought of the weakness of the governor's plan to install Sutter and his settlement as protectors against infiltrators in the north. Any man who had explored the inland country knew the futility of such a plan. Chard wondered, too, how Vallejo would take the news that Sutter, not yet naturalized, had been commissioned by his nephew to establish an outpost fort.

Vallejo might well be the key to the situation. He was the wealthiest and most influential of the native *californios*. He could trade heavily on the fact of his huge ranch and powerful military garrison in the Sonoma Valley. He openly favored immigration now as the only sensible way to establish a strong and independent Alta California, one strong enough to bargain on favorable terms with any of the three foreign powers who were unquestionably interested in California.

But it was sheer stupidity to believe that Alta California would ever stand united against a common enemy or welcome a friendly power for the common good. If Alvarado cracked under the strain, then Mexico City would appoint another weak man, another Gutiérrez, and that would mean another revolt in the south by Pico and his supporters. Pio Pico would never stop trying to bring the capital and the customhouse to Los Angeles. If that happened it would mean economic disaster to Monterey. To forestall that the merchants in the north would prefer a takeover by a responsible foreign power—annexation, something that Vallejo would also welcome.

The merchants in the south had built huge trading empires, too. They would have to defend them and they would fight unless the tapering off of the hide trade continued. Open immigration and annexation would be the only way left to build their markets and that had to mean new merchants in new markets. The vision excited Chard and hardened his resolve to find a way in.

John Lewis kept his journal faithfully. Through the fall and winter of 1839 he recorded the progress at New Helvetia.

December 3, 1839

The first Indian trapping party set out this morning. Captain Sutter believes fur will be prime by the time they arrive on the northern streams. The Indians assure him that many beaver will be found on the Rio De Los Americanos and the Rio de las Plumas. The Captain hopes to receive two thousand pelts worth four dollars each. The trash fur will be used for garments and covers here.

Señor Martinez finally sent about one fifth of the supplies the Captain ordered. He also released our two mission Indians. He had impressed them without pay for the past four months. The Captain's good humor and optimism are remarkable. We are sorely in need of everything but he refuses to be downcast.

February 10, 1840

Two deserters from the Hudson's Bay Company trapping parties arrived last night. One is a Frenchman who speaks several Indian tongues and may be useful. The other is from the Ohio Valley. They are not the most promising specimens but we welcomed them. We are now six whites and only six Kanakas. Four of the Sandwich Islanders returned to Yerba Buena with Captain Davis on the *Isabella* and will not return. Two of them were women and will be missed. The Captain believes we will lose the others if this cold continues but nonetheless he plans to petition the Sandwich Island King for more immigrants. His audacity may turn the trick.

Tomorrow we set out to study the pattern of high water in these parts. We are in danger of being washed away by spring floods if we remain here. Captain Sutter will study the situation and choose a higher location for his fort and the permanent settlement of New Helvetia.

March 4, 1840

Trouble! Several weeks ago the Captain banished four Indians of trapping party No. 1. They had returned from the streams empty-handed. The Frenchman, Octave Custot, who has joined us from Martinez rancho, learned the truth from the trapper, Matignon. The Indians had done well with beaver but had met a party of Hudson's Bay men north of the Rio Buena Ventura. The whites had given them whiskey in exchange for our entire catch. Sutter sent them packing north to their Korusi village.

Last night the Captain's Sandwich Island bulldog set up a terrible commotion. We sprang from our beds to find a party of our own Indians preparing to assassinate Captain Sutter. The dog, of a sturdy breed brought to the tropical islands by the New England missionaries, had fastened himself on the hapless savage leader and ripped him badly. The clamor sent the others fleeing.

Captain Sutter brought the wounded savage to his room, attended to him, then forced him to name his accomplices. Most had fled but we apprehended a dozen and fetched them back. Matignon advised the Captain to execute them forthwith as an example. But Captain Sutter refuses to deal with them as criminals. He seems to count them merely unruly children and disciplines accordingly. He did promise to deal severely with any further attempts. (I agree with Matignon. From this night on I shall not sleep easily.)

March 10, 1840

Our troubles worsen!

There has been much unrest among the Indian workers here despite Captain Sutter's Christian forbearance. We have discovered since the incident at the Captain's door last week that most of the Indians have been concealing weapons in preparation for a general uprising. Also, they have been stealing and slaughtering our precious livestock.

Two days ago we discovered that many had deserted New Helvetia. Our scouts found they had withdrawn twenty miles southeast to a position just beyond the Rio Consumnes. Thoroughly angered at last, Captain Sutter mounted an armed party and took after them.

We found them at dawn this morning and killed six of their number including their chief. Many more were wounded. After an hour they threw down their weapons and begged for mercy. The Captain was forced to restrain Matignon, Custot, Harrow, and myself for, though none of our party suffered so much as a scratch, we felt that unless a proper example be made of them we should never know peace.

I must count Captain Sutter a courageous man but a foolish one. Again he has promised the savages forgiveness if they will return and work. He also promised to improve their lot and to give them more glass beads and trinkets. We shall see if this is sufficient. I suspect it will not be since he is teaching them the rewards of blackmail and revolution.

Meanwhile, I shall watch this experiment from behind a loaded rifle and a well-sharpened knife.

In mid-June Captain Sutter sent John Lewis to Monterey with a letter for Governor Alvarado. The letter stated that Sutter would be arriving in the capital toward the end of August to receive his Mexican citizenship. There had been no time for John to advise Will Chard or Captain Cooper of his trip. When he arrived at the Cooper home minutes after sundown the Captain's greeting was cordial enough but Lewis sensed that the man was disturbed. "By God, John—come in! You're welcome, of course. But I'm not sure you'll be happy with the news I have for you."

Cooper helped him unsaddle and they turned the animal free in the corral.

Once inside the house, Cooper wasted no time on preliminaries. "Alvarado's shipped Will Chard and Isaac Graham off to prison in Mexico, at San Blas. About two score of Graham's men were sent with them. Castro put them aboard, in chains, by God, like animals!"

Dumbfounded, questions began tumbling from John's lips.

Cooper held up a restraining hand. "Lad, we think we know who's behind this but we can't prove it. The whole lot are charged with treason. Alvarado issued the warrant and Castro and his soldiers ambushed them in their cabins."

"Is Will all right?"

"He's unhurt. But it's a miracle. Two of the men were badly shot up and cut. That bastard, Castro, hamstrung Naile like an ox. He'll never walk proper again, if he lives."

"What about Harry Morrison? Did Castro go to Natividad?"

"Aye. They caught men there too, but not Morrison, so far as I know."

"Thank God for that!" But John was not reassured. Harry Morrison would never have deserted his men at the distillery, and it seemed unlikely that he would not be there.

Cooper continued his indignant recital. "They threw the lot of them into one little room at the old barracks. No food. No water. Tom Larkin and I protested and we managed to get a little to them. It's been five weeks now that Alvarado's refused to see us. He's refused to listen to anyone, even to Mariano Vallejo, who came down to protest."

Still incredulous, John struggled to curb his mounting anger. "I know those men! They have no minds for anything political. It would be contrary to Graham's plans to try such a thing. And you know Chard."

Captain Cooper made a placating gesture. "Aye. We do indeed. We've made the strongest representations, particularly for Chard. But Alvarado's still convinced that Graham was up to something. There was talk of a fake horse race that would be the excuse to bring all of his men into Monterey to bet on a new stallion Graham's said to have bought. The way Castro had it, the men would wait for the proper moment then pounce on the troops, kidnap Alvarado, and take Monterey."

"Take it for whom, for God's sake?"

Cooper shrugged. "That's another question that's not been answered, lad. But it's been suggested that the United States was behind it, as it doubtless is in Texas."

"That's bilge! I don't know about matters in Texas. But I'd stake my life that Graham and Chard are no part of any such plot here. I rode in with a letter from Sutter to the governor. When I deliver it, I'll speak for them."

Cooper took John by the arm and steered him to a chair. "You'll not do that, lad. Unless you want to risk chains and a trip to San Blas yourself. And it strikes me you were not very smart to be carrying the post for Sutter either, not to Monterey. It might be well for you to remember that it was the three of us who suggested you join Sutter. Not Alvarado."

John knew he was hearing the truth. Suddenly he felt foolish. In his effort to do an effective job for the merchants he had come to think of himself as their man, enjoying their immunity. Now, with the new turn of events, he realized how little immunity he really had.

Cooper held out a hand. "You'd best give me the letter. I'll get it to the governor. A schooner arrived from Yerba Buena this morning. As port captain I'd naturally receive the mail packets. I'll see that Alvarado gets the letter this evening, at his home."

A bit uncertainly, John removed the folded, wax-sealed paper from his pocket and handed it over. Cooper tucked it in his jacket. "Good. I'll tell Doña Encarnacion that you'll have supper with us. You'll stay here tonight. And I wouldn't show myself around the town too much."

Cooper left the room and returned shortly with two glasses of sherry. He handed one to John. "You'll be wanting to know what's being done for Will. Everything possible. The British consul in Tepic is looking into the matter now—acting for the United States too. David Spence got him onto it. Larkin's written to the Department of State in Washington and it's my opinion that Larkin will go to

Mexico City himself, if necessary. Also, we've forwarded some funds to the consul for the men's use, informally, of course."

Unable to believe that the governor could turn on the man who had marched with him, who had been responsible for sending the Mexican governor, Gutiérrez, into exile and insuring home rule for the *californios*, John began a bitter indictment of Alvarado.

Cooper cut him off. "It's treachery, right enough. But you're laying it at the wrong door. The root of it goes back to Castro's jealousy and his fear of Graham's riflemen. Goyo Robles and his friend Antonio Osio have cleverly encouraged it. But the perfidious act that brought about the sneak raid properly should be laid at the door of the church."

"The *church?*"

"Aye. Or at least at the feet of Father Varga."

Bewildered, John gestured helplessly. "But the church keeps away from politics now."

Cooper agreed. "True. True. It began with Goyo Robles. He was told that Tokoya, an Indian who had been one of Graham's men, heard Graham and Chard plotting to take over all of Alta California. Goyo wasted no time persuading Father Varga to seek out the Indian and administer the oath of truth to him." Cooper spread his hands. "Who is not to believe a priest? Anyway, it was sufficient to make Alvarado take action." He added slyly, "We have it on very good authority. Señorita Maria Robles, no less."

John was half out of the chair. "Robles' own sister? *Why?*"

"Because, lad, it seems she doesn't agree with her brother in all things." John thought he detected a suggestion of a twinkle in the older man's eyes. "I'm told by my good wife that Señorita Maria feels some Yankees should be excepted—particularly a young seaman from the *Reliant* who she thought was staying with Graham."

John hoped that he was managing to conceal his excitement. "Perhaps I'll have a chance to thank the lady for her concern."

Cooper nodded gravely. "Later perhaps."

Returning to safer ground, John asked, "Alvarado would take the testimony of an Indian, even under oath, against men who helped him to power?"

"Lad," Cooper's tone was sympathetic, "the whole affair is preposterous. But it's a fact. All we can hope for now is the triumph of justice, and soon." A vagrant thought caused him to chuckle. "As a matter of fact, some justice has been done already. The officials at San Blas also interned Castro and two of his officers and sent them to Mexico City. We do not know the reason for sure. The speculation is that Castro was so eager to get rid of his prisoners that he hustled them off without providing a bill of particulars or formal charges against them. The Mexican authorities would not look kindly on anyone dumping forty or fifty unwanted revolutionaries on them. The central government probably feels that since Alvarado makes so much of being a home-rule governor he should have taken the responsibility for sentencing and deporting them. And I quite agree. A fair trial here, without dealing with the practical matter of an illegal distillery, would probably have found the men innocent. My guess is, neither Alvarado nor Castro cared to risk that."

Thoughtfully, John resumed sipping his sherry. Cooper was right. It would be folly to attempt to intercede with Alvarado for Chard. It would be good to see Maria Robles again, to thank her for her concern. But that probably was impossible. The most important thing now was to find some way to rid himself both of the onus of fugitivism and of his known association with Graham and Chard. Until that was done there would be no security for him, even though the merchants might vouch for him privately.

"Sir."

"Yes, John?"

"In time, would you see any way that I might be able to move freely around Monterey? I'm not a fugitive. I was within my legal rights. I'm tired of skulking in the night. I intend nothing but good for California. I find it has great beauty and I'd truly like to stay on the coast without continual fear for my freedom."

As he spoke, John watched Cooper's expression change from mild interest to serious concern. Finally he looked up. "Yes, lad. There's a way. To tell you the truth, I hadn't thought of it when we sent you to keep an eye on Sutter." He nodded in the direction of an adjoining room. "Do you know the contents of that letter?"

"Yes, sir. I wrote it for the Captain."

"It is confidential?"

88

John considered briefly. "No, sir. It is mainly to advise the governor that the Captain will come to Monterey in August to receive his citizenship and to apply for land."

"Is that all?"

A slow grin warmed John's face. "He did add a post-script, sir, asking the governor to persuade you and Mr. Larkin, also Mr. Spence, to extend him more credit."

Cooper snorted. "By God, I could have guessed that!" He put his glass aside. "All right, John. Wait until Sutter's a citizen, then get him to vouch for you and countersign your formal application for citizenship. You'll get it if Sutter convinces Alvarado that you're indispensable to both of them."

Captain Johann Augustus Sutter, soon to be Don Juan Augusto Sutter, citizen of the Republic of Mexico, entered Monterey on the afternoon of a perfect August day at the head of a cavalcade consisting of an armed guard of honor of which John Lewis was the leader, two *vaqueros,* and some thirty horses.

The lookout posted by Governor Alvarado spied the party and spurred to a gallop to bring word to the fort. Then the hills around Monterey echoed with the booming of the old cannon. It was the signal the capital had been waiting for: Monterey had its excuse for a fandango.

Somewhat uncertain about his situation, John was careful to allow the gathering crowd to screen him from the governor. Some weeks before, Sutter had sent a letter urging the governor to grant immunity and to give citizenship to John Lewis, "this intelligent and courageous young man who has become my good right arm and without whom I should experience great difficulty in hastening the establishment of this fort so necessary to the defense of the interior."

John's anxiety had mounted until two weeks ago when Sutter received a note from Alvarado saying: "The young man may accompany you to Monterey on this happy occasion, certain that he travels under my protection."

Sutter's cavalcade arrived at the customhouse and the crowd pressed in to hear the governor's official speech of welcome. On foot, holding his own mount, John watched the people. He estimated there were over a hundred. In addition to the festively dressed Montereyans, the Indians, and *mestizos,* there were the crewmen from several of the ships lying at anchor in the bay. Once he thought he caught a glimpse of Goyo Robles and Antonio Osio down in front and he craned to see if Maria had come with her brother. He did not see Captain Cooper sidling unobtrusively through the crowd. "Welcome, lad. Why do you stay back?"

Startled, he turned to find the merchant offering his hand. He took it, somewhat surprised, for it was the first time Cooper had made the conventional gesture.

"I'm not much for ceremonies, sir."

Cooper moved closer, speaking softly. "Sutter is to stay at the Alvarado home. I could not be certain you would ride in. But on the chance, we've prepared a room for you. We'll expect you when this nonsense is finished." He waved in the direction of the speaker. "There's a fandango tonight. Tomorrow there'll be games and a bull and bear fight at the old presidio. At some point we'll make time for a little personal visit. We're anxious to know how things proceed." He looked at John closely. "Sutter has spoken for you, eh?"

"More properly you would say that I spoke for myself—on paper—and Captain Sutter signed."

Pleased at the forthrightness of the reply, Cooper said, "I'll wager that was the best you've ever written." He gave John's shoulder a pat. "If things work out, you'll find Spence, Larkin, and myself ready to speak for you, too, John." He moved away as unobtrusively as he had come.

Twilight had descended by the time the ceremonies granting Sutter citizenship were over. John waited with Captain Cooper for the arrival of the Spences and the Larkins, who would join them for dinner.

"We'll not be able to talk as freely as we'd like, lad," Cooper said. "Not that the women aren't dependable—if we threaten them judiciously—but if we bore them with business, they'll even the score and bore us with fashion. So tell me now, briefly, what you think Sutter's game is."

"It's too early to tell. There are two more trappers now. Nine of us in all. But we don't have enough of anything—not even good straw for bricks. None of the supplies the governor promised have arrived. If Sutter has anything in mind beyond setting up his fort and getting enough cattle and seed for crops, he's not shown his hand yet."

"If he got the items he needs for building and planting, do you think he'd make profitable use of them?"

Lewis nodded. "I think he'd try."

"Are you suggesting that we give him much more credit?"

"No sir. But I'm suggesting that unless he gets some credit soon, I'll be out of a job."

The fandango was held in front of the two-story government house overlooking the harbor. An area nearly fifty *varas* square had been broomed clean by Indian women and sprinkled down the previous night and again in the late afternoon. Surrounding the dancing area were dozens of pitch flares tied in place on high stakes. Strung between them on heavy cord were brightly colored pennants.

Dressed in their most extravagant finery, Governor Alvarado, Secretary of State Casarin, and their wives and the honored guest, Johann Augustus Sutter, emerged from the government house. The shabbily uniformed Monterey Military Band played earnestly, making up with determination what they lacked in talent. The official party watched as most of Monterey's men and women danced the *californio* variations of the *paso doble*, the *vals*, the *jota*, the *son*, and the bouncy *cortejo de las pulgas*, a favorite with the more daring young couples, whose pantomimed pinching gestures imitating the courtship of the fleas scandalized the older women.

Because he was not familiar with the dances, John watched from the sidelines. Most of his attention was directed to Maria Robles. Among a score of overly ornamented unmarried girls and young wives, most of whom were dressed in expensive silk gowns with daringly low cut bodices, Maria's beauty stood out. Her slender body moved with regal grace and then with fiery abandon through the intricate variations of the dances. She paired with Goyo to dance the controversial *cortejo*. Her delicately suggestive responses to the overtures of the male flea brought laughter and applause from all, including the governor.

Grudgingly, John acknowledged the grace of the *californio* men, who were equally at home in a saddle or on the *pista de danze*. Dressed in flaring pantaloons and fine cotton shirts with elaborately decorated black velvet vests, Goyo, Antonio, and a half dozen other young men deserved the admiration they were receiving from the female spectators. As he watched them, John recalled a comment Harry Morrison had made during a discussion of the trouble with Goyo. "Riding and dancing and plotting and gambling and fornicating. That's all they're good for, laddie! But ye'll find that knavery's their greatest accomplishment."

The dancing lasted until past midnight. When it was over, John made his leisurely way up the gentle slope to the Cooper adobe. Weary from the long ride to Monterey and the festivities, he slept until mid-morning, when Captain Cooper rapped on the door. "If you've turned out, John, there are some gentlemen here for a talk."

In the sitting room he was greeted by Larkin and Spence, who presented him to Don José Robles. Don José smiled warmly and extended his hand. "I have waited for the opportunity to apologize for my son's questionable hospitality. I was visiting Los Robledos. Otherwise, my friend, you would have had an entirely different welcome."

Surprised, John found himself at a loss for a graceful response. Don José changed the subject. "Señor Lewis, I'm afraid we are about to impose on you a second time." John Cooper indicated a chair.

"I hate to put you to work on an empty stomach, lad, but your employer, Mr. Sutter, has made a proposal to Don José and I took the liberty of suggesting that he speak to you about it."

"Señor Lewis, your Captain Sutter proposes that I sell him fifty quintales of wheat and barley on credit at nearly double the market price. I am anxious of course to do anything to assist the Captain in a project so favored by our governor. But the credit is the question. I am not a man of great means and the loss of that income could be of great consequence to me and my family." He hesitated. "I intend no disservice to Señor Sutter but we are all agreed that his credit is, well, perhaps not soundly established yet."

Had Don José not made a point of stating that an error in judgment would jeopardize his family as well, John would have leaned over backward to justify the extension of credit. But now the problem confronting John was how to answer fairly for all. Before he could frame his answer, Larkin broke in, "I think it's obvious, Don José, that our friend is troubled by some doubts. So I'll make an alternate proposal. I'll pay you market price, in cash, and take upon myself the risk of extending credit to Mr. Sutter on the terms he proposed to you. Since the governor has blessed the undertaking at New Helvetia I do not feel the risk unseemly. The man is already modestly entered on our books."

John saw Cooper's eyes widen with surprise, then crinkle with amusement. Little wonder, he thought, that Larkin, Cooper's half brother, had come to Monterey as his clerk and had managed in so short a time to become the leading merchant in the north.

With Graham's distillery all but shut down, Sutter would have a market for his spirits. Whiskey required grain. John wondered about Harry Morrison. In all likelihood he was no longer at Natividad. If Morrison was safe and could be induced to set up Sutter's still, there would be some justification for extending credit to make *aguardiente*. If the output reached Monterey, Larkin would market it. The local officials, for a price, had closed their eyes to Graham's illegal traffic. Surely, he thought, they would be stone blind to Larkin's. As it was, the merchants were able to land dozens of kegs of good Scotch whisky through the surf at night while the collector of customs conveniently found engagements elsewhere.

Larkin interrupted John's musings. "In order to insure my risk, Mr. Lewis, I would be willing to sell Captain Sutter the grain at a modest bonus if he will ⸻ t his entire output, beyond his household needs, to m, ompany. Do you think that is possible and practical?"

"It could be very fair for all, sir. And it could be practical if we can be assured of the try pots and copper for a larger still."

David Spence, silent until now, said, "We can assure Captain Sutter these items." He turned to the others. "Can we not, gentlemen?"

Cooper nodded. "Aye. No problem there."

Lewis wondered at the good grace with which they had apparently taken their outmaneuvering by the Yankee merchant until he decided that so far as the Monterey merchants were concerned, "One hand washes the other."

After the men left, John Cooper rested a hand paternally on John's shoulder. "A good start was made for everybody this morning. I am glad you did not endorse Sutter's credit too enthusiastically. That will count for you here, too." He gave the shoulder a thump. "Now get some food, son."

3 SHORTLY AFTER MIDDAY, John strolled slowly toward the arena where the bloody bull and bear fights, the favorite diversion of the *californios*, would take place. Deliberately, he had allowed Maria and her mother Doña Gertrudis, to move ahead of him. When they passed, Maria had turned, pretending a casual interest in the crowd. He made no effort to acknowledge recognition but determined to find a seat near her. The night before, her gleaming black hair had been pulled into a large bun worn low on her neck. This afternoon it was divided into two glossy braids into which had been woven bright strands of colored silk. Her elaborately embroidered blouse was gathered tightly around her tiny waist beneath a bright green sash. Her skirt was ankle-length, black and decorated with a bold design of yellow, red, and blue flowers and large green leaves. She was, John thought, extraordinarily beautiful. The risk with Goyo notwithstanding, he wanted more than anything to know her better. The memory of those hours when she had acted as his reluctant jailer had stayed with him through the months.

There were times when the need for a woman turned him restless and finally tormented him until he, or nature, had relieved the suffering. But during none of those times of faceless fantasy had the girl been Maria. "A mon's balls be a bloody burden to carry alone too long, laddie." Harry Morrison had observed once during a restless period at Natividad. "But it's nae good to risk the pox with a verminous savage." Sailors and frontiersmen as well relieved their sex urgencies as they relieved their bladders and bowels and that was the end of it until they could get ashore and find a woman. John had found tolerable women in South America and in the ports along the Central American coast and he had washed his parts with raw brandy and endured the frightful sting that could keep him

95

clean. But always the experiences had left him feeling anxious and somehow unsatisfied.

Now, as he neared the arena, a voice called his name. He turned to see Captain Cooper and Doña Encarnacion. "You'll sit with us, John." Grateful, he fell into step, hoping the Robles family would be seated nearby.

At the grandstand he helped the captain get Doña Encarnacion to a seat that commanded a view of the entire enclosure. John liked the kind, buxom, dark-eyed woman who, though she spoke little to him, made him feel welcome.

Finally seated fashionably but not much more securely than the common spectators opposite them, John looked around and discovered that they were two tiers above and a few feet to the right of the Robles party. When Captain Cooper and Don José exchanged greetings, Don José signaled up and called out softly, *"Muchas gracias, señor."*

Maria turned with studied nonchalance, then averted her eyes as John smiled and replied, *"De nada, señor."* He saw the girl turn to her father and question him. Don José's answer was interrupted by the release of the first bull. He was a handsome animal—a brown and white Mexican longhorn, heavy-necked and wild, one of the largest, most ferocious-looking range bulls John had seen. A cry of anticipation echoed from the stands as the animal hurtled from the *toril* and came to a braced-leg halt just beyond mid-ring. On the far side of the arena, Goyo Robles and Antonio Osio mounted their stallions. Moments later they entered the ring, holding *reatas* looped and ready.

In perfect accord, Robles spurred his animal and reined it to the left to distract the bull while Osio made ready to lasso a hind leg. The entire maneuver was executed so quickly that John found it difficult to follow.

The instant the bull began its charge, Osio's *reata* streaked out and snared a hind leg. The move required incredible timing. The hoof was clear of the ground for only a fraction of a second. To prevent his companion's mount from taking the full straight-line shock, Goyo Robles swerved his own mount to divert the charging animal into a turn. As he did so the yardwide spread of twisted horns grazed the stallion's flank. When Osio's braced mount brought the bull to a jarring halt, Goyo's *reata* leaped from his hand and the rawhide loop dropped over the deadly horns. While Osio's superbly trained animal kept the strain, the rider dismounted, rushed to the bull, seized its tail and began to twist it. Shouts of encouragement went up from the stands as the bull, caught front and rear, thrashed helplessly and began to fall. A final twist brought the animal crashing to the ground. At the same instant a helper, on foot, raced out dragging a long length of rigging chain. While Osio maintained the painful pressure on the bull's tail the links were secured to the animal's right rear leg.

On a signal from Goyo, two more horsemen entered the ring, their mounts plunging and straining to drag a heavy iron-strapped cage fitted with hardwood runners. A wave of excitement swept over those close enough to catch a glimpse of the bear inside the cage. John estimated the cage to be ten feet long by four feet wide and nearly as high. He was amazed that the animal appeared to fill it. Don José half rose, then turned to call out to Cooper. "See him! *Madre de Dios!* He is the largest I have seen in many years. Goyo and Antonio caught him near Gavilan. They say it took ten men to cage him. I believe it." He craned for a better view. "Goyo thinks he weighs six hundred kilos."

At roughly two and one fifth pounds to a kilo, John computed the animal's weight at better than thirteen hundred pounds—by any measure a monster.

While one of the riders dismounted, the helper dragged the free end of the chain to the cage door. The horseman removed a heavy pair of blacksmith's tongs from a saddle thong and waited until the kneeling helper had pried up the slotted cage door sufficiently for the tool to insert beneath it. After several attempts that enraged the grizzly the tongs were clamped around a forefoot and the stump-thick member was forced out far enough to secure the chain.

As the moment of the fight drew near, John found his excitement mounting. Because of the chains that linked them, both animals were at a disadvantage. In a natural confrontation, the battle might well cover a league or more. It would be a different matter in the arena. The bear, finding himself bested as often happened, might succeed in freeing itself and turn on the spectators in its panicked attempt to escape.

John had heard stories of the first bull and bear fight in

97

California. There had been no arena. The rawhide tethers had snapped and the retreating animal had clawed and slashed its way to freedom, killing or maiming a dozen people.

He wished now that he could see Maria's face in order to watch her reaction to the bloody encounter. He knew that his own sister quite probably would be sickened at the first sight of violence.

A hush fell over the crowd and John could see that the helper was preparing to raise the door. Goyo and Antonio were waiting to slip their *reatas* free. The other horsemen had fastened their *reatas* to the rear of the cage to pull it clear of the arena.

Osio increased the twist strain on the bull's tail as Robles' *reata* slackened. A flick of his wrist carried the loop free. Retrieving the braided rawhide as he moved, he urged his mount back in order to bait the bull into a charge as soon as it regained its feet. Then, in a series of moves executed so rapidly that they seemed to be one, Osio released the tail, freed his *reata*, and leaped into the saddle.

For a long moment the bull lay still, its rage-reddened eyes rolling wildly. Then, with the sudden realization that it had been freed, it convulsed, gave a great heave, and came up on all fours. Frothing, it charged straight at Goyo's mount.

A great roar went up as the force of the rush jerked the outraged grizzly from its cage. Fascinated by the raw brutality of the encounter, John forgot Maria for the moment. The grizzly, a deceptive monster who appeared awkward to the uninitiated as he was revealed in all his enormity, scrambled to his feet, snapped frantically at the chain around his foreleg, then saw the bull. Taking his natural enemy for his true antagonist, he sprang with incredible agility and landed full upon the bull's back. The chain thrashed crazily as both animals crashed to the ground. The bull, surprised from behind, struggled to turn its horns on the unseen adversary. A bucking heave sent the bear sprawling. In an instant it was on its feet again. Faced off, each sought the instinctive advantage needed for the kill. The bull wanted its horns in the bear's soft belly and the bear wanted its claws and teeth in the bull's thick throat. The bull charged first. The bear rose to meet it and the impact shook the ground and brought a wild shout from the spectators.

While the bear was still erect, attempting to get its fore-legs in position for a crushing embrace, the bull's head dropped and hooked up viciously. Another shout from those nearest the action brought the audience to its feet. The great curving horn had gouged deep into the bear's belly. Driving home his advantage, the bull continued to hook and each new thrust brought an outraged protest from the grizzly.

Suddenly the bear reared back and fell free. Blood pulsed in a thick stream from the gore wound. Men shouted and women and children screamed, calling for the kill.

Dazed, the bull stood with lowered head. On its feet again, the grizzly rushed in low and struck a clubbing blow at the bull's heavy cheekbone. The great head and horns snapped to one side. Quicker than any spectator's eye the bear's jaws drove in under the bull's muzzle and clamped high up on the throat. A vicious twist brought both animals tumbling to the ground. The grizzly's hind legs doubled and drove out straight again. Four-inch claws slashed into the bull's underbelly and laid it open down to the pendulous testicles. Burgeoning entrails, opalescent in the sun, bulged from the ragged rip. An agonized bawling filled the arena.

Through the screaming crowd, John caught glimpses of Maria Robles. She was watching, engrossed, her fingers pressed against her mouth as though to stifle an outcry. Another shout went up as the grizzly's claws ripped the exposed intestines and spilled their steaming feces on the ground.

In the arena again, Goyo Robles and Antonio Osio maneuvered their mounts into position to separate the animals. Seconds later, the stallions straining at the *reatas* pulled the combatants apart. The intestines that were still caught in the hooks of the bear's claws trailed from the open belly cavity in gleaming ribbons, tautened elastically and snapped apart as the bull began to convulse.

The helper loosened the chain around the bear's leg and secured a second *reata* to it. The free end was carried into the cage and threaded through the back bars. Osio therew two hitches around the saddle horn and dragged the mad-dened grizzly back into its cage. John, still watching Maria's reactions, turned back to the ring in time to see Goyo's knife slash across the bull's throat and plunge hilt-deep to the jugular vein. A font of blood spurted from the gash, soaking his arm to the elbow in crimson gore. Laughing, he pulled the knotted handkerchief from his head and wiped at it.

While wagers were being settled around the arena, the men at the pens examined the bear and decided it could fight again. The second contest was brief. An old range bull, no longer agile, did not survive the second charge and in less than fifteen minutes, Goyo and his helpers dragged its still twitching carcass into the street where, amid swarms of flies and a pack of wild street dogs, the first victim was being crudely butchered by the Indians.

The crowd, well pleased by the first fight but disappointed by the second, grumbled its way out of the stands. John helped Captain Cooper assist Doña Encarnacion down from the seats. The Robles family reached the ground first but were caught in the crowd making its way out. Without meaning to, Lewis found himself within inches of Maria. For the first time he saw her close up in full light. During the brief moment that their eyes met, he found himself trembling. Without warning, the idea of returning to New Helvetia with Sutter became unthinkable. Somehow he had to find a way to stay in Monterey.

His mind was whirling and he was scarcely aware that Don José was presenting Doña Gertrudis and Maria and her two cousins, Dolores and Secundino, or that Goyo had ridden up and was watching them from the end of the stands. John acknowledged the introductions awkwardly.

Don José was obliquely apologetic about the quality of the fights. "The second bull, that for certain would have finished the bear, broke its leg. The old one was all the men could find nearby at the last minute. We are sorry to perform so badly for our guest of honor." He glanced toward John Sutter, who was with the governor, talking animatedly. "But one day, here in Monterey, we shall have *corridas* as fine as those of Mexico City, Señor Lewis. Then you will not see just a contest between brutes. You will see man ennobled by the ultimate discipline," he turned toward Goyo, who was dismounting, "the triumph of reason over force. A great matador becomes almost a god when he also triumphs over man's fear of death. It is an ancient rite, not understood by all." He turned back and looked at John questioningly. "Have you ever seen such a *corrida de toros?*"

John shook his head. "No, sir. But I think I would enjoy one. I admire skill."

Out of the corner of his eye he saw Goyo pushing through the crowd to join them.

Captain Cooper cleared his throat and turned hastily to greet Goyo. "The bear was magnificent! Will he fight again?"

Goyo nodded curtly and made no effort to conceal his displeasure at John Lewis' presence. "He will fight again, captain, and he will fight well." His dark, narrow face broke into a malevovent grin. "He is a native bear. To him range bulls are intruders."

The gold flecks in Maria Robles' brown eyes turned to little points of fire as she glared mutely at her brother. She took her father's arm. "We are detaining Captain Cooper, papa." She urged him forward. "Besides, we should arrange to visit in a more comfortable place."

Goyo smirked at his sister. "Why not at our house? The last time Señor Lewis was there he found it very difficult to leave." The impertinence brought a gasp from Maria. Goyo pushed past John and went toward Governor Alvarado's party.

Goyo's mother, Doña Gertrudis, a slender, once-pretty woman in her mid-forties, looked after her son unhappily.

Don José said hastily, "I know Goyo. He feels he did badly at the morning games. And he blamed himself for the young bull's broken leg. He wanted things to go stupendously well today," he glanced toward the governor, "for his excellency."

A half hour of daylight remained but it was gloomy in the Coopers' big adobe. John helped his host light the lamps and accepted a sherry. Cooper, seated opposite, seemed preoccupied. Several minutes passed in silence before the captain set his drink aside. "This business with Goyo is not necessarily personal, lad. In time he'll come to accept you. Having you taken away from him by Graham was bad enough. But having you back here under Alvarado's protection is rubbing salt in his wound." He frowned. "And I don't suppose you've noticed, but his sister's disposition to be friendly hasn't helped him either."

John pretended indifference. "She seemed polite."

Cooper looked up, amused. "Aye, lad. That she can be. They're well raised. Don José's one of the few true gentlemen among the *californios*. The daughter's got a lot of fire like Goyo though. Ask the suitors who pester her with serenades. She can torment them unmercifully."

John suffered a quick stab of misgiving. Certainly he had seen evidence of her spirit at the fandango. But during his captivity and also at the bull and bear fight, he thought he had sensed another quality—an underlying disapproval of cruelty. At the arena she had averted her eyes during the worst of it and had not seemed to revel in the kill as most of the others had.

Cooper interrupted his thoughts. "When do you think Sutter will return to New Helvetia?"

"Within the week. Vioget is overseeing things, but the Captain doesn't trust him to handle the savages."

"I wouldn't trust *anybody* to handle them! Not even the *padres* any more since Governor Echeandía tied their hands with the secularization order nine years ago. Left to themselves, Indians will never work. If Sutter can get a day's work out of them, I doff my cap to him."

Lewis knew he was right. "Captain Sutter will never build what he wants at New Helvetia unless he can get good men to settle there."

"I wouldn't debate that point, lad," Cooper replied. "John, go on back with Sutter for a while longer. We'll ease his credit a wee bit and watch him. By the way, is he paying you as he promised?"

"Not in cash. I have no need for money up there. He's keeping it in his strongbox."

"You keep it in *your* strongbox, lad! Then you'll know it's there."

John felt foolish. "The captain's got the only one worth locking. I have no reason to mistrust him—so far." And he wondered then about the money the three merchants were crediting to him and whether or not he had better worry about that, too.

The formal ceremony investing Johann Augustus Sutter with citizenship in the Republic of Mexico was held in private in the office of Secretary of State, Jimeno Casarin. As soon as the proclamation was posted, Sutter began a drive to sign up men for New Helvetia. He bought dozens of drinks in the cantinas. Indirectly, he urged merchant sailors to desert. After two days of hard recruiting the best he was able to manage were six Spanish-speaking former mission Indians.

Late in the afternoon, John walked the dejected new citizen to the governor's home, where he had remained as a guest. A few yards from the entry, John stopped deliberately. For forty-eight hours he had done little but think of some pretext on which he could remain in Monterey. On the previous day he had met Maria on the Calle Principal. She had been with Don José and Doña Gertrudis. She had gone out of her way to speak to him and invited him to attend a *partida del campo*. He had declined with obvious reluctance, explaining that he was obliged to return to New Helvetia. There had been no mistaking the girl's disappointment. Casually, she had let him know that Goyo had gone to Branciforte for a few days. Don José, apparently still anxious to make amends for his son's behavior, had urged John to persuade Sutter to stay over and join them. John had been sorely tempted, but he decided against it because he was afraid of revealing his real purpose.

After a restless night, his strategy had come clear. Now bracing himself, he said to Sutter, "Captain, I haven't spoken before because I did not want to risk disappointing you at a time like this. But I believe it is possible that Captain Cooper and the others will extend more credit."

Sutter's china-blue eyes rounded. "*Wunderbar!* I shall write a list immediately! I shall present it tomorrow."

"Excuse me, captain, but I don't think that would be wise."

"No, why not? Why not?"

"I have taken advantage of my position as a guest in Captain Cooper's home to plead our case. But I have had to do it with great care. The merchants here do not have much confidence in your plan."

Sutter began to puff indignantly and John hurried on. "Only because they lack your imagination, captain, but if you will let me stay on here for a while, I think I know how we can win them to your way of thinking."

Mollified, Sutter was eager again. "*Ja? Ja?* How? Tell me—how?" When he was excited or angered, Sutter sprinkled his heavily accented English with German words.

"I am certain I can convince them of the importance of

103

your work at New Helvetia," John said as calmly as he could. "They ask me many questions. If I—"

Sutter's thick arms flung outward. "You have no more important work than this, Lewis. Stay. By all means, as long as necessary!"

A troubled expression clouded John's face. Sutter saw it. "What is wrong? Something is wrong, Lewis?"

"Sir, I am here in Monterey under your protection. When you leave I will have nobody to turn to—in case—"

Sutter dismissed his anxiety. "You have the governor's word. That is the best protection."

"But was it offered beyond this visit?"

"But of course it was! There was no time limit!"

Still unconvinced, John glanced toward the house. "All the same, sir, I'd feel better, I'd have a freer mind to work for you, if you could speak to him again—to make certain."

Sutter gestured expansively. *"Gewiss!* Certainly! I'll speak to him immediately." He stepped closer, smiling conspiratorily. "It is a magnificent plan, Lewis. Alvarado will be happy to agree. If my credit comes from the merchants, that will be even less he will have to pay from the treasury. It would be good business for him to agree. I shall speak to him immediately."

Sutter started to move away, then stopped abruptly. "These people are much friendlier after I asked to become a citizen." His voice dropped to a breathy whisper. "Have you ever considered this idea?"

Quite honestly, John replied that he had. He did not say that the thought had come to him at the same time he had been overwhelmed by Maria Robles.

"Good, Lewis. Good. When I ask for the governor's continuing protection for you I will be very clever. I will also hint that your great admiration for him inspires you to seek citizenship." He tapped John's shirtfront for emphasis. "And I shall tell him how important you are to his plans in New Helvetia—and how smart you are," he drew away a little, "and how much cleverness and courage awakened love can give a man." John felt his face drain and his guts knot and prayed that Sutter hadn't noticed. "Alvarado himself found such courage, my young friend, because of his love for California. And you and I have it too—because we share that love with him." He clapped

John on the shoulder. "Don't you worry!" He moved away. *"Buenas tardes, amigo!"*

That night, after dinner, John Cooper and David Spence were both aware of John's preoccupation. Puzzled, Cooper broached the matter. "You look like you've started a seam, lad. What's troubling you?"

It was the question John Lewis hoped to elicit and the one he feared. The outcome would probably depend on how successfully he had concealed his interest in Maria Robles. He said slowly, "Something unexpected has come up, sir. Captain Sutter wants me to stay in Monterey for a while."

The two merchants exchanged anxious glances. "What for, lad?"

"He does not feel that he's had time enough to impress upon the governor the importance of getting all of the supplies he needs and enough workers to do the job in time."

Cooper made a wordless sound of annoyance and fussed with his pipe. David Spence shook his head. "He'll never get the workers here in Monterey, even with Graham gone. As for the supplies, we're prepared to let him have modest amounts."

Lewis looked from one to the other, concerned. "I know for a fact that you and Mr. Larkin could not supply all he needs. Captain Sutter feels—"

Cooper exploded. "Just what in hell is this Sutter a captain of? I wish somebody'd explain that to me! If he was a captain in Charles the Tenth's Palace Guard I'll wager he went over to Louis Philippe's side after the first shot. As a drummer boy. Captain indeed!"

Spence laughed. "A good point. But never mind his title. I suspect it's like much else about him—subject to question." He turned back to John. "You were saying, 'Captain Sutter feels—'?"

"He feels that his best chance of getting the fort and the shops built in time to be effective is for me to convince the governor to appropriate a good sum for it and order some conscript workers north to get things done. He will suggest to the governor that I might make a good citizen."

Both men were startled by an idea that had not occurred to either of them. Spence said firmly, "Sutter must not suspect that you're our man. You'll have to stay here for a while, but that may not be bad in the long term. You may be able to make Alvarado see the urgency of Sutter's need, particularly if you emphasize the trappers who keep coming in illegally. If Sutter's credit is guaranteed by the state we would be happy to supply everything he needs."

Cooper was pleased. Spence's plan was perfect: they could have the business without the risk. But Lewis must not be allowed to meet with Alvarado until they had properly instructed him. Quickly, he addressed Spence. "David, I'm thinking—it might be wise if you spoke to Alvarado about prolonging Lewis' visit and possible citizenship before our illustrious new citizen does."

Spence rose immediately. "I agree, John." He moved toward the door. "Since I was on my way there on other matters, I'll speak privately with the governor this evening."

The Robles adobe, overlooking Monterey Bay, stood high on the wooded mesa at the upper end of the Calle Principal. Most of the year the family occupied the rambling, single-story structure in preference to the larger, more isolated *casa grande* at El Rancho de los Robledos on the inland side of the hills. Don José customarily spent ten days of each month there overseeing the cattle raising and the dry-farming activities. During these absences, Doña Gertrudis occupied herself with one of the finest gardens in Monterey. She had begun with seeds and cuttings brought from the missions at Carmel and Santa Clara, and in two decades had managed to grow grapes, oranges, lemons, a wide variety of vegetables, and a flower garden that was the envy of every woman on the north coast.

Maria found her there picking tiny, fiery *pimientas* for a hot sauce. Mechanically, she took the basket from her mother. Doña Gertrudis picked quickly for several minutes, then straightened, curious about her daughter's unusual silence. "Do you feel well, Maria?"

The girl shrugged listlessly. "Yes, *mamá*, I am well, thank you."

Doña Gertrudis frowned and peered at her more closely. "Then why do you look so," she fluttered her hands, "so miserable?"

"Because I am."

"Oh?" A knowing smile softened her thin, dark face.

106

"Does your unhappiness have anything to do with this?" She tapped the bosom of the long gray cotton apron that protected her dress and saw the quick little flash of surprise in her daughter's eyes. "Yes?"

"It is not my heart that is troubled, Mama. It is my conscience. I think Juan Lewis could have stayed a few more days. I think he did not want to because of Goyo. I am sure he believes we all feel the same way about foreigners."

Doña Gertrudis dropped a last handful of peppers into the out-held basket and slipped an arm around Maria's waist. "Your father has made it very clear that we are friendly. And I know at least six young men who would die joyfully if you would look at them the way you looked at Señor Lewis."

Maria pulled away to confront her. "I have looked at him only with sympathy."

Doña Gertrudis regarded the girl gravely and clucked. "What a pity. Truly a pity. Then you have not seen that this young yanqui giant is very attractive, that he is always neat and clean, even in his shabby clothing, that his hair is very dark brown—like Juan Alvarado's—and always trimmed," she reached out and turned Maria to her gently, "and that his eyes are the shadowy blue of the sea on a cloudy day."

Maria twisted away again and thrust the basket at her mother. Indignantly she braced her fists on the out-thrusting curves of her small hips. ". . . and that they always look wary—like an animal that is being hunted? Indeed, Mama, I have seen that look ever since Goyo, Antonio, and the others hunted him down like a bear, tormented him, and dragged him into this house. They forced him to the camp of that horrible Isaac Graham. And now they force him to hide in the wilderness with that ridiculous little *pisaverde,* Sutter. Juan Lewis wishes to stay in California and make a new life. He has risked much to try."

Doña Gertrudis lifted her hand soothingly. "And he will, dear little daughter, if that is his true desire. Have you forgotten how Goyo stormed all over the house shouting 'traitor!' after Juan Alvarado warned him that Señor Lewis was under his protection. That is a start."

Violently, Maria thrust her head forward. "Some day my idiot brother will call Alvarado a traitor to his face. Then he will be sent off to San Blas, too."

Doña Gertrudis gasped. "Watch your mouth, Maria. It is almost as though you wished it."

"I do, *mamá*! I do!" She faced her mother defiantly, then turned and fled to the house.

For a time Doña Gertrudis stood, smiling thoughtfully. She was certain now that her seventeen-year-old daughter, so much like herself at the same age, had fallen in love. It did not trouble her that the man was a yanqui. Among the girls in Monterey, Maria was outstanding just as Encarnacion Vallejo had been when John Cooper had chosen her, and Adelita Estrada when she had caught the eye of the much respected David Spence. Secretly, Doña Gertrudis had always hoped that Maria would fall in love with one of the foreigners. The Alta California girls who had married them in Monterey, in Santa Barbara, in Los Angeles, and in San Diego were the grand señoras now, the ones with position, the ones with the great homes and the fine things. But more important, they would be secure when the Americans came—as surely they would. Don José, who had spent long hours in futile argument with Goyo— who seemed determined to blind himself to the truth—had said they would.

As she moved toward the house, Doña Gertrudis decided to ask her husband to speak for John Lewis.

Spence returned to Cooper's home the next morning. Together they counseled John on his approaching audience with the governor. Spence was not optimistic.

"The governor is aware of you but I feel he neither likes nor dislikes you, lad. And the news that you would be interested in applying for citizenship did not exactly put him into a Highland Fling. He is under much pressure from Castro and Goyo. As I see it, you do not bring any special skill that could be useful to the governor at the moment and you can't count on much advantage from our sponsorship. So we must provide you with as much advantage as we can by giving you the essentials of Alvarado's background."

Spence rose and paced slowly. "Alvarado conceived the idea of an independent Alta California, but other, stronger, men, won it for him, too easily, I think. He heads the government because he is the only man capable of discharging the duties of office, except his uncle, Mariano Vallejo, who has other more practical ambitions."

"Alvarado was left fatherless at an early age. His mother, Josepha, was Vallejo's eldest sister. She was a great favorite of the royalist governor, Pablo Vicente Solá, who had sponsored the political career of her father, José Francisco Alvarado. Solá brought books to Monterey—against the wishes of the church—and personally tutored young Juan. Those books are still here. They are the best in California—the ones the priests didn't burn. You'll find them in Alvarado's library. They are his only true love. He is a scholar by instinct and an accountant and admininstrator by necessity. He is rather better at keeping accounts than at keeping civil order, but he does remarkably well with what he has to work with. He listens to Castro because in the larger decisions he lacks confidence in his own judgment. Castro, as military commander of the department, and Robles and Osio, exploit that lack of confidence whenever they can. They are directly responsible for the Graham affair." Spence frowned thoughtfully. "Alvarado is self-educated, but well-educated, I'd say. He's a realist with figures but an idealist with all else. He's a philosopher, not a politician."

The frown gave way to a compassionate expression that surprised John. "And above all, he's a very lonely man who was too long under the influence of doting women. Had his own father lived, or had Solá stayed in Alta California, he might have become the most effective statesman the *californios* could produce."

Cooper pulled a large silver watch from his waistcoat pocket and opened the case. "It's time to be on our way. Unlike most *californios*, the governor prizes punctuality." John rose somewhat reluctantly. He was disappointed. The information had been too general.

"Can you tell me his favorite books?"

A pleased smile lit Spence's angular face. "Well, I doubt it would be the Holy Bible. He was nearly excommunicated some years back for reading Fenelon's *Telemaque*. The bishop let him off with an official excoriation and he's had little to do with the church since. But I know he's read Cervantes and Gil Blas. *The Life of Cicero* is a favorite, I'm told, and Goldsmith's *Greece*. He admits to reading all twenty volumes of Buffon's *Natural History* and he admires Rousseau. I know he had a good translation of *Julie*. There are others, I'm sure, but I have seen these in his chambers."

John was familiar only with Cervantes and Rousseau and with some of Cicero's writings. There was little common ground there. The Bible would have been much safer.

Alvarado received them cordially and showed them into a small sitting room beyond his own austere office. A *mozo* brought a fine dry Spanish sherry and John sipped and listened to the polite small talk at which David Spence excelled. The Scotsman's Spanish was excellent. Spence had urged John to converse in Spanish, however haltingly. "Do it as evidence of your sincere intention to adopt their customs." Twice before, John recalled, Spence had referred to the Alta Californians in the third person. It was evidence that neither merchant truly regarded himself as more than a technical citizen.

The governor's large expressive eyes, mirroring each fleeting mood, commanded John's attention. He was so deeply absorbed studying Alvarado that he did not realize immediately he was being addressed.

". . . and we are always pleased when a traveler finds our land so pleasant that he wishes to remain with us. We thank you for such a sincere compliment. But may I ask, Señor Lewis, why one who comes from so favored a land as New England would wish to leave it and forfeit his United States Citizenship for a land as primitive as Alta California?"

Aware that David Spence was watching intently, tacitly warning him, John said, "Your Excellency, New England is a favored land for those who are in a favored position. As one who had no mother or father or close family other than a younger sister who lives in New York with charitable friends, I found my position difficult."

The governor's manner changed from polite interest to quick sympathy. He waited for John to continue. "I found that without sympathetic friends in important positions most doors were closed. So I chose the career of a sailor."

The governor smiled disarmingly. "That we know, Señor Lewis. We also know that your ship's master holds you in the highest esteem and places a premium on your services."

John's stomach muscles knotted. "Your Excellency, I am grateful to the master for the opportunity and for his confidence. I kept my part of the contract, but he was not prepared to do the same. When I give my word, it is given. I expect others to do likewise."

As he had from the beginning, David Spence continued to help John over the more difficult phrases. The governor smiled openly at the translation of the last part of the statement. "A commendable quality, my young friend."

Somewhat reassured, John thought "So far, so good. *Estoy con un pie en la casa*. I have one foot in the house."

"If it were possible to live where you desire, what work would you give your life to?"

John had no answer ready; he could not place himself in competition with his benefactors. Slowly he said, "First, Your Excellency, if I am permitted to remain in California I should like to travel more. I would hope to discover what my new home most urgently requires. Then I would try to learn to do that work as well as possible." John could almost hear Cooper and Spence breathe, "Well done, Lad!"

Abruptly, Alvarado changed the tenor of his questioning. "Señor Lewis, tell me please, what is your opinion of our friend, Señor Sutter, and his works at New Helvetia?"

It was not a moment for equivocation but John needed time. He smiled apologetically, and indicated to David Spence that he had not fully understood the question.

The Scotsman undertook a deliberate and unnecessarily long translation. John nodded and leaned forward earnestly to address the governor. "I cannot say, Your Excellency, that I am privileged to call Captain Sutter my close friend. But I have found him to be energetic and courageous. I think he is a good teacher for the Indians and he maintains military discipline and demands proper respect for the Mexican flag."

"Would you say that his first concern now is to build his fort and make it self-sufficient?"

"I think so, Your Excellency."

"Do you believe he can stop unlawful immigration from the north and east?"

Lewis recognized another dangerous question. "It is my opinion, Your Excellency, that Captain Sutter will be able to protect the frontiers better when more men can be spared from the building and planting."

Alvarado steepled his fingers. "Do you think, Señor

111

Lewis, that the captain, as you call him, will need a garrison of professional soldiers?"

Without hesitation, Lewis said, "I am certain of it, Your Excellency, particularly if there is trouble with the Indians from the north. But a garrison would not be practical unless the fort can sustain it, or unless supplies and arms can be sent from outside sources."

"Sources such as Monterey?"

Lewis spread his hands. "I was not suggesting, Your Excellency, I was expressing an inexpert opinion. I am not an experienced observer in such matters."

"Perhaps that is an advantage." The governor straightened to indicate that the interview was about to end. Spence and Cooper eased forward on their chairs. Alvarado remained seated and addressed the two merchants. "I am obliged to you for this opportunity to visit with Señor Lewis. I take your willingness to sponsor him as evidence of your high regard for him. I should think your confidence in this young man is well placed." He rose and shook hands with Cooper first, then with Spence. Then he turned to John. "We shall consider your wishes carefully, my young friend. I must tell you that in addition to these gentlemen you have the support of Don Juan Sutter, of Doña Encarnacion, also of Don José and Doña Gertrudis Robles." He moved toward the door. "But I think with at least one other in the Robles family, it is still necessary to do some winning."

After the meeting, John suffered a curious feeling of remorse. He was uneasy about the devious tactics he had employed and considered himself a poor finagler. Just before sundown, he climbed the hill back of Monterey. Below him, overlooking the great curving bay, was the capital of this new land that could become his home. Monterey's most imposing houses lined the west side of the principal street. Nearest, and directly below him, was the Robles house. Somewhere in it was Maria.

Monterey, as pueblo and town, was scarcely a half century old. In the mild coastal climate there was no need to build against sub-zero winters or blustery, hurricane-threatened autumns. John had felt the intense heat of the Sacramento Valley. But it was dry—garments could be washed and worn again within the hour. And he had felt the cold and broken skim ice along the edge of the river. The worst of California that he had seen, except for the great desert, was said by some to be kinder than the best of New England. And perhaps it was. But there were golden days in New England, too, days for adventuring along the streams, autumn days when the trees caught fire overnight with such color that their beauty made a body ache. There were crystal days when a glistening mantle of snow softened the land.

"Juan Lewis, Citizen of the Republic of Mexico." He spoke the words aloud, then repeated them. But the alien sound lingered. He thought of Maria and said, *"Don Juan y su esposa, Doña Maria."*

Restless, he rose and walked along the grassy contour of the hill until the twin belfries of the Presidio Chapel were directly below him. Two weeks had passed since he had last written to his sister in Brooklyn. He recalled, with a wry smile, the closing paragraph of the letter, now eastward bound aboard the Medford-built ship, *California*:

> . . . and so, my dear sister, there seems little to tie me to the old home and much to attach me to the new. I have been singularly fortunate in the making of connections here, not because I am extraordinary but because of the need here for any able-bodied man who is half literate. California will not be built by the timid, the stable, or the 'salt of the earth.' It will be built by adventurers who left nothing behind and for whom the excitement of an uncertain future is reward enough. Should the reward I find turn out to have been worth the seeking, I shall offer to share it with you in this new land, if such be your wish.

Three weeks after the meeting, John received a clue that he didn't recognize about the probable nature of the governor's decision. He had had a chance meeting in the afternoon with Maria and her mother. Afterward, Doña Encarnacion Cooper, listening as John talked with her husband, questioned him. "Do you remember exactly how Maria said it?"

"Oh, yes. She said, 'Father tells us that Governor Alvarado is well disposed toward your request for citizenship. He may grant it if he is convinced that you are willing to meet all of the usual qualifications.' She made a point of emphasizing the word 'all.' For some reason it seemed to amuse her."

Doña Encarnacion's plump brown face broke into a knowing smile. Cooper studied her suspiciously. "I know that look, my love. Let us hear the devious female logic that prompts it."

She turned to John. "What do you say most occupies the minds of men?"

His reply came without hesitation, "Business."

Still suspicious, Captain Cooper tried to anticipate his wife. "Aye, that would be true of responsible men. But what are you driving toward?"

Ignoring him, Doña Encarnacion countered with a second question. "And what do you think most occupies the mind of women?"

John frowned. "Well—their children, I suppose, and their homes."

The woman laughed sympathetically and shook her head. "No, no, my young man. Women's minds are most occupied by men. A married woman's mind is most occupied by *her* man. He is the beginning of everything else for her. She may deny it, but it is the truth."

Thoroughly confused, John turned from one to the other. Cooper still seemed bewildered. "Don't ask me, lad. I've been married to her for nearly a score of years and there is still much about her I'll never fathom," he extended his arms helplessly, "simply because she's a woman!"

Doña Encarnacion sniffed. "Simply because *you* are a man!" She lowered her needlework. "Maria understood what the governor meant when he said '*all* of the *usual* qualifications.' And she was amused because she knew that you would not understand until it had been stuck to the end of your nose. I think, Juan Lewis, that the governor chose a very clever and willing messenger."

A soft whistle escaped from Captain Cooper's pursed lips as an understanding smile spread over his weathered face. "Ah, yes. A year of probation and a promise of loyalty to country, to *family*, and to church." He braced his hands atop his knees. "By God, lad, I believe you've got your answer all right!"

That night, in bed, John tossed restlessly as he realized that the governor was attaching binding strings to his official consent. It was strange, he thought, even though he had admitted to himself his love for Maria Robles, Alvarado's almost mandatory condition that he embrace a *californio* woman and probably the Roman Catholic Church rankled him. He did want Maria. Everything about her appealed to him. In any female company she would be judged outstanding. From the beginning he had sensed in her a capacity for passion. When she gave herself the giving would be unrestrained. The thought of being with her had excited him to the point of distress every night since the fiesta. Suddenly annoyed, John threw off the Mexican blanket, rose, dressed quietly, and left the house.

The night was bright and clear. As he walked alone down the Calle Principal he heard the reedy wheezing of a concertina coming from one of the waterfront cantinas. On an impulse he started to enter the place for an *aguardiente*. As he reached the door, a figure moved stealthily from between the buildings. He braced for trouble. Then he recognized the *mestizo* woman known as *La Mofeta*, the Skunk, who sold the services of her temporarily adopted Indian daughters to visiting sailors. On several occasions he had taken one of her older half-breed girls to the beach. Afterward, he had cleaned himself painfully but effectively with strong brandy. But the rumor was current now that the girls had all been exposed to the Spanish pox. Some weeks earlier, sailors aboard an English bark had murdered and thrown overboard one of their shipmates who had caught the infection and threatened to spread it through the fo'cas'le. Lurid accounts of how the deadly Monterey Bay sharks had torn the body and each other in their greed to devour it were still heard on the waterfront.

The woman ignored his rebuff and called out. A heavily shawled girl emerged from the shadows and stood demurely, with lowered head. The woman pulled the girl in front of her. *"Nueva, señor. Limpia. Muy limpia. Por cinco reales, señor. Solamente cinco."*

Lewis peered closer and saw that the girl was indeed a new addition. If she was not as clean as the woman promised at least she was made bearable by a generous splashing of cheap perfume. It had not been his intention to look for a girl, but he paid and took her to a dune a quarter of a mile along the beach. When he tried to enter her she cried out pitifully and began sobbing. Lewis pulled away. "What's the matter? *Qué pasa?*"

The girl continued to sob, apparently unable to speak.

115

He shook her. *"Dígame. Qué pasa?"* Still there was no response but the sobbing. Puzzled, frustrated, and awkwardly hobbled by his trousers, he was propped on an elbow beside her. Impulsively, he pulled the shawl and loose fitting blouse away from her body. In the dim light he could make out the half-developed breasts of a child.

"Nina! Dígame! Cuantos años tiene? Dígame—pronto!"
The girl's reply was almost inaudible. *"Doce, señor . . ."*
Lewis gasped. *"Ay! Doce? Verdad?"*
Between sobs the girl managed to nod. *"Si, señor. Doce . . . "*

A wave of disgust engulfed Lewis. He struggled upright and secured his trousers. Then he pulled the sobbing girl to her feet and urged her gently toward the lights of the town. A block from the cantina he left her, still weeping, and returned to the Cooper adobe. Behind the house he relieved himself joylessly. It was nearing dawn when he finally fell asleep.

The first opportunity to spend time with Maria Robles came early in November. Doña Gertrudis invited the Coopers, the Spences, and the Larkins to share a wild boar that Goyo and Antonio Osio had killed in the hills behind El Rancho de los Robledos. While the animal was being roasted on a *barbacoa* constructed of green poles in the walled rear yard, John and Maria, grateful for the warmth in the chill night, stood back from the pit watching and talking.

"You have never eaten *jabalí asado*, Juan Lewis?"

"No, señorita. Only salt pork." His distasteful grimace made her laugh. "Goyo says it is the best of all roast meats."

John glanced toward the house. "I had the feeling when I arrived that Goyo would have enjoyed roast Yankee more!"

Maria said reproachfully, "You must understand, Juan Lewis, that my brother is not being personal. When Goyo understands that you wish to become a loyal Mexican citizen, he will be your friend."

"I would not depend on that, señorita."

"It is the truth. But let us talk of more pleasant things. Of course, you will stay in Monterey now. What will you do?"

"If the governor asks me to do the impossible I shall try

116

to find a berth on a ship sailing back to the United States."

He could feel disappointment settle heavily on Maria. "But, Juan Lewis, the governor likes you—very much. He would not ask you to do something impossible in order to become a citizen."

A curious perversity seized John. He nodded in the direction of the distant presidio chapel. "I'm told that I might have to convert and become a Catholic."

"But a man must have *some* church, Juan Lewis. The Catholic Church is the only one in Alta California. Señor Cooper and Señor Spence belonged to other churches when they came here. But they are Catholic now. Talk to them. They will tell you that it is a very beautiful religion. The padres would not expect you to believe everything—in the beginning."

Even though her growing anxiety pleased John, he still felt perverse. "But they took *californio* wives. They had to become Catholics in order to marry them. Is that not the truth?"

"But they loved their women. To please them they converted willingly, Juan Lewis. It is a small thing to do for a woman you love. Is *that* not the truth?"

"It is no small thing to take vows. But I have no need yet to worry about changing my faith, do I? Many things come before that. I must work. Then I must try to find some girl who could love me . . ."

Maria Robles drew herself up indignantly. "Juan Lewis, if you walk around with your eyes—" Before she could finish, the rear door of the adobe opened and Goyo Robles was silhouetted in the opening. Ignoring them, he approached with knife in hand and sank the long point into the boar's heat-swollen belly. Instantly, a stream of clear fat spluttered into the coals as Goyo examined the roast. Maria moved to his side. "I am very hungry, Goyo, will it be ready soon?"

Goyo pretended amazement. "My dear sister! What a surprise! Suddenly now, you have an appetite for pigs." He laughed derisively and strode away. Maria could feel John's anger as her brother swaggered past him. Silently she cursed Goyo and his *nationalistas*. The moment had been lost now and she cursed the big yanqui beside her who was not only blind, she told herself bitterly, but deaf and dumb, too.

117

The meal was the best John had ever eaten in Alta California. The roast wild boar was far more delicate than he had imagined it could be. Urged on by Maria and her mother, he ate shamelessly.

Goyo watched silently and spoke hardly at all. He and Antonio Osio, a strongly built, swarthy young man with unruly straight black hair, seemed to be listening and appraising everything that was being said.

The conversation was dominated by Thomas Larkin, who described his inland journey to Vallejo's Rancho Petaluma. Afterward the subject turned to Sutter. Goyo then concentrated intently, his narrow, sharp-featured face mirroring mistrust.

Larkin turned to Doña Encarnacion. "Your brother, Don Mariano was most hospitable. I spent almost one week at his *casa grande* and learned much from him. He met Sutter and Mr. Vioget in the Sacramento Valley surveying the land Sutter wishes to apply for. A considerable amount of land. He wants two very large grants reaching from the American River on the south to the Feather River on the north. Don Mariano said that Sutter has added several good French Canadians to his staff. Three of them are trappers. Also, he's hired that Morrison fellow who escaped from Natividad when Castro arrested Graham and his men."

A vast sense of relief came over John. The little Scotsman was safe. His attention returned to Larkin, who seemed to be speaking in the hope that his words would reach other ears. "Don Mariano's conclusion was that Captain Sutter is welcoming dangerous foreigners to the fort. Apparently he welcomes like brothers all who come, especially the French-speaking trappers. It seems to Don Mariano to be a curious attitude for one who was commissioned by the Secretary of State as the law-enforcement agent for the interior." He turned again to Doña Encarnacion. "Your brother hopes that His Excellency's trust has not been misplaced."

Absorbed as he was in the merchant's account, and in Goyo's reactions, John was still aware of Maria. There was no real need for it but she had taken over the supervision of the serving table, ordering the Indian girls to bring more of some dishes and remove the remains of others. Several times he saw Doña direct an approving glance at her daughter.

Maria whispered her orders a bit imperiously, John thought, pretending to ignore the guests but making it impossible for them to ignore her.

Shortly before ten o'clock, John took advantage of a lull to go to the *retrete*. When he returned he found the guests on their feet preparing to depart. As he stood admiring a tall, ornately carved Spanish chest, Maria appeared beside him.

"It is very beautiful, yes?"

John smoothed his palm gently over the dark oak. Its age-mellowed patina was warmed by the reflected glow from the fire. "It was not made here, I imagine."

"No, Juan Lewis. It is from Burgos in Spain. Governor Borica brought it to Monterey. He gave it to San Carlos Borromeo. My grandfather received it as a gift from the padres for his service to the mission."

Leaning closer, John let his fingers trace the carved door panels depicting four saints at their devotions. Maria watched him, smiling. "You love nice things, Juan Lewis."

He nodded. "We had some fine pieces in my home when I was a child. I remember them." He straightened and glanced around the room again. "You have many fine things here." He was referring particularly to the silver candelabra, to a large leather-bound trunk strapped with hammered brass, and to a long, beautifully made refectory table. Above it, in an oval mahogany frame, was a large portrait of a bemedaled, distinguished-appearing gentleman dressed in the court fashion of a half century earlier. The blue eyes and long copper hair arrested John.

"My uncle, Estevan Robles. He was the brother of my father's father. Charles the Third made him a special emissary to Mexico City." Maria clasped her hands beneath her chin and gazed up at the painting. "I used to think he was the most beautiful man!" She turned, frowning critically, and studied John's hair. "In the bright sun I think your hair is almost the same color. But your eyes are darker." She clucked sadly. "Too bad!" Lewis resisted an impulse to take hold of her regal little neck and shake her playfully.

"And my nose is thicker and my hands are larger, and my feet too probably, and in one thousand years I could never be a fine gentleman."

"Oh, but you are, Juan Lewis! Even your rough clothes ..." She broke off in confusion. "I mean, you cannot hide

119

what you are." She pointed to the picture. "If a good artist painted you, you would see that I am right."

John laughed. "If I paid him enough."

Doña Encarnacion interrupted to say good night. He excused himself and went to thank Maria's parents. For his host's sake, he was determined to say the conventional minimum to Goyo but when he turned to look for him, he discovered that he and Osio had gone.

At the door he said his formal thanks to Maria. She acknowledged them with an exaggerated curtsy. "Our house is your house, señor. We hope you will return soon. By the way, Juan Lewis, since you are learning Spanish, do you know the word, 'ciego'?"

He thought a moment. "I don't believe so, Why?"

Smiling mischievously, Maria curtsied again and disappeared. On the way home, he asked Doña Encarnacion what the word meant.

"*Ciega?* In English, Juan, you would say 'blind.' "

4 THROUGH THE WINTER and well into the spring of 1841, John, working as a clerk in Captain John Cooper's establishment, received packets of letters from Sutter. The tenor was always the same, extravagantly optimistic predictions for the future and petulant often angry, complaints that not enough of his basic requirements were being forwarded. There were increasingly urgent appeals to John to speak on his behalf. The most recent letter—John suspected Harry Morrison had written it for Sutter—told of a major invasion of Hudson's Bay Company trappers along the upper Sacramento River and its tributaries. Because of the consequences, Lewis showed the letter to Cooper. The merchant studied it carefully. "It's time to see if we can't move the governor to keep some promises. I'm still not sure what that poor fool is up to, but whatever it is he's trying to do it all himself. Until he gets some dependable whites up there, he's not going to establish anything that'll stand. Alvarado's going to have to dip into the treasury. Meantime, we can ship him enough to tide him over."

John refolded the letter. "What is the best way to handle the governor, sir?"

"The best way, lad, is to make him feel that his plans are being threatened. There are two conditions under which a man fights hardest—when he's scared for his life and when he wants something real bad. We've got a good straight haul on him both ways. I'll be stopping by there in a few minutes. We'll see what happens."

Shortly after Monterey's siesta was over, Captain Cooper returned to the adobe office. John looked up from an inventory sheet. "Lad, the governor's suddenly taken a notion that he'd like to chat with you in about fifteen minutes. Will you be ready?"

Surprised that an appointment had been managed so

121

quickly, John said, "I'll be there. Is there anything I should know?"

"Nothing, lad. Among other things, I happened to mention to His Excellency that you'd received some disturbing news from the north. For some reason, he got an urge to know about it. I told him he'd best hear it from you."

Alvarado's preliminary greetings were brief but cordial. He came to the point of the meeting quickly and said to John, "I am told there is great difficulty at New Helvetia. The government is fortunate to have you here in Monterey since you know our esteemed Señor Sutter's problems from personal experience," John caught the fleeting smile, "and quite possibly you would be less apt to exaggerate them. No? And, I understand he has written you."

"Captain Sutter feels a great responsibility—"

Alvarado lifted a hand to interrupt. "Perhaps Señor Sutter will also be a captain in Alta California, some day. Forgive me. Continue, please."

"*Señor* Sutter feels a great responsibility is resting on him. As Your Excellency's representative he fears he will earn your disfavor because he is unable to secure the simple things he needs to establish his fort and keep out the foreigners."

"Oh? But I have been told that Señor Sutter was able to get all he needs from the merchants."

"He has received less than half of the things he has tried to purchase. He lacks the money to pay."

Alvarado reached for a letter. "I have received letters, too, my friend. Sometimes I think our Señor Sutter has more trouble with our language than with our Indians. And I think he tries to frighten me into more assistance. He tells me he has reports of many groups of Canadian and American trappers on the waters above the Rio de las Plumas and he lacks sufficient strength to drive them out. Do you believe that is true?"

"Yes, Excellency. It is true. He has no dependable force."

The governor appeared to be lost in thought. After several minutes he looked up. "We are grateful to you, my friend, for telling us so many things. Sometimes it is difficult for an administrator to obtain correct information. Very little of the advice a governor receives is free of selfish interest."

John stirred uneasily, wondering how to interpret the remark. The governor went on. "If Señor Sutter is so short of good help, then he must have committed you to a very important task to spare you?"

John's uneasiness increased. He sensed it was no time for deviousness. "Señor Sutter feels it is very important for me to stay in Monterey to assist in getting supplies. It is his intention that I return to New Helvetia."

Alvarado's dark eyes saddened. "What a pity. I am sure there will be sadness in many of our houses. It occurs to me that your presence in New Helvetia could be useful to many people." Pondering, he returned to his chair. "For instance, if I were a merchant who had extended Señor Sutter much credit, I might find it useful to know how my materials were being used."

John's uneasiness verged on panic now. Obviously, the governor suspected he was working with the merchants.

Alvarado said slowly, as though to ensure complete understanding, "It could also be useful to the government to have loyal and experienced eyes watching our distant interests." He leaned forward. "Is it possible that you will be able to return soon?"

Although the room was chilly, John's hands were clammy. The extent of the duplicity he was involved in overwhelmed him. He struggled to keep from saying aloud, "First, the merchants sent me to spy. Then I schemed to come back and stay back. Now *you* ask me to spy." He longed to shout, to demand an end to his dual, now triple role. He wished to God now that he had not met Maria Robles and fallen in love with her. Without that he could find the courage to say what he wanted to say, then try to find a ship out of this accursed land, so beautiful on the outside and so rotten in its internal affairs—a land ruled by men filled with deceit, treachery, and selfishness, and Sutter was no exception. But he did love Maria. And it was no time to do what he had done so many times, let anger rule him and uproot him. "Excellency, it is possible for me to return to New Helvetia tomorrow. But I am in the captain's service." He made no attempt to correct Sutter's self-assumed title. "I have not accomplished what he expects. If I return now, I will have failed him."

"You will not have failed." The governor indicated the paper on which he had scratched notes some minutes earlier. "I have decided Don Juan Sutter needs practical assistance. The government will give him two thousand dollars in credit to be spent with our merchants and you, my friend, will be given an excellent reason to return. More than that, Don Juan Lewis, when you have enough information of importance to return to Monterey you will write me a personal letter and I shall demand your immediate presence here, to receive your citizenship."

John's sense of relief was so vast that the governor laughed. "I understand well, my friend! It is difficult to wait the outcome of critical things."

Early the following morning he intercepted Don José Robles, Doña Gertrudis, and Maria on their way to mass at the presidio chapel. Casually, he let them know that he would be returning to New Helvetia soon. Their disappointment was unmistakable. Maria appeared stricken until he added that the governor had indicated full citizenship for him, possibly within a few months. He accepted their congratulations gracefully and resumed his pretended errand to the customhouse.

During Monterey's two-hour siesta John had taken to climbing the hills back of the capital. It helped him think and gain perspective on his problems. Seated on a sun-warmed sandstone outcropping, he started as he saw Maria leave the Robles house almost furtively and hurry up the hill toward him. There was no doubt that she was taking pains to keep well concealed.

For the first few minutes he was able to follow her bright red and yellow wool shawl as it flashed between the tree boles and clumps of underbrush. And then he lost her.

Goyo, working in the compound, saw her too. It was not unusual for Maria to wander in search of wild onions and water cress. But he saw that she was hurrying now, half-running. Curious, he put a bridle on one of the horses and mounted. He circled to the west of the house so she wouldn't suspect that he was following. When he was certain that she could not see him, he turned southward and spurred his horse viciously into an uphill gallop.

John began working his way down the hill to intercept Maria. He caught sight of her, less than fifty yards below him, still climbing rapidly and obviously tiring. Moving toward her, he called her name. She froze when she heard his voice, a hand clapped over her mouth. He stepped into the open then and she cried out with relief. A moment later he found himself holding her as she braced against his body, supporting herself by clutching at the cloth of his upper sleeves.

"Oh, Juan Lewis, you frightened me!" The words came in one explosive breath. She took in another great gulp of air. "I saw you over there—I see you every day—but I did not see you leave."

Self-conscious, John freed her hands and urged her gently down onto a half-buried boulder. "Rest, Maria, get your breath first, then tell me what the trouble is." Annoyed with herself, she shook her head violently. *"Madre de Dios,* Juan Lewis! I ran too quickly. I am no longer a young girl, you know."

John burst out laughing. "You are an ancient hag, Maria. Even a blind man knows that!" He grasped her shoulder and shook her playfully. "Now tell me, what is the difficulty?"

Maria turned to him appealingly. "Oh, Juan Lewis, everything is wrong, everything!"

"Everything is *not* wrong. What are you talking about? Tell me!"

Seated close enough to feel the warmth radiating from her body, John looked down at her pale, oval face, at the luminous gold-flecked brown eyes, and the beauty of her made him ache.

"Juan Lewis—what is wrong is that you are leaving. It is not the proper time, because—because—"

"Because what? Why?"

Maria's face contorted with anguish. "Because you are blind and I am shameless."

"I am not blind, Maria."

Seized by a sudden fury she began beating on his chest with clenched fists. "Then you are cruel, Juan Lewis, because you force me to say it! You force me to say 'I love you!' Everybody in Monterey knows that I love you. Everybody but you!"

From his hiding place a hundred yards away, Goyo, choked with rage, watched his sister go into John Lewis' arms. He could feel the storm of their passion. He saw John rise quickly, lift her as though she were a child, stand her on the rock, and take her in a huge, hunched embrace. Sickened, Goyo watched Maria as she kissed the big American wantonly, urging herself against him until he was forced to thrust her away. Moments later, they were together again, down on the steep grassy slope. Maddened with hatred, Goyo Robles leaped down the far side of the hill toward his tethered mount.

Several hours later, at the Robles house, Goyo confronted Maria. His smile frightened her. "Well, my little maiden—or should I say, my little *'woman'*—did you have an interesting afternoon?"

Maria eyed him suspiciously and averted her eyes. "It was nothing unusual."

Goyo regarded her with mock amazement. "Nothing unusual?"

Maria cried out in terror as she was snatched to her feet and struck in the face. "Nothing unusual?" He struck her again and his palm left a broad reddened welt on her right cheek. "It is nothing unusual for a rutting whore to throw herself at a man and grovel around on the ground with him?" He struck her again and continued to strike with his open hand until she sagged and slipped from his grasp to the hard earthen floor. The cotton blouse that had ripped off in his hand he flung down on her naked torso and he jabbed the pointed toe of his riding boot into the flesh of her firm, outthrust breasts. "You like the ground, you dirty little whore! Stay there! Even *La Mofeta* would not offer your body for sale. That is how depraved you are. For a *californio* lover you do not even have a promising smile. But for a yanqui criminal you have everything and you beg him to take it."

Sobbing, Maria tried to protest. He abused her with his boot again and spat on her. "Weep, my little whore of a sister. Weep here and soon you will weep at the grave of your yanqui, too—if you can find it."

Caught up in turmoil, John excused himself after supper with the Coopers and went for a walk. The feel, the smell, and the volcanic passion of Maria still overwhelmed him. He cursed the caution that had made him keep his feeling to himself for so long. He wished that he had declared himself first.

His thought strayed again to the complexities of California politics, the jealous maneuverings that set brother against brother, California against her parent Mexico, Los

Angeles against Monterey, and Monterey against any group that coveted the customhouse. As darkness settled he turned inland to the San Jose road. Several times he heard rather than saw riders. Some were nearby. Finally, aware of the seeping night chill, he angled southwestward until he came to a meandering stream.

Midway across a narrow log footbridge, he heard the start of hoofs. Before he fully realized his predicament, he was confronted by a horseman spurring his animal to reckless speed. The bridge, scarcely four feet wide and without handrails, offered no possibility for escape other than over the side into the unknown darkness. John's warning shout caused the horse to shy when it was upon him. Instinctively his hand shot up to grab the bridle. As his fingers closed around the cheek-strap, the animal reared and its hindquarters slipped off the logs. An instant later, horse, rider, and intended victim plunged into the brackish water.

When he touched the muddy bottom John pushed to the surface and found the water came only to his armpits. The animal, screaming in terror, was thrashing on its side, struggling to keep its head above the water. Seizing the coiled halter rope, John pulled up until the horse gained its forelegs. From the darkness beyond the animal he heard a choking cry. Then silence. Its footing secure again, the big animal lunged at the slippery bank, driving its powerful hind legs wildly. John, caught between the narrow banks, had no chance to maneuver past it to help the man. After another series of futile lunges the horse wheeled and floundered off downstream in the darkness. Instantly, John began calling out as he searched for the rider. There was no sound. He made his way downstream until his leg struck a submerged object. Seconds later his fingers clutched at loose clothing and he pulled an unconscious form to the surface. Holding the man's head above water with his left hand, he groped along the bank with his right hand, seeking a place to climb out. Twice he tried to hoist himself up by the thick overhanging grass but the roots let go. Ten minutes of treacherous going followed. Several times John and his unconscious charge slipped below the surface. Finally he found that by driving his sheath knife into the slimy incline he could pull himself and the unconscious man up by degrees.

He gained the grassy bank and collapsed face down. He

lay there until his great heaving breaths began to subside. Then he realized that his hands were sticky and warm with fresh blood. He felt the rider's face and discovered that the temple and cheek had been laid open to the bone. Propping himself up, he grasped the clothing and turned the limp body over on its back. As he leaned close to listen for signs of breathing, he discovered that the man he had struggled to save was Goyo Robles.

Suddenly John understood the meaning of the hoofbeats in the darkness nearby and a murderous rage welled up in him. Grasping Goyo's long, coarse hair, he raised his knife intending to plunge its blade deep into the *californio's* throat. For a long moment the point trembled within inches of the bloody flesh. Then with an anguished curse he flung Goyo's head aside. An instant later the sound of voices reached him and he heard the muted thudding of hoofbeats moving nearer. John wiped his hands on the grass and replaced his knife. Then, running quietly, he followed the stream until he came to its small, thin-veined delta at the beach. There he turned west toward the town. An hour later, dry and fortified by strong Chilean brandy, he told Captain Cooper and David Spence what had happened.

Cooper, white around the mouth, glowered toward the bay. "That murderous bastard! I've a good notion to drag him up in front of Alvarado myself. He's a danger to us all!" He turned back to John, "You're sure he was alive?"

"He was breathing. I couldn't see but I think he was kicked unconscious by the horse."

Cooper snorted. "It would have been Divine Providence if the horse had killed him. God knows he's killed enough of them!"

David Spence, who had been listening with grave concern, rose from his chair. "Time enough to tell Alvarado about it later. I think I'll pay a little visit to the Robles adobe in my official capacity. If he was hurt as badly as it sounds, perhaps Providence will spare us much more of him anyway."

The *alcalde* departed and returned within the hour. "He's alive. Osio and the others found him. He's not very talkative at the moment but I gather his horse shied at something on the log bridge and they both went over the side. Osio says they found him about a hundred yards downstream. He thinks Goyo must have been dragged and worked loose when the animal leaped up the bank. Doña Gertrudis and Maria are going to make a novena to the Holy Mother for saving him."

Spence tried unsuccessfully to refrain from smiling and Cooper cursed half aloud. "He'll need nine novenas before I'm through with him! One way or another I'm going to keelhaul that rat!"

John drained the last of his second brandy and set the glass aside. "I'd like to attend to that myself, captain. I don't want anybody to go to the governor for me."

Cooper grumbled. "Good enough. How do you intend to handle it?"

The fact was that John had no idea how he would confront Goyo Robles. But he knew he would. "I'm not sure yet, sir. But you can wager that I will."

Ten days passed before John's opportunity came. He had managed to see Maria briefly each day. She seemed strangely subdued but through her John was able to follow the course of Goyo's surprisingly fast recovery. When he learned that Goyo would be visiting Juan Alvarado the following afternoon at five, he determined to confront him before the meeting.

During the morning he worked with Cooper on a list of basic requirements that he felt Sutter would need. As the afternoon wore on John found frequent excuses to go to the door. A few minutes before five he saw Goyo, his face heavily bandaged, emerge from the Robles house and walk slowly down the hill toward the adobe capitol. Ordinarily a *californio* would mount his horse to cross the street. John suspected that Goyo had been told not to ride until the flesh had joined properly. Quickly, John crossed the calle. Then he hurried to Cooper's house and entered through the back door. Seconds later, he left by the front doorway and waited, partially hidden behind a stand of tall willows that grew beside the railed footbridge leading to the governor's offices.

Goyo did not see John in time to avoid him. Smirking, he bowed slightly. "So. We meet on another bridge."

John blocked his way. "I did not know who I was saving, or you would be dead now. But if you or any of your friends ever make another move against me, I swear by our Lord Jesus Christ, I will kill you without mercy."

There was no fear in Goyo's fiery black eyes as he stared back at the yanqui towering over him. Inwardly he cursed the bad turn of fortune that had spared John. In his mind's eye he could see the yanqui and his sister again, lost in their passion on the grassy slope. At some place, at some time, he would be the one who killed. He eased back warily as John stepped closer. "Do you understand me, Goyo? Do you understand what I have said?"

The bandage distorted Goyo's attempted smile and made him wince. "I understand, Juan Lewis, yanqui defiler of virgins. And I swear also to the Holy Mother that I shall have the pleasure of seeing my sister weep at your grave."

Before John could respond, Robles slipped past him and strode across the bridge.

John was able to prolong his stay in the capital for another ten days. The last meeting with Maria took place in the untended garden of the presidio chapel after vespers. Doña Gertrudis had accompanied her daughter and had deliberately prolonged her devotions to allow them time together.

In the winter darkness Maria clung to John with her cheek pressed hard against his coarse woolen shirtfront. "Oh, Juan—I love you so much, and I will be like poor old Concepcion Arguello waiting for her Resanov. You will go away and I will never know what happened to you. I will wait for years and then I shall have to join an order!"

John chuckled mirthlessly. "And if I stay here your brother and his cutthroats will see to it that nobody else knows what happened to me also."

"Goyo will change in time, Juan Lewis. He does not know about love. He has never loved because he does not want the responsibility. He is filled with the political madness. He plays games and pretends he is doing the work of a patriot. But he will accept you when we are married. He will find someone else to suspect then. I am certain."

John slipped a finger under Maria's chin and lifted her face. "You are dreaming, dear little girl. Goyo would turn on me again just as he turned on Graham and Chard. He is treacherous. He would even turn on Alvarado."

Her eyes blazing, Maria pulled away. She had not spoken of the beating or the loathing for her brother that had followed his unfounded accusations, for when she learned that she had been seen a great guilt assailed her. She knew

130

that if John had persisted she would have allowed willingly all that he asked. She despised Goyo now, but for some reason she did not understand she felt compelled to defend him. "Goyo and Juan Alvarado are blood brothers."

"So were Cain and Abel. I will never trust your brother, Maria. Don't ask me to. To him I will always be an outsider whose hair and skin are the wrong color, who goes to the wrong church, if he goes at all."

To soften his words, John took her hands and put them around him. He kissed her tenderly and then with such fierceness that she protested and freed herself.

"Please, Juan Lewis! You will not be gone forever. You will return soon, I know. I will wait and I will write letters and when you return you can finish your instruction and we can be married here with my father's blessing and with the governor's too. His Excellency likes you, Juan Lewis."

"He doesn't really know me."

"He knows you through your friends."

John laughed bitterly. "He believes the last man who talks to him. Your brother makes certain *he* is that one!

Again Maria protested, "No! That it not true. The governor listens to Goyo, yes. But if he believed those lies he would not be trusting you in New Helvitia. There are times when Juan Alvardo has very much a mind of his own."

Doña Gertrudis, her knees sorely abused by the overlong devotions, appeared in the doorway of the chapel. Maria kissed John hastily and together they walked toward the Robles adobe. At the footbridge near the government house, John left them. Doña Gertrudis took his big hand in both of hers. "God will go with you, Juan Lewis. And He will keep you safe. We shall pray for you—Maria and I."

It was still dark when John, leading two pack animals heavily laden with personal clothing and some Indian trade goods for Sutter, rode out of Monterey along the San Jose road.

The trip to New Helvetia took four days. The second night was spent at the Peralta rancho on the east side of the Bay of San Francisco. The third night John spent at Doctor John Marsh's Rancho de los Meganos. He had heard about the penurious misanthrope but he was not quite prepared for the man. Apparently humorless and far

131

from hospitable by *californio* standards, the gaunt Marsh was said to have graduated from Harvard University with a degree in the liberal arts. He had arrived in Los Angeles in 1836 and was granted a license to practice medicine solely on his own contention that he was a skilled physician and surgeon. It was generally conceded that Marsh had treated successfully most of those who had come to him. Even on so short an acquaintance John found that he could believe the stories that Marsh had stocked his rancho by demanding that usurious medical fees be paid in livestock, seed, and equipment.

The suspicious Marsh ordered a straw bed to be fixed for John in the attic. He was to share the cramped quarters with two *mestizo vaqueros* who customarily slept there and acted as the owner's bodyguards. He had no doubt that Marsh had ordered them to keep a watchful eye on him as well.

When John climbed the ladder to stow his things he discovered that the walls below the overhanging eaves were perforated with powder-blackened loopholes. At supper that evening the doctor told him that the upper floor was often used for defense against bandits, marauding Indians, and renegade white trappers who judged the remote rancho to be an easy target. Marsh bitterly blamed Captain Sutter for attracting dangerous rabble with his compulsive hospitality.

The parlor was overrun with books. Among the rows of classics in English, Greek, and Latin Lewis found several impressive, well-worn medical volumes. There was no doubt that John Marsh, bona fide doctor or not, possessed an even more comprehensive library than Governor Alvarado. After supper John surprised his host by losing himself for an hour in a copy of Pliny's *Letters* printed in Latin. Marsh tested him by quoting long passages which John translated easily. The doctor seemed to mellow a bit then, but John knew that the eccentric *ranchero* was not one most men could ever warm to.

Marsh was quietly doing everything he could to encourage American immigrants to come West. He had been among those picked up in Castro's surprise raid and accused of plotting to take over Alta California for the United States. Cooper had told John that the doctor was released later after pleas from both Larkin and Vallejo. There was little doubt, John felt, that Marsh represented a far greater danger to Alvarado and the Mexican government than the illiterate mountain man, Graham.

Captain Sutter welcomed John Lewis as a prodigal son. Harry Morrison managed to conceal his own elation until he and John found a brief moment alone. "Oh, my God, laddie! What a relief it's going to be to have a two-sided conversation for a change." They had only minutes together before Sutter, jubilant over the news of his new credit, fired the small brass cannon to announce a celebration.

An old ox, well past its work prime, was killed and butchered to make a special feast for the Indians. In the Captain's quarters venison and several varieties of wildfowl and game birds were served for the dozen white workers along with vastly improved *aguardiente* from Harry Morrison's crude still.

At his request John shared a hut with the little Scotsman. They talked late and John questioned him about the raid that had taken Graham and Chard and the others and how he had managed to evade Castro's soldiers. "No credit to me, John, I was over bargaining wi' Butron for some malting barley. I took a demijohn of wally spirits and we talked and drank too late. So I decided not to ride back until early morning. Just before sun up, one of the half-breeds I had cutting wood for the stills come ass-spanking across the fields to tell me the soldiers were going to hunt me doon. Butron hid me in a bug-infested straw pile for two days. When it was safe again I rode east to the Consumnes River country and lived off the land until the damned savages got a wee bit too clubby. I did keep them calmed doon by cooking up a stinking brew of roots and berries mixed wi' a bit of abacadabra. When they finally caught the notion that it wasna' going to make them into eagles like I promised I reckoned it was past time to go calling on my dear friend Sutter."

John laughed sympathetically. "You've had me worried."

Morrison snorted and resettled himself in his blankets. "Nae half as much as I've worried myself, laddie. But this place'll do nicely until I can sniff the wind." He braced himself up on one elbow. "I'm afeared to ask, but what's happened to my still at Natividad?"

John did not have the heart to tell the little Scotsman

133

that he had not troubled to find out. "If I know anything about Alvarado he's got somebody running it at a profit to himself." John twisted on the straw pallet and changed the subject. "What do you think of the Captain by now?"

"Well, John, me young friend—if he gets one tenth of the things done that he's promising, then he'll have nae trouble getting himself crowned emperor of California. The only trouble is, like the bean stew he feeds us three times a week, I dinna ken how much is substance and how much is wind."

The first four months of 1841 passed quickly at New Helvetia. The merchants, certain that their bills would be paid directly from the treasury, forwarded to Sutter what was needed for the still and the blacksmith shop, and work had been started on the main building of the fort. John estimated the protected area would finally measure about five acres of hilltop. Sutter's plans called for walls fifteen feet high and three feet thick. Workrooms and shops were located around the inner walls and one of the bastions would house the prison. John noted in the journal he was keeping for Alvarado that Sutter intended to defend the walls with twenty cannon. He wondered what sort of invasion Sutter expected. The capital of Alta California itself had only eleven cannon, as defense against invasion by foreign fleets.

Early in May, Captain Sutter summoned John to a conference. Jean Vioget had gone down river to Yerba Buena to determine survey points on the proposed land grants. Sutter needed assurance that Alvarado would look with favor on the request for land grants. He planned to send John to Monterey with maps and persuasive arguments.

Sutter pointed to the crudely drawn map spread before him. "We do not ask for much land. Less than fifty thousand acres. In two pieces. Nine thousand acres here at the confluence of the American River and the Sacramento, and forty thousand acres here on both sides of the Feather River."

John studied the drawing. "Why do you not ask for this land?" He pointed to the great area of rich valley lying between the two parcels.

Sutter's shrewd little pale blue eyes twinkled. "Because, John, never ask for too much! This is a modest request. Alvarado will know it is the truth when I say it will be

134

easy to defend the state land between my two grants. We will have an armed outpost on the Yuba river and another on the Feather. With the fort here, intruders would be caught in the pincers. It is excellent military strategy." Sutter smiled conspiratorially. "And very good political strategy. When we have the two original grants, then we shall wait for the proper moment to ask for the land in between."

He spread his arms expansively. "And then, Johann Sutter will be the master of one hundred fifty thousand acres, the largest grant in Alta California. My fort will be the heart of a great center of commerce—the richest in the west." He pressed a cautioning finger against his lips. "But we will not speak about that to Alvarado. Take the map. Go tomorrow. Early. And you will see that Sutter does not forget to reward those who work well for him."

John Lewis did his work well. On June 18, 1841, Secretary of State Casarin confirmed to Don Juan Augusto Sutter eleven leagues of land in two parcels as described in the survey done for Sutter by Jean Vioget.

In Monterey again, Sutter was dumbfounded and then secretly elated to find that Alvarado had included in the terms of the grant a proviso that he in turn must grant to bona fide heads of families sufficient land to establish small ranchos for the purpose of guaranteeing stable manpower to protect the interior. The provision astounded Sutter because it seemed to be wholly illogical, a contradiction of all that Alvarado and Castro had espoused. Surely by now, Sutter thought, they understood that he would not be able to recruit native *californio* families to the interior. His most glowing predictions and most generous promises had failed to attract more than a score of undesirables. It must be obvious to the governor and to his advisers that any such settlement would have to be undertaken by the very immigrants from the north and east that the government seemed to hold in deadly fear. It was incredible. But now the success of New Helvetia was assured. He would be free to openly encourage settlers to establish families to protect the very land they would be overrunning. They would be his dependents economically; as Special Minister of the Interior he would hold the power of life and death over them. Sutter could hardly believe his own good fortune.

Two days later, shortly after daybreak, most of Monterey turned out to see the newly landed citizen on his way. From the moment of his arrival, Sutter again had started to recruit additional help for New Helvetia. He had combed every cantina in the capital, inviting, coaxing, and even indirectly threatening new deserters. This time he had managed to commit a dozen drifters most of whom the officials were openly relieved to see gone. Unmolested by responsible authorities in Castro's absence, these were men who roamed the capital at will, drinking, fighting, and stealing.

Captain Cooper saw the men assembled and turned to Sutter, his mouth agape. "God's cheek, man! How will you ever manage such a crew of rascals in the wilderness?"

Supremely confident, Sutter laughed. "It is very simple, my friend. I will allow them nothing stronger to drink than water."

One of the recruits was a big Negro who called himself Tennessee. Strong and amiable, he had been an expert blacksmith before he fled the slave compound and escaped to California aboard a trading vessel. Sutter learned that the man was a skilled craftsman and outdid himself at persuasion. He offered Tennessee a generous salary and promised him that he would be set down in "the great history books" as the first "darky" ever to hold a position of high responsibility in Alta California.

Diminishing his pleasure somewhat was the disappointment Sutter felt upon learning that John Lewis was to be detained in Monterey at the governor's request. But his mood changed immediately when John hinted that citizenship might be forthcoming. "Good! Very good, Lewis! When you say your oath, tell the governor that you wish to take up land near me. I will have Vioget measure off three leagues on the Sacramento north of the Feather River. We will work the land together. I will supply everything and we will share."

John professed to be pleased and Sutter, at the head of his motley *caballada,* marched grandly off to New Helvetia filled with plans more extravagant than ever.

Full citizenship in the Republic of Mexico was conferred upon John Lewis on the tenth of July. Following the ceremony in the governor's office, attended by the merchants and their families and by Don José and Doña Gertrudis, the head of the Robles family announced the betrothal of his daughter Maria to John Lewis.

For all but Goyo Robles it was an occasion for rejoicing. He managed, at his father's request, to endure the ceremony but refused to congratulate the couple.

Five days later, Monterey was plunged into despair by the arrival of the schooner *Bolina* from Mazatlán. Aboard were Isaac Graham, William Chard, and a dozen others of the company. All had been acquitted of treason, fully pardoned with promises of indemnity, fitted out with new clothing and arms, and returned to Alta California at the expense of the Republic of Mexico.

Stricken by the central government's affront to his authority, Governor Juan Alvarado retired to his inland rancho and left the government in the hands of the secretary of state and to *alcalde* David Spence.

The following day a dispatch arrived from Sutter addressed to Captain Cooper. It advised that a plainsman who had crossed the sierra reported a wagon party of two hundred men, women, and children rolling westward from the United States by way of South Pass. John, again in Cooper's employ, read the dispatch and was amused that Sutter could hardly conceal his jubilation. Sutter also demanded a great many additional supplies. John's computation showed that the order would exceed the governor's guaranteed credit by more than a thousand dollars. Skeptically, Cooper examined the list. "It's more of the same, John. We'll not be sending so much as one keg of nails until we've got our funds from the treasury. And with Alvarado away, no doubt nursing his injuries on a bottle, I'm more than a little apprehensive about receiving payment for what we've sent already."

"Suppose Alvarado should refuse to pay?"

"In that case, lad, we'll do as we've done in the past. We'll simply arrange to have our next cargo or two landed here free of customs duty." He smiled slyly over the steel-rimmed magnifying spectacles he had put on to read the dispatch. "As a matter of fact, if we've nothing more than profit in mind, I should think David and Tom would prefer such a settlement."

That afternoon John wrote a long letter to Sutter explaining Cooper's inability to extend more credit and urg-

ing him to do everything possible to help Harry Morrison
increase the size of the still:

> —for there is no faster source of cash revenue than
> that of whiskey. The Natividad distillery continues to
> produce, but only very small amounts. Even with
> Isaac Graham back it is doubtful that it will ever
> produce the quantity and quality of spirit realized
> under Morrison's direction. Most particularly since
> Will Chard wishes to forsake that activity and disas-
> sociate himself with Graham. So a ready and large
> market exists and established merchants here will take
> the product in fair exchange for credit.

John said nothing about the misgivings aroused by Alvarado's absence or about Graham's swaggering public
boasting that he would find a way to settle his score with
"Bautista."

John and Maria saw Will Chard only briefly before he
left for Branciforte. Though somewhat thinner than when
he had been taken away to San Blas, he looked thoroughly
fit. Maria found him an imposing figure. While Chard was
still angered at the injustice of his arrest, he was not as
bitter as Graham. Chard surprised them by revealing that
Thomas Larkin, working quietly behind the scenes, had
been a great influence in securing their release. Larkin,
without fanfare, had gone to Mexico to intercede. Chard
told them that Larkin, deploring the Mexican's inhuman
treatment of their prisoners, had managed to convince the
government that Alvarado and Castro had acted without
cause. No written charges had been filed and no proof offered. John wondered whether or not Spence and Cooper
knew of Larkin's intervention. He suspected not. Chard's
statements reinforced John's conviction that Thomas
Larkin was playing for far higher stakes than just a
preeminent position among the traders on the California
coast. His mysterious behavior in this matter, John felt,
lent credence to the persistent rumor that he sent confidential reports to high officials in the United States government.

Intrigue on all sides infested Monterey. Committed now
to assume the responsibilities of the head of a family, John
began to feel a deepening sense of anxiety. The realities of
the situation pointed to violent change in Alta California.

First, there was Alvarado's curious turnabout in the matter of settlers in the interior followed by Graham's release and the governor's irresponsible disappearance; Castro's continued absence; the presence of large groups of respectable family immigrants from the United States, not just mountain men and deserters who in the past had formed the majority of immigrants to Alta California. All of this was added to rumors that the United States would soon be formally at war with Mexico over Texas.

John was certain his best potential lay in becoming a merchant. But anything in Monterey would be limited by the tolerance of the established merchants, who were wary of anyone not working for them. Moreover, any upheaval in the government would be most acutely felt at Monterey. In Yerba Buena and Santa Barbara there were fewer merchants and fewer opportunities to trade.

Only one new merchant had managed to gain a foothold in Yerba Buena. William Leidesdorff had established a warehouse and forced Spear, Hinckley and Jacob Leese to accept him. For reasons he wasn't sure he understood, John found himself under a growing compulsion to travel to the Bay of San Francisco to visit Leidesdorff. Leidesdorff's reputation for charm and hospitality had already reached Monterey. Colonel Vallejo confessed to his sister, Doña Encarnacion, that his four attractive young daughters had been vying shamelessly to attract the newcomer's attention. Apparently, Leidesdorff's appeal was extraordinary.

On August sixteenth, Governor Juan Alvarado, appearing ill and much thinner, returned to Monterey to take over the reins of government. He had been brought back hurriedly by a report from Colonel Vallejo that an armed United States Navy flotilla had dropped anchor in the Bay of San Francisco two days earlier. Commander of the expedition, Commodore Charles Wilkes, immediately dispatched a party of sixty men in six whaleboats and a launch under the command of a Lieutenant Ringgold to explore and take soundings along the inland waterways and up the Sacramento River. Alvarado, commander of the capital's ineffective forces in Castro's absence, attempted to ready the Mexican Fort for a token defense. Next he called a meeting of Monterey's able-bodied men to form a militia.

Maria, clinging to John's arm as he got ready to attend the meeting, urged him to stand with the governor. "He needs help now, Juan, and he would rather die than turn to Graham again."

John laughed and slipped an arm gently around her. "I was one of Graham's cutthroats once. Do you really think they're so dangerous?"

"Do not laugh, Juan Lewis! They are dangerous now. There are wagers being made that Graham will try to kill Alvarado before the summer is finished."

John snorted. "All Graham wants now is his thirty-six thousand dollars indemnity. He will do nothing to risk that, I promise you." He brushed her hair with his lips. "And I promise you that I'll stand with the governor."

Speaking from the porch at Government House, Alvarado addressed the fifty-odd men. He had placed the capital's permanent garrison of thirty soldiers under the command of an arrogant non-commissioned officer named Chavez. As they listened, nothing about the plan reassured John Lewis or the other Anglo-Americans present. But in the end they pledged to defend Monterey. Muskets were distributed, most of which were rusty and bore French arsenal imprints dated during the Napoleonic campaigns. By common consent the men volunteered to use their own weapons and to provide their own powder and shot.

Later at a meeting with Spence, Hartnell, and John, Captain Cooper, acting as senior militia leader, summed up the situation. "It's no secret that the French, the British, and the Yankees all have warships on Pacific stations in case Mexico gives them an excuse to take over. But it will not be done this way. Save your powder for ducks and geese, my friends. The expedition is harmless and an accurate survey of the rivers emptying into the bay could be very useful information in the right hands. I'd a deal rather have those Yankee tars up there surveying the waterways than have them down here surveying our women!"

John listened and speculated about asking a leading question. Larkin had not been present at Alvarado's meeting. Rachael Larkin had sent word to the governor that her husband had been confined to his bed since the evening before but John had seen Larkin at work in his office earlier that day. Perhaps, if he could phrase it properly,

140

the question would reveal something of the thoughts of the other three. "Captain, the French and the British have had warships visit our coast much more often than the Americans have. Why do you suppose they have not undertaken such a survey?"

Half-smiling, Cooper answered, "John, lad—being mindful that I'm not blessed with occult vision—I'd hazard a guess it's because the French and the British have not had such far-sighted *citizens* in Alta California."

So there it was. A key piece to the puzzle. Given a choice, John had no doubt that both Cooper and Spence would favor the Union Jack flying over Alta California. He wondered if Cooper's oblique reply had been a tacit admission that the British had been outmaneuvered and that accurate inland water charts in American hands would be considered now to be "in the right hands."

Early in September, the unpredictable Sutter committed a serious political affront, this time an internal one. Governor Alvarado summoned John to his office and told him that the Russian commander at Fort Ross had sailed the schooner *Constantine* up the Sacramento River to New Helvetia for an unofficial visit with Sutter. Alvarado asked John to go to New Helvetia to check on Sutter's "progress in fortifying the fort." John understood that he was also to report on Sutter's relationship with the Russians.

Sutter greeted John like an affectionate father and presented him to Commander Rotscheff. The commander spoke no English and Sutter translated the amenities.

During dinner John tried to follow the animated conversation in French and managed to catch a few of the words that shared common roots with Spanish. From time to time, Sutter would provide a sketchy explanation. John gathered that the discussion related to Fort Ross and the Russian installations on Bodega Bay.

After the meal, Sutter indicated tactfully that he and Rotscheff wanted to talk in private. Lewis excused himself and returned to Harry Morrison's enlarged adobe hut.

Morrison showed him the distillery and Lewis saw that once again the Scotsman had managed a wonder of improvisation. The still was not as large as the one at Natividad but it was more efficient. Lewis found the whiskey raw but palatable. More to his liking was the brandy Morrison was distilling from wild grape wine. Later, in the hut where they could not be overheard, the Scotsman recounted the events of the last several months. They were largely a repetition of Sutter's endless promises and disappointing performance. Little was new. Martinez and Peralta had sent *majordomos* to try to collect unpaid debts. Doctor Marsh appeared in person to threaten. Sutter had not been able to mollify him and after his departure he had cursed the doctor and called him an unfeeling, money-mad devil. Vallejo would extend no credit. It was becoming apparent to Lewis that the Swiss who had talked himself in so readily was now in the process of talking himself out. The realization made it all the more imperative that he find out just what the Russian's visit portended. The potential possibilities were alarming.

Four days later, Rotscheff sailed aboard the *Constantine* for the Bay of San Francisco to reprovision before sailing north to the Russian outpost at Fort Ross.

John stood at the landing with Sutter as the vessel cast off. It was impossible not to feel Sutter's repressed excitement. "Such a good visit, Lewis. Such a good visit!" He rubbed his hands. "Very soon, my young friend, they will know that Johann Sutter will not be stopped by usurers like Marsh or by doubters like Martinez or Peralta and Vallejo. They will see!"

John and Sutter waited to ride back to the fort until the vessel disappeared around the bend. John debated the wisdom of prying. Sutter might welcome a safe audience for his boasting since he was extremely pleased with himself.

They rode in silence for some yards, Sutter astride his favorite mount, a leggy, ridge-backed mule that he called Katy. John rode beside him on a skittish, half-broken mustang. When he felt enough time had passed, John said, "The Russian commander seemed very pleased with things here."

"Ja! Ja! And why not? It was a very profitable visit for everybody. No?" The question was a deliberate lead. John felt Sutter studying him craftily and decided to wait and see if his apparent lack of real curiosity would egg the captain on. Minutes passed before Sutter eased his mule closer. "Lewis—you are one of the few people I trust. Always when I ask you to do something you do it very well for me. So now, maybe, I ask you to do something more. Ja?"

John smiled modestly. "I try to do what I can."

"Ja! I believe that, Lewis. So now I believe you can keep a tight mouth. Ja?"

"When it's best to be silent I can manage that, most of the time. But I prefer not to be told things if having such knowledge makes it dangerous for me and for others."

Sutter laughed gleefully and addressed the mule. "Did you hear what he says, Katy? He doesn't want to hear secrets if they are dangerous. But we can trust this young man, Katy. That is why we tell him that we have just purchased from the Russians all of Fort Ross and everything that is in it—livestock, tools, cannon, muskets, pistols, powder, shot—everything." Twisting in the saddle, he swept a strong, stubby arm back toward the river. "Including the *Constantine*—and I have bought it all, over a hundred thousand dollars in value, Lewis, for only thirty thousand dollars. Would you like to hear how I managed this?"

John's answer was a dumbfounded stare that made Sutter laugh. "Good. In my office I will show you. And when the time is proper I will reveal the purchase and you will see that Johann Augustus Sutter will very soon be the most powerful man in Alta California," he shook a stubby finger at John in good-natured warning, "and you will rejoice that you did not call me a fool and a *poseur* like some of the others!"

Alone with Sutter in his headquarters, John Lewis listened spellbound to Sutter's story. Sutter's ultimate purpose was to establish a personal duchy strong enough to dominate all of Alta California. If he could induce Isaac Graham, who bore a just grudge against the government, to join him, then Castro's pitiful army and Vallejo's irregulars would fall before the first charge. Suddenly John's fantasies seemed frighteningly real. Sutter could make any kind of a bargain he wished with the Russians, even have himself declared supreme commander of Pacific North America. Backed by his European military experience and by trained Imperial forces sent by the Czar, after he defeated the Mexican forces, Sutter could turn northward and easily defeat the token British garrisons along the Columbia. He could consolidate the entire Pacific Coast under the Double Eagle from Baja California to Russian Alaska.

The prospect made John's flesh creep. He tried to envision the sometimes ludicrous Sutter wielding such power and he wondered if Napoleon himself, in the beginning, had not seemed as ludicrous for the role of world conquerer as the fleshy, balding, mustachioed man recounting with childish glee how he had single-handedly outsmarted the Russians and the rest of Alta California.

Later that evening, John made careful notes on the details of the transaction. They included the promise of the incredibly small down payment of two thousand dollars in cash, bringing the total obligation to thirty-two thousand dollars.

The autumn of 1841 was a crucial one for Alta California and for John Lewis. He was spared the necessity for breaking his promise to keep Sutter's secret when word came to Monterey that Sutter had boarded the Russian vessel *Helena* in the bay of San Francisco and entered into formal contract with the Russian government.

Colonel Mariano Vallejo had been negotiating for the Russian holdings at Fort Ross and Bodega ever since Rotscheff's initial overtures. He was livid on hearing the news. He raced to the capital and arrived shortly after Castro's unexpected return from Mexico City. One of Santa Anna's high military commanders, General Manuel Micheltorena, had secured his release. Unlike Vallejo, Castro retreated into bitterness and displayed little interest in the threat that Sutter now posed.

John was present to confirm details as Vallejo stormed around his nephew's office and Castro slumped dispiritedly while Alvarado studied the figures Lewis had laid before him. Near hysteria, Vallejo broke out again. "Mother of God! I repeat. We are finished! My dear nephew—you must realize now what a traitor you have welcomed into our midst. By supporting this man Sutter you have delivered Alta California into the hands of its destroyer. You must realize," he leaned across the desk and rapped the paper viciously, "that this pompous buffoon now has more cannon, more powder, and more lead than the combined armed forces of all Alta California. More than that, my Indians tell me the first American immigrants are in the Sierra. Many of them! It was not serious before but soon now Sutter will have a hundred and fifty men there—all expert riflemen."

144

Straightening, Vallejo clasped his hands in prayerful pleading. "In the name of God, Juan, you must send a messenger to Mexico City immediately. Demand professional soldiers and money to garrison them. The immigrants must be controlled or in six months there will be no sovereign state of Alta California in the Mexican Republic."

Worn, and tortured by doubt, Alvarado closed his eyes. Finally, he rose slowly and walked to Vallejo. "I will send you, Mariano. No man can make stronger representations. No man is more respected."

Incredulous, the sleek, elegantly dressed *ranchero* backed away. "But that is impossible, Juan! Impossible! I cannot be spared from the rancho. It would be dangerous, even fatal to us all for me to be away for three months. My men are all that stand in Sutter's path if he should decide to move. Who knows what that fanatic will accomplish in three months with Russian assistance? Look at what he has done already, with no assistance. No, Juan, the very best thing I can do is to write a letter to Santa Anna. I will say that I support you in everything you do. Completely!"

John caught the veiled smile as Alvarado turned away. "Very good, Mariano. I will think. It is not a mission that can be entrusted to just anyone." He glanced at Castro. "I will think who will be the right man and I will tell you."

Castro's face mirrored sudden scorn. "There is no proper man! Santa Anna is a fool. No man of reason can talk with him. Do you know why I was humiliated? Because the Central Government was trembling with fear that our courageous act in banishing foreigners from Alta California would anger the Americans still more." He flung an arm outward. "Forget Santa Anna! You will see. Not one soldier will be sent. Not one!" Castro wheeled and stomped over to the window.

Castro wished that Vallejo would stop his stupid raving. He wanted help not because he feared an invasion but because he was afraid Sutter would build a stronger personal empire than he. But what difference? Alvarado was deaf and blind to the realities now. Mexico's only hope would be to sell Alta California to England in settlement of unpaid bonds. Or even better to establish a Mexican monarchy under French protection. France, too, was a Catholic

145

country. There were many in Mexico City who favored that course.

Castro pictured himself again in Alvarado's chair and a great frustration overcame him. How different history would have been if he himself had dared, as Pico once had, to declare himself governor general of the Department of the North. There would have been no waiting to act then. The foreigners would have been turned back or tried and executed as illegal immigrants.

A week passed and Alvarado had failed to make a choice. Filled with disgust, Vallejo returned to his rancho north of the Bay of San Francisco. Three days later a Chilean bark dropped anchor at Monterey. Aboard was Eugene Duflot de Mofras, the young attaché from the French Embassy in Mexico City. Acting under confidential orders from Paris, de Mofras was visiting the Alta California capital and other settlements along the coast, including the Russian installations, for the purpose of assessing their probable strength.

Monterey, knowing that such visits usually signaled a fiesta by official decree, began brushing up its best clothing. However, de Mofras departed for Yerba Buena two days later after no more than a coldly correct reception by Secretary of State Casarin and Governor Alvarado. Waves of speculation surged up and down the Calle Principal.

The truth reached John Lewis by way of Maria after she and her parents had endured another frightening tirade from Goyo. Bundled against the chill, the couple walked along the narrow tidal margin at sunset. Maria looked at John gravely. "I do not know what will happen, Juan Lewis. But it will not be good. Alvarado did not make a fiesta for the Frenchman because he believes that he came to Monterey to spy. The Frenchman asked to see the fort but Alvarado refused. Then he asked questions that were an impertinence. A young attaché does not innocently ask such questions of a governor. The Frenchman was very angry when he sailed yesterday. And do you know where he goes now? To visit Sutter. Do you know what he said to Alvarado? He said, 'It will be a pleasure to visit Señor Sutter who understands how to be courteous to the representative of a great friendly power.' Goyo is certain the Frenchman is here to spy. He has convinced

146

Alvarado." She tugged at Lewis' arm and they both retreated from the incoming tide. "It is not good, Juan Lewis. I am frightened."

He wanted to reassure her but there was nothing to say. As adroitly as possible he diverted the conversation to their own immediate plans. He knew that they too might well be swept aside by the mainstream of larger events. "No matter who dictates the operation of the government in Alta California, Maria, there can be no government without the trade that is controlled here by Cooper, Spear and Larkin, and by Abel Stearns in the south. Larkin and Stearns are partners in many ventures just as Cooper works with Spear and Hinckley and Leese too when it is necessary. Cooper needs me now just as Larkin needs his clerk, Talbot Green." He leaned down and kissed the end of her nose lightly.

Maria loved her big yanqui more than she had ever imagined possible. She reached up and put her arms around his neck and he half lifted her from her feet. A moment later she was kissing him with a hungriness that brought a muffled protest from his smothered lips. Before Maria realized what was happening he had carried her to the fine, dry sand beneath a low, grass-covered bank and had put her down gently.

There, in a timeless world, they lay together, talking, caressing, allowing themselves to imagine as much as they dared of that time of coming together when they would be coupled with no barriers of conscience and clothing between them and they could convey without words all that they felt, each for the other.

At about the same time, in Monterey's most imposing residence on the Calle Principal, Thomas Larkin was painstakingly phrasing a confidential message to the American President in Washington apprising him of the current French interest in Alta California.

Goyo Robles was confronting Juan Alvarado on the hillside high above the Mexican fort commanding Monterey Bay. They had ridden there at Goyo's request after he had pleaded so passionately for an opportunity to talk that Alvarado had not been able to deny him.

"The time for waiting has passed, Juan. There is no more time. You yourself have said there is nobody you can trust to send to Mexico City. Castro is finished there,

Mariano will not go. So, as ridiculous as it may be, Juan, you have no choice. You cannot go yourself. You must send me."

Alvarado rested a paternal arm across Goyo's shoulders. "Friend of my childhood, your passion makes a volcano of your mouth. In one moment you tell me you will die for me and in the next you call me a drunkard. But I understand you and even as I tell you that my heart is full of gratitude, I must also tell you that you do not have the qualifications. You do not know how to persuade. If a man does not listen and agree with you immediately, your temper flares." A thought made Alvarado laugh softly. "You would not be the first one to call Santa Anna a fool, but I fear you would be the first one to call him that to his face, if he did not agree with you." He shook his head sadly. "No. I cannot risk another Castro. And Castro holds his temper better than you do."

The outburst Alvarado anticipated did not come. Instead, Goyo lowered his arms slowly and turned away. When he spoke, after a long silence, his voice was strangely subdued. "So, Juan, the one who has the most need in his heart to help you has the least to offer here." He tapped his temple.

Alvarado moved close again. "Goyo, the man who goes to Mexico City must be one whose reason dominates his passion. He must have infinite patience. He must make indifferent men see the immense value of Alta California and convince them that a strong Department of the North is necessary to their own safety. Now, my dear friend, can you swear in truth that you are such a person?"

Another long silence passed, then Goyo shook his head. "I have not been such a person, Juan. I admit it. But I swear by the Holy Mother that I can learn to do it because it must be done. All we need is three hundred trained, well-armed men, a half dozen field pieces, a sloop of war, and enough powder and shot for our heavy cannon. For certain, Juan, the Republic of Mexico can spare that."

"Nothing is for certain in Mexico City, Goyo, except that the government will not act in time, and that it will do the wrong thing for Alta California. Remember the sixth of July, eighteen thirty-one, when Mexico secularized our missions and destroyed the only established order in the land? Do you think a government fearful enough of the church to destroy a state is concerned about a few deserters and trappers and an occasional foreign warship?"

"But, Juan, there are different men in the central government now. They know the American threat is real. Let me try, Juan. Please. I can do no worse than Castro. They will believe me and act or throw me in jail as they did Castro. You have nothing to lose, Juan. My father has many friends in Mexico City. He will help me, too." Goyo paused, waiting.

Alvarado knew that Goyo was correct when he said that his father could help him. In Mexico, Don José's reputation as an excellent military man still endured. His son would certainly meet men of influence. Perhaps, after all, it was not so important *who* told them and *how* they were told. If only he could rid himself of an abiding conviction that even now it was too late.

Alvarado straightened abruptly. "God help us all, Goyo, I have decided. If you wish, you may try." Alvarado regarded Goyo sternly. "But you must make me a sacred promise that you will do exactly as I ask. Can you make such a promise, Goyo?"

"Juan, the vow is made now, before God!"

On the eve of the new year, Goyo Robles and two companions quietly departed from Los Robledos with extra mounts and five pack animals carrying provisions for a long overland journey. Following Governor Alvarado's instructions, the party entered the San Joaquin Valley then headed south to the Old Spanish Trail. Alvarado hoped that this route would keep the south from knowing about the expedition. Once Goyo's mission became known to the Angelenos, they would race to Mexico City to protest help for the northerners. Pico would see in the move a direct threat to his own political ambitions.

On the morning of January twentieth, Goyo and his party crossed the Colorado, entered the state of Sonora, and began the long dangerous southward traverse of the *Gran Desierto*.

At noon on that same day, in the presidio chapel at Monterey, John Lewis and Maria Robles were joined in marriage. The event was celebrated by one of the gayest fiestas in the capital's recent memory. For three days old animosities were set aside and even the presence of a transformed Isaac Graham, scrubbed, shorn of all but his mustache and side whiskers, did little to dampen the festivity.

For seventy-two hours no doors were closed and no lights were extinguished in the Robles adobe, and Doña Encarnacion Cooper, with the enthusiastic approval of her husband, who had been John Lewis' *padrino de boda* at the wedding, opened her home to the overflow.

When at last the couple was escorted by serenaders to La Casita, a tiny two-room adobe presented to them by Don José, they slept exhausted in each other's arms.

John awakened from a sleep made deeper by endless responses to endless toasts to find Maria watching him. His brief befuddlement and start of realization made her laugh and she snuggled close, urging the warm contours of her naked body against his. Excitement, almost unbearable, filled Maria. And unfamiliar fear too, as she lifted to let her husband's left arm slide beneath her and felt herself being pressed closer still—face to face as they had fallen asleep. Her lips, moist and giving, moved to his as she felt him growing against her. For Maria, time lost both measure and meaning. If, in his eagerness, this man of hers who meant to be gentle caused her pain, then it was a pittance to pay for the pleasure she would give him, for the pleasure that she herself would be given, pleasure sensed beyond the pain. The end of frustration, the freedom to cling naked to the massive, hard-muscled frame of her man carried Maria to the unknown, far beyond the limits of her most vivid fantasies. She crossed the new threshold joyously, passionately; and John, for whom love always had been a taking, found in giving a depth of joy beyond expression.

Through the early part of the new year and on into the summer very little happened to ruffle the placid surface of the capital. At La Casita, John and Maria went about the engrossing task of settling into domesticity. In the process they learned much of one another that confirmed still further their conviction that each had chosen well.

Maria had become pregnant early in the winter. As often as he was able between summer trading trips, John worked at the addition to La Casita being built to accommodate the child. In early autumn, the expanded house was the scene of a celebration as Doña Gertrudis and the older wives brought their hand-made presents of swaddling clothes, down blankets, crocheted caps and boots, and a feeding spoon fashioned from a Spanish silver coin.

As Maria neared her time, John's concern increased. At least once each day he would look at his wife, rest a hand gingerly on her protruding stomach and regard her gravely. Once, when he had said, "But there's so little of you and so much of—*it!*" she had looked at him reproachfully. "—of *him!*" She had laughed to conceal her own mounting apprehension.

During the last week of September, Monterey's outward calm was shattered by the arrival from Mazatlán of the bark *Annie Gleason*. The ship's master, a gaunt, weather-worn New Englander named Enoch Blakely, brought the astounding news that Santa Anna had dispatched Brigadier General Manuel Micheltorena and three hundred prison-recruited irregulars to Monterey. Governor Juan Alvarado and Commanding General José Castro were to be replaced and their respective duties combined in Micheltorena as Governor-General.

Dumbstruck, John Lewis joined the merchants in the master's cabin aboard the *Annie Gleason* to hear Blakely elaborate on the sources of his information. Larkin, Spence, and Cooper hardly needed the New England ship's master to spell out their mutual dilemma. Even if Pio Pico moved the customhouse to Los Angeles, they would be better off. A Mexican military governor would be under instructions to squeeze every last penny of duty and tax from the merchants to help Santa Anna finance the war with the United States that was considered inevitable. Under the circumstances Yankee trading ships could expect the most stringent application of the regulations.

All of this John understood in those first brief minutes. What panicked him was that the new restrictions in trade would make it all but impossible to establish his own business. Moreover, the new order could multiply the obstacles already making it difficult to earn a proper living. John found some relief in the knowledge that he could, if necessary, take over the active running of El Rancho de los Robledos. Properly supervised, the rancho could keep the two families. But even that future could be bleak since the hide trade was beginning to diminish as new South American cattle markets closer to New England cut into the California trade.

Don José had seen clearly when he pointed out that Alta California's weakness lay in its dependence on a single economy. "This is a rich land," he had said, pointing to the lush natural growth in the valleys, "but we do nothing to use those riches but slaughter our animals who feed on them. Our valleys are like our cattle. We strip them and waste the greater inner riches." John recalled that Sutter had deplored the waste of fine land too.

After Captain Blakely's account of the essential facts, he turned to other equally disturbing aspects of the change. The assembled men struggled to find a way to work out an accommodation with Micheltorena. Blakely was no happier than they. "I have no need to paint it darker than it is, gentlemen. You'll find out soon enough, if you care to send someone south, that these three hundred soldiers of Micheltorena's are nothing but thieves and cutthroats that he either can't or won't manage. He had only one officer worthy of the name, a Safardic I believe, a colonel named Raphael Telles. The captains and subalterns are as bad as the rabble they're supposed to command. They are robbers and they committed cold-blooded cuttings in San Diego. They molest women on the streets in broad daylight. They are in Los Angeles by now, and I'll wager that the story's the same there." He looked from one to the other, ominously, and his flat Down-East voice sharpened. "They'll fall on this town like a plague, gentlemen, and there'll be no safety unless you take strong measures to defend what is yours!"

Thomas Larkin spoke up. "Castro gives Micheltorena full credit for securing his release. Through Castro we might have an avenue to the general's ear." He turned to Captain Blakely. "If what you say is correct—and I have no doubt that it is, sir—I can see Pico speeding him on his way to us posthaste."

Cooper expelled a long breath. "Aye! We can count on Pico's generosity this time. What concerns me now is what will happen when Alvarado and Castro hear this news."

At La Casita, John deliberately withheld the news from Maria. When she fell asleep he pulled on his watchcoat and walked down the hill. He wanted to think. The change that he had sensed was upon them now.

The moon, approaching its new half, cast a luminous glow over the mesa. At the customhouse boat landing,

John found one of the official dories with oars still in place in the lock pegs. On an impulse he climbed in. Sculling with one oar, he worked the small boat clear of the crude stone jetty and headed westward. It was the first time he had taken a boat alone out on the bay. It was the first time he had wanted to and he was not aware that the act was an unconscious manifestation of the desire to repeat an old pattern of escape.

Earlier, when he had been pulled out to the *Annie Gleason* in its boat with the other merchants, he had imagined himself an important merchant about to be entertained aboard. He had seen himself, the director of the John Lewis Company, dressed in the latest conservative Boston fashion, examining critically the great array of goods displayed on deck for his approval. He had walked along slowly, fingering samples of linen and colored cotton cloth and rich wool carpeting at one dollar and fifty cents a yard on which he would gladly pay seventy-five cents a *vara* duty—if necessary. He had picked his way through stacks of iron try pots that would bring a five hundred percent profit and past heavy iron hoes and picks and spades, cases of chinaware, turpentine, kegs of nails, stacks of Morocco-tanned calfskins that had been shipped raw from this very port two years earlier, and cases of boots and shoes made from California hides that had brought two dollars each at Monterey. Each hide represented a dozen pairs of footwear that would bring ten dollars a pair. He examined cards of lace and cases of rifles, tortoise shell combs from the Caribbean, barrels of coffee, ground rhubarb, almond oil, quinine, and cannisters of salmon from Nova Scotia. It went on and on, the array of items that were so prized on the California coast. Then he had climbed the *Annie Gleason*'s Jacob's ladder and that part of the vision became reality. It was spread out before him, and somehow the dream had assumed substance even though he was nothing more than a clerk for one of the merchants who would use him now but surely would abuse him later if his personal ambitions were to run contrary to theirs.

A half mile off shore John shipped the oars and let the dory drift. Off to his left he heard the deck watch strike eight bells aboard the bark. A few cables distant, to the northwest, the tolling couplets set a dog to barking aboard a coastal schooner out of Yerba Buena. Facing the shore, he could make out the dark outline of the customhouse and the pitch torch burning atop the pole in front of Larkin's new home. The merchants would be there, engrossed in more speculation, and he was glad he had not been asked to join them. He felt now that his guess was as good as theirs. Once again he fought off the dark specter of disaster. Half aloud he commanded himself to "hold her steady as she goes." If you are alive and well and have food to eat, he told himself, you are ahead of the game. And if you have a wife and an in-law family that regards you with affection and respect, you are in the way to become rich. He pictured the cargo again: the merchants trading sharply, taking advantage of Captain Blakely's inexperience in the California trade. Blakely had forsaken the China trade in the face of impossible competition from faster clippers to try the California hide trade as a commission master.

Soon enough, Blakely would learn the value of holding out for his price. Monterey merchants were flinty bargainers. John found himself more grateful than ever to them for the lessons he was learning. Making a place for himself would not be easy but it would be far less difficult than the challenge that had confronted him at Graham's camp. As he rowed back, he wondered about Will Chard. He had seen little of him since his release. Maria had said he was spending most of his days near Branciforte, ostensibly to look into the possibility of starting a water-powered saw mill but Maria suspected and hoped that the presence of her cousin, Dolores, was the real reason. In any event, Chard's earlier plans that had included him were over the side now. Somehow the thought relieved him. He liked Will Chard. He would always be his friend. But he knew now that the relationship would rest there.

The day after the arrival of the *Annie Gleason*, Joaquin de la Torre, chief customs clerk, received the packet from Captain Blakely and took it to Alvarado at his place at Alisal. Within hours Monterey was aflame with rumors.

"Alvarado is preparing a statement of resignation!"

"Castro is going to remove the guns and powder and shot from the fort and hide it in some inland cache where he will recruit a revolutionary army!"

"José owes his freedom to Micheltorena. He will become

154

the commander of all government soldiers in Alta California!"

"Isaac Graham and Will Chard are raising an army and will join Sutter in declaring California an independent republic." And so it went, endlessly.

Finally, a week after the news had been received and confirmed, David Spence volunteered to ride to Los Angeles on behalf of the Monterey merchants and petition the new governor-general to leave the capital and custom-house at Monterey.

A month later Spence returned and the merchants met at Cooper's house to hear about the trip. Reporting that he had met Sutter's new emissary, a German named Flugge, Spence turned to John. "You've been replaced in your friend Sutter's affections, I fear. The young fellow, Bidwell, is now his personal secretary and Flugge seems to be his ambassador at large." Somewhat apologetically, he braced his hands on the back of the chair. "I was not as successful in my mission as Sutter apparently was. The best the general would promise is to discuss the matter. Otherwise, I found him agreeable and very presentable, a pleasant surprise, I must admit. His second in command, Colonel Raphael Telles, is a thoroughgoing gentleman and professional soldier. But the description of the troops was no exaggeration. They are little more than legally armed criminals. I am told they have not been paid for months. Micheltorena has provisioned them from his own purse."

Larkin, appearing more dour than usual, asked, "What was Sutter up to? Could you find out from this Flugge?"

"The German is a very stubborn man, not given to talking. But it's fair to say that Sutter sent him to Los Angeles to speak well of New Helvetia before some of his enemies —Vallejo for instance—could speak otherwise. The best I could get out of Flugge was that Micheltorena has written Sutter a very friendly note assuring him that he will cooperate in helping to keep foreign immigration under control."

A laugh burst from John and the older men regarded him uneasily. "I'm sorry, gentlemen, but that's like setting the cat to guard the mice. To Sutter, keeping foreign immigration under control means welcoming all who come to the country and putting them to work at the fort for good wages and better promises. If Micheltorena criticizes him for that, Sutter will haul out the grant agreement

155

made with Alvarado stating he should encourage settlement by the heads of families. The governor-general will find a greased eel easier to take a hold on!"

The room was quiet until Cooper reached out to rest a hand on Lewis' knee and said, "Lad, none of us here likes the idea of keeping things covered too much. So, before you hear it spoken by others who may not wish you so well, I must confess that we've been wondering what part your brother-in-law, Goyo, may have had in bringing Micheltorena north."

Much to John's relief, Cooper had said it straight out. Despite the fact that his own ill-feeling for Goyo was well known, John had been suffering from a sort of guilt-by-association. Maria had told him about Goyo's mission to Mexico but had sworn him to secrecy. He had never believed anyway that Goyo would be able to convince any responsible official of the central government of anything. Alvarado must have been desperate when he sent him but the question had now been posed.

"I have only hearsay to go on. But if Goyo did go to Mexico City to ask for military help, he surely would not have suggested deposing his own blood brother. You gentlemen know him better than I. I would judge then that you'd give him even less chance to succeed."

Amused by John's artful dodging, Spence said, "We should try to discover upon whose recommendation he came."

John sought refuge in the obvious. "I'd wager a lot more on Castro than Goyo."

Spence nodded. "But it's unlikely Castro would petition Mexico City to replace him as commandant of the Department of the North.

"Any plea for help might be taken by Santa Anna as a sign of general incompetence requiring drastic changes."

"Aye! You've a point," Cooper said. "Why would Santa Anna send a distinguished general up here in command of a band of undisciplined ruffians?"

Spence snorted. "Either Mexico is far worse off for manpower than we believe, or its leaders lack common judgment and I do not rule out the possible existence of both conditions."

Larkin, listening attentively, made a mental note as the meeting broke up to transmit the reasoning to the United

States Department of State for whatever use it might be in making an evaluation of Mexico's condition.

On the way back to La Casita, John found himself wondering about the merchants. For some reason he was convinced that his relationships with them were changing. No single incident nor any overt action supported his conviction. But the change was real enough. John searched for a cause, perhaps he was assuming an unjustifiable burden of guilt because his marriage might have signified a possible shift in loyalty. Early in his association with Cooper, John detected an underlying anxiety. He had sensed it in Spence, too. Certainly Sutter troubled them. And Leidesdorff. In fact, anyone who could conceivably threaten their sinecures troubled them.

Only Larkin really worked at building his business. John was sure that Larkin's energy was impelled by interests far beyond trade and merchandise. He had become the government's principal banker. The Department of the North borrowed interim financing at high interest to carry it between the peak revenue seasons. Earlier in the year, Cooper had observed dryly to John that if Larkin chose to call rather than refinance the loans, he could foreclose on the government and own Alta California.

John found the governor's inconsistent attitude toward outsiders ironic. If Alvarado was truly concerned about a foreign takeover, he should not have wasted time on Graham and Chard or become involved with Sutter. Instead, he should have examined the motives of the Yankee merchant to whom he was now so deeply beholden.

Alvarado's reaction, when it came, saddened his friends and delighted his detractors. On the twenty-fourth of September he posted a proclamation that Micheltorena had come to Alta California at his request to be relieved as governor because of poor health. The explanation produced derisive laughter from those who knew about Alvarado's penchant for *aguardiente* when the burdens of state grew too heavy. John deplored the transparency of the excuse. The portion of the proclamation congratulating the people upon the appointment of a successor, "so well spoken of for heroic military ability and blessed excellence of character," disgusted him. He was certain that Alvarado did not lack physical courage. He had risked execution for treason when he overthrew the Mexican governor, Gutiérrez. He had been governor for six years and now it seemed he had suddenly become a weakling.

John voiced his doubts to Don José. "I foresee no future here now but confusion. There is no consistency in this government. There can be no salvation for us except in other than Mexican hands."

Don José laughed tolerantly and said, "Miguel de Cervantes wrote, 'It is a far cry from speech to deed.' Soon enough we shall find out Alvarado's reason. But do not become too quickly disillusioned. I have known Juan Alvarado since he was a child. He is deeply hurt now. But he loves this land and he will fight for it when the time is right."

Monterey's official business continued to be transacted with remarkable efficiency by Secretary of State Casarin. David Spence acted as both *alcalde* and justice of the peace, arbitrated civil controversies, and within a few weeks Alvarado's as well as Castro's absence was all but forgotten.

On the nineteenth of October, shortly after dawn, a lookout from the Mexican fort reported a sail on the horizon beyond Point Pinos. John and Cooper rode to the hilltop commanding the southwest to identify the ship. They saw not one but two sets of sails in addition to Captain Snook's coastal schooner, *Joven Guipuzcoana.* Cooper handed the glass to Lewis. "See what you make of them, John. One seems square-rigged and the other could be a sloop."

"I make out the one on the left to be a Cape Horner. The other is surely smaller but I can't put a name to her."

Cooper took the glass again. Without removing his eye from the objective, he reported, "Both vessels have altered course to the west. I can see the big one's—" he paused and looked at Lewis strangely "—and if you want to know something, lad, those stays'ls are a mite too square for a merchantman. She's flying no colors so I can't make her out, but she's a frigate, by God, as sure as she's a foot high. And that's a sloop of war with her. Those are not bogus gunports painted on her sides. Those are the real thing."

The words were scarcely out when they saw a puff of smoke erupt from one of the sloop's forward guns. A moment later, the muffled report reached them. Cooper fo-

158

cused on the smaller, faster vessel. "The sloop's put a shot across the *Joven*'s bow and Snook's coming about to lower sail." They watched in silence as the sloop of war approached the schooner, came about herself, and lowered a small boat.

"By God, lad, that's an armed boarding party!" The same fear struck both men simultaneously. A pair of privateers were on the California coast. While Cooper's eye remained trained on the smaller vessel, John had been watching the frigate, still holding a course that would bring her into the shelter of the Bay of Monterey. She had passed the sloop and its victim now and was standing inshore of her, no more than two miles off the headlands. Suddenly from the tip of her spanker gaff, the colors streamed. John saw them and called out. Cooper retrained the glass and let out a startled cry. "Mother of Jesus, lad, that's the Jack! She's British! Here!" Stepping aside, he held the glass in place until John grasped it. In an instant John confirmed the warship's identity. Quickly he swung the glass to the more distant vessels and saw that the *Joven Guipuzcoana* was preparing to make sail again. The sloop was staying outside of her, obviously intent upon convoying the captured craft back into port.

In less than a half hour all three ships were at the anchorage. Within the hour, John and Cooper watched with the stunned crowd that had gathered at the customhouse point. An outcry rose as the frigate struck the British colors and ran up the Stars and Stripes of the United States. Cooper, along with Spence and Hartnell, who had breathed private sighs of relief at the sight of the Union Jack, quickly made for the office of Jimeno Casarin. They learned there that Casarin had already dispatched a messenger to Juan Alvarado demanding his immediate return. Ashen, the frail Casarin looked from one to the other helplessly. "Governor-general Micheltorena's order commanded Alvarado to retain this office until he arrived in Monterey from Los Angeles. Under that order I have no legal right to act. He must come! And so must Castro—if he can be found. We have no defense!"

Unknown to Casarin, when the frigate first appeared in the harbor flying the British colors, Thomas Larkin had dispatched his own messenger to Alvarado demanding his return to organize defenses against a British takeover. Larkin's private information from the American chargé d'affaires in Lima had included an assessment of relative foreign naval strength in the Pacific. The United States had five vessels in its Pacific squadron totaling one hundred sixteen guns. The French had eight vessels bearing two hundred forty-two guns. But it was the opinion of both the United States officials and the experienced naval men that the British warships would be more than a match for either of the other two powers. Larkin knew Monterey could be taken from the sea, but if strong resistance was organized inland he doubted that it could be held, particularly if the United States Pacific squadron could be summoned in time to bottle up the British.

Larkin was in his office writing a hurried dispatch describing the action, which he hoped somehow to get to the United States, when word came that the vessels had changed their colors. He shredded the papers and burned them. Then he hurried to the customhouse and overtook the other merchants returning from the government house.

Cooper, his face a study in anguish and confusion, laid a hand on Larkin's arm. "What do you make of this, Tom? Two of your warships using the tactics of a privateer to take the capital?"

The inference annoyed Larkin. "I have no idea what to make of it, unless the United States and Mexico have gone to war. Who is the commander? Does anyone know yet?"

Cooper glanced up at the old Mexican fort. "No. We have no intelligence and no means to resist if their intentions are not peaceful and there's nothing very Goddamned peaceful about a shot over your bow—under any colors!"

By the time they had reached the customhouse a small boat from the frigate was seen pulling for shore under a flag of truce. At the landing, Cooper ordered the bystanders back as an American officer in full dress blues and cockade accompanied by his guard stepped ashore. He looked about, questioning, until Jimeno Casarin advanced timorously and identified himself in Spanish. The American saluted and introduced himself as Captain James Armstrong of the U.S. Navy, acting under orders from the Commander of the Pacific Squadron. With military correctness, he demanded a conference with responsible officials. An awkward pause ensued as the puzzled Casarin turned to those around him. Thomas Larkin stepped forward immediately, identified himself as a United States citizen, and offered his services as a translator.

"We are much obliged, Mr. Larkin. Will you please accompany us to a suitable place where I may transmit to the governor or his representatives the commodore's demand for a peaceful surrender. It is his wish to avoid the sacrifice of human life and the horrors of war." Larkin spoke briefly with Casarin, then led the official party up the slope to the government building. The apprehensive crowd strung along in its wake.

John Lewis, seated on the low stool beside the bed, tried to reassure Maria, whose labor seemed about to begin. Doña Gertrudis and the Indian midwives hovered silently in the background. Driven by duty, he had returned to La Casita when the ships were first identified. "There is no need to worry, *chiquita mia*. They are only British warships paying some sort of official visit. When your father returns he will tell us." Leaning close, he smoothed the moist hair from her temple and kissed her forehead.

"We have much more important welcoming to do here!" Maria managed a smile that did little to conceal her mounting fear. The first pains had begun just before dawn and she knew then that if these were the mild ones, as the women had said, then it would take all of her courage to face the ordeal ahead. She clung to her husband's hand and pressed the back of it against her neck.

"You are the president of this welcoming delegation. So you will be certain to be here when your son arrives?"

John smiled reassuringly and cursed the poor timing that prevented him from being with the others at the embarcadero. "I shall be here. After all, I am not Juan Alvarado." He regretted the joke instantly, but it was said. Maria closed her eyes and released his hand.

Doña Gertrudis tiptoed over to the side of the bed. "Let her rest now. I will tell you when to come in again."

John wandered into the parlor and stood in the doorway looking down over the pueblo. The sloop and the frigate were anchored a quarter of a mile out from the customhouse landing. Both ships were flying the United States colors from the gaffs but he could see them only as silhouettes against the lowering afternoon sun. Below him, a figure detached itself from a knot of people gathered before Thomas Larkin's house and he recognized his father-in-law heading with unusual haste toward La Casita. Minutes later, Don José, puffing from the exertion, broke the news of the vessels' real purpose. "Larkin is going out to meet the American commodore now. Casarin has sent him as interpreter. Pedro Navaez and José Abrego will arrange the terms of surrender. Alvarado will arrive by six o'clock. He has sent word that he wishes all to be at his home at that hour."

John followed Don José inside. Still short of breath, the older man settled gratefully onto a chair. "So, my son-in-law, you were first an americano, then a mexicano, and now you will be an americano again." He pointed toward the bedroom. "And whether or not it is an honor remains to be seen, but you may also be distinguished for having fathered the first new citizen born here under the United States flag."

By half past five Maria's pains seemed to have eased again. When he looked in she was sleeping. Doña Gertrudis took his arm affectionately and led him out of the room. "I do not think anything will happen for some hours, Juan. She still keeps her water. Go with Don José to Alvarado's home. If you are needed I shall send one of the women."

John slipped an arm around his mother-in-law's slender shoulders. "Promise?"

She crossed herself hastily. "I promise. You shall know when to greet your child."

John and Don José arrived several minutes after the frigate *Cyane*'s gig put Larkin and Casarin's two emissaries ashore. Obviously both weary and worried, Larkin greeted them on the porch. "This is a very unfortunate business. I have told Commodore Jones that I do not think a state of war exists between the United States and Mexico. He disagrees. But when I asked for proof he could present none except the considered opinions of his officers and some Department of State underlings in Panama and Callao. I am certain a grave mistake is being made."

It was almost dark when Alvarado appeared on the San Jose road. He greeted Jimeno Casarin and his staff and the principal citizens of Monterey, about thirty in all. Quickly, Casarin recounted the events, then handed Alvarado the penned draft of the United States provisional surrender terms. Alvarado read the single sheet scornfully and pushed it aside. "Jimeno—what is the state of our defenses?"

Casarin turned questioningly to Captain Mariano Silva, who had been given temporary command of the garrison in the absence of both Castro and the subaltern, Chavez.

Silva glanced around unhappily. "Our defenses are of no consequence, as everybody knows. We have twenty-nine unpaid soldiers including twelve officers and four subalterns. There are twenty-five volunteer militiamen—if all can be found. We have no more than one hundred muskets that will fire. And eleven cannon—" He paused. "And sufficient powder to fire salutes only."

A heavy silence fell over the room. Alvarado straightened in his chair and reached for the surrender terms. Holding the paper aloft in a hand that trembled as much from fatigue as suppressed rage, he looked around, then let his eyes come to rest deliberately on Thomas Larkin. "None who know me would doubt that I would rather sign my own death warrant than this paper. I have lived through no darker hour. I shall not rest in peace until those who would destroy us are themselves destroyed." He lowered the paper. "We shall agree to these terms to prevent the futile shedding of blood. Our situation is temporarily without hope. We shall agree because we are men whose compassion matches our courage. This surrender will be signed with our hands but never with our hearts. In the sight of God, I swear in your presence, gentlemen, that one day soon our terms for the retrocession of Alta California shall be written in their blood!" He took the quill from its stand and offered it to Casarin. "You will write first, Jimeno."

The acting governor accepted the quill reluctantly and signed. Alvarado inscribed his signature below. Then he looked up at those before him. "I wished to have you here to counsel me and to pledge your loyalty in the battle to drive off the invaders. For the present that is not possible so now there is nothing for me to ask of you. Under the flag of the United States some of you will find yourselves favored." His eyes roved the unhappy faces until they came to John Lewis. "When that day arrives I ask you who know our hearts to give to those whose land this once was the same consideration you received from them when you first came among us."

John returned the governor's level gaze and wondered

163

how Isaac Graham and Will Chard and the others would have responded. Chard would have been amused, he thought. But Graham would have gloated openly and hailed the just providence that evened the score for him. John supposed that he might be doing that already, with the help of a demijohn. Graham's revenge would be as sweet as Alvarado's defeat was bitter.

John could guess what was going on in Larkin's mind, too. There would be relief that the warships were flying the Stars and Stripes and not the Cross of Saint George. The opposite would be true of Spence, Cooper, and Hartnell. As for his own destiny, much would depend upon how the officers left to administer the country viewed adventurers who had given up their birthright.

At eleven o'clock on the morning of October twentieth, Commander Stribling and one hundred fifty spit-and-polish U.S. Marines and sailors stepped ashore at the customhouse landing and prepared to take formal possession of Alta California. As the band struck up, the Mexican colors were lowered to make room for the Stars and Stripes of the United States. Two men were notably absent: thirty-three-year-old Governor Juan Bautista Alvarado, who, unable to face the public humiliation of surrender, had ridden inland to Alisal before daybreak, and John Lewis, twenty-two-year-old father of an infant daughter, who had fallen into a deep sleep after the terrifying experience of witnessing his first birth. When the guns at the fort, manned now by U.S. sailors, answered the salutes from the two warships lying at anchor in the bay, John scarcely stirred. Don José told him of the ceremony, of the pride and gallantry of the ragged Mexican soldiers as they trailed their arms to surrender them at the government house, and of the courtesy of the American officers and men who disarmed them and assured them that not a single person in Monterey would be deprived of his rights of liberty.

John awoke shortly after two o'clock in the afternoon and went in to see his wife. Her appearance shocked him and filled him with a strange guilt. He wondered that any woman ever survived the ordeal of giving birth to a new life. He had heard tales of Indian women who paused during their labor in the mission fields, dropped their child in a furrow, and resumed their work within the hour. He could believe it of a broad-hipped, bandy-legged savage female but not of such fragile-appearing women as Maria and her mother or even his own sister, Alice. As he sat looking down at Maria's lips, swollen and bruised from teeth that had bitten through the thick, wet cotton labor braids, he resolved quietly not to expose her to such a trial again, not forever, but surely not for a long time. Holding his infant daughter, who would be christened Felicia Gertrudis Lewis, he looked up at Doña Gertrudis with frank disbelief as she reassured him that the wizened, beswaddled little creature in his arms was a faithful reflection of the best features of its mother and father.

At four o'clock, still heavy with fatigue, he walked down the hill with Don José to receive the congratulations of his friends in the upstairs sitting room of the Larkin house.

The merchant was cordial and generous with his good wishes and his brandy but he seemed distracted and hardly touched his drink. John was grateful to these men who had taken time in the midst of their own concerns to observe the custom. Ordinarily it would have been a long, relatively exuberant affair, but Larkin himself asked to be excused at five o'clock. The others soon departed, David Spence to write a long dispatch to the British attaché at Santa Barbara and another to Colonel Mariano Vallejo at Sonoma; John Cooper to continue reassessing his position as senior merchant; David Hartnell to ride to his inland college blessing his good fortune, for he knew that under American occupation, as under British, there would be a growing demand for the secular education of the young.

John returned to his new household, now so strangely rearranged. Alone, with only an oil lamp burning erratically above the adobe fireplace, he tried again to plan a future. Silently he thanked God that the war vessels lying at anchor were American. Immigration would come faster now, and with it a growing opportunity to establish himself in trade. Inadvertently, Captain Cooper had pointed the way when he had said, "There is only one great harbor on the entire California coast, lad, and that's the Bay of San Francisco. It is central and large enough for the greatest fleets. But the Mexicans will never make anything of it. Spain would have. But the Mexican government will not listen to the *californios* here who have vision and enterprise. Vallejo and Martinez and Peralta know what Yerba

Buena could be. So does Alvarado and Don José Robles. These men are done pleading with the central government. Their arguments are disputed in Mexico City by their own self-minded people in Los Angeles who mouth idiot dreams about a great harbor at San Pedro. San Diego, yes. But never San Pedro! There isn't a day the British don't kick themselves for having settled on the Columbia first. The future of this land lies in the great central harbor and in the rivers that empty into it from the lower valleys to the north and south. Those waterways are vital. Sutter understands that. In some ways that ridiculous little man is very clever. That's why he has chosen to fortify a position that commands them in every direction. But mark what I say, the key is the Bay of San Francisco."

John had recalled Cooper's reasoning often during his troubled ruminations over the past months. William Leidesdorff's name kept recurring in his thoughts; but each time he resolved to visit him some unexpected obstacle had intervened. Now, in the next room, he heard the hungry squalling of still another obstacle and smiled to himself as the muted cooing of the *mestizo* nurse reached his ears. Perhaps little Felicia should not be counted an obstacle at all. The infant and the war vessels in the harbor that portended such great changes might be the incentives he needed to rearrange his life.

Late in the afternoon of the twenty-first, Commodore Thomas Ap Catesby Jones made a tour of the Mexican fort and the customhouse, then he proceeded to the government building to meet with and reassure Monterey's leading citizens.

John Lewis and Don José fell in with Cooper and Spence and joined them. The Scotsman who would remain as *alcalde* indicated the streets and smiled wryly. "If you are looking for California officials, do not look in Monterey. This is a deserted town. Only Casarin remains at his post. A sorry spectacle, gentlemen. A sorry commentary."

Following a brief formal address to the small crowd gathered before the government building, the commodore asked to confer with Thomas Larkin. Embarrassed at being singled out, Larkin accompanied the officer inside the building. Captain Cooper remained grim and silent but David Spence laughed good-naturedly. "Before you think too harshly of Tom just remember that if the colors had not been changed, 'twould have been one of us to receive the dubious honor."

Cooper and Spence returned to their offices and John strolled down to the landing to strike up a conversation with members of the shore party standing by the commodore's boat. The few Boston and New Orleans papers that reached the California coast were so prized that they never remained long in anyone's hands. He wanted to hear the details of President "Tippecanoe" Harrison's untimely death. After only thirty-one days in office, Vice President Tyler's banking orders had succeeded in making all but Webster in the old cabinet resign. People wondered if Tyler could keep the country on an even keel. John was also eager to know about the cargo of slaves who had mutinied aboard the *Creole* and had sailed the American vessel to the West Indian port of New Providence. The Navy had been asked to intervene but he had read that the British had given the slaves asylum. And he wanted late news about the trouble in Texas. He was badly disappointed that the seamen he talked to could tell him very little. They had been on the Pacific station for many months.

At the customhouse he talked with the commodore's executive secretary, a man named Reintrie, and with the squadron chaplain, the Reverend Bartow. John answered their questions about Monterey and its people and thought he detected a touch of wistfulness in their queries. In answer to his queries about the probable future of California under American rule, Reintrie was composed and confident. He told John, "The commodore is convinced, and his staff officers agree, that California may well become as important as the Louisiana Territory. If there was any risk in taking Monterey, the commodore feels it was justified to insure that England does not lay claim to it first."

Their conversation was interrupted by a messenger from Thomas Larkin asking John to come to the governor's office as quickly as possible. After the briefest introduction to Commodore Jones, John was dispatched to get the latest editions of American newspapers making the rounds of the merchants' offices and homes.

Within a half hour he was able to find seven editions of Boston and New Orleans papers. None was dated more recently than mid-July. Lewis delivered them to Larkin and was asked to wait. He watched as the merchant and the commodore pored over the editions side by side searching for dispatches that would indicate the possibility that the United States and Mexico had gone to war. They found none. Commodore Jones, still unconvinced, pushed back his chair and looked up at Larkin. "I respect your opinion that a state of war might not yet exist, Mr. Larkin, but I cannot afford to risk letting Monterey fall into British or French hands in view of the fact that I have positive knowledge that Rear Admiral Thomas sailed with three British men-of-war under sealed orders from London. Moreover, the French Pacific Squadron left Valparaiso in June to cruise off the California coast. It is the sense of our attachés and of my officers, and I concur absolutely, that these fleets had been informed that war between the United States and Mexico was imminent and that they sailed under orders to take up positions enabling them to move against Monterey on a moment's notice. Buying our own continent back piecemeal from foreign invaders has become a fine proposition—for *them,* Mr. Larkin. It is my intention to forestall any more such unfavorable bargains."

Larkin peered at John. "Are you certain that John Cooper and David Spence have no later editions tucked away? It seems to me that somewhere I saw dispatches dated as late as the first of August that made no reference to a declaration of war."

John was unable to understand Larkin's curious behavior. He had been certain that the American merchant would have done all he could to support the United States' position. He replied with caution: "I did not see them myself, sir. But it is possible they've gone inland to Mr. Hartnell. Late news is very much in demand, as you know."

Commodore Jones stirred impatiently. "I think we've about come to the end of doubt-casting, gentlemen." He indicated a packet of papers. "I have here a letter from our man, John Parrott, in Panama, dated the twenty-second of June. It says without equivocation that war with Mexico can be expected momentarily. Parrott is very dependable. His view is supported by the June four issue of *El Cosmopolita* in which the Mexican Minister of State makes the most violent threats to Secretary Webster. These same dispatches were reprinted in the *New Orleans Advertiser.* They also appeared in the Boston papers in July." He gathered the correspondence.

"I appreciate your concern, Mr. Larkin, and I understand that it is exercised in our behalf. But on evidence, I feel we have acted prudently." He rose and prepared to leave.

Suddenly John remembered that he had seen a bundle of newly arrived dispatches from Mexico City at the customhouse, including copies of *El Diario* with new customs regulations.

"Mr. Larkin—"

"Yes, John?"

"If the commodore would wait, I may be able to find some late dispatches from Mexico at the customhouse. I don't know that they'll shed much light on the matter."

Annoyed that there could still be any doubt as to the wisdom of his action, Commodore Jones gestured impatiently. "Fetch them, Lewis! And don't bother us with anything not pertinent to the issue."

"Yes, sir." John turned to go but Larkin stopped him. "It might be best if one of the commodore's men did the actual searching." It took a moment for John to realize that Larkin was attempting to protect him from being in the position of a Mexican citizen who had given aid and comfort to the enemy.

Pausing uncertainly, he looked from Larkin to Jones. The officer scowled. "All right. That is proper. My secretary and the chaplain are at the landing. Ask them to do the deed, if you're timid about it."

Accompanied by Reintrie and Bartow, Lewis entered the deserted customhouse. On the second floor, in the room occupied by the collector of customs, Reintrie found a bundle of official communications in a metal box. He called down to Bartow and Lewis. "Come up here and have a look. Some of these papers are dated as late as four August."

In the most recent of them, dated in mid-August, John found several references to United States ships bound for Alta California. The documents warned the collector of customs at Monterey that certain items in the cargoes were to be taxed at new rates. Lewis translated aloud as best he could. Reintrie, unmistakably upset, took the papers. "I'll carry them. I think the commodore will be interested in these."

Twenty minutes later Thomas Larkin, doing his best to resist a smug smile, finished translating the letters and dispatches to Commodore Jones. "I'm afraid, sir, that if a state of war existed between us these communications from the Minister of Finance in Mexico City would not be reminding Señor Torre to be sure to collect duty at the new rate on American carpeting and iron try pots."

The commodore all but snatched the paper from the merchant's hand. "Damn it, Mr. Larkin, I do not need to be reminded of the obvious. Let me have the lot. I wish to take them aboard for study. We shall talk further."

At nine o'clock on the morning of October twenty-second, Commander Stribling stepped ashore and dispatched a runner to Thomas Larkin's residence. A half hour later Larkin dismounted at the customhouse and greeted the commander. Stribling came straight to the point. "I have here a letter from Commodore Jones to Governor Alvarado. He asks that you deliver it in person. I have been directed to inform you that it expresses the Commodore's deep regrets for any inconvenience he may have caused the government of Mexico, and the state of Alta California and its citizens. The commodore himself will sail for San Pedro this evening to deliver a similar letter to Governor-general Micheltorena. I have been instructed to arrange the ceremonial return of the government and of certain documents to Mexican officials and to strike our colors at four o'clock this afternoon. The commodore asks that you be good enough to so advise the responsible authorities here. Thank you, sir!"

Before Thomas Larkin could reply, Commander Stribling saluted, swung about abruptly, and ordered his men into the boat.

Late that afternoon, in the presence of a stunned citizenry, Secretary of State Jimeno Casarin, acting for Governor Alvarado, accepted the American commander's official apology. The United States flag was hauled down from the staffs at the customhouse and at the fort and Mexican colors returned to their rightful position. A salute was fired by the reinstated Mexican garrison and answered offshore by the sloop *United States*. A bugle sounded, commanders barked orders, drums ruffled, and two companies of disgusted U.S. sailors and marines marched back to their boats.

5 THE YEAR 1842 came to a close and Alta California moved into the new year—wondering. In the south, at Los Angeles, Abel Stearns, the merchant-banker who functioned for Pio Pico and his political *junta* in much the same manner that Thomas Larkin functioned for Juan Alvarado and therefore exerted much influence on local affairs, began moving carefully to hasten the departure of Governor-general Manuel Micheltorena. The outrageous behavior of the Mexican general's *cholos* had disaffected every decent citizen. As rumors of the excesses continued to filter northward, the Montereyans hoped against hope that the more agreeable climate in the south would tempt the general to tarry longer.

Micheltorena had received Commander Jones graciously, reciprocated with an official fiesta of his own, echoed protestations of friendship, and handed the American commander an exorbitant bill for damages. Commodore Jones had proceeded to the United States, where his action was creating a great controversy in Congress. He had been temporarily relieved of his command.

In Monterey the established merchants with the exception of Thomas Larkin went about their business as usual. Cooper had summed up their position in naval metaphor: "We're committed to a fixed course now, gentlemen. The Yankees have turned our battle line and the British and French are in a position to. No matter which way we steer we are in a fair way to take their broadsides. 'Tis only a matter of time—and whose shot you prefer to take."

Maria Lewis, fully recovered, had set about fixing up La Casita, renamed Casa Alta because of its sizeable addition and because it occupied the highest lot on the mesa. But John's activities in the capital had not expanded. He continued to receive thirty dollars a month from Captain

Cooper, most of which was taken out in trade at a favorable discount. As a consequence, the new family got by. In the spring of 1843 there was a flurry of excitement in Monterey. Abel Stearns had received a draft for three hundred and forty dollars from the United States Mint in return for a pouch of coarse gold nuggets he had forwarded for a *ranchero* named Francisco Lopez. Lopez had discovered the nuggets clinging to the roots of some wild onions in the San Gabriel Mountains. There were rumors that many citizens of Los Angeles were in the mountains prospecting along the streams and reports that traces of gold had been found in the Los Angeles river. At first, John was tempted to gamble a few months' time and try his luck but the sobering reality of his responsibilities soon put an end to that golden dream.

On the morning of April second, an American brig out of Charleston dropped anchor in Monterey Bay. The master lingered at the customhouse only long enough to ask the way to the home of Thomas Larkin. Two hours later all Monterey knew President Tyler had named Thomas O. Larkin as United States consul at Monterey. Well aware of the change this would work in his relationships with both Cooper and Spence, Larkin immediately went to Los Angeles to establish a commercial alliance with Abel Stearns, who he felt would be a dependable unofficial source of information useful to Washington.

In June, three fully laden merchant vessels, two from the United States by way of Honolulu and one from Peru, put into Monterey only long enough to secure permission to trade in Yerba Buena. To the consternation of both Cooper and Spence, the cargoes of the two American vessels were consigned in their entirety to William Leidesdorff. It was the first time that any major merchant vessel had failed to discharge the bulk of its cargo in Monterey.

On August thirteenth, Governor-general Micheltorena, having tired of Los Angeles, marched into Monterey. He was received with meticulously correct ceremony by Alvarado, who had assessed all those able to pay to raise the money for a proper official fiesta.

On the very night of the celebration, Micheltorena's *cholos*, officers and men, began confirming their reputations by molesting women at the cantinas and by stealing livestock. On the third day Monterey was outraged by the raping and knifing of a young Indian mother by two irregulars crazed with *aguardiente*. John, afraid for the first time to allow Maria and little Felicia to walk unaccompanied, even in broad daylight, joined in a general protest to the governor.

General Micheltorena was contrite. He promised there would be no repetition of the outrages. Within the week, however, two young Monterey girls were dragged screaming between buildings and were saved by sheer chance from assault by a group of sailors on leave. This incident made John Lewis resolve to go to see William Leidesdorff in Yerba Buena.

A pre-dawn start brought him to San Jose, a hot, unprepossesing pueblo. He reached Yerba Buena late the next afternoon and went immediately to the home of Jean Vioget. The Swiss, who had just returned from New Helvetia, was delighted to see him.

They talked late and John learned that Sutter, little by little, was seeing his dream materialize. The walls and bastions of the fort were finished and cannon were in place. Several thousand acres were under cultivation in wheat and a German named Theodore Cordua had become the first of several settlers to take up land under the requirements of Sutter's grant. Harry Morrison had turned over his distillery to one of the new immigrants and had begun the establishment of a pharmacy and dispensary, a task more to his liking. But credit problems still dogged Sutter.

Vioget felt that Sutter would not be able to meet his own needs and still make a payment to the Russians. John learned that twenty-two-year-old John Bidwell had taken over more and more of the clerical detail, freeing Sutter to oversee his field workers. John wished young Bidwell better luck than his own in collecting wages. Despite numerous letters, Sutter still had not sent the promised draft for nearly two hundred dollars. John asked Vioget if he should extend his trip and ride to New Helvetia to collect. Vioget laughed and said that he had never been paid for surveys and maps and his efforts to collect had been met with protestations of undying friendship, gratitude, stupefying hospitality, and an avalanche of promises.

The conversation turned to Leidesdorff then. Vioget said intently, "Do you know this man? Have you met him?"

"No. I have not met him properly. I saw him when he sailed into Monterey for his customs clearance."

"Then, my friend, you may anticipate an extremely rare experience. Leidesdorff—his father was a Dane and his mother a West Indian Negro—is one of the most dynamic and cultured men I have met in many years. He speaks three languages fluently and soon will have mastered Spanish. His enterprise is changing Yerba Buena."

Suddenly more hopeful, John decided to confide in Vioget. "I have described conditions in Monterey under Micheltorena. I must remove my family. The real reason I came here was to try to find employment with Leidesdorff."

Vioget's alert blue eyes brightened. "And you will. I am certain. Our friend Jacob Leese is not very happy about it, but Leidesdorff has constructed the largest warehouse in the cove." He pointed to the southwest. "And he is building our first real hotel. A very imposing one. Also, he is talking of a school and he and William Richardson speak of sawmills in the forests north of the bay. He has many enterprises, *mon ami*. And unlike our friend Sutter, he has the means to see them through. I shall be happy to introduce you in the morning."

The meeting with the thirty-three-year-old Leidesdorff took place in his cottage not far from the center of the little pueblo. Jean Vioget managed the introductions and excused himself on the pretext of business with Captain Richardson. Everywhere in Leidesdorff's home John saw evidence of the man's excellent taste, and here and there he thought he detected a woman's touch. After a very few minutes, Lewis was convinced that those who had proclaimed William Leidesdorff's charm had not exaggerated.

Somewhat shorter than John, the young merchant was a strong, active man with very dark, compactly curled hair. His broad face was open and friendly and his restless, wide-set topaz eyes mirrored a quick, searching intellect. Only the most subtle trace of the man's mulatto origin was evident to John. The well-moulded features suggested a Polynesian strain if anything. Leidesdorff wore his hair somewhat shorter than most, the modest side whiskers being his principal concession to current fashion. Except for a black mustache, he was clean-shaven. His skin was a luminous light brown, no darker than Maria's or little Felicia's. In a voice that was deep and rich, he beckoned Lewis to a back door. "When you visit me again, soon I hope, Mr. Lewis, I shall be able to invite you into our garden. Its principal distinction now lies in the fact that it is the first one to be attempted in Yerba Buena."

Leidesdorff traced the course of the paths between the beds that soon would be lined with ornamental stones. "California is an extraordinary land. It suggests the possibility of becoming all things to all men." He laughed and the sound was infectious. "I must have a profusion of flowers around me, Mr. Lewis. As a child in the Caribbean, my first recollections were of blooms. And later, in New Orleans, my uncle's garden was the delight of my school years. Flowers and music. For me they are life's only indispensables!"

Inside again, Leidesdorff indicated a chair. "Please sit. We shall have some good coffee, French coffee with a bit of chicory, and you will tell me what I may be able to do for you."

John reviewed his own background and was surprised that Leidesdorff seemed familiar with much of it. Before he could come to the point of asking for a position, Leidesdorff interrupted him with a gracious smile. "Mr. Lewis, you and I are two of the richest young men in Alta California." He lifted a long, symmetrical finger. "Ah, but you are the richer because you are younger. Shall I say why? Because it has been given to us to help build this land. I should think that no pioneer since Moses himself has been given such a glorious opportunity. A man born to wealth may be sorely tempted to take his riches for granted. He may abuse them. Perhaps that is the fault we find in most *californios*. Not in all, I must hasten to add. Our friend General Vallejo knows what nature has conferred upon us here. And there are others." He paused thoughtfully. "But we who have come more recently see it all more clearly than most. Certainly that is true of Captain Cooper, David Spence, and your own father-in-law." Leidesdorff paused again, frowning slightly. "You have been working for Captain Cooper and I've been told that you perform services for him well beyond the call of the average clerk. Am I correct?"

"My training as a supercargo is of some use to him. Buying and droghing are occupations conducive to quick learning."

Leidesdorff laughed. "Indeed, the latter can place a dan-

175

gerous burden on a man's brain and catch him his death of cold as well. But I interrupt. Go on, please."

"I know something of ships and stowing cargoes and the months I spent with Captain Sutter were an education."

"Yes. It is possible to learn much from Captain Sutter about grand enterprise, and equally to learn how not to undertake the financing of same." There was no suggestion of malice in the good-natured observation. "When you look ahead, Mr. Lewis, what do you perceive as your destination?"

The question was troublesome. Much had happened in short order since he had jumped ship in April a little more than four years earlier. There had been many plans and more dreams, but none had really promised viability.

"I think I have some talent for business, sir, but I'm afraid I've not yet thought of my particular niche."

Leidesdorff smiled sympathetically. "At your age, neither had I. But I was more fortunate than most. I was raised by an extraordinary man, an uncle. Quite early on in my rearing he was at great pains to make me see that the most favored place for a man whose bent is commerce lies between the producer and the consumer. My father was a planter. My uncle was a wholesale merchant. My father died in debt. My uncle died a man of wealth. The lesson he taught me was inscribed indelibly: If a man positions himself well between the producer and the consumer, he will seldom be unbalanced by the ill fortune of either and will most certainly be enriched by the good fortune of both. Indeed, if he manages his credit well, such a merchant may find both parties working for him!"

Leidesdorff set his cup aside and John sensed that it was time to make his proposal but the merchant anticipated him. "Mr. Lewis, I know you are well connected in Monterey. But I cannot help but wonder if someday soon we might not hope that you will see the possibilities in this most remarkable of all the world's harbors and decide to cast your fortune with us?"

At a loss for words, John sat desperately groping for some graceful way to answer in the affirmative. Smiling, Leidesdorff rose from his chair. "My hotel will be finished soon. I am expanding my warehouse and I plan to buy another schooner for coastal trade. I even dream of steam-powered craft on the bay so we shall not be at the mercy of wind and tide on our runs up the rivers. Those great interior valleys will be settled very soon now, Mr. Lewis. The trade will go to the firm that is ready. It strikes me that I could count myself extraordinarily fortunate if I were able to persuade one such as you to assist me in these ventures."

John Lewis scarcely saw his surroundings as he rode back to Monterey. For the entire journey his mind reeled with the bright prospects offered by Leidesdorff. He and his family would be given a house befitting the assistant manager of the William A. Leidesdorff Company. The salary would be seventy-five dollars a month with the promise of substantial increases as business warranted. Leidesdorff had also hinted that a successful association might also hold the promise of a partnership one day. Dazzled by new visions of a great merchandising empire, John rode into Monterey an hour after sundown.

Over dinner at the Robles adobe he recounted the details of his visit. Even the news that Goyo was rumored to be on the way home from Mexico did nothing to dampen his enthusiasm. Plans were made to move his family as early in the new year as possible. He explained that while Leidesdorff had set no definite time for the employment to start, it had been apparent that the earliest practical date would be the most agreeable.

It was decided that John would go north again after the first of the year to get established. No later than early March he would return for Maria and Felicia. These decisions having been settled, the family turned its attention to the coming holidays.

Monterey saw little of Juan Alvarado during the Christmas season. He had retired to Alisal swearing that he would never accept public office again. For a time an estrangement existed between the former governor and his military commander, José Castro. When Micheltorena came to Monterey he offered Castro the commission of lieutenant colonel and revoked the commission of colonel held by Mariano Vallejo. Alvarado expected Castro to refuse the commission. Instead he accepted with no apparent injury to his pride and pledged total loyalty to the new military governor.

More and more frequently word reached Monterey that parties of immigrants were on the overland trails from the United States. Early in January, Governor Micheltorena became so concerned about the situation that he discussed issuing a decree requiring each able-bodied citizen in Monterey to join the militia and undergo training. Worried that he might be detained in the capital, John made plans to leave for Yerba Buena immediately.

In his arms on the night before his departure, Maria whispered contritely and sought to reassure him. "But, Juan Lewis, it was I who kept you here. You should have gone two weeks ago." She snuggled closer and rested her cheek against his bare chest. "But I was selfish, no?"

Lewis cradled her head in his palm and looked down at her. "You were selfish, *yes*! And so was I. You are a very difficult woman to leave, Maria."

"But you will go now and I shall come as soon as you tell me. If it is dangerous to return, you will write to me and I shall ask father to make the journey with us."

"You will not make the journey alone. If necessary I will offer to serve in the militia in Yerba Buena. But I myself shall ride down to bring you to your new home." He drew her warm, willing body closer and moved his big hand down along the smooth, curving furrow of her back and up over the gentle swell of her hip. The specter of militia service and the separation paled and were forgotten.

John returned to Yerba Buena in mid-January to advise Leisdesdorff that he would be able to move his family north by mid-February and to inspect the house the merchant had written about. The house, made of plastered adobe, stood above Leidesdorff's cottage and commanded a view of the cove, the islands to the east, and the hills of the *contra costa* on the far side of the bay. Furniture for the new home would present no problem. A shipload was en route from New England to furnish the planned hotel. The few interim things they might require would be available in the Leidesdorff warehouse.

John stayed on for ten days, familiarizing himself with the stock and with the lists of merchandise on order. When he returned to Monterey he was certain no obstacles to an early move remained.

Captain Cooper continued John's employment until the first of February. When the day came to tote up the bill for the things drawn against salary, John found that very little cash was left. Cooper frowned over the balance sheet and clucked with concern. "I was afraid of that, lad. Yes, I was. A worthy reputation's mighty hard to come by. I believe I've a good one and I wouldn't care to lose it." He reached for the handle of a small desk drawer. "So, rather than risk being called a tightwad for sending a young father away with an empty purse, I've thought to provide you with this." He removed a fist-sized deerskin pouch and handed it to Lewis. "There's a month's bonus in silver in there, John. It's small enough to be a practical amount to give and large enough to be a respectable amount to receive. Take it with the blessings of the missus and me. If the good Lord had given us another son we'd have wished for the likes of you."

Surprised and touched by the unexpected generosity, John managed what he knew were inadequate thanks. That night, at dinner with Don José and Doña Gertrudis, he presented the pouch to Maria. To his astonishment her eyes filled with tears. It would have been more like his fiery little wife, he thought, to straighten indignantly and demand why her husband's worth had not been properly acknowledged by twice the amount.

In bed, after evening prayers, Maria snuggled her head beneath his chin and urged him to describe again their new home and the sort of furniture that would come from the United States. John obliged and wondered vaguely at her quietness.

Several times in the ensuing days he found Maria slumped on a chair resting. When he asked her if she felt ill, she pretended annoyance and brushed the query aside. "It is a very difficult thing for a wife to pull up her roots and organize everything that must go in the *carretas*. Men do not understand how fatiguing it can be. Now get out, my dear husband. Go talk to my father, who is going to miss you very much, because when I am busy I don't miss you at all."

The following day, Doña Gertrudis took John aside and asked if the trip north could be postponed for a week. Her reasons were not convincing. "Many things remain to be done, Juan. I am making things the baby must have for the trip. They are not ready yet. Would a week make a great difference to Señor Leidesdorff?"

"Probably not. He is anxious for me to begin work but I am certain he would accept a reasonable explanation."

The next morning, under questioning, Doña Gertrudis

told John that she was certain now that her daughter was pregnant again. "She is happy and sick at the same time, Juan. She is happy to have another child for you. A son this time. She prays for it. But she knows that it makes things very difficult. She will not tell you herself, but she is afraid to have her baby at Yerba Buena."

Completely upset, John struggled to control his voice. "In the name of God, *why*? It is not against the law. Babies have been born there."

"Indian babies and *mestizo* babies. But it is not like Monterey where there are many women who understand these things and know what to do. Maria had a very difficult birth with Felicia."

"Second births are easier. Everybody's said that. All my life I've heard it."

Doña Gertrudis shrugged. "It depends. Perhaps yes. Perhaps no. Only the Holy Mother knows. If you really wish it, Maria will go with you and have her baby there and I shall come with the women to help. But you must send for me in time."

John was still in a turmoil when Don José found him seated on an outside bench. "So, Juan, we are about to be blessed again. This is very happy news." He sat down beside his son-in-law and peered at him curiously. "But it comes at an inopportune moment. Yes?"

"In truth, yes."

Resting a hand on John's shoulder, Don José nodded sympathetically. "You have very strong ammunition, my son!"

"And your daughter is a very easy target!"

Don José's eyes widened and he threw back his head and laughed. "My boy, my boy, there are few things in this life more comforting than a passionate woman who comes to her husband's arms willingly and often. Do not curse your luck for that. Thank God that you are not married to," an impatient gesture embraced the town, "to a dozen women I can think of, and that in your old age you will have a loving family to care for you. That is the ultimate wealth." He rose and moved away a little. "May I tell you what I think you should do?"

John got to his feet with an exasperated sigh. "It would have been better if you had told what not to do!"

"That is counsel no man listens to, my son. But I will give you some now that you should listen to. Do not disappoint Señor Leidesdorff. Go to Yerba Buena. Begin your work. Finish your house. He is reasonable and sympathetic. Also, I am told that he is a lonely man who has known hurt. He will understand. Maria says the baby will come in September. Surely you will be permitted to welcome it and be with your wife. And then, when your family is able to travel, you will all go to your new home." His arms extended appealingly. "What could be better? Now you know what your new house must accommodate. You can prepare in time. It is a blessing, really."

John returned to Yerba Buena in mid-February and began his duties with William Leidesdorff. Soon he was at work devising a departmentalized system of storage that would make order out of the confusion of general merchandise stacked at random in the large warehouse. Leidesdorff ran one six-hundred-ton schooner regularly between Yerba Buena and Honolulu. He had several small bay schooners making frequent trips to landings along the bay. John was obliged to make these local trips during March and April to contract for hides and tallow. He looked forward to them since they gave him an opportunity to visit old acquaintances.

Leidesdorff had extended Sutter's credit to the limit and now refused further requests for supplies. But John exchanged letters with Harry Morrison and kept abreast of the progress. Morrison reported that the white population in and around New Helvetia had grown to more than fifty but there were still only a half dozen settlers on Sutter's land and most of them had not complied with the terms set forth in the grants. He wrote that Sutter "closed an eye and accepted as the head of the family any man with fortitude enough to take an unwashed squaw into his bed."

In May, John managed a three-day visit with his family when he sailed south to attend some customs clearances. He was shocked at Maria's size. She seemed to have grown large much earlier than when she was carrying Felicia. She laughed at his concern. "That is because I am making a very large son for you, Juan Lewis. All of the signs are right. The Indian women say so."

Privately, Doña Gertrudis was not so sanguine. "She is very uncomfortable much of the time, Juan. Don José and

I wish you were here. When the time comes she will need you."

"I will be here. I have already spoken to Señor Leidesdorff. There will be no difficulty. But you must send word to me in time."

On the night before he sailed, John and Maria dined at the Robles adobe and John learned that Goyo had been seen in Los Angeles. Don José also reported that President Santa Anna had formed a new constitutional government that called for the immediate expulsion of all Americans who were not naturalized. Governor Micheltorena, charged with executing the order, was extremely unhappy because of the obvious exceptions that would have to be made. A second order had followed barring all but naturalized merchants from trading in Alta California. Don José told John that the new edict had been met with outright derision by Monterey's merchants. Larkin suggested to Micheltorena that since he was unable to comply, as an official of the United States Government, he would be happy to dissolve his business if the central government would immediately pay up, in full, all of the loans he had advanced to the Alvarado administration, Micheltorena had chosen to ignore Santa Anna's directives as impossible to enforce without destroying the economy of Alta California.

Don José outlined the situation. "Santa Anna merely hastens the inevitable, Juan. By insisting on impractical conditions here he earns the disrespect of his own officials and shows the entire world the weakness of the Mexican government. It is an open invitation to those who would take us over. The next time we are captured our liberty will not be returned." He glanced around to make certain he would not be overheard by the servants. "And we do not deserve to have it returned. Who can respect us? Micheltorena is intelligent, but he has no backbone. He openly refuses to discipline his *cholos* and he has even made his only responsible officer, Colonel Telles, ill with the fever by refusing to support him when he disciplines the men. 'It is wrong to flog men whose bellies are empty because they have not been paid. They steal to eat. And so would we if we were hungry.' That is what he said. And so we do not walk about Monterey unarmed. Soon now, serious trouble will come."

Far from reassured, John Lewis returned to Yerba

Buena. He had been gone less than three weeks when Goyo Robles reappeared in Monterey. He seemed unmoved by his family's emotional greeting and he evinced no interest in his infant niece. Except for visits to the customhouse and the government buildings he kept to himself.

His son's appearance and manner distressed Don José. Goyo seemed to have aged. His lean body was travel-worn and his narrow, sun-darkened face had assumed an even more hawkish aspect. Traces of gray had appeared at his temples and the bravado that once had been appealing had been displaced by a surly arrogance. Each day at mass, Doña Gertrudis implored the Holy Mother to save him.

Goyo spent several days at the family adobe before riding inland to see Alvarado at Alisal. Within the week he returned, grimmer than ever. He stopped at his home for food, then rode to the government house to see Micheltorena. Two days later he left Monterey for New Helvetia carrying a letter from Governor Micheltorena commissioning Sutter a captain in the Mexican militia. The commission was accompanied by an order to form and train a company of soldiers under a promise that a government draft would be forthcoming to provide arms, uniforms, and wages.

Shortly after Goyo's departure, the French whaler, *Ganges*, put into Monterey late in the afternoon for provisioning. The second mate and six sailors on temporary leave from the ship visited a waterfront cantina. Almost immediately they were confronted by a group of Micheltorena's drunken *cholos*. Within minutes, one of the French sailors had three fingers lopped off, one of the *cholos* was killed outright, and another was impaled on a harpoon. Then the battle spilled onto the street and down to the landing.

Colonel Telles, still recovering from a fortnight of high fever, managed to get his men under control. Word of the vicious brawl reached Micheltorena and he accused the whaling captain of breaking the law by letting his crew remain after the sundown curfew. The Frenchman, convinced by reports from his own crew that the *cholos* had provoked the fight, refused to accept the responsibility.

David Spence had been present when the master faced down the Mexican general, accused him of laxity in discipline, and threatened to sail immediately to intercept the

French fleet cruising off the California coast and report the outrage. Spence persuaded Micheltorena not to press the charge and finally the matter was settled without creating an international incident. The *Ganges* sailed on the early tide the next morning but Monterey had had its fill.

At Larkin's home, Spence expressed his disgust to his fellow merchants. "We have reached the end, gentlemen. Every reasonable person knows that the *cholos* started it. They've been spoiling for weeks now. Micheltorena's been warned a dozen times. This is enough to bring responsible men to the edge of treason."

The statement was greeted by a chorus of "Ayes." Spence reached into his pocket and removed a folded paper. "As though we have not had sufficient trouble, Micheltorena has called the new departmental assembly into session here. They have chosen a slate for the position of civil governor that will be submitted to Mexico City. Then Santa Anna will choose one of the men for the post.

"But the trouble is Micheltorena did not notify Pico or Carrillo or any of the men from the south."

William Hartnell whistled softly and gazed at the paper Spence was holding. "Who was chosen for this exalted position, David?"

"Micheltorena is his own first choice. Alvarado is second—"

Spence was interrupted by expressions of disbelief. Cooper swore quietly as he got to his feet. "Micheltorena cannot be fathomed. He's about to make the only reasonably competent governor we've had a poor second choice. Who were the others?"

"Telles, Osio, and Casarin in that order. The general's tactic is obvious. By making certain he is named civil governor, he would no longer be responsible for his rats. Alvarado, as ranking colonel of the government troops, would have the responsibility."

When the men had gone, each to nurture his own misgivings, United States Consul Thomas O. Larkin went to his desk to pen a memorandum noting that the time was fast approaching when the United States should redouble its efforts to bring about a peaceful annexation of Alta California and the adjacent territory. Reasonable Californians, both native and naturalized, would favor it, he was certain.

In Los Angeles former governor *pro tempore*, Pio Pico, lost no time in venting his outrage in an official communication. Micheltorena offered the lame excuse that the dispatch to the southern delegates had gone astray. Apologies were made and the assembly was convened in August. In Monterey and Yerba Buena the merchants waited on tenterhooks the outcome of the voting.

Pico refused to approve a slate unless Micheltorena would agree that both capital and customhouse be transferred to Los Angeles. Evidently his memory of the *cholos'* depredations had paled before the personal advantage he could derive from having the customs money under his control. Reports came that the assembly was hopelessly deadlocked, the five northern delegates against the five southern ones. Micheltorena, as governor, could cast the deciding vote. The meeting was adjourned and rescheduled at a later date. John Lewis, in Monterey to see Maria, who had grown enormously, was present when word came that the matter of the customhouse had been put to a ballot and Governor Micheltorena had broken the tie by casting his vote to leave the office in Monterey.

There was high jubilation in the capital and a great tirade in Los Angeles. Pico charged fraud and collusion in the north and threatened to journey to Mexico City to have the decision reversed.

At the Robles house Don José sat musing aloud in the garden with Maria and John. "Pico will not go to Mexico City. Instead he will ask Alvarado and Castro to support him in a revolt against Micheltorena. It is his way. First a revolt against Chico, then Gutiérrez and soon, Micheltorena. No Mexican governor ever will be acceptable. But once they are driven out, it will be Los Angeles against Monterey again, and always the same issue, that accursed customhouse. Pico never has recovered from the grandeur of being governor, even for only twenty-two days, twelve years ago. He will never rest until he holds that office again. And no man can trust him because his personal ambition is greater than his love for California. He is a pompous little man, often generous, more often selfish, and still more often, ridiculous."

John was about to add an observation of his own when Maria reacted to a sudden, sharp discomfort. He put an arm around her anxiously.

"It is all right, Juan. It is only that your son grows impatient now," Maria said.

John wished profoundly for an end to the confusion that kept him from concentrating all of his energies on his new position. Things were going well in Yerba Buena. The house was completed and some of the furniture had arrived. He was well pleased with that aspect. But the disruptive politics of Alta California were having their effect upon Leidesdorff and also upon Leese, Richardson and the others around the Bay. Few cared to plan too far ahead. Only Sutter remained supremely confident about the future and continued scheming, blithely indifferent to the burdensome past obligations upon which his dreams were based.

John excused himself to go down to visit Will Chard and Josiah Belden in their new store. Part of the modest credit for its establishment had been advanced by Leidesdorff upon John's personal assurances. He paused behind Maria and rested his hands protectively on her shoulders as he addressed Don José. "More than one *californio* now wishes this fiasco could be put to an end. Even Vallejo told Leidesdorff that he has given up hope of keeping out the settlers. He has changed completely. He would welcome an orderly government under the United States. Most of us at Yerba Buena agree."

Don José smiled and lapsed into Spanish. *"Mas vale tarde que nunca, Juan.* The change should happen now, but better it happens late than never."

Maria's eyes darted heavenward and she whispered a quick prayer. "Thank God Goyo does not hear you. He is a *nacionalista* now. He would destroy us all."

Doña Gertrudis glanced at her husband apprehensively, then lowered her head to stare in unhappy silence at her folded hands.

On September 19, 1844, Maria Robles Lewis gave birth to twin boys. They were christened Steven Joseph' and William Eugene. The birth was difficult and no doctor was available. Skilled midwives and earnest prayer, plus liberal doses of laudanum, finally assured the twins' arrival. Badly torn and weak from loss of blood, Maria lingered in a comatose state for nearly a week.

John, fighting off panic induced by Maria's terrible outcries and her sobbing prayers, had wanted to ride to

186

Mount Diablo for Dr. John Marsh, but the men had intervened and convinced him that a doctor without proper qualifications would be far more dangerous than midwives who had successfully presided over a hundred difficult births. In the end, the weight of Doña Encarnacion Cooper's opinion dissuaded him. "She will live, Juan. We Spanish women have twenty children as easily as your woman have two. Now Maria has double the pain. But the Holy Mother is just. For all of her life, she will have double the pleasure also."

The midwives and Doña Gertrudis did not consider Maria to be out of danger until the beginning of October. Much relieved, John returned to Yerba Buena, where he was greeted by William Leidesdorff as a man of special distinction, the father of healthy twin sons.

Leidesdorff told him that forty-six more American men, women, and children had come into central California during his absence and that over a hundred more were on the trail south from Oregon territory. Few people had any doubt now that Washington planned to duplicate the Texas strategy when enough settlers arrived.

As autumn deepened, Micheltorena's two hundred *ratereos* grew bolder. Hardly a night passed without incident—another robbery, another woman accosted on the street, another drunken brawl with foreign sailors on shore leave, and endless internecine squabbles. The ultimate outrage came late in October when one of La Mofeta's prostitutes, a *mestizo* girl not yet sixteen, was found sexually ravaged on the beach. Before she died the next morning, she told Father Varga that she had been raped by seven of the *cholos*. One of them had paid and the others had been waiting in the darkness when she had accompanied him to the shore. Once again action was promised but not taken. Then La Mofeta herself attempted to stab the original offender and was disemboweled with her own knife in front of the cantina.

Goyo Robles, just returned from New Helvetia, learned that a delegation of *californios* who had stood with Alvarado had ridden inland to Alisal. These men were seeking Alvarado's leadership in a revolt. Goyo was torn between loyalty to a blood brother and a new and deep conviction that complete cooperation with Mexico was necessary to control the flood of Yankee immigrants. He returned to his father's house and prepared to ride to Alisal.

187

Goyo's brief presence at the family adobe occasioned nothing but hurt and anger. Once again he completely ignored little Felicia; but when he was forced by his mother's pleading to see the twin boys, he stood smirking beside the *doble cuna*, tracing his forefinger along the jagged scar that disfigured his temple. "Incredible! But I have seen that yanqui. He could not have made two sons at once without help!" Leaving his family mute with shock, he departed quickly.

He arrived at Alisal shortly before midnight and immediately confronted Alvarado. "Juan, I came to talk here because the whole town has ears. Do you know what is being said about you?"

"No. But nothing will surprise me."

"It may not. But it should worry you. Telles has been informed that you were asked to lead a revolt against Micheltorena. He has told that to the governor. They are saying that many *californios* and some foreigners have asked you to command an army to drive Micheltorena and his soldiers out of the country."

"Soldiers? Criminals!"

"What difference? I want to know whether or not they speak the truth."

Alvarado looked up unhappily. "I was asked if I would be governor again."

"And you answered?"

"Again I am administrator of customs. Also, I am colonel of the First Regiment. But most of all, I am tired. There is no persuasion in heaven or earth that could induce me to become governor again."

Sensing that Alvarado was being evasive, Goyo pressed his point. "Micheltorena respects you, Juan. It would be fatal to divide us now. What you must do is convince him of your loyalty."

Alvarado's eyebrows lifted. "And why should he doubt my loyalty with all of the honors he has conferred on me?"

"Because, Juan, he remembers that you led the revolt against his friend, Gutiérrez. Telles has told him that you would do it again."

Alvarado looked at Goyo incredulously. "Would I really? With no Isaac Graham? With no William Chard? I am a colonel without troops. From whom would I get help? Sutter? That one will march with the highest bidder—and only the governor can give him what he wants. Sutter is desperate for the *soberante* grant, all the land between the two grants I gave to him. Micheltorena could buy Sutter's soul if he promised him that."

Goyo was surprised that Alvarado seemed to be aware of Sutter's attempts to bargain with the governor for the additional land. "But Juan, if you know that about Sutter, then you also know that the governor has not responded to his maneuvering."

Alvarado nodded. "For now, yes. But if he needs Sutter, he will."

Goyo eyed him suspiciously. "Why would he need Sutter unless someone threatened him?"

"Goyo, for years you have stood with me for independence. You fought beside me when we drove out Gutiérrez. But now, I feel that you stand with a Mexican governor. Could it be, as with José Castro, that you also are in Micheltorena's debt?"

Goyo fought to control his voice. "I told you that I had no influence in the choice of the commander or the soldiers to be sent. I told Santa Anna only what you told me to say, that Alta California cannot be defended against the foreigners without many more troops."

Alvarado turned away and Goyo knew he was responsible for the undoing of his closest friend. On the journey home from Mexico City he had confessed to himself that he had been flattered into saying what President Santa Anna wanted to hear. Goyo's answers to questions about Alvarado's relationships with Pio Pico and Mariano Vallejo made it imperative for Santa Anna to place Alta California under central government domination. Santa Anna knew he was facing a war with the United States and his advisers were urging him to move before the Americans could muster a strong force.

Alvarado turned back again but avoided Goyo's eyes. "There is only one reason why Santa Anna would choose Micheltorena to come north with the troops instead of sending a detachment under a Telles, for instance." Then he looked directly at his friend. "Can you imagine what the reason is?"

Goyo flung his hands out. "There could be a hundred reasons! Who knows the mind of Santa Anna?"

"There is only one reason, my dear friend, just one. A

189

civil governor is replaced in time of danger only when the central government feels that he is incompetent."

"That is a lie, Juan. You have been governor longer than any other in our history. Six years. And we have prospered. I told Santa Anna there would be no foreign problems here now if Bustamente had sent soldiers when they were requested four years ago. I told him that you are a brilliant field commander. I said the same of Castro. I said that you hold the loyalty of every man in Alta California." There was a leaden silence. Then Goyo heard Alvarado asking the question he had feared for so long.

"Tell me, on your oath as my blood brother, did Santa Anna speak of Pio Pico and Mariano Vallejo? Did he speak of our differences?"

He forced himself to nod. "Yes."

The weariness in Alvarado's face gave way to a smile that at once was sad and triumphant. "He asked you about them because Pico had written to him saying that I was too ill to discharge my duties and that I had been a party to collusion in the matter of keeping the customhouse and capital here. Mariano has written many times complaining of my lack of military initiative."

Goyo seemed pale beneath his deep tan and the scar line on his temple and cheek shone dead white in the firelight. "He knows Pico. He cannot take him seriously. Pico has bombarded him with letters accusing everybody of collusion ever since the assembly. Most of all, Pico has accused Micheltorena himself. And he knows Mariano."

"Ah, yes, Goyo, I have no doubt of that. But the truth remains that Santa Anna was forced to conclude that men who fight among themselves while foreigners invade their land are not fit to defend the Department of the North because they are wanting in common patriotism."

Goyo hoped that the heat of his anger would obscure the light of Alvarado's truth. Santa Anna had tricked him into confirming the central government's suspicions that there could never be unanimity of purpose in Alta California, had tricked him into admitting the truth. "No man would accuse you of that, Juan. Your patriotism is a shining inspiration. Even in defeat Gutiérrez agreed."

"But the fact remains, Goyo, my friend, that the poor opinion of me is the one that prevailed. I am certain that you were asked if you thought I was fit for the responsibility of commanding federal troops in an action against the foreigners. I want to hear now how you defended me."

"You have heard. I have just told you. In God's name what more can I say?"

Alvarado's incipient anger had gone. His face reflected only the great burden of inner weariness and his voice was soft. "It is not necessary to tell me anything more if you can say again, on your oath, that you did not know Micheltorena would be sent to replace me."

Goyo all but leaped across the space that separated them. "I did not know, Juan, I swear it. Santa Anna said only that he recognized the seriousness of the situation here. He said only that five hundred men would be sent. He said nothing about a commander, for certain, nothing about a military governor!"

Alvarado dropped heavily onto the chair again. "It is the will of God. What has been done has been done. And because of that—*much more remains to be done*, again." He leaned forward to look deeply into Robles' eyes. "Where would you stand now, Goyo, if I were to ask you to join me in another revolt? Where would your loyalty be? And what would your counsel be?"

"For God's sake, Juan, is it necessary to ask? I would stand with you, always. But I beg you to go to Micheltorena first. Offer to help raise money to pay the men. Remove his suspicion by your loyal action. There is no other way now to save Alta California. It is too late for independence. We can survive only by cooperation with Mexico. It is our last hope. If we do not act instantly we shall be overrun by the yanqui pigs or by the British."

"You echo Santa Anna's words. Yes?"

"In the name of God, no. *He echoes mine!*"

Stunned by his own inadvertent admission, Goyo stood rooted. The implication in his outburst was irrefutable. In the past Juan Alvarado had led him to undo himself with his own temper. Now he had done it again. Goyo knew that in three thoughtless words he had revealed all that he himself had said in Mexico City. "Micheltorena will be your friend, Juan. Your friend, if you will permit him."

The questioning in Alvarado's eyes turned to reproach and then to sadness. "I have no friends, Goyo. I have only one well-intentioned, politically inept blood brother."

John returned to Monterey in early November to attend

the wedding of William Chard and Dolores Robles. Maria, radiant again and sufficiently recovered to take part in the festivities, danced the waltzes, the quadrilles, the jotas, and the boleros with all of her former abandon. Amazed, John sat out most of them, claiming less grace than a hamstrung ox.

The next morning, Don José returned from the calle principal. He was unusually perturbed. "It is very bad. Very bad. Sutter's serving boy, Pablo, rode in this morning and was seen entering the governor's residence. A messenger came for Goyo. He left me and went to Micheltorena immediately. Then both of them rode out of the pueblo. Goyo would not say where he goes. There is talk everywhere that Micheltorena has ordered Colonel Telles to arrest Juan Alvarado."

Before Don José could answer John's stream of questions, Will Chard pulled up in front of the house and strode unceremoniously into the parlor. "I'm not sure this is anything I personally will shed tears over, but Micheltorena is going to arrest Alvarado for treason. Telles is gathering his men at the presidio now. They will leave at dark." He laughed ironically. "I seem to recall that they excel at these nocturnal surprise parties."

Doña Gertrudis was aghast. "But Juan Alvarado has nothing to do with politics now. He has sworn it. If Micheltorena is arresting him, then it is only to save face—to invent some excuse to make us forget his own irresponsibility. Juan must be warned and someone must tell the truth to the governor."

She looked from Chard to John and back to Chard again. Chard warded off the tacit request with upraised hands. "Don't look to me. I went to prison for eighteen months for doing nothing. How long do you think Micheltorena would let me rot at Tepic if he knew I really had assisted a revolutionist leader? Alvarado's record is against him. Anyone who even pleads for him will be suspect."

Don José nodded in agreement and glanced meaningfully at his son-in-law. "A deputation has appealed to Alvarado to lead them. There is no question. That in itself is sufficient. Alvarado will never receive a fair trial from General Micheltorena. The only way he could clear himself would be to name those who approached him. Juan would never do that. It would put their necks in nooses

192

immediately. I know Juan. He would rather risk his own neck. He must be told."

Maria laid a hand on John's sleeve. "Juan, please? We cannot know this and not warn him. He has promised to be the godfather of our sons. And he has been your good friend, too. I know the danger, but please, Juan, please?"

At noon that same day, on the pretext of departing for Yerba Buena somewhat earlier than planned, John said his farewells to the merchants and left the capital by way of the *Camino Real*. When he was well beyond the pueblo he turned inland and rode toward a difficult short-cut cattle trail through the canyon that would give him a six- or seven-hour advantage.

Shortly before midnight, John, worn almost to exhaustion, dismounted heavily in the courtyard of Juan Alvarado's adobe ranch house and handed the reins to a sleepy servant. Moments later, Alvarado listened dumbstruck to the story of his blood brother's treachery.

"Incredible!" he murmured over and over as John filled in the details. When John finished, Alvarado stepped forward and embraced him. "Juan Lewis, it is not possible to repay what I now owe you. Until this moment I have not permitted myself to believe what my heart knows to be the truth. Goyo has become a *fanatico*. No man is his brother who will not believe as he does. For him it is easier to hate than to reason. He has no loyalty now other than to his passion. He will reject those who love him and embrace those who despise him if he thinks they will serve his cause. He has not the wisdom to know that his cause will be the end of Alta California. Now we must fight to save Alta California from our own brothers."

The following morning, just before dawn, Colonel Telles and one hundred *cholos* surrounded El Alisal and found it deserted except for servants who purported to know nothing until one of the officers took an infant Indian child and threatened to throw it into the blazing adobe oven. The terrified mother broke down and revealed that Alvarado and an unidentified man had left for Castro's adobe in San Juan.

At San Juan, Telles discovered that Alvarado and Castro had left for San Jose. He stopped only long enough to strip the adobe of supplies, then set out in pursuit well aware that he was certain to be frustrated still again, for

Micheltorena had ordered him to pursue Alvarado no farther north than the Rancho de Laguna some five leagues south of the pueblo of San Jose. Micheltorena's excuse was that he didn't want Telles and his men too far from the capitol. Telles arrived in a soaking downpour and made camp near some abandoned adobe outbuildings. There, fuming at the inconceivable stupidity of the governor-general. he and his men watched Alvarado supervise the establishment of his camp less than a half league to the north.

Alvarado invoked the protection of his personal saint and named the place El Lugar Seguro de Santa Teresa. John helped to set up a headquarters hut and reflected with grim amusement that poor Santa Teresa would be taxed to the limit should Telles and his men decide to attack.

After a miserable night the rain stopped and Alvarado, expecting Telles to move, alerted his little force. The day passed with no evidence of preparation on the other side. John, Alvarado, and Castro speculated that Telles must have sent for reinforcements even though he would be opposed by fewer than half as many men. Reconciled to his involvement, John agreed to scour the countryside to the north for recruits. Within the week he was back at Santa Teresa at the head of forty-eight well armed *rancheros* and their workmen, all of whom had suffered enough of Mexican rule under Gutiérrez and preferred a return to Alvarado's orderly but more lenient home administration.

Two more days passed and still there was no indication that Telles was preparing to do more than make his camp livable. Each side watched the other slaughter and butcher appropriated range cattle. Each side could see the silhouettes around the large bivouac fires at night. And each side could hear the laughter and occasional singing as the men sought to relieve their discomfort and boredom.

During the week Alvarado had added a small company of expert French Canadian riflemen to his army. He promised them liberal pay and the necessary supplies to return to the Oregon country. On the eighth day of the uneasy truce, a rider arrived from San Jose bearing news that Telles himself had not been in the camp for a week. He had left his officers under orders not to attack until he had protested to General Micheltorena and received permission to advance. Immediately Alvarado and Castro began plans for a surprise attack. Alvarado was elated. "Telles is the only able officer in the force. If we strike them very early and surprise them sleeping, it will be finished within the hour. We will force Micheltorena and his *rateros* to leave the country."

Castro was reluctant to move too hastily. "Telles can call on one hundred reserves in the Monterey garrison. How can we be certain that he did not return for them? Man to man we are better than they. But if they outnumber us two to one and bring cannon it can go very hard unless our first attack is a complete success."

Castro's resistance puzzled Alvarado. It was unlike him to argue for inaction. "But of course we shall have a quick victory, José. I do not understand your reasoning. Their reinforcements are not here. It is foolish to wait. After midnight we will deploy riflemen on both flanks, the best shots we have. Then we will rout the *cholos* at first light. We can move the flanking companies down the ravines on both sides while we charge directly from the front. That is why I chose this place. It is perfect. We must move now."

John, who held no official rank but was accorded the courtesy due an officer, witnessed the argument but avoided taking sides. Hoping that the confrontation would be over soon, he tried not to dwell on the possible consequences and on those that undoubtedly had already accrued. Unless William Leidesdorff had received word of the revolt from Larkin, who would understand the nature of his involvement, John knew that his employer would be at a loss to explain his overlong absence. He hoped that Don José would have had the foresight to advise Leidesdorff also, but these aspects of his involvement paled before the other possible consequences. He forced himself to face the truth that in revolts men must die and leave behind them weeping women, defenseless children, and a legacy of unfulfilled dreams.

Alvarado prevailed and covert preparations were begun in the late afternoon. Bores were cleaned. Powder and shot and wadding were checked and rechecked and the snipers were chosen for the two flanking companies and surreptitiously moved into position to deploy.

An hour before sunset, the sentry who had been posted at the top of the hill spurred his mount down the slope, pulled up at Alvarado's headquarters shelter, and passed the word that Micheltorena and twenty riders were approaching the Rancho de Laguna camp from the south-west.

Upon hearing the news, Castro proposed that he himself ride out to meet Micheltorena under a flag of truce and offer the general an honorable settlement. "It is the only sensible action, Juan. We must preserve Mexican lives to defend our land against the Americans."

Alvarado, facing Castro across the makeshift table on which was spread his battle plan, stared at his old revolutionary commander in disbelief. "I do not know you, José." He snapped his fingers sharply. "Like that, you have become a stranger."

Castro's face mirrored the conflict that had prompted his irresolute behavior. "I know Micheltorena. He has no stomach for battle, Juan. We can win honorably without wasting a man. The issue is clear. You were asked to lead this revolt to get rid of the *cholos*. If he will send them to Mexico we can place ourselves under his command. The problem will be settled. You do not wish to be governor again. Micheltorena enjoys the task. It is an excellent solution. Once more you will be a brilliant hero and every *californio* with us will return to his land and his family. Allow me to arrange it, Juan. Then you talk with Micheltorena. He is an honorable man, an intelligent man. He must accept our terms."

Alvarado tried to speak but Castro cut him off. "Do not forget, Juan, that Micheltorena's heart is with us in the north. When the vote was tied in the assembly, it was he who braved Pico's anger to cast his vote for us. He kept the capital and customhouse in Monterey. We *all* owe him something for that. Most especially you. It was not necessary for him to commission you a colonel—nor to make you administrator of customs. These general decisions were made out of consideration for your devotion to this land."

John watched Alvarado's surprise turn to suspicion. "How do you know these things, José? Tell me! How do you know Micheltorena has such great respect for me?"

"Because I have spoken with him about you."

"Ah! Then you *have* visited him in Monterey?"

"No. I have not."

"Then he had visited you at San Juan."

"No. I have not seen him since Mexico City. But when I was a guest at his home we often discussed Alta California. If he has tried to make good laws and establish schools, it is because I have told him what is needed here."

Alvarado found himself staring incredulously at his one-time supreme military commander. It was impossible, he knew, that Castro could not have understood the consequences of such discussions. Suddenly it was clear to Alvarado that his deposal as governor had far deeper roots than he had imagined. Trusted friends had praised him but none had protected him. If Goyo had done the reaping, then surely Castro had done the sowing. As he searched Castro's pained face, Juan Bautista Alvarado felt completely alone. Realization gave way to leaden hopelessness. "It is well, José. Take the white flag and go to your friend, Micheltorena." He nodded toward the men seen through the open doorway. "These men are loyal to me; but now I find it futile to ask them to shed their blood."

On the morning of December 1, 1844, Juan Alvarado met with General Manuel Micheltorena and the general agreed to send his *cholos* back to Mexico within ninety days. Micheltorena would continue as civil governor of Alta California. In turn, Alvarado agreed to place himself and his revolutionary army under the general's command as soon as proof was offered that the *cholos* had departed.

Monterey exploded in rejoicing. In Los Angeles, the relief was no less apparent. Pio Pico ordered his brother Andrés to begin immediate preparations to deport the small garrison of *cholos* still quartered there and a brig was chartered for the purpose.

At Santa Teresa, Alvarado and Castro prepared to move their troops to a winter camp near the mission at San Jose where Micheltorena promised they would be maintained at government expense until the ninety-day grace period had expired.

John, released from further duty, sent word to his family in Monterey that he would come for them as soon as he had made his explanations to William Leidesdorff in Yerba Buena.

Leidesdorff was generous and understanding, but he was far from sanguine about Alta California's future political stability. He spoke of it as he and John sat at supper in his cottage.

"At any rate, perhaps we shall know some peace.

Micheltorena does seem less concerned about immigration than he pretends to be."

John grinned. "And he has the questionable support of Captain Sutter."

Leidesdorff chuckled. "He wants immigrants and so do we merchants. He is a remarkable man with a remarkable lack of conscience, that may in the end serve our purpose."

Very shortly, the observations about the confused state of affairs in Monterey turned to business matters. Leidesdorff spoke of the need for an additional man after the first of the year, one whose duties would be to supervise his growing transportation operation. John, anxious to have Harry Morrison easily accessible to the family because of his wide knowledge of pharmaceuticals and his practical knowledge of simple medical procedures, recommended him. Leidesdorff knew of him and expressed interest and John agreed to sound him out. Satisfied that at last some stability seemed in the offing, he prepared to return to Monterey for the holidays.

During the previous summer, Sutter's long-time serving boy, Pablo, had visited Micheltorena. He was followed a few weeks later by Sutter's clerk, young John Bidwell. Both couriers had carried secret letters from Sutter, composed in grandiloquent French, pledging his absolute loyalty to the new governor. They emphasized the private militia Sutter was drilling and assured Micheltorena that these "perfectly trained" men were ready to march on any mission the governor might require.

In the government house, Micheltorena was reviewing those letters again. He was still smarting from the humiliating accusations he had endured from Colonel Raphael Telles. The colonel had called the general's conduct at Santa Teresa cowardly and disgraceful. He had charged the general with criminal stupidity in requiring that the pursuit be stopped at Rancho de Laguana.

News of the violent personal confrontation spread quickly through the capital. Micheltorena tried to save face by ordering Telles back to Mexico on the next ship. Monterey's citizens were outwardly polite but Micheltorena knew that he was a private laughingstock. Now he must demonstrate that he was not to be judged hastily, that he intended to enforce to the letter the central government's directives. The crux was Sutter and perhaps Isaac Graham also. Both men wanted land. Graham demanded a legal grant as part of his indemnity and Sutter wanted the vast *soberante* grant. Additionally, there was other land, huge stretches of fertile valley land in the interior that could be used to buy loyalty. Sutter's letters had the ring of sincerity. But against that Micheltorena knew that he must balance the evidence of the man's past performance. In the end, he realized that he had no choice but to trust Sutter and hope that promises compatible with the man's boundless personal ambition would constrain him to behave loyally.

Micheltorena dispatched Goyo Robles to New Helvetia for a second time with orders directing Sutter to form an army consisting of infantry, snipers, cavalry, and the brass field piece and march immediately to surprise Alvarado and Castro at San Jose. At the same time, he dispatched a letter to Castro. He reassured his "dear friend" that he was complying with the terms of the treaty and he was dedicated now to bringing a blessed peace to the hearths of every *californio*. Telles, he wrote, had been sent back to Mexico to arrange for the return of the soldiers. The letter ended with news that Sutter had reported a new immigrant train of eleven wagons and a hundred and forty men in the central valley and that still another party of sixty wagons was on the trail west. He urged Castro to send every soldier he could spare from San Jose into the interior to help Sutter turn back the foreign invaders.

On January 3, in response to a letter from John Lewis, Harry Morrison stepped ashore in Yerba Buena from the deck of William Davis' bay schooner. Morrison was overjoyed at the prospect of a position with Leidesdorff, but he also harbored some misgivings. When John heard them, he brought Morrison to Leidesdorff, who listened with mounting concern to the account of preparations underway at New Helvetia.

"Are you certain, Mr. Morrison, that Sutter is not raising this army to repel the immigrants as he is required by law?"

"Aye, sir. I'm certain. He's recruiting the settlers themselves to march wi' him, on the promise of a league of land."

The implications were unmistakable.

John whistled softly and looked across at Leidesdorff. "I know Sutter. He is the complete opportunist. But I cannot believe that Micheltorena would deliberately break this new treaty." He shook his head. "As a matter of fact, I even find it difficult to admit that Sutter would ever be an accomplice to such a vile plot."

Morrison gazed at them uncomfortably, then turned to John. "I hate to be the one to say it, laddie, but your own brother-in-law is there again. It's the second time in six weeks and he's making no bones about being there for Micheltorena. One of the reasons I was anxious to be coming here was to warn ye that I wudna be counting too much on Micheltorena's friendship. I mind well your realtionship wi' Robles. And I'll wager he's found occasion to remind the governor ye were wi' Alvarado. I'm not one for alarrums, lad, but I'd be a wee bit concerned aboot your family if I were you."

John had been worried about Maria and the children. His anxiety increased to near panic as he listened to still more evidence of Sutter's conniving. The family had agreed that in case of trouble they would accompany Don José to the pueblo of Santa Cruz at the north end of Monterey Bay. It was a quiet settlement, off the main road to Yerba Buena and relatively free from the possibility of trouble. There, with Secundino Robles and her father, the family would be safe. John decided to leave for Los Méganos the following morning.

At the headquarters adobe in San Jose, Alvarado stared at Castro. "You may take Micheltorena's letters for the truth. I do not trust him as you do. It is not reasonable to send Telles to Mexico by himself to arrange for the deportation of the *cholos*. That could have been done in Monterey."

José Castro patted the penned sheets. "Of course it is reasonable, Juan. How could Micheltorena explain to Santa Anna the sudden arrival in Mexico of his second in command, and his soldiers, at a time when it is well known that yanquis are pouring over the sierra?" He gestured violently. "Of course it is reasonable."

Muttering, Alvarado rose from the chair. "Then I suppose the rumor that Sutter is preparing his forces to march on us is unresponsible."

"I do not believe it. We have only the word of Doctor

Marsh's man, who said that Sutter had sent Pablo there to ask Marsh for supplies and to join him. I do not believe Sutter would ask an enemy to join him, and Marsh is his enemy."

Alvardo snorted. "I believe Sutter would ask the devil to join him, if he could profit by it!"

Deliberately, Castro changed his tactics and assumed the air of a tolerant elder brother. "Juan, you are tired. Now, you see an enemy behind every tree. Do not be suspicious. Micheltorena is glad to be done with his *cholos* and have an honorable army at his disposal. We have pledged that. He will send proof soon that the *cholos* have sailed. He has commissioned Sutter on the understanding that Sutter's men will be available to us to stand against the yanquis. Sutter likes to drill and maneuver. But he will not march and never against you, his benefactor. All he has, he owes to you."

Alvarado looked askance. "Paying debts occupies Sutter least of all."

The fruitless discussion ended with Castro complacent and Alvarado unconvinced. Alvarado had not told Castro about Captain John Gantt, a former United States military officer who had ridden for New Helvetia. Gantt had gathered together a private militia of long riflemen. Alvarado was sure Gantt would join forces with Sutter if he was promised enough. Gantt, by nature a mercenary, had for years been friendly with Isaac Graham. Alvarado himself had considered recruiting Gantt but dismissed it as unrealistic. Alvarado knew that if he had irrefutable evidence that Isaac Graham also had committed himself and his men to Sutter, the last shred of doubt as to Sutter's motives would be gone. He had secretly dispatched his own spy to look around Branciforte. Ostensibly the man had been released to return to his home because of ill health and Castro himself had been maneuvered into signing the release.

Several miles along the way to Los Méganos, John Lewis met one of Dr. Marsh's Indian *vaqueros*. Terrified, the man was fleeing northward. John stopped him long enough to hear that Sutter had marched into the ranch that morning, had requisitioned all of the usable horses, mules, and oxen and had given Marsh the choice of joining his army as a foot soldier or being imprisoned at the fort with the other Alvarado sympathizers.

John also learned that Sutter's personal courier, Pablo, and Goyo Robles were on their way to Monterey. If, as John supposed, Goyo's purpose was to coordinate a surprise move against Alvarado's forces at San Jose, then he had no choice but to try to reach Alvarado first. John rode straight south for San Jose.

Shortly before noon on the second day, five miles north of the eastern end of the Pájaro Valley, he saw a group of horsemen in the distance. Moving cautiously, he approached until he could identify the men as Alvarado's eight *exploradores* under Corporal Chavez. Relieved, John rode up to them at full gallop. He was about to hail the corporal when he saw the dangling body of Pablo, minus boots and pants, convulsing at the end of a *reata*. Before he could demand an explanation for the hanging of an apparently harmless young courier, Chavez thrust a paper up at him. "This stinking traitor was carrying this to Micheltorena. Your brother-in-law, Goyo, was riding with him. But his horse was faster."

John read the brief note signed by Sutter assuring Micheltorena that his army would be converging on Alvarado not later than the seventh of January.

"Why didn't you take him to Colonel Alvarado for trial?"

The corporal, who had made no effort to conceal his disdain for Yankees, smirked up at John. "Here, señor, I am the judge. He had the message sewn in the lining of his boot and he confessed that he knew it was there. He had a just trial and now he pays a just penalty."

John forced himself to look up. The boy's face had turned blue-black and red-flecked spittle was drooling from his blood-gorged tongue. "He is too young to hang."

Chavez shrugged. "He is too old to spank."

Turning away, Lewis pointed to the paper. "This boy's death gains nothing. Robles will be delivering that same message before sundown."

Chavez bowed with mock respect. "It is the truth, señor. He has an hour's lead because we attended to this business. And if you are dedicated to the cause of your sons' godfather, you will warn him of Sutter's approach with two hundred men," he smiled maliciously, "the best of whom are yanqui riflemen. Then, señor, you will continue to Monterey and attend to your wife's traitorous brother."

There was a murmur of agreement from the soldiers. John studied each in turn, then addressed himself clearly to the subaltern. "When I am ready to take advice, Chavez, it will not be from a fool nor will it be from a corporal." John reined his mount sharply and the livid Chavez stumbled and fell in an effort to avoid being struck by its plunging hindquarters.

At the mission headquarters in San Jose, Alvarado and Castro listened grimly to John's report of Sutter's activities. Alvarado wasted no time rebuking his duped second-in-command. Murderous rage smoldered on Castro's coarse-featured face and for the first time John felt that Alta California's military commander might actually fight without restraint.

Camp was struck, a messenger was dispatched to warn Pico at Los Angeles, and Alvarado's revolutionary army, numbering fewer than two hundred men, set off before dawn for the south. John Lewis was commissioned a captain and made responsible for the acquisition and transportation of supplies. He could also continue to help recruit men as they marched through the Salinas Valley for Gaviota Pass and Santa Barbara. It was Alvarado's intention to increase his strength to at least three hundred men en route. These, joined to Pico's force, which he estimated at one hundred men, would give him numerical superiority. The two five-pound cannon mounted on *carretas* would be supplemented, he hoped, by other pieces that could be adapted for the field in Los Angeles.

John rode to Santa Cruz to warn that community and to secure Secundino Robles' help in getting the family from Monterey. That accomplished, he cut back through the mountains and rejoined Alvarado and Castro at Santa Rita. Moving rapidly along the narrow Salinas River valley, the force paused at San Miguel, then turned southwestward for Gaviota Pass.

Amid the cheers of the populace, on the morning of January twenty-first, the insurgents made camp on the plaza in Los Angeles.

Pico embraced Alvarado as a brother and pledged the support of his troops and his people "to the last man."

On the twenty-ninth of January, John attended the extraordinary session of the departmental assembly and listened as Alvarado and Castro voiced the north's complaints against Micheltorena. It was obvious to John after listening to Alvarado's lurid predictions of the sack of Los Angeles that the people needed little convincing after their own experience with the general's *rateros*. He had gone to the meeting expecting an immediate declaration of revolution. Instead, after three days of deliberating, the Californians voted to appoint a committee of citizens to ride north in the hope of intercepting Micheltorena and Sutter and working out an accommodation short of war. Ignoring Alvarado's plea that any compromise would work to their disadvantage, the assembly stood by its decision.

On February seventh Micheltorena's combined regiments, totaling fewer than four hundred men because of desertions, reached Santa Barbara. Micheltorena, at Sutter's insistence, unequivocally turned down the commission's plea for peace. Defeated, they returned to Los Angeles. On February fifteenth, convinced at last that war was inevitable, Pico had himself declared temporary governor for the second time. He issued a call for volunteers to fight Micheltorena's despised *rateros* and elevated Alvarado to General of the Armies.

Meanwhile, Micheltorena, suffering from a nagging bowel ailment, had been so impressed with the strength and armament of Sutter's trained forces that the opportunistic Swiss had been able to secure approval of the *soberante* grant. In the absence of Telles, Micheltorena had also commissioned Sutter a full colonel.

Inflated with power, position, and wealth beyond his most extravagant fantasies, Sutter argued successfully against any further delay.

The proclamation announcing Pico's appointment as governor had scarcely been penned and posted in the plaza when a rider announced the arrival of Micheltorena's army in the San Fernando Valley. Governor Pico's brother, Andrés, an able soldier and commandant of the Los Angeles militia, departed immediately to place his men under Alvarado and Castro who were deploying troops in defensible positions on the hills overlooking the Plains of Cahuenga.

At daybreak on February twentieth the two armies found themselves face to face on opposite sides of the narrow southern end of the valley. On the previous night,

Sutter had chosen an exposed hilltop for his camp. The men had been bedded down less than an hour when the wind had changed and turned into an abrasive dust storm. All through the night, the men had struggled to keep their flimsy shelters intact. Morning, so long in coming, found them red-eyed and hungry.

Alvarado and Castro had deployed their men more sensibly. Sheltered in the lee of a spur of hills, they had spent a relatively comfortable night.

As the sun's upper limb shot its first blinding rays across the snow-dusted crests of the San Gabriel Mountains, John watched Sutter, in full regalia, mount his mule, Katy, and canter awkwardly to his forward artillery positions. Four cannon were visible, including the prized polished brass field piece. The other three pieces had been taken from the fort's battlements and mounted on ox-drawn *carretas*. Lewis looked down at their own positions and saw the gunners waiting with lighted linstocks beside the two cart-mounted ten-pounders. He was certain, despite his lack of experience, that the range was too great for either side.

Alvarado was deploying the skirmishers and the main body of infantry in much the same manner he had proposed at Rancho Laguna.

Castro and Andrés Pico were maneuvering their dragoons into position for a flanking sweep down across the flatter terrain, a move that would pen Sutter's cavalry between them and the sheer, crumbly banks of the Los Angeles River.

Pico and a small detachment of men, a dozen of whom were former American trappers and plainsmen, began to work to the left on the higher ground leading into Cahuenga Pass.

Sutter studied the maneuver anxiously, then jounced back on his mule to Micheltorena's command carriage. Moments later, John saw Captain John Gantt and his riflemen taking up positions to oppose a charge. To the north, a moving cloud of dust concealed a party of horsemen who appeared to be heading for Micheltorena's ranks. When the dust cleared, Lewis recognized Isaac Graham at the head of a column of men. He estimated their number to be about twenty. Alvarado also had recognized the trapper. He sent riders to call Castro and Pico in for a tactical conference. John joined them behind the artillery.

Alvarado inspected Micheltorena's position through his

glass, then handed it to Castro. Both men were remembering that during their revolt against Governor Gutiérrez, it had been the threat of action by Graham and Chard and their men that had decided the bloodless day. Together the Americans constituted a formidable force. Andrés Pico, short, tough, wily and without fear, watched them closely for a time.

"We have the advantage. We are higher. We must keep them on the defensive with cannon shot. I suggest that one gun be laid on them," he indicated the rise, "from a higher position."

Castro agreed and Alvarado gave the order. A yoke of oxen was brought up and the ten-pounder lumbered to the top of a low ridge. There it commanded the gullies and dry washes that would have provided cover for Micheltorena's men should they attempt their own flanking sweep.

John was directing the relocation of the ammunition cart that would serve the repositioned cannon when the first shot was fired by Sutter just after sunrise. The blast shocked the preoccupied men and panicked the animals. An instant later a warning shout went up and John, peering over the ridge, could see the ball from Sutter's Russian field piece. It struck short and began a series of erratic leaps over the hard-packed earth. Alvarado's loosely formed riflemen scrambled right and left as the ball continued up the slope, skidded past the main gun position, and smashed into the left front wheel of a commissary cart. The impact splintered the solid wooden wheel and the cart dropped down on its axle. The spent ball came to rest in some brush a few feet beyond.

John heard Alvarado order the gunners to prepare for action. Fifty yards to the left he saw the men swinging the newly positioned cannon back toward Micheltorena's battery. The first of their own ten-pounders shattered the silence and the wind blew the acrid smoke back into the faces of the men. John watched the ball arc, almost lazily, and strike the ground in a sandy explosion twenty yards in front of the enemy's position. Before he could follow its unpredictable course, Sutter fired one of his own ten-pounders. The heavy charge jumped the gun off line and the ball went short and wide. Deflected by the slope, it skittered harmlessly in a great curving path and came to rest in a nearby ravine, scattering a score of jackrabbits and raising a cloud of brush birds. Castro's high cannon fired then, slewing the makeshift cart carriage in a half circle. But the gun had been well laid. The ball fell a bit short, skipped high, and killed the mount beneath one of Sutter's dragoons. John saw men rush to the fallen cavalryman but he was unable to tell whether or not the man had been injured. Just then a shout went up from Castro, who was pointing toward the positions occupied by Gantt and Graham. It appeared that Graham and his men were trying to block any possible retreat to Los Angeles through Cahuenga Pass.

John ran to the higher gun and helped swing it toward the riders, who were partially concealed in a shallow defile. Castro ordered a dangerously heavy powder charge and a number of short lengths of iron chains rammed into the muzzle. The linstock touched the fuse hole. There was a deafening crash and the chain, clustered at first, began to separate into writhing, whirling metal serpents that could cut a man in half. They rained down among the riders, who broke ranks and sought cover behind the sage and the scrub oak. Convinced now that Alvarado's well-placed guns could reach them, Graham and Gantt gathered their force and circled to the rear out of range.

Rattled, Sutter began to spend his ammunition unwisely. When he elevated the guns, the balls fell short and imbedded harmlessly in the sandy soil. When he depressed them, the balls skipped and skidded past the men, who had ample time to avoid them. Sutter fired ten shots to every one ordered by Alvarado and Castro. The fruitless exchange lasted for an hour before Sutter's firing slackened. Lewis saw John Bidwell come running to Sutter. The pair talked earnestly for a time, then the young American and a party of men rode toward the nearly dry riverbed, pulling two *carretas* with lariats. Through the glass he could see that they were searching for cobblestones small enough to load into the muzzles. Alvarado also watched, then smiled and ordered another shot from his own lower ten-pounder. He laid the gun himself, aiming it for Sutter's prized Russian field piece. The ball carried over the gun position, forcing the men to throw themselves flat, and crashed into the brush behind. Above the reverberating echoes, they could hear Sutter shouting hysterically in bad Spanish and thick, broken English. He was ordering his men to drag the cannon back to safer positions. For the first time in months,

Alvarado laughed outright. "Splendid!" He turned to John. "We have nothing to fear from them now. I will have our riflemen give your men cover. While Sutter shoots stones at us, let us gather his iron shot and prepare to return it with our compliments."

John took a detail of men to retrieve a half dozen five-pound balls and three times that many ten-pounders. Several times musket balls from Sutter's snipers whooshed dangerously close. But answering fire from Alvarado's men on higher ground kept them pinned down and hurried their aim.

The rest of the morning saw only desultory firing. John watched as Sutter deployed and redeployed his men, seemingly uncertain as to how to mount an attack. Well to the rear, Micheltorena, suffering from the intestinal ailment that had become aggravated by anxiety, remained in the carriage that had brought him from Santa Barbara. He was apparently more than willing to let his new colonel improvise the field strategy.

Shortly before midday, with one horse killed and one cart wheel smashed, both sides suspended action and prepared to eat. From time to time John would see a small puff of smoke and hear the delayed report as a sniper tried for a target at long range. Alvarado's men returned the fire but neither side scored any hits.

The Battle of Cahuenga Plains wore on through the afternoon with only sporadic small-arms fire. Knowing Sutter, Lewis was able to tell from his antic dashing about that the man's anxiety was mounting. One minute he was examining the stones that had been gathered to supplement his ammunition. The next minute he was conferring with the officers commanding his various units. Then he was at the new gun positions again, inspecting them and gesticulating officiously.

Late in the afternoon, as the sun was beginning to lower, some of Graham's men, unarmed, appeared on foot and began advancing cautiously up the shallow draw toward the left side of Alvarado's position. John and the others watched curiously and could see no purpose in the maneuver. One of the men—John thought it might be Bill Dockey—moved out in front of the others with a hand raised in an obvious gesture of truce. They could hear him shouting but could not make out the words. Then they heard an answering shout from their own ranks and two unarmed men, each with a hand raised, moved out of their cover cautiously. While Castro, Alvarado, and the officers and men watched in astonishment, the three men ran toward one another. They met on the open slope, embracing, slapping one another on the back and shoulders and whooping with the uninhibited delight of plainsmen reunited with old friends.

The first exchanges had scarcely taken place when Pico came charging along the contour of the slope and pulled his bloody-mouthed mount up, rearing. He leaped from the saddle with an arm outflung in the direction of the men who were being joined now by others from both sides. There were close to a hundred of them and in their midst was Dr. John Marsh.

"These gringos are deserting! They have seen friends. They will not fight them." Before Alvarado and John realized what was happening, Pico leaped to the gun trail and tried to pull the piece around so he could bring it to bear on the exposed Americans. John seized the linstock from the startled gunner and tossed it out of reach as Castro restrained the cursing Pico. "We are men of honor. We do not shoot unarmed men."

Pico continued to struggle, protesting in a torrent of unintelligible Spanish. John Marsh, holding both hands aloft, called for silence. Leaving Alvarado and Castro to restrain Pico, Lewis ran toward the gathering. Others were still joining it. At Marsh's request the men began squatting in a semicircle. An eloquent man, the doctor was in his element now. "Boys!" We are a hundred or more here and every one of us has two important things in common. We were born Americans and we have suffered the hardships of plain and mountain to get here. That binds us together as brothers."

An exuberant chorus of approval followed.

"We have been tricked into this war with promises that will not be kept. None of these posturing generals or colonels would dare fight a battle without us. They declare the wars and bribe us to fight. And if we do fight, do you know what the end would be? We'd kill each other off and leave them this land, which may be their true purpose!"A growl of agreement rose from the crowd.

Isaac Graham, dressed in buckskins agains, climbed laboriously up the short slope and stood beside Marsh. He was still armed. "I heard ye, Doc, and ye're very learned

209

and sensible, like always. So I ask ye, boys, why don't we just go back and shoot them? That'll put a proper end to all of the trouble."

The men guffawed and Graham, eyes glittering with malicious humor, raised a hand and turned his snaggle-toothed grin on them. "Only thing is, I'm a selfish man as ye know, but I'd admire to reserve to myself the honor of exterminating Alvarado and Castro."

A chorus of sympathetic expressions went up from all who knew of the trapper's imprisonment. Graham looked around and his eyes fell on John Lewis squatting on the periphery of the group. He pretended great delight. "Wa'l now! Damn me, if I don't pleasure myself from seeing another old friend." He pointed to John and the men craned to look. "Boys, if ye're ever in need of a smart runaway sailor who's as handy with his hands and feet as he is with his tongue, then I'd be pleased to recommend him to ye." Graham hooked a thumb in his broad hunting belt and smiled. "Course, I'd be a mite more quick to do that if the lad were a little choosier about his friends lately—"

John sensed that silence might lead to difficulties. He decided to put an end to any baiting before it could begin. He stood up, "Captain Graham, I judge that I don't want a part of this war any more than most of you. It isn't going to settle anything that'll make for lasting peace of mind for any of us. If our side wins, the same things will happen."

Dr. Marsh, who had been sizing up the temper of the men, interrupted. "Young Lewis is right, boys. I came here with Sutter's gun in my back. How many of you came here on promises of free land?"

Half the men raised their hands. Marsh looked at the others. "Why are you here?"

When no immediate response came from the Americans on Alvarado's side, John spoke up for them. "Some of us with families prefer the bickering of Alvarado and Pico to a general from Mexico City whose troops rape and steal."

Shouts of confirmation came from a number of the men who had been recruited in and around Monterey. Marsh nodded, smiling smugly. "Before I'd take promises too seriously, boys, I'd remember that Micheltorena promised Alvarado he'd send his *cholos* out of the country. Then he tried to trick Alvarado into sending his men against you in the Sacramento so he and his *cholos* could stab Alvarado in the back."

Isaac Graham hooted derisively. "Ho! That makes him an evil one all right! But I'd say he's fair matched with Alvarado, who promised Will Chard and I his undying brotherly love just a few months before he sicked that mad dog Castro on us in the middle of the night and carted us through town in chains." He spat viciously. "I'm not trusting the best of them as far as a frothing wolf."

Marsh moved a half step forward. "Isaac may speak the truth. I hold this war to be none of our business. Thomas Larkin in Monterey would agree. He is the American consul now. He thinks that very soon we'll all be American citizens again without stirring a foot from here. So why fight for these men who are soon to be put aside? Land you buy with an eye or an arm or a leg is not *free* land. Have you thought that Sutter, who is really asking you to die for him, may not have the authority to grant you land?" Marsh asked. "Micheltorena keeps his promises no better than Alvarado. And Sutter is worse than either." He stood silently searching their faces, then turned away.

The men sat musing—Graham as silently as the others. He had seen enough of Micheltorena to judge him both incompetent and too ill to deal with troops. As for Sutter, nothing he had seen of the man and nothing he had heard about him changed his conviction that Sutter was no more than "a big blow of sour wind." Sutter had been many times a failure and there were numerous stories about the way he had cheated partners in the past and failed to pay his debts.

Graham, roused from his musing, rose and rested the musket in the crook of his arm. "You boys'll be making your own judgments. I reckon it won't surprise ye none to learn that I come a helling down here because I saw a change to weigh out accounts with Bautista. But I figure now that what I'm risking for what I'd likely be getting just ain't worth the aggravation. So I'm calling on my men to light out for Branciforte with me at first light if they be of a mind to."

Several rose to leave with him. John could see Sutter standing halfway down the slope, watching them through his glass. On the opposite slope, Alvarado and Castro were also watching. Hoping to avoid having to make an imme-

211

diate decision, John started to leave but Dr. Marsh challenged him. "Tell me, John, where do you stand?"

"I want no part of this either. But I promised Alvarado I'd help see Micheltorena and his *cholos* gone. I promised my family that too. I guess I'd best say to you that I stand on my word."

Marsh smiled thinly. "That is your right, John, but I think you'll find it lonesome territory to stand on just now."

John rejoined Alvarado and the other officers and watched all but a few Americans on each side retrieve their arms and mounts and retire from the field. Sutter brandished his sword and screamed threats at them. When they ignored him, he mounted Katy and jogged stiff-legged down the slope in pursuit. In the dim light, Andrés Pico slipped away and whispered to four of his dragoons. Moving quietly, they mounted and pretended to ride to the upper gun position. Alvarado glanced at them questioningly and continued to watch the main force of his American recruits in the act of deserting. Minutes later, Pico and his men dashed down the hill in a reckless gallop, caught Sutter by surprise from the rear, and made him their prisoner. It had happened so quickly that Sutter's men, unable to believe their eyes, stood by without lifting a gun. Graham and his men had gone. Gantt and his men had joined them.

Confronted by two simultaneous disasters, General Micheltorena left the comfort of his carriage and rode to the forward positions. For an hour, with no real hope for success, he did what he could to reorganize his stunned officers and men.

Alvarado established his headquarters in a nearby adobe. Sutter, stripped of his sword and pistols, was taken there, protesting tearfully that his captors were rough and were not observant of the rules of war pertaining to the capture of distinguished officers.

Shortly after dawn on February twenty-first, Alvarado ordered the batteries to begin firing Sutter's own ammunition at Micheltorena. The blast of the first round was still reverberating in the pass as Andrés Pico and José Castro led twin flanking attacks with their companies of dragoons.

Micheltorena's men, working frantically, succeeded in loading one ten-pounder with cobblestones. The blast knocked the cannon off its mount and the stones disintegrated in a spray of small gravel and showered down on the slope no more than a hundred feet to the front. A cry went up as one of Alvarado's ten-pounders, well aimed, sent a ball whistling between two of Micheltorena's guns to crash into the wagon carrying the water jars. A second ball from the higher gun landed short, peppered the front line troops with sand and small stone, then screamed down the far side of the hillock smashing brush and cactus until it came to rest within yards of Micheltorena's carriage and field tent.

Frantic officers relayed a cease-fire to the few disorganized skirmishers who were still trying to shoot down the hard riding dragoons in the process of outflanking them.

Desperate and in severe pain from his outraged intestines, Micheltorena untied his large white silk neckerchief, secured it to a ramrod and hastily waved it aloft. For several minutes Alvarado's troops continued to fire. Then suddenly the truce flag was seen and a victorious shout went up along the battle line. A few more shots echoed across the barren plain and the bloodless Battle of Cahuenga was over.

John Lewis spent ten days in and around Los Angeles before returning to Monterey in mid-March. The evening after the emotional reunion with his family he was asked to Thomas Larkin's home to describe the happenings at Cahuenga.

Over coffee and sweets the merchants and their wives and friends listened raptly as John recited the first eyewitness account of the battle. Taking pains not to exaggerate, since the bare facts alone were strange enough to tax the credulity of the most gullible, he told his tale matter-of-factly to the moment of surrender and indulged in personal speculation only when he came to the summing up: "So, under the circumstances, I would say that Alvarado treated Micheltorena with uncommon consideration. The general was escorted to Don Abel Stearns' adobe. When he tried to surrender his sword, neither Alvarado nor Castro would take it. But our friend Sutter was quite another story." In spite of himself, John smiled. "They took his sword on the field. And his mule. Then Pico put him in manacles, the same ones, by the way, that Sutter had boasted he would lock on Alvarado." The irony delighted his listeners.

"Castro was really rough with him. He trussed him up like a pig and I do believe it is the only time anybody has heard Doctor Marsh laugh. In the cart, all the way to the Los Angeles jail, Sutter kept crying, 'I am innocent! I am the pitiful victim of another man's ambition. I am the pitiful victim of my own loyalty and patriotism. I had no choice but to follow the command of my governor. Any of you who love California would have done likewise.'

"I thought Andrés Pico would slit his throat, but Alvarado, and in the end Castro too, were very tolerant.

"They seemed to pity the man more than hate him for what he revealed himself to be, an unscrupulous fool whose vanity had endangered the lives of nearly a thousand men.

"In the end, Sutter asked me to plead with them to allow him to keep his sword so he could break it in honorable surrender."

There were more involuntary exclamations and Thomas Larkin lifted a hand in protest. "Surely they did not permit it?"

Struggling now to keep a straight face, John shook his head. "No. Castro came to see him, all solicitude, and explained that Governor Pico would not permit him to break the sword over his knee for fear he might injure himself."

An explosive roar of laughter went up.

"The man was truly a pathetic sight," John said, "and if the people of Los Angeles had been his judges, they would have hanged him within the hour. They saw Sutter as the cause of all their trouble. It's not a just charge, but strangely enough they do not blame Micheltorena. Both of the Picos behaved very honorably; some will say too honorably. They have pardoned Sutter and he is now on his way back to New Helvetia under orders to disband his army and never take up arms again."

Captain Cooper threw up his hands. "By God, we deserve what we get. And we deserve what we're about to get, too. Aye. And it won't take a mystic to divine it either." He rose so abruptly his brandy glass slopped over. "Pico will have himself voted constitutional governor again, the capital will be moved south and the customhouse with it, and until Divine Providence or the United

States saves us from our folly, we'll be the commercial mendicants of Alta California "

John Lewis disagreed. "I do not think we will lose the customhouse, Captain."

Cooper challenged him. "Pray tell us why not, lad?"

"Because Castro has promised Alvarado that he and his men will take the Monterey customhouse and hold it. He means to do that."

The news was greeted with both relief and apprehension. William Hartnell and David Spence foresaw the possibility that Andrés Pico would march north.

Cooper disagreed. "No, gentlemen. There's an easier way. Pico can open a customhouse at San Pedro or San Diego and drain off a good half of our comerce. We're in for some trying times—but I discount civil war."

Thomas Larkin rose to indicate the evening's approaching end. He seemed to be in an unusually good mood. "So, ladies and gentlemen, it would seem that in some respects we have concluded a very satisfactory war. No lives were lost save a horse; Sutter has been chastised and shrunk to size; Micheltorena and his rabble are to be deported immediately, and," he smiled cryptically, "Alvarado will no doubt continue as collector of customs and continue to interpret impractical law in a most practical manner."

John and the merchants suspected that the light, almost gay recapitulation would be couched in more sober tones when it was reported, as it certainly would be, to the Department of State in Washington.

A letter from William Leidesdorff to John said that everything was in order for his return to Yerba Buena with his family and thanked him for the account of events at Cahuenga. Leidesdorff concluded by writing, "Now, more than ever, most thoughtful Californians agree that the historic schism between the Picos and the Alvarados will never be permanently bridged and that the United States of America, by virtue of its geographic and political disposition, is the logical successor to the beleaguered central government of Mexico. Should American warships arrive carrying the prospect of peace and stability it is conceded without exception hereabouts that they would be welcomed with huzzahs."

Since Sutter's despicable behavior at Los Angeles, few

people regarded him seriously even though his fort, in itself, was an impressive accomplishment. He was thought of as a charlatan with a flare for grandiose schemes. But in early June this tolerant attitude suddenly changed. Still smarting from humiliation, Sutter perpetrated a brutal act that outraged the north.

Some immigrants had settled on an Indian tribe's traditional hunting ground. In reprisal, an Indian named Raphero led a party of braves against the settlers and killed one of the immigrants and stole some livestock.

Sutter took a squad of riflemen in search of Raphero and his Indians. When they caught up with him they killed most of the war party. Raphero was taken alive and returned to the fort. There, in a grisly ceremony presided over by Sutter, Raphero's head was hacked off with an ax and impaled upon a sharpened pole outside the gate as a reminder that the days of benevolent justice in New Helvetia were at an end.

Within a fortnight, Cooper's pessimistic predictions were beginning to came true. Pico had designated Los Angeles the capital and opened a competitive customhouse at San Diego. He sent messages to the New England traders inviting them to direct their principal cargoes to that port, where he promised they would find a plentiful supply of hides and tallow. He had drawn up a new set of ordinances prohibiting the import of all intoxicating beverages for five years and threatened to put the local distilleries out of business by holding them strictly accountable for their gallonage and placing a new, heavier tax on it. He exempted only the importation of fine liqueurs for which he had a personal preference. Monterey laughed when Isaac Graham, hurt by the new restriction on alcohol, publically rued his decision not to have stayed on long enough to whip Pico's forces.

However Pico's detractors grudgingly conceded the wisdom of demanding more teachers for the inclusion of both French and English as required studies. The teachers would be paid from the public treasury and schools established in all places were there were sufficient pupils to justify one. Parents would be required by law to send their children.

Pico also issued regulations prohibiting the destruction of the forests. He was aware of a survey that attributed the devastating series of droughts and floods to indiscriminate denuding of the mountains and hills. The Yankees, who were felling Monterey's great redwoods as fast as saws and axes could swing, derided the new law. The state government had no means to enforce it, so they continued to construct even more efficient sawmills.

John Lewis prepared at last to take his family to Yerba Buena. On the eve of their departure they had dinner with Don José and Doña Gertrudis. Will Chard and his wife Dolores joined them. One of Micheltorena's last official acts had been to give adjoining grants of land in the upper Sacramento Valley to Chard and Josiah Belden. As soon as the store and boarding house in Monterey began to show a profit, both men planned to build on their land and establish their families there. Chard, who had persistently urged John to apply for land, could not resist reminding him that his last chance was fast fading. "Micheltorena would not have approved your grant. But Pico will now, if you ask for it. Certainly he must have felt some gratitude when you refused to desert with the others. Remind him of that."

"Take Will's advice, Juan," Don José agreed. "Ask for the land. We are now attending the death vigil of our beloved Alta California. This beautiful land is dying and we are responsible. Mexico has tried every form of government from absolute monarchy to dictatorship. And now, Santa Anna is in prison too. It is too late. Mexico does not know what to do with us. We are remote. We are an enigma. The signs are unmistakable. Already an American flag has flown here. Do as Will says, Juan. Apply for a grant."

Don José's angular face saddened. "Goyo was wrong about many things, but he was correct when he predicted we would be strangers in our own land. I do not know where he is now, or even if he lives. But I hope that the men he tried to warn in Mexico City will remember and credit him for that, at least.

"But we were speaking of land, Juan. You must have a grant now. Another government will not be so willing to give away its wealth. Write to Pico now."

After they left the Robles adobe, John and Maria climbed to the scene of their first meeting alone. Maria linked an arm through her husband's. She loved this strong Yankee who was her man, a mate, a lover, the father of

217

her children. "What do you think about, Juan Lewis?" she asked.

John continued to reflect a moment longer, then smiled down at her. "I was thinking of my sister in the United States and how I wish she could know you and our children."

"Once you told me, Juan, that you would send for Alicia. We'll be in Yerba Buena soon. It is no longer necessary to wait. Why not write to her now and ask her to come?"

He considered briefly. "There are two good reasons."

Maria scoffed. "I can think of none!"

Lewis put his arm around her and brought her closer. "Dear one, you California women are accustomed to all this commotion, this changing of governments with every new moon. That is one reason. The other? You and I are accustomed to our adobe houses with no proper doors and few glass windows. But Alice is twenty-three years old now. She has been raised differently, in a great city. I do not know how she would take to our primitive ways."

Maria glared at him indignantly. "You speak as though we are Indians! We are *gente de razon*." Lewis chuckled indulgently, then mocked her.

"Indeed we are the best people. The very best. We have almost as many servants as we have fleas. And we live on the cleanest dirt floors. And we walk on Spanish tile to our elegant outhouses. Also we eat food only with clean fingers after we've set it afire with the hottest red pepper that sends its fire from one end of us to the other. Even so, my precious one, I would like to be able to do still better for my sister when I bring her here. I would like to show her that I have been able to provide for my own wife and children as much comfort as any man in this country. So, we will wait. There is time. Next year perhaps."

Maria did not argue, for she had come to understand the nature of her husband's quiet pride and she loved him all the more for it. They sat until the night chill began to seep through her shawl. Then they picked their way back down the slope to Don José's adobe.

While Maria was tending to the children, John stood in the doorway gazing down the length of the Calle Principal. Twice before he had thought he would be leaving Monterey. Twice before the internal troubles that plagued the

218

capital and the state had diverted him. He did not doubt that still more disruptions would plague him and his family in the future and he tried again to guess what they might be—from what quarter they might come and when.

That night in bed, John thought about the future of Alta California. Larkin would figure prominently in any future change. He knew there would be increased sub rosa involvement on the part of the United States. Lieutenant Charles Wilkes' assessment of California's inland waterways was said to have prompted Senator Thomas Benton of Missouri to suggest the Frémont surveys. These took place in 1842 and 1843. Frémont had led a party of United States government surveyors westward to the Columbia River country and down the length of Alta California. His reports to Washington were said to be a factor in Commodore Jones' premature decision to take Monterey. Unquestionable, the United States was moving to prevent Britain from expanding its influence along the Pacific slope. The Republic of Mexico owed the British Crown twelve million pounds in bonds. Many felt the British bankers who held the obligations would be willing to accept repayment in California land.

This brought up the question of the loyalties of the merchants. Larkin, through his personal loans to the Alta California Government, had been trying to minimize the economic influence of Cooper and Spence that might conceivably prejudice Alvarado and Castro toward Britain. Cooper and Spence both had deep Anglo roots; Hartnell would be a realist about events beyond his control. As for Vallejo, his hero was George Washington and his hobby was the United States Constitution. Sutter had forfeited his right to any influence and Castro would accept France but, like Goyo, he would die before swearing allegiance to the United States.

John did not know the men in the south well. But they were predominantly Yankee. Whatever they might decide, the balance was tipping slowly toward Washington and its doctrine of Manifest Destiny.

Weary from a long day and what seemed to be an endless, perhaps hopeless, attempt to sort out the future probabilities, John tried to push the specter of the future from his mind. At daybreak they would say their last farewells and begin the slow journey that would take Maria and the three children to their new home in Yerba Buena.

219

6 San Francisco, Alta California
August 31, 1847
(Until this past January 30,
Yerba Buena!)

Mr. and Mrs. Edward James
Number 3 Washington Mews,
Manhattan Island,
New York State, U.S.A.

My dear sister and brother-in-law:

It is beyond my capability to express the joy I felt upon receiving the news of your wedding last June. From your letters, Alice, I suspected that ever since Ned delivered my first letter to you an eternity ago, you two had enjoyed each other's company. I am sure now that Ned would have resigned from Bryant-Sturgis to pursue you if his firm had not transferred him from Boston to the Battery. My congratulations, Ned, on becoming head clerk.

On my table here in Mr. Leidesdorff's new City Hotel stands my most prized possession, the Daguerreotype made at your wedding at the Gladwyns' home in Brooklyn. What a beautiful bride my old shipmate Ned has! Ten thousand blessings on you both. I can only wish for you the deep happiness Maria and I take in each other and in our offspring.

You say that the news journals there are filled with accounts of the varying fortunes of the Mexican War but that little of California finds its way into print. The same is true here since our two journals, *The Star* and *The Californian* (the latter first published as a weekly at Monterey), are scarcely a year old and consist of only four pages. Two of the *Californian*'s pages are printed in Spanish. Both journals are devoted to small kernels of late news that have been winnowed from the embellished adventures of overland immigrants plus some editorial opinion of dubious value.

In answer to your request for personal news I'll try to tell you all that has happened since I left Monterey and started with Mr. William A. Leidesdorff.

I could not have chosen a more unsettled time, for California itself has now embarked on a new course. As a result, I find myself being swept along in its wake.

Previously I told you about Captain Frémont and his company of men who set out to map the western portion of the continent. It now appears that the Captain (who rose to Lt. Colonel in a matter of months) was really mapping plans for the conquest of California. I believe his personal ambitions overburdened his judgment because last week we heard that he is being returned to Washington under arrest for refusing to obey the orders that would have deposed him as governor of California. He had aspired to that post with great passion.

Personally I would not regret his conviction for a legend has been growing, as a result of Frémont's own self-advertisements, that he and his crew of mountain men are superior beings. History will be the judge of that but if history judges Frémont's right bower, Kit Carson, other than a cold-blooded murderer then it will be in flagrant disregard of the facts.

Without elaborating, just let me say that during the infamous Bear Flag Revolt, Carson and two of his men shot down in cold blood the adolescent twin sons of Francisco de Haro, former Alcalde of Yerba Buena and one of the most respected men in California, on the pretext that they were carrying secret messages to Vallejo from Castro. The twins' uncle, Don José Berryessa, was also killed as he stepped from a small bay boat with his nephews. None of the three were armed. It was purely and simply an act of vengeance, the viler still because Don José was shot through the heart as he was pleading for the life of his nephews, offering proof of their innocence. If there is such a thing as Judgment Day, this man Carson may expect no more mercy than he has shown.

Maria, with Felicia and the twins, are still with her ailing father for whom I have the greatest affection. I have managed several visits with them to satisfy myself of their safety and comfort.

Late in January, shortly after Will Chard (now the father of a fine boy), left to investigate the Santa Clara quicksilver mines, this fellow Frémont appeared in Monterey with eight of the roughest plainsmen imaginable, including the infamous Kit Carson. Frémont's declared purpose was to petition General Castro for permission to rest his men in Alta California before undertaking the return journey to St. Louis.

Castro, who is capable of passion which occasionally verges on valor, met him under the most correct auspices and granted him permission. But hardly had the meeting ended when word came that several of Frémont's ruffians had made vulgar overtures to two native girls who fled in terror.

Moreover, a *californio* contended that two of the mounts ridden by Frémont's men bore the brands of his ranch and had been stolen. Castro naturally tried to investigate but Frémont arrogantly dismissed him. Whereupon Castro summarily ordered Frémont and his men from the department.

The captain, who by this time had augmented his company to sixty-odd, marched his men from Monterey to Gabilan Peak, that overlooks the mission at San Juan Bautista. In a fury, he threw up a breastwork of logs, raised the American flag (the second time this has occurred in Alta California), and dared Castro to dislodge him.

Castro marshaled several hundred heavily armed soldiers and the chastened Frémont, acting something less than a hero, slipped away in the night and beat a hasty retreat to New Helvetia.

Sutter, ever the complete opportunist, greeted him warmly, repaired his outfit, and sent him on his way to Oregon from whence the party planned to return to the United States.

Then, unexpectedly, a mysterious stranger entered the scene. This was Archibald Gillespie, a Lieutenant in the United States Marine Corps, traveling incognito, who was carrying dispatches for Frémont from his father-in-law and from President Polk and Secretary of State Buchanan. Immediately after Gillespie intercepted Frémont's party, Frémont turned right around, marched to New Helvetia, and commandeered Sutter's entire establishment.

Sutter protested and was threatened with confinement in his own fort. Frémont has no respect for Sutter since the fiasco at Cahuenga although it appears to many that

Frémont himself was wanting in both strategy and valor at Gabilan.

Our impression is that Frémont is an ambitious and arrogant adventurer, fortunate to be the favored son-in-law of Senator Thomas Hart Benton, who has expedited his career. However, Frémont's impudence and mutinous insubordination have seriously aroused General Kearny and Senator Benton may have to salvage his son-in-law's career. Kearny is demanding his court martial.

In spite of Frémont's bickering over power and position, California is secured for the United States under the military governorship of Colonel Mason and is now, for practical purposes, one of its territories.

Frémont, who appears to have some instincts in common with Sutter, may, like that remarkable Swiss, not only survive but thrive. Both seem to have a rare gift of survival—of turning adversity to advantage.

I visited New Helvetia several weeks ago. Sutter seems to have totally forgotten about his inglorious defeat at Cahuenga and still insists upon the use of the title "Captain." He is playing the role of benevolent Lord of New Helvetia to the hilt, demanding near papal fealty from all who depend upon him. *"Qui se laudari gaudet verbis subdolis, sera dat poenas turpes paenitentia,"* was not spoken of Johann Augustus Sutter.

In spite of everything, Sutter is a most extraordinary fellow whose enterprise has wrought a miracle. There is a veritable city at the once primitive New Helvetia now, and another city is growing at nearby Sutterville. I counted nearly fifty structures and six mills, two distilleries, two heavy forges, and one blanket mill. There are several commercial shops and a large tannery. Also, Captain Sutter has an agreement with a New Jersey man named James Marshall. He is under contract to build a sawmill on the American River at Culuma, an Indian settlement about 40 miles away from New Helvetia.

Since most lumber is whipsawn by hand in the Bodega forest and brought by schooner to the Bay of San Francisco and then up the river, it is exceedingly hard to come by and very expensive. Sutter plans to raft the cut lumber from the mill most of the way to New Helvetia, then ship it by water down river to San Francisco. There is a growing demand for it here. Our interest lies in the possibility of acting as agent for the resale. Mr. Leidesdorff has a spacious warehouse on the waterfront where a substantial quantity of prime material can be dry-stored. But to return to Sutter, taken with 12,000 head of cattle, 200 horses and mules, 15,000 sheep and 1000 hogs, and several hundreds of workers, he must be a wealthy man even though I know from our own account books that he owes substantial amounts on which little if anything has been paid in recent years.

He is also said to be badly defaulted on his debts to the Russians. However, a year or two of clement weather and political tranquility may well see his great dream fulfilled. Since in this land one man's victory is every man's hope, we can do naught but wish the captain well.

A tremendous transformation is taking place in San Francisco. The mere change of name seems somehow to have exorcised the spirit of lethargy from the entire community. We know, of course, that the prospect of orderly government is the true cause. There is more construction and bustle here than anywhere else in California. Some speculators are paying as much as $100 cash for lots in favored positions along the waterfront. Mr. Leidesdorff owns several well-situated plots including some on the lane that bears his name. His residence stands on one of these.

As I gaze down the hill to the Bay I can see the *U.S.S. Portsmouth* lying at anchor surrounded by a fleet of naval transports and several sloops of war. Indeed, Commodore Stockton seems to prefer this bay to all other harbors in the Pacific. He has said repeatedly that he will urge Washington to establish a major military installation here with a naval yard to rival the one at Boston. It is only rumor but it sends a fever of excitement burning through all those whose faith in Yerba Buena has been constant during the long, lean years.

I see also three deep-water merchantmen at anchor. Two are Boston ships and we hear on good authority that many more have San Francisco as their destination.

And now I hope that one day before many more months pass I shall be standing with Maria and the children watching the arrival of the vessel carrying you both here. How appropriate that you both, whose love so brightens my heart, should arrive through the Golden Gate, the entrance to the great bay quite aptly named by the controversial Frémont.

(some hours later)

Maria and Felicia are now at Santa Cruz with Dolores Chard, attending the latter's mother whose days seem to be nearing an end. The twins, William and Steven, remained at Monterey with their grandfather, Don José, who is doing his best to make *californios* of them and is succeeding. His *vaqueros* carry the 3-year-old boys in front of them in the saddle.

I must go now to visit a merchantman with Mr. Leidesdorff. More and more he depends upon me to bid in the cargoes that we need for resale here in the north.

With enduring affection, I am,

Your devoted brother and "in-law"
John

San Francisco, Alta California
February 14, 1848

Señora Maria Robles Lewis
El Rancho de los Robles
Monterey, Alta California.

My dearest wife and family:

Harry Morrison is returning to Monterey on business for our firm so I am writing again rather sooner than I had intended.

I regret to say that Mr. Leidesdorff has been suffering from an indisposition which the doctors diagnose as "an imbalance in the system" caused by a fall from one of his racing horses on the flats near the mission several weeks ago. Unfortunately, he struck his head sharply on a corral railing in an effort to save himself.

Both he and the doctors are predicting a full recovery soon. In the meantime a great deal of additional responsibility has devolved upon me. I welcome it both for the opportunity to learn by administering the more complicated aspects of international trade and for the additional salary. He is surely one of the most considerate and gracious of men and one must forciably remind one's self that he is of Negro extraction. My admiration for him and my feelings of fellowship are unparalleled. His strength of character commands the respect of all men and his unusually attractive personality have set many a feminine heart aflutter.

I happened to be at Rancho Petaluma with General Vallejo when a rider brought a startling letter to the General from Captain Sutter. Sutter claims to have discovered an extraordinarily rich gold mine near his fort. That should be the best of news, particularly to a long-time and unsatisfied creditor; but General Vallejo fell into a thoughtful silence. When he spoke he just kept shaking his head and muttering, "*!No es bueno. No es bueno!*" He refused to discuss the news beyond saying that gold has been the downfall of nations of men and that in a fertile land such as ours the only true wealth is in the crops and in the herds. He was really much disconcerted.

Your last letter was most reassuring, my dearest wife. Your account of the children's progress is gratifying. I am pleased that Will's family is enjoying his presence again and that he will not start to drive his livestock north until the spring. The failure of his store and boarding house was predictable but it will yet prove to be a blessing both for him and for Josiah Belden.

Harry is impatient to be on his way so I shall seal this now, knowing you understand that it contains not just a modicum of news but the full measure of my affection.

Your devoted husband,
J.L.

San Francisco, Alta California
June 8, 1848

Mr. and Mrs. Edward James,
Number three Washington Mews
Manhattan Island, New York State,
U.S.A.

My dear Alice and Ned:

I suppose one should not reckon it news that in a topsy-turvy world a man is apt to find himself upset and unsettled. Scarcely a month ago disaster struck our city. The Mormon apostate, Sam Brannan, fired with avarice (and other raw spirits), rode through the streets displaying a bag of nuggets and shouting like a banshee that gold had been found on the American River. In a matter of hours he had emptied the town like some infernal Pied Piper. Every able-bodied man, including several preachers of the Gospel (who apologized for their desertion by saying they were going to gather golden riches to erect still greater cathedrals to the glory of God), has departed this town leaving only the timid, the skeptics, the infirm, and a

226

handful of others such as myself who are bound to their posts by conscience.

And now I have a personal tragedy to report. My benefactor, William Leidesdorff, is dead. He died on May 18 after having lain in a coma for several days. The doctors have said the cause of death was "brain fever." He was 38 years of age, in the prime of his life, on the threshold of accomplishments that would have enriched this city beyond measure commercially and culturally.

Some measure of the respect in which he was held during the brief time he lived here may be judged from the fact that his mortal remains have been interred in the actual Mission itself, an honor accorded only to the highest churchmen and the most revered California Catholic families.

Mr. Leidesdorff spoke little of his own early life, but papers discovered by the executors indicate that he was actually the ward and heir of the man he referred to as his uncle. The executors are presently trying to establish the legal heirs, if any, since Mr. Leidesdorff, who could have indulged his fancy among the most beautiful women of the region, charmed all but apparently favored none. Mystery shrouded him in life, and the shroud is gathered still closer in death. It is rumored that he left his one true love in New Orleans when her father objected to the union with a mulatto. A delicately made lady's gold and jeweled crucifix was found among his personal effects and it was apparently intended as a gift, for it was still in the original vendor's silk-lined box. Enclosed with it was a card in Mr. Leidesdorff's fine script on which were inscribed the words, "To my beloved Hortense." There were also several extremely tender notes from the lady.

I sorely miss Mr. Leidesdorff and my plans once again are in a state of confusion. Sometimes I despair of ever finding my proper place in this land.

Several days after the uproar about the gold, Mr. Leidesdorff ordered me to get his schooner, *The Rainbow*, ready for a trading trip to Sutter's embarcadero. Sam Brannon reported that Sutter's store was stripped of everything of use by the men rushing to the mines. Judging by those who left here, most have undertaken a dangerous journey ill equipped. Indeed, most lack even elementary knowledge of mining.

If it's true that unlimited quantities of pure gold may

actually be garnered from streambeds with one's bare hands, then I may have the opportunity to establish my own trading firm. It would be possible for me to pay full market price here for supplies and still turn a handsome profit by transporting the material to or near the mines. One man is said to have been paid $100 a barrel to pack in two barrels of flour and one of salt meat.

Another received $4.00 a pound for flour, the same price for poor quality sugar and the cheapest chicory and coffee. Sardines sell for $5.00 the tin and a hundred-pound wheel of New York common yellow cheese sold for $500! Shovels, picks, and rakes and knives are in great demand as are pans of all descriptions, particularly frying pans and shallow winnowing pans with which the particles of gold apparently are separated from the lighter overburden by washing in some fashion.

I am singularly fortunate in that the executors have allowed me to pursue this trip on the same generous terms agreed to by Mr. Leidesdorff. Also, I am doubly blessed by having my old friend Harry Morrison, a most competent Scotsman, as my companion and assistant.

We leave for the Sacramento and American Rivers tomorrow morning. I shall try to keep in communication with you during these coming weeks but long silence is not to be construed as a mute harbinger of trouble since it may well be impossible to find a dependable person who is journeying back to civilization.

God grant us all safety and may He bless you both and grant me my most cherished wish, to greet you and embrace you here as,

> Your affectionate brother and in-law
> John.

San Francisco,
Alta California
February 10, 1849

Mr. Edward James,
Bryant-Sturgis & Company,
The Battery,
Manhattan Island,
New York.

Dear Ned:

We have just received word of President Polk's confirmation of the gold strike in his Congressional Message. The reports reaching us from the mining regions east of Sacramento are so extravagant that I would not have believed them if I hadn't witnessed the spectacle with my own eyes.

I have seen an entire land in turmoil. I have seen the gentlest of men turn monstrous with greed and the strongest of men weep with disappointment. Prudent men gamble away a fortune on a turn of the cards with the thought that another fortune might be plucked from the earth on the morrow. And on all sides men vie with one another to hand over their pokes of gold dust and nuggets for the simplest necessities of life—an ounce of pure gold worth $16.00 in exchange for a 25¢ washing pan; $20.00 for a simple physic; Laudanum at $1.00 the drop and pills for any ailment man is heir to (and some not yet discovered) at $1.00 each. Potatoes and apples, when available, bring $2.00 to $5.00 *each*. A poor shovel brings two ounces of gold. A pick the same. Any knife or usable piece of metal for seaming or sniping brings an ounce of gold or more. I saw an Indian exchange a half pound of gold for a half pound of raisins and if he had not done so an equally savage appearing "white" would have willingly done the same.

All civilized instincts seem to have been stifled except one. Curiously enough, there is almost no dishonesty among the miners, it being as easy to glean a fortune from the streambeds as to steal it. I have seen $3,000 in gold nuggets left unattended in a miner's lean-to with never a qualm for thieves. Precious tools left overnight in the claims are unmolested, as are the claims themselves.

At the end of last year it was estimated that ten thousand men were digging and had recovered $10,000,000 in gold. But the price exacted by nature for this bounty is dreadful to contemplate. Men suffocate of pneumonic lung congestion with no one to care or help. Others die raving of ague and burning fever, with malnutrition the cause, abetted by lack of shelter and hours upon hours soaked to the waist in icy water in their quest for a "strike."

The proven diggings now extend well north and eastward along both the Feather and American Rivers and along a number of lesser streams. The same is true to the south of Culuma where the first strike was made. Some miners have worked well up into the Sierra and found exceedingly rich pockets in the alluvial washings. One company of men mining have regularly taken up to $1,500 per day in the finest specimens of coarse gold. All this I have witnessed with my own eyes. And it is upon this evidence that I wish to make the following proposal:

I enclose a guarantee of credit for $5,000 signed by Messrs. Spear and Hinckley. I should like you to purchase and forward by the fastest vessel the appended list of tools, iron rod, and strap. If you cannot find copper washing pans resembling the slope-sided one indicated in my rather poor sketch, then I shall take any approximation of same in any durable metal whatever. Should some of the listed items be found in short supply there, make up an equal dollar value in the more plentiful items requested.

I should like you to act as my purchasing agent on a full and equal partnership basis. At present the gold seems inexhaustible. The mines will surely produce for another five years or more. I have talked with General Vallejo and also with Dr. John Marsh, who made $40,000 in trade and mining before ill-health forced him from the diggings. Both men agree that the wasteful methods presently employed will leave fortunes for those willing to mine more scientifically. But the number of farmers-turned-miners who have become discouraged and turned to the land hereabouts will increase as will those who made their stakes in order to purchase choice valley land. This will greatly speed up the process of settlement.

In this event, the firm of Lewis & James (it has a true ring to it) could well adapt its imports to farm implements and other vital necessities.

Poor Sutter is quite overwhelmed by events. He made a fortune as a trader and supplier but the first gold strike emptied his factories and fields of all help. In the end he himself was forced to try the mines. But his mining expeditions ended in defeat and his properties have now been signed over to his son, John Augustus Jr., to keep all that remains from being foreclosed by claimants. This occasions some embarrassment for me since Mr. Leidesdorff acted as collection agent for the Russian transactions on which, like all others, Sutter was in arrears. His trustees are unforgiving and somehow the captain—he seems to have aged greatly and has quite fallen apart from ill-fortune and brandy—connects me with his misfortune though heaven knows he found a far abler clerk and general factotum in the conscientious Bidwell than ever was to be found in the restless Lewis.

Sam Brannan has established a mercantile store and so has Thomas Larkin, who admits quite freely that his profits from supplying miners along the Feather River exceed 300%. (Knowing Mr. Larkin, I suspect him of undue conservatism in this connection also.) Bidwell has opened a store and somehow manages to keep a few men working at the fort's forges making improvised mining tools. Only the distillery continues unabated.

The warehouses here are stripped of merchandise since everyone who could garner a dollar or wheedle credit marched off to the mines with items to exchange for gold dust. Transient opportunists arrive each day and anyone who sets up his trade in a business-like manner will thrive.

I would not presume to tell you how to come to a decision on my proposal and I freely confess the underlying selfishness that motivates me for I see in this venture an opportunity to bring you and Alice, and my as yet unseen niece, to California, here to make a permanent home.

A man named Peter H. Burnett, lately a territorial judge in the Oregon country, has come to the new Sacramento City to supervise its sale and development for John Sutter Junior. Since the announcement on December 16th last, the lots have been selling like johnny cakes at $500 each.

Commercial situations along the river bank are going for well over $1,000. I have taken the precaution of securing a splendid lot directly opposite the embarcadero and adjacent to the new hotel for the firm of John Lewis and Company in the event Lewis and James is unable to use it. I have also placed options on a number of other sites well back from the water since my experience at Sutter's Fort has made me respectful of these rivers during the spring.

Again, poor Sutter. His plans for a city around the fort have come to naught and Sutterville lots are selling at half the Sacramento City price. Sacramento is becoming a hub of commercial activity in the central interior.

I shall try to curb my impatience and shall pray for a favorable reaction to my proposal. If you decide not to gamble in this uncertain land I will understand and harbor none but the most sympathetic attitudes along with my own keen disappointment.

Tomorrow I return to the mines with a schooner filled

with the most varied merchandise procurable. I shall pack merchandise into the lower hills where most of the mining is now concentrated due to snow above the four-thousand-foot level. It is bitterly cold, even in the lower reaches. I far prefer gold from merchandise than from marrow-freezing labor in the icy streams.

We send expressions of deepest affection to you; and how Maria wishes to embrace the distant un-met in-laws for whom she has quite as much affection as I.

Ever thine,
John Lewis

San Francisco, State of California
October 29, 1850

Mr. and Mrs. Edward James
13 Monroe Street
Brooklyn, New York
My dear Ned and Alice:

I hope I do not risk immodesty by reporting that the partnership of Lewis and James now holds in deposit another 1000 fine ounces of gold represented by 16,000 in certificates. These comprise the net proceeds of Harry Morrison's recent trip to the mines. In the appended list I have requisitioned supplies that will seem somewhat different, occasioned by a change in mining methods. The "easy pickin's" of the past seem to be exhausted. For months now fortune seekers have filled and emptied this city every twenty-four hours. No sooner are they off the ships that now clog Yerba Buena Cove than they find transport to Sacramento City. The same streams now support five times the number of prospectors, but the increase in profitable strikes is not proportionate. Many now make their way 200 miles north to the Trinity River country where new alluvial deposits are being found. But in the old diggings it is now necessary to search every nook and cranny that might conceal a nugget. These miners, now called "skimmers" and "snipers," still require the conventional picks, shovels, etc. But men are now engaged in a new form of burrowing called "coyoting" after the dens dug by that animal. It is still another technique introduced by the industrious Sonoran Miners from Mexico from whom we have learned most of our tricks.

It is extremely dangerous work but often results in high

yields. It is for this hazardous tunneling along the bedrock that the men need the smaller tools I have specified since most of these men live (and too often die) on their hands and knees in dark, wet passages seldom more than three feet in diameter. We anticipate no difficulty in disposing of all you can supply at from 1 to 2 ounces of gold per shovel or pick.

Harry Morrison made an arrangement with a blacksmith to make sniping irons from scrap metal scavanged from the abandoned ships that rot in this harbor. Even these primitive tools sell instantly for ½ oz. each. They cost us no more than $1.00 to make and transport, giving us a net profit of $7.00. Harry disposed of 500 in two days at Mormon Island. We now have three blacksmiths engaged full time manufacturing them for us. The "sniping irons" are used for seaming—scratching in the deep cracks in bedrock along streambeds where some of the finest nuggets are often trapped.

In July, I tried my hand at sniping on the Feather River. I located some likely looking seams and gouged deeply into the cracks with the spatula end of the iron. In a matter of minutes I had scraped out several handfuls of gritty clay which I then deposited in my washing pan. I kneaded the mass until the clots were broken up.

Even before the final washing I was able to pick out several beautiful nuggets the size of my fingernail. When I finished (and ineptitude doubtless cost me many small particles), I had over a half ounce of beautiful gold. I confess that the ease of obtaining it gave me a touch of "the fever." But a few minutes of sober reflection dispelled that.

That gold, by the way, will shortly reach you in the form of two rings, one for each, which your local goldsmith can adapt for correct size.

The spring floods that inundated Sacramento City earlier this year did little damage to our supplies stored there. Thanks to my experience with Captain Sutter, I took the precaution of making a heavy dry-storage loft in the back of the building a good ten feet above the floor. I stored all articles that might be damaged by moisture there.

I must say that while others were wading chest deep in the muddy swirl trying to rescue floating cases and barrels I felt inclined to smugness. The envious looks of some who earlier had scoffed at my precautions more than made up for the discomfort suffered from their derision.

Despite the annual inundation, optimistic merchants continue to repeat the old mistakes. Sacramento City may not have any secure future without a series of enormous levees or dikes to contain the rivers. Even old Sutter, now living at his new Hock Farm on the Feather River, even he, often called a "fool," had sense enough to heed the advice of the Indians when he chose the site for his fort.

Fire and flood! Sometimes it appears that Almighty God is displeased with our stewardship of this land. Since early May of this year five great fires have consumed over 500 houses and countless flimsier structures in San Francisco. This is despite valiant efforts of the new fire brigades and elaborate precautions that require each dwelling to have on hand at least five water buckets filled at all times. (We have profited by supplying these too.)

I do not think it an exaggeration to count the fire losses at close to $10,000,000 during the past six months alone. While carelessness (usually drunkenness) caused one or more, others may have been set by incendiarists bearing malice toward some gambling hall or saloon.

A great fire that destroyed over 100 structures was still smoldering when we turned out for the official Admission Celebration on October 29th. If these fires continue to destroy our flimsy structures, we may find that there is more true wealth in bricks of clay than in bricks of gold. A ship arrived here last month with 50,000 Belgian paving blocks as ballast. They were sold for $1.00 each. Such stones are hard to plumb and mortar but they won't burn.

You, of course, know all the details of California's admission to the Union, at long last, and about the seating of John Frémont and William Gwin as our first senators. We did not think statehood would come this soon because of Southern opposition to the anti-slavery provision in our new state constitution.

There is much dissension here still. Many from the slave states are sympathetic to that obnoxious system. Senator Gwin himself quietly favored slavery for California; but since political ambition overbalances his Southern conviction he "ran before the wind" most agreeably. Even so, the Southern sympathizers will leave their mark on California.

We have seen the passing of an era, and while my cheers were loud when the *S.S. Oregon*, all dressed in pennants, sailed into the bay on the 18th inst. carrying the glad tidings, I could not help shedding an inward tear for General Vallejo and the 6 other *Californios* who sat with 41 Anglo-Americans at last year's constitutional convention. They were forced to expedite their own extinction. Vallejo's vast holdings have suffered the severest depredations and still he was the first to urge that California's constitution contain nothing inimical to the United States Constitution that he holds so sacred.

And Juan Alvarado. As I sit here in this thriving city in which so much has been accomplished in so short a time, those days ten years ago seem to belong to eons past. Alvarado the idealist was not proposed for the convention because (the kindlier said) he was intractable. The truth is he was ill from disappointment and from the spirits he took to assuage it. In recent years his uncle Vallejo told me he had persuaded Alvarado of the hopelessness of unifying an independent California and the inevitability of union with the United States. He would have added great insight to our deliberations. History must not be allowed to rob him of his place or give more to those who, through selfishness or short-sightedness, would not support him. The bromide "while Alvarado and Pico fought over the pail, the Yankees stole the cow" is a cruel jest.

Perhaps California is destined always to be split asunder, for even now, only 11 days a confirmed state, there is a group of separationists led by Abel Stearns who would petition Congress to divide us into Upper California with the capital to remain at San Jose, and Central California with the capital at Los Angeles.

The Angelenos deny it, but they are jealous of our gold, our harbor, our energetic population and of our leadership in social and political affairs. They are divided from us by both the Tehachapi and the Santa Barbara Mountains. Perhaps they should go their own way, for surely they provide us with little but distraction.

As you know, a company of Mormons sailed here from N.Y. with Sam Brannan, now a competitor merchant. Brannan, whose capacity for hard liquor is exceeded only by his rapacity, has been cut off from the tithes he had been collecting from the faithful. The money, long since diverted to his personal use, should have been forwarded to the Deseret Colony at the Great Salt Lake to sustain the Mormons there. The story goes that when Brigham Young said that it was God's money and demanded that it

235

be sent forthwith, Brannan replied, "I shall forward it instanter upon receipt of a draft signed by God."

It is Brannan, by the way, who is now attempting to organize here a vigilance committee to insure law and order. But the lay Mormon is a devout, skilled, hard-working, and honest man and there are those who regret the departure of many of the original Brannan group to their settlement in Utah Territory. At the worst, one may say that these Mormons are a mixed blessing.

As you know, Peter H. Burnett was selected as the first civil Governor of California. Earlier, Burnett assumed the responsibility for selling Sacramento City lots and in so doing established a personal fortune solely upon his ability to spellbind. He is a persuasive man, indeed. It was he who sold me the embarcadero lot and others on J Street. At $750 I overpaid by a third. But I did haggle him down from $1,000.

I do not impugn him. His commission was only 25% of the purchase price. (We customarily make far more than that.) But most of the city lots sold by Burnett will be worthless when the gold fever abates, for surely Sacramento City must go the way of Sutterville. The miners are now reduced to scarcely an ounce of placer gold for a day's digging and inevitably they will return to their homes in the East or drift back to San Francisco. Many are skilled in the crafts, arts, and sciences and have the potential to enrich the California economy and culture once the powder-flare of greed and adventure has subsided.

Though we build them up and burn them down as fast, we are hopeful that theaters, hotels, schools, hospitals, a library, and an art museum will soon outnumber the saloons and bordellos that thus far have provided the principal diversions for our restless society.

What a commingling we have here. Every race, religion, vice and virtue. But still, through the strange alchemy, these disparate elements are slowly harmonizing. Unfortunately, the unusual trust displayed at the mines has given way to general crime and violence. This, paradoxically enough, may prove to be the making of our society. I see in the conflict around me a principle, that extremism in any form carries within it the seeds of its own destruction. Even an engaging rogue like Brannan calls upon the "decent element" of San Francisco to establish an orderly and safe society. Crimes of violence lately have rendered our streets a jungle. We need more virtuous women, more families, more teachers and preachers to demonstrate, by example, the blessings of the good Christian life.

One bit of news that I pray for Maria's sake and her father's is only erroneous assumption: you remember that my brother-in-law Goyo disappeared shortly before the so-called Battle of Cahuenga. Word has reached us that one of the bandit leaders harassing settlers from San Fernando to San Diego may be Goyo Robles. He (the man reputed to be Goyo) and his men are known as *Los Lobos*, the wolves. A vigilance committee riding after them lost one of its men to an ambush. An unseen assailant snared him around the neck with a *reata* and strangled him before he could utter a sound.

The only rancho victims of *Los Lobos* are *californios* who have lately sold to Yankees. Their cattle is taken, women and children are terrified, and loyal Mexicans and Indians are often murdered. There are a number of such outlaw bands operating, mostly in the south below the Tehachapis. Many raid and plunder indiscriminately, choosing as their victims both native and Yankee alike.

We have highwaymen here also but they seem to operate singly for the most part and attack messengers and the few stagecoaches that supply transport to mining areas.

This is the result of the great abuse that obtains against the Mexican miners. With the end of easy diggings, gangs of Yankees are falling upon peaceful and industrious professional Mexican miners and driving them off their rightful claims. Several hundreds have been illegally evicted in the past month. They have gone south of the Tehachapis and are joining outlaw bands to wreak vengeance on all Yankees wherever they find them. It is a tragic situation.

Knowing of the bitterness of my brother-in-law against all "foreigners," I fear there could be more fact than rumor in this news. We have taken the greatest possible precautions not to let it reach Don José in Monterey, for lately he has been in poor health.

He entertained such lofty aspirations for Goyo. But his son has remained a hotspur, a victim of irresponsible patriotism that he uses as an excuse to avoid the responsibility of managing his father's holdings. I can only pray that the apparent similarity between my brother-in-law and the leader of Los Lobos is merely cruel coincidence.

Maria and the children question me impatiently with each letter, so eager are they for word that you will at least visit us in California. Their concern helps to bind us all with love and affection in which I pledge I shall never be found wanting.

John

Book II

The Steven Lewis Story

7   CALIFORNIA WAS CHANGING. Its principle wealth was no longer founded on its mining claims, even though millions were occupied in the hard rock and hydraulic works and in new dredging operations that had superseded the ragged companies of men with picks and pans. The drifters and snipers of fifteen years earlier were now dead of privation or dying in the Comstock's fetid, silver-lined labyrinth. Some were freezing beside a remote stream in Colorado's new strikes.

In the beginning, California's wealth had been its land. Then had come furs, hides, and gold. In that era the merchants had prospered. Now the Central Pacific Railroad was lining its pockets with federal money. Huntington, Hopkins, Stanford, and Crocker had forced Theodore Judah, the scrupulously honest engineer whose concept the railroad had been, out of the corporation. Crocker, a ham-fisted, bull-necked slave driver, mercilessly pushed his huge army of Chinese coolies. It was true that Crocker and his coolies were chipping away at the granite escarpment of the Sierra but most men claimed this was merely a gesture. "The Big Four" were milking millions in taxpayer dollars by awarding the building contract to their own construction company. Both John Lewis and Billy Ralston doubted that Congress would continue to pay forty-eight thousand dollars a mountain mile for a road that progressed eastward less than a dozen miles a year after the first easygoing valley miles had been completed.

Steven Lewis was convinced that the transcontinental railroad was a necessity at any price. He was sure it would absorb or drive out the California Central, push northward toward Oregon and southward down the San Joaquin toward Los Angeles and San Diego. He remembered the persuasive argument by an old river captain who had seen it happen in the East.

"By the time you're as old as your father, Steve, there

won't be a freight wagon left, and there'll be damned few river boats. This ain't a frontier any more. This here's a civilized place with hotels and art museums and opera theaters and saloons and Turkish baths and gambling halls and fancy whorehouses with velvet settees. My God, they even got staterooms on the *Queen City*. You can sleep all night for five bucks and wake up in Sacramento. There's even a floating barber shop aboard. If you're looking for frontier in Californy, son, go to Los Angeles. They ain't come alive yet down there. But those cow counties are going to pretty quick now. There are thousands of Confederate folks that lost everything in the war heading west across Texas and New Mexico by now."

Steven had heard the same prediction the year before, the second year of the present drought. Most of the huge ranchos whose titles had finally been confirmed by the California Land Commission were delinquent with tax payments or mortgaged at usurious interest rates. Pasture land was being offered at ten cents an acre in the San Gabriel Valley. There were few takers. The best cattle were being sold for one dollar a head. Thousands of range cattle were sold for half that price and those not already dead were slaughtered on the parched ranges for their hides. Steven remembered Governor Low's recent wry observation: "The Almighty is punishing the *rancheros* for their indolence and for the willful squandering of His riches. The southern counties will never amount to a hill of beans until good small farmers come in who know what to do with land."

If the rumors were true, Steven thought, then before long the southern part of the state would come into its own. Most Southerners from the defeated Confederacy were, above all else, good small farmers. In southern California they could find modest parcels. Unlike his father and twin brother, Steven Lewis wanted land.

In his father's office, Steven broached the matter that had occupied most of his waking hours for nearly a year. John Lewis smiled across the polished expanse of walnut table. "Now, Steve, what's on your mind? Land again?"

"Yes."

"Where now?"

"In the south. Around Los Angeles."

John regarded his son unhappily. "Still Los Angeles? I thought I had convinced you that John Lewis & Sons has no opportunity there. It's too late. Phineas Banning's trying to do there what we're already doing here, and he has to build his own harbor to do it. I know that south country, son. Nothing will ever come of it until a railroad connects it to us, and that's at least fifty years away, in my estimation."

"A lot of people don't believe that, father. When Crocker blasts through the Donner Pass summit, it will go fast. Once Central Pacific rams through those mountains, freight and passengers will start moving overland at twenty miles an hour instead of ten knots at sea. We can steal land in the south now, and hold it for taxes."

John spread his hands. "To what purpose?"

"I have no definite purpose now, father. I want to go to Los Angeles and San Diego to look around. If the company does not want to invest in land there, I should like to borrow money from it, at the usual interest, and take up a league or two on my own account."

John was grim now. "Only eight thousand people in Los Angeles. Only five thousand in Santa Barbara. Half that number in San Diego with the second best harbor on the Pacific Coast. Arid mountains with little timber. Arid plains with fewer streams. No minerals of any account and some stinking black ooze called brea that the Mexicans smear on their roofs. A history of droughts. Right now, this minute, thousands of cattle are dying. Two *years* with no rain."

John bent forward, almost pleading. "Can't you see, Steve? Man must not only remake the land down there, he must control the climate as well. Nothing of any consequence grows without rainfall. The south is a desert. I've known it for twenty years. It has not changed, except in small patches where a few men have scratched out colonies."

There was a suggestion of tried patience in his tone as he continued. "No Steve. I'll give you *ten thousand* dollars to buy land in the Sacramento Valley, or anywhere else in the state, except south of the Tehachapis. You'll run afoul the same problems there that Will Chard and I had here twenty years ago. And what's more you'll have to bend God to your will to boot."

Short, stocky, elegantly groomed, delicately manicured Francis L. A. Pioche, the French-born financier and *bon*

243

vivant, sat across from Steven in his new three-story Stockton Street mansion.

Pioche's obviously admiring appraisal made Steven ill at ease. He seemed to be devoting the same degree of intensly personal attention to him that he might lavish on a young lady. Steven had the feeling that Pioche was listening with two distinctly separate minds. One noted his request for a cash loan and the other was weighing the business merits of the request against the personal satisfaction Pioche might derive. Even the voice—women described it as "charmingly accented"—seemed to caress rather than question. *"Mais, mon ami, combien faut-il payer?* And what shall I ask of you as security for a personal loan?"

· "I need a credit draft for five thousand dollars. For security you have my hand and my word and a deed for half of the land I purchase, with the understanding that I may buy it back from you at the market upon satisfaction of the entire loan."

Pioche's small shrewd eyes widened, then he threw back his head and a delighted laugh echoed through the room. *"Sacre bleu*! You will give me half of the land you buy with my money *if* I promise to trade the deed for the satisfied personal note." He leaned across the table and rested a hand on the younger man's knee.

"Steven, my dear young friend, if I am as shrewd as my competitors credit me with being, I should pay you fifty thousand dollars to desert your family, move in here with me, and become my business protégé. We would soon have M'sieur Ralston for our office clerk, would we not?"

Pioche gave Steven's knee an affectionate squeeze and leaned back to contemplate the fragile snifter of Sazerac poised in his left hand. "Let me ask you another question. Why did you not go to your father?"

"I did, sir. He will give me any amount I want to purchase land north of Monterey, but none for Los Angeles or San Diego."

"Then why did you not ask M'sier Ralston? Many times on the Champagne Route when we have discussed the new generation of promising young men he has had flattering things to say about the Lewis twins."

"Sir, my father is financed by Mr. Ralston now. I prefer to act independently of my father's business associates."

"Most particularly since you act in opposition to his wishes?"

"Yes, sir."

Pioche sniffed the Sazerac. "You wish to be your own man, then?"

"Yes, sir."

"And, forgive me, you find it doubly difficult being a twin."

"My brother and my father see with the same eyes. I don't say they are wrong. I don't say I am smarter."

Pioche nodded. "But you are different, Steven. Even I, who will never have sons, can see that. Somehow, at your tender age, you have concluded that great opportunities are to be found in solutions to great problems. *Très bien! Vous avez perception.* But what will you do with the land?"

Steven considered his answer. "It is possible, sir, that I will not make a purchase at all. I do not want just any land."

"So?"

"I want cheap land. And I want land that controls the headwaters of a river or a year-round stream with a good flow."

Incredulousness shone in the financier's eyes. "But my dear young man, you will sooner find virtue in a *demimonde* than abundant water in the south. What you are really asking me to do is finance an outing."

Steven Lewis answered by taking from his pocket a folded paper. "I have sufficient personal funds to finance my own journey and a stay of several months, sir." He unfolded the paper and revealed a crude hand-rendered map of the area from Santa Barbara to San Diego. The map showed outlines of the confirmed Mexican grants, the direction of the principal mountain ranges, and the approximate courses of their few known dependable streams. Pointing to the general area of San Diego and San Bernardino, Steven moved his finger along the base of the mountains whose slopes drained onto the coastal plain. "There are two dependable streams here."

The finger moved toward sprawling Los Angeles County. "And there are three more here. The ranchos with ranges in the foothills are best off. Even so, much of that rough land is for sale. That is what I propose to buy."

Recently Pioche and Bayerque, the name of Pioche's

trading firm, had speculated in several huge tracts of land for subdivision including hundreds of acres in San Francisco's Visitation Valley. Pioche had had a hand in building the San Jose Railroad, the line on which hordes of settlers traveled to buy home sites for ten times what Pioche and his partners had paid for the raw acreage. Still other Pioche money went to subsidize and eventually control cattlemen in Monterey County and Santa Barbara County. He was said to have as many fingers in as many pies as the dynamic banker Billy Ralston.

Steven Lewis watched him studying the map. The man was an enigma. He pretended as much interest in hunting and fishing as he did in San Francisco's blossoming arts. In contrast to Billy Ralston's preference for male companions in his favorite saloons, Francis Pioche preferred artists, writers, actresses, and singers. He was adored by women of the theater for his lavish gifts of jewelry. He asked nothing in return but their companionship, always in the company of others. No whisper of scandal ever touched him. His gifts were understood to be precisely what they were, expression of the donor's gratitude for the distinction, and occasionally the notoriety, the performers lent to San Francisco. If William Ralston called San Francisco "his city" Francis Pioche could make the same claim with equal justice. Their civic rivalry was amiable.

Steve's disquieting personal appraisal of Pioche was interrupted by a sudden question. "Tell me, Steven, where did you get the notion to control water?"

"From my grandfather, Don José Robles, and from my father's partner, Harry Morrison. When I was still in school Harry took me on a trip up the American River. I saw the ditches and flumes there. The men who brought the water from the high country and sold it by the inch made more money than the miners who used it for washing gold."

Pioche tapped the map. "And you propose to corner the market in liquid gold?"

"I propose to control a good share of it, sir."

"To what purpose?"

"For whatever purpose the people below will buy it."

"Have you thought out what some specific purposes might be?"

Steven Lewis met Pioche's questioning gaze for a time, then lowered his eyes. "Not exactly. They want water for

246

their cattle and their gardens, and everything else water's needed for."

Steve knew that he had replied lamely, because he had acted too hastily. His arguments in favor of the loan should have been thought out in more detail. He should have financed his own exploratory trip to Los Angeles and San Diego, seen the streams and the lower lands dependent upon their water. The map should have been drawn from personal observation. He was about to confess his dereliction when Pioche leaned back and laughed softly.

"Do you know something, my dear Steven? I am twenty-six years your senior but I am not so old that I cannot remember my own impetuosity, my own errors of haste." He lifted a hand. "Oh, I made them. I made them, *mon cher ami*. Some of them were *maqnifique*. I remember, while suffering from a multitude of youthful misjudgments that had compounded themselves into a *désastre*, the advice I received from Victor Hugo, who was my dear mother's close friend. He said, 'Great blunders are often made, like large ropes, of a multitude of fibers.' *Il y a du vrai*. But it is also true that strong ropes are made of many fibers well laid. Your concept is excellent. It has daring and majesty. What it lacks, my dear boy, is research and order. Not only must you see the opportunities for yourself, but also you must anticipate the problems. I do not refer to mechanical problems. Engineering brains and strong backs can be hired. I refer to the curses that are certain to accompany the blessings you propose to confer upon the southerners."

Pioche leaned forward earnestly. "Do you know anything about human nature, Steven?"

"Some, sir."

"Have you learned that the most feared and detested man is the émigré, the outsider, who would exploit the opportunity the natives have failed to see?"

Suddenly his father's warning whispered across the intervening days. "You'll run afoul the same problems there that Chard and I had here twenty years ago." Steven understood that while the situations were not precisely analagous the underlying principle was the same. The Anglo-Americans now outnumbered the native *californios*. They controlled the politics and economy of the state. Steven understood that he could expect no consideration from his own, most particularly if he seemed to threaten their dwindling supply of lifeblood. In an instant he anticipated all that Pioche would say. But he listened attentively.

"The trick, *mon ami*, is to convince people, while you are gaining control over them, that you are their benefactor, that you have anticipated their need and you have come to help. Do that successfully and you become a hero. Fail and you become a corpse. There's only one principle. *Écoutez bien*, Steven. All men secretly desire something for nothing. But offer it to them and they grow suspicious. So? How do we take advantage of this human perversity? We do *not* offer them something for nothing. We offer them something of value, at a bargain. *C'est tout!*"

For a moment Pioche regarded his young visitor with undisguised admiration. "Of course, *mon jeune protégé*, there are other more obscure aspects of human nature that concern man's relationships, especially where the passions are involved. But that is another lesson. *N'est-ce pas?*"

Pioche removed an ornately carved gold watch from the pocket of his brocaded waistcoat and snapped open the diamond inset cover. "Forgive me, Steven, but my valet, Louis, will be reminding me that I have dinner guests this evening."

Pioche walked around the small table to guide Steven by the elbow. "I'll see you to the door and make you a proposal, yes?"

Steven's mouth twisted into a wry grin. "You'll propose that I have all of the facts before I waste your time again?"

Pioche linked his arm affectionately through Steven's. "You have not wasted my time, Steven, or yours. Invest your own funds in an exploratory trip, make a decision supported by facts. If I find it attractive you and I shall become partners, *equal* partners in the venture."

Steven turned to face his host. "But I am already a partner in Lewis & Sons . . ."

Pioche laughed. "My dear young friend, I am a partner in twenty ventures. That is how one covers his wagers."

He opened the door and extended his hand. "Thank you for choosing to come to me, Steven. I like you very much. The world deals kindly with smart attractive young men. You will do well. You shall see. *Au revoir, mon partenaire.* And if you do not sail for the south too soon I should like you to join us at a little *soirée*. I think my friends might amuse you. And I know that you will prove devastatingly attractive to the ladies."

The invitation was extended as Steven made his way down the flight of marble stairs to Stockton Street. He acknowledged it awkwardly, from the walk. As he turned down the hill he sensed that Francis Pioche was still watching him through the half-opened door.

On the cabin deck of the thirty-three-hundred-ton side-wheeler *Persia,* Steven wondered if he should not have managed a more considerate family leave-taking, one that would have spared them all the unhappiness of the past few days.

Since, in business, Pioche was known to be a man of his word, Steven had not hesitated to tell his father and brother in detail the conditions of the agreement. They had listened in disapproving silence and his father had spoken first. "You are a goddamned fool, Steven. You will not be Pioche's partner. You will be his prat boy. He will flatter you and bend you around his fat little fingers and you will wear out a dozen pairs of boots running for him and pay for the privilege from your own purse."

His brother had been hardly less direct. "Pioche doesn't mix with our kind, Steve. He's too fancy. If you won't listen to father, the least you can do is talk to Billy Ralston. He's our kind. You don't have to ask him for money. Ask him for advice. Tell Pioche you've changed your mind."

The scene with his mother and sister at the big house in the country out near Mission Dolores had been the most difficult.

Doña Maria, withdrawn, graying but still lovely, in her forties, enlisted the assistance of twenty-two-year-old Felicia who, four years earlier, had married Lambert Lee, a San Francisco lawyer fifteen years her senior. Most of his practice had come to relate to the manifold affairs of John Lewis & Sons. It was understood that a partnership was in prospect.

Steve's brother-in-law, a tall, humorless man, had come in during the most turbulent moments with Doña Maria and Felicia. The scene had not been helped by Steven's nephew and niece, two-year-old Lewis Lee and six-month-old Emily. Sensing the emotional conflict, they added to the clamor. The hardest thing to bear had been his mother's quiet weeping. *"Por que? Por que, Steven?* Why do you leave us? You are of the north. The south is not good. *Es una tierra abandonado, un gran desierto.* Only death lives there. You will never return. I know. A woman knows these things about her own."

Felicia's pleading, done apart from the others, had been more subtle. "It is not that you shouldn't go, Steve. You are a man now. You have a right to make a man's choice. But wait until after the holidays. I know how you feel. Lambert and I have talked about your place in the company, about how Will seems more suited to work with Father."

Steven could not resist a retort. "I do not think your Lambert will shed many tears if I vacate my place in the company."

He had endured the torrent of angry denials but he knew it was true. There was still another truth to be faced. Steven had long sensed his twin brother's rivalry for parental affection. Will would make, indeed had made, a great show of protest too. But however convincing it had been to others, Steven knew that his absence would relieve rather than grieve his brother. He did not understand his own compulsive need to move out, to pit himself against the brotherhood of selfish giants who were shaping California. In five years, perhaps less, steel rails would bind the Atlantic to the Pacific. That meant the railroads would hold the entire continent in a gleaming skein.

After a half hour on deck a chill drove Steven below to the main saloon. For the most part the passengers were an affluent-appearing group.

In the dining saloon he was seated to make a fourth with a Reverend and Mrs. Lathrop and their daughter, a young woman in her mid-twenties whose pallid face was saved from the commonplace by arresting, long-lashed, slightly up-tilted peridot green eyes. During the discreet mutual questioning initiated by the preacher, Steven found those eyes disconcerting. He would not have called the young woman's gaze bold but certainly it was more than the polite pretense of attention usually accorded him by genteel, match-minded young ladies.

At twenty-five Arlene Lathrop Baker was a widow. Her

mother had volunteered the information. "It has been very difficult for her and I think she is very brave."

The daughter disagreed firmly. "I have not been brave, mother. Gerald's untimely death was part of his karma, just as it is part of mine. It does not require bravery to accept the workings of Divine Law. One needs only faith and understanding."

She turned to Steven. "I hope, Mr. Lewis, that I do not sound callous, most particularly since my late husband was taken from me by his own hand just a year ago. I do make the conventional concessions. I did go into mourning, of course. But I feel a bit of a hypocrite since only a person wanting in understanding would indulge in such self-pity."

The Reverend Lathrop laughed nervously. "I must say, Lewis, that my daughter and I do not see precisely eye-to-eye on this matter. I tend to stay with the literal word of the scriptures. I see no need to question their intent."

Arlene Lathrop Baker directed a benign smile at her father, then patted Steven's hand lightly. "The eternal schism between the generations, Mr. Lewis. Father only recently heard his call to the ministry and founded his own church against all of the remonstrances of his own father. But now that I've heard my call he uses all of the arguments that he himself renounced."

She laughed for the first time. The sound was gay and musical. Suddenly her face seemed quite beautiful. Then she was serious again and Mrs. Lathrop's expression of hurtful reproach faded, but the Reverend Lathrop continued to make soft lamenting sounds. "My daughter does not believe in sin, Mr. Lewis. She calls it the 'immutable law of cause and effect.' But I say a sin by any other name—"

"Oh, father!" Arlene raised long white fingers to her temples. "You will never understand. Of course I believe in what you call 'sin.' Almighty God knows I saw enough of it first hand with poor benighted Gerald. And he paid his penalty, didn't he? The law of cause and effect. He was punished on earth, not in Heaven. His hell was here."

Suddenly contrite, she turned to Steven and rested a cool hand on top of his. The sensation was not unpleasant. "You see, Mr. Lewis, I believe we learn our lessons here. Life is a classroom. If we do not learn here, then we are sent back a grade, reincarnated and made to face the same problems over and over until we solve them. Then and only then are we sent on to higher, more noble lessons."

Jabez Lathrop snorted. "Nonsense!"

Arlene was not to be stopped. "Only through the cultivation of true understanding, Mr. Lewis, can we make our bodies perfect instruments for the joyous expression of God's Will."

She punctuated the statement with a little pat and removed the hand that had rested on Steven's. The discussion unsettled Steven. He turned the conversation to more familiar matters. "Sir, will you start your church in Los Angeles?"

The preacher placed the palms of his hands together and bowed over them.

Arlene gave Steven a knowing smile. "Even though father denies its existence, father is using the Great Inner Eye—the symbolic term for Divine Perception. Yours, Mr. Lewis, by the way, is very marked. That means you are a very highly evolved soul in this incarnation."

Jabez Lathrop groaned and shot an appealing look at his wife. "Dammit, Arlene!"

Mrs. Lathrop gasped and lowered her head as he continued: "It's all right for you to spout that heresy in the privacy of our home. But not here, not in public!"

Mrs. Lathrop lifted a hand in a wan, helpless gesture. Arlene smiled triumphantly. "Father, the very fact that you can lose your self-possession in public and that I can keep mine, even when my deepest convictions are being attacked, is that not proof that my understanding is as great as yours?"

"Why don't you say, 'greater'?"

Arlene smiled compassionately. "Because I understand, dearest father, the misgivings felt by parents even though I was not fulfilled as a woman by poor Gerald."

It was obvious that the Reverend Lathrop could not cope with his daughter's forthrightness. He turned, almost desperately, to Steven. "You asked if I am going to found a church in Los Angeles? The answer is yes! I am going to found a church, somewhere in or around Los Angeles. I will call it the Tabernacle of Truth, a name I put together from the Scriptures by searching them with the *only* two eyes I'm certain the Almighty gave me." The Reverend's daughter smiled with long-suffering forbearance.

Warming to his subject, Lathrop's long, knob-knuckled fingers clutched at the satin-faced lapels of his frock coat. "Through no desire of my own, Mr. Lewis, I prospered during the late war. I resolved I would show my gratitude to the Almighty by devoting the rest of my days to His service."

Before he could launch into a full dissertation, Arlene interrupted. "Father—forgive me, please, but I do think the sea is getting a bit tippy." She patted her brow and looked about apprehensively. "I really feel the need for some fresh air, rather quickly, I fear!"

Steven's chair was back before she had finished. "It is cold on deck, Mrs. Baker. You'll need a wrap."

"I have one in my cabin, Mr. Lewis. If you would be good enough to see me there, then show me to the upper deck, I'd be most grateful."

Steven guided her into the main saloon and onto the weather side of the deck. Clutching his arm tightly, Arlene led him past several staterooms as she rummaged in a small bag for the key.

Steven let her in and stepped aside. "Do come in, Mr. Lewis. I shall need help getting this heavy old coat around me."

On deck again, Steven guided her to the ladder leading to the top of the deck house. So far as he could tell there had been no noticeable change in the sea. Even so, Arlene seemed very unsteady and he found himself supporting most of her weight whenever the vessel heeled. At the railing forward of the stack she realized that he was not wearing a topcoat. "Oh, Mr. Lewis, I'm so sorry. How utterly selfish of me. You'll take a chill."

"I'm quite all right, really, Mrs. Baker. You'll feel better in a moment and I'm used to the sea air."

Arlene turned, rested her hands against the front of his coat, and looked at him contritely. "I have a confession, Mr. Lewis. It was not the motion that made me ill. It was the thought of another hour of listening to father's pious pretensions. Oh, *I* could endure it all right. But I saw no earthly reason to ask an intelligent young gentleman like you to suffer through it."

She turned away. "Besides, it is so beautiful up here, so clean." She turned back to him. "I'll be all right alone for

253

a moment. Do get your coat and come back and talk with me. I'm hungry for intelligent conversation, Mr. Lewis."

He returned in several minutes and they found a seat on the frame of a closed skylight. Seated close to him, Arlene was silent but Steven could feel her studying him. The ship's bell sounded and she shivered and inched closer. Without warning, she laughed a bit wildly and turned to Steven. "It's amazing! Truly amazing," Puzzled, Steven looked around the deck.

"Nothing here, Mr. Lewis. I meant meeting someone such as you." She leaned closer. "Don't ask me to explain. As much as I know, there is more I do not know." She continued to search his face. In the starlight, framed by the soft knitted shawl that protected her smooth dark brown hair, Steven thought her face was serenely beautiful, almost madonna-like.

She smiled and seemed about to rest her cheek against his shoulder but changed her mind and looked away again. "It isn't necessary to talk, Mr. Lewis. Communing in silence is the highest form of communication."

She seemed to retreat into herself then and Steven watched her from the corner of his eye. Daughter of a well-to-do food processor, undoubtedly a war profiteer, offspring of a self-ordained minister of a nonexistent church, a free thinker, and a new widow to boot, all this troubled him far less than it intrigued him.

Neither he nor his twin brother were strangers to young ladies, proper ones and some not so proper. But this woman beside him did not conform to familiar patterns. He could not put a name to the curious quality in her that seemed at once both prim and promiscuous. In the midst of this speculation, she startled him again.

"I don't believe in senseless convention, Mr. Lewis. I can only hope that you find me direct but not bold." She turned to him. "For some reason I cannot explain I feel the need to be very truthful with you."

Uneasy, Steven started to protest but she cut him off. "I must say it. Father did not heed God's Call, so to speak, until he was tried and found innocent for want of sufficient evidence in the death of ten Union soldiers. They died of poisoning after eating food tinned on our factory.

"The prosecution proved contamination was present. But it could not prove that the contaminants had been present in the unopened tins. Father won the case because there is always some spoilage in tinned foods. The jury agreed that the army cooks were negligent in not examining the contents before they emptied them into the common mess.

"But the boys' deaths shocked father. So he is trying to find his way to self-forgiveness by devoting all of his very great energy to God's work as he understands it. I see through him, Mr. Lewis, but I admire him. Most men would do nothing to make amends. And I share his burden of guilt."

Steven frowned. "I doubt that somehow. Why do you say it?"

"Because I often helped in the canning house. Several times I had the feeling that the tins were not being boiled long enough before the women filled them. And I often saw poor work in lidding and waxing. I did speak on these things. But not insistently enough."

"That's ridiculous. We are merchants in San Francisco. We handle thousands of cases of tinned food. I would say more pickled salted and dried stuff spoils. You are too hard on yourself."

His indignation seemed to touch the young woman. Gently, she captured his upper arm between her hands. "Dear Mr. Lewis. May I ask how old you are?"

The question took him by surprise. "Why I'm twenty-one, almost twenty-two. Why?"

"Oh. I would have said older. I'm sorry. I never should have started this dull personal conversation."

"It isn't dull. It's interesting. Do you mind if I ask you a question?"

She laughed softly and let her cheek brush against his shoulder. "Heavens, no. I'm flattered by your interest."

"It's about your late husband."

"Gerald?" She drew a deep breath and gazed upward. Her large eyes seemed luminous and her profile was lovely. "What do you want to know about poor Gerald?"

Steven struggled. "I can't guess why a man married to a wonderful woman like you would want to—to—"

She finished the question for him. "Take his own life?"

After a troubled silence, she released his arm, turned and folded her hands in her lap. "Are you certain, Mr. Lewis, that you will not find it too much if I speak with utmost candor?"

He nodded. "Quite sure, Mrs. Baker."

She moved an inch away and sat up very straight. "I married Gerald when I was nineteen. Our families had been friends for years in Springfield and in Pennsylvania before that. I guess we all just took it for granted that we would always be together."

"From the very moment the vows were taken, Mr. Lewis, something happened. We had always been comfortable with each other. Suddenly we were strangers, or at least Gerald was. We went to Lime Rock Springs for our honeymoon."

She paused and looked directly at Steven. "It was never consummated, Mr. Lewis. Whatever had happened between Gerald and me not only made us strangers, but almost enemies. We went back to Springfield and moved into the house father had built for us. I thought perhaps there, with our own things around us, it would be . . ." she shrugged, ". . . better.

"I thought perhaps I had been too aggressive. I wasn't timid because our theosophy teacher in Chicago taught me that there should be nothing but joy and beauty in all natural relationships. So I took the initiative and let Gerald know that I was eager to receive him. But my honesty seemed to make him withdraw even more and he found excuses to stay at his father's hardware store where he worked later and later.

"We went on that way for a year. He avoided me as much as possible and I made excuses and pretended that I was bursting with pride in my industrious husband. But some people saw through it. In time even mother began to wonder why I did not become pregnant."

Arlene broke off and turned away. When she was in possession of herself she continued. "I sublimated my passionate nature in the making of a home. I worked long hours in the canning shed. I even got a citation from our mayor for outstanding patriotic war assistance. Gerald signed up with the Illinois Volunteers and went into training and that helped with appearances. He was gone a year but he didn't see any fighting. When he came back I welcomed him, Mr. Lewis, I welcomed him eagerly and without shame."

Again Arlene paused and turned away. "When Gerald returned from the war he was often in his cups. Sometimes it was so bad he could not work. Had he known combat it might have been taken as a reaction to the horrors of the battlefield. But he had no such excuse, Mr. Lewis.

"Then one night when he had been drinking heavily I felt I had to be completely candid with him. I asked him if he did not find me attractive, as a woman, as a sex object. He—he smirked in a most revolting way." She stopped for a moment. When she continued her voice was subdued. "He told me that he found *all* women physically revolting, and that he always had. He told me that his needs were taken care of by others who felt the same way."

There was a long silence. Then Arlene rose abruptly. "On the first day of January he was found in a thicket out near the lake. The ball from his gun had passed upward and blown away the back of his head. It was set down as a hunting accident, Mr. Lewis. But it was not. It was suicide. Gerald was not a hunter. He took his own life. But he did it in a manner that left doubt. And in so doing he spared all but me the pain of absolute knowledge. A family can learn to live with the grief of an accident. But a suicide? No!"

Without quite realizing what he was doing, Steven reached out in an attempt to comfort her. She avoided him.

"I must go now, Mr. Lewis. I do not know how I shall ever thank you for your sympathetic understanding. I have needed," she closed her eyes tightly and her voice seemed near to breaking, "my God, how I have needed to say it all out loud to some compassionate soul. We were led to one another, Steven Lewis. Believe that."

Before he could respond she had kissed him full on the mouth and was hurrying toward the ladder. He overtook her and helped her down to the main deck. There, without a word, she brushed past him and ran to her stateroom.

Steven saw the Lathrops briefly when the launches from the new San Pedro pier carried them ashore. Since he was not delayed by a wait for luggage, he was able to take the first Banning stagecoach to Los Angeles. After a wild three-hour ride the shaken passengers alighted at the Bella Union Hotel advertised as "the finest hotel south of San Francisco." It wasn't, Steven observed as he let himself into a small third-floor room, much of a recommendation. Former governor Pio Pico's promised "great hotel," Pico

House, was still only a rumor. That afternoon he arranged for a saddle horse for the following morning.

When he returned to the hotel, the stagecoach bearing the Lathrops had just pulled up. Smiling, he walked over to them. "Allow an old-timer to welcome you to Los Angeles. I've been here for three hours."

Arlene laughed and gave him her hand. Mrs. Lathrop greeted Steven with a bleak smile. Jabez Lathrop looked about critically, studying the dung-littered, unpaved street, the motley ranks of pretentious two- and three-story brick buildings with arched windows overlooking low, flat-roofed, fly-infested adobe cantinas. "The Promised Land does not look full of promise, Lewis."

Steven was about to agree when the stage driver cut in. "You're dead right, Reverend. And some folks are thinking of suing the Almighty for *breach* of promise!"

Arlene Baker turned to Steven. "I'll forgive this land anything so long as I can enjoy this wonderful sun. And in November. It's a miraculous land, Mr. Lewis."

Steven nodded. "Perhaps. But I'm reserving my opinion until I've looked around a little."

"How long will you be here?"

"Long enough to ride out to the San Gabriel Valley. And perhaps down to San Diego."

Arlene pouted. "I envy you your adventures." She indicated the hotel. "Is this place at all bearable?"

"It's reasonably clean and a lot quieter than its namesake in San Francisco."

The stage driver spat and chortled. "You sure wouldn't have said that if you'd been here last July sixth, mister. No, sir! You would have been cut down by a dozen slugs when Bob Carlisle shot it out with the King brothers." He wagged his head. "Carlisle dead. Frank King dead. Sam King still hanging on with three slugs in him and likely to die from rope poisoning if the lead don't get him first. I don't think you folks up in Frisco get much noisier than we do, what with ordinary friendly shootings and lynching greasers and chinks. Last week them Lobos outlaws rode down from the hills and shot up two squatter shacks outside of El Monte, killed the men, stole the stock and the women, and set fire to the whole shebang."

Mrs. Lathrop listened with oval-eyed horror. Steven was puzzled by Arlene's smile until she explained. "Violence al-

258

ways results when man frustrates his true nature. Hatred is simply dammed up love."

Frowning, the perplexed driver examined Arlene and said, "Then there sure must be a lot of damned love in this here town, ma'am!" He looked expectantly from one upturned face to another. He saw a twinkle in Steven's eyes and slapped his thigh, succumbing to a paroxysm of self-appreciation. Arlene Baker shot a scornful look up at him and rested a hand on Steven's arm.

"I hope you will join us for dinner this evening, Mr. Lewis. It would seem strange not to have you with us now."

After the dinner, which Steven Lewis insisted upon hosting, the Lathrops retired to their rooms to finish unpacking. Steven went to the bar and struck up some easy conversations over a brandy. The information he gleaned was consistent: the entire southern region of the state was verging on disaster unless the rains came quickly. Even so, the rains would probably cause as much damage and suffering as the drought itself. They always had.

"It's the nature of this country," an older man with holdings in the Santa Ana River Valley volunteered. "There's not enough cover on these mountains to hold back a heavy run-off. It's been a plague on the land ever since earliest times. We've all seen it. A heavy rain comes, the run-off starts in the canyons, then all of a sudden a wall of mud and water flashes down onto the plains. Nothing can stand up to it. I've seen boulders as big as Phineas Banning's coaches come bouncing down a wash, smashing trees and houses and squashing cattle and horses like sow bugs. A river of liquid mud can pour out of a canyon and sweep everything away, completely burying houses without a minute's warning to the folks inside."

The man next to him nodded gravely. "What this country wants is dams to slow down the run-off and save the water for irrigation. Every time a flood comes it contaminates the drinking water."

The bartender's eyes turned limpid with exaggerated sorrow. "The pathetic part is, it drives a lot of otherwise temperate folks to come in here to disinfect theirselves and ward off the fevers. 'Course I admit we get a few such folks that prays for floods."

The customers laughed but there was no mistaking the anxiety underlying the levity. The drought was in its third year and if the rains were going to come they would come soon. They were, in fact, seven or eight weeks overdue.

After the second raw native brandy, Steven said his goodnights and climbed the stairs to his room. His window overlooked the Church of Nuestra Señora la Reina de Los Angeles de la Porciuncla. The original pueblo was founded in 1781 and it stood next to the Los Angeles River. The river had rampaged over its banks a dozen times.

In 1800, following a two-year drought, the floods had destroyed most of the thirty original adobes and washed away sections of the pueblo walls. The plaza had been moved then to its present location on high ground, but the river still took its toll in the outlying regions. No one dared to predict that it would remain in its present course for more than a season. Like a great, sandy serpent, it writhed over thousands of acres, brimful for weeks at a time, then diminished to a trickle, often so slight that people were forced to dig holes in its bed to find water.

Steven heard an echo of the stranger's words. "What this country needs, mister, is dams to slow down the run-off."

He lowered the shade and began emptying his pockets. As he was about to light the coal-oil lamp he heard a soft tapping on the door. For a moment he thought he'd been mistaken but it came again, more insistently. At the door he hesitated.

"Who is it?"

The whispered reply, so close it startled him, came through the ill-fitting jamb. "It's Arlene. Mrs. Baker. May I talk with you for a moment?"

Steven unlocked the door, intending to open it sufficiently to look out, but he found himself being moved backward as Arlene pushed into the room and closed the door behind her.

"Forgive me, Steven, I know my behavior must shock you, but I need your help desperately. I knew you'd be up and gone tomorrow before I had time to see you alone."

Flustered to be found undressing, he moved toward the lamp again.

"No. Don't bother with a light or your coat or tie, Steven. I'll just stay a moment. I realize what my presence

260

here could do to both our good names, but I simply had to risk it."

Steven turned back to her. "I'll put up the shade a bit."

The room lightened sufficiently to reveal that she was still dressed in the embroidered gray silk blouse and the mauve wool skirt she had worn at dinner. But the jacket was missing and her hair, usually pinned in a severe roll at the back of her head, now hung in loose soft curls that spilled from a band of ribbon secured low on her neck. The disconcerting eyes seemed wide and curiously luminous as she moved close and rested a hand lightly on his upper arm.

"I warned you, Steven, that you and I are old souls who have been through much together in other times. But as candid as I was on deck last night, there simply wasn't time to confide all that needed saying."

Steven flopped his hands awkwardly.

"I hope you don't mind if I call you Steven and you must please call me Arlene. Steven, I can't explain it, but once you must have been very dear to me for I still feel the light and warmth of that earlier relationship. Perhaps we were brother and sister, or husband and wife, or perhaps just sweethearts."

She looked around, obviously seeking a chair. Steven pulled a small cane-seated rosewood rocker from beside the washstand.

"You sit on that, Steven. I'll just perch here for a moment."

Before he could protest, she seated herself on the edge of the bed. In doing so the braided hem of her skirt hiked above the tops of her expensive shoes, revealing the curves of her surprisingly full-turned lower calves. She made no effort to conceal them and leaned toward him urgently.

"I told you father had decided to devote the rest of his life and his modest fortune to God's service. What I did not have time to tell you last night is this: I too am going to dedicate my life to the service of mankind. I told you what I believe in, the free expression of Divine Love with man and woman its perfect creative instruments. I am determined to found a colony for Free Thinkers, an earthly paradise where others who believe as I do may devote their lives to the passionate pursuit of the true Truth!"

Less uneasy and frankly curious, Steven controlled a smile. "I didn't know there was any other kind."

"Of course there is. Have you never heard of a half-truth?"

"Yes, ma'am. I've even heard myself saying a few."

Arlene Baker frowned. "Be serious, Steven. We have very little time."

"I am serious. But how can I help? What can I do?"

"While you're looking around for whatever you're after, Steven dear, you can seek a likely place for me to found my colony. I will call it Brindavanam."

Steven fidgeted on the small chair and it creaked alarmingly beneath its six-foot, one-hundred-eighty-pound burden. "But I don't know what you need."

"You'll be led to it, dear Steven, a beautiful secluded location, a place of beauty with trees and meadows and a stream of cold pure water."

"But you'll have to buy the land. You'll need buildings."

"And they will all come, Steven, everything I need."

Arlene Baker's long fingers explored the narrow waistband of her skirt. Steven watched amazed as she removed an envelope, opened it and slipped out five one-thousand-dollar bank notes.

"I brought these to you for a start. I have much more on deposit with Lazard Frefes in San Francisco, enough to purchase Brindavanam, build our first temple, and our first fifty residences."

She rose from the bed and handed Steven the notes. "I want you to take them. I have perfect trust. I want no receipts or any evidence that I have given them to you."

Steven tried to return them. "But Arlene, this is a lot of money. I can't take it. Suppose I lose it or get held up or suppose I'm really just a crook. You don't know anything about me, really."

She put her hands behind her in a gesture of stubborn refusal. Steven stood up and reached around to force her to take the money. Laughing and protesting, she stepped back quickly. As she did the heavy wooden bedframe struck her behind the knees. Uttering an alarmed little cry, she began to topple backward. Caught off-balance himself, Steven tried, too late, to steady her. They fell together on the bed.

Arlene, lying with her sparsely fleshed, naked body flattened along Steven's upper belly and chest said in a whisper, "Are you shocked knowing I have no shame, Steven?"

262

He rolled his head away to look at her in the half light. "If you're not shocked, why should I be?"

"Because I let everything happen so fast, dearest one."

Steven smiled inwardly and thought that *"made* everything happen so fast" would have been more accurate. The time with her, whatever its length, had been a dark fantasy, a *tentación del diablo,* a fulfillment of all those hebetic, libidinous longings that had so often been vented in an agony of repression lest his twin brother, sleeping nearby, might hear and suspect. Now in this strange bed this voracious, man-hungry woman had twice drained him with her insatiable demands. Steven felt her hands move up the sides of his head. The thin fingers found the thick tangle of his dark brown hair and probed sensuously.

After a time, Arlene inched her body up along his side to kiss him. For several minutes he failed to respond to the new assault of caresses. Annoyed, she stopped. "Steven—"

"Yes?"

"Kiss, darling. Do things. Anything. Make me feel."

Before he could reply she was on his lips again, first probing in his mouth with her tongue, then once more moving her body urgently against his. She clung to him, pléading, coaxing him up and into her. For the third time, Steven could feel himself responding and then, too quickly, he came. Her narrow hips started to batter his and she began to plead again, "Stay—stay—stay—stay, Steven, oh—stay, darling."

They remained locked together until Steven heard her gasp, suck in a huge breath, then felt her body, cold with perspiration, collapse on his. After that he became aware of a new wetness, on her cheek. He touched the tears lightly and she began to quiver in his arms.

Holding the thin, vibrant body close, Steven struggled to sort out from the welter of feelings the dominent one that had possessed him for the past hours. There had been, still was, excitement, passion, tenderness, and a strange uneasiness too. Steven had never been in love. There had been, on several occasions, the not unwelcome pain of a brief infatuation early in his teens. But tonight something new had been awakened, some feeling he could not put a name to.

He had shared two wracking orgasms with Arlene Baker. After them had come an unaccountable tenderness.

263

She had satisfied him deeply and he wondered if what he was feeling might be the beginning of love, but he mistrusted his emotions. Certainly what he had felt was not what he had felt for the prostitutes who had taught him well. And it was not that added something he had felt for the fresh young whore who had claimed she had fallen in love with him and offered to renounce the profession if he would marry her. It was strange to remember her now and remember Harry Morrison's earthy observation: "Sometimes whores make the best wives, laddie. Aye. They say the first ladies of two of our states were madams who worked their way up. If you want a wife that knows how to meet a mon on his own terms ye couldna do better than a good clean professional lady."

Steven felt Arlene lift her head to look at him. When he opened his eyes her face was inches from his. "I could feel you thinking. Would a penny buy your thoughts?"

He smiled and attempted to bring her face closer, but she pulled away. "Please don't, darling! I've waited so long to find you and gotten so hungry in the process. You'll think I'm insatiable!"

She let her body roll from his then and curled up beside him. "Were you worried about," she rested a palm lightly on her lower stomach, "about complications?"

Steven lied. "I should. But I guess I wasn't."

The palm moved to his face and two fingers pressed against his lips. "You shouldn't. So don't. It is too late to explain now. I must dress and get back down to my room before it's light. But one day you'll understand."

She cocked her head quizzically. "By the way, when will I see you again?"

Steven pushed half upright. "It depends on when I get back. The night after tomorrow, maybe. I came here to find some land, remember?"

"And you promised to find me some, too."

He nodded and swung his legs off the bed. "What was the name of that place I'm going to be *led* to?"

Her eyes rebuked him. "Brindavanum." She repeated it slowly. "Brin-*dah*-van-um. It's ancient Tamil for Garden of Love. I first heard the name when I was studying Oriental theosophy in Chicago. I love the sound of it."

She saw Steven eyeing her narrowly. He grinned and said, "It sounds like Greek to me."

Arlene wrinkled her nose at him and without a trace of

false modesty stepped into the first of several petticoats thrown across the back of the little rocker. She finished dressing in silence. After a final deft poke at her hair she moved to the door, listened, then opened it a crack to peer out. Before Steven could say a word, she had slipped into the hall and closed the door behind her.

8 A FOUR-HOUR RIDE brought Steven Lewis to Anaheim, a communal German settlement. It had been founded by a group of emigrants from San Francisco, under the leadership of George Hansen, who had become discontented with the life there. It was the most successful new community in southern California.

Over a thousand acres were divided into a forty-acre townsite and twenty-acre plots. The cooperative Los Angeles Vineyard Company was the heart of the colony. The neat homes were entirely surrounded by a dense living willow thicket. It was as effective a barrier as John Sutter's adobe battlements.

Steven stopped at one of the four gates and asked permission to ride through. Hoping to find a bed for the night, he attempted to visit with several of the families preoccupied with pruning. Identifying himself as a San Franciscan warmed them but little. He inquired about the nearest stopping place and was told that travelers usually could find a bed at the Garcia y Perez Rancho de Los Nidos fifteen miles to the southeast. The vinculturist at the winery warned him that in any event it would be easier to find food for himself than from his mount.

Saddle-weary and aching to the marrow, Steven pressed on along the base of the eroded, tinder-dry foothills of the Santa Ana Mountains. By dusk he was within a mile of a large hilltop, tile-roofed adobe surrounded by lacy pepper trees.

He crossed the yard-wide trickle of the sluggish Rio Claro. He had been told that the usually dependable river disappeared into the sand now several miles before its waters reached a confluence with the larger Rio Santa Ana.

All along the way, he passed heaps of bleached bones, unending evidence of the disaster that had overtaken the once great herds. The third year of the drought had extinguished the *rancheros'* hope that they could replenish their herds and find a new market in the north.

Steven knew well the futility of that hope. The northern California market no longer held much promise for the local ranchers and it simply had ceased to exist for those in the south.

Steven passed several mounds of smoldering carcasses from which hides had been stripped. The *vaqueros* had had to cremate the dead and dying animals in an effort to discourage the plague of flies, the scavenger birds, and the hordes of nocturnal carnivores.

Following a worn bridle path, he came to twin ranks of scrubby native junipers flanking the graveled driveway. At the top of the hill a leathery old *vaquero* stepped from the doorway of an outbuilding. Steven waved, reined up, and called to him. *"Buenas tardes. Dígame por favor. El patrón? Está en casa?"*

"Si, señor." The man pointed to the house and indicated that Steven should ride on.

Several minutes later, he dismounted. The house was impressive. Except for Mariano Vallejo's Casa Grande, it was the largest and most carefully made he had ever seen. It was one-story, planned in the classic U-form with the wings enclosing the sides of a patio. The thick walls were clean white and well-plastered. Hewn rafters protruded from beneath a red tile roof. The wooden window casements, two feet deep, shone with the gleam of hot tallowed oak and the door, placed in the center of a tree-shaded main facade, was much larger than most, at least six and a half feet high and four feet wide. Steven saw that it was beautifully constructed and divided into twelve carved panels, each representing some heraldic symbol that he assumed pertained to the Garcia y Perez families. The hinges and ring bolt were forged of hammered black iron.

While he was tying the halter lead to a ring post, a slender, fine-looking man in his late forties appeared in the doorway and addressed him in excellent English. "Good evening, my friend." He approached, smiling, and extended a hand. "You are a welcome visitor. I am Emilio Garcia y Perez." With his left hand he swept the horizon. "The owner of this *carniceria* that once was El Rancho de los Nidos. But whatever we have we are happy to share with you."

267

Steven found the proffered hand hard and good to the feel. "Thank you, sir. My name is Steven Lewis. I am from San Francisco."

Don Emilio's eyebrows lifted. "From San Francisco? Why would one leave that blessed land for this desert?" He laughed apologetically. "I do not intend *impertinencia*, my friend. It is only that in these times we are seldom visited except by worried money-lenders and neighbors who need to share their own troubles."

Steven smiled sympathetically. *"De nada, señor!* The whole south has my sympathy. But I assure you, I am not a worried money-lender."

As he spoke, Steven was aware of Arlene Baker's folded banknotes in his pocket. A money-lender, no. But perhaps in the end something worse, a man who would steal land that the unfortunate owner could not hope to recover.

"Pedro will care for your horse, Señor Lewis. Come in. Meet my family. Share our poor table. And we shall find you a bed. Should you bring us any news at all, we shall be in your debt."

Doña Paula Garcia y Perez was a slender, elegant woman not much younger than her husband. The only child in evidence was their fifteen-year-old daughter, Anita, a shy, extremely attractive girl who was built along her parent's finely drawn lines.

Steven wondered if there were other, older offspring, but the couple volunteered nothing beyond the name of the majordomo, Pedro Morales, whose wife, Gracia, headed a modest staff of household servants.

During the exchanges he managed a casual examination of the house. Its interior appeared to be as impressively built as the exterior. Inside the rafters had been squared and the ceiling carefully plastered between them. The effect was a finished interior, unusual in California ranch houses. A long, rectangular, tile-floored room was divided in two; the area to the right was a study filled with expensively bound volumes. A highly polished oak table dominated the center of the room.

The twin room in which they were standing was elaborately furnished with fine tables, sofas, and chairs that had come around the Horn from Spain. At the end of the room was a huge stone fireplace ornamented with inset Talavera tile. Logs were in place on heavy andirons and a small caldron hung from its hook at the end of a soot-blackened bracket.

Steven could see into the *comedor* with its long dining table, chairs, and side board. And on beyond in the *despensa* that adjoined the *cocina* he could hear the animated chatter of the women at work preparing food.

The evening meal was a simple dish known locally as *carne en camisa*. It consisted of inch-thick strips of lean barbecued beef wrapped in large corn tortillas and generously garnished with a fiery concoction of peppers and tomato that sent Steven repeatedly to his wine glass.

After the meal they retired to the far end of the room, where Pedro and an Indian helper had set a log fire. Purposely, Steven kept his chair well back in a futile attempt to combat a numbing drowsiness.

When he told them that he had Spanish blood and that his mother was of the Robles family, the last of Don Emilio's reserve melted. For more than an hour the ranchero described in detail the plight of the drought-plagued south. His realistic grasp of events and their inevitable consequences surprised Steven.

"We are finished, my friend. We *californios* had our time in the first half of this century. Fifty years in *paradiso*. That is what God gave us. But as it was in Eden, we abused His trust." The *patrón* of El Rancho de los Nidos extended his hands in eloquent resignation. "So now we dance at the Devil's fandango and feast on brimstone and bones."

His dark eyes challenged Steven. "Do you know how it will end? The great *ranchos* will be shattered like *ladrillos* in a *temblor de tierra*. The *yanquis* will pick up the pieces to make *ranchitos*. The traders who own the south, men with money, will bring water to the land and plant it with orchards, grain, and vineyards. They will take over. That will be the end and, *quien sabe*, perhaps a beginning too, but not for us."

Doña Paula and Anita excused themselves and the two men continued to talk over brandy. Steven had provided news of San Francisco and the beginnings of the railroad. His news from Los Angeles was meager. He could only confirm something Don Emilio knew: the migration of Southern farmers ruined by the Civil War had already begun to arrive in San Bernardino. They were coming in droves with their wagons and their meager belongings, searching for cheap, fertile land. Nomads, living out of boxes and buckets, foraging for food, seeking work that did not exist. Both Steven and Don Emilio understood that out of the poor, polyglot mass would come whatever future southern California would have. Such a migration had been the strength of the north. But there was a vital difference and the *ranchero* stated it clearly:

"The miners who came to California were young and strong and single and free and filled with hope. These new émigrés in the south are not the same. They are defeated men. Even a drowning man has hope as long as he struggles. But hope without confidence makes nothing. So, we shall wait and see what these people make of our land."

Although he longed to collapse on a bed, Steven forced himself to stay alert. Don Emilio had provided the opening he needed to broach the matter of land acquisition. "The purpose of my visit is to buy some good land. For cash."

Don Emilio's face did not betray the sudden flicker of hope. "That should not be difficult now."

Steven smiled sympathetically. "Perhaps not. But I am looking for special land. Land with a guaranteed year-round supply of irrigation water."

Don Emilio's head rested against the chair back and he traced the contour of his lower lip thoughtfully with a forefinger. "That is more difficult."

"I am told it may even be impossible. But I felt I should ride out and see for myself."

"It is not necessarily impossible, Señor Lewis. We have land below the mouth of our canyon that receives water regularly, even in dry years. This year is unprecedented. But there is still some sub-surface water."

"Would you yourself sell such land?"

Don Emilio considered briefly. "Perhaps—"

"How many acres would be available?"

The question seemed to trouble the *ranchero*. "That would depend upon what a buyer planned to do with them."

Steven was evasive. "For the time being I have in mind an investment in fertile land that will support agricultural crops. I do not know just what crops yet. I do not want range land. I have little interest in cattle."

"And you have no market for agricultural crops, Señor

Lewis. You may have to wait until you are as old as I am to see such a market develop here in the south."

"I am in no hurry, Don Emilio. I wish to buy land at the lowest possible price and hold it. If enough of the right land was available, I would even be glad to buy it and let the original owner continue to use it, perhaps for just the taxes."

Don Emilio could no longer conceal his interest. His eyes narrowed thoughtfully. Steven decided to press a bit more. "Of course I would wish some assurance that the water would not be diverted, perhaps by a new owner of the headwaters."

"That will never happen as long as I live to control this rancho, Señor Lewis. The water and awareness of its value are my only real assests."

Suddenly less hopeful, Steven realized that he had been naïve to entertain even a small notion that any *ranchero* would part with the life source of his holdings, regardless of the pressures imposed by drought and economic set-backs. Those who were managing to survive were those who still had some water. But there might be some way. Billy Ralston had said often enough that there always was, for the man who wanted something badly.

"Perhaps tomorrow I could ride over the land you have in mind, Don Emilio."

"Indeed. If you wish we can ride to the source of the river and follow it down so you can reassure yourself."

"I would like that. Would there be as many as two thousand acres available, along the lower river?"

"It is possible. Yes."

In spite of himself, Steven yawned and Don Emilio smiled sympathetically. *"Ahora, dormimos, amigo!"* He rose and indicated the doorway. "I will show you to your room. Tomorrow we will leave early and we will have the day for questions."

That night Steven slept in a dreamless, timeless void. The barking of dogs awakened him shortly after sunrise. When he had washed and dressed, Don Emilio knocked on the door and escorted him to a breakfast of coffee, beans, and tortillas.

Young Anita, petulant with disappointment, watched her father and their guest mount and, followed by Pedro and several dogs, begin the ride into the wild *Cañada Laberinta* in whose upper reaches rose the Rio Claro.

271

For a mile or so the trail was well defined. They left it from time to time when Steven expressed curiosity about some of the side canyons that showed evidence of flash floods in the past. El Rancho de los Nidos suffered no less than the others from the uncontrolled run-off that continually changed the semi-barren canyons.

As they picked their way up the boulder-strewn Rio Claro the water became abundant. Two miles from the ranch the canyon widened abruptly and they came to the first of the *nidos,* the nest-like meadows that characterized the rancho. *Nido Mejor,* the largest, measured nearly forty acres. Despite the third year of drought, it was a beautiful spot, a miniature sheer-walled valley whose once lush grasses had been grazed to bare earth by wild cattle and deer.

The dogs, frustrated by a plethora of scents, went yelping off in every direction, then converged on a tangle of brush. Steven and Don Emilio rode over. There they found the half-eaten carcass of a doe. Pedro glanced at the carnage and grunted. "Pumas!"

One of the dogs began nosing the bluish blob of fly-covered entrails and Pedro sent it howling with a blow from a rawhide quirt. Don Emilio shook his head. "The big cats do not feed on dead cattle, but they are so bold now they come within a few yards of the main house to kill the dying." He turned to Steven with a sad smile and indicated the carcass. "Perhaps there is a lesson here that we *californios* should remember. No?"

As he relaxed in the shade, admiring the beauty around him, Steven recalled Arlene Baker's prediction that he would be led to Brindavanam. During the morning he had scarcely given her a conscious thought. But now, as her words echoed almost audibly, he was aware of a growing eagerness to be with her again.

Don Emilio had said there were many things to be seen within the eight square leagues of the rancho. Moreover, the Rio Claro's headwaters appeared to fit perfectly into a subdivision plan that had begun to assume real substance when he had visited the Anaheim colony the previous afternoon. There he had seen dramatic proof of the value of careful planning and the miracle of water at work in this arid land.

It was well past midday when they returned to the big

adobe by way of a series of lesser *cañadas* where Don Emilio had shown him other, smaller *nidos*, several of which were watered by dependable springs during normal years.

After the noon meal, Steven asked if he might ride over the lower ranges. Don Emilio, eager to prolong his visitor's stay, readily agreed after extracting a promise that his guest would not leave until the following morning.

A whispered family conference ended in a delighted squeal when Anita was permitted to join them. Instead of the circumspect side-saddle, and the full skirts usually worn by female riders, she appeared in full-cut brown woolen *pantalones* and beautifully handcrafted boots. Before Steven could assist, she was mounted astride a small, spirited gelding.

A wind, unseasonably warm, was blowing down from the mountains. Off to the south, beyond the low hills that concealed the ocean, Pedro called their attention to a formation of cirro-stratus clouds.

Don Emilio dismissed them. "How many times can a man's heart leap with hope?" But Pedro insisted the dry Santa Ana wind was the sign of a major weather change.

A half mile beyond the point where the Rio Claro disappeared beneath its bed, Steven dismounted and dug. Less than a foot down, moisture began to seep into the hole. The *ranchero* nodded. "It is there. The coyote dig for it. But there is not enough water for cattle. We have dug waterholes for two years now. But it is useless. The animals trample it full of sand again in five minutes. So we no longer try."

Steven frowned. "Couldn't you put a dam across here to hold back water when the stream runs?"

"Yes. It would be possible. But not for us. We do not have the tools or labor or the skill to build the stone dam required to hold against flash floods. And who is to say that the water might not make a new course? Look." He indicated the meandering streambed and the evidence of older watercourses that had scarred hundreds of acres of good land on either side. "These rivers are like temperamental women. With every storm they change their minds."

Steven laughed with Anita as Don Emilio turned his horse. "Come. Let us go back now. We have seen it all. One pile of bones looks much like another."

By five o'clock, darkness was closing in and Steven was relieved to be out of the saddle. Bootless, he stretched out on the laced rawhide bed and wished that he had brought another change of clothing.

Early the following morning, remounted and provisioned by Doña Paula and Gracia, he repeated the instructions given by Don Emilio. After sincerely meant expressions of gratitude, he reined his mount down the steep, tree-bordered lane.

El Monte, where he spent that night as a paid guest in a settler's home, disappointed him. The location was beautiful but it lacked the planning and order of the Anaheim colony. But even in the third year of the drought it was an oasis filled with promise. Several small orchards had been set out and there was evidence that the trees were being regularly irrigated from the main *zanja* that led down from the mountains. Here again he found confirmation of a pattern for the future.

Steven arrived at the plaza in Los Angeles shortly after noon the next day. He resisted an urge to ask the hotel desk clerk if the Lathrops were in and went directly to his room. There, filled with impatience, he stripped off his dusty clothing and managed an effective but unsatisfactory cat bath from the large porcelain basin. Clean and changed, he went to the bar and ordered food to be served at a corner table.

Arlene Baker's five one-thousand-dollar banknotes were still safely tucked in his pocket. No commitments had been made. But he was certain now that El Rancho de los Nidos offered the brightest promise despite its remoteness. Arlene had said that the right place would attract her followers regardless of its location. He wondered if the same principle, if that's what it was, would apply to the settlement that was beginning to assume detailed form in his mind.

While he was waiting, Steven tried to anticipate the questions Pioche would ask. Even if he could assure Pioche that they could effectively control the source of the water, transportation was a vital need before a country could really boom. The southland seemed years away from that. He would have to convince Pioche that immigrants could be diverted to the south by the lure of an easy living from some of the cheapest, most fertile land on the continent.

Steven tried unsuccessfully to keep his thoughts from straying to Arlene, to the part she might now be playing in his determination to produce answers that Pioche could accept. He both welcomed and resented her intrusion.

His introspection was interrupted by the flat, abrasive voice of Jabez Lathrop calling from the doorway. "There you are, Lewis. They told us at the stable that you'd come back sooner than you expected." As he crossed to the corner table, Lathrop glanced distastefully at the card players and the men drinking at the bar. "My daughter and I would like to talk to you. I wonder if you'd care to join us in a more genteel atmosphere in the dining room?"

Concealing his eagerness, Steven managed a token show of reluctance and agreed. The first course was being served when they joined the two women. Mrs. Lathrop favored Steven with her usual bleak smile but Arlene was flushed and effusive.

"Oh, Mr. Lewis. How fortunate for father that you were here. He wants so badly to ask your advice about some lots the real estate person showed us this morning."

The broker was a young man named Warden whose office consisted of one dingy room and a sidewalk bulletin board.

Nonetheless he had impressed Lathrop. "Mr. Warden seems like an honest Christian."

Steven smiled blandly. "If the real estate profession is beginning to attract *good* Christians, perhaps there's some hope for the country after all." The mild sarcasm was lost on Lathrop.

"When I get my ministry started, Lewis, I intend to see to it that all so-called Christians within the sound of my voice become good Christians. Mr. Warden is unaffiliated, it seems. He has already promised to be one of my deacons. He assures me he will concentrate his company's sales effort in the area to help me build our congregation."

Steven made a mental note to look up Warden. Obviously he was bringing to his profession some unusual imagination. Arlene leaned forward. "Mr. Warden was kind enough to interest himself in me, too, Mr. Lewis. He said that he lives with his sister and they would be happy to put themselves out to see that I am introduced into the proper young circles in Los Angeles."

Steven suffered a pang of anxiety mixed with jealousy. "I shouldn't think that would take much putting out."

Arlene glowed with appreciation.

Lathrop flopped his napkin, "Let's get on with this real-estate proposition. I'm imposing on Mr. Lewis as it is."

"It is no imposition, sir. Where is the property?"

"It's south, about a mile out of town where Main Street and Spring Street come together."

Steven shrugged. "I don't really know, but the other evening I heard one of the natives betting that Los Angeles would grow toward the south. He said in the beginning towns usually did."

"The price seems right and the places across the road are all about to get city water. Warden is offering me eight quarter-acre city lots at a hundred dollars an acre. He says I can hold it for a couple of years and sell off half of it for more than I paid for the whole shebang."

Steven nodded. "That's been happening in San Francisco too. But there's a lot more going on up there."

Lathrop laid his fork aside. "Warden says he'll guarantee title at the courthouse. As to taxes, I don't really care."

Steven spread his hands expansively. "Good, I envy you. Sounds like southern California has a useful new citizen, sir. My mother's people would say: 'Viva aqui en buen salud.' Live here in good health."

For the first time during the discussion, Mrs. Lathrop spoke. "I didn't know you were Spanish, Mr. Lewis."

"I'm not. I'm half Mexican."

The woman attempted to conceal her stricken expression.

Arlene relieved the awkward silence. "Live here in good health. What a civilized benediction. Thank you, Steven."

Jabez Lathrop pushed back his chair. "Lewis, I have a feeling that if anything had been seriously wrong, as I've related it to you, the Lord would have moved you to speak out."

Steven stirred uncomfortably. "Sir, I'd feel a lot better if you took my silence for ignorance of the subject."

Arlene placed her napkin in its ring. "Nonsense, Steven. I want to hear about your land. Would you like to walk in the plaza and tell me about it?"

Several minutes later they were strolling in the warmth of the winter sun. Taking his arm, Arlene said, "I'm dying

276

to know whether you found anything approaching my Brindavanam."

Steven described his journey and the effects of the drought. Deliberately, he emphasized the negative aspects of the search, devoting only a brief comment to the Anaheim and El Monte colonies, avoiding entirely any mention of the vital part ample water was playing in their success. "There was only one place that looked promising, Arlene. But it's at least forty miles southeast of here, in the Santa Ana Valley."

"Forty miles? Is there nothing closer? Surely you can do better than that."

It was less rebuke than disappointment but it annoyed him. "Why not ask Warden? He's your official real-estate agent. He'll probably be able to do better. I'm just an amateur looking for land for myself."

Arlene Baker lowered her head. "I deserved that, Steven. I'm selfish and impatient. Please forgive me? And Mr. Warden is not my real-estate agent. He's just an eager young man who will promise anything to make his sale."

She studied him intently for a time. "Steven, I do believe you're jealous. Are you?"

His lips compressed stubbornly then twisted into a sheepish grin. "A touch, maybe."

Arlene looked around quickly and leaned close to brush her lips against her ear. "Darling Steven. Do you know what you've done to me, here?" She indicated her heart. "You have so unsettled me that I haven't slept a wink since you left. I've created the most wondrous fantasies about us." Arlene was tempted to tell him and watch his face as she described them. She had lain naked on her bed in the warm, dry night and with her hands had brought her nipples to hard little points and then aroused all of the senses in her body until she had been forced to cry out his name. Instead, she leaned away and regarded him gravely. "Do you know something else, dearest, darling? The only peace I've ever known was in your arms and I would rather die than never to be there again."

His annoyance faded as quickly as it had flared. He was seized by an overwhelming urge to be alone with her again, to shed the last of his reserve. But he remained frustrated and inarticulate. He could feel her, waiting, almost able to hear his unspoken words, but they were the wrong words and he could not bring himself to say them.

"Steven, if you can, please tell me one thing. Do you feel perhaps even a little of the same thing I feel?"

He nodded. "I do."

He heard her whisper something to herself. A moment later she drew in a deep breath and sat up straight. "One place looked promising. I said you would be led to the right place, Steven. If I suggest that it is the wrong place simply because it is not close by I shall be denying everything I profess. Tell me about it. Please."

Steven described El Rancho de los Nidos and spoke warmly of Don Emilio, Doña Paula, and their young daughter, Anita. He described *Nido Mejor*. But again he did not emphasize the water beyond saying it was adequate for limited use even after three years of drought. He said nothing about Don Emilio's reluctance to sell and omitted any mention of the Rio Claro. The ambivalent nature of his feelings distressed him. He wanted to be open with Arlene, to confide in her the tremendous possibilities he saw in the land. But when his own enthusiasm brought him to the verge of superlatives he restrained himself and did not know why.

"The *cañada* may be too wild and remote for you. The whole little valley might become a trap. And you may have trouble getting your followers to travel that far."

Arlene refused to acknowledge obstacles. "Oh no, darling. If it's the *right* place I shall know in an instant. They'll follow me. Why don't we go there together and look? We can hire a surrey and leave in the morning."

"It's not possible, Arlene. There are no proper places to stay between here and there. It's a two-day drive."

"Surely, if we say that I am your fiancée something decorous could be managed. I'm a farm girl, remember, darling? I can make do with very little, really."

"It won't work. We would have to drive it in one long day and Don Emilio would have to know we are coming. There may be more rooms but I saw only three bedchambers."

"I could share a room with the child. Gracious, Steven, I shared with three others at college in Chicago."

Steven remained adamant. "There's no guarantee that he will sell any land."

Arlene's eyes widened. "You didn't even discuss the possibility?"

"Not openly. Not the first time. The best way to run the

fact that President Washington and General Lafayette, and Benjamin Franklin too, were all happily married men. But history is replete with their peccadillos. Come with me on the Champagne Route, my young bridegroom, and I shall show you a dozen restaurants and saloons filled with happily married men and those *other* female companions with whom they are more often happy. And I presume that you would not be overly shocked to find your father among them from time to time."

Anger flushed Steven's face but Pioche dismissed the matter with a wave and continued. "*Ce n'fait rien*. What is done is done; what is not done concerns me much more."

He indicated some sheets of paper on the marble coffee table. Steven recognized them as his own written prospectus and the estimates of how the work would progress.

"Shall I be concerned now, my young friend, that you will be so preoccupied with your marital obligations that you will lack the time and perhaps the energy to implement these?" He tapped the papers with the back of his perfectly manicured nails.

Still smarting at the allusion to his father's occasional but well-known infidelities, Steven determined to stand firm. "I say that everything will be done as promised and barring acts of God—"

Pioche interrupted, smiling. "Such as children?"

Steven controlled himself and continued. "—barring acts of God, everything will be done on time despite the fact that funds were two weeks late arriving in Los Angeles."

Pioche was amused and Steven detected a trace of admiration in his shrewd little eyes. "*Bien. Bien*. Go ahead. I admire a man who makes his points."

"Don Emilio is hiring men. A good blacksmith shop is being built and I have ordered steel strap for scraper boxes, new harness, picks and shovels, crow bars and heavy tools." He pointed to the papers. "Everything in there is either on the job or on order. And I have a line on a good engineer. He is one of the men who planned the water system for El Monte."

Pioche spread his hands. "*C'est ça!* I am reassured. Now then, as my junior partner I am going to assign you a duty. Tomorrow night I am having a modest soirée in honor of Signor Guido Morelli of the Carlo Rosa Opera Company whom I hope to entice to San Francisco this coming year, There will be a cosmopolitan group of guests. I want you to meet some of them. I have in mind your education in cultural matters and even more practical considerations. If our sphere of influence in the south is to grow in all civilized respects, you should be making contacts in the arts." He paused with a questioning look. "One hopes that the new Madame Lewis has interest in this direction too?"

Steven realized that he didn't know the answer. "I think her chief interest lies in religion."

Pioche closed his eyes and touched his fingertips to his temple. "If this is true, my dear boy, I promise you that many a night you shall know cold feet!"

Steven managed a smile. "So far she seems to have a very warm heart." The attempt to relieve the tenseness with humor failed to move Pioche. "Remember, tomorrow night. Seven o'clock. Did you bring formal clothing?"

"No. But unless my brother has a formal engagement I'll manage to be presentable."

Pioche nodded slightly and rang for the butler. When the imperturbable German appeared, he rose and indicated the hall. "Louis, will you please show our young bridegroom out."

Steven could give only a day to visiting his family. The steamer *Goliath* sailed on the midday tide and he expected to board it without sleep after the Pioche soirée.

He found his mother suspended between delight and desolation. Doña Maria's tears of joy at seeing her son were mixed with those of anguish over news of his marriage. She seemed unable to comprehend the need for a ceremony that did not include the family. Nothing Steven could say seemed to assuage her hurt.

His brother-in-law, Lambert Lee, had been blunt. "The family considers this marriage a disaster!" His long arm had swept the city. "There are a dozen young ladies from splendid and affluent families here in San Francisco who have set their caps for you. And one of them would have been a brilliant match and useful to your career. But a preacher's widowed daughter nearly four years older than yourself? Great God!"

Steven stunned Lambert by telling him to "go fuck himself."

Reluctant to attend though he had been, Steven was

caught up in the unconventional gaiety of the Frenchman's party. Many of the guests were members of the Parisian *Tableaux Vivants* troupe currently at the California Theater. In white make-up, some of the women entirely nude, the artistes simulated masterpieces of Greek and Roman sculpture. Ignoring the Eastern taboo against movements on stage, the members changed poses in full view of the audience. Steven had seen the performance several times. One of the girls had appealed to him. He met her now and was disappointed. Offstage she seemed much older and the seductiveness that projected across the footlights had vanished.

Several of the men in the troupe were professional acrobats and two of the younger ones appeared to be Pioche's favorites. He insisted that the guests admire their well-developed physiques as they obediently struck a number of poses.

At four o'clock the serving staff was still icing and uncorking champagne. Steven sought out Pioche and, pleading extreme weariness, thanked him and said his goodnights. The little Frenchman, mellowed by wine, feigned desolation.

"*Alors. Je suis inconsolable, mon cher ami. Mais, c'est la vie.* The best part of my soirée begins now. And later we all go to breakfast at Le Coq Rouge." One of the financier's sycophants laughed. Pioche frowned and raised a finger to his lips. Then he pointed to Steven. "It is demanding work, this new career as a husband. *Bon nuit, mon ami. Dormez bien et bon voyage.*"

Arlene greeted Steven passionately when he arrived and promptly announced she had a surprise for him. The surprise was the house that Tom Warden had found. Warden's attempt at humor was less than convincing. "I've got to admit, Steven, that I hadn't expected to hunt out a house for Arlene and somebody else." He grinned. "But that's life in the Far West. I hope you like it."

They climbed down from the surrey and entered a small brick cubicle with a mansard roof. Warden's gesture encompassed the fenced-in dust-dry yard, two scraggly saplings struggling to survive, the woodshed and the outhouse.

"It is not Mr. Temple's Los Cerritos, but it does have an attic, if Steve doesn't mind stooping a bit."

Arlene slipped an arm around Steven. "I saw it the other day, darling. Tom took me to a half dozen houses. But I think this is the best one for us, for now."

Inside Steven found a parlor, a small dining room, a kitchen with a narrow attic staircase and one bedroom. It was hardly enough space for an expanding family. Arlene read his disappointment.

"Darling, for the time being this is all we need. The attic is quite adequate. It is warm and snug and I can fix it up very nicely as the extra bedroom."

Warden regarded Arlene with mock concern. "Remember, Mrs. Lewis. You've married a native son. These Californians have a tradition of large families."

Arlene smiled archly. "I know. Steven and I have agreed that we'll limit our family to twelve children."

Charlotte Lathrop Lewis was born in the Hill Street house shortly after midnight, October 11, 1866. The birth was not difficult even though the infant exceeded eight pounds.

Steven had arrived home from El Rancho de los Nidos in time for the birth. He had been working harder at Los Nidos than ever before in his life.

The days at home were trying. For practical reasons Arlene and the child were bedded in the single sleeping room and he had taken the makeshift attic. As much as he delighted in his first-born, Steven wanted to get back to the rancho that had become his second home. He felt responsible for overseeing the more than one hundred Mexicans and Indians who were laboring on the ditches and flumes to bring water to the new reservoir. Arlene, aware of his unrest, urged his early return. Apologetically, after ten days, he did.

From *La Cueva de Los Lobos*, the cave to which Goyo Robles and his followers retired after each successful plundering expedition, the *bandido* and his men watched the work proceeding far below.

"Don Emilio tries to outwit nature. That is good. But I wonder where he gets the money?"

The lieutenant, a pockmarked Sonoran called Bruto, patted the stock of his carbine. "From the gringos. There are two there now, both *jefes*. We Mexicans work. They boss." He spat. "And we are the ones who taught them how to transport water at the mines."

Goyo smiled tolerantly. "Perhaps they are Don Emilio's engineers. There are no *americanos* here. We'll wait. We have time. If the *zanja* is for the gringos, the more work, the greater the loss."

As he continued to study the figures below, a plan began to evolve. "Bruto."

"Yes?"

"Cinco and Tito tell me they pay one dollar fifty, American, each day for work on the *zanja*. Perhaps one of them should work for a week and listen."

The lieutenant scowled. "I know a faster way to get their money."

Goyo laughed. "Those are Sonorans working. If we take their money on payday we take from our brothers."

A crude oath escaped from Bruto's lips. "If they work for gringos they are not *my* brothers."

Goyo nodded. "Let us be certain first. Tell Cinco to come here."

By the twentieth of December the main ditch had been pioneered to the mouth of *La Cañada Laberinta*. In several places it had become necessary to use black powder to remove boulders. Because of the scarcity of lumber, Steven was trying to hold the use of flume to a minimum.

After Christmas at home, Steven returned to his work on the aqueduct. Don Emilio and Doña Paula, enthusiastically supported by sixteen-year-old Anita, urged him to bring Arlene and the baby back with him.

"They will be much more comfortable here in this big house, Steven. They are as welcome as family."

Don Emilio agreed and offered a most convincing argument. "It will not be an imposition, as you suggest. It will be a great pleasure for all of us. But most important, my friend, Doña Arlene should be here when we begin your house. She must be here to help us bless the lintel. Pedro has already cut it from oak."

Despite Arlene's concern that they would have little or no privacy as guests, she found the arrangement agreeable. Her resilient body had returned to normal, and physical contact with Steven was resumed with undiminished passion. Although the idea repelled Arlene at first, she

303

came to enjoy the peace of mind that resulted from the moistened square of finely scraped lamb's intestine that Steven insisted they use to guard against a second pregnancy before he could provide a suitable home. Also, it seemed to intensify the sensation for her.

"But darling," she made a distasteful face, "we must find another name for it. I refuse to think of it as a 'gut bucket.' "

Privately, Steven agreed. At fourteen, he had first seen the sporting-house girls hanging their newly washed diaphanous membranes on roof lines and the explicit answer to his question both repelled and fascinated him.

The weather favored Steven's work. When word spread that the new *zanja* at El Rancho de los Nidos needed more workers at one dollar and fifty cents a day and found, men began drifting down from as far north as drought-parched Santa Barbara. By June two hundred Sonorans and Indians were at work building the stone sub-surface dam and the twenty-five-foot earthen embankment on top. It would be the first of three such dams that would, it was hoped, keep the river from rampaging over the lowlands during the flood season.

Several times during the summer, parties of horsemen stopped nearby to watch the work. Each time, after brief consultations, they rode off without attempting to identify themselves.

Quite by chance, on a visit to San Pedro Bay, Steven discovered that the anonymous visitors were ranchers from the Santa Ana River. He ran into Senator Phineas Banning, the dynamic pioneer developer. Banning was responsible for the huge Wilmington pier and there was a rumor that the road Banning's men were grading from his Wilmington slough to the south end of Main Street awaited only city and county approval of a two-hundred-and-twenty-five-thousand-dollar bond issue. It would then become the first railroad in southern California. Steven believed the rumor. Nobody had taken Banning seriously when he said that mankind would have to create what nature neglected. Now the Wilmington Harbor at San Pedro was a fact.

Banning told Steven that the ranchers at the lower end of the Santa Ana River, Steven's unidentified visitors, were afraid that Steven's project might cut into their water supply. Steven went out of his way to reassure Banning that this was not so. Banning also said that while the water situation in Los Angeles was bad, farmers in the San Gabriel valley had hit artesian flows at sixty feet. Both the Danes and the British were looking for farmland for their settlers who were finding it easy to borrow in order to buy. This meant abundant new farm settlers and cash customers for Steven's parceled land.

There was no question about it. A feeling was in the wind. A good feeling.

By October most of the exterior work on their home in *Nido Mejor* had been completed. It was the first of the redwood and native stone structures designed for Arlene Lewis' cherished Brindavanam. Arlene became defensive when Steven cautioned her about expounding her unorthodox beliefs in the presence of the Garcia y Perez family. Don Emilio, at great trouble, had sent for the Catholic father at San Juan Capistrano to bless the lintel. In a heated scene, their first, Steven got her promise to endure "that barbarous ritual" on the reciprocal understanding that he would join her in their own private dedication. He wondered why she suddenly had become so intolerant. The religious ceremony was a small concession in view of the lavish hospitality they had enjoyed for months at the rancho.

Her fanaticism, gone briefly after the birth of Charlotte, had returned and increased in intensity. The compulsive drive was back. On the slightest pretext Arlene would turn the conversation back to Brindavanam and her plans to attract a congregation. Steven tried to forewarn her that Southern "hard shell" Baptists might resist, but she dismissed the possibility.

Arlene's financial independence added to Steven's uneasiness. Her funds had built their home; her funds had paid for the plans depicting an architectural potpourri of Egyptian and Oriental structures. She would also pay for the materials, many of them exotic even for a cosmopolitan community. In subtle ways she used her independence as a goad.

Arlene suggested that Steven appoint Tom Warden exclusive Los Angeles sales agent for the forty-acre tracts. Steven did so with some reluctance and found Warden surprised and obviously pleased. The sales would begin from surveyors' plats immediately after the new year.

Arlene hugged him when he told her about Warden's acceptance. "Oh, darling, I'm so glad. I had no idea that Tom would be interested, really. But it's one less responsibility for you. That's my only concern. I didn't mean to butt into your business, dearest one, but I've been so worried that you are overdoing. And I couldn't bear to see you go on. Forgive?"

Moments later, in her arms, he forgave her.

Another irrigation project was started on the Rancho San Pasqual, ten miles northeast of Los Angeles, by the rancho's new owners, Benjamin Wilson and Dr. John S. Griffin. "Wilson Ditch," as it was being called, was an impressive feat. It represented new competition for *Los Nidos* and the defeat of Don Emilio's old friend, Manuel Garfias, who had lost the rancho. Don Emilio looked at the construction of the ditch and sighed. "God forbid, but what you see here is the story of our ranchos, *Esteban!* We will see it repeated many times. The land belonged to Manuel by right of inheritance but taxes and loans forced him to sell. He sold it all to Wilson for one thousand eight hundred dollars."

Steven whistled softly. "My God, that's thievery!"

Don Emilio shrugged. "Some would call it charity. A drowning man does not inquire into the motives of his rescuer."

Sad as it was for the *ranchero*, the trip to the project was useful, for it confirmed the soundness of their own project. While Steven conceded that the Wilson-Griffin development offered the attraction of proximity to Los Angeles, he felt that El Rancho los Nidos, by offering greater arable acreage and in normal seasons more dependable water, would be able to offset the competitor's advantage.

The main ditch at Los Nidos was completed in February of 1868. It was christened *Zanja Paula* in honor of Don Emilio's wife. The central reservoir, also completed, was named Lake Arlene. From it would radiate sub-canals designed to carry water to the various parcels of land. Arlene, who was pleased, did not resist the dedication ceremony.

A week after the dedication, during a three-day rainstorm, Steven and the engineer, Monteith, opened the head gates in *El Nido Mejor* and diverted the flow into the long ditch. They followed the course of the controlled floods as fast as horses could travel the rough service trail. In less than an hour, first water from Rio Claro flowed into Lake Arlene.

Steven had deliberately chosen the rainstorm as the best time to divert water. The anxious downstream ranchers who had watched the work would see no appreciable change in the level of the flooded Santa Ana River below its confluence with the smaller Rio Claro.

In a week the lake was full and the excess water was released over the dam's cobblestone spillway. Another week found the surface of the big reservoir black with waterfowl—the tag end of the winter migration. Don Emilio, looking at the newly shot mallards and the brace of Canadian geese hanging from the side porch, was moved to silent thanks for the events that had brought this new bounty so close to home.

Steven had managed to postpone a meeting with Pioche on the plea that he wanted to wait until he was certain that the basic engineering was completed and sound and he had worked up a carefully audited set of books. The ledgers would show the banker that the work, thus far, had come in substantially below the original estimates and, due to the continuation of the drought, well ahead of schedule. On the basis of Tom Warden's leads, he could safely predict the lease of twenty or more parcels to the new bee farmers on a sharecrop arrangement.

Over a thousand double-supered beehives had been set out the previous October. Assuming a normal spring, the total harvest of fine comb honey would exceed one hundred thousand pounds. The rancho's share was twenty-five percent of the gross profits. It would be a fine report and he was eager to make it.

The trip would also be a chance to introduce Arlene and Charlotte to his family. Steven was sure Arlene's bright charm and little Charlotte's promise of great beauty would overcome any family resistance. To Steven's dismay, Arlene refused to leave until the house was finished and more work was done on the cottages and the temple.

"Dearest Steven, I have subordinated my own wishes to yours because of that ditch and the lake. It was not a sacrifice. It was an act of love. I ask you to repay me in kind by not insisting that I make that dreadful journey now. I promise that we shall make it in the fall. Nothing will be allowed to stand in the way. I do want to meet your family and show off my little lovely one. But I cannot go now, please don't insist."

Steven refused to allow her to stay alone in *Nido Mejor*. She agreed to go back to the main ranch house for the three weeks that he would be away. Disappointed and morose, he left for Los Angeles.

Warden and his sister asked him to dine and stay over with them. The following morning Tom drove him to the Bella Union to catch the stage. "Isobel sensed that you're worried about leaving Arlene and the baby alone."

"They won't be alone. They'll stay with Don Emilio until I get back."

"Would you feel easier if Isobel and I drove down and looked in on them?" When Steven did not answer immediately, Warden slipped a folded paper from his inside pocket. "Actually, I will have to go down there within a week or so anyway. Three deals look certain, but I want the parties to see the land first. I promised them their pick."

Steven thanked him for his thoughtfulness and wished him well with sales. Warden's optimism was unshakable. "Wait until spring, Steve. When the wildflowers are out and the ranges are green again we'll have to arm ourselves to keep from being stampeded by customers."

Aboard the northbound sidewheeler, *Golden City*, Steven concentrated on the report to Pioche. He wanted to tell him that his original investment would be returned within the following year—that the partnership would then begin operating at a profit. But he was leery of "supposings" as Harry Morrison called them. In this case, however, the odds seemed to favor him. Phineas Banning's new road would be a railroad all right. He was promising a spiking ceremony before the end of the coming summer, with free train rides to Wilmington and return and a huge barbecue, "all on the road."

Good transport had always been the magic, and the great magic was yet to come. Word from the Sierra said Charley Crocker's horde of coolies was successfully leveling every obstacle God and man could place in their path. Central Pacific was predicting a link-up with Union Pacific, probably in eastern Utah territory, within a year. Montague, the chief construction engineer, would have chosen an earlier date but the carnage from mishandled nitroglycerine was too much even for tough Charley Crocker. He ordered "the damn stuff buried" and a return to black powder and Oriental persistence. Relieved, Montague revised his date and the mangled bodies were replaced by other Chinese shipped into California, despite popular outcry, under a new treaty negotiated by Ambassador Anson Burlingame. The terms unmistakably favored the railroad.

Steven did worry about the effect of the transcontinental railroad on his father's business. Billy Ralston had suggested that Lewis & Sons hedge its bets by starting a chain of warehouses. His father and Will had built three. But there was little doubt in Steven's mind about the effect of the railroads on the southland.

At 806 Stockton Street, Steven was confronted by valet Louis Reiff. "Mr. Pioche is ill. He asks that you return at the end of the week."

When Steven did get to see the little Frenchman, it was only for a few minutes. Pioche was pale and distracted. He dismissed the proffered report: "It is commendable that you are meticulous, my dear boy. If you say things go well and we shall be even within a year, *c'est ça.* That is quite enough assurance for the present. You are doing your work well. Write me. Later, I shall ask you for a full report when I am less pressed."

Unsettled by Pioche's sudden turnabout, Steven went down to the Bank Exchange bar to meet his father and brother. He knew that Pioche was involved in a great many businesses, all successful. He had also finally arranged an appearance of the famous Carlo Rosa Opera Company in San Francisco in the fall. Whatever the Frenchman's problem, it did not seem to involve those aspects of his unusual life.

Steven was diverted from his preoccupation with Pioche by Will's announcement of his impending marriage to Mary O'Dwyer. The bride-to-be was the daughter of Sean O'Dwyer, who had brought a considerable fortune to San Francisco and had added to it through his successful foundry operations. The vows would be taken before Christmas in the Mission Dolores. Steven promised his twin that he would bring Arlene and the baby to the wedding and that he would be Will's best man.

As eager as he was to return to the south, Steven took advantage of an enforced wait for the old sidewheeler, *Senator,* to visit family and friends and to get caught up on news.

Harry Morrison, who had been north assessing business possibilities for the freight lines, had attended the ceremony transferring Alaska from Russian ownership to the United States. The half million square miles had been officially proclaimed a Territory on the previous October eighteenth. As usual, the Scotsman's cogent observations amused Steven.

"I dinna ken the reason for calling it 'Seward's Folly.' The Secretary of State stole the world's largest curling court for seven million two hundred thousand dollars, which reckons doon to aboot tuppence an acre!"

Neighboring Canada had become a British dominion three months earlier and Steven, along with most Californians, felt easier with Alaska secured. He listened to a great deal of speculation about the refusal of Congress to concur in President Johnson's suspension of Secretary of War Stanton. There was a lot of wagering along the Champagne Route that Johnson would be impeached.

John Lewis joined with Harry Morrison in some anxious speculation about the machinations of the New York speculators, Jay Gould and Jim Fisk, and their domination of major railroad stock. But in the end, they agreed that the Big Four were more than a match for the most ruthless manipulators.

Steven was particularly interested in the impending transformation of the College of California at Berkeley into a state university to be known as the University of California. The move was long overdue in the north and a similar move was needed in the south. John Lewis quoted Governor Low on the subject: "Now, here you have scholarship, system, organization, reputation, everything but money; but we, the state, have none of these things, but we have money. What a pity they cannot be brought together." However, John had one misgiving. "I personally see nothing wrong with the plan, but a lot of good people, your mother included, see danger in allowing young men and women to study side by side in the same classes. It could make for distraction. For instance, when I was

courting your mother I had the devil's own time keeping
my mind on business and it was a matter of life and death
that I should."

Steven found himself impatient to be back in the southland again doing what he could to help it move forward
toward new progressive ideas in whose implementation
San Francisco seemed always to stay ahead.

When the steam lighter came alongside the *Senator* in
San Pedro Bay, Steven heard an urgent voice calling his
name. He located the man and hailed him from the deck.
Minutes later he was handed an envelope.

"The Reverend Lathrop sent this, sir. And I'm instructed to get you to his home by carriage. It's been terrible,
waiting, sir. I've met the last three steamers."

Steven broke the wax seal and ripped open the message.
Numb with apprehension, he read: "Steven: You will
need all of the courage God can give to a mortal to bear
up under the news you are about to receive. Hurry, you
are desperately needed."

Tom Warden and Isobel had journeyed to El Rancho de
los Nidos three days after Steven sailed for San Francisco.
They were welcomed and settled for the night. Arlene Lewis, who had seemed depressed and impatient after Steven's departure, had been driving herself and the workmen
at Brindavanam. With the Wardens' arrival her mood
brightened and Doña Paula concluded that company and
diversion were the best remedies for a lonely wife.

The following morning, full of enthusiasm for her own
project, Arlene insisted that Tom and Isobel ride into
Nido Mejor to see the new home. The three spent the
night there, talking until late. Tom promised to help build
her colony as he had built her father's congregation, but
urged her to tell him more about it. "Farmers are sort of
peculiar philosophers, Arlene. I'd better know what you're
going to promise them. If you can give me a story that'll
scare them real good you'll probably have more converts
than you need. They won't admit it but they like that sort
of excitement. The threat of hellfire and damnation is
working wonders in your father's Tabernacle."

Arlene laughed. "I'm afraid you've got your work cut
out for you, Tom dear. I promise them nothing but peace,
understanding, and Divine Love."

The following day when the brother and sister were ready to leave for the return trip to Los Angeles, Tom admonished Arlene. "You know I'll do anything I can to help. But you still haven't told me enough to go on."

She laughed and winked at Isobel. "I'm not certain that a man who sells real estate can be trusted with the truth."

Two weeks later Tom Warden reappeared alone, ostensibly to check progress for Steven. When he returned from the subdivision with Don Emilio shortly after noon, Arlene called him aside. "Tom, were you serious about wanting to help me?"

"Never more. What can I do?"

"It's difficult to talk here. Will you ride up to Brindavanam with me? I want to see after things at the house. We can talk on the way."

Tom Warden's apparent hesitancy caused her to reassure him. "If you are worried about appearances, Tom dear, don't be. I have already told Doña Paula and Don Emilio that you promised Steven to counsel me while he was away."

They spent the afternoon walking to the springs and meandering along the headwaters of the Rio Claro while Arlene explained, a bit cautiously at first, the philosophy she would espouse at Brindavanam.

Warden did not appear surprised. On the contrary, he seemed to follow easily and agree completely with her reasoning. His rapt attention and discreet questions encouraged her. By the time they had returned to the new house Arlene was deep in the persuasive yet somehow defensive justification of her beliefs.

"All religions talk of love of God or Gods and love of fellow man. They all have their commandments. They are all the same, Tom." She regarded him closely. "And do you know why man has made no real progress—except in the art of annihilating his own kind? Because he has never learned the meaning of true love. Frustrated love becomes hate. We are ashamed of love, Tom. We are ashamed of our bodies. How monstrous. Our bodies are God's own temples of love."

Arlene's voice had become strident and her eyes glowed with a fanatical intensity that excited Tom. He noticed the strange whiteness around her mouth and the fine beading of perspiration on her forehead and at the corners of her eyes. When he dismounted to assist her from the side-saddle her body was tense.

Inside the house she busied herself at pretending to see that things were in order. "I'm dreadfully nervous about leaving everything unattended like this, Tom. I don't trust our workmen as Steven does."

Warden chuckled. "How about using a little of that love on them?"

Arlene stiffened and turned to face him. "Oh, Tom Warden, I hope I've not misjudged you."

Embarrassed, he grinned. "I didn't mean to poke fun, Arlene. I know it didn't sound serious, but I meant it to be. You told me that like begets like. I took that to mean that love begets love." He managed a woebegone smile. "But I ought to know it doesn't always work, oughtn't I?"

Arlene moved closer. "Indeed you should not, dear Tom, if you're talking, as I presume you are, about my choice of Steven, even after you made your intentions clear."

Warden laughed with unconvincing good humor as he recalled his frustrated courtship. "I did everything but paint 'Tom loves Arlene' on the courthouse walls."

Arlene rested a hand on his forearm and looked up at him. Reproach turned to sympathy. "Poor Tom. Did you really think I was blind? Of course I could see. And how I loved you for caring. How lucky I was, two wonderful men in love with me."

The doleful expression on Warden's face turned to a wry smile and he shrugged. "So, the best man won. That's as it should be."

Arlene pouted. "Not the *best* man, but *another* wonderful man." She looked up at him intently for a moment then sighed. "Who can say what might have happened if it had been you on that boat? You and Steven have so many of the same fine qualities. Who can say? Who, really, can say? For I do love you both."

The words were half whispered, wistfully, and then unresisting, she allowed Tom Warden to take her in his arms.

Numb with shock and rage, Steven Lewis stood by the side of the bed in Jabez Lathrop's new home looking down at the sleeping Arlene. Dr. Rebecca Foley, a severe-visaged,

313

competent physician in her early fifties, touched his sleeve.

"She's been sleeping like this for three days now, Mr. Lewis. I have given her heavy doses of laudanum. I want her under sedation until some of the outraged tissues begin to heal." She indicated the door. "Let's go downstairs now. I want to talk with you."

Alone in the sitting room with the doctor, Steven listened. "The events are substantially as reported in unnecessary detail in the newspaper." She nodded distastefully at the issue of the *Los Angeles Evening Star* spread open on the side table.

Jabez had told him of the graphic coverage but he had not had time to read it.

"If you would prefer to hear this from a male physician I can arrange it, Mr. Lewis. Dr. Hoffman assisted me."

"No. You tell me. I want to know everything, right now."

Dr. Foley nodded. "All right. I'll tell you what I know for certain. The rest you'll get from Mr. Garcia at the ranch. When the Morales man rode here trying to get word to you, your father-in-law and I immediately followed him back to the ranch in a fast rig. There was nothing we could do for Mr. Warden. But Mrs. Lewis was still alive.

Dr. Foley paused. "Are you sure you want to hear all of the details, Mr. Lewis?"

Steven exploded. "Goddammit, yes! I want to hear it all. Every last word of it. Now tell me and quickly. Enough time has been lost already."

"Very well, Mr. Lewis. Your wife and Mr. Warden were found in the house. Both were naked. Mr. Warden had been emasculated in the crudest possible manner. He died from loss of blood and one can only hope that the brutality rendered him unconscious quickly. Mrs. Lewis was ravished and left for dead. There was no way to tell how many men used her. Speaking medically, I can only guess from the washings I was able to obtain that there must have been several. Perhaps as many as a half dozen. She was badly torn. I am sure she too was unconscious, very early on.

"Jabez has told you that Mr. Garcia and his men have been looking for the outlaws who did this for several days now. Deputy Sheriff Jim Bowdon took six men down there the day before yesterday. Mr. Warden's body was brought here this morning and interred in the Protestant Cemetery on Fort Hill."

She nodded toward the staircase. "There is no way for me to tell for certain how long it will be before your wife recovers. She may never recover fully, Mr. Lewis. You must be prepared for that. She is blessed with a strong young body. Physically she may recover in time. Dr. Hoffman and I have done all of the surgery possible. But there may be other after-effects, mental damage. What she has suffered, Mr. Lewis, is the most traumatic experience a woman can endure. How she comes out of it will depend on factors we doctors simply cannot judge. I tell you this quite honestly. Be prepared for the worst and hope. Your daughter is safe. She is being cared for at the ranch and I would suggest, Mr. Lewis, that you leave her there for the time being. Your in-laws are too distraught to attend to her here."

Later, when the doctor went upstairs for a final look at Arlene, Steven read the lurid account in the newspaper. Its innuendo enraged him.

> "It would be unfair to conclude that the victims were surprised in *flagrante delicto,* for it may well have been the intention of the leader of the murderous gang to leave precisely that impression for some evil motive of his own."

The account sickened Steven, all the more for the pernicious doubts that he couldn't exorcise by his rational attempts to counter them. Every aspect of his life with Arlene argued against deliberately contrived circumstantial evidence—her erratic behavior, her unashamed aggression, her eroticism and insatiable physical need, the open almost eager admission of her unconventional moral code, the abortion, and, hardest of all to admit, her obvious attraction to Tom Warden and Tom's scarcely concealed interest in her. True, as husband and wife they shared a common affection for little Charlotte. Even so, Steven recalled that he had often thought that Arlene regarded the baby daughter as a possession rather than a part of herself. And it had been at Arlene's insistence that Tom had become the sales representative for the development. Steven recalled his strange uneasiness when she said, "Oh darling,

I'm so glad. I had no idea that Tom would be interested, really. . . ." And there was the matter of Tom's eagerness to look in on Arlene and the baby, a friendly service perhaps, one he himself would likely have offered in similar circumstances, but again, there had been the uneasiness. Tom had left him no reasonable excuse to object, by reassuring him that business would be the prime reason for the trip.

Steven flung the paper aside and went upstairs again. For a time he stood looking down at his heavily drugged wife. Then, after advising Jabez Lathrop of his plans, he drove to the livery stable to arrange for a pair of fast saddle horses at dawn.

At El Rancho de los Nidos the shock of the rape and murder was evident in everyone. Don Emilio and Doña Paula had greeted him mutely while Pedro and Gracia and the other help stood back and watched with impassive faces and lowered heads.

Later, when he had settled in his room and washed, Don Emilio led him outside. "Before we eat, I want you to see this. Pedro found it on the nightstand in the sleeping room of your new house, when he found them."

Steven took the torn paper. He recognized it as half of a sheet of the notepaper that he had brought to Arlene from San Francisco on an earlier trip. The scrawl in Spanish was hasty and ink splattered. Half aloud, he translated: "Thank you, señora, for accommodating us as you accommodated your gringo lover."

Don Emilio watched as Steven's eyes remained fixed on the paper. "Only Pedro and I have seen this, Steven. Pedro does not read. It is the most despicable perfidy. I do not believe it. I was uncertain about showing it to you. I wanted to burn it immediately, and then I thought perhaps—"

Steven crumpled the paper and handed it back. "Burn it now, and forget you ever saw it."

While they were still at the table, Deputy Sheriff Bowdon rode up with six men. Some minutes later Los Angeles Marshal Bill Warren joined them with eight more men. Despite the fact that at least a score of lesser bandits continued to roam the state, raiding ranches and holding up coaches, the outrage in *Cañada Laberinta* was credited without a single dissent to *Los Lobos*.

316

Deputy Sheriff Bowdon reported. "We've been over the country for two days now. There's no way those men could have ridden into *Cañada Laberinta* without being in sight of this house. Pedro and his men have sworn on the Bible that no horsemen rode anywhere near the mouth of the canyon on the afternoon of the killing. They were working on the ditch all day. And there's no way that riders could get down into *Nido Mejor* from the east. Even deer keep away from those slopes. Whoever did this thing came in on foot. That don't square with the habits of most badmen around here. There was no fresh prints or signs around the house that could not of been made by Don Emilio's own men."

Don Emilio stiffened. Quickly, Bowdon raised a hand. "Don't take me wrong. I'm not trying to put a doubt on anyone. I know all your men. I'd as soon suspect the *padres* at Capistrano. There was no robbery as far as we could tell. Only the cutting and the—" He glanced at Steven and blinked in confusion. "—and—uh—the terrible thing with Mrs. Lewis. And there was the burning of the outbuildings."

Steven had learned earlier that three of the nearly completed residence cottages had been put to flames and an attempt to burn the main house had apparently been interrupted, for no flame had been touched to the leaves and sticks that had been heaped under the wooden front steps.

"The reason has to be revenge for something. And so far as we can tell there isn't a soul could have cause to hate Mr. Warden or the Lewises. There just ain't sense to it. If they were after livestock or money or food or clothes they would have struck this place here, not a house that wasn't even properly finished yet."

Steven, controlling hurt and cold rage aggravated by impatience, forced himself to listen. Don Emilio and Pedro had persuaded him not to ride into the canyon at night.

They were right. No purpose would be served. Much more sensible would be a coordinated search beginning before dawn. He prayed that the night would pass quickly.

The men spent an hour planning and checking their rifles and pistols before spreading their blanket rolls wherever they could. Shortly after four o'clock, Gracia turned them out. A half hour before daylight they were on their

317

mounts, breakfasted and provisioned with bundles of ropy, peppercoated dried beef.

Steven, Don Emilio, Pedro, and Marshal Bill Warren with four men rode along the *zanja* trail to *Cañada Laberinta*. Jim Bowdon with his own men and the remainder of Warren's men turned north along the base of the mountains. At Diablo Canyon they would divide into two smaller groups to comb the area for signs. At midday they would work their way south again and converge at *El Nido Mejor* to report their findings and coordinate further actions.

They let Steven go alone to look at the evidence of violence in his home. Upstairs in the bedroom that he and Arlene had shared, he stood gazing mutely at the big bed and its rumpled confusion of coarse sheeting and downfilled quilts. Just inside the door, where Tom Warden had been mutilated, the floor and the circular rag rug, a wedding gift from his mother-in-law, were covered with a yard-wide stain of dried blood. The room was permeated with the flat acridity of a charnel house. Steven walked to the bed and examined it briefly. Disgusted, he pulled the covers back in place. His throat was constricted and suppressed rage blurred his vision. Nothing seemed to be missing. Arlene's dresses were still in place on the peg hangers. Tom Warden's clothes were neatly folded and draped on the chair. The Congress gaiters he affected were side by side beneath it.

Steven forced himself to stay in the room until every detail of its condition was fixed in memory. Then he went downstairs. Things were also in order in the living room. But in the kitchen he noted that several utensils were missing as well as some containers of preserved food. The old Sharps rifle had been taken from its pegs over the hall door.

Outside again, he confronted Don Emilio. "When you and your men were here did anybody touch anything? Was anything moved or rearranged?" He indicated the house. "In there, or upstairs?"

Don Emilio, understanding the implications in the question, responded with an emphatic denial. "Nothing was moved, my friend. We brought Warden's body out of the house. Then we went back for your wife. Nothing else was touched. Absolutely nothing was rearranged."

When Steven continued to search his eyes appealingly,

Don Emilio lowered his head. "I am sorry. But it is the truth. Nothing was disturbed. Everything in the room is as we found it. *Verdaderamente. Lo siento mucho.*"

At the headgates there was evidence that several men had investigated its works. Pedro examined the footprints with two of his Indian *vaqueros.* After several minutes he called to Don Emilio and Steven. "These tracks were made by Mexican boots. But the men did not wear spurs. They came in on foot. We will look for more signs along the stream." He pointed to the steep slope between the two springs. "There are fresh slides there. Probably from animals. But we will look."

Shortly after noon, Jim Bowdon returned to *Nido Mejor* with all but two of his men. Seated on rocks beside the streams, they gnawed on the tough jerky and speculated on the absentees. "Merlhof and Parsons are good men. They're on to something. They'll show up."

Two hours later, just before the now uneasy Bowdon was about to go searching for them, the two men appeared. Parsons was excited.

"We found something all right, in that little canyon south of Diablo. There's a slide trail on the south slope so it's hard to tell one track from another. We could read the game and cattle droppings real clear. But what couldn't be seen was the horse turds, some no more than two days old. We didn't see them because all of them was kicked off the trail down into the brush, on purpose. Max and me went more than a mile up the slope. Droppings has been kicked off the trail for months now. Whoever's using it for damn sure don't want to be follered."

Bowdon looked around. "Anybody here been up that little canyon?"

Pedro nodded. "*Si, señor.* That is *Cañada Ciega.* In the first dry year we used to ride in looking for cattle. It only goes maybe two miles. It cuts down from a small mesa. There used to be feed there and a little spring."

Parsons nodded. "We didn't cross the mesa. The trail splits to a couple of other little canyons. But it was late. We didn't want to go up them alone. We figgered they's got to be six or eight men up there somewhere."

Steven tensed as he recalled Dr. Rebecca Foley's words: "There was no way to tell how many men used her, Mr. Lewis . . . perhaps as many as a half dozen . . ."

He rose and addressed both men. "Did you see any

319

place where they could have left horses if they did come in here on foot?"

Parsons shook his head. "Nope. We looked for that, too. The trail cuts southwest over to the river. If they were going to ride down out of the hills and fetch up, then walk here, they'd leave their animals close by. There are no signs that's what they done. We looked real good."

Jim Bowdon listened carefully, then turned to Pedro. "If anybody's holed up in those canyons they got to have water for themselves and their animals. Are there any other springs back up in there?"

The majordomo shook his head. "There is no other water. Only the little spring on the mesa above *Cañada Ciega*."

Pedro shrugged. *"No sé, señor.* There was not much in the summer. Maybe enough for men, if they dig."

The deputy tugged at his ear thoughtfully. "But maybe now with snow on top there's enough for men and animals?"

"It is possible señor."

Bowdon grunted and squinted at the sun. "We've got three hours of light. Let's take a look."

Pedro and his four men stayed with Don Emilio and Steven. They would rejoin at the rancho at dark. By tacit agreement Steven was left alone with his thoughts. For the first hour he wandered around assessing the damage to the cottages. Don Emilio watched him standing in the midst of the ruins and understood the conflict in him.

"He belongs to the yanquis and to us," he had said to Doña Paula. "There will always be a tempest in him. It is in his blood."

Anita disagreed. "He is more like us, father." Don Emilio had laughed. "To believe that, *hijita mia*, would be to make a grave mistake!" He had sensed from the beginning that while Steven Lewis might have inherited his mother's dark good looks he had also inherited his Yankee father's compulsive need to acquire, to build, and to innovate. No *californio* would have done or even cared to do what had already been accomplished by Steven at El Rancho de los Nidos and by the other yanquis at Anaheim, El Monte, and San Bernardino.

"Seedlings do not produce good wood or good fruit," he had observed. "They grow stronger and more fruitful when they are crossed with other stock. It is the same with animals and with men."

After a second visit to the new house, Steven wandered back toward the springs. On his right he caught a glimpse of something that brought a quick stab of recognition. It was the fallen log against which he and Arlene had leaned on their first visit alone to *Nido Mejor*. It was the place, bathed in warm sunlight, where Arlene's emotion had overwhelmed them both. It was the place where Charlotte had been conceived. Steven turned away and the pressure of tears that would remain unshed blurred his vision.

A few yards along he stopped abruptly. For a moment he stood thinking. Then he made his way back to the log, leaned his carbine against it, and sat down. For a long time he rested his chin in his palms. Then he looked up at the steep, brushy slope that formed the vast north wall of the hidden valley. Something had disturbed him on that first afternoon. He remembered now. It had been a stabbing glint of sunlight on some bright object. The flash had endured for mere seconds but it had been bright enough to attract his attention.

Without taking his eyes from the slope, Steven pushed his back up against the smooth weathered log until he was seated on it. For several minutes he studied the mountain side, too steep in most places for a man to find secure footing. What could have caused a flash up there? A slab of gleaming basalt disturbed by an animal? But basalt is dark. The flash would have been muted. The one he had seen was intense enough to have come from a bright reflecting surface, a piece of mirror, a bottle or a piece of metal. It seemed preposterous to suppose that such items would be found several thousand feet up that precipitous slope. And still there was no ready explanation for the flash and he had not imagined it. He rose suddenly, picked up the carbine, and walked a hundred yards or so to the place where Don Emilio was standing with Pedro watching the action of the water on the large bend in the ditch.

"Do you have a telescope at your house?"

"I do. But it is very old."

"May I get it?"

Don Emilio was puzzled. "But of course. Pedro will get it for you. But why a telescope?"

"I want to look at something on that mountain." He

pointed well up the slope. "I remember seeing something up there when Arlene and I first came here alone. It's probably nothing, but I'd like to look anyway."

In a half hour Pedro returned with a tarnished brass ship's telescope bound in cracked leather.

Steven located a tree near the log that would give him approximately the same point of view and rested the instrument on a limb. Methodically he began scanning the slope from the top down, moving the lens across the narrowed field, then lowering it to sweep a new area directly below. For some minutes he continued the scrutiny. Don Emilio grew curious enough to question him.

"What do you see?"

"Nothing . . . ground squirrels mostly."

"What do you expect to see?"

Steven folded the instrument and shrugged. "I don't know. I recall seeing a strong flash of sunlight up there."

Don Emilio gazed up thoughtfully. "It could have come from water seeping down the face of a rock."

Steven nodded. "I thought of that. But Pedro says there is no water up there."

Don Emilio gazed at the patches of snow still visible in the rocky clefts at the summit. "There is melting snow up there every year, as there is now. Sometimes the water wil trickle down." Steven nodded. "That's possible. But if the sun was catching a wet surface it would shine on it a while. What I saw flashed quickly and disappeared." He pointed. "As I remember, it was up near the top of those big rocks, better than halfway up."

Both men studied the steep terrain. Don Emilio was skeptical. "It could have been many things, a big bird, a condor perhaps, turning into the sun just right." He shrugged. "Who knows? But if you wish, I can send the men up there."

Steven shook his head. "Let's hear what the others say first." The recollection was vivid now, even to the start it had caused. But there was no question that the flash had come from some highly reflective surface, not from the fleeting iridescence of plumage. Perhaps he and Arlene had been watched. The possibility produced a stab of guilt and embarrassment even now. And perhaps too he was attaching to it far more importance than it deserved.

At sundown, Steven and Don Emilio remounted. Followed by Pedro and his *vaqueros*, they wound westward along the ditch toward the *casa grande*.

As they emerged from the tortuous canyon they saw Marshal Bill Warren approaching across the mesa that led up to the base of the hill on which stood the Garcia y Perez home. He was riding flat out. Don Emilio, a superb horseman, spurred his mount and motioned the others to follow. The trio intercepted the marshal about a mile from the main trail. Warren shouted as he pulled up.

"We found them! By God, we found them! We stumbled onto their *caballada* in the south canyon just off the little mesa. Three men were fixing to take the animals to water. We got two of them and hazed their horses out of the canyon. I think we nicked the third one. I'm not sure. But there's more of them up there. Jim's got the men strung out but it'll be black dark tonight. We couldn't guarantee that someone who knows the lay couldn't slip through afoot. We need more men."

Don Emilio dismissed the possibility. "It will take until tomorrow afternoon to get more men here. By that time the matter will be settled. My men know these *cañons*. Let us talk with Señor Bowdon and see what it is possible to do."

A twenty-minute ride brought them to the mouth of *Cañada Ciega*, where the chief deputy was waiting for them. After Don Emilio explained the problem of getting settlers to leave their families alone at night in the scattered *ranchitos* Jim Bowdon agreed to make do. In all they were twenty-three men. Most carried Colt pistols in addition to an assortment of single-shot rifles and some repeating rifles. Steven was best armed. In San Francisco he had paid a premium for a new .44 caliber Henry Repeating Carbine.

While the men were planning, Pedro Morales moved beside Steven. "Señor Lewis, I think the *bandidos* came down the mountain into *Nido Mejor*. The prints go out of the cañada but none come in."

"You and your men saw slides. But you said animals made them."

"*Si, señor*. It is possible. But I looked again. There are little slides from those big rocks all the way down to the springs almost straight down. Animals move across a slope. There are many such trails."

"What about a rock falling down? That would make slides."

"It is possible. But a small rock would not come all the way down. A large one would make more marks. No, I think maybe two or three men came down."

Steven knew that if he accepted Pedro's theory the conclusion was inevitable: men barred from escape by the usual route would resort to any alternate route, no matter how difficult. He motioned to the majordomo. "Stay with me. Let's listen to Bowdon's plan first."

The deputy was an imaginative strategist. "It's going to be cold and black tonight. If they can see us I want them to think that we're going to wait until daylight to make our move. We'll make two camps—one here on the south side of the canyon mouth and the other on the north side. If they're cornered, they'll probably try to sneak out after midnight. They'll figure we're split, because of our fires, and they'll try to slip between us down this draw or they may try to angle up over the north rim and head for the San Gabriels.

"After dark I want four men with repeaters to split two and two and sneak up on both rims. Stay fifty feet or so above the trail. I want one man down here at each fire and keep moving around. Make it look like many men. If they're going to try to come out afoot this way, they'll either try the ridge or come straight down the draw. If you hear anything, challenge it. If it don't talk right, shoot it."

Bowdon began deploying his men and Steven moved beside him. "Pedro thinks some men came down the mountain into *Nido Mejor.* He may be right. Anyway, I want to go back up there with him tonight and wait. If they do try to come out that way and there's nobody there to stop them they could get to the ranch, steal horses and food and God knows what else, and be gone before we know it."

Bowdon was skeptical. So was Bill Warren. "If they're in those caves, they'd have a sheer drop of fifty feet or more to get to the slope. It'd be hard enough to make it down through the slides and brush in daylight let alone pitch dark."

Bowdon looked reflective. "But I wouldn't want to be the one to say a desperate man wouldn't try it."

Steven nodded. "And I don't like the idea of leaving the women alone at the ranch with no men around."

The deputy grunted. "All right. We'll make out. Let Don Emilio go back to the house with the women. You and Pedro go on up to the *Nido*. But leave the Indians with me."

Under protest, the *ranchero* agreed to return to the *casa grande*. Steven and Pedro rode with him. There they checked ammunition and ate a hasty supper. Then amid protestations and prayer, Steven and Pedro left for the hazardous night ride into *Cañada Laberinta*.

By eight o'clock the canyon was enveloped in velvet darkness. The sheer wall of the Santa Ana escarpment was a presence felt rather than seen. They tied their horses in the shelter lean-to and as an added precaution they hobbled them. Then they entered the big house.

In the kitchen Steven found some short tallow candles and a container of Allin matches. Working with a hooded light, he located two boxes of Sharps cartridges that the marauders had overlooked. These he gave to Pedro. After thinning the wax shipping lubricant on his own metal cartridges and making certain both weapons were clean, he extinguished the candles and took two ponchos from their pegs by the door.

"Let's go up to the springs. I'd rather be early and freeze than take a chance."

Thoroughly familiar with the trail, they made their way on foot to the upper pond and climbed over the rubble of boulders at the base of the slope. The mountain was referred to by the natives as *La Colema*, the beehive.

Steven had questioned Pedro about it. Now, as they huddled for wind shelter behind a large boulder, he visualized the three-thousand-foot slope rearing above them and pressed Pedro for more details. "Could men get to those caves by climbing up here?"

"No, señor." He pointed to his left. "It is necessary first to go over that ridge into *Cañada Ciega*. Above the *mesita* men can climb to the west face of La Colema and follow the shelf around to the caves." He pointed into the darkness above them. "Pumas used to live there. I have hunted them."

Steven reviewed what little he had seen of the mountain from the canyon to the north where the lawmen were now deployed. From experience he knew that it was easier to scale than descend a very steep incline. If the killers had managed somehow to come down several thousands of feet of rubbled, cactus-studded slope, then they must have devised some way to get down the sheer, fifty-foot cliff.

"If men came down this way, how did they get to the slope from the caves?"

"Who knows, señor? There must be some way. I am certain they did come down."

"How high would we have to climb the south slope to see across to the caves?"

Pedro considered briefly. "Perhaps five or six hundred *varas,* señor."

That meant a fifteen- to eighteen-hundred-foot climb. Under ordinary circumstances it would not be too difficult. But the plan he was formulating would call for the climb to be made in total darkness and in absolute quiet.

"If you were Los Lobos, Pedro, and you knew men were coming after you at first light, what would you do?"

The majordomo laughed softly. "I have been thinking of this, señor. Unless I had enough food and water and bullets for a week, I'd be trying to go away."

"What would you try first?"

"I would try to come out by *Cañada Ciega* and get by the men. Then I would steal horses from Don Emilio and take my chances."

"If you were El Lobo himself, would you be the first to try?"

"No, señor. He is the leader. He will be the last man."

"What happens if his men do not get out of the canyon tonight?"

"Probably they will try to come down this way, later when they can see."

Steven grunted. "That's what I think too."

He reached over and rested a hand on Pedro's forearm. "*Amigo.* I am going to climb until I can see the caves."

Pedro started. "No, señor. If they see you they will have a great advantage. They will be able to shoot across and down at you. Much better to wait here."

"They won't see me, Pedro. I'm going to climb now. By daylight I should be high enough."

The audacity of the decision left the Mexican momentarily speechless. "It is not possible. You will fall. You will break bones. You will be cut by a thousand cactus spines."

Steven peered around him, reaching out to touch nearby objects. He called each by name. "I can see well enough. My eyes are accustomed to the night now. I will

326

go one step at a time. You stay here. When it gets light you can cover me."

"Señor. It is not possible. When you are on the mountain they can shoot across at you and I will never see them from here. If you go, I go too."

Steven concealed his relief. "All right, let us go."

Goyo Robles, haggard and increasingly aware of his fifty years despite a spare, rawhide-tough physique, knelt on a sandstone ledge overlooking *Cañada Ciega*. Beside him was his second-in-command, the Sonoran, Bruto. Behind them were the remaining five members of the nine-man band.

Below them was the small mesa and the spring at the head of the blind canyon. Also below them were the bodies of their dead companions. The sloping plain was a mile or more beyond. In the distance two fires flickered, one on the north side of the dry *barranca*, the other on the south.

At first the loss of the horses and the two men had seemed to present an insurmountable obstacle. But the more Goyo thought about it the more hope he found. With horses, the temptation to try to run the cordon might prove irresistible. Goyo knew that would be fatal for most of his men.

Softly, he called them closer. "They expect us to come out on foot. The *barranca* will be guarded. If we follow it we will be slaughtered like pigs in a ditch."

He tapped Bruto's leg with the back of his hand. "Take Diego, Lucio, and Frasco. Go down along the top of the ridge almost to the mouth of the *cañada*. They'll be spread out, waiting. So go down the south face of the ridge and make your way over to *Los Nidos*. Wait down the road from the corral. Tito and Cinco will come down the *reatas* with me into *Nido Mejor*. We will take horses and food from Don Emilio and meet you."

Bruto grumbled unhappily. "You are going down the cliff in the dark. What if you don't make it?"

"Wait a half hour after first light, then take horses for yourselves. Ride to our place in *Cañada Santa Margarita*. If we do not meet you there in one week," he paused, "then, my friends, good luck and go with God!"

Bruto was reluctant. "Let us all go down the *reatas* as we did when we entertained the gringo woman."

A murmur of agreement came from the three who were chosen to go down the ridge. Goyo silenced them. "It will take too much time. You know that, besides, it is possible that Morales and his *indios* are waiting there. Already that one is suspicious. I have watched him studying the signs."

Still not convinced, Bruto pressed his point. "Everybody believes there is only one way out of *Cañada Ciega*. They will all wait for us." He pointed toward the mouth of the canyon. "We will have no chance."

Goyo turned to face his lieutenant. He spoke quietly and coldly. "Bruto, my friend, I will make a bargain with you. You and your men go down the *reatas*. Tito, Cinco, and I will go this way. But if you are not waiting with the horses after one half hour, then you and I will use these," he patted the haft of his knife, "to decide who leads *Los Lobos*. Yes?"

In the strained silence no sound was heard but the breathing of the men. Then abruptly, without a response, Bruto began to climb to the ridge a hundred yards above. Reluctantly, the others followed. When the four had disappeared Goyo called to the remaining men. "We go now."

Although he was burdened by pockets bulging with ammunition and handicapped by darkness, Steven climbed quietly and well. At times Pedro was forced to plead for a respite.

Except for the occasional rattle of light rubble that a listener might have taken for the sound of small night animals scurrying across the slope, the pair did nothing to arouse suspicion. After an hour Steven paused. "How high do you think we are?"

Pedro sucked in several labored breaths. "Not high enough, señor. Maybe two hundred *varas*."

Steven was about to speculate aloud on the time remaining until first light when the majordomo tapped his arm and signaled for silence. For a long moment neither man seemed to breathe.

"What was it?"

"I don't know. I thought I heard something." Pedro pointed upward and across to the invisible opposite slope. "It was a voice maybe." He listened again. "I am not certain."

They resumed the climb. Several times they barely avoided placing their free hands in stray clumps of low pincushion cactus. Once when Steven attempted to steady himself by grasping the branches of a scrub mesquite the shallow roots gave way. Only Pedro's instant reflex spared them both a painful slide.

For another half hour they struggled for each foot gained. Finally they rested, listening intently. Nothing could be heard but the muted rush of wind moving up the steep, flue-like ravine.

As they were about to resume the climb, Steven clutched Pedro's arm. "Look!" He pointed across the ravine somewhat above their position. "There's a fire. You can see its reflection on the rocks above."

For a long moment both men strained to see, but whatever Steven had glimpsed seemed to have disappeared. Then, just as suddenly, the dull red reflection flickered again. Taut and still, they watched until the flare subsided. Pedro moved closer.

"It is a little mesquite fire in one of the caves. Somebody put more wood on it. What we see is the light on the roof of the opening. Quick. Let us climb higher. A few *varas* more and we can see it."

They climbed for another ten minutes, pausing every few yards to peer across the narrowing ravine. In several more minutes the flames themselves were visible as were the silhouettes of three men who appeared to be busy at some urgent task.

Steven estimated his own position to be approximately three hundred line-of-fire yards from the cave. The men were well within the killing range of his Henry carbine. Even so, a moving man was a small target, especially in poor light. While Pedro Morales watched in mute disbelief, he raised the weapon, rested it on the slab and sighted along the barrel. After a moment he relaxed.

"I could pick off one of them."

"No, señor! If you kill only one, the other two will get us. We have no good cover here. They can stay on the mountain longer than we can."

Steven grunted. "Unless Bowdon's men follow them up, which they'll do at first light. They'll be in a cross-fire then."

Pedro remained adamant as Steven considered the options. *Los Lobos* must have some alternate route out of their hiding place by way of *Nido Mejor*. He turned to Pedro. "What do you think they're doing?"

"It is too far, señor. The fire does not make enough light. But I think they are tying something."

As Pedro spoke, two of the distant figures moved a bulky object to the edge of the outcropping and a third began securing something to it. Shortly afterward the object disappeared. The obvious explanation struck both watchers at once.

"They're lowering supplies. They're going to try to get out this way." Steven blurted the words half aloud and silenced himself instantly. Pedro confirmed his observation. "I think it is blankets and rifles. It may not be possible to carry anything down but their pistols."

Fingering the Henry carbine as he watched, Steven wished for the greater accuracy of the more cumbersome, long-barreled Henry rifle.

Pedro, sensing his impatience, again urged caution. "It is not possible for them to go in the dark, señor. They will go at first light and pick up their things at the bottom of the cliff. Then we can get all of them, before they have their own rifles. Let us wait and be ready."

Steven pressed his right cheekbone against the smooth, oiled stock and lined the sights on the distant silhouettes. "Why take a chance? They may get away. They'll still be dangerous with pistols. And they're sure to take our horses. Nobody will be there to stop them."

As he spoke, Steven could see the fire lowering again. The once clean silhouettes were becoming diffused. In a matter of minutes there would be no target. His thumb moved atop the hammer and forced it back. When it clicked into place, a sound of protest escaped from Pedro and he swung down the trigger guard on his own single-shot Sharps. Into the breech he slipped a linen-cased ball and powder charge. The block, sliding up into place again, sliced the tip off the powder bag exposing the charge to the primer.

The two rifles discharged almost simultaneously. The echo of the double blast drowned out the cries across the ravine as the man who had been standing erect in the center of the group threw up his arms and fell backward. The blast reverberated between the sheer walls and died in the upper reaches of the canyon.

No other sound was heard but the startled screeching of a night-bird and then a silence, so deep it was oppressive, settled over the *cañada*.

Steven saw Pedro reloading. His own repeating carbine,

with second cartridge chambered, was already sighted on the spot where a waning flicker still marked the mouth of the hideout. But no target remained.

Protected by their meager cover, they waited, expecting return fire. Instead, the glow of smoldering embers died suddenly, leaving only the deep, pre-dawn darkness. A large owl brushed the air nearby and startled them. Steven leaned close to whisper. "You were right, Pedro. They must have lowered their rifles down the cliff."

"Perhaps, señor. But I think they did not see where our shots came from. It is possible they are afraid to shoot because we could mark their position again. We wait now, until it is light."

They had scarcely settled down for the cold, cramped vigil when the flat splat of distant rifle fire reached them. The reports were coming from the northwest, across the rocky spine separating them from *Cañada Ciega*.

"They're trying to get out the other way. They've run into Bowdon's men."

Before Pedro could reply, they heard more shooting. The rapid fire of repeating rifles was unmistakable. "That sounds like fifty-six caliber fire from Spencers. I don't think we have to wait up here now. I think it's finished. Listen."

The fusillade had diminished to sporadic firing. Steven nudged Pedro. "Come on. Let's start down."

After a few steps they discovered that it had been much easier to ascend than descend the slope quietly. Heels, rammed into loose shale, gave way and started alarming cascades. From there on, neither man made a serious attempt to move in silence. Above him, Steven could hear Pedro's quiet cursing. Within a half hour, they had descended more than halfway. Below, they could hear the distant spill of water from the large pool at the head of *Nido Mejor*. Several times on the opposite canyon wall that reared to the foot of the cave shelf, they heard the running rattle of small stones. Pedro guessed that the noises came from animals moving down to water.

Well below the base of the opposite cliff, Steven paused. "We should have cut across higher up and picked up their blankets and guns."

Pedro glanced up at the gray seam of pre-dawn light that was beginning to outline the high, ragged ridges to the east.

"Nobody will take them, señor. Let us get the horses first. It will be light soon."

At the rim of the upper pool, both men flattened on their bellies to drink. Pedro rose first and, moving with care, he began to follow the path around the pool, moving toward the ruins of the three burned cottages and the animal shed beyond. Steven sheathed his knife and set out to catch up. He had gone only a few yards when Pedro called out, Señor Lewis! Señor! Our horses are gone. Someone has cut the halter leads."

For an instant, Steven had trouble understanding. Then, vaulting over the boulders, he began to retrace his steps up the slope. It was growing light now but he knew there was no need for caution. In long, driving strides he forced his way up the steep incline, losing a foot for every two he gained. When he was close enough to the base of the cliff to see clearly, he paused to look around.

Several more minutes of reckless climbing brought him to the base of the cliff and then he saw it, the slack rawhide line dangling from the lip of the ledge far above him. What had happened was obvious now. His shot had driven the bandits down the slender line. They had recovered their weapons, stolen the horses, and headed out of the canyon, probably as much as an hour before he and Pedro had been able to descend.

Also obvious was the manner in which *Los Lobos* had entered *Cañada Laberinta* the afternoon they had mutilated, raped, and burned.

Steven whirled and started back down the slope in reckless leaping strides. When Pedro met him he gasped a brief explanation and ordered him to follow. On foot, they reached the *casa grande* just as the sun broke over the ice-glazed crests of the Santa Ana Mountains.

Inside, they found Doña Paula unconscious on the tile floor. Anita, racked with sobs and bleeding from a head wound, was crouched over her mother as though to protect her.

Don Emilio, dazed and rigid, sat at the table clutching at a blood-soaked gash in the left shoulder of his short jacket. Before him were the scattered contents of his strongbox. When he saw Steven and Pedro he attempted to speak but no sound would come from his gray lips.

A moan sent Pedro diving for the kitchen door. There he found Gracia and her three Indian *cocineras* sprawled on the floor. Pedro's outcry brought Steven to the door-way just as he dropped to his knees appealing to his wife.

Another groan followed by a heavy thud sent Steven racing back to the big room. Don Emilio had fallen forward on the table. A film of blood had begun to stain the edges of the scattered papers. Steven pushed them aside, propped the *ranchero* upright, and ripped away the vest and shirt. What he saw sickened him. A blade had slashed from the top of the left shoulder across the base of the neck just above the collarbone. From deep in the wound a finger-thick stream of blood was pulsing from a severed artery.

Bill Warren and two of his men found Steven trying to staunch the flow with a balled-up remnant of Don Emilio's cotton shirt. The marshal pushed the cloth aside gently, studied the wound, and shook his head. "I doubt if a surgeon could fix it, Lewis. It's cut through under the bone. You can't get at it. Leave him now and let's get the women to another room. It'll be over in a minute or two."

They carried Anita and Doña Paula to a bedchamber and returned to the kitchen, where the Indian women were beginning to stir. Still on his knees, Pedro was blotting blood from his wife's left temple. When Steven knelt beside him, he nodded. "Thank God they live! For that thank God!"

Warren leaned over and placed a hand on Pedro's shoulder. "Pedro, my men will stay with the women for a few minutes. I want you and Lewis to come with me. We've got two of them tied up down at the corral. Jim Bowdon wants you to see if you know who they are."

As they rode down the knoll from the *casa grande*, Bill Warren explained the capture. "We heard your two shots so we started over. When we came up out of the riverbed we saw two men riding like hell southeast from the house. They had a big lead so we shot their horses. When they went down we couldn't figure out why they didn't shoot back. But we found out soon enough. One of them had three rifles wrapped in blankets. The other one had a bag of food and some gold money and jewelry. They both had knives but no pistols. They claim they don't speak English."

He looked across at them. "By the way, what were you shooting at?"

Steven recounted the events in the canyon and Bill Warren grunted. "I thought there was only six. We got four killed and two hogtied. If you hit him, you left one on the shelf. You better come with us for a look after Pedro sizes up these men."

At the corral they looked at the two trussed Sonorans who were squatting with their backs to the adobe wall. Beyond observing that both men were half-breed *yaquis* Pedro could do nothing to identify them. After another futile attempt at interrogation during which the Marshal's vicious kicks had no effect, Pedro returned to the house and Steven and the Marshal rode to *Cañada Ciega* to join Jim Bowdon and the others.

The bodies of the four who had attempted to escape down the south ridge were laid out by the nearest of the fires. Merlhof and Parsons wore pleased expressions as they contemplated their handiwork. Merlhof chuckled and kicked one of the lolling heads. "Now, lads, there's the perfect picture of three good greasers!"

He guffawed with the others and kicked the corpse again. "We gotta do this about three thousand more times afore the score is anywheres near even."

Bowdon snapped an order. "All right! Leave 'em be now! There's one more up the canyon. Lewis thinks he hit him. We're going to have us a look."

Bill Warren and several of his men accompanied them to the edge of the little mesa. From there Bowdon, Steven, and two of the marshal's deputies started up the trail. They climbed along the rocky spine until they reached a sandstone projection that led to an adjacent ravine. After several hundred feet, the treacherous path turned sharply eastward. Steven could see across to the rocks that hours earlier would have shielded them in the event of a rifle duel. He called to Jim Bowdon, who was in the lead. "The cave is just around the next shoulder. Maybe another fifty yards."

The ledge was no place for a nervous man. At times it was scarcely more than two feet wide and the drop, in most places sheer, was at least one hundred feet. The first wind cave they came to was not more than five or six feet deep with a portal a scant four feet high. A few yards farther along they found another cave. Moving quietly, Bowdon edged around the shoulder, then signaled them to follow. Certain that they were within a few yards of the hideout, Steven tapped the deputy on the arm. "Not far now. Be careful."

They moved a step at a time until they were able to look directly across to the opposite slope. Steven studied the canyon wall and marveled that he and Pedro had managed to scale it at all, much less in the black of night. Jim Bowdon had eased back the hammer on his seven-shot Navy-model Spencer rifle. At close range its heavy ball could blow a man to pieces. Crouching, he moved to the projection of sandstone and peered around it. After a few seconds, he stood upright and beckoned to them. "Come on, boys. He's there all right and he ain't going to hurt anybody now."

They found the man sprawled in the mouth of the cave. He had been struck high on the right side of the chest. The slug had entered cleanly but the lead had mushroomed against the inner surface of the shoulder blade and ripped out of the body through a ragged six-inch wound. Slight but strongly built, the man appeared to be well into his middle years. The black hair had gone gray. The tanned skin was deeply lined from years of exposure but the features were clean and strong. Even the *serape* and the much-patched clothing could not conceal the unmistakable evidence that once this man had been of the *gente de razon*, a well-born *californio*.

He had died neither quickly nor easily. After his companions deserted him, he had managed to crawl into the cave. The blood-stained floor indicated that he had lain beside one of the two water *jarros*. Then later, perhaps in an attempt to reach the warmth of the still smoldering fire, he had tried to crawl back outside. Death had come within the present hour.

Bowdon made no effort to conceal his exultation. "By damn, Lewis, right through the lung at three hundred yards. But before we give you the sharpshooting medal I want to see you do that again with my own eyes."

Though he took little pleasure from it, Steven smiled as the others added their grudging admiration. He had never wanted to kill before Arlene's rape and Tom Warden's emasculation. These bandits were the ones who had done it, and still, kneeling beside the man who surely was their leader, he found no satisfaction in retribution. When Bowdon extended a foot to turn the face in order to get a better look at it, Steven fended off the boot.

Bowdon's smile was puzzled. "I wouldn't dirty my hands on these murdering greasers if I was you, Lewis. If you can keep remembering what they done at your house maybe you'll start cursing God for not letting you get here in time to uncock the son of a bitch while he was still alive."

Steven did not attempt to defend his action. It had been impulsive. If Bowdon did not understand it, neither did he. Somehow the dead bandit did not look evil and he did not look strange. In his mid-years his own grandfather, Don José, had been such a man, finely made, well-proportioned, differing very little in appearance. He would have found it less disturbing had the man resembled the two captives and their dead companions. They were villainous and looked the part.

A Colt Dragoon revolver had fallen from the bandit's belt. Bowdon shoved it with his boot. "It's yours if you want it, Lewis. You earned it right enough. I'm going to have a look around this place before we fix to carry this bastard out of here."

A brief inspection of the cave turned up a small buckskin bag containing some Mexican pesos and an oiled skin envelope containing several papers. Bowdon tossed the packet to Steven. "They're written in spic. You speak their lingo. Why don't you look at them?"

Of the four papers, three were personal notations and comments on conversations with various officials in Mexico City, Tepic, San Blas, and Mazatlán. All were dated in the mid-Forties. The fourth sheet, carefully folded in its own inner wrapper, was an official document dated Monterey, Alta California, 20 Septiembre, 1841. It was a single page. Steven started when he saw the governor's seal and the signature of Juan Bautista Alvarado. Quickly he translated to himself. The document commissioned Gregorio Robles as special envoy to Mexico City whose duty it was to convince General Santa Anna, President of the Republic of Mexico, that he should bolster the garrisons in the Department of the North.

Unmindful of the activity around him, Steven seated himself on a small boulder and studied the paper. In the prolix, formal prose, he could follow Goyo Robles' mounting frustration as one after another apathetic Mexican official temporized with him.

Frantically, Steven raked over the past. The possession

of the papers would not necessarily prove that the man he had killed was his uncle. There had never been any hard evidence that the man called *El Lobo* was actually Goyo Robles. For as long as he could remember, the family had believed that Goyo, while on a vital mission for his blood brother, had fallen ill or had been murdered. Alvarado himself had done little to dispel the assumption. Indeed his tacit agreement seemed to reinforce it.

Steven glanced at the men who were using *reatas* to lash the body to a carrying pole. He felt empty. There was no remorse, just a strange emptiness and a sense of deep futility. The body looked almost frail now, far older than its years, as the men bound the neck to keep the head from hanging. He had resumed his study of the papers when Bowdon approached. "What do you make of them?"

Steven shook his head. "Nothing. Just some personal letters."

Bowdon frowned and pointed to the separate envelope. "What's that fancy one?"

"Nothing important, some sort of commission, army or something. Written before I was born."

Bowdon glanced back at the body and grunted. "The son of a bitch was probably respectable once, huh? I saw a name on it, didn't I?"

Steven nodded. "Governor Alvarado signed it."

The chief deputy snorted. "*That* drunken greaser!"

Without intending to, Steven Lewis stood up abruptly. The move startled Bowdon. "What's eating on you?"

"*That* 'drunken greaser' is my godfather."

Bowdon's mouth slacked open. "*Your* godfather? Bullshit, Lewis, You ain't no spic."

For a long moment the two eyed one another. Then Steven brushed past him. At the fire he squatted, stirred the gray to uncover the glowing coals, and touched the edge of the papers to them. Bowdon watched but made no attempt to interfere as the yellowed papers cindered to brittle black flakes. "Why did you do that?"

Steven smiled deceptively. "No use keeping papers signed by a drunken greaser, is there?"

The chief deputy flushed, then addressed his men. "All right, boys. Let's get that bastard out of here. Maybe we can tease his two friends into telling us who he is."

The man supporting the rear end of the pole looked at Bowdon. "Jim?"

"Yeah?"

"In view of the shortage of trees and all, do you suppose we could arrange a little horizontal hanging for them other two?"

Bowdon glanced at Steven before he answered. "We just might save the state the nuisance. But killing seems to upset our friend here, so I figure we won't invite him."

As the trail narrowed, the ledge angled abruptly to the right. The eight-foot pole with its cumbersome burden created a dangerous problem. As the lead man began the turn, his companion lost his balance. Bowdon jumped to assist him but too late. The man released the rear end of the pole as he cried out. "I'm letting go, Pete! Dry gulch the bastard before we go with him!"

A fraction of a second apart, they heaved the pole over the edge and braced themselves against the cliff. Mutely, all four men watched the trussed body vault end over end down the gorge. Halfway, the corpse tore loose from its bindings and began a series of grotesque, loose-jointed cartwheels until, a broken thing, it came to rest in the jagged boulders far below.

Filled with an unexplainable outrage, Steven leveled his rifle at the men, then lowered it. If Bowdon saw the move he gave no evidence of it. Instead, he broke the taut silence with an unconvincing rebuke. "That was a wrong thing, boys. You should have clung on." He looked down at the partially visible body. "But I guess it ain't killing when a body's already dead."

An hour later, at the rancho's corrals, City Marshal Bill Warren, satisfied that the job was finished, ordered his own men to mount. "We can get back by sundown if we go now. Besides, Jim, this is your job—rightfully." He indicated the prisoners.

Bowdon looked at the two bound men propped against the adobe barn wall. "Did you get them to talk?"

Warren shook his head as he mounted. "We didn't try. None of my boys speak their lingo." He turned his horse. "Shall I noise it around that you're bringing them in?"

Bowdon straightened and dismounted slowly. "I dunno, Bill. We're all pretty tuckered out. If I decide to, suppose we let it be a surprise?" He considered a moment. "If we do come in, though, I won't show favorites. We'll stretch

338

one on John Gollar's gate and the other at the lumber yard."

The men rode off laughing and the deputy turned to Steven. "All right, Lewis, you savvy their lingo. Súppose you try and get a little testimony about what happened to your wife," he paused intentionally, "and her friend."

Steven slipped Goyo's Navy Colt revolver into the saddlebag and walked over to confront the prisoners. Addressing them in Spanish, with the Henry repeater cradled in his hands for added emphasis, he asked a series of blunt questions. When it became obvious that the men would not answer, Bowdon dismounted and kicked them viciously. "You talk up, Goddamn you, or I'll snap your fucking heads off right here." He delivered two more kicks. "Now talk."

Steven motioned the deputy away and tried persuasion, holding out hope but not promising leniency, if they would identify the men who had committed the atrocities. But the two *yaquis* maintained their stolid silence. They would not so much as nod in answer. When Steven saw them look past him, he turned to find Bowdon uncoiling a lariat. Three of the men were doing the same. He pointed to them and questioned the *yaquis* again. *"Saben que van ahora?"*

The men's eyes remained expressionless. Bowdon dismounted. "They savvy all right! Let's pick a couple of good posts. This trial's over!"

In Los Angeles, lynchings and vigilante hangings were both tourist attractions and social events. Steven had witnessed several and if formal trials had preceded the execution he had not heard about them. Once, when the hanging of a minor outlaw was announced for a time two hours later than the newspaper was scheduled to go to press, the editor earned the admiration of the entire community by publishing the event in accurate and lurid detail forty minutes before the execution took place. The doomed man's terror and the audience's enjoyment was made all the more exquisite when he was forced to stand and listen to a reading of the gruesome account of his own hanging.

Whatever mercy Steven may have felt for the pair at his feet was dissipated by a new tide of revulsion as he looked at them and envisioned their filthy bodies on top of Arlene. Hang them and be done with the whole rotten

339

business. There were a dozen stout rafter poles protruding from the sheds that would serve very well.

To Steven's surprise, Bowdon ordered the men dragged to the corral fence. There they were laid out face up with their feet toward the rails. Quickly the men lashed their ankles securely to the bases of the posts. Before Steven realized what was intended, lariat loops had been tightened around their necks and the free ends tossed up to the two riders. Ten feet of slack was left coiled on the ground. Bowden raised his revolver to signal and said to Steven. "You best back off some too. This kind of neck snapping can get a bit squirty!"

Steven saw Bowdon's finger begin to tighten on the trigger. In an instant he foresaw the horror about to happen. He heard Bowdon's revolver crash above him and the riders whoop at their mounts. The Henry repeater jumped to his shoulder. Its first slug tore the back off the head of the *yaqui* farthest from him. The second ripped into the skull behind the ear of the man at his feet. A split second later both bodies seemed to leap into the air as the horses reached the end of their tethers. Steven heard the inhuman groan and the sickening rending that followed as the heads parted from the bodies. Suddenly ill, he turned away and staggered to the fence.

He did not know how long he'd been standing with eyes closed and his body bathed in chill sweat when he heard someone move up close beside him. Bowdon's voice echoed both pity and scorn. "You know something, Lewis? Fer a young fellow whose wife was ruined by these son-of-a-bitching animals, it seems to me you hold a lot of pity fer greasers." He smirked and wagged his head. "Fer the life of me, I can't figure you out."

Steven fought down a dry heave and turned to face him. When he spoke, his voice was little more than a whisper. "Maybe you'll savvy, Bowdon, when I tell you that I'm half greaser." His voice grew stronger. "And maybe you'll savvy that even to a half-breed like me, bastards who can do what you've just done are worse than animals."

He spat out the words and dizziness overcame him. Grasping the top rail, he cradled his glistening forehead in the crook of his arm. As he did he caught sight of the nearest headless body twitching. A fit of nausea seized him and the men laughed as dry heaves convulsed him.

340

10 EARLY IN JUNE, on a warm afternoon, Steven sat with Francis Pioche on the veranda of Pioche's mansion. He was there to tell Pioche about the tragedy at Los Nidos.

"In the opinion of the doctors, Mrs. Lewis has been afflicted mentally by her experience. She and the child are with her parents in Los Angeles. Recently she has turned devoutly religious, which seems to help. Her life now is wrapped up in her studies and speaking selfishly that is best for me too. There's much to do. Doña Paula insisted on my being the trustee of the ranch even though I have, we have, a proprietary interest in the estate. Legally, I am accountable to Judge William Vance, an old friend of Don Emilio's, and of course, to you."

Pioche smiled blandly. "Very interesting. Very interesting. All at once now you have much responsibility for a young man of—how many years now? Twenty-four?"

Steven nodded. "In September, sir."

"So, my young friend, I hope you will not think me insensitive if I also express concern over the state of our business affairs? I gather the late Mr. Warden had concluded some transactions. Correct?"

"Yes, sir. We have twenty-two leases for apiaries and leases, with water contracts, on fifteen forty-acre parcels."

If the Frenchman was impressed, he gave no sign of it. "Who will replace Mr. Warden?"

"For the time being I will, sir."

"Perhaps now, dear Steven, that you have learned the folly of haste in matters of the heart you are ready to listen to mature counsel."

Steven nodded.

"Good. Then I suggest you engage a competent salesman. Save your energy for administration. I shall add another ten thousand to your account. Do you have a prospective sales person?"

"Yes, sir. There is a new man named Widney. He is five or six years older than I. I had thought about interesting him." Pioche frowned, apparently searching his memory. "What is Widney's first name? Could it be Robert?"

"Yes sir. Robert M. Do you know him?"

"*Oui*. I know of him. He read the law here. Also in Sacramento. I recall that he made an excellent impression on men of judgment. But he does not strike me as a candidate for land salesman."

The extent of the little Frenchman's knowledge never failed to disconcert Steven.

"He has opened a law office in Los Angeles, sir. But I think his first interest is real estate. In the past several months he's ridden over most of southern California. I have not met him formally, but I shall. The Hellmans are kindly disposed toward him."

Pioche inclined his head and pursed his lips. "*C'est bien. C'est bien.* By all means talk to him."

The steamer schedule allowed Steven only two days with his family. Again, it was a difficult visit, made more so by the hurt in his mother's eyes, his brother's studious indifference, and the avoidance of any reference to Arlene. Hardest of all to endure were the congratulations tendered on all sides for what was considered his heroic part in the extermination of the *Los Lobos* gang. The San Francisco newspapers had made much of the story.

Billy Ralston had treated him like a hero and had insisted on standing drinks for all at the Bank Exchange Bar. It was an uncomfortable experience. While most of the men took his reticence for becoming modesty, he knew his father suspected that more lay behind his reluctance to disclose details not reported in the press. Steven's evasive reply to the obvious question had been the same to everyone. "There was no way to positively identify the man. Apparently he had been in Mazatlán and Mexico City some years ago. His men were all *yaqui* Indians, Rock Wolves, they call themselves in Mexico. Even the Mexican government has a bounty on their heads."

He knew that while his parents would always deny the possibility that Goyo and El Lobo were one and the same, nonetheless, their lingering doubt could never be dispelled.

In Los Angeles again, Steven, made contact with Rob-

342

ert Widney. But Widney's reaction to his proposal was somewhat disappointing.

"I'm very flattered, Mr. Lewis. I know the Los Nidos *ranchitos*. I have already surveyed your development and given it a high rating. There is no doubt that I could make much money with you. But I do not want to commit myself to any one area.

"There is such variety of land in southern California. When its richness is discovered, people in the East will want to use it in many different ways. I am now acting as a consultant as well as a broker and will publish a journal called the *Real Estate Advertiser* to circulate throughout the East. I will solicit inquiries for certain types of land and attempt to supply it. You may be sure that I'll sell many parcels for you, unless, of course, you do decide on an exclusive agent."

Steven was so impressed with Widney that when he engaged Henry Vance, a cousin of Judge Vance, to head sales, he did so on a non-exclusive basis.

Henry Vance, a man in his forties, had been in land sales in Missouri for some years. Borrowing a page from Robert Widney's plan, he prepared a prospectus and had copies printed and mailed to his acquaintances back home. The response was immediate. By the first of September, Steven was able to report to Pioche a substantial number of leads.

In October, he moved Arlene and little Charlotte to a larger home on Fort Street where he hoped to resume a normal relationship, if indeed, he thought, it ever had been normal. The physical damage did not preclude a union. But Arlene made it clear that the thought of being entered by a man, any man, under any circumstances had become utterly repugnant.

"God, in His Divine Wisdom, often demands terrible sacrifices so that we may grow strong in spirit. Earthly pleasures are given to be taken away. I have grown from this ordeal, Steven, far beyond what I thought I could."

He smiled bitterly at the bleak prospect his marriage held for him when his need finally drove him to visit the best new house in town.

Steven found himself spending more and more time at Los Nidos. As trustee for Doña Paula and actual head of the ranch, he had to supervise its operation.

Anita Garcia y Perez, now seventeen, was, as Doña

Paula observed somewhat sadly, "a beautiful young lady when she isn't masquerading as a *vaquero*." Pedro Morales was devoted to her. "She knows how this rancho works. She is a better majordomo than I." When Anita was with Pedro, Steven was forced to agree that she was as effective on horseback working with the *caballada* as she was at the *casa grande* playing a gracious hostess.

Since Don Emilio's death, Doña Paula had gone into semi-retirement, preferring to leave most of the day-to-day decisions to Anita and to Gracia, who had mothered the girl since infancy. There was no filling the void left by the tragedy. But a very real happiness prevailed at the big ranch when Steven was there. Neighbors had taken to coming by more often. The Yorbas, Lugos, Bandinis, Serranos, Sepulvedas, Del Valles, members of all the great southern families, were frequent visitors. Some came out of friendship and concern. Some came to see the new land usage and to learn. By late fall most of them had accepted Steven not only as a member of the family but as its actual head.

Steven came to think of himself as an integral part of the rancho and his ties to the north hardly seemed to exist as a part of his present.

He was forcibly reminded when Will's letter arrived setting the date of his marriage to Mary O'Dwyer. Steven had promised his twin that he would be the best man and that he would bring Arlene and the baby to meet the family.

After a consulting the doctor, who found Arlene well able to travel, Steven booked passage to San Francisco. The fact of the actual departure date made Arlene retreat into deliberate vagueness. Steven reminded her of her promises, but she denied any clear recollection, indeed, seemed to have forgotten that her in-laws even existed.

"I cannot possibly go. I am not up to it. Neither is Charlotte. It's very dangerous for her to travel by ocean this time of year. The doctor will agree. And more than that, I'm far behind with my studies. There is so much to learn before I am fit to teach others and that is to be my life, a life of service."

Arlene resorted to hysterics when Steven threatened to take the child without her. Alarmed, he called the doctor, who placed her under sedation. On the fifteenth of December he sailed for San Francisco, alone.

Even in the midst of the wedding confusion, Steven found it impossible to rid himself of the nagging problem of Arlene, a problem in which the Lathrops had been no help at all.

However much he once resented his brother-in-law calling into question the legality of a union performed by a self-ordained minister, he now found himself grateful when Lambert Lee broached the subject: "In the name of God, Steve, you've got to get out of this mess. Even when you stood up with Will yesterday, you were somewhere else. This situation is preying on you. We all see it. Call me presumptuous, but I've half a notion to return to Los Angeles with you and confer on your behalf with Judge Vance. There are legal remedies for your difficulty. Also moral and ethical ones. You've got to find them before you are destroyed."

It was strange, Steven thought, but he would have jumped at the offer had it been made by almost any other person. "I appreciate the family's interest. I suppose it's been discussed?"

"It has. But only with your father and brother. If your mother dwells on it, she does so in silence. She does not confide in your sister or in me. But I'll wager it occupies much of her introspection. Really you must do something."

After a moment, Steven said, "I will. I'll talk with the judge when I return home."

As soon as he returned to Los Angeles, Steven arranged a meeting with Judge Vance. As he sat in the judge's outer office, Steven wondered at the restlessness he felt when he was in Los Angeles and the deep contentment that came over him whenever he was at the ranch. He sensed a profound rightness in it. In the midst of his introspection, Judge Vance loomed in the doorway and motioned him inside. "Sorry to keep you waiting, Steven." Indicating a chair, he returned to his own behind a formidable, carved oak desk. "Now then, lad, what are we discussing this morning?"

After a full review during which he kept virtually nothing from the judge, including the reason he had moved into the marriage so hastily, Steven spread his hands. "That's it. I'm at some sort of crossroads. I don't know which way to turn. There's no use denying it."

Judge Vance leaned back and clasped his long fingers across a belly surprisingly flat for his years.

"It's a familiar problem, Steven. You are not lost, my boy. Your brother-in-law was correct when he said there are legal remedies. But you need some emotional remedies too. Before we undertake any steps, have you been completely candid about your feeling for this marriage?"

"So far as I know, yes."

"When Cervantes talked about 'absence, that common cure of love' he was not talking about the sort of love I have known with Mrs. Vance for thirty-five years. If I thought you and Mrs. Lewis shared something like that, I'd urge you to stay with her through all adversity. But from your commendable candor I suspect your relationship was principally grounded on other important, forgive me, earthier emotions."

Steven nodded. "I am not looking for any easy excuses."

"Nor am I putting any in your mouth, my boy. Go on."

"I'm here with my guard down, Judge Vance, because I'm only certain of one thing. Whatever happened was at least half my fault."

Judge Vance laughed softly. "In someone else I might take that as a sign of spurious virtue. In your case it is the reaction of a responsible person. But it's not necessarily true. You were pursued, were you not? You haven't said so in precisely those words, but—"

Steven interrupted. "Let's just say that I was a willing victim."

Judge Vance nodded. "Most men are. You were in the hands of a somewhat older, very attractive, highly experienced woman who wanted you and who knew how to get you. I doubt that any single young man in your position could have resisted her.

"Also I have no doubt that her extraordinary needs drove her to exert those same wiles on poor Warden. That is not a cruel observation, Steven. But you were not dealing with what your church and the law consider a moral young woman."

Steven started to rise. "Look. If we have to drag Tom Warden back from the grave to witness her guilt, to hell with it. We'll let things ride."

Judge Vance smiled compassionately. "Easy, lad. Easy. We'll do no such thing. But I want to make certain that you carry no unjust burden of guilt if we decide to dissolve this marriage, which, by the way, was never legal in the eyes of the law or the church. You know that, don't you?"

Reassured, Steven settled back. "I've wondered about it."

"And now you hope I'm right. Is that it?"

"To be honest, yes."

Judge Vance plopped his big palms flat on the desk. "All right. Let's see what can be done. Obviously, we can't leave your daughter in the position of having been legally born out of wedlock. I will need testimony from the two attending physicians and one other. If they agree on the probable permanent nature of your wife's aberrations, we may be able to arrange a divorce with proper provisions for the child and your wife's expenses and so on. As to where this will leave you with your church in the event you wish to remarry," he shrugged, "I shall have to have a talk with your bishop."

When Steven grew concerned again, Judge Vance smiled reassuringly. "A discreet one, of course."

The settlement and dissolution of the marriage was arranged so quietly that several months passed before it became common knowledge in Los Angeles.

In San Francisco the news was greeted with vast relief by the family, including Doña Maria who had never considered them truly married anyway. Felicia wrote that Lambert had begun laying plans to introduce him to San Francisco ladies of acceptable social status. Both Felicia and Lambert were at pains to let him know that, as a divorced man, he would no longer have *carte blanche entré.*

Annoyed at the prospect of having to resist Lambert's maneuvering to reinstate him socially, he wrote to the family and to Francis Pioche delaying his promised visit several months because of difficulties in constructing the expanded irrigation system at Los Nidos.

By June first, 1869, Robert Widney's *Real Estate Advertiser* was able to report land sales of one hundred fifty thousand dollars with sales of two hundred thousand dollars a month predicted as soon as California began to feel the full impact of the completed transcontinental railroad. The joining of the Central Pacific and the Union Pacific Railroads had demolished the last barrier to the opening of the west. Few southern Californians understood this better than Judge William Vance and Steven Lewis.

The judge pushed a sheaf of land contracts across the desk to Steven and said, "When Banning gets his railroad finished we're going to see the beginning of the biggest migration since the Gold Rush. You have enough contracts now to more than carry your notes, Steven. Mind if I make a suggestion?"

"Certainly not."

"While there are still large parcels of distress acreage around, buy more land. And from here on out consider going back to your original plan of long-term leases on a minimum cash and maximum share crop basis with the Los Nidos Ranch Company furnishing water and seed and perhaps, in some cases, basic tools. Of course, your share of the percentages would increase with the services rendered. This tenant farmer idea is not new to Southerners. They may not like it. But the ones without capital or credit will settle for it. If they're good farmers, everyone will prosper. Be fair with them. If you are, they'll go along. But remember human nature too. Make them feel like partners, not tenants. Make their stiff-necked Southern pride work for you."

Steven outlined the plan in a long letter to Pioche, in which he did not credit Judge Vance with the concept. Pioche replied immediately and arranged for a new line of credit with Hellman's bank. By mid-July the company had purchased five thousand acres on the northwest boundary of San Diego County at two dollars an acre cash and had secured an option on another three thousand.

The engineer, Monteith, solved the water problem by using a new redwood stave and hoop pipe to transport it. Steven ordered enough for a half mile test run through John Lewis & Sons in San Francisco. The pipe was among the first freight transported from the harbor to Los Angeles on Banning's new Los Angeles-San Pedro Railroad.

Steven brought Doña Paula and Anita into the Bella Union as the senator's guests. In his private coach they made the gala inaugural trip with Banning from Los Angeles to the harbor and return and participated in the great barbecue and ball at the combination freight terminal and passenger station.

A late Indian summer, with dry, unusually gentle Santa Ana winds, expedited the work of expanding the irrigation projects. Steven found himself spending more and more time at Los Nidos. He seldom went to Los Angeles except for his monthly visits to little Charlotte, a duty made painful by Arlene's growing jealousy and overprotectiveness. As much as he loved the child, Steven was relieved when Arlene told him that she and her father had purchased land in Santa Monica canyon where they would establish a philosophical study colony.

In early November, Steven brought Pedro and a crew into *Nido Mejor* to begin the careful demolition of his former home. Anita, in her unconventional masculine riding habit, watched the first cart load of furniture began its journey down the precarious ditch road. Steven studied the expression on her face, then rode over and dismounted beside her.

"*Chica mia*, I'd rather share happier days with you. Why don't you stay with Doña Paula and learn how to make a dress?"

Anita looked at him sternly. "I know how to make a dress. And if you had watched the gentlemen at Señor Banning's fandango you would have seen that I also know how to wear one."

"I watched them, Chica. I watched them. And men who look at you that way are not gentlemen."

Anita grinned wickedly, "In that case, Señor Lewis, it is not very flattering to me that you consider yourself to be such a grand *caballero*."

She narrowly avoided an ungentlemanly swat. But she had made him laugh, a difficult thing to accomplish these past few months.

After Steven had shown the men how to pry the priceless redwood siding from the front of the house without damaging it, Anita moved beside him. "What will you do with all of this?"

He shrugged. "Store it for now. Then sell it, perhaps, to recover some of the money."

She winced as a hand-forged nail screeched loose from a stud. "Store it, Esteban. Someday you may wish to build another house."

The words were spoken innocently enough but something in her tone made Steven turn to look down at her. For a long moment he returned her deliberately ingenuous

349

gaze and it annoyed him that his own eyes were the first to waver.

"Mind your own business, *Chica*, or I may use those boards to build a *calabozo* just for you."

Later, at the dinner table, Steven was aware again that the now eighteen-year-old girl he called *Chica*, because it annoyed her, was much more woman than she appeared to be in her practical riding clothes. He wondered whether his hearing had tricked him. Had her retort, half spoken as she had turned away, really been, "If you were my jailer, it's possible I would like it."

In late June the test section of redwood pipe had been completed on the new agricultural subdivision and filled with water to swell it tight. For Steven, now twenty-six, and called, *"El Patrón,"* the burden of past troubles began to give way to a sense of well-being and accomplishment.

One great sadness marred the summer. Word reached Steven that Harry Morrison had died suddenly in Sacramento. He prepared to leave immediately to attend the funeral in San Francisco.

Anita, in a scooped-neck Mexican blouse and embroidered skirt, stood in the doorway to Steven's room. She was carrying his freshly laundered clothing that she insisted on taking to him herself.

"How long will you be gone, Esteban?"

He motioned her to bring the laundry over to a heavy cowhide *maleta*. "I don't know, *chica*. It depends on the steamer schedule. If I can't get one immediately, I'll take the stage."

The girl grimaced. "That is so difficult and so dirty. And much too slow."

Steven took the shirts from her and dropped them on top of the other clothing. Anita let out an anguished little cry. "You'll spoil them, clumsy." She pushed him aside gently and rearranged them.

A half smile tugged at the corners of Steven's mouth and there was an expression in his eyes that she had not seen before. A flush spread upward from the expanse of smooth tanned skin above the flattering curve of the low neckline. She retreated to the safety of indignation. "Why do I trouble to pack them so nicely? When you come back you'll just throw them in again."

Steven grinned agreeably. "That's right, *chica.*"

She stood her ground with her fists braced against her hips. "You are like a child. You need somebody to look after you. Every man does. So if you're smart, you'll ask your sister to pack for you."

Steven reached out, captured her head gently between his hands and pulled her close. It was the first he had touched her deliberately. The jet hair, parted in the middle and drawn back in a glistening knot low on her neck, felt silky and warm. The young flesh of her cheeks was petal soft against his palms.

"Do you know something, *chica*?" His hands dropped to her half-bare shoulders. "I've a mind to . . ." He broke off and released her. "Never mind what I've a mind to."

After the funeral and a sad visit with his family, Steven sent a note to Pioche asking for a meeting. Pioche was morose, distracted, and uninterested in the affairs of Los Angeles. Steven had been told that Pioche was under increasing pressure by both the Central Pacific Railroad's Big Four and his own partners to sell out his interests in the Placerville–Sacramento Valley Railroad and the San Francisco–San Jose Railroad. Similar pressure was being put on Billy Ralston in an effort to gain control of his steam navigation interests on the bay and rivers. Clearly, Stanford, Crocker, Huntington, and Hopkins were determined to dominate all transportation in the state.

Steven persisted in attempting a progress report. Pioche cut him off. "*Mon vieux,* it should be clear to you by now that so long as each new operation is profitable I shall make funds available. *C'est tout.*"

Steven left the three-story Stockton Street mansion, troubled not so much by the Frenchman's brusqueness as by something strange that he detected beneath it. This time there had been no unsettling personal overtures and none of the annoying petulance.

On the top deck of the *Goliath* that was taking him back to San Pedro, Steven's thoughts turned back to the night four and one half years ago when he had met the Lathrops. Thoughts of Arlene and her uninhibited performances in bed still excited him but there were other equally vivid, more painful ones: the frustration, the hurt, and the futility of their union.

He banished the ghosts of those times by deliberately

thinking about Anita. He was startled to find that he had whispered *"Chica"* aloud. He could see her now, in the doorway of his bedchamber, her arms loaded with his fresh shirts. He smiled as he remembered how she had tried to mask her embarrassment with indignation. He could feel again her silky hair beneath his fingers and could see again the serious little face and the huge, luminous eyes, half eager, half defiant. The vision made him laugh silently and he spoke her name again with great tenderness.

"*Chica, amorita.* I miss you. I'll be damned if you haven't grown very dear to me."

Judge Vance attended to the complicated matters with the church. The bishop had been understanding and eager to return to the fold a stray as promising as Steven Lewis. One week before Christmas, after signing an agreement that their children would be raised in the faith, Anita Garcia y Perez and Steven Eugene Lewis were married in the family chapel at El Rancho de los Nidos.

The impetus of Robert Widney's real-estate publication, in addition to the Eastern promotion efforts by both the Union Pacific and Central Pacific railroads, was starting to give Henry Vance more business than he could handle. Vance was hampered though by Steven's refusal to sell the land in fee simple. "Hell's bell's! If we could let them buy outright, I could make five times as many deals."

Since he was limiting Vance's income, Steven asked Widney if Vance could help sell the new land Widney had bought in the San Fernando Valley. A few months later, Vance's anxiety to earn more money was explained by the arrival of his wife, a woman twenty years younger than he, and their five-year-old son Thomas.

For a while Vance seemed content. Then, using money borrowed from his cousin, Judge Vance, he asked Steven if he could buy twenty acres outright to start an experimental lemon grove. Partly to repay the Judge, Steven agreed to one last exception to his policy and soon afterward, Vance moved his family to a modest prefabricated house. It was one of the first, sent by ship from Oregon.

It seemed to those around Henry Vance that each boat brought packs of literature to him from the United States Department of Agritulture. One communication particularly interested Steven; it described a new, seedless orange from Brazil that government horticulturists felt showed great promise. It was described as somewhat larger than the native Spanish or Mission orange, with a navel-like aperture at its apex.

Steven was excited by the possibilities in the new product but realized there would be a problem in the lease-partnership agreements. Since they did not own the land, farmers would be reluctant to invest in orchards that took years to bring to maturity. This meant that if orchards were to be set out in large numbers, they would have to be undertaken by the Los Nidos Ranch Company itself.

Steven began to study the situation with Pedro. Together they rode the highlands above the fog belt that were usually free of killing frosts. In less than two weeks they had staked out several likely eighty-acre parcels.

On September 30, 1871, Alicia Paula Maria Lewis was born at El Rancho de los Nidos. In a matter of hours the *casa grande* was filled with more joy than it had known since the arival of Anita herself.

Within days, Anita was up and around the house and grounds. In less than a month, to Steven's dismay and to the amusement of Gracia and her *cocineras*, Anita was astride a horse again, eager to be shown the new work.

In October, Steven persuaded his mother and father to come south for the holidays. John Lewis was eager to see his son's new family and wanted to catch up with the market in the south. He and Doña Maria arrived late on the afternoon of October twenty-third and went to Pico House, the former governor's elegant new eighty-room hotel. In addition to a fine restaurant and bar, it was the first hotel to offer inside plumbing with hot and cold water piped to the rooms.

Steven put an arm around his mother, saw his parents registered, and conducted them to their second-floor room. A short time later, as he freshened for dinner in his adjoining room, he heard the sound of horsemen and loud voices. Below, he saw a lighted, heavily guarded hack being driven westward toward Spring Street. In the lantern glow he could see that it was surrounded by pigtailed Chinese in their loose black trousers and jackets. He raised the heavy sash window to get a better view and saw his father peering from the adjoining window.

353

"What's going on, Steven?"

"I don't know. Let's go down and find out." Then Steven caught sight of Sheriff Frank Burns and his chief deputy coming out of the Lafayette Hotel with City Marshal Bill Warren. They were moving quickly toward the center of the disturbance.

In their haste to reach the staircase, Steven and his father nearly collided in the hall. On the street they were caught up in the surge of curious citizens hurrying toward the corner to follow the progress of the surrounded hack that was now moving along the south side of the Plaza.

In the crowd Steven saw Jesse Yarnell, one of the men who had just founded a newspaper called the *Los Angeles Evening Express*. Motioning to his father to follow, he forced his way across the street and caught up with him. "What's the trouble, Jesse?"

"They're bringing that Chinese slave girl back from Santa Barbara, the one Wong Lee's Chinamen charged with stealing jewelry."

A man behind Steven spoke up. "She belongs to Lum Fong's Chinaboys. They been claiming they'll take her back by force."

By the time the carriage reached the southwest corner of the plaza the local law-enforcement men had converged on it with rifles and drawn pistols and the Chinese had begun to disperse. Most of them were retreating toward the old Corónel adobe, the central structure in the labrynthine slums, known locally as Nigger Alley. Steven and his father returned to Pico House just as the carriage turned the corner on Spring Street.

They were about to order dinner when a man burst into the dining room shouting for Judge Widney. "If anybody knows where he is, get him! Those 'slants' just shot Jesus Bilderrain and Bob Thompson in Nigger Alley. Thompson's dead and the boys are fixing to lynch every chink in town. Burns, Warren, nobody can stop them."

By the time Steven and his father reached the street, hundreds of men were converging on the plaza. All were armed. Many were carrying ropes. In a matter of minutes every hitching post and rail in that area was jammed with mounts abandoned by their owners. Above the angry clamor some shots were heard. Sporadic at first, the firing soon turned into a barrage.

John Lewis grasped his son's arm. "This crowd's losing

its head, Steve. Let's keep back. Pretty quick they'll be shooting at each other. I've seen it happen before."

Steven dismissed the advice. Followed by his father, he had managed to move about halfway across the Plaza when a shout went up. Moments later several small groups of men, each dragging a terrified Chinese by his pigtail, began clubbing their way back through the crowd.

"Get out of the way, boys. We're going to start hanging the slant-eyed bastards." The cry was taken up by the onlookers, who began clearing a corridor. Soon, well over a thousand men and boys were screaming for a mass lynching. Beside Steven a man shouted, "Here he comes." Turning to look back, Steven saw Robert Widney's tall, powerful figure forcing a way through the crowd. In his wake were several members of the Law and Order Party. All were armed.

Steven pushed in behind Widney. Sheriff Burns and four deputies with guns drawn were retreating slowly as they shouted orders to disperse. The hysterical crowd ignored them.

Steven could hear Widney offering the lawmen the services of his civilian group. At the same time, Robert Widney's younger brother, William, forced his way through followed by a man named John Lazzarevich and a half dozen more armed members of the Law and Order Party. The younger Widney recognized Steven and shouted. "Steve? Are you armed?"

"No. My gun's at the hotel."

William Widney thrust a Colt Navy revolver into his hand. "Come on. Help us break this up."

Ignoring his father's warning, Steven disappeared into the crowd. The worst of the shooting had stopped but scattered fire continued to come from the north side of the low compound where a new mob was now intent upon a mass lynching. Behind him somebody yelled, "They're stringing up the first ones at Slaney's Shoe Store!"

There was a moment of uncertainty, then the more timid turned back and began running toward the intersection of Commercial and Los Angeles Street. Steven estimated that half the town of six thousand had gathered. Several times each minute small bands of shouting men dragged shrieking Chinese to the lynching sites. Somewhere off to the side, Steven could hear Sheriff Frank

Burns shouting, "It's too late to help those. Just keep them from taking any more."

Steven was beside Captain Cameron Thom and Sam Caswell. Behind them was the principal access to Nigger Alley. Captain Thom took up a position with his back to the opening. His new Winchester repeating carbine was leveled at the crowd. He motioned Steven in beside him. On the far side of the plaza an ugly cheer went up each time another writhing Chinese was hoisted from the awning braces at Slaney's store or from the gate post at John Goller's Wagon Shop. Every place that could accommodate a mob became a killing ground and every support that would hold a body became a gallows. In the flickering lantern light the contorted faces reflected mass hysteria bordering on madness. Hoarse voices were demanding the life of every last one of the one hundred seventy-five Chinese men, women, and children in Los Angeles. Steven guessed that a score were already dead or dying. The mob had no single ringleader. In each group at each possible access to the Chinese quarter smaller mobs formed around the loudest of the rabble rousers. The leader of the group confronting them now was the known troublemaker, Jack Pollard, whose chief delight was testing the courage of newcomers at Buffum's Saloon.

Pollard, mean drunk and flanked by his gang of sycophants, confronted Captain Thom. "We got no fuss with you, Cap. When chinks shoot down decent men and the law won't do nothing about it, then it's time we learned them." Pollard was seconded by a shout of agreement but the clamor subsided when a familiar voice boomed behind them. Judge Widney, followed by his brother, came pushing through and motioned Steven to follow. They held drawn revolvers. The judge shoved some bystanders aside and faced Pollard. Those nearest began edging away from the possible line of fire.

"Stand where you are. All of you!" Widney's voice was calm but clearly audible for fifty feet around. "Pollard, I've never used a pistol to take a man's life. But I promise you, the first one who tries to go into Nigger Alley to get another Chinaman is going to die. What's been done in this town tonight is the worst disgrace ever to happen here. And every one of you standing here is guilty of aiding and abetting it. You are under arrest, Pollard. Take his gun, Steve."

Steven moved to obey. Pollard's fingers locked around the grip and began to tremble.

The judge raised his pistol. "Don't try it, Pollard."

Steven, hoping his knotted gut wouldn't betray him, took the weapon and stuck it under his belt.

After that, Pollard's men were the first to turn away. Others followed on their heel. It was past midnight when the last of the ringleaders had been jailed and the corpses cut down. Twenty Chinese had been lynched at John Goller's Wagon Shop. Nineteen had strangled on gallows improvised in front of William Slaney's Shoe Store. Four more had died suspended from the stakes of a freight wagon on Fort Street. The next morning three more bodies, one a badly mutilated female Chinese, were found dumped in the *zanja* that still supplied most of the Los Angeles city water.

John Lewis, helpless and unable to stop his son, had returned to Pico House. Steven had come in for a few minutes shortly after three in the morning. His clothing was dirty and torn from working with the Widneys, Frank Burns and Bill Warren, and their men. Burns had sworn him in as a deputy on the spot and charged him with protecting the remaining Chinese. Now, over coffee and brandy, Steven and his father listened as eyewitness fragments were fitted together into a picture of unprecedented mob brutality.

Sheriff J. Frank Burns and his men had done what they could but everyone agreed that Judge Robert Widney and his Law and Order Party were the force that had turned the tide. The shoe merchant, William Slaney, was toasted as a hero. Even though the mob had used his iron awning support as gibbets, Slaney himself had saved the lives of his own Chinese employees and their families by locking them in his storeroom and defying the lynchers with a shotgun.

Some newspaper accounts of the Los Angeles Massacre were so incomplete they amounted to distortions. Others were deliberately slanted to discredit Los Angeles and leave the city in the position of sharing with other cities around the country equally deplorable records of mob violence.

Forty-six Chinese had died. Nearly one hundred Caucasian ringleaders had been taken to jail. Of these only a dozen were being held. The solid, law-abiding segment of citizenry was confident that justice would be done and Los Angeles would redeem itself. Their optimism was based on the foregone conclusion that the men indicted would be tried before Judge Robert Widney.

John and Maria Lewis' visit to Los Nidos was marred only briefly by the mob violence in Los Angeles. As Steven had anticipated, Doña Paula and his mother were in immediate rapport. Anita was embraced as a daughter and the child as an "angel." He could not remember ever having seen his mother so happy and animated. As for Doña Paula, the visit had a miraculous effect. For the first time since the days with his grandfather, Steven experienced a keen sense of family. He was relieved that his parents had resigned themselves to his commitment to the southland.

Shortly after the beginning of the new year, Steven escorted his mother and father to Los Angeles and saw them safely aboard the steamer for San Francisco. Before returning to Los Nidos the following morning, he stopped by Judge Vance's home to pick up some books and pamphlets newly arrived from the East.

The judge handed Steven a book by a Charles Loring Brace.

"Widney's been accused of being too optimistic in his *Advertiser*, but compared to this man, who was here two years ago, for only one week mind you, Robert's an incurable pessimist."

Steven opened the book to the foreword and found himself laughing. "Why he uses the Holy Bible to prove that southern California is the New Palestine. According to this, we've got everything from mustard to Moses with the hot springs of Tiberius thrown in."

The Judge snorted. "Sodom and Gomorrah maybe. But the Holy Land, never." The judge thrust another book at him. "And try this one. The eminent Dr. Edwards, whoever he is, credits our 'salubrious ozone' with curative properties that even our Lord Jesus didn't have."

Disbelief spread across Steven's face as he read aloud: "—and also incipient phthisis, tuberculosis, liver disease, constipation, enlarged glands, scrofulus infections, scarlet fever, diphtheria, kidney malfunctions, jaundice, and most female disturbances." He shook his head. "It is a bit far-fetched, all right."

"Far-fetched? Southern California has a clear-cut case

of defamation of character chargeable to these boomers. Sooner or later we're going to have to do something to counteract this, Steven, or these rascals will turn us into the world's largest sanitarium and asylum."

The optimism of the land boomers was infectious, but it was predicated on the completion of a railroad down the San Joaquin Valley from San Francisco to Los Angeles, a difficult engineering feat, not due for at least five years. Immigrants found their way south by steamer and stage-coach but they were not arriving in the great numbers predicted.

On the ride back to the ranch, Steven reflected on the need to temper optimism with caution.

In early April, Steven saw Judge Vance again to show him a letter from Pioche. Pioche had written:

> I watch with apprehension the increasing imbalance between your credits and debits. I fear you have undertaken more than you can manage. Or perhaps, having again assumed the responsibilities of a family, you find yourself without sufficient energy to devote to my interests. I will not be reassured until you present me with a practical plan for reconciling this disparity between receipts and disbursements. Meanwhile I urge you not to commit my credit to more acquisitions and have so advised Messrs Temple and Hellman of my wishes in this regard.

Judge Vance studied the letter, then laid it aside. "You've got to do what Widney suggests, sell them when they get off the trains before they get switched into the Sacramento and San Joaquin valleys. We're getting the dregs down here now. You've got to sell them on the idea of coming straight south to take up a going thing. Think about sending Henry up to San Fransisco to open a land office there."

The solution was obvious and Steven damned himself for not having thought of it. But he did not want to send Henry Vance to San Francisco immediately. "I have to talk with Pioche myself anyway. Let's not bother Henry now. I'll stay up there a few days longer and see what the prospects are."

He arrived in San Francisco on the last day of April, surprised his family, and sent a note requesting a visit with Pioche. For the second time in their association the Frenchman sent word that he was indisposed and would be unable to confer for several days.

Steven spent a day visiting land offices along Market Street. He found a firm advertising San Bernardino and Los Angeles land. When he asked about it, the clerk was vague. Steven discovered the vagueness was due to the man's pretense of not knowing the location of the holdings because he wanted to divert sales to land in the north near San Jose.

The time had been well spent. That evening, with his father, his twin, and his brother-in-law, Steven outlined a plan whereby John Lewis and Sons could diversify and open a land office exclusively representing the Los Nidos leases. Fearful that Pioche would summon him before the plan could be committed to paper, Steven sat up late with Lambert drawing up a prospectus.

He was in the office ahead of everyone else the next morning to review the plans. At a quarter of eight his father burst in. "Steve! Steven! Have you heard? Pioche is dead! He killed himself less than an hour ago."

Without waiting to hear more, Steven charged past his father, raced to the corner, and ran westward three blocks to Stockton Street. At the three-story mansion a crowd had already gathered around the steps. Two marshals were keeping the entrance clear. Steven recognized a surrey belonging to Pioche's personal physician whom he had met on several occasions.

Questions produced a variety of rumors ranging from a heart seizure to a lurid murder. Someone said the valet had killed him. Another said a jealous companion had stabbed him.

Shocked at losing his benefactor and filled with apprehension over the possible consequences, Steven was about to leave when Louis Reiff appeared at the doorway escorted by two men. Steven tried to force his way close enough to question the valet but was stopped by a policeman. Then J. B. Bayerque appeared. As Pioche's partner reached the bottom of the stairs, Steven shouldered through him.

"Mister Bayerque, I'm Steven Lewis. We've only met once briefly, but—"

Bayerque cut him off without stopping. "I know you, Lewis. Glad you're here. You may have to testify at the coroner's inquest. We'll be in touch with you."

Steven left the Stockton Street mansion as the black morgue van arrived and made his way back to the John Lewis & Sons offices. His father, flanked by Will and Lambert, listened with deep concern to the news that he might have to appear as a witness. Steven knew that his brother-in-law was struggling to resist saying, "I told you so." Instead, Lambert paced the office, thinking aloud. "There is no earthly reason why Steven should have to appear. We all know where he was when the man killed himself and there's little doubt that it was a suicide. That much seems clear.

"The point of the matter is this. The motives behind Pioche's suicide, which I suspect were purely personal, could be messy. Few people know of Steven's *business* association with Francis Pioche." Lambert Lee deliberately emphasized the word. "But if he's forced to take the stand at the inquest and reveal that the business connection also included some social obligations, his soirées and so forth, then," he threw up his long hands, "God alone knows what may come out. Never mind that Steven knows nothing of Pioche's private life. He might very well suffer guilt-by-association with those who did."

John Lewis rose suddenly and reached for his hat. "They're not going to call Steve. I don't give a goddamn who I have to buy off. He had no connection with Pioche's private affairs and he's not going to be made a party to a Roman circus."

At the door, Lambert laid a hand on his arm. "Where are you going to start, John?" John angled past him. "I'm going to start where the power is, with Billy Ralston."

A half hour later Steven edged through the crowd at the Bank Exchange Bar and joined his father at Ralston's table. Billy Ralston, profoundly unhappy, rose to greet him. "Sit down, Steven. And don't worry about being called to testify. That will be taken care of. There's little doubt that whatever drove Francis to take his own life was a personal matter, if he *did* take his own life."

Ralston ordered a coffee for Steven and continued. "I do not have full information about Pioche's dealings, of course. There may have been pressures on him that we

361

don't know about. But as far as his financial situation in California is concerned, we can rule out money troubles. Pioche and Bayerque is one of the most solvent financial houses in the state and I do not except my own Bank of California."

Billy Ralston worried the heavy links of his gold watch chain. "I simply don't understand it. He was an impeccable business man. He was that above all, no matter what else he may have been called by lesser men. I personally have heard Francis express himself on the subject of suicide. He did so at Bleyer's funeral and at Wexler's, when they checked out of the game after the Silver Queen stock mess. He called suicide 'cowardly and unchristian.' He said a man should fight life's battles, that he has no right to kill himself."

Ralston exhaled heavily. "I'm a man who deals in facts. I can accept a proven one. But I still find it hard to believe that Francis Pioche would blow his own brains out." He looked across at Steven. "In any case, you can rest easy, Steve. I don't think Pioche has any family in this country. But nonetheless I intend to see that the newspapers don't make a sensational thing of this. I would like Francis remembered in this city for his contributions to it, particularly to the colleges of medicine and law and to the museum and the theater. Francis Pioche was the real successor to Leidesdorff, no matter how much I may blow about what I've done."

Steven smiled at the banker's oblique modesty, for he was certain that no single man had done more for San Francisco than William Ralston.

Ralston rose to return to the bank. "If this leaves you in a bind down south, Steve, let me know. Perhaps we can help tide you over there, too."

Later, at his father's office, Steven listened and was grateful for the family counsel. He had wanted to go his own way, to be a loner, but it was good now to have them on his side. He was particularly grateful to Lambert, who was reasoning with his unusual impersonal clarity.

"One thing you can expect now, Steven, is a power struggle to see who takes over Pioche's assets. The paper he holds on Los Nidos may be a very small factor. But Bayerque, or whoever comes out on top, will be just as greedy to acquire it. Do you have an idea how much your obligation is?"

362

Steven reached for a folded paper tucked away in an inside pocket. "About eighteen thousand dollars."

His father settled back, relieved. "Not as much as I thought it would be."

Steven smiled ruefully. "It's about half as much as it would have been if I'd seen Pioche before he died."

Lambert settled on the edge of a chair. "Work up an exact statement. It may be a blessing that most of us up here have little faith in southern California. Pioche's successors might be willing to make an accommodation on those debts." John Lewis agreed.

"And Billy will not be discommoded by eighteen thousand, if you need to refinance with him."

But what troubled Steven the most was not the immediate cash. What he needed was the continuing enthusiasm and willingness to go along that Pioche had displayed. Ralston could not be expected to share that. But perhaps Isaias Hellman would.

In Los Angeles again, Judge Vance listened while Steven recounted the Pioche tragedy and analyzed his own position: ". . . that's why I feel I'd be better off trying to work something out with the Hellmans. They know the land and they know me. What I do would be important to them. To Billy Ralston I'd be little more than a favor to my father."

"Hellman's your man, Steven. Your head's on straight. But there are times when I'm not so sure about Ralston's. He's keeping some very questionable company when he partners with that Kentucky scamp, Asbury Harpending."

Steven had forgotten about the flamboyant young soldier of fortune. "I remember the name all right, but that's all."

Judge Vance grinned and rubbed his nose. "Well, he's the lad who formed the private army and damn near got away with a plan to steal the whole west coast and hand it over to the Confederacy. He got put in Alcatraz for that."

Steven laughed. "They accused my father's good friend, Will Chard, of trying to steal California from Mexico. He was put in prison too, but now he's one of the most respected ranchers in the Sacramento Valley. And look at poor old Sutter. He plotted against everybody and wound up being honored by them all. I'm not sure a little insurrection counts much against a man in California."

"It didn't used to, son. But today it's a different game."

Steven's examination of his financial position proved that income from leases and the ranch's share of profits from partnerships fell short of covering overhead and note obligations. Enough new leases to cover the discrepancy could not be negotiated immediately. Steven would have to borrow or some land would have to be sold. He agreed with Judge Vance that a decision to spin off acreage should be kept as quiet as possible.

"Have a confidential talk with Robert Widney. He'll understand your situation. Set a bargain price on some good acreage and he'll probably see you out of trouble."

Widney was sympathetic but not helpful. "I would undertake the purchase myself, Steve, but I'm committed heavily in the San Fernando Valley. You need cash and I doubt that any of my prospects would be in a position to do you much good. But I'll be glad to speak with Isaias and see what he can do."

Hellman was also sympathetic but not interested in a small parcel of a few thousand acres. The only way Steven could get his hands on enough cash to satisfy the Pioche notes would be to mortgage the entire Los Nidos holding to the new Temple-Hellman bank. He was unwilling to do that even if Doña Paula agreed.

He could see nothing but trouble from the men who took over from the dead financier. If they demanded an immediate liquidation, it could mean the passing of Los Nidos from his control. Another down-turn in the southland's economy could have the same result if he was beholden to John Temple or Isaias Hellman or for that matter, even Billy Ralston, for all of his outward show of benevolence. After a pride-damaging reappraisal of his situation, he decided to seek help from his father.

Steven could imagine his father sitting at his big roller-top desk examining the projections he had set down and agreeing with them. But he knew that his father would not break the promise that Lewis & Sons would not lend him any money to buy land south of the Tehachapi mountains. So while he tried to give the request the appearance of a routine business proposal, it was actually a request for a personal loan. He could only hope that his father wasn't cash short because of recent purchases of Comstock shares as an expression of confidence in Billy Ralston.

Several anxious weeks of waiting passed before the steamer brought word from San Francisco. Two letters arrived. A brief but friendly note confirmed his father's cash short position. A longer letter from his brother-in-law was far more encouraging.

Lambert's business associate, Moses Berwin, had been considering the purchase of good agricultural land in the southern part of the state against the day when the population boom would materialize. On a long-term investment basis, he was offering six dollars an acre for the three thousand acres of El Rancho de Los Nidos land.

By mid-July, somewhat apprehensive because Moses Berwin had not been able to come south to see the land, Steven had Judge Vance attend to the final details of the sale and to the transfer of the eighteen thousand dollars to the late Francis Pioche's executors in return for a release from all obligations to the financier's estate plus a covenant not to sue.

As the year 1872 neared its end, Steven Lewis had good cause to thank God a thousand times that he was not beholden to the bankers. There was grave concern over the failure of the completion of the Central Pacific Railroad to San Francisco to produce a boom and mounting anger over the high-handed tactics of the Big Four. In spite of the fact that they held title to millions of acres of Federally deeded land, the railroad was blackmailing important farming centers along the San Joaquin Valley into donating land and pledging bond issues to pay for the construction of depots and rail yards. Communities that refused would be by-passed and left without means of getting their produce to the major markets.

The presentiment of trouble spread over the entire country. The Union Pacific's involvement in the Credit Mobilier scandal had repercussions that reached all the way to Congress. Speaker of the House James G. Blaine had ordered an inquiry.

As a result, the expulsion of Congressman Oakes Ames of Massachusetts and James Brooks of New York, who was also a government director of the railroad, was recommended. The report named several Congressmen and demanded the impeachment of the Vice President.

In the end the cynics were right. The two Congressmen

were merely reprimanded and the impeachment proceedings against Colfax were dropped.

To offset this, San Francisco morale received a big boost from the new Clay Street tram line. Suddenly the steepest hillside lots became the most desirable.

Steven managed to keep the development going along at Los Nidos and continued to send cautiously optimistic reports north to his family. He was concerned because land values had not risen as quickly as predicted and as grateful as he was, he could not rid himself of regret over the need to dispose of acreage. A dozen times Anita had heard him say, "I'll buy that land back one day or die trying!"

Twice during the first half of the year Steven and Anita thought they were to have an addition to their family. Gracia blamed the false pregnancies on too much horseback riding. *"Tu tienes el corazón del vaquero!"* she would say when she saw Anita going off to ride with Steven and Pedro.

Late in the summer, reports began reaching the Pacific Coast that a number of banks in the East were closing their doors. Steven's anxiety over the family's interests brought reassuring letters from Will and from Lambert. "The Bank of California is prospering as never before." They said, "Now it virtually dominates the Comstock mines and the stamp mills."

Then on the twentieth of September the transcontinental telegraph flashed the news that the New York Clearing House was closing its doors for ten days. Panic spread across the nation and gripped California. By the end of the year a dozen Los Nidos leases were in default. Cash from the partnership crops dwindled and dried up altogether. Steven had to slow down work on the subdivisions to conserve cash. For the time being, he would trim and retrench and produce working capital, if possible, through resale of the foreclosed parcels.

A score of times Steven recalled his father's gloomy assessment of the southern part of the state. He could not deny that when times were poor in other parts of the country they were worse in the southland. For the first time, he found the bright flame of faith in his dream beginning to flicker. He could only hope that San Francisco's banks, heavily involved in the Comstock's precious metals, would remain solvent.

11

PORTLY, HEAVILY BONED MERCHANT Moses Berwin, president of San Francisco's Congregation Emanuel, left the temple fifteen minutes later than he had intended. He set out on foot for the Dupont Street offices of his wholesale grocery business, the Golden West Processors. Half running, sometimes skipping with a curious grace, Berwin hurried along and was annoyed that in the seven years of his association with the punctual Lambert Lee this would be the first time that he was late.

In the outer office, before he could attempt an unaccustomed apology, Lambert greeted him with a placating hand upraised. "I was late too, Moses. I stopped to check another rumor that Stanford and Huntington and Hopkins are selling the Central Pacific from under Crocker."

Berwin, puffing a bit, showed his new corporate counsel into his office. Indicating a chair, he walked around his own cluttered desk and sat down. "When Charlie Crocker said he'd trade his interest in the Central Pacific for a clean shirt, believe me, it would have been safer to take the shirt instead of personal notes from his partners." Berwin laughed. "So why am I feeling sorry? Crocker's made four million dollars on construction profits alone. And I'll tell you something else, Lambert, he's the only man in the country who knows how to build a railroad through the mountains. When they start to build north from Redding, Sam Montague will need Charlie again. Anybody else will go broke trying to drive crews through the Siskiyous. You'll see."

His mood sobered. "But we have troubles of our own." He picked up a letter and handed it across the desk. "It's from your father-in-law's friend, Will Chard, at Tehama. Read it."

After Lambert had scanned the letter, Berwin's eyes flashed with indignation. "Would you believe it? In a free country? Would you believe the nerve of those *gonovim?*

367

Those thieves?" He retrieved the letter, searched out a paragraph and read aloud.

> The only way the railroad can set realistic freight rates for its customers in the Sacramento Valley is to have as thorough an understanding of production costs for your various field crops as we have of their marketing costs. Consequently we are asking our division freight agent to call on each agricultural shipper so that he may go over your books first hand and give you the benefit of our experience.

He slammed the letter down. "Thieves! Damned, miserable thieves." Berwin punctuated each epithet with a hard fist. ". . . . the benefit of our experience! Do you know, Lambert, that they even asked to see *my* books? Would you believe that?"

Lambert smiled. "It doesn't surprise me. They asked to see our books too, so they can offer what they call a 'fair price' for our two freight boats."

"I know. Yesterday I saw Stanford at Bancroft's book store. Such a bad trader, that man. Huntington should keep him quiet." He paused. "I want to talk about that offer, Lambert. Already you and John have sold the long overland freight lines. What's left?"

"We still have the grain warehouses and the short freight lines from Red Bluff and Redding into Shasta, Whiskey Town, and Trinity mines."

Berwin's eyes narrowed. "Tell me. Do you think John would sell his boats?" Lambert considered briefly. "I don't know. When it looked like Congress would give the entire San Francisco waterfront franchise to the Central Pacific we thought we'd have to. But we're all right for now."

Berwin seemed relieved. "Lambert, there isn't a damned thing anybody can do to help Chard or Tyler or Thomas or Wilson or Kimball and the other ranchers up in the Sacramento Valley. So long as they have to ship by rail, they're going to pay with blood. Those monopolist bandits squeeze and leave men like Chard just enough to stay alive. Even me. They do it to me. From day to day I never know what I'm going to pay to get produce down here. The reason I want to talk is to find out if you think John will sign a two-year shipping contract with Golden West at the present rates? If he will, I'll guarantee that everything I buy in the valleys will be shipped here on your boats. What do you think?"

A long silence ensued. Lambert Lee knew that the man opposite him understood the alternatives. The mere rumor of such a contract, if noised around Montgomery Street, would place John Lewis & Sons in a more favorable bargaining position with the Big Four. If an improved offer should be refused, it was inevitable that the railroad would undercut the competitors' rate, thereby leaving John Lewis & Sons and Golden West Provisioners caught in an unfavorable contract. Eventually competition would force the Lewis rates down to impossible levels and Berwin would be obliged to seek a release and ship with the Central Pacific to maintain his own competitive position.

The proposal puzzled Lambert. He prided himself on his ability to see through obscure tactics and he was certain that Moses Berwin was thinking well beyond the immediate consequences. He always did. Whatever they were made Lambert wary. "Moses, let's dispense with obvious answers. Why do you want John Lewis and Sons to go out of business?"

Berwin didn't hesitate. "Because, Lambert, John Lewis is my friend. Things are stirring that could break his company. When men like Newhall, Ralston, and poor Francis Pioche sell their railroads and steamship lines to the Central Pacific," he gestured in annoyance, "or the Southern Pacific or whatever they call their railroad today, then you have no one to stand with you to fight them. John is fifty-four now. If he gets out at his price he can live very well for the rest of his days. The longer he waits the lower the price will be. He's got to think of himself. He shouldn't worry about the twins. The foundry business has a great future. If Will had a choice, he would go to work for his father-in-law. He's as much as told me so. And Steven is on his own."

Lambert waited expectantly as Moses Berwin frowned and seemed to gather his thoughts. "So now I'll tell you what I'm up to, Lambert. But first, if you wouldn't mind, I've got a personal question. How big a stockholder is John in the Bank of California? Would he get hurt if Billy got hurt?"

Lambert knew the question was not as ingenuous as it sounded. He hedged his reply. "If you mean would he get hurt like Ralston got hurt when Sharon touted him off

Consolidated Virginia, yes. He'd get hurt for well over a hundred thousand. That's a lot for John. Why?"

"We'll get to 'why' in a minute. How close is John to D. O. Mills?"

"Mills is president of the Bank of California. He and John are original stockholders."

Berwin verged on impatience. "This I know, Lambert. But are they close otherwise? Do they drink together or womanize?"

Lambert frowned. "If you mean do they talk off the record, no. You know John. He's not a social man. He doesn't inspire confidences. Look, Moses, what in hell are you driving at? Come out with it. Please."

Moses Berwin opened his arms. "All right. All right. I'll come out. I was hoping maybe you and John had heard the talk, then I wouldn't be spreading rumors. God forgive me if I'm wrong."

Alerted, Lambert leaned forward as though unconsciously bracing himself against an impact. "What rumor, Moses?"

"That Mills is forcing Billy to buy him out. He wants out of the Bank of California before it's too late."

Lambert settled back, remembering the long list of men who had lacked the courage and vision to play in Ralston's league. He smiled with relief. "Moses, how many times have we attended funerals for Billy only to find out that the corpus delicti has turned the predicted disaster into another fortune and he's gone for a swim in the bay?"

Berwin agreed. "I know. I know. I'm not exactly sitting shiva, Lambert. A professional mourner I'm not. But always in those times Billy had a mountain of Comstock ore to back him up. It's different now. They say he's tearing scrap paper into little bitty pieces again. That's a bad sign. He only does it when he's got deep trouble. Everybody on the street knows that. It's how Billy tips his hand." The merchant nodded, hoping that he was wrong. "Sure, he's got assets, the New Montgomery Street Real Estate Company," a thought struck Berwin and he threw up his hands in horror, "with that mad man Asbury Harpending for a partner. And he's got the woolen mills and the carriage company. Good businesses, maybe. But he doesn't have a mountain of gold and silver—and he needs one just to keep up that nice cozy little Belmont place of his, a nice little country house with rooms for a hundred guests yet, and solid marble stables. And now, God help him, the Palace Hotel. Two years he's been building it and no roof yet. Do you know what it will cost? Give or take a few hundred thousand? It will cost five million."

Berwin closed his eyes and groaned. "Five hydraulic elevators. Eight hundred rooms. Eight hundred toilets. Four hundred and thirty-seven bathtubs. Thirty thousand special dishes."

Berwin paused for breath and reached for a paper at the side of his desk. "Personally, Lambert, I'm not complaining. This is Golden West's bid to supply the kitchens. And I'll get the business but believe me, it will be C.O.D."

Lambert frowned. "Mills doesn't make many mistakes. I admit that, Moses."

Berwin stifled a small belch. "Look, Lambert. A deal is only good when everybody makes out. It's only a matter of time, two years, three years, before the railroad puts the squeeze on John. They can bleed him and force him to sell at their price. Also they'll squeeze me because I can't figure freight costs for my goods. I need two years to get my packing plants built near the crops so I don't have to ship perishables so far. What I want John to do is make a contract with me, at today's top rates. If he does that, I'll have a guaranteed freight cost for the two years I need and he'll have another asset worth a quarter of a million dollars that he can use to boost the price of his business to the Central Pacific. They're still dickering, aren't they?"

Lambert nodded. "Stanford talked to John again the other day."

"Good. Good for everybody. Especially for you, Lambert. For you I've got some very exciting plans."

Moses Berwin was one of the few who anticipated the railroads' stranglehold on the economy. Lambert stated the case clearly. "It's still cheaper to ship fabricated and processed goods around the Horn from the east coast than it is to ship overland by rail. And no doubt, when we're ready to ship canned goods down here to the city, the railroad will invent a new higher rate for that, too."

Berwin's concept of distributing by growing and packing in close proximity to major markets was extremely profitable. Berwin had used John Lewis to good advantage to buy the time he needed to establish his packing plants and, as Berwin predicted, John prospered. In the fall of 1874, independent at last, and tired by the unequal battle for survival with the Central Pacific railroad, John retired. He planned to take Doña Maria to Europe for the Grand Tour.

So far, Berwin's operation had not helped Steven Lewis. The sluggish southern economy made it impractical. Furthermore, the Southern Pacific was fighting the congealed seismic agony of the Tehachapi barrier. Engineer William Hood was driving four thousand of Charlie Crocker's China Boys through tunnels and over torturous summits. Steven was amused when Berwin growled, "California isn't one state. It's two *countries*."

In the summer of 1875 Moses Berwin expanded by constructing the first flour mill near Chico and a new packing plant in the Santa Clara valley. He arranged the financing through individual investors; he did not trust the Bank of California.

Rumors of trouble around Ralston were rampant. Ralston's South Montgomery Street real-estate project was in jeopardy because Ralston had committed huge sums to extend the street to the waterfront without acquiring all the rights of way. The owners of two key parcels waited until nearly two million dollars had been sunk in excavations before they announced their flat refusal to sell.

Ralston had given Lucky Baldwin a personal note for three and a half million dollars for shares in the Ophir mine and he had been forced to borrow two million in gold from William Sharon, who had demanded the New Palace Hotel as security.

Berwin was bluntly suspicious. "I told you. Sharon never gives up. Ralston can't keep him from buying a Senate seat this time. Billy had better watch out. That beady-eyed little rat is liable to dump his stock."

Lambert Lee was incredulous. "For God's sake, he wouldn't dare. He'd squeeze Ralston, but he'd never risk wiping out the Nevada legislature. Most of them invested their personal fortunes in the Ophir on his say-so."

One week later, Nevada's U.S. Senator-elect, William Sharon, wiped them all out. Ralston, desperate for cash, began selling his remaining holdings in distress.

The exchange collapsed and once again panic pervaded San Francisco's financial district. Lambert and Moses watched in disbelief as one hundred and ten million dollars in paper value in the Ophir and other Comstock mines disappeared in the Eastern money markets and small investors went broke by the thousands.

Lambert Lee supposed that there wasn't a man in San Francisco who wouldn't pay for the chance to murder Sharon in cold blood; but he had concealed his stock manipulations so well that no proof of them existed.

Within a few short weeks, Golden West Processors was beset by nervous investors. Reassuring them as best he could, Moses called Lambert into a private emergency meeting.

"I told our investors that we'd be slowed down for a while, not to worry, that the state is built on more substantial assets than the Comstock."

Lambert smiled bleakly. "The state is, but not San Francisco. Damn near everybody here has a few shares of some mine."

"Sure, I got some too, but to me it's only a poker game. What I'm worried about is not the Comstock. I'm worried about Ralston's bank. If his investment ring starts cashing in its stock, Billy will have trouble like he's never seen." Berwin fingered his cravat. "Tell me, Lambert, do you have power of attorney for John's bank stock?"

The question surprised Lambert. "Yes. Why?"

"I'll tell you in a minute. Also, how much cash can you raise? Your own, I mean?"

"Fifty thousand, I'd guess." Immediately Lambert knew what Berwin was driving at. "You're going to ask if I would act to protect John by selling him out of the Bank of California?"

"Would you?"

"I would."

"If you did, could you recommend that John come in with us?"

The query troubled Lambert. He did not relish the responsibility it would place on him. "I don't know. Why?"

"Because I want to pay off our notes. I got maybe eighty thousand. You got fifty and maybe with something from John, we could do it. Our investors are asking too many questions. When I don't have good answers, I don't like questions." Berwin rested a palm on his breast. "Believe me, it hurts to use our own money. But I think we should buy them out. So maybe we'll expand a little slower. This morning I heard Ralston's sold his interest in the San Joaquin ranches, too. I don't like what I'm hearing, Lambert."

That afternoon, after telling Moses that he would sleep on the proposal, Lambert spent several hours on San Francisco's Champagne Route drinking moderately and listening.

Ralston had gained control in the city's Spring Valley Water Company. He had bought up the necessary shares with a three-and-a-half-million-dollar loan engineered through his wife's father, Colonel Fry. It was puzzling news because Ralston had always called his interest in the water company philanthropic; he was happy to subsidize it for San Francisco's benefit. But now it could be Ralston's most valuable asset, one for which he could demand any price. Still, such a tactic seemed uncharacteristic. Sharon might try it but not Billy Ralston.

Lambert also heard a rumor that William S. Chapman, California's largest rancher, had advanced funds that would indirectly bolster the Bank of California. Chapman, owner of a million fertile acres in the San Joaquin valley, did most of his financing through the bank.

That afternoon, with Will Lewis' consent, Lambert took John Lewis out of Bank of California stocks.

The next morning Lambert and Berwin stared at the morning newspapers. There it was, in print: William Chapman Ralston was accused of attempting to bribe the city council in order to insure the sale to San Francisco of the Spring Valley Water Company. The price Ralston was alleged to have asked was just under fifteen million dollars.

Repercussions in San Francisco and in the Eastern money markets were immediate. Lambert, with John Lewis' endorsed stock, did his best to be inconspicuous as he presented the certificates at the cashier's cage. He was relieved when Ralston, preoccupied at his big desk in the glass-enclosed corner cubicle, did not look up. Screened by two clerks from Golden West who had accompanied him to help transport the gold proceeds from the sale, Lambert did his business quickly.

For a week or more San Francisco financial circles were riddled with rumors. Some said Fisk and Gould had raided the Central Pacific, that Collis P. Huntington, the railroad's actual head, was mortally ill in New York. Another rumor said the Ophir had made a secret strike and

374

was keeping its miners underground, well-fed from the best restaurants and well entertained by the most accomplished prostitutes, to prevent word from leaking.

A few days later, a new rumor swept along California and Montgomery Streets. The silver kings were quietly unloading shares in some of their holdings. The veins had petered out. Was the Consolidated Virginia in trouble? What about the California? Nobody knew how many of the various Comstock shares Ralston still held, but most of the mines on Mount Davidson were said to be in deep trouble. Now, they were saying, even Adolph Sutro's tunnel could not save the Comstock. If Mackay and Fair were selling out, the mines were finished.

What that could mean to San Francisco was clear to Lambert and Moses. Banks that had invested heavily in the mines and mills and the ore-transporting railroad were finished, too. One hopeful report had it that the once rich California mine had struck a new vein. But San Francisco's attitude was negative now and Mackay and Fair would say nothing to dispel the gloom.

The rumors persisted through July and on into August. Billy Ralston continued to present his usual cheerful front to the city. At the Bank Exchange Bar he presided at his corner table exuding the same durable optimism. When questioned about Spring Valley, he replied, "There's lots of room for misunderstanding in a complicated deal, especially when politicians are involved." Questions about the bank were parried with a cryptic smile. "I think I'm known in this city. I have taken all of the precautions necessary to protect my depositors. I have an obligation to each one of them. After all, they are also my friends."

On the morning of August twenty-fifth, word came that the Bank of California was overextended. By noon every depositor in San Francisco and a number of correspondent banks on New York's Wall Street had been alerted. Nearly two million dollars had already been withdrawn. Stock certificates were being endorsed and presented for sale. By mid-afternoon the anxious customers had become a panic-ridden mob. In a frenzy, men and women charged the lobby and crushed against the huge bronze doors. Police were called as scores of carriages continued to arrive. Horses and vehicles were left unattended for blocks around as their owners raced on foot to withdraw their money.

At a quarter past four a great shout went up and the doors, each manned by a dozen club-wielding guards, began to swing shut. By four-thirty, the Bank of California had failed.

On Saturday morning Billy Ralston was seen entering the bank with William Sharon and other directors. The restaurants and bars were filled with men who had gathered early to speculate on the meaning. Ralston's deserted table at the Bank Exchange Bar somehow seemed an ominous portent and the rumors Lambert heard changed in tone. Gone was any hint of underlying optimism.

At three o'clock that afternoon, Ralston emerged from his massive neo-classic California Street Bank alone, entered his carriage, and drove northward toward the Golden Gate Straits. A half hour later, Sharon and the others pushed through the crowd with police help and departed in their carriages.

Shortly before five o'clock, word flashed through the city that Billy Ralston was dead. An hour after he had plunged into the Bay for his usual constitutional swim in the rough, icy currents, his body washed ashore a few yards east of the pier.

Lambert, Will, and Moses Berwin joined the incredulous crowd that rushed to Neptune Beach at the throat of the "narrows." They kept hearing the word "suicide" whispered, but they refused to believe it. Although the weather had been unseasonably hot for a week, the San Francisco Bay never warmed.

Berwin was indignant. "He was overheated. He had a seizure. A big man in his fifties should slow down, but Billy didn't know the meaning of the word. He'd never take his own life. Never."

On Monday the suicide theory gained some credibility. Sharon, already sole owner of the Palace Hotel, had also acquired ownership of Ralston's fabled Belmont country estate with its dining room that could seat three hundred guests. In addition he had forced Ralston to sign over every last personal possession including the great Pine Street mansion, his furniture and art collection, and his stable of one hundred thoroughbred race horses. In the name of depositors, Sharon, the conscienceless bachelor and manipulator, had left the grieving, much respected Mrs. Ralston a destitute widow.

In the office of Golden West Processors, Lambert Lee paced before his partner's desk. "That son-of-a-bitch. That miserable, ruthless, immoral, benighted son-of-a-bitch. There's got to be a special hell for him or I'll stop believing in an Almighty."

Moses Berwin studied the papers he held without really seeing them. When he spoke, it was softly and to himself. "Where is it written that in California the bad ones are always punished? Francis Pioche a suicide, and who knows the name of his tormenter? Now Billy Ralston dead and with him dies part of San Francisco, and Sharon winds up with everything Ralston built."

Hatred for Sharon reached an exploding point when San Francisco learned that Ralston had pleaded for a chance to pay off the bank's creditors with four and a half million dollars that had been promised to him, but Sharon forced the directors to refuse. Sharon fled San Francisco. There were reports that he had gone to Virginia City in Nevada where the power of his money remained undiminished.

Doña Maria and John Lewis, returned from their European Grand Tour, were profoundly shocked by Ralston's death. They too refused to accept the suicide theory. Grateful though he was to Lambert for saving what amounted to a fourth of his modest personal fortune, John Lewis declined to take an active part in Golden West. But he arranged confidentially to purchase for twenty thousand dollars in gold the three thousand Los Nidos acres Berwin had bought. In a secret holographic codicil to his will, he left the land to his son Steven. The cash gave Moses and Lambert the one hundred fifty thousand dollars needed to buy out the dissident stockholders and bring Golden West completely under their control. In the end, John Lewis bought one thousand shares of stock and accepted a seat on Golden West's board of directors.

The first evidence that the entire Comstock was in serious trouble reached San Francisco's exchanges in mid-January. Consolidated Virginia failed to pay a dividend. The silver kings had quietly disposed of their Consolidated and California shares at the top market price the moment they learned the rich veins were pinching out. To secure their own huge fortunes, they ruined the market.

No disaster that had ever befallen San Francisco could match the disruption caused by the failure of the Consolidated Virginia and the California. "Gentlemen" fought like savages on the floors of the exchange to divest themselves of shares at any price. The repercussions were felt up and down the entire state. Small businesses were the first hit. Then the companies that supplied the mines. Throughout all of California men were being laid off.

Even Moses Berwin felt pinched. Bitterly, he complained to Lambert and John Lewis. "Look at this city. In three weeks, millionaires are standing on breadlines. A professional whore can't find a patron because waitresses and chambermaids are servicing them for two bits to buy a dinner."

John tried to interject a note of optimism he did not feel. "Maybe it's not as bad as it looks. Will says there is good ore still coming from both mines. The speculators are the ones who got hurt."

There was no humor in Berwin's laugh. "My friend, that's all of San Francisco and half of Wall Street in New York."

For the average man, the future seemed to hold little. On the classic assumption that things must be better elsewhere, the philosophy that had brought many of them to California in the first place, a number of San Franciscans began to go south. The majority were defeated families with few assets beyond a determination to never again speculate in mining shares.

It was a time of disillusionment and many were forced to return to the East. They departed, filled with bitterness, and Eastern editors printed their experiences in full and lurid detail.

Steven Lewis' Los Nidos parcels began to lease well even though farmers in general were going broke. Guaranteed water and liberal share-crop terms attracted the most far-sighted among the newcomers and Steven was careful in his choice of landholders.

New orchards and groves were set out. Henry Vance did not get the new Brazil navel orange first. But he was among the first. His avocado trees were bearing but new growers were wary of the fruit from Central America that they called "the vegetable that grows on a tree."

As often as time permitted, Steven visited eleven-year-old Charlotte, but the child had been completely absorbed by Arlene. Jabez Lathrop and his wife had moved to Arlene's Santa Monica colony. She had abandoned the Oriental in favor of Greco-Roman. The faithful in evidence appeared to be in their late middle years. All affected togas and sandals.

Steven enjoyed his visits when he was alone with Charlotte. He tried bringing along six-year-old Alicia, hoping a friendship would develop, but he felt a return of Charlotte's earlier restraint. On the next visit, Arlene made it clear that she did not want "a confusing emotional problem" to develop between Charlotte and her half sister. "Divided loyalties are very damaging, Steven dear. I know your motives are the noblest but I must forbid any more such visits."

Steven welcomed the business responsibilities that diverted his thoughts from his personal trials. In San Francisco, things worsened. The Southern Pacific, pursuing its policy of squeezing the last cent the traffic could bear, had raised freight rates down the valley to the point where it was cheaper to order mine machinery shipped around the Horn. The bulk of the business had gone to Eastern agents.

Earlier, Moses Berwin had made contacts in Los Angeles through Steven to supply canned goods to the Cerro Gordo silver and lead mines in Inyo County's Owen's Valley. Remi Nadeau's freight lines provided the transport. That portion of the business allowed Golden West Processors to weather the Comstock debacle.

Things had changed in the city by the Golden Gate. It had built, burned, and rebuilt on an average of once every five years since it had cast off the humble name of Yerba Buena. Now, with a wild Irish teamster named Dennis Kearney shouting for "bread or blood" in the streets, with William Coleman back again at the head of a vigilante group armed with pick handles, there were those who said the city named for the gentle saint would have been more aptly named for Satan since San Francisco was "in a hell of a fix."

A Los Angeles news editor remarked with questionable civic loyalty that no change would be needed in the southland. "The City of the Angels is quite appropriately named in view of the fact that it's dead!"

The new opera *Carmen*, for which the late Francis Pioche had planned a gala for the history books, failed in an excellent production at the Baldwin Theater. Despite the international stars, Marie Rose and Anna Louise Carey, in the leading female roles, the presentation went twenty thousand dollars in the red. San Francisco had no stomach for grand opera. It needed plain bread.

In 1882, the Lewis twins lost their godfather, and California lost its first native-born Mexican Governor, Juan Bautista Alvarado. Several months later, the state lost another symbol of its pastoral days when their grandfather, Don José, died. For the Lewises and the Lambert Lees, it was a sad year relieved somewhat by the pleasure of growing children but by little else.

In 1883, optimism began creeping back. With typical ambivalence where Leland Stanford, Mark Hopkins, Charles Crocker and Collis Huntington were concerned, San Francisco celebrated the news that the Southern Pacific's two-way construction crews had met on the west bank of the Pecos River. Finally, the transcontinental rails of the SP's Sunset Route were joined, linking the South with the West.

The Berwins and the Lees went to Oakland to cheer the departure of the first train from California to New Orleans. Once again the Big Four were given conditional absolution in the expectation of another boom. Moses watched Stanford's Palace Car pull away from the terminal shed. "Every sabbath I do *bruchas* that the Santa Fe Railroad will get into Los Angeles first. What that *momser* Huntington needs is competition. That's the best steam for any man's engine."

No discernible good resulted from the completion of the Sunset Route in 1884; but as 1885 approached, a definite aura of hope was in the air. Even Santa Barbara, twice wooed and twice jilted by the railroad, felt a resurgence of hope as some of the immigrants made their way down the coast by steamer and stagecoach. As mid-year approached, there were other more significant indications that the corner had been turned. At a directors' meeting, Lambert Lee speculated aloud.

"We're bound to the rest of the country now by hundreds of miles of steel rail. In another couple of years we

380

should have California fruit and vegetables under our labels in every important city in the country. While we're damning them, we can thank the Big Four for that." Berwin and his son Samuel, who had just joined Golden West Processors, nodded in agreement.

Moses Berwin, speaking of Leland Stanford, wagged his head compassionately. "He's not the smartest of the Big Four, but Stanford has more heart. To found a great university in memory of Leland Junior is a wonderful thing. By this, he does for us all. He's cost me, this Stanford. But I like him." Moses looked across at twenty-four-year-old Samuel. "To have a son live and turn out, there's no greater blessing for a father. Believe me, for Stanford, I can weep."

Samuel Berwin smiled uneasily and wondered what his father and Lambert would say, or think privately, when they heard that he and Lambert's daughter, Emily had fallen in love and wished to marry. Samuel Berwin and Emily Lee had anguished singly and together over the ancient customs that divided them when they had fallen in love. Samuel had told Emily firmly, "I don't think I'd go as far as Benjamin Disraeli's father, Isaac, and turn Christian, Emily, but I do not intend to let my faith stand in the way even though our decision may disappoint my parents and yours."

Emily had tried to reassure him. "We both pray to the same God, darling Samuel. And we use at least half of the same book. I really think I shall be able to spare you for an hour on Saturday if you do the same for me on Sunday."

At first both families were deeply concerned when Emily and Samuel told them. In the end, convinced that Emily and Samuel knew their own hearts, they reconciled their prejudices by refusing to acknowledge them. Cheerfully, they made plans to celebrate the engagement at the Poodle Dog in early November. The parents admitted their decision had not been made free of all reservations but it was one that had been unselfishly made.

At the engagement party, Moses raised his glass and the other parents followed. "*Shalom*, dear children, *Shalom!* Together you had the chicken pox, the measles, and a thousand runny noses. Now, together may you have a lifetime filled with happiness and good health and with charity for all who have less!"

12 The invitation read:

SOCIETY OF CALIFORNIA PIONEERS
You are cordially invited to attend
a formal banquet and testimonial
honoring our beloved founder-member and native son,
STEVEN EUGENE LEWIS
on the occasion of his Eightieth Birthday,
Friday evening, September Nineteen,
One Thousand Nine Hundred and Twenty Four,
at Seven O'Clock.
Hotel Lankershim
Seventh and Broadway
Los Angeles, California

R.S.V.P.

Twelve hundred copies were mailed. Over six hundred responses arrived at the Founders' Parlor of the Society. Steven Lewis' widowed daughter, Alicia Lewis Vance, and her son Steven and daughter-in-law, Catherine Coulter Vance, were in charge of arrangements for the head table. Steven was still a remarkably rugged and active man despite his approaching eightieth birthday. He leaned forward and peered at the guest list and the names of the family members and others who had promised to attend the testimonial. After a brief inspection he grunted in mock displeasure and said to his daughter Alicia, *"Hijita mia,* if the object of this affair is to praise me, the job had best be left to them who don't know me." Alicia started to dispute him but he dismissed her. "All I ask is that the family be seated down front so they can't see the guests behind them smirking at the pack of lies they'll be hearing."

Alicia smiled indulgently and kissed him on the temple. "All right, father. I promise."

Steven reached up and cupped his hand around the cheek of the daughter who resembled so much his own beloved Anita, who had died of cervical carcinoma in 1892—"from riding like a vaquero instead of a lady!" old Gracia had insisted to the day of her own death three years later.

For the most part, the guests at the banquet were in their middle to late years. Here and there were tables of young people whose parents birthright entitled them to attend. From his seat to the right of the podium Steven could catch glimpses of some of the younger guests surreptitiously pouring the contents of silver hip flasks into the Prohibition punch. He did not disapprove; in fact he found himself amused and somewhat pleased that several of his livelier contemporaries were also spiking their drinks. A lot of things had happened since the turn of the century that had not pleased him. Foremost among them were the involvement in the European War and the passage of the Eighteenth Amendment while the country was preoccupied with something that was "none of its damned business." Once Los Angeles had been the toughest town in the nation. Now Steven reflected on what it had become—a city of blue noses from the middle west who had opened two churches for every saloon they closed. San Francisco voted ninety thousand strong *against* Prohibition. But what did this damned town do? It voted a hundred and forty-five thousand *in favor* of the Eighteenth Amendment and voted its vineyard industry, the biggest in the state, right the hell into bankruptcy.

While the guests were still occupied with their breast of chicken Mornay, Steven gazed thoughtfully over the room. Southern California had changed with the coming of the Santa Fe Railroad and the "Boom of Eighty-seven." It had changed again with the beach boom. They'll talk about all that tonight, he thought, but they won't say it like it really was.

The change had been very profitable for the Los Nidos Ranch Company and also for the state-wide Golden West Processors. With the help from Amadeo Gianinni's new Bank of Italy, the packing firm had thrived under the management of his niece's husband, Samuel Berwin, after Moses had retired in 1902.

Both Moses and Lambert had been gone now for more than twenty years. Their bones were resting in San Francisco. But at the long family table below him were their offspring, that once new generation which had taken over and the present newer generation that was in the process of taking over. Steven Lewis gazed at them now and smiled to himself. There it was, the history of California, spread before him, recorded in the blood and sinew and aspirations of as diverse a population as ever had gathered into one society—or was it in danger once again of succumbing to its repetitive pattern and dividing into two separate societies?

The nine persons seated along one side and at the ends of the long table directly in front of the dais were his family, Will's, and Felicia's.

Felicia had died three years earlier, but her daughter Emily and son-in-law Samuel and their son Lee and daughter-in-law Lillian Cohn Berwin, were there. He thought about Lambert now—humorless, a bit stuffy, but completely dependable, as he had proved again when he had straightened out the tangle left when no wills could be found after the deaths of his father and his twin brother. They had died on that April morning in 1906 when most of San Francisco had quaked, buckled, and burned and much of what had been left had been deliberately destroyed to halt the spread of the flames.

After the first quake shock his father and twin brother Will had rushed downtown to try to save the records in the modest family office they had rented after the company's sale. An exploding gas main had trapped them on the second floor of the building. Later the family had held a memorial service. There had been nothing left to inter. He recalled how he had stood disbelieving at the top of the hill on Valencia Street with his mother and Emily at his side and looked down along the contorted cable car line that ran for twenty buckled blocks through devastation no city in modern times had known. City Hall had become a twisted skeletal dome and the Nob Hill mansions were gutted. The after shocks and the distant detonations of dynamite signaled the final destruction of the tottering, fire-blackened walls that were destined to take the lives of a score of rescuers searching the rubble for victims. In time the dead would number four hundred and fifty-two. But ten times that many had fled the cremated ruin that once had been the most boisterous, recklessly speculative, and ingenuously culture-conscious city in the world. Many of San Francisco's pioneers seated in the room to pay homage to Steven's years had been among the great scoffers and deriders. From the security of their small estates in outlying districts, they advertised the ambivalence of their loyalty by defining Los Angeles as "six suburbs in search of a city." But it was all *habladuria*, empty talk. If any of the palaver he was about to hear concerning his own accomplishments was deserved it would be that which acknowledged his devotion to southern California.

Southern California could be spelled with a capital "S" now, thanks to fellow pioneers and believers like the Chaffees and the Smiley twins and the Norths—and later Henry Huntington—expiating the sins of old C.P. who had died eight months into the new century and had never enjoyed a penny of his railroad millions that had not been spent in trying to add to them—and Van Nuys and Lankershim and Eli Clark and William May Garland and General Harrison Gray Otis—and Harry Chandler, William Randolph Hearst, and the Workmans. And E. L. Doheny who had drilled his damned stinking oil wells right in people's front lawns! And C. C. Julian who just might be the biggest of them all if he kept on going. He could put a name to every older face in the room and to some of the younger ones, too—Spanish, Mexican, and Anglo names—and many Italians—names that identified a living history more distinguished than his own, Steven thought.

On the left side of the room, he could see Guillermo Morales and his family. Guillermo was thirty-five, the youngest of four sons born to Pablo Morales and Gracia Lopez at the ranch. Pablo was the son of old Pedro and old Gracia, now long gone. The parents were at the table, self-conscious in their borrowed formal wear, unable to conceal their pride in Guillermo, who had earned his law degree, and immensely flattered because Don Esteban had said there would be no party without them.

There had been some resistance. Young Steven's wife, Catherine Coulter Vance, who would always remain a patrician from New England, had questioned the propriety of having servants present as guests. The twenty-two-

year-old bride had acknowledged begrudging admiration
for the Mexican American's achievements but seemed disconcerted to find dignity, intelligence, and innate grace in
a person in whom "the Indian still shows." Those qualities,
she had inferred, were reserved for "one's own kind." Steven smiled inwardly, remembering his grand-daughter-in-
law's consternation when he had reminded her that she
had married a *mestizo*.

The room quieted down and the president, Anthony La
Barbera, was beginning to spout those ceremonial platitudes
that always annoyed him if they did not lull him to sleep
first. He would have to guard against dozing. The older he
got, the easier it had become. He would try to listen now.

"... a man who, in the eight decades of his life so
far—and I know we'll be here to celebrate his hun-
dredth—has seen California progress from an unexplored
wilderness in the north, and in the south a land of *ranchos*
that provided their few hundred Mexican owners with a
fine living, to a state with better than three and a half million souls who have dedicated their lives to making this
the greatest state in the union ..."

Steven's gaze wandered to his grand-niece, twenty-four-
year-old Maria Carla, now Mrs. Maylon McCarrell.
Young Maylon had already become a promising San Francisco investment banker and Republican state commit-
teeman. Steven liked him well enough but he resented the
young man's cocksure attitude where the south was concerned. "You southern Californians will never get over
your inferiority complex. With money you can imitate but
never duplicate what God has given us up north." Annoyed
all over again, Steven forced his attention back to the
speaker.

"... Steven Lewis' story is the story of our glorious
state. Born in Monterey five years before the Gold Rush,
he moved to San Francisco. Very early, he saw his mistake and came to Los Angeles. And from the time Steven
Lewis set foot south of the Tehachapis, he moved unerr-
ingly toward his goal ..."

Steven's eyes continued to wander along the family table. There should have been at least two and possibly four
more chairs there. But some mistakes cannot be undone—

"... and his devotion to civic duty from the time he
stood with Judge Widney and his brother against the lynch-

386

mob that decimated our great Chinese community right
where this great hotel now stands . . ."

Inwardly, Steven Lewis snorted. And they hung the
wrong goddamned men! Not one of those murdering
bastards was punished. Oh, yes, one man was fined one
hundred dollars by Judge Widney because the jury would
not bring in a conviction against men who had done what
each jury member himself had wanted to do.

Trivial human errors? How trivial is an error a man
pays for privately for the rest of his days? He raised his
head to look at the table again and wondered where Charlotte would be. In another month, she would be fifty-eight.
After Arlene had died from an overdose of the laudanum
she'd been taking for years, Charlotte had disappeared. He
had tried for years to locate her, had spent thousands to
no avail. One tracer had her in South America with a mis-
sionary group. A second indicated that she had died there.
But somehow a part of him rejected the idea of her death.
The thought of it brought back an old pang of guilt. He
managed to rid himself of it as he usually did—like
mother, like daughter. Arlene had done her work well on
Charlotte all right and there was nothing anybody could
do, no matter how much . . .

La Barbera's measured intonation separated again into
meaningful thoughts. ". . . he has walked among us, sharing with us, blessing us with his compassion and wisdom
. . ."

Steven Lewis jerked his head up and fixed the master of
ceremonies with an incredulous stare. He wished he could
say "Bullshit!" after each new extravagance. What about
those sixty lease partners the judge and I dispossessed
when all of the damned subdivision foolishness busted in
our faces? In two years, from Eighty-seven to Eighty-nine,
those "Escrow Indians" platted sixty new towns on eight
thousand acres of land, some of it right in the middle of
the Los Angeles River. I sold them a few thousand acres of
that land. And that pious son-of-a-bitch, Jabez Lathrop,
had made himself another fortune with Island View Harbor, boasting that he preached the Promised Land on Sunday and sold it on the other six days. Two thousand lots at
five hundred dollars apiece and all he gave them was a
church and a bathhouse. He had bought five thousand
dollars' worth of lumber and bricks and had salted a bunch
of lots so people would think homes were being built on

them. Later, the boys who promoted Hollywood used that same trick. At least, by God, he could say with a clear conscience that every man who did business with him got a fair shake.

While La Barbera droned on, Steven pondered the state of affairs in Sacramento. The population balance was moving southward but political power remained in the north. For forty years the Democratic Party had been in a decline because the stupid bastards kept fighting among themselves. It started back in "Seventy-three" about the time William Sharon began to double-cross Billy Ralston. That's when the People's Independent Party got hot enough under the collar to have a convention and publicly damn the Southern Pacific's corruption.

Both old-line parties started singing the same tune: "Get the railroad and its graft money out of politics."

La Barbera was winding up. "... it is my pleasure to introduce the President of State College, Dr. James Denton Boyce."

Steven applauded obediently and smiled at the distinguished educator. How long had it been? Twenty years?

"... that was the year I first met our honored guest. If I have made some progress in understanding our complex society, a good part of the credit must go to my first practical instructor, the man who ..."

Steven remembered. Who taught you that you don't help people by feeling sorry for them? Who taught you how to use a shovel on an irrigation ditch? A derisive snort escaped Steven. He pretended to clear his throat, muffling the sound with a napkin.

"... I had a lot of thinking to do about the whole relationship between labor and management and what I learned from Steven Lewis in those days has colored my thinking down through the years."

Old misgivings made Steven shake his head and a newer worry sent his glance to where Guillermo Morales sat. He gazed at the young lawyer who was concentrating with the intentness of a well-disciplined mind, evaluating, agreeing, rebutting. What was going on in that smart brown head of Guillermo's just might stir up trouble someday.

Two weeks earlier, Guillermo had finally won his client's suit against the East County Land Company. A Mexican-American laborer had lost an arm in a bean thresher. Negligence, they said. But Morales took the whole damned jury out into the field and showed them. The jury agreed that a safety screen should have been bolted around the conveyor chain pully and they set the price of an arm at ten thousand dollars. Los Nidos wouldn't order machines without them. More than that, the foremen had always been careful about the men they put on those platforms.

". . . a man's earnings are directly related to the quality of his training and in the case of agricultural workers, his basic education."

Steven Lewis tried to resettle himself on the chair and hoped to God that the remaining speakers didn't run on and on. This whole business about educating workers was fine in theory. But how often had he argued, "so you educate them to want to do something else. Then who in hell is going to work in the fields? Even stoop labor takes more than a strong back and that's why Los Nidos has always paid a few cents more and seen that they have a little better housing. Of course, in time, machines are going to take care of all that and farm laborers are going to agitate themselves out of jobs."

". . . that is why I have chosen this occasion to announce that next Saturday State College with confer upon Steven Lewis an honorary degree in economics."

Steven blinked in genuine surprise. Well, now. What do you know about that? It was difficult to swallow and the expression that had set on his face felt like a stupid grin. He was glad when Jim Boyce stopped the applause.

The next speaker was Harry Rhoades, a fellow rancher who with Steven had lived through the boom of "Eighty-seven" and the collapse that followed it.

Harry described the real beginning of growth in southern California shortly after the turn of the century. The "Pullman Crowd" arrived and bought up the orange groves along the sheltered citrus belt that runs from Santa Barbara to San Diego.

Quite properly, Rhoades credited J. W. North's pioneer experiments at Riverside in the Seventies for the citrus boom. North had proved with oranges what Anaheim had proved with grapes and what Los Nidos had proved with field crops: If you bring water down from the streams you can turn land that people call "nothing but desert" into profitable acreage.

"The point was—and Steve saw it—diversification. Steve had the acreage, the water, and the variety of terrain to prove the point. If you wanted insurance against crop failure you planted a variety of crops, you didn't put all your oranges in one basket. The ones that did got cleaned out in the big freeze eleven years ago and most of them wouldn't have had a dime if Steven hadn't offered to buy them out for cash."

Steven shot a baleful glance at his old friend. He wanted to remind Harry that he had bought them out for ten cents on the dollar because the little operators couldn't stay in the citrus business any more. It was a two-hundred-million-dollar industry now, no place for the little guys. If Harry had been really honest he would have reminded them that the others around the country accused him of stealing the ruined groves, even spread the rumor that he had sent his Los Nidos boys around with cash and loaded guns to force them to sell. It was a damned lie but it was the sort of thing you had to expect when you got big.

As the rancher continued to talk of the old days Steven watched him through heavy-lidded eyes. Rhoades had come from Idaho to work in sugar beets with the Spreckles interests. There were some things in southern California that Harry just never could adjust to. To himself Steven said, "You're a hell of a lot better rancher than a speaker, my friend, unless you're chewing the ass off your Mexicans. You never will learn how to handle a Mexican. You always figure they're talking behind your back in their own lingo. It ought to be a state law in California, Arizona, New Mexico, and Texas, by God, to have every kid learn both languages. We had to learn their language when we came here to steal California from them."

He glanced over at the table where Guillermo was seated. Maybe, by God, they'll steal it back some day.

Steven's musing was interrupted when Harry Rhoades turned to address him.

"So, Steve, nobody will argue much when I say that you and Los Nidos showed this part of the state how modern ranching works. And finally, I want to say this: You're not always lovable, Steve, but by God, we love you!"

There was another ovation and Steven flushed, trying not to look pleased. Then he entertained the futile hope that the next speaker would be brief and end his misery.

Anthony La Barbera brought the room under control and introduced State Senator George Kenny. Steven looked at the lawmaker with some affection. A good Democrat, a winner in a losing party, a realistic politician who knew what the trouble was.

"If there's anything scarcer in California these days than a genuine native son it's an honest-to-goodness Democrat. Our honored guest today has always voted for the man, not the party."

Steven nodded his approval openly and thought, "That's a very respectable way to get around the truth. But what I really voted for was a chance to let southern California catch up with San Francisco's forty-year head start."

". . . so I guess it shouldn't surprise us that politics in the state of California just don't seem to follow the old classic blueprints. My father told me that when President Lincoln was assassinated, San Francisco went into mourning and Los Angeles staged a celebration."

The statement brought back a troublesome memory for Steven. Not everybody celebrated. Only the Confederates. I didn't see any black man in that parade. And I didn't see any brown men, slant eyes, or otherwise. But I did see a hell of a lot of men who would have started the Civil War all over again if the police hadn't stepped in. And every one of them was an outsider, with his own set of notions. Steven wondered why people always seemed to bring their pet peeves to California. The place could only get built by pulling together. Lately they'd been doing a little better, but the friction with San Francisco was getting hotter with all of the "Keep the White Spot White" open-shop business and the growing harbor competition.

". . . We are a state of individualists. We are a state filled with immigrants and some of us brought our eccentricities with us. If you don't believe me, then listen to Sister Aimee on your crystal set—"

The reference to Aimee Semple McPherson turned Steven's thoughts momentarily to Arlene and an old sadness settled on him that the senator quickly dispelled.

"So that's all the more reason for paying homage to our few remaining, stabilizing old-timers who did the pioneering so that the rest of us can enjoy the most turbulent political climate and the most salubrious geographic climate in the United States. Now I want to extend to Steven Lewis the gratitude of the California State Senate in the form of this official resolution."

Senator Kenny held up a large plaque bearing the state seal at its top. The chairman whispered to Steven, who rose stiffly to receive it.

"Whereas the Senate of the State of California, being mindful of the valuable and unselfish services rendered to the state by Steven Lewis. And whereas . . ."

It felt good to stand. If it took a load of official horse manure from the boys in Sacramento to get a man to his feet, then it was the first useful thing that legislative body had done in some time.

Then, almost before he realized it, Steven Lewis found himself accepting the rarely given honor from the California State Senate and it was time to say some of the things that he'd been thinking about.

His words would be reported in the press, not all of which was friendly. But whether the press liked it or not he intended to set the record straight about what kind of men it took to build a country. There is no progress and opportunity without doers. California found that out from men like Ralston and Sutro and Huntington and Stanford and Crocker and Widney and Irvine and Newhall and Chandler and Hearst and Earl and Mulholland and Hellman and Gianinni, especially Gianinni, who was showing guts enough to buck Governor Richardson. He might have let the church get mixed up in his Bank of Italy as rumor had it. But he wasn't about to let the state stand in the way of expanding his branches to serve the little merchants and farmers in every small town in California.

All along the line you've got to fight the people you're trying to help, unless you promise to do it for nothing and give them all of the profits, like that damned lanky, starry-eyed dreamer, Upton Sinclair.

". . . so, if I were to say now, Steven Lewis, that you needed no introduction, it would be the truest thing I've ever said in public or in private. Ladies and gentlemen—Steven Lewis."

Steven Lewis waited through another ovation, then deferred briefly to those on either side of him.

"Mr. Chairman, honored guests, fellow members, and friends, I've had a lot of praise heaped on me tonight and you can see that I'm flowering under it. It also happens when we heap the same stuff on the beans down at the ranch." The deliberate scatalogical jibe brought raucous laughter from the men and subdued tittering from the ladies. He could see that Alicia was flushing as she exchanged horrified glances with Catherine.

"First, I want to say that no man deserves all this praise. But I bow to my peers in this decision because, after all, I'm only a doctor, not a judge." The laughter which had not quite subsided swelled again and was interspersed with a scattering of applause.

"And before I get down to speaking, I want to say that any man who would risk making me a doctor has got to be desperately sick."

Steven Lewis knew that he could keep them laughing and they would go away chortling over his bucolic humor and repeat it in clubs and in speakeasies. But it was time to try to put into words some of those things that he had been thinking about while seeming to listen. He would set the record straight and he would tell them that even in the free swinging year of 1924, they would have to fight for survival.

Book III

The Howard D. Goodwyn Story

13 FOR SEVENTY MILES in either direction there was nothing but the blinding, furnace-like heat—searing, bone-drying heat that had made the wasteland an unmarked graveyard for unnumbered millennia. And with the heat there was the wind. Day and night, the hot desert wind.

Engineers on the Santa Fe trains that roared and rattled along a roadbed made treacherous by the shifting sands swore that tumbleweed, racing the wind, had passed their locomotives going better than a mile a minute. No one who knew the land doubted it.

Howard Goodwyn, encumbered by shabby high-heeled cowboy dress boots, ran awkwardly across the sage-tufted flatland. He still had several hundred yards to travel when he heard the deep whistle of the westbound locomotive. A moment later the headlight stabbed the darkness as the train emerged from behind a range of low dunes.

He reached the right of way a scant thirty seconds before the ten-wheeler lumbered by. Crouching behind some scrub sage, he watched the passing string of dark cars. Despair turned to hope when he realized the train was slowing. Keeping low, his left hand gripping the black leather guitar case on which faded sequins spelled out "Howdy" and clutching a suitcase in his right hand, he came to within three feet of the moving train. His ankles turned dangerously in the heavy rock ballast as a rush of hot night air flapped his jacket. Then hope turned to despair again when he realized the box-car doors were sealed.

The train was traveling slowly enough for him to keep pace. Squinting anxiously into the darkness, he searched for the tell-tale darker rectangle that would mean an open box-car door. Finally he saw it—an automobile car with both doors wide open. If he could toss his stuff inside, he felt certain he could catch the rear edge of the opening and hoist himself in.

Ignoring the danger, he began to run, staying opposite the door. Just as he was about to swing his suitcase up, a silhouette appeared in the opening. For an instant he thought it was a trainman. A harsh voice called out: "If you're gonna hop it, Willie, toss me your bindle!"

Howdy swung the suitcase up. The guitar case struck the steel door guide, knocking him off balance. Recovering his footing in the treacherous ballast, he caught up again. The man was shouting something but his words were lost in the hiss of air brakes bleeding off. The couplings clanked taut down the line as the freight train began to gather speed again.

Panic knotted Howdy's guts. His clothes were in the car, everything he owned except the guitar. He had to get aboard. Running wildly now, he reached out, shouting. "Gimme a hand, pardner! Gimme a hand!"

"Heave your other stuff in first, pal. Hurry on!"

"I can't! It's my guitar! It'll smash! Just gimme a hand——" Racing along inches away from the rails, Howdy's right hand groped frantically for something to hold on to. His fingers found the cloth of the man's trouser leg and closed around it. Instantly there was a warning shout. "Let go, you goddamn fool! Let go."

Ignoring him, Howdy clung desperately and tried to pull himself up. "Christ—gimme a—"

The words were cut off and the cloth tore free from his grasp as a heavy work boot crashed into his left temple.

Howdy heard the man's curses but the voice trailed away, lost in the din of clanking trucks and couplings. His body seemed weightless and the night closed in around him black and silent.

The old man who ran the only filling station in the one-hundred-and-forty-five-mile stretch of Mojave desert that went from Needles, on the Arizona border, to Barstow, California, had been in bed for an hour when shouts awakened him. He got out of bed and with the aid of a flashlight found Howdy collapsed beside the water tank. He managed to get the injured stranger on his feet and into The Oasis, as he called the furnace-hot little wooden structure that also doubled as his home.

It took an hour and most of his meager first-aid supplies

to patch up the tall, thin, redheaded youth who managed between winces to explain that he was an out-of-work cowboy singer from Guymon, Oklahoma, trying to get to the West Coast.

When the deep abrasions and gravel scratches were finally bandaged, Howdy managed his sincerely felt thanks.

"I figured I could hop another freight like I been doing and get to Barstow tonight. Most often I can find a place that'll swap me some food and a place to flop for a few songs."

"Why a place like Barstow?" the old man asked. "Ain't nothin' much there—"

Howdy made a noncommittal gesture. "The way things is going I gotta take one town at a time. But I sure want to get to L.A. as fast as I can. They got a lot of radio stations there and I figure to catch on with Stuart Hamblin or the Sons of Pioneers or one of those outfits." He glanced down at his badly torn trousers and managed a grin. "You might say I'll be starting from scratch—"

The old man cackled. "Y'also might say that you haven't lost your sense of humor, son."

In the morning, Howdy stripped down to his boots. Clad in a grubby towel cinched around his lean middle, he washed his things in an iron tub. When they were hung on the line, drying almost visibly in the hundred-degree morning heat, he returned to the shack and studied his reflection in an unframed mirror. His left eye had purpled during the night and the worst of the abrasions had begun to scab over. A soundless laugh made his shoulders heave. "Howdy boy, you got nowhere left to go but up!"

During the morning, two trucks, both eastbound, had stopped to fill their radiators. The only westbound traffic had been a 1930 Buick bearing Arkansas license plates. It carried a gaunt man and wife, four worn children, and an unbelievable load of poor household articles. Howdy did not even consider asking for a lift. The old man said it all as the car pulled away after buying a dollar's worth of gasoline. "That car's so loaded that if one of the kid's ate a square meal the axle'd bust. They're all the same. More Arkies going west. Heading from bad to worse."

In mid-afternoon a gleaming passenger train blurred eastward but Howdy didn't even bother to look up. Then, during the hottest part of the day, around four-thirty, a middle-aged couple in a dust-covered touring car drove up.

The old man filled the car with gas and walked to the front of the car. The red fluid in the Moto-Meter on the radiator cap warned that the motor was dangerously close to boiling. The driver, a slightly paunchy man, opened the door and climbed out stiffly. "Better let her simmer down a little. Been pushing right along at forty for the last hour."

The old man glanced at the empty back seat. "You folks going as far as Barstow tonight?"

The driver nodded. "We live there. Been up to look over Hoover Dam. Decided to come home by way of Kingman."

The old man nodded, "I'll get some fresh water."

As he moved off toward the faucet Howdy came out of the small dug toilet a few yards behind the living quarters. The old man motioned to him urgently. "There's a couple out front going to Barstow. Whole empty back seat. Better go ask them."

Howdy moved instantly, but stopped a few steps away. A hand explored the bruised left cheek and temple. The old man urged him on. "Tell them the truth—you tripped and fell. They look like nice folks."

A few minutes later, Howdy and his guitar were in the back seat. As they pulled out onto the highway the woman, a comfortable, motherly type, turned to give Howdy a concerned inspection.

"Sure you didn't break anything?" she asked.

"The only thing I broke, ma'am, is a string of good luck I had finding rides. But you good people put that back together by taking me in. I thought for a while the Good Lord didn't want me to get to Barstow—or anywhere else, for that matter."

The husband called over his shoulder. "You got folks in Barstow?"

"Nope. Never been there."

The man nodded and probed again. "I expect you've got a job waiting for you."

There was no way to avoid an answer. "I have prospects."

The woman, still turned on the front seat so she could keep an eye on Howdy, frowned. "Way things are these days, I sure hope your prospects pan out." She looked at

400

the ornate guitar case and unaccountably began to giggle. "Frank and I saw a gangster picture in San Bernadino last month. Fellow had a violin case with a machine gun in it."

"I've got to tell you, Mrs.—" Howdy left the words suspended in a question.

"Persons. Melba Persons. My husband's Frank."

"I've got to tell you, Mrs. Persons, that if anybody looking like me asked for a ride, I'd be a touch skittish, too. But I sure appreciate your taking me in."

Melba clucked, "Well, my goodness, decent folks don't expect to be paid back for simple Christian charity. Truth is, it's nice to have company. At home we just sit and read and listen to music on the radio mostly on KNX and KOA and WLW."

Howdy rested a hand on the guitar case. "What's your favorite song, Mrs. Persons?"

"Mine? Oh, well, mostly old ones. But I like that new song the Crosby boy sings, 'How Deep Is the Ocean?' "

Howdy unsnapped the latches on the case. "Would you and Mr. Persons like a little music now?"

Melba looked at him, wide-eyed. "Well, my goodness." She watched, fascinated, while Howdy positioned the instrument and tuned it softly.

"Now then, I'm not up to the regular popular music. But I know a couple of new hillbilly songs that just came out. Ever hear 'I like Mountain Music'?"

Without waiting for an answer, Howdy went into a rhythmic vamp and started to sing. When he finished and looked up, the rapt expression on Melba Person's face made him chuckle inwardly. It never hurt to have an edge.

For an hour Howdy held the couple with the same spell he had cast on audiences in Texas and Oklahoma as the young featured soloist with Spike Spangler's Radio Rustlers.

The long summer twilight had fallen and in the distance Barstow's first lights were visible as he finished the last song. It was a new cowboy ballad by Billy Hill called "The Last Roundup."

Howdy smiled to himself as Mr. and Mrs. Persons awkwardly attempted to thank him. Some minutes later, in the heart of town, Frank Persons angled the car into a parking space in front of a grocery store. "Is there any particular place you were going, son? Soon as Melba picks up some food, we can drop you off."

Quickly Howdy decided what his approach would be. "No. No, thanks, sir. This'll be fine, right here."

Melba Persons was fussing with the door handle. Before she could move it, Howdy was out and helping. The attention embarrassed her. "My goodness, Mr. Goodwyn. I'm not used to all this fuss."

Howdy handed her down from the running board to the street and helped her over the curbing. "Well, that makes us even, Mrs. Persons, 'cause I'm not used to all the kindness you folks showed me."

Frank Persons got out and walked around to join them. "What are you going to do now? You said you don't know anybody in town. That right?"

"Yes, sir. I figured I had such good luck singing for my ride that I might look around for a likely café and see if I can't sing for my supper, too." He hoped he had gauged correctly the amount of casual bravado needed to elicit sympathy.

Melba reacted instantly. "Frank, this boy isn't going to look for a place to sing for food, for heaven's sake! You keep him right here while I go inside and get some things."

The Persons home was a neat one-bedroom cottage well away from the highway and the railroad. The screened front porch was furnished with weathered wicker chairs and a couch covered with faded green burlap. The interior consisted of a small living room with an adjoining alcove fitted out as an office, a small dining room, a good sized kitchen, and, down the hall, a double bedroom and bath. Howdy could easily have predicted the cretonne-covered overstuffed furniture, the plum-colored silk shade on the mahogony floor lamp, and the occasional tables with their assorted trinkets, dishes, and momentoes that included a piece of polished wood from the Petrified Forest and a winter scene captured in a crystal ball.

During the half hour it took Melba to throw together a salad of cold meat and hard-boiled eggs, Howdy sat on the porch with Frank. Choosing his words carefully, he answered most of the older man's queries about his past, but was grateful when Melba called them to the table.

After supper, when he offered to dry the dishes, she

shoo'd them both out. Pleasantly full for the first time in almost two weeks, Howdy would have been more than content to return to the cool porch. Instead, Frank diverted him to the tiny alcove.

"I want to show you that lots of good people got caught in this damned depression bind."

Three years earlier, Frank Persons had closed his downtown real-estate office, sold the furniture he couldn't get into the alcove to a San Bernadino dealer for ten cents on the dollar, and transferred his California real-estate-broker's license to the wall above the alcove's roller-top desk.

In the early Twenties, when Wall Street was heading toward its zenith, Frank had been one of the most active brokers in the country. There had been a lot of "new highway talk" and "railroad talk" and "new industry talk" and everybody around town agreed that Frank had been pretty damned smart to tie up pieces of land near the town for well under a hundred an acre, even though that was four or five times more than it sold for when the war ended.

In the end, at Melba's insistence, Frank had sold for cash the land that was to have become his ideal subdivision—"Garden Estates"—put the money in Postal Savings and thanked God that he'd had sense enough to listen to his wife. But Frank kept the dream alive by talking about it every chance he got and this unexpected young visitor offered the first chance in some months.

Laden with tubes of blueprints, Frank led Howdy back to the dining room table, where things could be spread out. For half an hour Howdy listened quietly, interrupting from time to time to ask questions that surprised Frank. Howdy's interest was no token act of politeness. Frank reluctantly rolled up the fading prints when Melba, carrying a pitcher of cold lemonade, joined them.

"All I ever wanted was to give young folks a subdivision with decent streets and good square lots with common sense restrictions on building." Frank sighed the sigh of a contented man who has been privileged to have a good listener.

Looking at her husband and Howdy with indulgence, Melba said, "You two talk a while longer and I'll make up the porch couch."

Howdy started to protest but Melba shushed him and

said, "Look young man, you don't have a bed and Frank and me are not going to turn you out to sleep under a bridge like some common hobo."

Melba left and after a brief reflective silence, Frank looked up. "I was thinking, Howdy. I know everybody in town. Maybe I can turn up a job that'll get you a few dollars for new clothes."

For once Howard Goodwyn had no calculated response. He mumbled his thanks and tried to cope with an unaccustomed pang of conscience. How could he keep his edge with people like these? Remembering Al Phelps advice, he said to himself silently. "Bet on human nature. It don't never change. That's your edge, kiddo!"

Bathed and freshly bandaged, Howdy stretched out in the first clean bed he had slept in for weeks. Ten hours later, voices—deliberately raised a bit—roused Howdy from his slumber. He pulled up the sheet as a screen and slipped into his B.V.D.'s. A clatter of dishes being scraped and stacked came from the back of the little cottage. He reached for the trousers that he had tossed on the chair the night before and found them neatly folded over its back.

Puzzled, he discovered that the ripped leg had been repaired with remarkable skill. Frank Persons appeared in the doorway as he was stuffing his shirt tails beneath the broad western belt.

"Thought I heard you. How'd you sleep?"

Howdy blinked in woozy wonderment. "Like a babe." He pointed to the trouser leg. "And while I was sleeping some ministering angel mended me."

"I know. The wife said if I was going to take you job hunting she'd better get you fixed up. Come on, chow's ready." In the kitchen, Melba was bending over the sink running water into a pot. Self-consciously, Howdy placed an arm around her shoulders.

"Thank you, ma'am, for putting me up—and patching me up." He turned to Frank, who was grinning at Melba's confusion.

Melba moved away, settling her hair, then shook her apron at him. "You two sit down. Things are getting cold."

After coffee they talked for an hour. Grown expansive, Howdy responded openly to most of their questions. He told them about Al Phelps and how Phelps had promoted him as a teenage cowboy singing star with Spike Spangler's Radio Rangers.

Frank Persons' eyes gleamed as he listened to the story of Phelps' rise from an eighteen-dollar-a-week operator of a pill-stamping machine to the creator and distributor of the famous Phelps' Formula.

The patent medicine had become a household word by the simple expedient of promising listeners everything short of eternal life. The pills, mostly bismuth subcarbonate and bicarbonate of soda flavored with mint, cost Phelps fifty cents a thousand to manufacture, bottle, and sell. He sold bottles of one hundred for five dollars.

Howdy explained that Phelps had spread the news that he was going to build a big plant a few miles out of town to manufacture medicines. Phelps bought up four sections of land fronting on the highway for less than $25 an acre. Next, he had large amounts of building materials dumped near the highway in full sight of all passersby. After that, he put up signs indicating where the "town's" churches, market stores, and club houses would go. Even with the advertising, surveying, engineering, and the land cost that had been split with a partner, Phelps had less than fifty dollars an acre invested.

"And," Howdy continued, "he sold quarter-acre homesites like tortillas for nine hundred and ninety-five dollars with only one hundred dollars down."

The older man whistled. "Six hundred and forty acres to a section—makes at least ten thousand quarter-acre sites—"

Howdy nodded. His expression clearly spelled out appreciation of Phelps as an operator. "—makes better than ten million dollars."

Phelpsville had collapsed with Al himself. On the eve of his biggest promotion, Al had dropped dead of a coronary. After the funeral, a large sign appeared on the site of Phelpsville. The crude lettering read: "TO ALL US PHOOLS WHO BELIEVED IN PHELPS' PHOLLY."

Frank really tried to find work for Howdy, but there were no offers beyond a vague promise of some garden work "for two bits an hour." Apologetically, he reported to Howdy and then said, "Look, I've got to put a new roof on the porch. If you can stick around to help me, I'll pay you six bits an hour plus room and board."

Howdy sensed that he would risk nothing by being honest. "I don't know a thing about shingling, Mr. Persons."

Frank laughed. "Name's Frank. Neither do I. We'll figure out how to do it together."

Late Friday afternoon, Melba Persons ended her anxious vigil at the bottom of a ladder as Frank and Howdy locked into place the last square of green asbestos roofing. She backed off and examined their work. "My goodness—what a difference!"

A pleased grin warmed Howdy's face as he stepped off the last rung. "Well, between singing at night and shingling by day I oughta be able to pile up a fortune."

Quickly, Melba said, "Don't ever give up your music, Howdy. I know two people right on this street that wouldn't be eating right now if they hadn't stayed with their music."

Frank Persons, still cautiously descending the ladder, said, "You talking about Angie and her mother?"

"I'm talking mostly about Angie Woodward. She may be playing piano in a saloon, but she's earning an honest living."

Howdy directed an amused glance at Melba Persons. "Playing in a saloon sounds like she's teetering on the brink."

Melba ignored the remark. "Angie's mother is the one that made the girl stay with her music. She's been teaching piano for twenty years or more—ever since Ralph went to war and never came back. He wasn't killed, either. He just plain deserted her and little Angie."

The men carried the ladder around to the side of the house and Melba followed, still talking. "That two-story place on the corner is theirs."

Howdy was surprised that it looked so well tended. "Except for yours, it's the nicest house on the street."

Later, when Howdy had pocketed the eight dollars earned for the work on the roof and they had settled on the porch, he asked, "Where's the place the girl's playing piano in?"

Melba pointed west. "Right outside of town—on the highway. Food's Italian and so are the owners. Rosa and Mike Rinelli. They call it the Roadside Inn."

Standing in the shade on the scraggly lawn at mid-morning the following day, Howdy said his farewells to Frank and Melba. Tucked inside the guitar case were a pair of Frank's socks and a change of underwear they had insisted he take. As the couple watched him stride down the street, Melba shook her head. "If anybody'd told me I'd cotton to a total stranger I'd of said they were crazy."

Howdy headed westward toward San Bernadino. On the opposite side of the highway, less than a half mile distant, he saw the Roadside Inn. He decided that the best way to get a ride would be to invest in a beer and strike up a conversation.

Blinking in the darkness, he made his way to a small bar at the right of the entrance and rested his guitar case against a vacant stool. He asked the small, wiry, work-worn woman who tended bar for a beer. He assumed she was Rosa Rinelli. As Rosa poured his beer, a young woman entered. The man at the bar nearest to Howdy swung around on the bar stool. "Hi there, Angie, how are you doing?"

Obviously, this was the girl Melba Persons had spoken about. Without appearing to, Howdy tried to get a look at her. As she exchanged easy banter Howdy was aware that her voice was low and pleasant. She seemed a bit taller than average—a good figure with wide, well-turned shoulders. Her hair was light brown, probably tending toward red in the sun. Unobtrusively, he tried for a glimpse at her legs but the guitar case leaning against the stool blocked his vision. He didn't catch the remark that made her laugh and step back but as she did, her leg struck the unseen guitar case. Too late he saw it start to topple. An instant later it slammed to the floor with a reverberating crash.

Stricken, the girl whirled around. "Oh my gosh! *Please* excuse me. I didn't see it."

"My fault, ma'am. I shouldn't have left it there."

"You mean, I should have looked where I was going." She glanced at the case. "It made an awful whang. Maybe you better look at it."

The other men had slipped off the stools and were moving toward the door. The younger of the two paused. "See you tonight, Angie. You got some new ones for us?"

Still upset, she replied over her shoulder. "Unless that piano tuner gets here we won't have any music."

Howdy had opened the case and quickly stuffed the

spare clothing out of sight beneath the instrument. The girl turned back and looked at the guitar, first with concern, then with admiration. "That's a beauty! Golly, I hope nothing broke—"

"It's okay. It's been banged around before—worse." He had positioned himself between the case and Angie when he picked up the guitar. He could see that while she wasn't a beauty she was certainly more than attractive. He liked her hair—the soft natural curl and the way she had it pulled back and caught at the nape of her neck. Apparently preoccupied with a bass string, his eyes focused briefly on her legs. From what he could see of them, they were clean-lined and symmetrical. But it was really her face that held him—an open face with regular features—a straight nose with a suggestion of an uptilt at the tip, and an agreeably full mouth. He assumed that in the light her wide-set eyes would be more green than gray.

After a moment he looked directly at her and smiled. "I could use a new bass string. But that didn't have anything to do with the fall." Effortlessly his hands drifted into position on the frets and he struck a soft chord. Listening critically, his fingers moved through a series of intricate rhythmic progressions.

Angie raised her eyebrows, "Mister, you certainly get around on that thing."

Howdy lowered the guitar and turned on a modest grin. "Let's say I did once, ma'am. But my fingers are sure out of practice."

She eyed him skeptically. "If yours are out of practice, then mine," she raised her hands for his inspection, "are in plaster casts."

They laughed together and Howdy put the instrument on top of the case. The girl sighed with exaggerated relief. "I'm sure happy nothing happened. By the way," she extended her hand, "I'm Angie Woodward. You must be the one Melba Persons was telling us about. You've been staying with them—helping Frank? Howdy Goodwyn. Right?"

Her hand had a good feel. "I was up on the roof with Frank, all right—but I don't know how much help I was."

"Don't be so modest. Melba told Mom you're one of the best workers they've ever had. And the best musician they've ever heard." A wistful note crept into her voice.

Howdy released her hand. "Well, from what I hear, you haven't got anything to worry about, Miss."

Rosa Rinelli returned from the dining room. "He's-a no come yet?"

Angie glanced outside unhappily. "Nope. He said he'd be here by lunchtime and work on the piano first thing this afternoon so I can practice. I want to run down some new things."

Rosa's eyes glowed with black malevolence. "He's-a no come last time too. If he's-a no come this time he's through. *Ecco! Finito!*"

"If he doesn't come this time I'll be through, too! Who's going to sit through an hour of me playing out-of-tune hits?"

Howdy craned to see the piano. On the way in he had caught a glimpse of the battered old upright in the far corner of the big dining room. "Is it just out of tune or is something busted?"

"Like everything and everybody around here, Mr. Goodwyn, it's dried up and coming apart." Outside, the sound of a car slowing made Howdy turn. The girl watched him curiously. "Melba said you're heading for Los Angeles."

"If I can find a ride." His fingers touched the bruised flesh beneath the gauze on his cheekbone.

Angie smiled sympathetically. "Melba told us about your accident. The only thing is, Mr. Goodwyn, if you're looking for an entertainment job I hope they told you things aren't very good in Hollywood either." Howdy nodded glumly and rested the guitar on the bar. "You've got my curiosity up. Would it hurt if I looked at the piano?"

"It's impossible to hurt it. Come on. I'll show you." She led him to the rear of the dining room where a bilious green lattice had been constructed. The whole graceless effect was punctuated here and there by great clusters of apoplectic artificial grapes. An old, ornately carved upright piano sat in the corner.

Angie executed a skillful arpeggio. Half a dozen notes were all but toneless. Howdy winced. "Mind if I look inside?"

He swung out the front panel and examined the strings, hammers, and pin block. "Could you fool around a little and let me see if I can find the worst ones?"

Angie began improvising. Working together, they iso-

409

lated the worst of the offending strings and in half an hour managed passable repairs to more than a dozen of them. Angie let a tinny chord sustain. Satisfied, she turned to him. "Such versatility! First shingling, then piano tuning." She began the opening vamp of the "Peanut Vendor." Automatically, Howdy reached for his guitar and joined her in a series of improvisations. They traded the lead back and forth until finally, in complete accord, they went into a deliberately corny ending and burst into laughter.

Angie studied him appraisingly. "You *are* good."

Howdy bowed with mock dignity. "Likewise, ma'am." With the guitar braced on his knee, he began to sing. Angie turned back to the keyboard. Toward the end of the chorus Howdy saw Rosa Rinelli and her husband move quietly into the hall doorway. At the end of the song, Angie whirled around on the stool and began applauding. "Wonderful! Wonderful!" Rosa and her husband Mike joined in. Rosa was so pleased she lapsed into excited Italian superlatives. *"Bella, Bella. Que bella canzone. Que bella voce. Mi piace molto. Moltissimo."*

Mike Rinelli, grinning broadly, simply said, "Sing more."

By the time Howdy and Angie got through "Tiptoe Through the Tulips," Nick Lucas' huge success from the talkie, *Gold Diggers of Broadway,* the Rinellis were overcome with enthusiasm. Glowing from the excitement of working with her first professional, Angie got up and linked her arm through Rosa's. "Excuse us a moment, will you? I want to talk to the Rinellis privately. We'll be right back."

Within minutes they returned and Angie said, "Mr. Goodwyn, I hope you won't think I'm a butinsky—but I had an idea while you were singing. Tonight and tomorrow night are our big nights—Friday and Saturday always are. I know you're anxious to get into L.A., but I told Rosa and Mike that I thought our customers would really go for a little change—something like you and I working up a few more of the things we just did for a sort of special weekend show. I don't mean for nothing, of course. Anyway, the Rinellis are agreeable—if you are. How about it?"

Howdy had trouble concealing his relief. "Well—I sure am obliged to you." He wagged his head. "But you don't have to pay me. I know all about hard times. I'd be plenty glad just to sing for my supper."

"You no sing fo' you suppa!" The woman's work-corded

arm swept the room. "You sing for money. Understand? Atsa only way people work for Mike and Rosa Rinelli." She jabbed a forefinger at Howdy. "Atsa *only* way. You get food and you get five dollars—two-fifty each night. Okay? And you get a room back there." Her tightly pinned, gray-streaked head jerked in the direction of the kitchen. "Okay?"

Softly, Howdy expelled a held breath. "Mrs. Rinelli—nothing has been this okay for months."

More than a hundred persons jammed into the Roadside Inn for the special show. By the time the second duet ended the customers were keenly aware that they were witnessing an unusual performance. Angie was their favorite and they were loyal to her. But the tall, spare, somewhat shabby young man with the scuffed-up forehead and the shy, ingratiating manner possessed a quality that not only compelled their attention but seemed to inspire Angie as well. His two solos produced an unprecedented hammering on glasses.

Later, seated on the front steps of the Woodward house, Angie summed up the opening. "Howdy, we need a lot more material. I'll bring everything I've got here at the house and you try to remember some of the new ones you lost in the suitcase."

Howdy got up, moved down a couple of steps, and faced her. "I think I can remember three or four. I'll let you turn in now and I'll start picking my brains."

Angie would have preferred to sit in the warm night air longer, re-living their success. Reluctantly she said, "See you tomorrow," and rose to go inside.

Saturday night was a standing-room-only repetition of Friday's triumph. Howdy and Angie had worked hard for most of the day adding new numbers and polishing the old ones. Howdy was at a disadvantage when it came to reading music, but Angie had managed to improve the harmony in his simpler chords with a number of tactful suggestions. For Angie, Howdy found himself feeling something akin to affection. It troubled him in a way that he did not comprehend because he sensed that she threatened his edge.

After the show, Howdy returned a wave to the last of the patrons and was about to step outside to join Angie and the Persons when Rosa called him to the bar.

She came right to the point. "Hey, Howdy. You want to work one more week?" When he made no immediate response, Rosa added, "Bed, food, and twenty dollars, including Saturday."

It was a windfall and Howdy accepted as gracefully as he could. With a little more luck, he would be able to stretch his stake to a job in L.A.

It was nearly one in the morning when Howdy undressed and stretched out on the bed in the stuffy little room at the rear of the Inn. At peace for the first time in months, he thought about Angie and how friendly she was—how good she looked—how fresh and sweet she smelled. Suddenly he gave his head a violent shake. "Screw that stuff, Goodwyn! That's how it always starts. You got other fish to fry."

Angie had asked him if he wanted to go to church with her. Howdy thought about church—what it would be like—and begged off. He could still see his own mother and father anesthetizing themselves with a simplistic, do-nothing faith in God when the first of the real hard times hit the small ranchers in Oklahoma. The recollection brought a bitter half-laugh in the darkness.

He remembered the day his father's faith had failed and he had left the ranch to search for wage work—a search that soon ended in death from exposure and pneumonia. He recalled the old man's words just before he left: "God's turned his back on this land. The Dust Devils is stealing it. If I set here and wait for Him to see what's going on, the Devil himself will steal the lot of us, too."

Drowsy, Howdy forced his mind back to the present. "No church," he told himself. "I'll just thank God for every day I'm alive and well."

That weekend Howdy and Angie repeated their previous success before an over-capacity audience. Customers unable to find a table or a place at the bar jammed the doorway and lined the walls. The last customers drifted from the bar shortly after midnight. Rosa and Mike asked Howdy to stay on for a second week. Gratefully, Howdy accepted but he knew that would be his last.

Once again, Howdy and Angie sat on the porch at the Woodward home, talking about the performance, and speculating on new material.

Suddenly Angie laughed. "Just listen to us. You'd think Mike and Rose had signed us to a five-year contract."

There was an uneasy silence that Howdy broke by rising abruptly. "It's getting late. I better go now."

Controlling her voice, Angie nodded. "When are you going to leave? Town, I mean?"

"Tomorrow, I suppose—I've got almost forty bucks now. I better move on before I wear out my welcome."

Angie struggled against the nagging sense of loss. At times during the last few nights the feeling had come close to desperation. Before, she had never really measured the monotony of her life. The word "love" had not entered her mind—but Angie had come to understand Howdy's appeal. It did not incite romantic fantasies, but when she was close to him she was acutely aware of him and the feeling was akin to excitement.

Reaching up, Angie rested what she hoped was a comradely hand on his shoulder. "Well, Howdy, I'm lousy at weddings, funerals, and farewells. So," she removed her hand and offered it directly, "I want to thank you for everything and—and—good luck!"

Before Howdy could respond, she gave him a quick peck on the cheek and hurried inside.

After he left, Angie castigated herself for the fool she had been. Dismally, thinking of the success of their performances together, she felt she was stealing the ten dollars Rosa and Mike were paying her. The thought of going back, to face that relic of a piano, chilled her. Even more chilling was the realization that Howdy had ignored her as a female. Against all reason during the two weeks Howdy stayed, bright hope had displaced drab uncertainty—the same uncertainty she knew would prevail even if she did break down and marry one of the several steady and dull suitors who really wanted to take care of her.

14 HOWDY GOODWYN STEPPED DOWN from the electric car at the corner of Hollywood Boulevard and Vine Street. He had boarded the loaf-like street car at the Hill Street Station in downtown Los Angeles thirty minutes earlier.

For several minutes he stood looking around, a tall, lean young man dressed in worn show-business cowboy clothing, clutching a scuffed, sequin-embossed guitar case. He was inconspicuous among the regulars who haunted the notorious corner—an old-time fighter whose kneaded dough face and erratic speech and movements betrayed a lifetime of more punishment received than given, a dilapidated one-time silent-screen bathing beauty whose orange hair seemed about to burst into flame, a ferret-eyed taxi driver who augmented his uncertain income by pimping, a part-time, toga-wearing recluse known as the Hollywood Holy Man, and a benignly visaged eccentric with flowing white hair who claimed to be the incarnation of Edwin Booth.

The human menagerie made Howdy uneasy. He headed for a filling station on the Boulevard and asked the attendant where he could find a cheap boarding house. He was directed to one on Franklin Avenue, run by Georgette Follansby, where he took an attic room for six dollars a week. The price included breakfast. After he paid for his room Howdy returned to the filling station on the pretext of thanking the attendant and got directions to the radio stations he planned to start visiting the following morning. The man also told Howdy about the principal points of interest along the Boulevard.

It took him an hour to walk the circuit. Except for Grauman's Chinese Theater and the older Egyptian Theater, the Warner Brothers' Theater and the Pantages, which also boasted a stage show, he found the celebrated Boulevard shoddy. The famed Hollywood Hotel seemed little different to him than a dozen turn-of-the-century resort hotels he had seen in the South and Southwest. Beyond the Broadway-Hollywood, the only stores that attracted him were The Columbia Outfitting Company and the "Walk-upstairs-and-save-ten-dollars" men's store, Foreman and Clark. By the time he climbed the hill to Franklin Avenue it was nearing eight o'clock.

Lingering on the broad front steps, he gazed out over the carnival sprawl that is Hollywood and Los Angeles after dark. The day had been hot, but sundown had brought a cool breeze from the ocean. It moved like a benediction over the coastal plain, bearing a trace of salt freshness and the perfume of numberless flowers and trees. A transformation had taken place in both the land and its beholder. He was responding to a magic well known to natives and frequent visitors—a phenomenon not to be ignored and never to be taken for granted. Commonplace by day, the squat stucco "California Cottages" and the newer, uninspired box-like brick apartments and commercial buildings had undergone a metamorphosis with the setting sun. Evening did for the city what candlelight does for a once-beautiful woman. The illusion cast its spell on the young man from the Southwest and he fell in love.

Breakfast was served at seven in the dark-paneled dining room across the hall from the sitting room. It was a gloomy room suffused with the odor of greasy cookery and dominated by an old oak dining room suite.

Of those at the table only one old man seemed to possess any animation or interest in his surroundings. Howdy watched him test the grease-curled margin of over-fried egg white. In a remarkably young, vibrant voice the senior boarder pronounced judgment on the temporarily absent landlady's cooking. "This egg, dear fellow sufferers, is not fried. It is ossifried!" He detached a portion, maneuvered it onto a wedge of limp toast, and regarded it philosophically.

Howdy glanced around at the two middle-aged women and the other two men, waiting for a reaction. There was none. At his father's funeral Howdy had seen several other corpses awaiting interment. These people reminded him of those dead ones—empty human husks. He smiled across at the old man. "The only time I eat worse eggs is when I cook 'em myself."

The old man lifted the paper napkin to stifle a small

415

belch, murmured an apology, and looked up at Howdy again. "What perverse fortune brings you here—if I may ask?"

"Prospects for some radio work. I play guitar—and sing a little."

"One of those, eh? Well, it's honorable work. I concede that—even if it does strike a blow at my livelihood."

"What do you do, sir—if I'm not prying?"

"Son," the word filled the dining room with a commanding resonance, "*I*—am a voice coach. Name's Neville Newton. When the Brothers Warner introduced their Vitaphone process and poor Jack Gilbert's career came to a squeaking end, I left Chicago and caught the express west to make a fortune salvaging the careers of silent stars." His expression turned forlorn. "However, during the past two years most of my energy has been devoted to an attempt to salvage my own career."

The two women looked at him reproachfully and excused themselves. Amused, Neville said, "They've heard this before a time or two. But it will be new to you."

"I'd be glad to hear anything about this town that'll help me get next to it."

"In that case, son, why don't we put my counsel on a professional basis?"

Howdy looked startled. "I could use the help but I can't pay for it. Anyways, not right now."

A resigned sigh deflated the old voice coach. "Well, like FDR said on the radio—the only thing we've got to fear is fear itself."

Howdy watched the old man closely, for what he was hearing induced in him pity not unmixed with fear. Abruptly, he rose from the table. "'Long's you got hope you're not whipped." He indicated the street. "And if I want to stay alive I'd better get hitched up and start peddling me."

Neville nodded. "Good luck, my boy."

In three days Howdy visited five radio stations in Hollywood and Los Angeles. At each, the answer was the same, "We're not putting on any new acts now, thanks." His attempts to talk with the leaders of the established groups were frustrated by receptionists, switchboard operators, and gate guards. It seemed to Howdy that the minute they saw him coming with his guitar, they automatically slammed the door.

For all his determination, Howdy's financial situation became acute. The condition was aggravated by the need to spend some of his meager cash to have his boots half-soled and to spend five dollars and change for a pair of frontier trousers at a Western outfitter's shop on Santa Monica Boulevard patronized by the cowboy actors and stunt men who appeared in Poverty Row's quickie Westerns.

The owner of the shop, a man called Harry, gave Howdy his first solid encouragement. "I know most of those producers. I'm carrying two of them on the books now for costumes. If you don't care how busted up you get for five bucks a day, I might be able to get you in. Can you ride?"

"I'm no bronc buster. But I know one end of a horse from the other."

"Know how to take a fall?"

Howdy smiled ruefully. "I've taken my share."

An hour later, wearing refurbished boots and carrying the new trousers in a bag under his arm, Howdy entered the shabby Sunset Boulevard office of Running Iron Productions. The producer, Bronc Bronston, who had been pressured by phone into seeing him, did little to hide his antagonism. "What do you want to do, kid—get paid to learn how to act?"

Howdy's smile lingered but his reply was flat. "What I want to do is eat. I don't know a solitary thing about acting, but I can ride a horse and do what you tell me. Is that good enough?"

The producer let Howdy endure a long, resentful appraisal. "Okay, kid. What's your name?"

"Goodwyn. Howdy Goodwyn."

The man made a note on a slip of paper and shoved it aside. "Okay, Goodwyn. You get three days at five bucks a day with grub on location."

Howdy tried not to show his relief. "Thank you, sir. I appreciate it."

"You better. When you pick up your dough just remember you took it from one of them pro's out there on the street who needs the job."

Howdy's eyes glazed and he had a hard time keeping his voice even. "Where do I show up? What time?"

Bronston jerked a stubby thumb at a cast notice tacked to the wall. "Six A.M.—Monday—out front. The bus don't wait."

As Howdy turned to leave, the man stopped him. "What work clothes you got?"

"What I got on—plus some pants."

"No Stetson? Or Levis?"

Howdy sensed the producer was about to find the out he had been looking for. "Hell, yes. I got them—if that's what you want."

Bronston smirked. "That's what I want."

Outside, Howdy walked through the knot of gaunt movie cowboys waiting by the door. He could feel their eyes following him—questioning. Edging through them with a friendly nod, he turned west and then south toward Santa Monica Boulevard and the Western outfitter's store. Harry greeted him expectantly. "How'd you make out with Bronc?"

Howdy laughed mirthlessly. "Like a skunk at a picnic. But I got the job—if you'd go me a little credit."

The clothier's pleased smile grew a bit strained. "What do you need?"

"A hat. Some Levis. That's all."

Harry shrugged. "So pick 'em out."

Howdy left the store in debt for eight of the fifteen dollars he had hoped to collect for the three days' work.

The Reo bus left Running Iron Productions at six in the morning. Howdy was among the last to board. Behind him during the long ride to the San Fernando Valley the men, all veterans of a hundred quickies, talked in the flat-voiced, nasal jargon of the movie cowboy. There was no laughter and what humor he could overhear in the rattletrap transport was grim.

When the bus pulled up to the false-front Western street the wranglers had horses saddled and ready to work. Immediately it was apparent to Howdy that each man had his favorite mount. The two stunt men had their own personal horses.

"Pick yourself out one, kid." Bronc Bronston indicated the corral with a jerk of his beefy head. Most of the other men were mounted and waiting.

Howdy walked over to the remaining half dozen animals. He knew Bronston and the others were watching.

Affecting the easy nonchalance of a man used to saddle animals, he moved smoothly from one to the other, sliding a gentling hand along each neck. He chose a sorrel mare who had the compact look of a good cutting mount. He led the animal into the clear, checked the bridle carefully as well as the cinches and the stirrups. Satisfied, he swung up easily and waited.

Some minutes later the director called for attention. "You men follow Charley." He indicated the assistant director. "You ride up that draw over there until you get to those big rocks, then keep your horses out of camera sight until Charley gives you the signal. We shoot all the long chase scenes this morning. I don't want more than one take or any busted animals. So don't bunch up—and watch the slide on this side. Most of you hands have been over the ground a hundred times."

He waved them away. "Okay, men—take your cues from Charley."

It took an hour to show the men the chase route and mark the paths the two stunt men would follow. At the top of the ridge the assistant marshaled the riders. "We'll run it once, real easy now, for Bronc and Lou. Let's go."

At the end of the line of horsemen, Howdy urged the sorrel into an easy lope down a long and sloping trail. The stunt men stopped at the point where they would take their falls. The others continued another hundred yards then pulled up on the brink of what seemed to be an almost vertical fifty-foot slope of loose rubble. The assistant director raised an arm, cavalry fashion. "Hold up here! No use going down now." He motioned to one of the men. "You and I'll ride down it for the camera, Joe. The rest of you guys go on back to the top."

After half an hour of tedious waiting, Charley and Joe rode back and joined the others behind the rocks at the top of the hill. Dismounted, Charley waited for the action signal. It came quickly, a puff of smoke followed by the sharp report of a forty-five. Charley wheeled and thrust an arm at the waiting men. "Okay—action!"

Howdy was not prepared for what followed. The riders—a dozen of them—urged their mounts into leaping starts and plunged headlong down the ridge. There was no time to think. All around him the men were yipping and rebel-yelling, oblivious of the dangerous mesquite, the manzanita brush, the loose rocks, and the choking cloud of dust. Off to his right he saw the two stunt men separate and crash with their mounts in the prepared areas. He was dimly aware of scrambling bodies and thrashing animal legs and then they were behind him.

Seconds later, the men and animals immediately in front of him began to go over the edge. An animal on his left dug in stiff-legged and balked at the brink. The rider cursed and spurred it over. His own animal held up and tossed its head wildly. Howdy gouged his heels into its flanks but before he could regain control there was a shout behind him. Nearly blinded by dust, he half turned to look just as the animal behind him crashed into his own mount's hind quarters. He saw the rider leave the saddle, saw cartwheeling arms and legs disappear over the edge and then he, too, was on his way down in the heart of a sheer hell of sliding rock and ochre dust. Twice the mare's hind legs buckled so badly that his stirrups dug into the slope. The rubble flared out a bit and then he was on hard level ground again. Without thinking, he wheeled the animal and turned to look back. Through the ochre dust he could see the two stunt men running across the slope toward a riderless horse floundering in the brush.

In the distance he heard a voice bellowing. "Keep coming, you stupid son-of-a-bitch! Keep coming!"

Unaware that the order was intended for him, Howdy urged the mare into long leaps back up the slide. When it was no longer possible to find footing, he jumped off, dropped the reins, and scrambled toward the fallen man. The stunt men reached the fallen rider first. One of them turned to him. "What kind of jackass are you, pulling that mare up short at the top with Foy here right behind you?"

Howdy looked up from the unconscious rider. "I didn't pull up. Even if I wanted to, I couldn't. I couldn't see the drop. He was riding too close onto me."

The man spat. "Riding too close? Shit!" He pointed at the downed rider. "This man was a rodeo champ when you was still setting down to pee!" He spat again. "Riding too close. Shit!"

Howdy was still kneeling helplessly beside the man when Bronc Bronston came scrambling up. Without warning, he kicked Howdy on the thigh with the side of his boot. "Get off this goddam hill and wait for me, you dumb bastard!"

Howdy restrained an impulse to strike out at the man and scrambled back down to the mare.

It took ten minutes to get Foy off the slope. As far as they were able to tell, his most serious injury was an ugly gash on his forehead but he was still unconscious when Charley drove off with him to the doctor in San Fernando.

As soon as the car was on its way, Bronc Bronston turned to Howdy. He jabbed a blunt forefinger into Howdy's shirtfront. "You get the hell out of here. You get in that goddam bus and sit there. Then you collect one day's pay and I don't ever want to see you around a movie company again. You lied to me, you bum. You said you knew how to handle horses."

The regret Howdy felt was submerged in a wave of cold anger. "Before you start calling me a liar, you better remember I told you I can ride a horse and follow orders and that's *all* I said."

Bronston thrust his face into Howdy's. "What you cost me today could break this picture. When a man asks me to pay good money to handle a horse, I expect him to know all there is to know about it."

"Look, mister, I was raised on a ranch outside of Guyon, Oklahoma. I been around animals all my life. If you expect a guy to know a new animal then you better give him time to learn it before you tell him to jump it off the edge of the Grand Canyon."

Somewhere in the crowd a man guffawed. Bronston, his face purple, struggled to keep from smashing a fist into Howdy's impassive face. He jerked a thumb toward the bus. "Get your ass over there and keep out of the way."

He turned on his heel and Howdy continued to stand. He wanted to make it clear that he had not been intimidated and would take his time getting to the bus.

By mid-afternoon some of the anger had leached out of Howdy. One of the cowboys had told him the report on the injured rider had been encouraging—some stitches and a possible concussion.

In the producer's office Howdy waited while Bronston drew a check for five dollars. Bronston shoved it to the front of the desk without blotting it. "You ought to give me five hundred. That's what you cost me today."

Howdy picked up the check, blew on it, and smiled pleasantly. "You claim to be an expert on lies, so you ought to know one when you tell it."

Bronston's eyes widened. Suddenly he laughed. "If you could ride as well as you talk, kid, you'd make one hell of a cowboy. Just get the hell out of this office."

On the corner of Hollywood and Vine an old man was handing out leaflets. Absent-mindedly, Howdy took one and was about to throw it in the gutter when his eye caught the phrase, "Free Refreshments." It was an announcement of a meeting of the Utopian Society, a secret fraternal organization being founded "to acquaint southern Californians with the New Economic Order that will guarantee every American a life of plenty."

The private residence on Fountain Avenue below Hollywood Boulevard, where the meeting was held, proved to be more impressive than Howdy had expected. More than thirty persons, most of them past middle age, listened to one of the three organizers, a persuasive man named Rousseau, expound on the society.

Rousseau exuded an infectious brand of confidence. "We have friends in high places—enough friends to unseat the 'Power Gods' downtown and their political machine in Sacramento. Their days are numbered. Today 'Plenty for All' means plenty for them and *nothing* for us. But we're going to change all that. We're going to end this depression. There is more than enough wealth in southern California to take care of every man, woman, child—*and old person*—in the entire state—when it's distributed fairly. We aim to see that done by exercising our power in a truly democratic way."

Rousseau went on to reveal a well-kept secret: the notorious Socialist, Upton Sinclair, was changing his political stripes and becoming a Democrat. His intention was to organize a new wing of the party that would support him for governor.

"I know Sinclair. He wants the same things we want. We foresee the possibilities of combining forces. Then, my friends, you will see an end to the Republican stranglehold on the politics of this state—an end to the domination of Harrison Gray Otis and his newspaper—and end to the Merchants and Manufacturers' lobby—an end to greed and an end to want!"

Rousseau spoke for thirty minutes and painted such a convincing picture of Utopian possibilities that every person present donated as much as he could spare. Even

Howdy put in two dimes while making mental note once again of a fundamental principle of salesmanship: *"Find out what they don't like and be against it. Then find out what they want and promise it to them."*

The free refreshments turned out to be watery, sparingly sweetened orange juice squeezed from fruit donated from the backyard tree of one of the charter members.

The Utopian hostess apologized: "It's not very thick, but it's a lot thicker than the milk of human kindness that flows in the veins of those Scrooges downtown."

Howdy managed to slip away unobtrusively after a half glass of the indifferent refreshment. Several minutes later he joined a crowd of people at the corner of Hollywood Boulevard and La Brea Avenue which had gathered to attend a radio show called *The Hollywood Barn Dance* featuring The Crockett Family, The Stafford Sisters, and Sheriff Loyal Underwood and the Arizona Wranglers. The largest letters on the banner across the front of The Hollywood Woman's Club Auditorium spelled out ADMISSION FREE.

The KNX radio show was one of the best country and western presentations Howdy had seen. After the show, he lingered with autograph seekers and managed a word with the Master of Ceremonies. Something about Howdy caused Sheriff Loyal Underwood to listen instead of smiling sympathetically and dismissing still another out-of-work musician. Without quite knowing why he did it, Underwood promised to arrange an appointment for Howdy with KNX's program director, Dave Layne.

Monday morning Howdy retraced the familiar route to the Western outfitting store. Harry was surprised to see him. "Hey! How'd it go, cowboy?"

Howdy slipped the check from his shirt pocket and handed it to the puzzled merchant. "I'll sign this over to you now. As soon as I get a job I'll pay you on the balance —with interest. I have an appointment with the program director at KNX."

Harry ignored the check. "What happened with Bronston?"

Howdy shrugged. "He's your buddy. You better let him tell it."

"You tell me. Bronc and I do business and we go to the same temple. But that don't make him a buddy. You can't

423

keep friends when you make pictures on his budgets. What happened?"

Simply, without rancor, Howdy recounted the events leading up to his dismissal. Harry listened, nodding silently. Then he took the check from the counter and stuffed it into Howdy's pocket.

"Bronston's going to eat tonight and so am I. I'll digest better if I know you're eating, too. Pay me a buck or two every so often and I'll do better with you than I do with most of them—including Bronston." He indicated the door. "So go get something to eat and Mozl-Tov with your audition." Howdy's puzzled expression made Harry chuckle. "Kiddo—'Mozl-Tov' is good luck the hard way. Now go eat."

Howdy's second break came when he persuaded Dave Layne to at least let him audition. Later, Layne like Underwood, was at loss to explain why. But Howdy knew he had his edge back when he saw the amiable, one-time Irish tenor waver.

"Okay, Goodwyn. Go ahead and sing. But I'm not making any promises."

When the first song was over Layne motioned through the glass of the control room for another. After the third song, a hymn, he returned to the studio.

"Remember. No promises. But I may be able to fix you up singing hymns on the Reverend Matt Simon's Wednesday prayer show." In spite of the program director's caution, Howdy's heart leaped. While waiting for Layne to arrange the studio he had seen the big, burly revival preacher in the front office counting an impressive stack of greenbacks sent in by the grateful radio congregation. To Howdy the sign augered well.

Howdy got his start and his first break when he persuaded David Layne, the program director for KNX, to let him audition. At the time, KNX had a money-making property in the Reverend Matthew Simon. Simon, an unctuously pious man in his forties, had assiduously studied the lesson implicit in Sister Aimee McPherson's spectacular success.

Howdy had his first glimpse of Simon sitting at a desk littered with mail. On his right side was a shoebox filled with currency, on his left was the lid, brimming with coins. The Reverend was busy slitting open envelopes and emptying their contents. His appearance repelled Howdy as surely as David Layne's engaging Irish face had attracted him.

David Layne literally coerced Simon into taking Howdy on his program as the hymn-singing guitar player. The Reverend put up with Howdy for exactly four weeks and then insisted on booting him off. As a man used to a recently achieved spotlight, who over the past two years on the air had acquired "a more suitable residence in which to meditate on the Word of God" along with a new La Salle touring car, he was not in a position to welcome anyone who might compete with him on his own program. Further, he was terrified of anything that might interfere with his tidy arrangement with KNX. The station made unproductive radio time available in return for a portion of the "Free Will" offerings.

After the Matthew Simon impasse Layne was hard-pressed to find anything for Howdy. But he had an innate faith in him and he finally succeeded in giving the young singer his own show when Howdy solved the problem of the Urinex commercial. Urinex wanted radio listeners with bladder trouble to send a specimen and twenty-five cents to Little Rock for a free urinalysis. The purpose was to hook the specimen-senders into buying the product. KNX's owner had shown an unexpected conservative streak by flatly refusing to permit such advertising on his station. Even David Layne admitted it took guts to turn down $500 a week during a depression. Howdy's solution, arrived at by poring over the ads in a cheap movie magazine, consisted of couching the ad in delicate terms, never quite coming to grips with specifics and asking the radio listeners to write in for "a personal symptom and diagnosis chart" at a cost of a dime. The chart, not the station, would suggest that the recipient send the specimen to Little Rock.

The news that Howdy would have his own radio program flabbergasted Angela Woodward. She was reading the Sunday papers and glancing through the entertainment section noting reports of the success of the Ballet Russe de Monte Carlo in the East and the proposed dramatization of Erskine Caldwell's controversial novel, *Tobacco Road*. There were several reviews of new radio programs. The *Romance of Helen Trent* was dismissed as "sentimental dime-novel trash" that would, mercifully, be short-lived. *The Woman in White* was given a better chance because of its noble central figure. *The Lady Esther Serenade* was promising and Walter Winchell would reveal some earth-shaking news on Monday.

Angie turned to Carol Nye's column. Her eyes moved down to an item about Lanny Ross, Showboat's singing star, to a paragraph about a radio series starring "The old Maestro, Ben Bernie." Then a name jumped out of the page at her. An instant later she was running upstairs calling to her mother.

Ana Woodward stopped struggling with an awkwardly placed hook and eye. "For pity's sake, Angie, you'll have an attack!"

"Mom! Howdy's in Carol Nye's column. Listen!"

She gulped in a deep breath and began reading: "Dave Layne, progam director for Station KNX, tells us that new singing star Howdy Goodwyn, an import from Oklahoma and Texas, where he was featured with Spike Spangler's Radio Rustlers for three years on Station KALP, is going to be given his own show on Wednesday evenings. Will Thatcher and the KNX staff orchestra will support the personable young performer."

Angie gasped through the rest of the column. When she finished, she flung the paper aside and said dramatically, "*I* have discovered a star!"

Ana nodded indulgently. "I wouldn't brag about it yet. Wait a few months and we'll see. But I don't mean to dampen your enthusiasm just because I seem to have lost mine."

"How much proof do you need? Wait for what? You heard him on one of those dreadful religious shows. He was wonderful."

Ana smiled tolerantly and moved toward the door. "All right, dear, he was wonderful. Come on now, let's go. I want to run down the hymns before the service."

Angie was still standing outside the church when Melba Persons came bustling up, waving a folded clipping. "Did you see the news?"

Inside, they talked in excited whispers until Frank, who had arrived late, hushed them as the service began. Afterward they resumed their speculations. Angie swore that she would not work that night. Melba suggested they all listen at their house.

Frank Persons, who had been secretly sharing their pride and excitement, broke in, "Maybe we could find out if there's an audience and drive to L.A. to see the first show. But you better remember it'll make it a late night. Very late."

Excitedly they agreed to try it. There would be five of them; in addition to Frank and Melba, Angie and her mother, Rosa Rinelli was asked to join them.

Frank and the four women pulled up to the studio at ten of eight. It was twenty after eight before they found a parking place and began the walk to the auditorium. When they turned the corner they were confronted by a line of several hundred persons.

Melba stared at the scene open mouthed. "For heaven's sake! I wonder if we can get in."

Angie urged them on. "Let's get in line quickly and we'd better all stay together."

The front doors opened and by the time they were inside, the only unoccupied chairs were scattered singles on the sides and a sprinkling of two's and three's well toward the rear. Angie steered her mother and the Persons into the ones at the rear. Then, taking Rosa Rinelli by the arm, she hurried to a pair of singles one behind the other midway down the side. In a matter of minutes the auditorium was filled to capacity. Disappointed people lined both side walls. Others were still clogging the lobby. The house lights snapped off and a spotlight suspended from the ceiling projected a blazing circle on the drab monk's cloth curtain. The chatter subsided at once. A moment later an attractive young man slipped through and stepped out onto the apron. There was a scattering of applause, which he silenced with a good-natured gesture.

"Good evening, ladies and gentlemen. My name is Tom Smith. I'm your announcer and it's my pleasant duty to welcome you to the première of the Howdy Goodwyn Show."

A cheer went up all over the auditorium. The announcer consulted his wrist watch and held up his hand. "We have only three minutes until air time. Before I introduce our orchestra leader and our star, I just want to tell you that we hope you will applaud after each number. Let's try it now."

The engineer checked sound levels and signaled his okay. The musical director, Will Thatcher, appeared followed by his four boys. The audience applauded as Tom

Smith beamed his approval. "And now, ladies and gentlemen—the brightest new star in our Western skies——Howard D.——Howdy——Goodwyn!"

The din of cheering, applauding, stomping people filled the auditorium. It continued as Howdy deliberately delayed his entrance. Then, pretending he'd been unavoidably detained, he came running onstage with his guitar, glancing apologetically off into the wings.

For a full minute he stood acknowledging the ovation with the same underplayed engaging shyness he had affected in front of audiences in Oklahoma.

The Persons, Ana Woodward, Rosa Rinelli, and Angie sat open-mouthed, trying to reconcile the tall, well-groomed young man with the scarred, bedraggled hitchhiker they had first known two months earlier.

Rosa turned to Angie in the chair directly behind her. "*Mama mia!* Wotsa hoppen to Howdy?"

The girl leaned forward and grasped the older woman's shoulders. "Oh, he looks *wonderful*, Rosa! Look at him! He looks like a star already."

"He looks pretty good, all right. Beautiful."

Angie let her chin rest lightly on Rosa's shoulder. Her voice was scarcely audible. "He's not beautiful, honey, but he looks better than any man I've ever known."

Rosa Rinelli leaned away and twisted to look Angie in the eye. "Oh, ho, ho! *Amore*, eh?"

Howdy began to speak: "I only got about thirty seconds, but I want to thank you all for coming out tonight." He looked offstage, received a warning signal, and acknowledged it. "I have to go now. I sure hope you like what we do and I'll talk to you some more later."

From the wings an unseen cue was thrown to Will Thatcher and the theme song began. It was a bright, catchy original opening number entitled "Howdy" that had been composed by Thatcher several days earlier as a welcoming signature song. Accompanying himself on the guitar and backed by an infectious arrangement, Howdy smiled over the footlights and addressed the simple lyrics directly to the audience. When the theme ended the reaction was so enthusiastic that Howdy had to help Tom Smith quiet the house. The theme had performed its intended function perfectly. Dave Layne summed it up halfway through the show: "That kid could blow his nose onstage and get an ovation. I may send in a dime myself."

Compared to the big network musicals, or even to the *Saturday Night Barn Dance, The Howdy Goodwyn Show* was a simple affair. It relied on Dave Layne's pet formula—"Good shows are made by good performers, not gimmicks." Howdy proved to be a better performer than any of them had suspected.

Neil Carlson, the station's sales manager, listening to Howdy's Urinex pitches being delivered with such deceptive ease and confidential sincerity that they seemed to be the spontaneous after-thoughts of a dear friend concerned for the welfare of an intimate, shook his head in disbelief.

When the show was over, the front aisles were clogged with eager fans. Howdy, flushed with elation, scarcely saw individual faces as he squatted on the apron greeting acquaintances and strangers with both hands, scribbling autographs on proffered scraps and soaking up adulation. After ten minutes his legs began to cramp. Apologetically, he struggled upright and rubbed his knees. It was his first real chance to look out into the auditorium. The crowd had begun to thin as Howdy's eyes swept across it to the aisle on his right. Suddenly the set smile turned to amazement. An instant later, with a joyful whoop, he leaped into the startled crowd and began pushing his way toward the Persons, the Woodwards, and Rosa Rinelli. Halfway up the aisle Angie was in his arms. Too full of emotion to trust her voice, she clung to him. When Melba reached them, blinking and daubing her nose, Howdy freed an arm and reached out to embrace her too. Finally he pushed Angie gently from him and grasped the hands of each in turn. Over and over he kept expressing his wonderment.

"I don't believe it! I don't believe it! I just don't believe it . . ."

Angie, smiling broadly, said, "You'd better. Frank drove like Barney Oldfield for five hours to get us here on time."

Neil Carlson, looking apologetic, came up and tapped Howdy's shoulder. "Sorry to interrupt, but the boys from the agency want to talk to us over coffee at the Roosevelt." Sensing Howdy's keen disappointment, he added, "You come along when you can. We'll wait for you there." Before Howdy could introduce him he slipped into the crowd.

Frank Persons took out his pocket watch. "If we don't have a flat tire, it'll still take us until after two in the morning to get home. So we'd better hit the road. And besides—Howdy shouldn't have anything but business on his mind right now."

They left the auditorium and walked down La Brea toward the car. Angie clung to Howdy's arm, visibly at least more elated than he at the obvious success of the first program. At the car, Melba, enthusiastically supported by Angie, urged Howdy to come down for a weekend. The rest of them took up the coaxing. Rosa Rinelli's invitation was more of a command. "You coming down, Howdy. That's all! We make you *pranzo speciale.*"

Howdy slipped his arms around Melba and Rosa. "As soon as I know what'll happen next I'll mail you a card and see when's a good time for you."

Melba patted his back maternally. "Any time's a good time for us, young man. Your bed's waiting on the porch." At Frank's insistence they got into the car. As it started to pull away, Melba leaned out. "And you bring your mending too."

Howdy watched them depart and returned their waves until the car disappeared around the corner. He did not envy them the one-hundred-twenty-five-mile drive and he was more grateful than he had been able to say that they had come.

As he walked back to Hollywood Boulevard to join Dave he wondered again at the curious loneliness he felt.

Howdy's success on the Urinex show was sufficient to make other sponsors interested in signing him up. But none of them wanted any part of him as long as he was connected with a product whose commercial catchline read, "Make your bladder gladder. Use Urinex." The agencies bluntly told KNX "Get rid of Urinex and we'll give you more quality business than you can handle."

As a result, KNX offered Howdy a five-year contract—with a catch. The station had the right to terminate at the end of each twenty-six-week period but the contract for five years was firm as far as Howdy was concerned. Throughout the meeting with the KNX executives and David Layne, Howdy seemed to be understanding, even agreeing. At the end of the session, he nodded to himself and grinned amiably. "Everything's clear now. But I was just wondering if I could have a little pondering time in view of the fact that you good folks are taking the gamble and all you're asking me to take is the risk."

The next night David Layne surprised Howdy by asking him to stop by his apartment. The invitation carried the sound of urgency. Dave's apartment turned out to be a cottage in one of the ubiquitous garden courts scattered throughout Hollywood. Through Neville Newton Howdy had found a professional whore whom he used once or twice a week. David's place depressed Howdy because it reminded him of the cottage Renée occupied. There was the same shabbiness and cheap hominess about them both. Dave indicated a ratty easy chair and said, "How about a beer?" He disappeared into the kitchenette and returned in a moment carrying two bottles of Miller's High Life, and two jelly glasses. "Thought I'd better break out the family crystal. This might be a momentous meeting."

Howdy's wondering gaze made him grin.

"I may sound like Benedict Arnold when I tell you what I have in mind, Howdy—but that's a chance I'll have to take."

Howdy poured the beer without looking up. "Never did hear Arnold talk—so I wouldn't know. Shoot."

"Ever since you talked me into listening to you sing I expect you've noticed that I have done all I could, consistent with my job as program manager, to help you along."

Howdy confirmed the truth with a nod.

Dave paused to light a cigarette. "I told you I used to be a performer—a legit tenor. For almost six years I was a pretty big name on WLS in Chicago. I got signed to the same kind of contract our station is offering you. And I signed it—gladly—for security. Then along came a guitar twanger named Autry and the next thing I knew I was off the air. I couldn't find another show so I did what I could. I sang leads in *The Student Prince* in high school auditoriums and sang 'Danny Boy' and 'Mother Machree' at Women's Club luncheons. I got so damned hungry I had to lean on the piano. In the middle of all that my wife left me."

Dave smiled bitterly at the recollection. "Finally I got a job in the chorus of *The Desert Song* and wound up out here. Three years ago I started singing on the station for nothing and selling electric heaters door to door. Have you ever tried to sell an electric heater in Los Angeles in August—during a depression? My best month I made

431

sixty dollars but I guess God must have been listening because a local dairy bought my quarter-hour *Sunset Serenade Show* across the board and I got paid five bucks a program—twenty-five a week. I did every mother song, every sweetheart song, every dying child song and every non-denominational hymn in the books. I wrenched more hearts than Little Eva. Then one day, for another twenty-five, Neil Carlson asked me if I wanted to take over his programing duties. He'd been holding down both jobs.

"The rest is easy—I don't sing much anymore—I get seventy bucks a week—and if I'm lucky I may get up to a hundred bucks a week someday. And this, my friend, is not what Dave Layne calls a future."

Dave paused and gave Howdy a searching glance. "Look, do you think you should sign that contract?"

Howdy examined his guitar calluses. "I don't know."

Thoughtfully, Dave lit another cigarette. "First, the radio business is changing. The change is going to make a fortune for a few people who understand it and break those who don't. Those big advertisers may buy participation with Urinex out, but you've got Urinex now and they bought you awful damned cheap. Right now there are two things you ought to think about—upping the ante and holding the contract down to one year. Then everything possible should be done to build Howdy Goodwyn—releases, public fund raising appearances, phonograph records, later pictures, westerns . . ."

"To hell with that!" Howdy's explosive dismissal of the idea produced a surprised laugh.

"What's the matter?"

"Just put it this way, Dave—*I hate horses!*"

For the moment Dave could think of no rejoinder. Howdy filled the breach. "Also—I hate movies."

To Dave the statement had the shock impact of heresy. "Movies too? Why, for God's sake?"

"I tried 'em. I wound up on my ass, out of a job. I'm not that good a rider and I sure as hell can't act."

"What the hell do you think you're doing on stage when you turn on that bashful bumpkin charm? Don't tell me that's the real you."

"Shit, no. But it ain't acting either."

Dave gestured impatiently. "Quit crapping me, Howdy. If that isn't acting, neither is Will Rogers' cow-licking, turd-kicking bit. All you need is a little time, a little slick-

432

ing up ... you do for Billy Hill what John Charles Thomas does for Oley Speaks, what Lanny Ross does for Jerome Kern. I'm not a very bright man, Howdy, but this I know—it's a safe gamble that I can build you into a star. I'm willing to put my job on the line that I can build you into America's 'pop *corn* king.'" He fixed Howdy with a speculative look.

The silence that followed was long enough to make Dave uneasy but he waited. Finally, Howdy spoke. "I'm listening. Keep talking."

"All I need is enough percentage of the gross to live on. But our deal wouldn't start until you're making at least seven fifty a week. Then we can start with ten percent, plus reasonable expenses to pay for the buildup and you can approve every dime in advance."

Dave stopped long enough to let the point sink in. "First I want you to package your own radio show. Next we should look into syndicating a recorded radio show. Third, I want you to start making phonograph records of your best songs like Bing Crosby, Donald Novis, and Russ Columbo are doing. I've got a friend, a genius, Danny Mayer, who has a little recording studio. We set up Danny with a mail-order department and plug these records on your show. After a while the big distributors will be coming to us to make deals.

"I say 'we' because I expect to be an equal partner with you in all of the subsidiary enterprises. That means I'll work my butt off for ten percent of the radio show because that's what makes the rest possible."

Dave paused and looked at Howdy expectantly. "Well—that's about it. How does it strike you?"

Sprawled in the big chair, twisting a sandy-red forelock, Howdy was silent for almost a minute—a minute in which Dave's misgivings began to mount. He wondered if Howdy was hesitating because he felt that a man who would double deal with one employer might in time do the same with a partner.

Abruptly Howdy got up from his chair and stood looking down at Dave. He stepped close and extended his right hand. "I'd say it strikes me just fine."

15 SINCE THEIR VISIT to the premiere of Howdy's show in early October, Angie Woodward had been struggling against the run of emotional tides that left her alternately exhilarated and exhausted. Even though Rosa Rinelli, with a repressed romantic's perception, had diagnosed the symptoms correctly, Angie herself dared not acknowledge either infatuation or love as the cause. Scores of times she had shaken her head viciously to dispel the fantasies, not all of them pleasant, and had scolded herself half aloud in those wakeful pre-dawn hours.

Howdy seemed to have built an invisible wall between them. Still, Angie could reassure herself when she thought about her ability to help Howdy. "He's been using those chords and combinations I taught him. I didn't really begin to teach him all I can. More than that, when I ran down the aisle and threw myself into his arms like a simp, he hugged me like he was glad to see me. It wasn't just a friendly hug. Something happened because—anyway, he put as much into it as I did."

Some hours later she awakened and grimaced painfully. Downstairs one of her mother's beginning piano pupils was committing musical mayhem on "The Jolly Farmer." After a meal eaten mechanically, she bundled up against the gray December chill and went out onto the porch. Across the street Melba Persons was walking homeward burdened by two large food bags. Angie waved and called out. "What's the matter? Car broken down?"

Melba shook her head. "No. Frank's out looking at land with some fellow from San Bernardino. Say—come on over when you can. I want to talk to you about something."

Angie ran down the steps and crossed the unpaved street.

"Let me have one of those bags. I need the exercise."

Over coffee in the Persons kitchen Angie tried to con-

434

ceal her excitement as Melba revealed her plan to invite Howdy down to spend Christmas.

Howdy seemed glad to receive Melba's telephone call but reluctant to accept her invitation. When she persisted, Howdy explained that his partner, Dave Layne, would be alone, too. Melba promptly invited them both.

Angie was waiting with Frank and Melba at the railroad station in Barstow when Howdy and Dave stepped down from the train Saturday evening. Melba's greeting to her guests was motherly and effusive. Frank's welcome was warm and a bit self-conscious. Angie's greeting was restrained. She linked her arm through Howdy's, smiled warmly at Dave, and pressed her cheek fleetingly against Howdy's shoulder. "Everybody's so anxious to see you. Rosa and Mike have invited us all to a special dinner tonight."

Frank Persons reached for Howdy's valise. "But Rosa won't let you sing, Howdy. You're her guest and she and Mike would just feel awful if you thought they'd invited you so you'd entertain."

The Rinellis' uninhibited greeting became a minor ovation. Howdy was certain he had never seen many of those who pushed through the crowd at the bar to clutch his hand. The Twenty-first Amendment had gone into effect two and a half weeks earlier so the hard liquor Mike dispensed now stood in open array on the back bar. Mike leaned across the bar and indicated Dave standing down from Howdy with Frank Persons. "He's your boss, eh?"

Howdy nodded.

"Good. He's a nice guy."

After the most elaborate Italian dinner Howdy and Dave had ever eaten, they followed Angie into the main dining room to listen to the show.

The show was difficult for Angie. Since mixed drinks had been legalized the crowds had become noisier and less attentive. To counter their expansive good humor she had added more rhythm numbers to her repertoire only to learn that they produced the exact opposite effect. She had sent for new sheet music. Among the selections was a piano solo arrangement of Duke Ellington's biggest hit, "Sophisticated Lady." She had worked on it at home perfecting the harmonies and rich modulations.

Angie played it beautifully, impressing both Howdy and

435

Dave with her complete competence. She was not a natural performer but she was an accomplished one.

Christmas dinner was to be held at the Woodward home. The house was all Melba and Frank had said it was. A well-kept old frame structure, it had been planned along the generous lines of the two-story family homes misleadingly labeled California Cottages. The front door led directly into a spacious, wainscoted, high-ceilinged living room. Directly opposite the front door stood a large red brick fireplace topped by a massive oak mantel.

An old, carefully preserved Knabe grand piano dominated the plain, turn-of-the-century furniture. The floor was covered with a worn but clean pseudo-Persian carpet. To the right of the entrance, through a square-pillared archway was the large dining room. A flight of banistered stairs led to the bedrooms and bath on the upper floor.

Howdy realized that most of the Persons' bright, homey little cottage down the street could have been placed in these two main rooms. But somehow the place depressed him. Then he remembered that he had felt much the same when he had first entered Georgette Follansby's old Franklin Avenue boarding house.

After welcoming Dave and Howdy, Angie and her mother excused themselves and went out to the kitchen. For the moment, Howdy and Dave were alone. Dave gave Howdy a knowing look. "Now I understand why you wanted to come down here. Nice! Very nice people. Especially your friend Angie."

Howdy avoided his eyes. "They're all nice. They sort of feel like family."

Dave fixed Howdy with a skeptical look. "Don't try and tell your Uncle David that she's your adopted kid sister."

Howdy was spared an awkward reply when Frank Persons appeared in the doorway.

They completed decorating the Christmas tree a few minutes before midnight. The garlands of cranberries and popcorn, Melba's Santa Claus cookies plus an assortment of old German tinseled globes resulted in an old-fashioned Christmas tree that filled everyone except Howdy with pleasant pangs of nostalgia. It was the first such tree he had ever known.

Dave Layne lit a cigarette and leaned against the mantel inspecting their work. "You know—for about three hundred years I've been telling myself that I didn't miss all this fuss." His pleasant Irish face grew pensive. "And you know something else? I'm a liar! I'd forgotten how nice it can feel to be domesticated."

His mood brightened again and he took Angie by the hand and led her toward the piano. "As long as I'm getting maudlin, why don't we do it up right with a quick chorus of 'Silent Night'?"

Acting as conductor, Dave led off with a downbeat and, somewhat timidly at first, they all began to sing. As Dave's clear lyric tenor began to dominate the other voices, Angie glanced up, her face mirroring surprise and admiration. When the singing ended Angie clasped her hands at the base of her throat. "Dave! You're wonderful! Tomorrow you've got to sing for us." The others took up the demand until he held up his hands in surrender. "I will. I will. In fact, I insist on it."

Sometime later, as they readied for bed on the Persons' porch, Dave looked up from undoing a shoe. He seemed unusually serious.

"Howdy—thanks for insisting I come down. This is the best medicine for me that you can ever imagine, pal. Your friends are great. And that Angie. She's for dreaming about, that one."

On Christmas Day, they were at the table for almost two hours before they pushed back their chairs and the men were sent to the living room to wait until the dishes were stacked. Good food and easy conversation spiced with Dave Layne's lively humor and interesting anecdotes of his days as a would-be musical comedy and operetta star produced an aura of well-being.

Ana Woodward, a bit less withdrawn, wondered at her daughter's radiance. She wondered, too, at the transformation that had taken place in the old house. Happiness was not a state a person could trust.

Shortly, everyone settled into a state of euphoria. Bored by the drowsy, sporadic talk, Angie moved inconspicuously to the piano with the package of new lead sheets Howdy had brought. Without striking the keys, her fingers sought out the chords as she went leisurely through the copies, putting aside those that appealed to her the most.

Dave Layne, slumped luxuriously in the Morris chair beside the fireplace, puffed on his cigarette and watched the play of light and expression on Angie's face as she responded to the beauty of silent harmonies. Behind her, the rickety wrought-iron bridge lamp created a pale halo that accented the highlights in her red-blonde hair. His eyes moved languidly to Howdy, who was listening with somnolent patience to still another of Frank Persons' land deals that "looked good." There comes a time in a man's life, Dave thought, when most dreams become absurdities—as unattainable as the mill donkey's dangling carrot. For at least a third of his thirty-five years, Dave Layne had followed the dangling carrot of his own unrealistic ambition until—blessed day—circumstances had cornered him and forced him to face the fact that his true talent lay in recognizing in others the ability he himself lacked. He was determined that time would not turn this new dream into an absurdity. The partnership with Howdy was the first move to use his own talent realistically. Nothing in Howdy's manner, or in Angie's, had suggested that the girl was to be a part of that dream. And still, as he watched her, he could not rid himself of the unsettling notion that somehow she would be. A compulsion brought him from the chair to the piano.

"Louder, lady! The customers in the back row can't hear."

Startled, Angie looked up, returned his broad grin, then compressed her lips and grimly began to play Mendelssohn's "Spring Song," deliberately interpolating into it a number of sour notes. Dave winced and plugged his ears. Imitating the New York Capitol Theater's famous Major Bowes he droned, "All right! All right!"

Angie made a defiant face and positioned her hands over the keys. "All right then, try this."

Her fingers began flying through her own arrangement of "Twelfth Street Rag." Ana Woodward's expression of shock turned to reproach. "Angela! Not on Christmas night, honey—please."

The sudden barrage of rhythm interrupted Frank Persons' aimless monologue and gave Howdy a chance to escape. In the hall he uncased his guitar and joined Angie and Dave at the piano.

For a half hour they went through old familiar numbers while Dave Layne listened and watched closely. His initial expression of pleased surprise faded a bit but did not vanish entirely as Angie and Howdy moved easily from one number to another. After Melba had coaxed Angie to play her version of "Sophisticated Lady," Dave's expression changed to open admiration.

"Bravo! Pretty good for a backwoods kid from Barstow. In fact, pretty good for Hollywood and New York, too."

Angie grimaced. "Flattery will get you nowhere. But I love it. Anyway—Howdy and I have done our act. We want to hear you sing, Dave."

Angie pulled out a large paper-covered album and set it on the music rack. Dave moved in beside her and together they flipped the pages until they came to one of the favorite ballads from Sigmund Romberg's operetta, *The New Moon.* The show had opened in New York in 1928 and after five years it was still playing in road-company productions around the country.

Dave placed his hand over a page. "One of my fondest dreams was to sing this song in the show. I never got beyond the chorus—but—you will now confirm operetta's tragic loss as David Layne sings, 'Softly As in a Morning Sunrise.' "

The room filled with spontaneous applause as Dave ended the last note. None was more enthusiastic than Angie's. "You're wonderful, Dave! I can't imagine why on earth you quit your career."

"I quit my career, young lady, because I have the voice of a romantic leading man and the appearance of an underweight bartender."

Later, when the dishes had been done and they were all gathered in the living room, Dave Layne spoke of something that had been on his mind most of the evening. "Angie, have you ever thought of training your voice?"

The question was greeted with an incredulous stare. "Heavens no!"

"I don't mean studying to develop a 'legit' sound. I mean coaching and learning phrasing so you can develop a popular sound, actually not a great deal more than you've been doing here tonight."

Angie looked astonished. "Me? Another Ruth Etting? It's never entered my mind."

"Well, it should. You don't have a big voice—but with the new amplifying equipment you don't need one. All you need is a pleasant sound and a good sense of rhythm. A coach can take care of developing style. Think about it. Like Howdy, I have a hunch you may be a natural."

439

Angie gave him a narrow, sidelong look. "I have a hunch Melba put too much brandy in the hard sauce."

The matter rested there until Howdy and Dave were getting ready for bed.

"Hey, Dave—were you serious about Angie singin'?"

"I sure as hell was. Why?"

Howdy settled himself beneath the covers. "Nothing. Just wondered."

"We've got to be ready to make our move by March first."

Dave Layne flipped to the month on the desk calendar resting on the arm of the easy chair at his apartment. "The brass wants national prestige sponsors and these new station sales representatives are promising spot business from people like Ford, Chevrolet, Nash, Franklin, and the soaps like Fels Naphtha and Gold Dust."

Bootless, Howdy was sprawled on the sofa. "How much time do we have?"

"A month—at the most. We've got to start right now figuring out what we want in the show."

Howdy stifled a yawn and reached for his boots. "If the station doesn't go for our idea—then what happens?"

"We're not even going to think about that. You've proved you're a talent that can draw. Chaffee isn't going to like our proposal, but he's going to have to buy it. You've got the hottest western family show on the air now."

He pushed the calendar aside and leaned back. "—and we're going to make it easy for him to keep you—for the time being. Now then, let's start building a basic family around you for the air. I don't mean a Crockett Family where one of the sisters is really that youngest Stafford kid, Jo. I'm talking about a group of friends who get to be as close as family—like you and the Persons—and Angie."

Dave broke off and frowned thoughtfully. "How would you like to have Angie on the show?"

For a long time Howdy stared at the program director without blinking. Then he broke into a slow grin. "Well, hell, yes. Why not?"

During the ensuing week the program director put together, complete with suggested music, three sample programs.

"There's nothing new about a family group in show

business, Howdy. The Foys, the Stones, the Barrymores are real families. The new radio shows are beginning to use the family idea too. Rudy Vallee, Fred Allen, Burns and Allen, Jack Benny."

He rattled a sheaf of papers. "Here's what I have in mind. A basic musical group of eight men called The Golden Westerners. Next a good singing chorus—The Campfire Choir—seven voices, four men and a girl trio. We'd call the four guys, 'The Menfolk,' and the girls, 'The Womenfolk.' They'd start the show off with a theme song probably built around the Golden West. Together they'd sing as a chorus to back you up in addition to their own ensemble.

"Then I'd take a guy like Steve Stone—the best harmonica player—and call him something like, 'The Maestro of the Mouth Organ.'

"The last regular on the list would be Angie. If you still think it's a good idea, I suggest we sound her out. If she wants to go along on a tryout basis we can bill her as, 'Our Lady Angela, Queen of the Keyboard.' Angela—Queen of the Angels—the thing works subjectively with Los Angeles—our Lady, the Queen of the Angels," he dismissed the idea with a wave, "etcetera. It may have some memory value."

Howdy had made no comment during the explanation. Dave watched him closely now as he studied the pages. There was a hard-headed, stubborn thoughtfulness behind the easy-going onstage personality. As Howdy's continued silence showed no sign of letting up, Dave became openly uneasy. To break the mounting tension he went to the kitchenette and returned with a bottle of cheap bourbon. He set a glass in front of Howdy and poured himself a stiff jolt. "Look, Howdy—if you and I are thinking in opposite directions all of a sudden, we can throw that out and start all over. But goddamn it, we better do it tonight. I want to break the news to Chaffee on Friday. That will give him the weekend to think it over."

Howdy nodded. "There's only two things I'd do to this show, Dave—"

"What are they?"

"I'd want me and the Campfire Choir to end each show with a hymn—and I wouldn't look for a new theme song. I'd keep the one Will did—'Howdy.' "

A broad, relieved smile spread over Dave Layne's face. "Is that *all* you'd change?"

Howdy looked up. "That's all. I think you've done a hell of a job. I think we're going to have a pissing winner with this show. But I wouldn't say anything to Angie 'til we know we got a deal. I'd sure hate to get her all riled up then have to call back with bad news. Okay?"

"Hell *yes!*"

Later, alone with a third drink, Dave spoke aloud to himself. "So far so good. But just protect yourself in the clinches, Davey. If this Okie's got what it takes to be a star, he's also got what it takes to be a son-of-a-bitch."

At four o'clock Friday afternoon Dave met with station owner Roger Chaffee. The meeting was not long and Chaffee was not happy. Dave had braced himself for recriminations and charges of ingratitude that did not come. Although the executive would not have admitted it, one of the reasons he had chosen Dave Layne to be program director was the very initiative that the man was demonstrating.

Chaffee kept them waiting until the following Wednesday, Howdy's show day. The delay had not been intentional. It was occasioned by the need for meetings with Neil Carlson and the treasurer of the company. He had told them, "I want the best deal I can drive them into—but I don't want to lose them. Also—I want a long-term contract—a tough one. I don't want to build up *The Howdy Goodwyn Show* just to have the networks outbid us at option time."

Dave Layne, with Howdy's approval, brought a lawyer into the negotiation. Everett Moses had been chief counsel for a group of independent stations in the Chicago area but illness had forced him to bring his wife to southern California.

"He's as smart as they come," Dave told Howdy. "He negotiated for the station when they signed me in Chicago—so I know. Also, he'll string along with us until we've got money coming in."

It took ten days for the contract to be finalized and signed. Moses secured all that Dave Layne had asked for—ownership of the package for Howdy and a guaranteed

442

basic fee plus an override on sales above a specified base figure.

Howdy and Dave waited until they were certain Angie would be home before they phoned. The effect of the call was just short of cataclysmic in the Woodward home, the Persons' home, and at the Roadside Inn.

Angie arranged to commute by train each Tuesday morning to Los Angeles and return to Barstow on Thursday. The show would pay her transportation and her room at the Hollywood Roosevelt. She would continue her job at the Roadside Inn, at least until it was certain that the tryout had proved successful.

The opening of the new show was set for Wednesday, March nineteenth. The only person not happy over the prospect was the Reverend Matt Simon, who had been put on notice that any evidence of a substantial increase in his audience would automatically result in a larger percentage of his take for the station. He blamed Howdy for the turn of events that he refused to concede were inevitable.

The Howdy Goodwyn Show got off to a good start. Carroll Nye of the *Los Angeles Times* thought the show was "the equal in entertainment value of any variety hour on the air." Bernie Milligan of the *Los Angeles Examiner*, usually harder to please, was equally enthusiastic and singled Angie out for special mention. Zuma Palmer, whose column in *The Hollywood Citizen-News* reflected the women's point of view, found Howdy and his radio family "—an engaging, wholesome group, talented, well-mannered, and a credit to the medium." Several radio fan magazines asked for picture stories and Dave Layne engaged a part-time public relations man named Don Bellew.

Georgette Follansby was stricken when Howdy told her that he and Dave Layne had taken a two-bedroom furnished apartment. She offered them her two best rooms, but Howdy explained that the bachelor quarters in the new seven-story building on Las Palmas and Hollywood Boulevard would also serve as their production office.

From the beginning, the one-hundred-dollar-a-month apartment was more office than home. After a week of wading through their own confusion, by mutual consent they budgeted another twenty dollars a month for a part-time maid.

At the end of the first thirteen-week cycle in mid-June,

there was no doubt about the future of the show. The demand for seats was so great that tickets had to be printed and holders admitted on a first-come first-served basis.

Howdy's first recording on his own HG label was a double release featuring his theme song "Howdy" on the A-side and Billy Hill's "The Last Roundup" on the B-side. Copies of it were sent to every radio station of consequence in the eleven Western states together with a personal letter from the star saying they could expect other records to use for "program fillers." The letter made a point of thanking the station program directors for using them. The innovation caused a flurry in the trade and brought some angry press comment from the big record companies who saw the move as a threat to their retail market.

Dave, working with Everett Moses and Danny Meyer, set up a distribution company to service retail music stores with HG records. When the first sales returns became generally known in the trade, Dave Layne's prediction proved correct. Several national record distributors contacted them, offering distribution deals. The attorney looked at the offers and compared them with their own costs for doing the job. "Let's hold off a while. Their offers aren't that good yet. Let's get more records out and plug them on the show. If we can't handle the job as cheaply as they can, we'll do business."

Ev Moses brought to HG Enterprises a big-time knowledge of business practices and a shrewd understanding of the temper of the times. Howdy, applying lessons well learned from Al Phelps, understood how to relate his talent to the most cherished hopes and aspirations of the common man. Dave Layne's intimate knowledge of the performer's problems and a sure grasp of radio's mechanics and its new national dimension completed the know-how necessary for a firm foundation. Radio prospered and the new company prospered even though the country as a whole did not.

Upton Sinclair provided the nation's incredulous reactionaries with a shocking lesson. He fully demonstrated the power of radio as an educational medium by creating a wave of lower-middle-class white-collar discontent with the status quo. Eight hundred EPIC clubs, determined to End Poverty In California by implementing Sinclair's doctrine of "Production for Use," listened intently and heard

444

not only promises but something they had yet to hear—and never would hear from the pleasure-loving Utopians—a definite plan.

In one of the dirtiest campaigns in California's brief and turbulent political history the reactionary establishment defeated Upton Sinclair by slightly more than a quarter of a million votes. No sooner had the socialist retired from the arena than the lugubrious Dr. Francis Townsend appeared on the scene in Long Beach with his Old Age Revolving Pension Plan. The doctor had received the blessings of Governor Frank Merriam during his campaign and no less a literary great than Kathleen Norris was endorsing him. Everett Moses saw the meaning behind the repetitive pattern of these something-for-nothing movements.

"Every penny we can divert to building the show and your subsidiaries should be spent right now. There are three hundred thousand unemployed people here in Los Angeles. And God knows how many there are in the state. I saw figures this morning showing that, all told, fourteen million people are out of work in the country. Figure out what it costs to get into a movie. Radio's free. That should tell us where our audience is. If you entertain them now and make them forget their troubles for a while, when times get better they'll remember you. Keep giving them more and tell them you're doing it. You're never going to get the Park Avenue crowd in New York, Howdy, or the Wilshire-Beverly Hills crowd here. There are a hundred of your kind of people for every one of them. Right?"

Howdy agreed. But he kept to himself certain reservations that he would never quite be able to articulate.

Frank and Melba Persons and Ana Woodward came to Hollywood as company guests for the Wednesday show preceding Thanksgiving. The next day a special dinner was arranged at the hotel. On an impulse Howdy invited Neville Newton. He had run into Georgette Follansby on the street and, in making a routine inquiry, had found out the old man was despondent.

After the old man left, Angie looked saddened. "I feel so sorry for that sweet old man, Howdy. I can't tell you why, but when he talks about going back to coaching movie stars I get a lump in my throat."

Howdy's noncommittal "Yeah—" troubled her.

445

Christmas came on show day, making it impossible for Howdy and Dave to accept the Persons' invitation. The cast and engineers had a tree onstage and Howdy initiated a custom that would endure through all of his years as a performer. He gave each member of the show a personally inscribed gift. In return, members of the cast pooled their money and bought him a handsome new guitar case.

Angie spent New Year's eve with Howdy and Dave at the Moses' modest hillside home in the Silver Lake district midway between Hollywood and downtown Los Angeles. Throughout the three-and-a-half-hour vigil during which they listened to Ben Grauer describe the arrival of the New Year in New York's Times Square, Dave Layne drank constantly. He dominated the conversation, speaking with amusing and, to Angie, somewhat pathetic self-depreciation about his years as a singer on radio and in road-company musicals.

Shortly after twelve-thirty, following the ceremonial New Year toast and a thickly emotional prediction of good fellowship, they said their thanks to Ev and Miriam Moses and made their way from the front porch to the car.

On the way home, Dave slept with his head on Angie's shoulder. After they had put him to bed, Howdy drove Angie back to the Roosevelt Hotel and parked at the side entrance on Orange Drive. As he was about to open the door she rested a hand on his arm. "Howdy—"

"Yes."

"Would you think I was crazy if I asked you to do something?"

His puzzled expression made her laugh. "My goodness! All I had in mind was a little drive."

She peered through the windshield into the perfect night sky. "Ever since the show started I've always wanted to go up on top of the hills and look down at the city. Could we drive up there tonight—please?"

They drove out Hollywood Boulevard to Laurel Canyon, followed it to the summit, and turned onto Mulholland Drive, passing a dozen parked cars before Howdy found a place to pull off.

Spread below them like a random display of unset gems were the lights of Hollywood, West Los Angeles, Beverly Hills, Inglewood, and half a dozen other suburbs. On beyond were Culver City and Sawtelle and in the extreme distance, strung along the edge of the Pacific, they could see the lights of Santa Monica, Ocean Park, and Venice. For a time the spectacle held them speechless. Angie slipped her arm through Howdy's. A moment later her fingers laced through his and he felt her shiver.

"You cold?"

"No. That did it."

She indicated the panorama of lights with a nod. "It must be the most beautiful sight in the world."

Angie saw only the beauty below them. She did not relate the twinkling points to homes still ablaze with party lights, to blinking signs above sleazy clubs, cafés, and restaurants or to the moving headlights of homeward-bound revelers.

Howdy saw only a sprawling city over which he was rapidly getting an edge. The smallest of the suburban clusters scattered below him was larger than Guymon, Oklahoma. If things kept going the way they were, there wouldn't be a person in any one of those houses that wouldn't know the name, Howdy Goodwyn. The same would go for the thousands of other cities and towns within reach of the station's powerful transmitter.

He was not aware that Angie was speaking until she gave his sleeve an impatient tug. "I said, What are you thinking about? Or is it none of my business?"

Howdy looked at her and smiled. "Sure it's your business, Angie. Why wouldn't it be? If you hadn't spoke for me with the Rinellis—"

" 'Spoken.' "

"What?"

"If I hadn't *spoken* for you . . ."

She laughed apologetically and pressed her cheek against his shoulder. "I'm sorry. But sometimes those words hit me just like a sour note. Go ahead. I didn't mean to interrupt."

Howdy chuckled. "You taught me an awful lot about music, Angie. But I don't know if you can teach me your kind of English. I figure if folks can understand me, that's good enough."

Angie slipped her arm free. "They understand—but they'll respect you even more if you get rid of some of the worst of those back home-isms. They're not very classy, you know."

Howdy studied her for a moment then turned back to

the panorama of lights. "I'm trying—like I told you I would."

Something in his tone made Angie uncomfortable. "Forgive me, Howdy. Here we are in a perfect place after a perfect night and I'm sounding like a prissy old school teacher."

When he did not respond she reached over and turned his chin toward her with a forefinger. "Forgive? Please—?"

For a long moment he looked down into the appealing face and then they were together, Angie so eagerly that her lips and caressing fingers brought a muffled protest. Tears that had welled up an instant before trailed down her cheek and across the back of his left hand. When he felt them he eased her away, questioning but she freed her head and pressed it hard against his chest. "Oh, darling— I'm sorry. I'm sorry. But I thought it would never happen."

Renée's hands pressed upward frantically against Howdy's lean, hard shoulders. "Hey! For God's sake, what's the matter with you?" His teeth found the soft fold of flesh at the base of her neck and she cried out again. "For Christ's sake—what are you trying to do, screw me or kill me? You'll split me open, you goddammed savage! Howdy! Howdy—"

Her plea died in a long, anguished moan as she felt him start and clamped her full legs around the small of his back to share with him a pain more to her liking.

Later, after she had done what she could to ease her own discomfort, she returned and slammed the wet towel onto his relaxed belly. "What the hell got into you tonight?"

"Nothing got into me. I got into you. Remember?"

Renée snorted. "Look. This may come as a big surprise, buster, but you're not the first man I've known. So don't crap your Aunt Renée. You weren't laying me. You were fucking some other dame—to get even for something. Right?"

Howdy shook his head. "Wrong."

Renée eyed him skeptically and started to sit on the bed. The edge buckled and she gave his hip a shove. "Move your cracker-ass!"

When he complied, she inspected him unhappily and using the towel still wadded on his belly, absently finished

448

the task he had left uncompleted. Viciously, a long polished nail flicked against the offending part. His pained outcry made her look apprehensively toward the living room. An instant later she yelped as he flicked her protruding left nipple. Before she could defend herself he had pulled her on top of him and locked her in a suffocating embrace. When her fingernails threatened to draw blood he released her and she rolled over beside him. For a time they lay panting, their faces inches apart. Renée broke the silence and her voice was strange. "I'm a professional whore—and you play with me like I was your girl-friend. How come?"

Howdy yawned. "Don't know, Reeny—I feel easy with you."

She pulled away and sat up. "Get out of here now. I've got to sit on an ice bag or take the night off."

She started to get up and Howdy caught the back of her wrapper.

"Hey. I'm hungry. Why don't we both go out?"

Renée jerked the garment free and turned on him. "You stupid yokel. If you start running around this town with me you'll be off the air and back on that freight train faster than Sam Hayes can say, 'That's thirty for tonight!' Now scram! Get out of here and leave me *alone* for a while, will you?"

Dave Layne was still at the desk working on a Lincoln's Birthday program when Howdy let himself in. He looked up and whistled softly. "Boy, you sure look relaxed! What did you do—get your gonads emptied?"

Smiling, Howdy collapsed in an easy chair and draped a leg over the arm. "Pumped dry—right down to the gravel."

Dave shook his head unhappily. "I told you to have the girl come here. Just let me know and I'll fade out for a hamburger, like you do for me. I don't think it's a good idea for you to be seen going into that place."

They sat in silence for a time, then Dave held up a memo slip. "I don't suppose this is the most appropriate time to tell you that Angie called about an hour ago? She wants you to phone her at the hotel."

Howdy looked at his wrist watch. "It's too late now."

She said any time you came in would be okay."

Clearly, the message annoyed Howdy. Dave studied him

briefly, pushed the papers aside, and got up. "Howdy, is this a good time to talk to you, about Angie?"

The singer looked up slowly and shrugged. "Sure. Good a time as any. Go ahead, only—"

"Only what?"

"Only don't start pacing like a caged cat. Just come right out with it."

Half defiantly, Dave began. "Look, Howdy. I'm your friend, not your keeper. We both understand that. So what I'm about to say has nothing to do with you or me personally—but only with the show and our business plans."

Howdy pulled himself erect. "You trying to tell me you want to can Angie?"

"Hell, no! Don't you read the mail? She's getting to be one of the best attractions on the show. What I'm trying to say is—everyone connected with the show—and some who aren't—knows the girl is nutty in love with you. And they know something else, too—"

Howdy's eyes challenged him. "What?"

"They know that you don't give a two-bit shit about her that way."

"That is a fucking lie! I never did think as much of any woman as Angie. And that's the by-God truth."

Dave waved his arms helplessly. "Then why don't you let *her* know—even just a little? Goddammit, Howdy—she stays in town—she comes over here and cooks for us—she tidies up the place—buys curtains—even buys flowers—for *us*—"

He broke off, frustrated by words that wouldn't come. "Why, Holy Mother! I'd get out of here and leave you two alone—but if I did, you'd probably walk out with me."

Howdy relaxed and the promise of a smile played at the corners of his mouth. "Dave, old buddy, I been wondering how long it would be before you and me got around to this, so lemme just tell you how I feel about things. Okay?"

Dave Layne braced himself against the desk. "Okay."

"I know how her hair feels—I know how she smells—I know how her mouth feels—and I know how her body feels—"

Pretending he had not, Howdy saw Dave stiffen. "—and I know that she loves me—she told me so—early New Year's morning—up on the mountain where she asked me to take her. We stayed up there in the car until almost light—talking," he broke off and his eyes appealed for understanding, "and I could have done anything I wanted with her—right then. She didn't say so—but I just could . . ." He compressed his lips and shook his head. "But I didn't . . . I couldn't. I'm a son-of-a-buck if I know why . . . but I couldn't. Why, Goddamn—I slept with a woman back home that I respected. It didn't stop me. But with Angie it's different."

A thought remained suspended in silence and Dave Layne, his voice tight, prompted him. "Why?"

"I don't know!"

"Because you think of her as a sister?"

If Howdy had not been deafened by the clamor of his own conflict he would have detected the note of hope in Dave Layne's question. "Sister? Crap, no! Boy, I'll tell you something—when she come into my arms that night and kissed me with her mouth all loose I rassled with the Devil to keep from spreading her on the seat right then and there."

Dave was unable to conceal a pained grimace.

"But, like I said, I couldn't do it . . ."

"Because you respect her too much?"

Howdy deliberated, then looked up. "That's right. She's wonderful, Dave." He vented his frustration in an explosive sigh. "Oh, shit. I don't know why."

"I know why, Howdy."

"Sure you do. Sure you do."

"I do. I'm serious. You like the girl and you're annoyed with yourself because it gets in your way right now—and you've got too many other things on your mind that are more important. Right?"

Howdy jumped up from the chair with jaw out-thrust. "You're fucking well right! We're just getting a good start now—thanks to you." Howdy began pacing between the chair and the desk. "I know Angie loves me—but I don't know if I love her. I don't know what love feels like. So far I been able to get along without it. But I can't live without singing, and money, and what money gets me. I *know* that."

He turned to face Dave. "And I know something else too—I know I can't even think about love until we get everything we planned done. Angie can go back home if she

451

doesn't like it. We don't have to waste any more time discussing it because that's how it's going to be."

Dave stared at Howdy. "Jesus, Mary, and Joseph! And I was the idiot who suggested she join the show . . ."

Howdy crossed to the desk. "Dave, if you hadn't I would of."

A year slipped by. Howdy Goodwyn was too absorbed in achieving his own objectives to be aware of the national travail. He knew about President Franklin Roosevelt's "Brain Trust" and that it was radically altering the old order because Ev Moses was concerned about the possible effects on the radio business. The original Federal Radio Commission had been replaced with a seven-man Federal Communications Commission that promised far more stringent rulings about programing and commercials to protect the public interest.

When John Dillinger was shot to death outside a Chicago theater on July twenty-second the news reached the Pacific Coast while Howdy and his troupe were entertaining at a rodeo in Bakersfield. The announcement over the public address system brought a medley of cheers and boos from the stands.

In September, when the Morro Castle fire cost one hundred thirty-four lives off the New Jersey coast, Howdy joined the others in deploring the tragedy, and when three Army balloonists set a new altitude record of sixty thousand six hundred thirteen feet over Rapid City, South Dakota, Howdy was rebuked by Angie for saying, "That's almost as high as old Dave was last Saturday night." Only the continuing dust storms in Oklahoma, Texas, Arkansas, and in the middle west seemed to trouble him seriously. "Son of a bitch, I think God must have it in for us Sooners."

Then, when the full force of the Okie migration began to spill over the state line into California, Howdy reacted positively. "Good. Pretty quick we'll outnumber the tight-assed bastards that run this state. Dave—find out where my people are camping and let's give them a show to cheer them up."

Howdy's new La Salle sedan was loaded with cases of canned food, coffee, and candy bars. They entertained where they could and the stories they heard brought tears to Angie's eyes and a bitter set to Howdy's mouth. In an unplanned comment, he vented his outrage on the air: "Seems to me that a country that can find money to send a flock of seaplanes flying from here to Hawaii and set up post offices at the south pole could find a few dollars to help dustbowl farmers."

Later, Ev Moses cautioned him. "God knows, Howdy, we understand how you feel. But don't get into that problem on the show. The sponsors are raising hell. And another thing—if you start championing causes you won't be able to turn any of them down."

Dave Layne concurred. "Keep out of controversy. Our job is to entertain. That's the best way we can help everybody."

When Howdy came to understand that his emotional involvement with the Okies, displaced by long years of soil abuse, could jeopardize everything he was trying to build, he contented himself with unpublicized appearances, with modest gifts of money and generous gifts of food. Angie, matching her own interest to his, worked beside him. Before Howdy realized what was happening, they became identified as a "couple."

Between Christmas and the New Year Howdy took the entire show to Barstow to entertain at the Roadside Inn. The decision was made when Frank Persons called to say that Mike Rinelli had suffered a heart attack.

After the party, Rosa clung to Howdy in a mute effort to convey the fullness of her gratitude.

Angie's Christmas present from Howdy and Dave was a new contract for one hundred dollars a week. Shortly afterward, Ana rented the old house in Barstow and moved into a Hollywood cottage with Angie. Aside from a few personal belongings, the only furniture taken to the new home was the grand piano. Before long Howdy and Dave found themselves eating several meals a week at the Woodwards' place. And quite often, without premeditation, they also found themselves involved in building shows with Angie helping at the piano.

Twice a week for almost a year Angie had been investing part of her earnings with a vocal coach. Dave had been right. Angie was a natural. Her first duets with Howdy and as a soloist on the show proved the point. Confirmation had come immediately in the fan mail. Very soon the duets with Howdy were established as a regular feature.

453

By early autumn six duets had been cut on the HG Record label. On-the-air promotion sold them out all over the West. Such new songs as "When I Grow Too Old to Dream," "Red Sails in the Sunset," and "East of the Sun and West of the Moon" were instant hits for them.

The Golden Westerners scored a regional triumph with their version of "Tumblin' Tumbleweeds" and Steve Stone's harmonica arrangement of the nostalgic ballad, "I'll See You in My Dreams" brought ovations and shouted demands for encores. The Howdy Goodwyn radio family was growing and prospering.

The longest new step ahead, the one that filled Howdy with the most misgivings, came early in 1938. Marty Wolfson, an engaging energetic fellow in his forties, owned a chain of independant movie theaters in the Northwest. He was an old friend of Harry Liebowitz, the clothier to whom Howdy remained loyal. Liebowitz arranged to have Marty and Howdy meet at his store but the meeting was to appear coincidental.

Wolfson's conversation was casual. He complained about current movie making. "The trouble is they're going to keep on making *Golddiggers, Broadway Melodies,* and *Big Broadcasts* until nineteen thirty-nine. All we're getting is Winnie Lightner, Eleanor Powell, Ruby Keeler, Dick Powell, Jack Benny, Fred Astaire, Ginger Rogers, Deanna Durbin, Shirley Temple, Bing Crosby, and the rest. They're great in cities but we need more product for our kind of audiences. They like westerns and they'd eat up western musicals. The outfit who starts making them is going to have a gold mine."

Howdy, apparently preoccupied with the fitting, nodded mechanically. "Maybe. But where can you show westerns with a lot of singing and dancing—Texas, Oklahoma, Arkansas, California, Washington? There isn't enough audience to make it worthwhile."

"That's the argument I've been getting from the majors. But they're asleep, like they are when they say their stars going on radio hurts box office." Wolfson pulled a folded paper from his coat.

"Take a look at these figures, Mr. Goodwyn. I'm in the theater business. I can't afford to kid myself about what my audiences want even if the big studios think they can."

He interpreted the figures as Howdy glanced at them

casually. "In forty of the forty-eight states most people outside the cities like country entertainment. Look at the *National Barn Dance*. And your show. The group I represent has put up hard cash to finance a couple of western musicals to prove the point. Most of the names we've approached don't have the imagination to see the potential. It's not classy enough for them. If Dick Powell put on a ten-gallon hat and Levis and made a western musical the sales would break records." He wagged his head mournfully. "But they won't let him! All they want him to do is stand in front of a bunch of wet bathing beauties and sing, 'By a Waterfall.'"

Wolfson reached for the paper. "I'm sorry, Mr. Goodwyn, I didn't mean to bother you with my troubles. Someday I'll be able to sell this idea."

When Marty Wolfson left after making a minor purchase, Howdy walked up behind Harry Liebowitz, who was on his knees measuring a trouser length. "Thanks, Harry, for plotting that accidental meeting."

Harry looked up, all innocence. "So what are you talking about?"

Howdy's reply was an unblinking stare and a disconcerting smile. Harry maintained the deception briefly then broke into a sheepish grin. "Okay, so I'm a fixer."

He rose and held a stubby finger under his star customer's nose. "But don't laugh, Howdy! I wasn't wrong about you and I'm not wrong about Marty. What's it gonna cost to talk to him?"

Howdy gave Harry's arm an affectionate squeeze. ". . . a nickel, if *I* call him. Ask him to call Dave in the morning."

It took Ev Moses and Dave Layne a week to work out a preliminary agreement with Marty Wolfson. Wolfson's group would provide fifty thousand dollars worth of financing in return for distribution rights. Howdy and Dave would form a corporation—the Rolling-O Corporation—that would sign a five-year agreement with Wolfson's company, Northwest, and Howdy would agree to appear personally in two out of every five musical productions. Choice of stories and stars to be vested in Rolling-O.

At the end of that week, Dave Layne came in with a contract for Howdy and the Golden Westerners to appear at the National Orange Fair in San Bernardino. In addition there was a bid for the cast to appear at the Roundup in Pendleton, Oregon, during the coming summer with the provision that Howdy would also serve as Grand Marshal of the parade.

"Son of a bitch! This on top of the pictures." Howdy tossed the contract across the desk to Dave. "This means I haul my ass up on a horse. Does that have to be part of the deal?"

"Thirty-five hundred dollars and all expenses for five songs and a quarter-mile jog around the track. What do you say?"

Howdy jammed his hands into his pants pockets. "I say for thirty-five hundred bucks plus expenses I haul my ass up on a horse."

Early in March Howdy received a telephone call from Georgette Follansby. "I hate to bother you. I know how busy you are—but could I come and see you this afternoon? I'm in the neighborhood."

Several minutes later the boarding-house keeper met Howdy at the apartment. She was distraught. "I don't know what else to do. The old man's just plain down and out. I don't know what happened to the income he's supposed to have, but I know his daughter's husband has been out of work for a long time. She hasn't been able to send money for two months now. I've been carrying him. But I just can't any longer. I'm barely making ends meet myself."

For a time Howdy seemed to be studying the papers on his desk. "What about relief?"

Mrs. Follansby shook her head. "He's not eligible . . . some technicality. I called and asked. He's got so darned much pride he wouldn't do it for himself." She spread her arms. "How can I turn him out on the street? I even offered to borrow money and pay his bus fare back to his daughter but he wouldn't hear of it. I just don't know what to do, Mr. Goodwyn. I know it's none of your business but you're the only one . . ." The words trailed off.

Howdy rose from the chair. "Where is he now?"

"At the house. He just sits in his room."

"Okay. You go on back and tell him I want to see him. Ask him if he can come here just before noon tomorrow."

The change in Neville Newton shocked Howdy. The durable optimism that had made the old man seem younger than his years was gone. Howdy made an effort to greet him optimistically. "What I want to know is—why haven't I seen you all year?"

The old man kept his eyes averted. "You're a big star now, son." For the first time since he had known him, there was bitterness in the old man's voice. "We're pretty stupid, most of us. If we weren't we'd understand that the possibility of success should be more frightening than the possibility of failure."

Howdy, envisioning Al Phelps, smiled ruefully. "That's the damn truth. Every time I think I need a larger Stetson I try to remember the time I got a hobo's boot in my face."

Exploring the still visible tracery of scars along his left temple, he asked, "What are you figuring on doing now?"

The old man shrugged. "For a while I kept telling myself that I'd find some voice or speech coaching at the studios. But they don't want an old has-been . . ." He broke off and lifted his head and looked Howdy directly in the eye. There was no self-pity in his voice. "I don't know what I'm going to do, son, I just don't know."

Howdy nodded. "When you heard I wanted to see you, did you think maybe I could help?"

Neville Newton replied without hesitation. "I could try to save face and say, 'No, it didn't occur to me.' But it did, Howdy. I'm ashamed that Mrs. Follansby had to speak to you. I thought about asking you to see me but I didn't have courage enough to come begging."

There was more than a trace of satisfaction in Howdy's smile. "You wouldn't call it begging if you come to offer your services, would you?"

"Of course not, son. But what on earth could I do for you?"

"The first thing you can do is get paid up with Mrs. Follansby. Then you come back here and start teaching me how to talk the English language better'n I do. Angie says I got everything but class." Howdy reached into his pocket.

The old man stared blankly at the proffered bills. His mouth slacked open and his lips began working in a futile attempt to form words. Howdy spared him the need. "If you think you can do anything to change a hopeless mess like me, then you got a job for thirty-five bucks a week for as long as it takes. How does that strike you?"

The old man forced his eyes back up to Howdy again. They were oddly glazed. "Son—I think it would be a mistake to change you very much."

When Angie heard about the addition of Neville Newton to the staff from Dave, she waited until they were alone then hugged Howdy and rested her cheek against his chest. "You are a most surprising man. Just when I think you're made of ice you go out of your way to do something like this."

She looked up at him in the way that made Howdy want to take her face in his hands. "I love you for doing that for the old man."

She went up on her toes to kiss him. When their lips parted he held her away and grinned down at her. "I done it—I mean, 'I did it'—for you so you wouldn't have to go around holding your ears when I say more'n ten words. I'll get me some class if it kills me."

Angie looked into his eyes and spoke in a half whisper. "You've already got class, Mr. Goodwyn, but you're a faker. You're really as sentimental as a lace valentine."

Neville Newton tried hard to earn his money by disciplining Howdy to regular sessions. Inevitably the phone rang or Dave called him to discuss an urgent matter. In the end the old man was reduced to following Howdy around and recording in a notebook the worst of the singer's lapses. At odd moments he would try to point out the errors and correct them. Though Howdy's patience was often tried by the old man's persistence, he was never short with him.

Early in April, Rolling-O Productions got underway with its first western musical. It was completed in ten days and was moderately successful. Preview comment cards proved there was no question about the popularity of Howdy and Angie. People wanted "the songs Howdy and Angie sing on the radio show."

This led to the start of the HG Music Company, organized at Ev Moses' suggestion to avoid paying huge music royalties to other publishers. The company would hire its own song writers. Howdy and Angie would push their material on the radio show and use it later in the motion pictures. The increase in staff made it necessary to take new offices and the apartment became a deserted place used only for sleeping and occasional love-making with professional call girls. Howdy had taken Dave's advice and allowed Renée to come to the apartment. But he wasn't happy about it. He told David, "I don't like sleeping where I've been fucking."

David's reply had not amused him. "That could create a hell of a problem when you get married, buddy."

The second picture, openly exploited on the radio show, was a hit. Rolling-O Productions expanded. Dave urgently recommended hiring an executive producer and once again Liebowitz had a suggestion. "Look, Howdy, a sweetheart you're not looking for. Only a son-of-a-bitch can run a production company like that. And who's a bigger one than Bronc Bronston?"

It took Harry's logic a week to triumph over Howdy's prejudice. Bronston had been out of work for almost a year and pride had kept him from coming to the extra he had once fired. When they met, Bronston smiled crookedly. "Okay, Mr. Goodwyn, it's your turn now."

From the beginning Bronston ran an efficient operation. One of the pictures was based on Howdy's early career and filmed in Barstow. To save the Persons from hurt feelings, Howdy and Dave stayed with them during the shooting. On their last night, from his cot on the porch, Howdy watched a new street light cast a vivid moving tracery of cottonwood limbs on the wall. He was disturbed by a feeling that the clock had turned back to August of 1933 and nothing had changed. Dave interrupted his reverie. "We've got five pictures working for us. I predict this will be the biggest grosser of them all. We've got to find something to do with our money. I never thought I'd say this, but we're suffering from an embarrassment of riches."

Dave spelled out their sources of income ". . . and the radio show, bringing in over two thousand a week. . . . Howdy, you can afford about any damn thing you want right now."

At breakfast the next morning with the Persons, Howdy surprised Frank. "With your license, can you buy real estate anywhere in California?"

Something in Howdy's voice made Frank begin to hope again. "Sure, I'm licensed in the whole state. Why?"

"Just thinking."

Despite Melba's warning look, Frank began talking about the questionable land outside the city limits.

Howdy stopped him. "I don't want any land this far away. But if I do decide to buy land someday, maybe you could handle it."

After the picture was finished Howdy brought the subject up to Ev Moses. Ev was emphatic. "There has never been a better time to buy. There is good distress land close in. Use cash and you can probably get it for half its present market value."

In November, Howdy made his first purchase, a five-acre peach orchard in the San Fernando Valley. The land lay close to the main state thoroughfare to downtown Los Angeles. Frank Persons handled the transaction.

The year had been a good one for Rolling-O Productions. *The Guy From Guymon*, the movie based on Howdy's career, was a box-office success and a turning point for old Neville Newton. He was given a small part and although he had never been a professional actor, he had a flare for comedy. As a result of his performance, "Judge Habeas Q. Corpus" would become a regular in Howdy's and Angie's musical westerns. The old man's ecstasy in his late-in-coming success was pathetic to witness.

Don Bellew, the publicity man for Rolling-O Productions, was responsible for a three-page photo story in a national magazine featuring Howdy and Angie and their "radio and screen sweetheart relationship." As a result, a number of fan magazines and columns began conjecturing about the "*real* relationship." Don Bellew, quite honestly, denied any responsibility for the rumors and innuendo.

"I don't give a shit how you do it," Howdy exploded, "but I want those lies stopped. They're trying to dirty us up. If you can't get them stopped, then by God I'll find me a man that can."

Several weeks later Bellew was fired when in desperation he attempted to stop the rumors of an illicit relationship between Howdy and Angie by leaking to a nationally syndicated woman gossip columnist an exclusive story that the co-stars were secretly engaged.

In the meeting that followed the firing, Ev Moses summed up the situation to Howdy and Dave. "You can't deny the story. If you do you'll just confirm it. For now, play it cool. Keep smiling and don't say anything. As long as the people think you two are secretly engaged they'll read a lot more into your relationship on the air and on the screen than there really is."

After a long, unhappy silence he added, "Of course, if Angie were to actually fall for somebody else and get engaged or married, that would be another kettle of fish altogether."

Dave Layne's grim rejoinder said it all. "That, my friends, will be the day."

Renée raised up on an elbow and let her breasts, grown still heavier, spill over Howdy's naked chest. When he refused to look her in the eye, she reached down and gave him a painful jerk. "Cheer up, lover boy. Either marry her or fire her. What's so tough about that?"

In the end, it was Angie who brought up the problem. They had appeared together at a hospital benefit. On the way home they stopped at a drive-in for sandwiches and malts. Angie twisted on the seat to face him. "Let's talk about it, Howdy. Most of it's my fault, you know."

"There's nothing to talk about, Bellew's gone. He was a damned fool. Things'll die down."

Angie sighed impatiently and rested a hand on Howdy's shoulder. "I don't care about those lies, honey, but the more things we do together the more people are going to wonder about us. If we just go on like we have been, the gossips will say they were right. And if we don't go on the way we are—then—well—"

"Well, what?"

Her hands flopped down to her lap. "Nothing, really. In a situation like this the girl doesn't have any alternatives." Angie straightened and let her head fall back against the seat. She could feel Howdy eyeing her and she waited for the question she had made inevitable. It came quickly.

"Angie, I wish you'd talk straight. You're talking in circles and I'm not bright enough to follow you. Just tell me what's bothering you."

"Not here, Howdy. I didn't mean to bring it up here but I do want to talk to you. Could we go up to the mountain again, where we first talked?"

Twenty minutes later, the car pulled off Mulholland Drive and stopped on the crest of a hill worn barren by countless tires. Outwardly composed, Angie curled a leg beneath her and leaned against the door. "Howdy, I don't want to go over everything between us. I helped you a little bit and for one reason or another, perhaps gratitude, you helped me a lot. But something else has happened and

461

that is, I've become a problem . . . because I went and fell in love with you and had the shameless gall to tell you so."

She turned away to look out over the panorama of lights diffused beneath the thin blanket of low fog. When she turned back, Howdy saw the determined set of her jaw. "When this next contract cycle ends, Howdy, I'm leaving the show. You can make it sound like I'm just taking a vacation, that I'll be back. But I won't. I'm not being heroic. You don't need me. I've screwed up enough courage to say this tonight, so please just accept it. I'm more grateful to you than I can ever say. I always will be. You've never made any demands on me but I've made a lot on you. I told you how I felt," her arm swept across the horizon, "right here, where we are now . . . and I took a dirty lowdown sneaky female advantage of you. I'm sorry about that."

She paused and extended her hand. "Forgive me?" An instant later, Howdy's hand shot out and clamped around her wrist. He pulled her to him so roughly that her half reclining body slammed against his. His right arm locked her to him and she could feel the fingers of his left hand working deep into the thick tangle of her hair. And then his mouth smashed against hers so viciously that his teeth bruised her lips and brought a muffled cry. As eagerly, her arms moved around him as his hand cradled the back of her head.

"Little Angie—you're my luck, honey. You ain't goin' no place. I need you. Hear me?"

16 No ADVANCE ANNOUNCEMENT was made. Howdy and Angie were married in November in a quiet ceremony at the church in Barstow. Dave Layne stood up for the groom and Frank Persons gave the bride away. A small luncheon reception for family and old friends was held at the Roadside Inn. In mid-afternoon Dave drove the couple to the San Bernardino airport where a chartered four-place Beechcraft was waiting to take them to Palm Springs.

Dave had made the arrangements for everything—the wedding, the honeymoon and the Hollywood apartment. The latter was a large new place on Hollywood Boulevard at the east end of the county territory known familiarly as The Strip. It lacked nothing, including a Steinway grand piano.

In a private cottage at the Desert Inn, they were surrounded by evidence of Dave Layne's thoughtfulness. The flowers, the fruit, the refrigerator filled with champagne, guest cards to fashionable La Quinta and a letter of introduction to the management of The Dunes, the gambling resort and restaurant south of the town.

Howdy and Angie, inconspicuous in a town frequented by the great and near-great of a dozen arts and industries, dined quietly at the Inn then strolled along the picturesque Palm Canyon Drive.

It was after nine when they walked back along Indian Avenue. The town and all that was in it seemed miniaturized by the overwhelming, snow-mantled presence of eleven-thousand-foot Mount San Jacinto. Dead-black against the luminescent night sky, it sheered straight up from the neo-Spanish winter homes.

As they walked through the gardens of the Desert Inn, Angie tugged at Howdy's arm to stop him. "I wish we could climb up there sometime and just look down on things."

Howdy reached out and turned her to him. "No more mountains for a while, Angie—please?"

They laughed and went inside.

Howdy skinned out of the cashmere pull-over, tossed it on a chair, and went to the refrigerator. "Mrs. Goodwyn—would you like some bubbly?"

"What year is it, Mr. Goodwyn . . . darling?"

Howdy frowned. "What year is it? It's nineteen thirty-eight. November eleventh. We got married today. Remember?"

Angie giggled. "I mean the champagne, silly. What's the year printed on the label?"

Howdy examined the bottle. "It says, 'Piper' something or other and the date is nineteen twenty-eight. Why?"

Angie shrugged. "Because you're supposed to ask. Anyway, that's a perfect year—if we drink it right now."

They sat diagonally across from one another. Howdy, dressed in a sport shirt and gray flannel slacks, had one leg slung over the arm of the easy chair. Angie, in a new silk negligee that covered her slip and bra, sat curled on the near corner of the sofa. The bottle and two glasses stood on the end of the coffee table between them.

After the second glass, she patted the sofa beside her. "If you don't come over here and prop me up, I may just keel over from happiness."

She held up the glass to watch the bubbles rising from the hollow stem. For no apparent reason she giggled. "That's what I feel like—bubbly."

When he settled beside her, Angie made an elaborate ritual of cuddling. "Nineteen thirty-eight is a good year too, darling. You'll never know how good."

She put the glass down and a moment later, in his arms, her fingers had undone the buttons on his shirt. Inside, her hand explored the smooth skin of his rib cage and moved up to the hard pectoral swell and the small, protruding nipple. She disengaged her lips long enough to tease, "You've got a goose bump, darling," then twisted her waist to ease the way for the hand that was groping for the hook on her bra.

They undressed each other on the sofa, scarcely parting their lips. Angie found him first. Her fingers explored his length and girth, then closed around him and her thumb began smoothing the lubricious secretion in small circles. When she felt him responding, she quickened and widened the movement, sensing and seeking out the pleasure points until he began to protest. Her free hand urged him to find her and when he did, she encouraged the fumbling fingers and guided him into her. For a moment she lay motionless—feeling. The wanting, the imagining so short of reality came flooding against the long-built barrier of sublimation. Howdy felt Angie's body, flushed and moist, begin to convulse beneath him. He called out and tried to control her—called out again. Seconds later, unable to hold off, he succumbed to a racking orgasm.

Rigid, Angie lay beneath him, her arms locked around his rib cage, her senses congealed in the penultimate agony of frustration. When she began to stir he moved as though to leave her.

"No darling! No! Stay with me. Stay with me. It's all right, darling. You were wonderful. Just let me feel you."

Howdy lifted his face from the soft wedge of her neck and shoulder. He wore a stricken expression. "I'm sorry. I shouldn't of let you horse around so long. I just couldn't hold back."

Grasping him in place, Angie tried desperately to reassure him. "Its all right darling. You were wonderful. Really. You were wonderful."

Ever since Dave had chartered the Beechcraft for the honeymoon flight, Howdy had been toying with the idea of learning to fly. Over mild objections from both Angie and Dave, he took a trial flight. Howdy found his medium in the air. After six and a half hours of dual instruction at the Grand Central Air Terminal in Glendale, he made his solo flight. Six weeks later he qualified for a private license.

For good luck he bought the plane he had soloed in but in midsummer he traded it for a new four-place Stinson. Every hour he could spare was spent in the air. On two occasions Howdy and Angie flew to Barstow and landed on a dirt road just outside of town.

Frank Persons was as enthusiastic as a boy when Howdy took him up and let him handle the plane from the right hand seat. "Damn! If they'd only got these things perfected while I was young enough I might have joined the Lafayette Escadrille." But Frank's principal preoccupation was the great living relief map spread out below

465

them. "You can see tomorrow from up here, Howdy. You can see tomorrow."

He pointed southwest to the ribbon of Union Pacific tracks snaking over Cajon Pass toward San Bernardino and Colton. "It doesn't take much to figure out how real estate gets valuable."

Off to the west they could see the barren summit of Mt. San Antonio. "Old Baldy," the natives called it. It was the peak whose snow-shrouded crest and slopes provided dramatic contrast to the myriad rows of manicured orange groves at its base.

In the distance random mile-square patches of pasture and rich grain and bean fields—some green and some fallow—stretched away to the low, ocherous hills bordering the sea. Beyond shone the haze-screened silver sheet of the Pacific. Dimly, they could make out the mountainous profiles of Santa Catalina and San Clemente Islands.

Northeast of the mountain range, the oven brown expanse of the Mojave Desert disappeared into the distant shimmering scrim of late summer heat. At eleven thousand feet, as they prepared to cross the San Gabriel Mountains, Frank Persons' breathing became labored. Howdy's concerned look brought an apologetic smile. "I'm glad we're riding, not hiking. Air's a little thin up here." A moment later the craft's nose dipped below the horizon as they began a slow descent.

Reassured by the older man's grateful nod, Howdy studied the terrain. No map could depict southern California's growth as graphically as the panorama below them. Certainly no book could recite the decade-by-decade development of the fertile plain reaching from coastal ranges to the sea. It was all there—the groves turned to towns, the towns turned to cities, the cities spreading their suburbs outward along new arterials to merge with neighboring cities—an amorphous metropolis-in-the-making that Howdy could put no name to. But he understood, instinctively, the nature of the miracle and the opportunities inherent in it.

Risking some turbulence, he crossed back to the desert side of the mountains by way of a low saddle and made a big circle toward the southeast. Coming in over town, he landed on a hard dirt street less than two blocks from the Persons' cottage.

On the return flight, Howdy's preoccupation troubled Angie. When a half hour had passed with little more than a token grunt or the briefest laconism she made no attempt to conceal her annoyance. Surprised, Howdy looked away from the controls. "Nothing's wrong, I was just thinking about Frank and why that promotion of his never had a chance."

The inference seemed unfair to Angie. "He got caught in the depression, Howdy—that's all."

"Nope, that isn't all. Frank didn't bother to figure out the facts and work with them. He worked backward. He bent the facts to fit his idea."

"Oh? How do you know?"

They had recrossed the mountains. Ahead lay the neat cross-hatch pattern of the pioneer community of San Bernardino.

"It's all spelled out down there. Everything's growing along the highways leading toward L.A. People are going to fill up the good land between here and L.A. and from the beaches in toward L.A. before they start moving out from the edges. Barstow's way out beyond the main edge now. It's on the wrong side of the mountains, too. Most folks'll want to stay in close to the city like we did." He sensed Angie was beginning to bristle with hometown loyalty. "I'm not knocking Barstow. It's just that in the San Fernando Valley the towns are spreading together already. So far nothing's spreading around Barstow except sagebrush and it won't until a hell of a lot more people settle in southern California or unless some big industry comes to the area. If the railroad didn't do it for the town, then nothing will, not for years."

Howdy's logic was too clear to admit reasonable rebuttal. Her hometown was out on the edge, the ragged, hot, windy, sometimes icy edge, with none of the allure that brought people to southern California. Southern California really *was* the land on the ocean side of the mountains. But someday that would change.

They flew westward into the wind. Angie wondered now at Howdy's unusual interest in the southern California growth pattern. As well as she thought she knew him— "I'm not sure anybody'll ever really know him," she had confided to her mother—she was unprepared for this new preoccupation. In a strange way she feared it.

In September, when Hitler's armies invaded Poland, Everett Moses began to stockpile product in the recording division. He presented, and had accepted by Howdy and Dave, an accelerated overall schedule. A research division was incorporated and staffed and by the end of the year, Meyer Laboratories had applied for patents on a system of turntables and pickups with new amplifying circuits that was efficient in truly portable equipment. Shortly afterward came a portable field radio telephone.

When the first Nazi bombers dropped their explosives on Britain the U.S. Army Signal Corps contracted for an experimental order of one hundred field units. This was followed by an order for five hundred portable play-back units to be used for audio training. Meyer Laboratories became one of the most profitable of the several H.G. Enterprises.

In February Howdy and Angie moved into their new ranch-style home built on the five-acre peach farm in the San Fernando Valley. Fan magazines covered every aspect of the showplace, the house, the swimming pool, the stables and tack room, the corrals, the one-acre peach orchard saved for family use and the private airstrip and hangar that ran along the back line of the acreage and extended into additional acreage that Howdy had acquired the following year.

In April, Angie, three months' pregnant, suffered a miscarriage after a riding sequence in a picture—a sequence that she had insisted upon doing herself. After two weeks in the hospital Angie was permitted to complete the shooting. When Hedda Hopper revealed the reason for her absence, Dave Layne was forced to hire three temporary secretaries to answer the thousands of notes of condolence and to acknowledge the dozens of crocheted bed jackets, home knitted sweaters, afghans and shawls and the "lucky baby clothes" that were sent to insure a successful second attempt to establish a family. After what Angie insisted was a "decent time" the clothing was given anonymously to local charities.

John Steinbeck's novel, *The Grapes of Wrath*, had attracted attention to the plight of itinerant families: the crop followers. The state legislature passed restrictive immigration legislation aimed at stopping the mass migration of dust-bowl immigrants, the so-called "bum blockade," and the farmers and ranchers, to whom the unexpected cheap labor pool was a boon, often obstructed real help by minimizing the problem in Sacramento through their lobbying organizations.

"We're taking good care of them. It's the goddamn commies that are riling them up," was the explanation most frequently offered. Howdy himself succumbed to the propaganda after he and Angie attended a rally in a neighborhood school one evening. During the meeting an agitator berated capitalism for an hour and they were shocked to discover that a huge Soviet hammer and sickle flag hung opposite the American flag.

Howdy summed up his disenchantment: "If they're dumb enough to swallow that crap then they're too dumb to bother with. To hell with them."

For Angie, the edict brought both relief and disappointment. She watched the man who was the dearest person in her life, so often now a stranger, and realized that despite the western clothing and the more than residual speech mannerisms, Howard Dennis Goodwyn, the genial "Howdy"—star of radio, screen, and rodeo—had crossed a border and in doing so had renounced any real identity with the "back home folks." She understood also that her husband would continue to give lip service to his background, but it would be done deliberately out of promotional need rather than emotional necessity. To her his repudiation was, in its way, an act of "honesty" but the answer did not satisfy her. More and more there were areas in their relationship in which she, too, was becoming an outsider. She assumed her husband's disenchantment stemmed from an absolute lack of sympathy for any person who would not fight for what he wanted. She knew that Howdy felt that his own circumstances seven years earlier had been no more promising than the least fortunate Okie of Arkie who got dusted off his land. Howdy had often talked of those places, incredibly poor spreads, on which a man and his family thought of security only in terms of an unlikely prayer answered or a patient creditor at the store, a little stringy meat on the hoof, and a patch of dry-land hay.

"If he ain't bedridden, any man can do better if he'll just get up and go. Better to die trying than die crying," his father had said. That was the son's philosophy, too.

Angie knew what Howdy wanted and she knew what she wanted and the price of keeping what she had was helping her man get where he wanted to go. If getting there meant closing her eyes and echoing his "To hell with them!" that would be part of it too ... if she could forget the scrawny, shivering, snotty-nosed kids in tar-paper lean-tos. A gentle, unsolicited observation from Dave Layne had surprised her on the set one day, shortly after she returned to work: "It's tough to be married to two men, Angie."

Three hundred and thirty-seven thousand British, French, and Belgian troops were a part of the miracle of Dunkirk that took place between May 28 and June 4. The Royal Air Force's pitifully outnumbered, haywired Spitfires took on the German Luftwaffe and were killed at the rate of four to one. In southern California Douglas and Lockheed became the cornerstones of the free world's airpower. The state's immigration laws tumbled and the itinerant fruit pickers and stoop-crop harvesters traded clippers and hoes for rivet guns and wrenches and a lot of consciences eased and a lot of money flowed.

Rolling-O Productions completed two musicals and three straight westerns during the year. Meyer Laboratories won state and Federal approval to go public and two hundred thousand shares of common stock were issued.

At the initial stockholders' meeting, coming after Roosevelt had been elected President for a unprecedented third term and the Lend Lease act was signed into law, Howdy wore a dark blue chalk-stripe flannel business suit. Angie, straightening his four-in-hand tie, found herself forcing a smile. "From now on I'm going to call you 'Ty.' That's short for tycoon, darling."

Neville Newton, doggedly persisting in his frustrated attempt to keep his end of the bargain between parts in pictures, shook his head and made no effort to conceal his misgivings. "Behold. We attend the rising of an industrial colossus. You fairly reek of class now, son—until you joust with the King's English. But I warn you, in the Jonathan Club it would be better to drop your pants than your G's."

The stockholders were impressed by President Daniel Meyer and Secretary Everett Moses, who projected an upcoming clutch of new government contracts. Moses surmised that the book value of Meyer stock would, within two years, increase to ten times its present market value.

Howdy surprised the officers of his companies by not

staying with the script. He indicated the printed reports that each person had been given as they entered the convention room at the Ambassador Hotel. "You can look at it. Study it. It's a pretty good job of work for something under six years. The only thing is—except for Meyer Labs—it's all entertainment."

Behind him on the platform Ev Moses leaned unobtrusively toward Dave Layne. "We didn't talk about this. What's he up to?"

The partner shrugged. "I don't know. Whatever it is, it's too late now. He keeps a lot to himself these days."

Assuming his professional mantle of humbleness, Howdy grinned shyly at the gathering. " 'Course, I don't mean to downgrade entertainment, because that's how this all started. I just want to assay it for what it's really worth in times like I'm sure we're coming to."

He half turned and directed an apologetic little smile at his officers. "If the boys behind me are fidgeting a little, it's because we didn't rehearse this part of the show."

He watched them until the ripple of laughter subsided. "I've always been scared of big business because I thought it was like high religion—something only preachers could understand. But thanks to Dave and Ev and others, I found out that good business is just good horse-sense."

There was an instant murmur of approval throughout the big room. Dave and Ev smiled dutifully too, and tried to conceal their growing apprehension. "So, after looking at what Dan Meyer has been able to do with his amplifiers and communications gadgets and knowing that the government will spend billions on lend-lease war material, I figured it would make sense if everybody who's got a stake in our operations started to look for ways that we can catch some of our own money on the first bounce and keep it at home."

Howdy paused and pretended to ponder his next words. "What I'm trying to say—and you stockholders are probably way ahead of me—is that we should welcome suggestions about other things we can do—like certain kinds of defense work—to help the war effort along. We can't build shipyards and steel mills and things. But we can build electrical equipment and I figure there must be a lot of real smart guys around that have other good ideas but don't have the money to get 'em going yet."

Howdy concluded his impromptu remarks with a request that stockholders submit the names of any small companies interested in products geared to the war effort who might welcome an assist from H.G. Enterprises. Although they were taken by surprise, in the end Dave Layne and Everett Moses could find no fault with the request. The attorney summed up his reaction? "What he's doing is telling the stockholders that we are flexible and progressive, that our credit can be put to work for them—if they'll go to work for us. It's not the usual way to handle things—but then Howdy's not the usual man."

When the meeting ended, an attractive man in his early forties approached the platform and extended a hand. "My name is Vance. Steven Vance, Mr. Goodwyn. Our family votes twelve hundred shares of Meyer Laboratories. It's reassuring to hear management ask stockholders to do something more than sign proxies. I'd like to make a date with you gentlemen to tell you about a small company I've been watching that has a tremendous potential if this war business spreads. I think it could be taken in under the Meyer umbrella or as another subsidiary. It has a government contract but needs financing and management. About an hour of summary would give you enough background to decide whether or not it's worth exploring."

A luncheon meeting was set up for the following week. Steven Vance turned out to be a man of considerable means, the direct descendant of the California pioneer family that still owned the huge Los Nidos Company. He explained that he had come across the Lucifer Flare Company in Santa Ana. "Louis Siefert has been running a little fireworks factory there for years. He had a Coast Guard contract to make emergency flares and last year he went to Washington and got a Navy contract for an advanced type. But he's a scientist. No business man. I considered buying in, but aside from looking after our ranching operation and teaching the children something about it, I don't want any managerial responsibility. I find this sort of investing more fun, frankly."

After two months of meetings, H.G. Enterprises acquired controlling interest in the Lucifer Flare Company, incorporated it, and installed Steven Vance on the board of directors.

In July, Howdy and Angie spent a weekend with the Vances at El Rancho de Los Nidos some sixty miles southeast of Los Angeles. The house, most of which incorporated the original Garcia-Perez adobe built by the peons and Indians in the 1840's, was a spacious one-story U-shaped California-Spanish structure with heavy tile roofing. It was situated on top of a large knoll bordering the Santa Ana Mountains. The property, almost ninety thousand acres of it, reached from the serrated mountain slopes to the shoreward lowlands whose southern boundaries were obscured in the coastal mist.

Nineteen-year-old Steve, Junior, and thirteen-year-old Jennifer became the Goodwyns' principal guides. While the father watched with transparent pride, young Steve explained the complicated operation of the ranch.

Jennifer, an olive-skinned, arrow slim, violet-eyed tomboy, wore her glossy black hair in double braided "Indian pigtails" and rode like a Comanche. At the corral Howdy and Angie watched her throw a hackamore on a half-broken cow pony, leap on bareback and drive the animal to a lather. The girl was fearless, but not reckless.

Steven Vance regarded his daughter with wonder. "I think she's a throwback to her paternal great-grandmother. My own mother told me that Grandmother Anita Lewis was one of the best horsewomen in Southern California. She used to scandalize all the proper ladies by riding astride with the *vaqueros*," he indicated the backlands, "over these same hills."

They watched Jennifer pull her mount to a dust-exploding stop, dismount, slip off the rope, and whack the subdued animal on its glistening rump.

"Sometimes Catherine is convinced that they got the babies mixed up at the hospital. But one thing *is* for sure—she's a lot harder to break than any cayuse in this corral."

Catherine Coulter Vance, a somber beauty who seemed to resist smiling, though she was properly cordial to her guests, nodded. "Steven Junior runs truer to my New England breed."

Although her husband understood the oft-repeated observation for the veiled reproach it was, Howdy and Angie took it for another manifestation of the usual mother's-pride-in-handsome-son syndrome.

Later, alone in the guest room, Howdy and Angie discussed the younger Vances. "I thought you avoided having to demonstrate your horsemanship very gracefully, darling."

Howdy balanced on one leg and tugged at the bottom

of his narrow frontier pants. "I don't know anything about clay feet. But I'd rather have one of them than a busted back."

Angie laughed and returned to the mirror. "That's all right, she adores you anyway. I think you've made another conquest."

After a reflective silence she turned to him again. "But I'm not so sure either of us made a hit with Catherine Vance. She's very nice, but a little too," she shrugged, "I don't know—a little *too nice*, I guess."

Howdy finished removing his trousers. "She's all right. Cold-assed—but all right."

A surpressed explosion of mirth came from the dressing alcove. "Good God! I hope nobody ever describes *me* that way!"

Howdy took a shade too long to reply. "Not a chance."

They breakfasted in the patio on Sunday. After much urging, Howdy got into a pair of young Steve's trunks and joined the others in the pool. Both he and Angie felt naked white in contrast to the glowing, sun-bronzed bodies of the Vance family. Howdy was uncomfortably self-conscious about his color and about his awkwardness in the water. He could swim with a thrashing sort of stroke that Angie described as a "drowning dog paddle."

The senior Steven Vance was an excellent athlete, still quite lean despite his forty-three years. The boy was a beautifully coordinated natural athlete who performed matter-of-factly with no trace of exhibitionism. Jennifer was equally at home in the water and, again, she was the unabashed show-off on the diving board. Catherine Vance neither dressed for swimming nor made any explanation. In a smart sun dress she presided over after-breakfast coffee, asked all the correct questions, listened to Angie's replies with apparent interest, and turned the conversation to books and the theater. When Angie confessed that she had little time to read because of rehearsals, Catherine recommended the new Martin Dies book, *Trojan Horses in America*, which warned of the subversive forces at work in the land. She also spoke highly of Thomas Wolfe's newest outpouring. *You Can't Go Home Again*. Angie fibbed and said she had heard fine things about both books and intended to read them.

They toured the principal units of the ranch and at four o'clock returned to the main house for a patio barbecue prepared by Rosita and Pablo, the Vances' Mexican house couple.

"They are absolutely devoted to us," Catherine explained. "They're such jewels. Their grandparents worked for Steven's grandparents so they are really family, you see."

Later in the afternoon, rolling leisurely through the citrus groves that lined most of the highway to Norwalk on the first leg of their two-and-a-half-hour drive home, Angie and Howdy compared notes.

"I like Steve Senior and those kids, but frankly, Howdy, even if business depends on it, I can't warm up to Catherine. We sat there smiling—or rather I did—talking about all those silly la-dee-da things. I was bored stiff. She made me feel like a yokel when she talked about books and plays: *The Male Animal, Separate Rooms, Johnny Belinda, Charley's Aunt!* She must have done a cram course the last time they were in New York."

"Guess we'll just have to go get our brains gussied up too. Why didn't you put her on about pictures and music?"

"I did talk about music. She's up on that too. I didn't exactly feel uncouth, but I sure as hell felt uncultured."

Howdy was amused. "I'm a country bumpkin from Guymon, but it doesn't bother me. If you want to get a quick culture job, why don't you go on back to New York this winter? Maybe you can catch some culture for both of us."

Angie put her left arm along the backrest so her fingers could trace affectionate little figures on Howdy's shoulder. "I'd love that, but not without you."

At 7:55 A.M. Hawaiian time, on December 7th, one hundred Japanese carrier-borne aircraft and a school of vest pocket submarines changed the plans of one hundred and thirty-two million Americans. In order to directly involve the United States in Europe and divert defensive forces from the Pacific, Italy and Germany joined Japan by declaring war. In a matter of weeks the Allies were engaged on a half dozen fronts in two hemispheres. The United States became the world's largest military hardware manufactory and training camp. California became one of its most vital elements. President Roosevelt and General Hershey began sending their official greetings to ten million young Americans, among them Steven Vance, Junior, and Howard D. Goodwyn.

When the classification card arrived placing Howdy in 1A, Everett Moses undertook a series of legal maneuvers to keep the young star-businessman out of service. But Howdy had other plans.

Company pilot, Chad Chadwick, a major in the Army Air Force Reserve, was called up for duty with the Second Air Force and assigned to Lowry Field near Denver. He had been on duty for less than two weeks when Howdy received a call from the commanding officer offering him a position as civilian instructor. On February 10th, 1942, Howard D. Goodwyn received orders to report to the base for indoctrination by midnight, March 15th.

During the scant five weeks a multitude of decisions had to be made. The practical business of running H.G. Enterprises would be left with Dave Layne and Everett Moses. Bronc Bronston was elected a vice president. Meyer Laboratories and Lucifer Flare remained under the active management of Layne and Moses with Danny Meyer and Louis Siefert running the companies. None of these men understood Howdy's decision. The most persistent protests came from Everett Moses and it was to him that Howdy addressed the blunt explanation that silenced them all:

"I know that strings can be pulled to get me reclassified 2A or 4B. I'm an entertainer, not really a business executive or an official. H.G. Enterprises is first and foremost an entertainment operation. I'm it's chief product and I'm twenty-nine years old. I don't intend to stand up there looking healthy in a cowboy suit singing back-home songs to a couple of hundred thousand guys in uniforms. If I was too old or had one leg or one eye that'd be different.

"When this war is over I don't want anybody to remember that I took the easy way out. When I come home I know I can hold my head up and there'd better not be any crap from anybody. That's how it's going to be and I'll thank you to just take it that way and keep on doing a great job.

"Just in case I don't come back, everything's been arranged by you, Ev. But I'm coming back. And I'll tell you why. Because any kid that gets into an airplane and can't do what I tell him the first time is going to get busted out of the Army Air Force on his ass and put in the infantry."

476

At the going-away party after the last radio show with Howdy as star, Angie tried to convey her feelings to Melba Persons. "I don't know how to say it."

She rested moist palms beneath her rib cage. "I feel so empty in here. But it isn't really empty because I'm filled with fears, Melba. Awful fears."

The older woman who had been trying to reassure her reached over and placed her fingertips over Angie's lips. "Honey, let me tell you something about men like Howdy. They live in another world that has another set of rules. They make them. So when he tells you he's coming back you better believe him because it's true. He *will* come back."

"I know he's coming back, Melba. I feel that. It's something else. I don't know what it is."

The written examination arrived. For Howdy it required little more effort than the completion of a form. At Lowry Field, as one of six civilian instructors who received officers' pay, allowances, and privileges, he was assigned to Bachelor Officers' Quarters. In his element and oblivious of his fame as a show-business personality, Howdy Goodwyn immersed himself in the demanding routine of training cadets. Seven days a week, fourteen hours a day, Howdy drove his four charges to the limits of their endurance. Consistently they were in the top ten of the class. Most pleased of all was Major Chad Chadwick. The major summed up his staff's appraisal of Howard Goodwyn. "That drawling Okie son-of-a-bitch can pound more flying savvy down their throats, into their ears, and up their trembling asses than any flight instructor I've ever seen . . . and for this we pay him less money a month than his corporations make for him every sixty seconds. That's what I call dedicated service."

As well as he knew his former boss, Major Chadwick could be forgiven for underestimating the true nature of Howdy's dedication.

At the end of the first two months of training, during a bull session in the BOQ, Howdy found out, inadvertently, that Gene Autry had made plans to establish a contract training school for military pilots at Gilpin Field near Phoenix, Arizona. As he lay awake, too tired to sleep, Howdy went over the advantages of such an arrangement. Half aloud, he voiced his conclusion: "God love him, that Gene's really got an edge."

Two nights later, Howdy was sitting in the bar at the Brown Palace Hotel in Denver with Dave Layne and Ev Moses: "I want you to look into every angle of this flying-school deal. Find out what Autry and his partner had to do, then get back to me in one hell of a rush."

The shy smile that misled or concealed so much from those who didn't know him tugged at the corners of his mouth. "I figure if we had our own school we could pay me more than three hundred and twenty-six bucks a month, and turn out more good combat pilots one hell of a lot faster than I'm turning them out here. If we can do the job better, it's unpatriotic not to do it, isn't it?"

A week later, Ev Moses telephoned. "I have the figures, Howdy. There's no question about getting a contract with either the Army or the Navy and maybe both. We have to acquire the right land, get priorities on material and equipment, and satisfy Stimson and the War Department."

"What about financing?"

"We can get Federal funds."

"How much of our own dough do we need to get going?"

"Whatever the payment on the land turns out to be."

"You and Dave do any thinking about locations?"

"Not yet. But that won't be a problem. Good land's going begging. Incidentally, we keep hearing rumors that the Navy is going to establish a major air base for the Marines on the Irvine Ranch back of Santa Ana. Some place called El Toro."

"Isn't that near Vance?"

"Not too far."

There was a thoughtful pause. "Ev."

"Yes?"

"Get hold of Steve. Ask him if he can fly over here with you this coming weekend. And bring Angie, too."

Steven Vance, Everett Moses, and Angie flew to Denver the following Saturday morning. Bone-tired and still in his flying clothes, Howdy met them that evening at the hotel. Angie was shocked by his appearance. "Honey, you've lost *pounds*! You look awful."

Howdy grinned. "You ought to see the kids I'm teaching."

Angie slipped an arm around his waist and rested her

head on his shoulder. "I don't care about them. I bet you're working twice as hard as they are."

Howdy tousled her hair. "Four times'd be more like it. Come on. I need some coffee."

For two hours Howdy drove himself through the details of his plan, describing what he felt would constitute an ideal training installation in terms of location, hangar facilities, classrooms, commissary, quarters, flight line equipment, and aircraft. ". . . But the key to the whole shebang is location, Steve. What I want to know is, have you got a square mile of land on your ranch that I can buy? I'll lease it if I have to, but I'd rather buy it."

"We have a lot of square miles, Howdy, but I can't answer that offhand. The best bottom land, the level stuff, is under tenant lease on crop percentages."

The spectacle of the tidy mosaic of fields and groves spread before them as they stood on the terrace of the Vances' Casa Grande was as vivid in his memory as it had been when he was there. Howdy understood the problem he was posing. "I don't mean the best bean field you got, Steve. What about some of that fallow stuff lying next to the hills? That's still lease-free, isn't it?"

Steven Vance nodded. "We have about six sections along the edge of the hills. But that's no place to build an airport."

Howdy chuckled mirthlessly. "By the time I get through with these kids, if they make it, any place they can get a ship into will look like an airport. All I need is two strips of about three thousand feet with enough room for a tower, hangars, and offices."

Later, when Vance had promised to see what he could do and Howdy and Angie were alone, she sagged on the edge of the bed beside him. "Does this mean you'll be coming back home instead of me coming here?"

Howdy yawned and began unlacing a shoe. "It sure as hell does."

He kicked off the other shoe and collapsed backward with his legs dangling. "There's no point in you coming. You'd be sitting alone all day and half the night in some dump here in Denver. You stay put. We'll have our own operation going in ninety days. You and I can start living like white folks again."

Angie undressed him and all but led him to the shower.

479

Later, in bed with him for the first time in eight weeks, she cuddled his head in the crook of her arm and watched him sink into the deep sleep of the exhausted. It was well past midnight before she slept.

Steven Vance agreed to lease, with option to buy, two contiguous half sections. The strip ran for ten thousand feet along the base of the low hills.

Early in August, when Howdy's first four cadets graduated from Lowry as numbers one, two, four, and five, respectively, most of the paper work had been processed and assurances had been received from Washington that the field as planned would be approved. On December first, when Howdy's second group graduated, again in the top ten, his own release was expedited by Chad Chadwick, now a Lieutenant Colonel.

Once again Howdy and Angie spent Christmas with their adopted family. The celebration on Christmas Day at the ranch house in the San Fernando Valley was the happiest gathering in several years. Only one thing marred the holiday—the worsening condition of Neville Newton. With grim humor the old man sought to dismiss his ailment. "Son, if you will forgive my indelicacy, whether it's sick or well man's prostate gland is a pain in the ass. It would seem that it's now exacting full payment for the alleged pleasure it has given me during the past sixty years."

The ground-breaking was celebrated on January fifteenth and the first group of cadets reported for primary training on June 20. Five weeks later Benito Mussolini resigned as Premier of Italy following the Albanian and North African debacles.

On June twenty-first a race riot broke out in Detroit. When the toll of 34 dead and 700 injured had been tallied, Howdy glowered at the newspaper story then tossed it aside. "I can tell you right now who's behind it. The commies. They'll never miss a chance to stir up trouble inside the country and they'll always wait until we're in some other big trouble. Just like they stirred up the fruit pickers right in the middle of the depression. It isn't easy to be a nigger. But I sure wish they'd wise up. As bad as they got it, it's better here."

Ev Moses smiled sadly. "We have a long way to go, friend. A long way. Everybody's motto seems to be:

Howdy shook his head. "It isn't just the color. They think different too."

Ev Moses braced himself against the chair back. "My brother was the only Jew in medical school in San Francisco. Some of the guys gave him a bad time because they thought he was 'different' until the doctor in charge of dissection straightened them out."

Concealing his surprise, Howdy listened intently as Moses continued. "The surgeon got three hearts from the cooler and laid them on the table. Then he pointed to them and said, 'One of these came from a Catholic, one from a Protestant, and one from a Jew. I'll give any student a passing grade in the course who can tell me positively which one is which.'"

The attorney laughed softly. "That settled that."

Without knowing why, Howdy was suddenly self-conscious. He tried to conceal it with an elaborate casualness. "Hey now, I didn't know you were a Jew, Ev."

Ev smiled sadly and shrugged. "I didn't either until I was six."

During a July Fourth exercise Lt. Colonel Chadwick and a Navy cadet, simulating a carrier take-off from a marked area, encountered a dust devil in their AT-6. The ship stalled, sideslipped into the ground from fifty feet, and crashed. The left wing absorbed most of the impact. The cadet went on to combat duty but Chad was given a medical discharge after an operation on his smashed left hip. Two months later Chad was placed in charge of operations at Vance Field.

Howdy's growing preoccupation with the flying school made it impossible for Angie to keep her apprehension to herself. He was so deeply involved he was seldom home. Loneliness drove Angie into confiding in Dave Layne.

Dave's own status in H.G. Enterprises had changed. He was still involved in the recording business and the film productions but the top-level business decisions had fallen on Ev Moses. Dave had also begun to feel a nameless uneasiness. To avoid spending long, idle days alone at home, Angie continued to come to the office and three nights a week she helped out at the Hollywood Canteen but even so she found herself welcoming the impromptu cocktails with Dave and Ev. As time went on she found more often than not that her evenings were spent with Dave alone. Since neither had home obligations, the cocktail hour was often prolonged to include dinner at the Vine Street Derby.

Angie refused a third martini. "No more. I'll start getting little blue veins in my nose."

Dave looked at the waitress. "One more, and a couple of menus, please."

He turned back to Angie. "Is Howdy going to stay at the Vances' again tonight?"

The answer was a glum nod. "Yes. That'll make four nights this week. He might as well have his mail sent there."

Dave impaled the martini olive and ate it. "In a way it's a good thing he can stay there. I'd hate to make that drive twice a day."

"I know. I know. But that doesn't help much when I'm alone in the house."

"Why don't you go down and stay with him more than you do?"

"Two reasons. I can't impose, and I don't feel easy with Catherine Vance." She worried the doily. "There's another reason too, Dave. I don't want Howdy to think that I'm always under foot. I compromised my pride enough when I threw myself at him."

Her eyes challenged him. "I *did*, you know."

Dave shrugged. "You went after something you wanted. There's no law against that."

The waitress returned with the drinks and the menus. Several minutes passed in silence as they studied a bill of fare they both knew by heart. Finally Dave folded the menu.

"Steaks are back on tonight. Want to splurge?"

Angie nodded and recited by rote: "Medium. Baked potato. Sour cream. Cobb salad. Same old routine."

Dave frowned. "I think you need one more drink."

"One more drink and I'll start crying on your shoulder."

"Unless I beat you to it and start crying on yours."

Angie smiled crookedly. "No, Dave, you wouldn't, I know. I can depend on you."

"Dear old dependable Dave." He emphasized each word disparagingly. Before Angie could protest he held up a hand. "I know. I said it. You didn't. Actually, I don't mind the 'dear' or the 'dependable'—it's the 'old' that gets me."

His eyes rolled upward. "Forty. Holy Mother!" He shuddered. "A terrible thing happens to a man about to be forty, Angie. It's called 'middle age' and it scares the hell out of me."

Angie studied him sympathetically. "Dave . . ."

"Yes?"

"Why do you go on like this?"

"You mean—a bachelor? Well, for one thing my first wife walked out on me. For another, you know perfectly well that if I had met you before you met Howdy, I'd have given him one hell of a run for his money."

Angie rested a hand lightly on top of his. "I know that, Dave, and I hope you know how important it's been to me. But tell me something—why did she walk out? Do you know?"

"Not really. I loved her. I did everything I could for her . . . I thought we did everything well together."

Angie finished the thought. "But she didn't love you, and love doesn't work when it's a one-sided affair."

Dave Layne smiled cryptically.

"You loved a girl who didn't love you—and—" Angie broke off briefly. "—and I love a guy who doesn't really love me—and—"

Very gently Dave shook her shoulder. "Wait, Angie. Don't jump to conclusions about Howdy. Remember when I said that it was tough being married to two men?"

Angie nodded.

"I thought you understood what I meant then."

"I did, then."

"Well, it means the same thing now. When you say Howdy doesn't really love you, you're wrong. I suspect he loves you as much as he can love any woman. But you're not in competition with something as simple as another woman. You're in competition with—oh hell, 'dream' is a corny word—but that's what he's in love with—his dream of who and what Howard Goodwyn is going to be."

Angie smiled sadly. "I know. I've known that for years. But I always thought I fitted into that picture."

"You did and I did as long as the radio show was the

big dream. But he's dreaming bigger now, and that's going to call for some understanding, and some compromises, too."

Angie looked at him sharply as he continued.

"That means that you, as his wife, and I as his partner, will have to accept the fact that our roles are less important and may get even less so as time goes by."

Angie sat rigidly while the truth of Dave's words hammered her insides to pulp.

Howdy called early the next morning and asked Angie to come down for the weekend. She protested but Howdy told her the Vances expected her and that he had to be at the field both Saturday and Sunday.

Angie arrived at El Rancho de los Nidos at mid-afternoon on Saturday. It was blustery and a cold dry Santa Ana wind streaming from the northeast drove Angie and Catherine Vance indoors.

Catherine served tea before the fireplace in the study. The masklike beauty of her face remained undisturbed as she spoke. For the first time, Angie began to sense the undercurrent of loneliness in the woman. But Catherine Coulter Vance let no one see what lay behind her impassiveness. Beyond saying that she had been born in New Canaan, Connecticut, and had met Steven on a ski holiday at Mount Mansfield in Vermont, she revealed little. Perhaps, Angie thought, there was a clue in her statement that Steven had really planned to make a career in finance in the East. From Howdy, Angie had learned that the accidental death of Steven's father, Thomas Vance, in 1922, three years after his own marriage to Catherine Coulter, had necessitated the return to California to share the management of the Los Nidos Ranch Company with his grandfather, Steven Lewis.

By nature Steven Vance was neither a rancher nor a gentleman farmer. Even so, after his grandfather's death in 1930 at age eighty-six, he could not bring himself to dispose of the huge holdings. The dilemma deepened for Steven and Catherine when the depression made it impossible for them to return East even for the prolonged visits that Catherine thought would make her California stay endurable. So they stayed on at Los Nidos, telling each other that perhaps in a year or so they could return East, until so much time had passed and Steven had become so deeply involved that a second major uprooting was impossible.

As they talked about trivial, impersonal things Angie began to understand the older woman's disappointment and some of her resistance melted. She made no effort to encourage Catherine to reciprocal confidences. To do that she would first have to admit and then define her own dilemma. For the time being all she could do was admit that for those who compromise, time can become a relentless trap.

Always unsure on the slippery surfaces of small talk, Angie was relieved when Jennifer came home from the Glenborough School for Girls in Los Angeles. She greeted Angie with a friendly wave and gave her mother a perfunctory kiss. "Where are Dad and Howdy? Still down at Vance Field?"

Catherine felt no need to answer the obvious. Instead she countered with a question of her own. "How did your examinations go, Jennifer?"

Jennifer made a distasteful grimace. "If I told you, Mother, you'd wash my mouth out with soap. The only subject I got A in was dressage."

Catherine raised her eyebrows. "I do not want to hear any of those earthy protests from you when your father orders you to start tutoring on weekends once more."

Jennifer curtsied and smiled with vicious sweetness. "Yes, Mummie dear. You shan't hear a single four-letter word out of me. But you may hear one heck of a yowl from the frustrated tutor." She turned and marched out.

Howdy and Steven returned from the field at six. Jennifer launched herself at her father and gave him an affectionate kiss. She hugged Howdy quickly and pushed him away at arm's length. "If you have any excuses, sir, I refuse to hear them. Tomorrow, sick or well, you take me up in one of the new Stearmans and wring it out. Right?"

Howdy extricated himself and tousled the girl's neatly combed pageboy bob. The way he did it, and the girl's playful protest, brought a stab of loneliness to Angie. Howdy didn't answer and Jennifer persisted. "Howdy Goodwyn, you promised." She backed off, eyes snapping. "I've forgiven you for hating horses—almost. But I'll never forgive you for breaking your word. You made a solemn promise to Stevie and me. And by God, sir—you'll keep it." Her mood changed abruptly and she stepped close to him, wheedling. "Won't you? Please?"

Howdy looked helplessly at the others. "I'll keep my promise if the mechanics keep theirs. If they don't, you'll get a nice straight and level ride in an Interstate. But, if you don't stop being sassy, you might get grounded for the duration."

He took her shoulders, turned her around, and whacked her backside. Howling with mock indignation, Jennifer whirled on him. "I'm pretty old to do that to. I'm beginning to shape up a bit, in case you hadn't noticed."

She assumed an exaggerated pose with one hip jutted out provocatively and her small, well-shaped bosom thrust forward beneath the loose cashmere sweater.

Catherine Vance gasped. "Jennifer!"

The girl held the pose defiantly then stalked contemptuously to the big oak coffee table where she scooped up a handful of small Spanish peanuts. Child-like, she crammed them into her mouth and brushed away the salt. Steven Vance laughed indulgently and moved toward the sideboard bar. *"Amigos! Beberemos! Vamos a beber!* What will you have?"

Young Steven arrived in the midst of cocktails. He was dressed in Levis and boots and an old corduroy field jacket. After booming greetings and placing a quick kiss on the cheek that softened Catherine's face for a fleeting moment, he poured himself a Coke and pointed to the residue of mud and straw on his heels. "Fine thing! Future Rickenbacker mucking around in manure."

Howdy chuckled. "I don't know if it's any kind of a recommendation, Stevie, but that's how I got my start."

Catherine Vance smiled bleakly as the others laughed outright.

Dinner was planned around a magnificent standing rib roast butchered from one of the ranch's prize steers. Steven Vance was apologetic. "I feel a little unpatriotic, knowing that most of us have to save about three weeks worth of stamps for this." He paused, smiling guiltily. "But I don't intend to let that spoil my enjoyment."

The dinner conversation was good. Steven Vance was proud of his California heritage and he understood it well. "We don't have any rickety salt-cellar houses with DAR plaques in front of them saying, 'George Washington Slept Here,' and we don't have a Grant's Tomb or a Lincoln

Memorial or a Jefferson Memorial. But we do have a Mount Whitney and a Mount Lassen and a Mount Dana and a Frémont Peak. I'd call them rather imposing monuments to some remarkable men, wouldn't you?"

Catherine Vance protested. "You know, dear, I think I rather resent the implication that your Western monuments are more imposing and therefore more important than ours. It is a sort of *nouveau snobisme,* really."

Steven laughed. "You can take the girl out of New England but you can't take New England out of the girl."

"That's not true. I consider myself as much a Californian as you. It is just that I refuse to become parochial about it. It's very important to remember and honor the traditions of our forebears no matter where they may have come from. After all, your own great grandfather, John Lewis, came from a very good family in Middletown, Connecticut. He was a direct descendent of Welsh royalty."

Steven Vance looked at his wife in astonishment. "He was a rabble-rousing merchant sailor who jumped ship, and if he hadn't got all hot and bothered about the sixteen-year-old Mexican girl who was my great grandmother, he probably would have ended up a jailbird like his friends, Isaac Graham and Will Chard."

For the first time since Angie and Howdy had known her, Catherine Vance displayed something close to animation. "Your great grandmother, Maria Robles, was not a *Mexican.* She was a *Californio*—and there's a vast difference, as you should know. Her people came to Monterey from Burgos in Castille—*by way of* Mexico City."

Her husband winked at Howdy. "I defer to you, darling. But I prefer my version. It makes them all seem more colorful."

Catherine Vance was not amused. "You are quite colorful enough for the lot of them."

Jennifer, who had been listening with a vixenish smile, giggled. "You two remind me of the girls at school." She mimicked them. " 'My family came over on the Mayflower.' 'Oh, really? So did mine.'—'Pipe down you two. My family *sold* it to them!' "

She looked from one parent to the other. "I think the only thing that's important is that they got here, and married fertile women."

Young Steven applauded his sister. "Bravo. If that's

what they're teaching you, Pop's getting his money's worth."

"The only thing I've learned in girl's school, brother dear, is how bitchy females can be."

For a moment Catherine Vance's mouth clamped into a bloodless line. When she spoke her repressed outrage was evident. "Jennifer. You are to be excused from the table . . . immediately."

In spite of herself a small sound of protest escaped from Angie. The girl returned her mother's chill stare then turned appealing eyes to her father. Steven Vance seemed to waver. Then he nodded almost imperceptibly and Jennifer understood that the edict had been sustained. Slowly, defiantly, she left the table and went to her room. Young Steven broke the strained silence.

"You're pretty rough on her, Mom. After all, she's no kid any more. And she's heard you use a word or two."

Catherine Vance glared at her son. "Never in front of strangers."

Howdy and Angie exchanged startled looks, then Howdy scratched his head and turned on his shy country boy smile. "Stranger? Well dawgone, Mrs. Vance," the drawl was exaggerated deliberately, "we're sure hoping to work up to being acquaintances, at least, right after the bookkeepers get done with the half-year profit statement."

Suspended somewhere between mortification and amusement, Steven Vance busied himself with his coffee. As quickly as it could be gracefully managed, he terminated the strained evening.

Sunday dawned bright and clear and Jennifer with it. She paced the family room like a caged cheetah until the others appeared for the buffet breakfast, then hovered over Howdy so persistently that he felt obliged to chide her. "Miss, one of the first things you learn about flying is not to take off until you get into the airplane."

Jennifer was ready with her own ingenious logic. "It's not that I'm impatient, Howdy. It's just that the weather report says 'variable cloudiness' and this time of year a clear morning can turn into a typhoon or something by ten o'clock!"

All but Catherine Vance arrived at the field shortly after nine. For twenty minutes Howdy wrung out the trainer, putting it through every aerobatic maneuver he and the ship were capable of. Before each one he called

488

through the gosport to the girl in the front cockpit to alert her. On the ground Angie, Steven Jr., and his father watched as the craft sequenced from power-on and power-off stalls through spins, a single loop, three linked-up loops, chandelles, snap rolls, and finished with a half loop with a roll out at the top.

The altimeter read six thousand feet when Howdy finally called through the gosport. "Had enough?"

Jennifer twisted in the harness to look back at him. Her face glowed and Howdy could see her eyes literally dancing behind the big goggles. She shook her head and her lips formed an emphatic No.

Howdy laughed. "How would you like to fly it?"

He headed the ship out across the crazy quilt of cultivated fields in the direction of the Newport-Balboa area. Jennifer followed his instructions to the letter. She made predictable control errors causing the ship to dip and meander but Howdy was forced to concede that in an unusually short time Jennifer Vance would probably be as much at home in the cockpit as in the saddle.

On the ground, Howdy smiled at Jennifer and gave her neck a playful squeeze. Watching, Angie was annoyed again by the little twinges of jealousy she always felt when Jennifer monopolized Howdy. She would not have admitted it but increasingly his frequent affectionate little gestures toward Jennifer had produced painful stabs. She could count on the fingers of one hand the times she herself had been the object of such gentle demonstrations.

On D-Day plus two Ev Moses called a general meeting of the executives, announcing that the recent good war news made it necessary for the company to have a reappraisal. They would have to prepare to phase out some operations or fit them into a peace-time economy.

None of the operations was in immediate jeopardy except the flight school. Chad Chadwick put it bluntly: "Vance Field will be a dead duck as soon as the war is over. We can look into civilian light plane sales and into surplus and salvage. But whatever happens, I don't think we should exercise our option to buy the Vance Field land."

On the way out of the meeting Ev Moses stopped Howdy. "Has Angie told you about Neville?"

"Nope. What's the trouble?"

"They found a malignancy in his prostate. He's got to have an operation."

After a brief silence Howdy nodded. "It figured. The old guy's been drawin' his cards from a stacked deck all his life. It's that way with some people."

The attorney's eyes narrowed inquisitively.

Howdy tapped his chest. "The old man had something I needed so I used it. Now it looks like we've got something he needs so let's make sure he's got enough money to pay for things from here on out."

"From here on out?"

"That's what I said. If those sawbones are right, they just gave the old boy his last piece of bad news. I want to make it easy for him, if there is such a thing."

When the attorney appeared reluctant, Howdy brushed past him to enter the room. "You work it out, Ev, with my dough."

Chadwick's recommendation to drop the option on the land made Steven Vance uneasy. He had hoped that Howdy would exercise the option for a sizeable chunk of cash and relieve some of the financial pressure that had been mounting ever since the depression.

Nineteen forty had seen a little easing. Crop control and allotments had helped meet interest payments and taxes. But the war-time freeze had caused both the Vance operations and those of their tenant farmers to slow to a virtual standstill. Some tenants' taxes were in arrears, taxes that the main ranch was obligated to pay to avoid a lien. Steven Vance could see little to be hopeful about even after the lifting of war-time freezes.

He had given vent to his private worries to Catherine shortly before D-Day, "The damned trouble with our kind of ranching is very simple: when you have no crops to sell, you borrow on land to pay taxes. Then you sell other land to pay off the loans. In California the process is historic and self-defeating."

On July Fourth Howdy and Angie did their first show together since the war had begun. The appeal had come from Major Sam Garrett, thirty-two-year-old holder of the Victoria Cross, the Distinguished Flying Cross, and two Air Medals received for his exploits in the European Theater. The major had been fished from the Channel with a shattered left arm and sent back to the States for

490

more corrective surgery. Finally, with a minimal disability, he was assigned to the Santa Ana Air Base as regional public relations officer—"A hell of a letdown, you'd better believe," he said, openly admiring Angie, "not without its compensations!"

Dave Layne, filled with his old efficiency and enthusiasm, assembled many of the original radio gang and pulled together a ninety-minute show that was received with the deafening cheers of five thousand overworked, yearning-for-home recruits.

Acting on an impulse, Howdy asked how many of the airmen had come from out of state. More than three fourths of the crowd raised hands. When he asked how many would like to return to live in California after the war, the show of hands was virtually unanimous. Howdy filed the information in the back of his mind, unaware at the time of its eventual importance.

The huge success of the Santa Ana show, presented under the auspices of the USO, brought requests for performances at other installations. Major Garrett turned on his own brand of persuasiveness and Howdy finally agreed to do two more shows, one at March Field near Riverside and another near Sacramento.

Each time the response was overwhelming. But when Sam Garrett suggested a half dozen more appearances for the *Howdy Goodwyn Show,* Howdy balked.

"I got a flying school to run, and a flare outfit and an electronic outfit. I'll do some more if I can but you better not count on it for a while."

Garrett had anticipated the refusal. "What about letting Dave revamp the show around Angie? The boys will settle for a beautiful girl any time!"

Angie gasped and broke into surprised laughter. "Beautiful girl? Me? At thirty-three?"

On August first the *Howdy Goodwyn Caravan*, with Angie and Steve Stone as the stars, left in a chartered bus for a tour of a half dozen bases extending as far north as Chico. Major Garrett, traveling with the troupe, coordinated the transportation and living details with the public relations officers of the individual bases.

Shortly after Labor Day, Angie received a request to fly to Smoky Hill Army Air Field near Salina, Kansas, to entertain the men of the Second Air Force. After a futile attempt to induce Howdy to appear, she resigned herself to the four-day tour that would also include the bases at Great Bend and Walker.

Angie and Sam Garrett took off early one morning in a war-weary B-17 Flying Fortress. They were squeezed down through the hatch behind the pilots' seats into the bombardier's "greenhouse." Hunched against the chill, they sat on their chutes and tried to play cards. When Angie's hands grew too cold to manage the cards they sat close together in their makeshift flying clothes and talked. The Major revealed a great deal about himself. There was an engaging wistfulness about him as he told Angie about a girl who had thrown him over just before he went overseas, first with the RAF then with our air force.

Angie studied him as he talked and was struck by a curious similarity to Howdy. Not feature by feature but they both possessed a certain reserved boyishness and while Howdy tended to be self-conscious around women, Sam was not. Sam was still young and had kept his dark good looks, the kind Angie was sure some women would call "sexy." In subtle ways, he appeared older than his years, the price for having endured some of the most vicious aerial combat in history.

When he finished the story of his abortive romance, Sam rumpled his hair and regarded Angie with an uncertain smile. "You're one of those warm, lovely females with big sympathetic green eyes and an understanding heart who doesn't have sense enough not to ask a man not to talk about himself. Now, what about you?"

Deliberately Angie tried to look mysterious. She was aware that she was responding to flattery. Casting her eyes down, she said, "Honestly, there's not much to tell. I grew up in a small town and married an entertainer. I'm, well, not very fascinating."

Sam gazed at her intently. "No woman can have as much wisdom and as much sadness in her eyes as you have without having felt things deeply and without having understood them. I know that, even though I'm an ageing boy who's done a lot of superficial feeling and not much thinking."

"That's a bid for sympathy if I ever heard one. I suppose you're going to tell me you haven't thought about the war you've been fighting either?"

Sam's expression was bleak. "Of course I have, Angie.

492

That's what scares me. I think this war may have taken the hope out of me just like it has for a lot of men in my old squadron. I can't explain it—but maybe what's happened is that a lot of us who have been living from day to day for so long are not going to be able to break that pattern. Maybe by now we're like the professional soldiers who say they hate war but die of boredom if they aren't fighting one. I don't know, Angie," he shrugged, "sometimes everything seems pointless."

"I think I understand. Women can feel that way too."

Abruptly, Sam changed the subject. "Ears pop yet? We're beginning to descend."

On the strip at Smoky Hill, the B-17 taxied to the administration building. It took an hour to get the men and women assigned to quarters. Angie was to be the guest of Colonel and Mrs. Price at their home just off the base. The others were quartered in the BOQ and in the WAC's barracks.

The show that night was held on an improvised stage set up in a huge hangar doorway facing a semicircle of portable bleachers. Although scheduled to run for just under two hours, the entertainment-hungry troops kept the performers on stage until they were literally out of material. It was close to midnight when Angie said good-by to Sam and the others and got in the car with Colonel and Mrs. Price.

When she finally climbed into bed in the little guest room she felt happy and pleasantly exhausted. For a time she stared up at the ceiling thinking about Howdy. Then, unaccountably, her thoughts drifted to Sam Garrett. As she thought back to their conversation in the plane she smiled sympathetically. "Poor baby," she said to herself. The thought made her laugh softly. "Poor *baby*? At thirty-two?"

After her third appearance with the troupe at the air base Angie called Howdy. When she could not reach him at home or at the Vance's ranch she called Dave Layne.

"He's up in Sacramento, Angie. He and Steve flew up to see Mr. Berwin this morning. He won't be back until Sunday afternoon. Can I pick you up somewhere?"

Angie hesitated. "No. No thanks, Dave, we're coming into Lockheed. Major Garrett's arranging for an Air Force car. He'll drop me off, then drive back down to Santa

Ana. We'll be in around noon tomorrow. You can take me to dinner tomorrow night if you haven't anything better to do."

From the corner of her eye Angie saw Sam's frantic signaling. "Hold it a moment, Dave."

Placing her hand over the mouthpiece she turned, questioning. Sam jabbed at his chest with a forefinger. "*I'm* taking you to dinner. That's an order."

Angie turned back to the instrument. "Dave, I'm sorry, but I forgot. I promised the Army Air Force they could do the honors, do you mind?"

After a brief silence Dave's voice grated in the earpiece. "Of course I mind. But that's not going to do much good, is it?"

Early the next morning, short of sleep and somewhat worse for the revelry at the farewell party given for them the night before, the troupe climbed aboard the Flying Fortress for the return flight to California.

Again occupying their exclusive place in the bombardier's greenhouse, Angie settled down for the six-hour flight. Sam tried to keep up a conversation but soon was dozing with his head on her shoulder.

Colonel Price, checking on his passengers as an excuse to stretch his legs, peered down through the greenhouse hatch at the couple. A minute later he was back in his seat at the controls wearing a cryptic smile. Lieutenant Colonel Sharpless glanced at him quizzically. "Why the Mona Lisa puss?"

The colonel grinned broadly and indicated the greenhouse with a nod. "Young 'Major Makeout' is pulling the sleepy boy bit again."

The two pilots exchanged knowing looks. Colonel Sharpless made a move toward his pocket. "I'll bet you twenty he doesn't make it this time."

The commanding officer shook his head. "Not with me you won't. I'm betting the same way."

The B-17 touched down in L.A. at 2:47 P.M. Both Angie and Sam were ravenous. When they got to the lunch counter in the terminal building, G.I.'s with duffle bags were three deep. Garrett was annoyed. "We'll have to try the one-arm joint across the street."

Angie glanced at the clock. It read twenty after three. "I've got a better idea. Let's go home and have Helga fix

494

us some sandwiches. It won't take any longer to drive out there than it will to find another place."

Twenty-five minutes later the staff car pulled into the long, secluded driveway. Sam began unloading baggage as Angie rang the bell. After several rings that produced no response she fumbled in her purse for the key. She called through the open door but the house was empty. Then she remembered. "Oh, for heaven's sake. I forgot. I gave Helga the day off."

In the hallway she pointed to the wall. "Leave the bags there, Sam. Helga will unpack for me later. Come on. Let's see what we can find in the kitchen."

From the well-stocked pantry Angie threw together a salad of avocado from their own trees while Sam, perched on a breakfast stool, watched her and made no attempt to conceal his admiration.

Moments later she placed the salads on the counter. "Let's eat out by the pool." She indicated a patio table and umbrella visible through the large sliding window-wall. "Think you can get them out without a disaster?"

"Just open the door for me, ma'am."

Angie followed, bearing a tray with place settings, rye crisps, and tall glasses of ice tea. It was hot in the patio. Occasionally the lightest breath of a breeze ruffled the peridot-green surface of the pool and rattled the tattered leaves of the travelers' palms. Sam slipped his cotton tie through its knot, opened the top two buttons of his khaki shirt, and heaved a huge sigh of relief. "Hope you don't mind?"

"Of course not. Why don't you roll up your sleeves too? In fact, you can take off your shirt if you want. We don't stand on ceremony around here."

Sam looked longingly at the pool. "Then I wouldn't be out of order if I invited myself for a swim after lunch? We've got to do something to work off this food, you know. We have a dinner date tonight. Remember?"

Her woeful expression alarmed him. "Don't tell me you forgot."

"No, I didn't forget—really. I just forgot how late it was."

"Lady, we have four hours of daylight left. An hour in the pool and I'll be ravenous again."

Angie was dubious. "An hour in the pool and I'll be three hours fixing my hair."

"In that case you'd better just go wading. I can't face three hours alone."

Angie clucked sympathetically and shook her head.

A white brick, tile-roofed dressing cabana and shower stood at the deep end of the pool. She pointed to it. "There are some shorts and towels on the right hand side. Help yourself and I'll join you after I clear off these things."

Ten minutes later she found him seated on the edge of the pool, smoking. His left shoulder was covered with a gaudy towel. He smiled at her apologetically. "You know, every once in a while I forget." He tapped the covered upper arm. "The surgeons patched this wing all right, but it's not the prettiest thing to look at." He saw the fleeting look of sympathy as she knelt beside him and removed the towel. The incision, less than a year old, still bore traces of proudness.

Angie slipped her hand beneath his arm and moved it toward her. As her free hand traced the course of the surgery she became aware of the ridges of scar tissue on the soft underside of the biceps. Lifting his arm, she peered at the second scar.

"That's where the slug came out. It ripped across the front of my flying suit, smashed the right corner of the instrument panel, and went clear through the fuselage on the other side."

She released his arm and shuddered. "My God! It missed your chest by inches."

"By millimeters. That's why I figure that no matter what happens to me from here on out, I've got it made."

She stood up and looked at him sternly. "Well, don't be silly about that scar, Sam. It has a very neat, business-like look to it—nothing to be self-conscious about. Now go and swim. I'll be with you in a few minutes."

"I'll wait for you. When you come out I'll demonstrate my world's championship one-arm Australian crawl."

"That's a blatant bid for sympathy. I watched you carry my bags in. Remember?"

"Okay, lady, but don't shoot me down for trying. I like a little sympathy."

When Angie reappeared and slipped off the thick white terry robe, Sam surfaced at the pool's edge. His wavy dark hair was plastered in water-set bangs and the thick matting that spread across his muscular chest veed into a gleaming curtain of dripping curls that divided his hard brown belly and disappeared beneath the drawstrings of Howdy's snug-fitting trunks.

Grinning, he subjected her to a deliberately impertinent appraisal. With the assurance of a woman who knows that an attractive male finds her desirable, Angie took more time than necessary to tuck her red gold hair underneath her bathing cap. But she kept her gaze cool and aloof.

After a long moment Sam let out two sibilant whistles. "Are you ever beautiful! I've always known you had a face for breaking hearts, but this," his hand swept the length of her, "this is more than mortal man can bear."

Angie tucked the last stray strand beneath the cap and regarded him archly. "You are an accomplished liar, Major."

"And you are Miss America. That girl Jean Bartel is an impostor."

"You *are* shameless." With that Angie entered the water with a flawless shallow dive. Turning seal-like beneath the surface, she emerged beside him.

"All right, Major, I'm ready to watch a demonstration of your world famous one-arm crawl."

"I'd rather watch you."

Angie splashed at him with the heel of her hand and an instant later found herself being pulled under by the ankles. They surfaced together spluttering and laughing and to Angie's amazement Sam pushed off and headed toward the deep end propelled by a powerful kick and a curious sort of circular one-armed sculling stroke that carried him along faster than she could swim using both arms. When he reached the end of the pool he executed an expert racing turn and swam back. Clutching the spill gutter, he drew in several deep breaths. "This is wonderful, Angie. But I'm out of shape. I used to be able to do fifty laps without puffing. Next to beautiful women swimming pools are the world's greatest inventions. I envy you and Howdy . . . a lot of things."

Angie let herself drift away a few feet and treaded water. "I'm afraid the pool is my pet plaything. Howdy doesn't have much use for it."

Angie swam several laps with Sam pacing her. On the last lap she veered to the ladder and climbed out. "Go on.

Swim as long as you like. I'm going inside and rest a bit. If you want to shave you'll find everything you need in the cabana. If you want to snooze in the sun, use the mats."

"If you're going to desert me I may do that. By the way, do you like Chinese food?"

"Love it."

"Okay. I know a place on Vineland near San Fernando Road."

"But that's way out past the terminal . . ."

"I don't care if it's east of the sun and west of the moon, I want to share it with you. I know the family. I'll phone and tell them we're coming. They'll really shoot the works."

It was dark by the time the staff car pulled up in front of Fat Lee's restaurant. When Sam introduced Angie, both the husband and the wife recognized her immediately. The obsequious flurry embarrassed her.

During the course of the dinner that was delicious but endless, she signed autographs on menus and odd slips of paper brought from the kitchen by the apologetic proprietor.

It was after ten when they left for Angie's home. The night was unusually still and warm and a hot, dry Santa Ana wind was promised by the forecasters. The valley-ites could feel it. Always, before it began to blow, something happened. The air seemed to have an ominous, positive electrical charge that made them restless. Some Californians called it "earthquake weather" but it was really fire weather. If the dry wind prevailed for more than a day or two the dehydrated foothills and mountains would be certain to suffer a series of disastrous blazes.

When the car pulled into the driveway, Angie rolled her head toward Sam with a satisfied smile. "It's been a wonderful day. Thank you for taking pity on a deserted wife.

"They've given medals to people for doing less than you've done for my morale these past few days."

He reached over to take her hand and she made no effort to pull it away. "You're something special, Angie Goodwyn." He looked at her intently for a moment. "I'm going to see you to the door now. I don't want to forget that all officers are supposed to be gentlemen."

He got out and ran around to help her. At the front

door Angie inserted the key in the lock and paused. "Sam, what time do you have to report back to Santa Ana?"

"Not until morning. Why?"

"Would you like another swim and a nightcap?"

Gently Sam took her by the shoulders and they walked through to the patio without turning on the lights. The night was so clear that the stars seemed three-dimensional. A host of cicadas pursued their raspish courtships and the frogs continued croaking with mechanical monotony. They listened in silence for a while, then Angie shivered. "I love it."

She started back toward the house. "Go change if you want. I'll get our nightcaps."

She returned with the drinks shortly and sat down beside him on the grass by the pool. She had changed into a two-piece swim suit. Conversation that had come so easily before now seemed forced.

Tacitly, Angie recognized their self-consciousness and said, "I'm sorry. It's my fault. I have a guilty conscience because I've been having so much fun."

"You? Guilty about having fun?"

"Oh, it's not fair to say it but even with all the things Howdy and I have, we don't seem to have—just fun. We enjoy a lot together but we don't . . ."

He clasped her face gently between his palms. "Angie, I've known a lot of women but you've got something they didn't have. I don't know what it is but it makes me feel like the high school boy who finally has a date with the girl he's been admiring all year and then when he's alone with her he gets all fouled up and tongue-tied."

Sam's eyes were serious. "If I said the things I want to say, Angie . . . Well, I can't. Not to you. Anyway, I'm suspect as a single officer. That means I'm automatically on the make."

Angie lowered her head. "And I'm a married woman who's alone tonight and I asked you in. What does that make me—automatically?"

The silence between them felt far longer than it was. Sam broke it. "Lonesome? Like I am . . . ?"

Angie looked down at the hands covering hers. After a moment she nodded almost imperceptibly. An instant later she was kissing him willingly. When she finally drew away he forced her head beneath his chin and pressed her cheek against the coarse cushion of hair that covered his chest.

The strange feel of it shocked Angie at first; but as he gently forced her head closer the sensation grew pleasant. She felt secure. Her left hand withdrew from beneath his right arm until the fingers found wiry hair. Like sensuous shuttles, they began to weave random patterns and her mouth, gone moist and slack, pressed against him.

Certain that she had been wanted ever since their first moments alone after the show in Kansas, Angie cast off the last of her reserve and allowed compulsion to drive back anxiety and guilt. Beneath the clinging shorts she could feel him growing and the realization started a burning between her legs. The sensation, pervasive and pleasant, was not unlike the slow beginning of the auto-erotic release to which she sometimes resorted after Howdy, consumed by his own spasmic pleasure-pain, had ground himself empty and withdrawn, convinced that his own coming was reward enough for both.

When it happened now, whatever it was, Angie knew that it would be more than she had known before. Her hand slipped between them, seeking the drawstring, and he twisted away to help. While she inched the cold, clammy cloth down over his hard buttocks, he unhooked her bra top and pulled it free. When the soft coils of his chest hair touched her erect nipples an involuntary little sound welled up. Angie's right arm tightened around his neck to pull her upper body closer still. Half recumbent, she began to undo the buttons at the side of her shorts. Quickly, Sam shucked off his own and kicked them free. He pushed Angie's hand aside gently and took over the task.

She lifted her bottom to free the shorts, slipped them down, and let him pull them over her ankles. Naked and free, their bodies came together in eager collision. For a time they clung to each other. Then Sam lowered them until they reclined on their sides on the mat, still embracing. Angie opened her eyes and lifted her lips to find his but he avoided them and his own lips brushed her cheekbone and her ear and moved down to the base of her neck. He felt her shoulders hunch against his mouth and his right hand caressed the smooth blade of her left shoulder. When his palm, surprisingly soft and gentle, reached the swell of her hip, Angie's left hand began to move down the muscled rib cage, out beyond the splay of dark hair that began at the base of his strong neck. She shifted to free him and cupped his testicles. Suddenly

Sam's head was up and his mouth was hard on hers. When his fingers found her and pressed slowly inward Angie began to move against them as she did during those tortured times alone when she was forced to fantasize a faceless lover. Sam's tenderness and finesse were bringing her close. She arched her back away urgently. "Sam, darling! Slower! Slower! Slower! please . . ."

Ignoring her plea, his lips moved down to her breast. Angie flung her head back and struggled to control the pulsing waves of electric sensation that seemed about to engulf her. Sam continued until she cried out again. Then he stopped suddenly and caught her face between his palms. "Angie . . ."

"What, darling?"

"Don't hold back, sweetheart. Let yourself feel. Feel clear into your guts. Don't be afraid. You've built up an awful debit. I'm going to pay it off in full now for that insensate idiot who doesn't know what a feeling, giving, out-of-this-world wonder you are."

Before Angie realized what he intended, Sam had swung his body around so that his lower belly was pressed against her face. She felt the stubble of his beard moving down along the soft swell of her middle and the abrasiveness excited her in still another way. She began to shiver. An instant later came the shock of realization. Her entire body went rigid. Her hips heaved in a violent spasm and she felt his arms locking hard around her to hold himself in place. She cried out and her head rolled frantically against his thighs. She felt him moistening against her cheek and still caught in the terminal tension of her own first uninhibited orgasm, Angie groped frantically, found him, and forced him to her mouth. She worked at him hungrily until he reached down to push her head away. Controlling himself, he persisted until the last of Angie's convulsions had subsided. He released her then, straightened, and took her in arms again. "That one was for you, darling Angie, so you can learn to feel all there is."

She buried her face against his chest. "Oh God, Sam, I didn't know there could be such a feeling. I didn't know . . ." Her voice trailed off and tears began to trickle down her face. Lovingly, he cradled her, caressing her cheek and kissing her hair, whispering reassuringly.

From the very first Sam had promised himself that sooner or later he would sleep with this woman. But there had been no intention to make it more than that, no intimation that it would not be just another lay. Angie was different.

In the warm, luminous Southern California night, Major Sam Garrett, decorated pilot, dedicated cocksman, held Angela Goodwyn in a way he had not held a woman since his first love. For a reason he did not fully understand, he wanted to make up to her for those numberless nights of frustration that he had been able to read out so clearly in all that she had said and had left unsaid. Without obstacles, with no sense of urgency, he would, in the next hours, bring them both to orgasm several times until no unfelt ecstasy remained. Then his own silent voice began to mock him. He heard it saying, "Bullshit, you greedy humpmaster!" He tried to squelch it and reaffirm as truth the strange conviction that after this neither of them would ever be quite so alone again.

Her fingers closed around him gently. "Oh, Sam, I'm in the world's most exquisite agony and I don't want it to end for hours. I want to do it all, everything. With you. I've never wanted to before, like this. You've let me out of my own jail. I used to dream of something vaguely like this and then I'd masturbate and feel sick with guilt and pray for forgiveness. But it's different now. I want to do it for you, Sam. Howdy uses me. He doesn't mean to but he just does. He doesn't know how a woman feels, that she's got to give back. It's not his fault. He is what he is and part of him is wonderful—his ambition, his determination, his courage, his loyalty to his friends. But he could never love me like you do because he could never stop thinking about himself long enough."

He searched her face for a moment, then braced himself, half reclining, and Angie moved down over him. He endured the torment of her body straining onto his until he was close to the limit of endurance, then, reaching down, he caught her face and forced her away until he could turn, inverted, to her again. Moments later the darkened patio was filled with the suppressed sound of his wordless outcrying.

Naked, they lay in a rigid embrace until a breath of breeze made Angie shiver. They sat up then, saying nothing, and slipped into the water. There, they played together like two satisfied, unashamed animals. When they were through swimming, Sam supported her with an elbow hooked onto the rung of the ladder, kissed her, and moved to bring her to him again. Angie let herself come to him willingly. As her arms went around his neck a light blazed in the upstairs room at the far corner of the patio.

Howdy crossed the Santa Monica Mountains at ten thousand feet and called the Burbank tower. Seven minutes later he touched down the Lodestar and let it run out to clear the following traffic.

It was three-thirty P.M. when he called Angie from the public phone outside the hangar. Helga answered. "She's not here now, Mr. Goodwyn. She called Mr. Layne early this morning and they went to lunch someplace to talk about the new camp shows, she said."

Howdy glanced at his watch. "When did she get back from Kansas?"

"Late Friday, I guess. She and Major Garrett were swimming when I got home just before midnight."

A brief silence followed. There was an edge of annoyance in Howdy's next question. "Did she say when she'll be back this afternoon?"

Helga nodded vigorously at the phone. "Yes, sir. She said she would be home by the time you got here, Mr. Goodwyn. She wants to cook out on the patio tonight."

"Okay, Helga, I'll be home in about an hour."

"Yes, sir. I tell her, Mr. Goodwyn."

"You do that."

Howdy checked the logs in the operations office, made his own entries in his personal log, and called a taxi. Dave and Angie had driven up to the front door moments before. The intensity of Angie's greeting puzzled and embarrassed him. He disengaged himself and put her away almost roughly. "You going to give me time to get showered and cleaned up before supper?"

Angie pouted indulgently. "Honey, I'll give you all the time you need. I've been trying to urge Dave to stay and have a steak with us."

Howdy turned a questioning look at his partner.

Dave smiled apologetically. "I'd love to but I can't. See you tomorrow, Angie."

A short while later Angie was sitting on the edge of the bed watching Howdy change. "I missed you, honey. I don't like doing out-of-state shows without you."

Howdy worked off the second Wellington flying boot.

"You don't have to do it any more. Trouble is, you let Garrett con you."

The accusation was innocent enough but it made her start inwardly. She laughed. "Is it con when he says those kids in camp need entertaining?"

Howdy turned to face her. "What time did you get back Friday?"

Angie frowned. "Late. Why?"

"Nothin'. I just happened to check the traffic log in operations and it showed Army 402 down at two forty-seven."

A quick stab of panic unsettled Angie. She knew she sounded defensive. "When I said 'late' I meant a lot later than we planned. You know we had a bad engine going over. Colonel Price wanted to be sure everything checked out."

Howdy gave her a long, penetrating look and resumed undressing.

Angie stood up. "You're acting funny. What's the matter?"

"What?"

"I said, 'What's the matter?' You're acting like I'm keeping something from you. I promised Sam he could take me to dinner because you weren't home. We didn't have any lunch so I fixed something here about three-thirty and he borrowed your trunks and had a swim while I took a rest. Then we went to a Chinese place on San Fernando Road. I signed a dozen autographs, we got home late, Sam jabbered about himself for a while, then we had a swim and he drove back to Santa Ana. What on earth is wrong with that?"

His amiable grin made her uncomfortable. "Nothing's wrong with *that*—but as of now no more shows. You've done your share of boosting GI morale. You tell your major that for me. Right?"

Guilt fueled a sudden indignant flare-up. "If that's how you want it, you tell him. And while you're at it, you might give him a good reason." She stalked to the door and turned back. "And you might give *me* one too!"

Howdy's grin faded until only a suggestion of a smile lingered. "What the hell do you mean by that crack?"

"Just what it sounds like. I've been out there in the sticks grinning like an idiot, pounding my fingers to stumps, shouting myself hoarse for the good old USA

504

while you've been doing," she tossed her hands, "God knows what! Then all of a sudden you cut me a new set of orders. I want to know why? Is that too damned much to ask—after ten years of saying, 'Yes, sir'?"

They studied each other coldly, then Howdy exploded in forced laughter. "God love you, honey, I expect I've been leaving you too much alone." He started toward her to take her in his arms and for the first time in the decade they had been together, Angie experienced a spasm of revulsion. "Howdy, I told Helga to start a fire—"

"Honey baby, you just tell her to hold off with her fire until we get this one put out." Slipping the silk tie free of the miniature gold guitar she had given him on their first anniversary, he reached out for her.

Angie backed away. "Howdy."

"Yes?"

"Couldn't we wait until after supper? I, well . . ." She continued to retreat and gestured helplessly. "It might be better. I mean without Helga sitting down there waiting."

Howdy unbuttoned the neckband of his expensive Western shirt and pulled her close. She was stiff and unyielding but he seemed not to notice. "Baby, what she's got'll keep. What I brought home ought to be used while its fresh."

Almost frantically, Angie pushed away from the embrace and resisted an impulse to cry out. Controlling herself, she managed a contrite smile. "Howdy, I'm afraid it's going to have to keep. I'm really in no condition."

Puzzled, his hands stopped manipulating the ornate silver buckle. "What the hell's eating on you?"

Angie grimaced. "Nothing's *eating* on me, as you call it. But please don't make me go into details. Later, Howdy, later."

Before he could protest, she fled from the room.

As the war drew to a close the housing shortage on both the east and west coasts became acute. In California huge industries such as Kaiser and Lockheed had increased over a thousand percent in the past five years. The government was anxious to persuade private industry to construct emergency housing. The President's special assistant on emergency housing had approached H.G. Enterprises. Howdy, along with Ev Moses, Danny Meyer, and Louis Siefert, agreed that as tempting as "cheap" government loan money was, the risk was great. When the war was over, what would happen to the hordes of people out of jobs? Would they wander back East and if so, how many of them would go. Certainly, historically, Southern California could expect a large number to stay but how many workers would be willing to return to their old pursuits, in agriculture for instance, for far less money? And of those who stayed, how many could survive the readjustment period without defaulting on their new home mortgages?

During lunch at the Vine Street Derby, Ev Moses summed up his position: "There's no question about the need or the fact that it's nice to have cheap government money. But if we get into this on a long-term basis and the war ends in a year or so, we'd be caught with an unsettled market and thousands out of work."

Howdy turned to Danny Meyer and Louis Siefert. "What about you guys?"

Meyer responded without hesitation. "I see a great new market for electronic gadgets in this housing, but about the housing itself we better be sure the market is there and what kind. If we're going to build more civilian barracks like most of this emergency housing, then I say, no dice."

Abruptly, Howdy turned to Angie. "What about you, honey? Got any of that female intuition you always talk about?"

Angie was not amused. "I defer to all of this executive judgment. I don't have any feminine *intuition*. I do have a female *opinion*. I've been in a lot of that emergency housing. It's all around the bases we play. The women hate it. If that's what you have to build, then I wouldn't bet that many wives can be sold on buying."

Howdy listened with half-closed eyes, then sat up straight and pushed his steak sandwich aside. "Okay, I'll tell you what we're going to do. We pass this government deal and find out where folks really want to live if they get to stay. And we find out what kind of houses they want. Then if it adds up, we'll buy some land and try a few with our own dough."

He looked at each in turn. "We're going to get Steve Vance to work. He's a native. He knows what outsiders want in California. He told me once that, except for oil, the land is getting to be worth more than anything you can raise on it. I want to know which land and why."

On October twenty-second the first contact was made in the battle for Leyte Gulf. In the three engagements that took place during the next six days and nights the effective power of the Japanese navy was destroyed. Experts felt optimistic about a victory in the Pacific and Howdy was glad that he had not succumbed to the temptations to get into Federally financed emergency housing.

At a Sunday barbecue in the patio of the Vances' Casa Grande, Howdy was fired with enthusiasm. The first surveys on probable migration patterns after the war had come in. They confirmed Howdy's hunch that G.I. home financing would, in time, create a huge market for better housing. Angie was annoyed by Catherine Vance's supercilious amusement as she watched Steven being caught up in Howdy's plans for the future development of H.G. Enterprises' land purchased from the Los Nidos Ranch Company

"Hot damn, Steve! If these projections are only half right we're going to build a whole new town right where we're training those kids to fly now. By golly, we might even call it Vanceville." Aiming a finger at a large artist's rendering propped on a chair, he continued to articulate his dream. "We'll give them two-bedroom, two-bath houses with a double garage on a quarter acre of flat ground. The whole place'll be fenced and seeded for lawn and we'll throw in an orange tree, a lemon tree, maybe even a peach or apricot tree and a bunch of rosebushes and things. And no two houses will be alike—on the outside, at least. There are all kinds of jimcracky tricks that can make a basic house look different."

Howdy walked to the end of the patio. "As soon as priorities are lifted on building materials we'll go into production with the first hundred houses. Ev will set up the subsidiary and I want you to head it, Steve, with Lloyd Wilson. He's the best city planner and architect around."

For an hour Angie watched and listened as Howdy carried Steven Vance along by sheer force of enthusiasm. Nobody she had ever known could conjure such an arresting vision with so few basic words. Even Catherine's thinly disguised skepticism seemed to have dissipated somewhat.

Seated on a cushion with legs crossed and chin propped

on clenched fists, Jennifer listened too. From time to time her violet eyes would widen with wonderment. The jet-haired girl's devoted concentration fascinated and troubled Angie. Try as she would, Angie could neither ignore nor dismiss Jennifer's girlish infatuation for Howdy. In another age in California, Angie could see the darkly beautiful Spanish-speaking girl eagerly awaiting the arrival of the New England traders from the far-off United States. Dimly she recalled her mother's occasional references to such girl-women in her own family. And they had been women—setting out to catch their men—often as early as fifteen—Jennifer's age—bearing their first child at sixteen. Perhaps they had not all been as beautiful as Jennifer Vance, Angie thought, but their blood, undiminished in passion and intensity, clearly coursed through this girl's veins.

Late that night, in the guest suite, Angie sat propped up in the oversized Spanish bed watching Howdy sprawled face down in deep slumber. With each new move away from show business, where she could participate, her anxiety had mounted. It was not for material reasons. She was, in her own right, a wealthy woman. It was not the disparity in their ages. She was three years older than Howdy but she had kept her figure and her good looks.

For a long time she studied the man who had always been more stranger than husband. She tried again to will more meaning into the present and the future by recalling the times in the past that had really been theirs together, refusing to acknowledge them as times of mutual need. She was deathly afraid of the terrible emptiness she had watched her mother become a victim of when her father left—the kind of emptiness that even a Sam Garrett could fill only momentarily. Cautiously she bent over Howdy until her lips brushed the unruly hair on his temple. "Slow down, honey—please," she breathed. "You're going too fast. I can't keep up—"

Alone in the family room well past midnight, Steven Vance studied the artist's rendering of the first unit of Howdy's proposed subdivision. After a minute or so he moved to a nearby window.

Midway across the dark expanse of fields were three scattered patches of light. Well within the heartland of the ranch, they marked the parcels that had been sold by his grandfather, Steven Lewis, during hard times in the Eighteen sixties. They were the only areas within the original boundaries that still lay beyond ranch control and they had changed the nature of the ranch, for with the growth of population they had become the first urban incursions.

Steven Vance could visualize the shape of the future and the change he would preside over would be the most far-reaching of all. The proposed airport and commercial complex were irresistible magnets for urbanization. There was no doubt the plan would be successful—everything Howdy Goodwyn touched was. It would grow and consume hundreds of prime agricultural acres. In this vision of the future Steven Vance could see clearly the pattern of California's past.

Steven's great-grandfather, John Lewis, had had the same kind of pioneering instinct and shrewdness of vision that marked Howdy Goodwyn. Both had started with nothing, both were immigrants to California, and both would bend the land to the making of their personal empires.

Book IV

The Howard D. Goodwyn Story

(Continued)

17 AT THIRTY-EIGHT, after seventeen years of marriage to the man she had vowed to get from the time she was sixteen, Jennifer Vance Goodwyn was, by any measure, still an unusually attractive woman. Gleaming black hair framed large violet eyes. Her figure was usually described as sensational. Her weight hadn't varied by more than a pound or so in the fifteen years since she had added several pounds following the birth of their son, Howard Junior.

Seated alone in the bar in Sacramento's imposing new Eureka Tower Hotel, she was a familiar and welcome distraction both to the waiters and to the confidentially hunched huddles of lobbyists. The waiter, Joe, whom Jennifer addressed by his correct given name, José, glanced solicitously at the nearly empty brandy snifter. *"Desea Usted mas, Señora?"*

Her grateful smile was like a benediction. *"Nada mas ahora, gracias, José. Estoy esperando a mi esposo. Mas tarde, por favor."*

She had downed two and a half doubles already. Her Spanish, spoken infrequently now, was alcohol-thick and Yankee rough. It saddened her that she was losing it and she wondered morosely if it was going the way of certain other inherited advantages that she had taken for granted. In the midst of her moody introspection she saw Howdy's silhouette appear in the doorway. He was straining to penetrate the gloom.

"Over here, darling."

Howdy maneuvered onto the banquette beside her. Jennifer scarcely had time to give him a perfunctory little peck on the cheek when José appeared with a bottle and a set up.

"Buenas tardes, Señor Goodwyn." He indicated the tray. "We got your Crown Royal in this morning. Straight? With the water back?"

Howdy looked up, smiling. "Hi, Joe. Make it a double on the rocks and skip the water. You know us southern Californians. We'll save water for you northerners every chance we get."

Flattered to be a party to the joke, José laughed. He filled an Old Fashioned glass to the brim. When he turned questioning eyes to the snifter, Jennifer capped it. "Let's let Mr. Goodwyn catch up first."

Howdy waited until the man was beyond earshot, then gave Jennifer a searching look. "Catch up with you? God love you, Jenn, lately I'd have a better chance of catching up with Dean Martin." He put his glass to his lips and drained it.

"That wasn't a drink, darling. That was first aid. What happened at the hearing?"

Ignoring the question, Howdy reached for the check. "I'll tell you upstairs. I want to take a shower and stretch out for a while. Lew and Myra are going to pick us up here at seven."

A quarter of an hour later, wearing an oversized towel, Howdy came out of the bathroom. In spite of the air-conditioning the suite was hot. With less than three hours of daylight left, the nearby downtown buildings and streets were still shimmering in the mid-August heat. In the distance, trees and rooftops danced fluidly, distorted, apparently disconnected from the earth. The distant ones were all but obscured in the brown smog smear. Somewhere beyond was Sutter's Fort, reconstructed now as a state museum. Still farther to the east were the soaring peaks of the Sierra Nevada. The despised immigrants had crossed them. Many, like the Donner Party, who had waited until too late in the autumn, had died in them.

Howdy liked Sacramento. Much of the frontier spirit still lingered in its mixture of old and new. In a vague way Howdy wished that he could have shared the turbulent early times when Sacramento City's population exploded from several hundred adventurous trappers to five thousand permanent residents in less than three years. He envied Jennifer's great-great grandfather, John Lewis, who had founded this fortune there.

Jennifer wasted little time in the shower. Glowing from the sting of icy jets and the rough toweling, and still pleasantly high from the brandy, she stood beside the bed studying her husband's spare, long-muscled frame. He was

514

too white. He always had been, except for his forearms, neck, and face. She called it his farmer's sunburn and had long since given up trying to persuade him to swim. He was a Gemini, complex, mercurial, not one to be penned in. Her father had warned her of that. "A bird bath for Kiwis!" Howdy called the pool. It penned him in the same way a home penned him in. Lately, even a ninety-thousand acre ranch, Los Nidos itself, seemed to pen him in. The only time he seemed completely at ease was in one of their aircraft.

Cautiously, Jennifer lowered herself to the edge of the bed and sat with legs tucked under, watching him sleep. In repose Howdy's face seemed remarkably young. It betrayed almost nothing of the strain of responsibility that he seemed to absorb so well.

She let her eyes wander in critical approval from the wiry, short-cropped hair, shot with gray now, along the bridge of the clean-lined nose and slightly prominent cheekbones that betrayed a trace of Cherokee down to the well-formed lips, determined even in repose. Upon occasion they could widen into a wonderfully open smile or compress into a grim line that revealed a streak of latent cruelty.

She resisted an urge to wake him up with a kiss. Lately she had spent too little time with him. She had even had to ask to accompany him on this trip. The excuse had been a chance to visit with Lew and Myra Berwin, their closest friends.

Lew was the power behind the Association of California Grower-Packers. He had made Howdy listen to their pleas that the only way the state's five-billion-dollar agribusiness could survive was to put a man in the United States Senate who knew how to help. George Murphy was trying, but he needed help and the industry could settle on nobody until Lew suggested Howdy. At first the idea had seemed exciting. But now she was suffering misgivings.

At her dressing table she studied herself in the mirror and undertook, without enthusiasm, the minimal things her face required. Beyond her own reflection she saw Howdy beginning to stir. She'd let him have another ten minutes. The thought produced a smile. Another ten minutes? She'd let him have anything he wanted, just as she always had from their first time together after the messy divorce from Angie. To her mother's horror and her father's secret delight, she had taken the initiative then and the conquest had been easy.

It had been a good bargain, Jennifer reflected, this marriage that so few had held out hope for. Howdy had brought to it the tough-minded determination and vision that her father had lacked. And she had brought to it the elements that Howdy had needed to extend his own considerable success. She had brought to it also a savage passion and loyalty that awakened in him a latent ability to love. When Jennifer thought about the word love she was never certain that anyone could define it. Mutual need? Selfish need? "Whatever the hell it is," she had told herself a thousand times, "if it works, it's love."

Above all, Jennifer needed to see that the bargain endured. Family and friends had been far from unanimous in approving the romance. Catherine Coulter Vance's objection had not been based on anything more substantial than what she termed Howdy's lack of "Family Continuity." That had always been a favored euphemism for social background. Unlike Jennifer and her father, Catherine seemed to find more shelter beneath the spreading branches of the Vance-Lewis family tree than she found security in their huge ranch that straddled three county lines.

Catherine Vance's attitudes had imposed some painful burdens on the family. At the fashionable Glenborough School in Los Angeles, Jennifer had been in trouble from the outset because of her mother's insistence upon good form and her antipathy to the predictable nickname "Jenny."

Jennifer dubbed the whole business a "pain in the rump." She rebelled by standing rock-like against the current of the social swim, bringing her mother close to distraction. She had derived a perverse satisfaction from the knowledge that a girl less prominently placed would not have got away with it. Her satisfaction was short-lived, however, when she realized that her mother also derived a sort of inverse satisfaction for the same reason. The tacit competition had endured throughout the years.

In June of Nineteen fifty-two, with her own successful pursuit of Howard Goodwyn had come the crowning victory of her long rebellion. Jennifer made it secure by conferring on her successful but socially controversial husband all of the acceptance he really needed in California, a potential net worth, including her own certain inheritance, of a half billion dollars.

From the moment of her engagement, Jennifer had worked to interest Howdy in the operation of Los Nidos Ranch Company's varied activities. Under her father it had managed to survive. Under Howard Goodwyn it had begun to reach a potential that nobody but her own great-grandfather had ever envisioned. Jennifer expected the process of indoctrinating Howdy to take years. Instead, the wartime death of her brother and the tragic death of her father and sixty others in a commercial airline crash placed the responsibility in her husband's hands overnight.

Quitely and surely, much to the dismay of some ranch officials whose long-tenured sinecures had been tolerated by her father with characteristic forebearance, Howdy cut away the dead wood. Within a year the huge operation had come completely under his control.

Jennifer had come to accept as inevitable the eventual erosion of their prime agricultural holdings in Southern California by the tidal bore of new space-age immigrants. It was California's history repeating itself for the fourth time. But this time the change would be as profound as the one wrought by the original Forty Niners. The optimists said the destruction of the present California would take fifty years. The pessimists gave the state twenty-five years. After that there would be no large agricultural holdings left. Jennifer knew the man on the bed would never accept the inexorable change that was coming unless he could control it.

She suspected and feared that Lew Berwin would finally convince Howdy that direct political action was the only way to control the state's future. The continuing urbanization of Southern California's best land had shifted the power to a new breed of opportunistic politicians, men untroubled by tradition. Jennifer knew it would take a knowledgeable and secure man to assure leadership of such a group. Howdy was both.

The question was where would all of this leave her? She recalled a frightening dream she had suffered through several nights earlier. Howdy was taking an unnamed oath of office and she was standing only slightly behind him, smiling bravely but her face had changed. She had aged and there was a haunted look in her eyes. It was the same look she had seen in the tired eyes of those other once young, pretty political wives who stood in the glare of the television lights.

A restless thrashing on the bed made her turn, Howdy was sitting up, befuddled and blinking. "I musta corked off . . ."

Jennifer walked over to him. "That's what you musta did, honey. But I've been watching the time. You've got twenty minutes to get dressed."

He yawned and rubbed his head roughly between his hands. "Thanks."

Jennifer reached out and tweaked his ear. "Ever wonder what you'd do without me?"

He looked up at her, confused, then broke into a broad grin. "Nope. But I'd think of something."

In the private dining room at Sam Lee's Restaurant overlooking Sacramento's historic waterfront, Jennifer relished an array of Cantonese dishes along with the Berwins. Whatever Myra Berwin may have been, Jennifer agreed with Howdy that she liked her. The dinner was fun.

Myra had married Lew in 1952, the same year she and Howdy had been married. Both marriages had sent mild shock waves through their respective social strata in Los Angeles and in San Francisco. The marriage of long-divorced Lew Berwin to an obscure actress twenty years his junior had caused the most comment. The general tone of it was summed up by an older, unfulfilled actress who was reputed to have been a part-time occupant of the commodious Berwin bed. "That Mansfield dame's got sprocket holes in her back from so many continuous performances."

Privately, Jennifer conceded the possibility that Myra might have tripped an occasional producer and beat him to the floor, as one gossip columnist put it. But so far as she was concerned, Jennifer could find no fundamental difference in the tactics she herself had used to commit Howdy. Whatever the facts of Myra's former life, Jennifer had quickly accepted her as an ideal mate for Lew, an outgoing, "no crap" female who was doing her job. Watching Myra now, she acknowledged the uneasy kinship that exists between women who know what they want, know how to get it, and hope that they know how to keep it.

In the beginning Jennifer had been afraid of Lew. The balding, stocky, hard-handed, fifty-seven-year-old packing company president who drove head on at everything he undertook seemed dangerous to her in ways that she did not comprehend. He had expanded the packing company founded in San Francisco by his great-grandfather, Moses Berwin, in the post Gold Rush days until it had become a hydra-headed complex of related businesses under the Golden West trade mark.

Once, when Lew had been particularly insistent about Howdy's participation in a deal, she had expressed that fear. Howdy had made her dismiss it by saying, "Honey, you don't ever have to be afraid of people who need you. It's the ones *you* need that you've got to look out for." Howdy had also pointed out that Lew Berwin's companies had a vital need for the great variety of produce grown on the ranch. Los Nidos could do business with many packers but there were too few large, diversified ranches close in to the big markets to give the packers any real independence. Lew Berwin's extensive company-owned ranches were not sufficient and economic pressure to spin them off for suburban homesites was increasing. South of San Francisco, five hundred acres of Golden West's richest artichoke land had been over-run by a new suburb-city. The survival of all that both men had built had to be protected. That would mean they would have to fight. Dimly Jennifer feared that she and Myra could become casualties of that war.

At thirty-six, Myra was still a very desirable female. The startling resemblance to Rhonda Fleming that had been a disadvantage in Hollywood had become an asset in their segment of San Francisco's society. Her engaging informality disarmed the socially orthodox in the Berwin circle of friends and the conquest had become complete when her love for the children she could not have led to the discovery of a latent talent for portraiture. She had worked hard to develop it and over the years her pastels of friends' offspring had brought in an impressive number of commissions. Myra had accepted the money gladly and promptly endorsed the checks over to the Children's Hospital.

The dinner conversation managed to stay away from business until the subject of increased assessments and the Farm Workers Organizing Committee came up. Scowling,

Lew Berwin gestured impatiently. "That's all we need! Reassessment and Chavez. The goddamned fools. They'll put us out of business and themselves too. Their leaders don't tell them that. They don't tell them that you can't fill warehouses full of perishables and then negotiate while the inventory is being depleted, like they do with steel. All they say is, 'Screw the big big boys. Screw the growers.' And those soft-headed liberal politicians who brown nose them keep egging them on. What the hell do those Ivy League dudes care about agriculture? All they want is votes. And if they have to crawl in bed with those red-eyed liberals to get them, believe me they will—no matter who get's screwed!"

Myra gave Lew a pained look. He ignored it. "It's pretty clear now that we've got to have more help in Washington. If we don't get somebody back there who understands California's special ag problem, you and I are going to wind up in the real-estate business in another five years."

A long ash from his cigar cascaded down his shirtfront. Before Myra could stop him, he had brushed the mess away, leaving a long gray smudge. Moaning, she closed her eyes. "I hate those damned cigars!"

Lew shot her an annoyed glance and resumed his tirade. "And we're going to be put there by a bunch of brown-skinned idiots. On your ranches and on ours they average a hundred and twenty-five bucks a week each. Fifty weeks a year, with free permanent housing, free language schools and bonuses. That's pretty goddamned good for a bunch that can't write their own language and probably haven't bothered to learn to speak ours."

Despite the certain knowledge that Lew could never be either chauvinist or bigot, Jennifer found herself growing angry. In his frustration she knew that what he was really asking for was a willingness on the part of the present-day minorities to work as hard as his own immigrant forebears had, not only at their jobs but at the task of getting an education, pulling themselves up to positions of importance. She understood Lew's and Howdy's anger at the short-sightedness of the uneducated and uninformed workers who listened to the emotional appeals of Cesar Chavez. Chavez promised them power. But the workers would lose if they listened and in the end Chavez would be killing the patient to cure the ailment.

520

Much later Howdy and Jennifer lay naked watching their reflections in the mirror-wall beside the bed. Jennifer stirred first, rolled her head toward him, and kissed the end of his nose. "You're very good, darling, when you've saved up for a week."

Pulling away, Howdy peered down his nose at her. "What d'ya mean, a week?"

"I mean one week. I keep track. I used to be your CPA. Remember?"

He laughed suddenly at the half-forgotten private joke. In the early months of their marriage CPA had stood for "Cute Piece of Ass." Howdy studied her and thought that seventeen years and one kid later she still was. "You're not trying to tell me that I'm hanging you up these days?"

She nodded curtly and affirmatively.

For a long moment she returned his defiant gaze. "You're oversexed."

"I know. But we'll just have to try to live with it. Won't we?" When Howdy didn't respond, she frowned. Suddenly her mood changed from playful to serious. "It's not that I get hung up in the hay, darling. It's some other kind of damned hangup that's bugging me."

"Like what?"

"I don't know." She shook her head. "It's almost like I'm getting lost or falling by the wayside." She turned to him, appealing. "I can't put my finger on it."

Troubled now, Howdy pushed upright. He reached down and squeezed her neck gently. "You drink too much. You're beginning to imagine things."

Jennifer freed herself and gazed at the empty brandy snifter on the bedstand. "I won't deny that I've been slurping a little more than usual lately. But you've got it backwards, Howdy. I'm not feeling lost because I'm drinking. It's the other way around." Pushing herself up beside him, she appealed for understanding. "I don't know what it's all about, except that I don't feel it when we're buried in ranch problems and figuring things out together."

She was silent for a moment, reflecting. "In a way I'm to blame for this political thing. It sounded exciting when Lew first started working on you. It seemed like the best way to fight off those damned annexations and all the rest. Maybe it still is, but—" She broke off and groaned. "Oh damn it, Howdy. If you do run, you'll win. You always do. So I guess what I'm trying to say is, 'Where will that leave me?' Lost in some sort of a middle-aged female limbo?"

Jennifer's tanned body sagged and her eyes lowered to her hands. They had fallen, upturned, cupped between her thighs. Suddenly they seemed like beggar's hands, supplicating. She laughed half aloud and the harshness of the suppressed sound made Howdy turn to look at her closely. Jennifer slipped her hand beneath his upper arm and curled her fingers around his biceps.

"It's asking a lot of you, Howard Goodwyn, to expect you to know what it feels like to be alone. I haven't felt this way since boarding school when I used to sit alone in my room trying to get myself together after Mother and Father took off on another of their trips." She reached up to lace the fingers of both hands over the still hard muscle of his upper arm.

"I'm sorry, honey. How on earth can I expect a man like you to know how it feels to be—" she searched for the right word and settled again for "—lost."

With unusual gentleness Howdy reached for the tangle of dark curls and rumpled them. "I expect I don't know. But do you want to know what I think about it?"

Her eyes narrowed suspiciously. "I'm not sure I do, if you're going to tell me that it's self-pity and I ought to be ashamed of myself."

"No. I'm not going to tell you that. But I am going to tell you again that you're imagining things." He grasped her neck gently and pretended to shake her head. "There's never been a time when you weren't part of everything I do. And there never will be. No matter what I do, here, in Sacramento, in Washington, and down at the ranch. You'll be with me, doing it with me, Jen. Now go to sleep. You've had too much of everything, but rest. And so have I."

Howdy slid down flat again. A moment or so later Jennifer worked her long, sun-browned legs beneath the cover and inched over beside him. Within minutes she slept.

As he watched her, the possibility that Jennifer would ever find herself in any sort of limbo struck Howdy as ludicrous. Still, her plea had betrayed genuine anxiety. It troubled him. There was a pattern to it, something familiar. It reminded him of Angie during those months following the end of their radio show and the beginning of the war years. She had complained of a lost feeling too, of being out of it, not needed. Howdy stirred restlessly at the thought and wished that he could turn his head off. Making love to Jennifer stimulated him with a sense of well-being. Other men said sex wound them down and caved them in. But it never had with him, except perhaps after a twenty-dollar session with Renée. But that was different. Renée's job was to take the pressure off. With Jennifer, sex added something. As he lay still, staring up into the lumimous darkness, Howdy wondered why it had not been that way with Angie. She had been loving and giving, but in her giving she had been strangely demanding, as though the gift of her body had carried an implied obligation to appreciate. An old twinge of guilt returned. He dismissed it with a silent curse. He had no reason to be concerned. Angie was a wealthy woman. For almost ten years she had been Mrs. David Layne. The infrequent pangs of conscience he felt about Dave were quickly allayed by the knowledge that what he had paid for his partner's share in Goodwyn Enterprises, added to Angie's settlement, more than compensated them for the fact that both had run second best. He had been generous despite the fact that if he had used what Helga had seen from her window that night as evidence in court, he could have gotten off with a quarter of the offer Angie finally accepted.

After the first angry sting of wounded pride, Howdy convinced himself that Angie's need for another man was less physical than emotional. After the separation he had moved to an apartment in Hollywood's Sunset Towers and was surprised to find how little he had really needed Angie for anything. He welcomed the relief from a burden that had been unrecognized until removed.

Howdy looked down at the youthful nude body beside him and marveled again that Jennifer could have produced a child and kept herself in such lean-hipped, flat-bellied shape. That was something they had given each other, a son and heir. Howdy wondered at times if it had been a mistake not to have had another child, but one child seemed to have fulfilled Jennifer. Any number of times she had complained good-naturedly, especially as Howie entered his teens, that he was more than enough for one mother to handle.

At fifteen, Howard Junior was a rawhide lean, handsome boy with the easy grace of a dedicated surfer.

Howdy had once confided to Ev Moses, "The kid's well hung."

It troubled Howdy that he had so little time to spend with the boy. Politics would leave even less. He had convinced himself long since that in the main he was discharging his principal responsibilities as a father. He had discussed it with Ev Moses, but for once the attorney had not been so sanguine.

"A good-looking kid like Howie could become a mark for some scheming mother, somebody who knows how to figure the angles. It can be worth a lot to a prominent family to avoid a paternity suit." But the kid had kept his pants zipped and his nose clean. At least so far, Howie's dedication to surfing seemed to absorb most of his energy. Jennifer had said, "After those kids have been out there freezing their little ornaments off they don't have enough pizzazz left to get into trouble." Jennifer had forgotten just how much raw energy kids have. At Howie's age, Howdy could remember no time when sheer physical fatigue had not suddenly given way to a surge of new energy at the prospect of an imminent piece of tail.

Unable to will himself to sleep, Howdy let his mind drift to the ranch. His involvement in Los Nidos had begun immediately after Angie's Mexican divorce in the winter of Nineteen fifty-one. He had flown Jennifer up to Monterey. They had wandered along the same streets that her paternal great-great-grandfather, John Lewis, had known as a young man. Jennifer had just turned twenty-one that September. From the time she had been thirteen he had never been able to deny her anything and the trip was another promise kept.

He reserved separate suites, amusing Jennifer by his propriety. Later, when she knocked on the adjoining doorway and he opened it somewhat timidly, she laughed at the expression on his face. In a matter of minutes, he discovered in his arms the most intensely passionate female he had ever known. Howdy wondered again as his hand involuntarily reached out to touch her whether or not the decision to marry had really been his or hers.

The next step had been to exercise the option to buy the airport and to develop an ambitious light industrial complex there. Reluctantly, Steven Vance had accepted the move as inevitable. In the midst of the industrial development Steven Vance had died in a take-off crash at New

York's Idlewild Airport. Within weeks, as Jennifer's husband, and with Catherine's grateful consent, Howdy had taken over Los Nidos.

Quickly he had perceived one underlying principle: In a population explosion and in the sellers' market it produced, it was far better to own land than to have to bid for it. His marriage to Jennifer had placed ninety thousand acres of California's best diversified land under his control and it was located in the heart of the state's fastest-growing area.

When it was developed it would easily be worth a billion dollars. Los Nidos' position was very different from that of the smaller ranches. Almost without warning, residential developers had become the new sharecroppers with middle-income housing the most profitable crop. Howdy couldn't blame ranchers, beset with rising taxes, threats of annexation, and soaring labor costs, for taking their capital gains profits and heading for the nearest cruise vessels. Unexpectedly, the farmers had won economic survival but California's agriculture was the victim.

Subdivisions ate up more than one hundred thousand acres of the state's best agricultural land every twelve months. Much that remained of the state's arable land was polluted. And nobody seemed to give a damn. Mass builders who had learned from the Levitts cared about nothing but profits. They were being helped at every turn of the bulldozer by vote-hungry local politicians with an eye to new families in their districts. Howdy knew there was little chance that agribusiness executives could stand against the tide. California had become the only place on earth where bulldozers customized the land so builders could rubberstamp their houses.

Howdy had commissioned the architect and city planner Lloyd Wilson to update Los Nidos' original master plan. Wilson had recommended developing a revolutionary new plan whose guidelines would anticipate the urbanization of the entire southern California coastal basin. Lloyd Wilson was due at the ranch the following afternoon to demonstrate his preliminary concept.

Howdy damned the ambient thoughts that were keeping him awake. At three A.M. sleep finally came while he was still trying to reason a safe way into the future.

Lloyd Wilson and two associates arrived at Los Nidos

shortly before two P.M. Ev Moses, Jennifer, and Catherine Vance were all on hand to attend the conference.

Wilson wasted little time on preliminaries. He immediately set up aerial photographs with overlays and spread a rough plat of the general plan on a large table. Using a pencil, Wilson indicated the meandering boundaries of nearly twenty thousand acres of rich agricultural land that lay between the mountains on the northeast and the coastal hills on the south and west.

"This is the land that must remain in highly diversified agricultural production for at least twenty-five years before it can be rezoned."

The pencil moved to the foothills. "This land, currently producing citrus, avocado, oats, and barley, remains as is until it is moved to the company's new acquisitions in the San Joaquin Valley. When the demand warrants, it can be released to private developers working within our guidelines for single-family and multiple residences. Eventually there will be about twenty residential complexes, each accommodating about twenty thousand residents."

Wilson turned to indicate a large cardboard tube. "Now we're going to show you our artist's visualization of the entire project as it could look about the year Ninteen ninety."

While the others watched with growing wonderment, Wilson helped his men unroll a huge mural visualization and pin it to the top of a drapery valance. When the men stepped aside, Jennifer's hand went to her mouth. "My God, Lloyd. It's ... it's stupefying. It makes Reston and Columbia look like crossroads villages."

Wilson allowed himself to be cautiously encouraged. He would wait to believe that Jennifer's reaction signified approval. What he was visualizing for her was the end of El Rancho de los Nidos. She might call the rendering "stupefying" now, for it was a daring piece of exhibitionism, but he could hardly expect her to wholeheartedly accept this metamorphosis from Los Nidos to MICROPOLIS 2000.

Howdy ran the operation but when the chips were down it was not likely that he would do anything that was seriously contrary to her will. Wilson glanced at Howdy, whose face betrayed no visible emotion beyond concentration on the painting. Neither could he guess Ev Moses' reaction. He decided it would be wise to anticipate some inevitable questions.

"Our rough figures show income from real-estate leases and sales matching net earnings from agriculture in three years and leveling out at about four times the agricultural gross within ten years. After that we'll need computer projections on the cost of finance money and rising labor and material costs." He waved a hand. "And all the other factors. We feel it can be made economically sound because it has to be. The only alternative is to fight a losing battle against annexation and urban sprawl to tract-built super-slums."

Then Lloyd went on to interpret the remarkable rendering. In addition to the twenty complete communities with their own service centers and regional shopping centers, there were schools, a two-year junior college, a neighboring state university, and two private vocational schools. One was for general training and the other for training maintenance mechanics needed for the sophisticated new automatic farm equipment soon to replace much of the field labor.

The Casa Grande would still stand, with the adjoining hill and mountain country, undisturbed by the proposed development. The reservoir-lake would remain, surrounded by a naturalistic public park just as it had during Steven Lewis' time.

Reversing what he considered an idiotic modern concept, Wilson would build as many communities as possible on non-food-producing land. They would be built on otherwise useless hills. There would be no single dwellings, only apartments. There would be no streets for vehicles in the conventional sense. The steep, stone-paved streets that would provide access to the buildings were to be used mainly for walking. Only vehicles needed for heavy deliveries, emergencies, and services would be permitted. Residents would park private cars in disguised common garages engineered into the face of the hill and take moving side-walks along a tunneled subway to a point directly beneath the hill towns. There they would use express elevators that would let them off at various levels. Then, through common passageways, they would reach the lobbies of their respective buildings. Wilson's sketches created the aesthetically pleasing impression of an ancient tile-roofed Spanish balcony village constructed mainly of stone and great hand hewn beams.

Connecting all the MICROPOLIS 2000 communities

and serving the two major shopping centers would be a high speed monorail. Shoppers would leave their automobiles in underground parking lots beneath the central plazas of each community and walk under cover to the stations. The shopping centers themselves would be climatized and the monorail coaches would enter, discharge, and receive passengers in a fully protected environment.

Wilson planned a cultural center with an amphitheater for summer musical productions, a civic playhouse and auditorium, and, on a mesa at the extreme top of the coastal hills, a great circular convention center with exhibition galleries for the arts and crafts. A spectacular cantilevered restaurant was located on the top floor. The complex would be reached from parking areas at the base of the hills by escalators.

Wilson turned from the physical layout of MICROPOLIS 2000 and its main design innovations to the large forest that had been created by the artists. "One of the most exciting aspects of this concept to me is this reforestation project. If we can prove the practicability of the plan on Los Nidos land, I'm sure we can secure the cooperation of conservation groups and the Federal government. What we are proposing could radically improve the bionomic state of Southern California's coastal shelf. It could control the fire and flood cycle that has plagued this land. Wildlife would be preserved to proliferate again. In another generation, Southern Californians would not have to travel hundreds of miles to campsites only to find them jammed."

Grinning, Howdy pointed to the illustrated mountains. "If you start covering our national forests with trees, you're liable to confuse a lot of natives."

Jennifer shot him an oblique glance. "That's our normal state, darling."

Howdy ignored her. "Lloyd, if you and your boys have invented a new rain-making machine that really works, I'll buy the trees for Los Nidos and the whole damned national forest around us, too."

Wilson smiled and pointed to a network of light blue broken lines. "These are all sewage. About twelve acre feet of fluid per day per twenty-five thousand population, would be processed to potable purity, pumped to these storage reservoirs, then repumped to these plastic line sprinkler systems deployed along these mountain slopes. In time they would cover five thousand acres of our highland.

528

In case of a brush fire, that particular sector could be turned on and fires brought under control. Our plan proposes that we plant a million trees that were indigenous to the area hundreds of years ago. We know the trees will root if they receive water. We provide irrigation with our portable treated sewage. The solid waste from the treatment plants will pay for itself as fertilizer, both for the reforestation project and for certain Los Nidos crops.

"In short, we are proposing to return this land to the pristine state that geologists and ecologists say existed up until several thousand years ago. If the surrounding cities could be induced to join in, perhaps with state and Federal grants, we could begin to transform Southern California's coastal shelf by the year 2000. The Israelis have done it with their tamarisk and eucalyptus forests and with cedar groves. They've planted over a hundred thousand acres. Why can't we?"

Lloyd Wilson looked intently at his listeners for a moment, then tossed the pencil onto the table. "That's it in sketchy form. There's a lot more detail to come. I'd like to leave this material here for you to go over. If this concept is too far out, we'll haul back a little. I'm not married to anything here except the basic premise that Los Nidos is not going to be able to survive much longer unless it beats the invaders to the bridge. Protect your best agricultural land at the heart of your township and phase it out according to your own time-table."

Jennifer was waiting for Howdy when he returned from the office at half-past six. As he entered the family room, she handed him a bourbon and water.

"I've got a glorious piece of news for you, darling."

Howdy gave her a perfunctory kiss and flopped into his favorite chair. "I could use some."

She perched on the chair arm and began massaging the back of his neck. "Well, see how this grabs you. Mother's coming here for the holiday, and—"

Howdy glanced up, frowning, and said, "That's news?"

"—and darling, she's bringing me a new step-daddykins who's only five years older than I and you're getting a new father-in-law who's only twelve years *younger* than you." She leaned away and looked down her nose at him.

Howdy had arrested the drink at his lips during Jennifer's revelation. He lowered it untouched. "Well, I'll be a son-of-a-bitch. So she went and did it?"

"That's right."

Howdy took a good swallow. "I never thought she would." He looked up, questioning. "Rob?"

"Yup."

"You met him in New York, didn't you?"

"I did."

"What's he like?"

Jennifer pursed her lips thoughtfully. "He's like, well, charming, attractive. in an *Esquire Magazine* sort of way. Got gobs of his own sun-bleached hair, his own Ultra-Brite teeth, good New England background, plays excellent tennis and squash, golf, sails, flies light planes, knows all of the important maitre d's—" She pantomimed empty pockets. "—and hasn't got a pot to pee in."

Howdy rumpled his hair in annoyance and Jennifer smoothed it, clucking. "Everything'll be all right, darling, because mother's only sixty-six and has forty million dollars. That should be enough for them to get by on if they're careful." She kissed the end of his nose. "So now you know. And while I'm at it, I might as well tell you that Robert Westbrook Williamston III also expressed an interest in Los Nidos. He's absolutely champing at the bit to be given the short course in how to make millions at ranching between golf games and other urgent engagements."

While Howdy sat slumped, immersed in his own forebodings, Jennifer went to the bar, poured a brandy, and resettled on the chair arm. Howdy swung the ice in his drink. "I never took the bastard seriously."

"Neither did I, baby. But we better start now."

He slapped the left chair arm. "Yeah. But what stalls me is how your mother, who's a reasonably sensible woman, could fall for a lounge lizard."

"Mother is a reasonably sensible, very *lonely* woman, darling. And Rob's not a lounge lizard. He's got all of the right credentials. His grandfather had blanket mills in New England. His father was very well off but got wiped out in Twenty-nine. He went to all the proper schools and graduated from Yale. After college he dabbled in the brokerage business, just like Dad did. Then he tried gentleman farming in Virginia, like Dad did. I think he was also involved in banking and oh yes, he was a male model, for a gag, he says. Mostly he's made himself a very attractive and acceptable odd man, the kind hostesses dote on. That's how Mom met him. I was at the same dinner. In fact, he squired us both."

Deliberately, Jennifer needled a sore spot. "And, darling, I almost forgot, he's a divine dancer."

Howdy's muttered obscenity made Jennifer laugh. She patted his cheek. "Don't worry, sweetie. I promise not to dig his type until I'm a hundred and sixty-six. Meanwhile, back at the ranch, we've got ourselves a fox in the hen house, as your senator friend, Clair Engle, used to put it."

A clatter in the adjoining room interrupted their musing and young Howie appeared holding a soft drink bottle tipped up to his mouth. When he lowered it, some of the fluid spurted on the floor. He swabbed it with a bare foot and collapsed on the sofa. Jennifer regarded him critically and sat down beside him. "Cat got your tongue?"

Puzzled, Howie looked at her, then grinned. "Oh, hi, Mom."

"Hi." She indicated Howdy. "That man over there is your father. Say something nice to him, son."

Howie hoisted the bottle. "Hi, Dad." When Howdy grunted an acknowledgment without looking up, Howie turned from one to the other curiously. "Wow. You two are sure breaking it up. What's the matter?"

Jennifer answered, "We got a little surprise today. Your grandmother got married Saturday in Connecticut."

A broad grin spread over Howie's tanned face. "Hey. How about that? Grandma got stoked on some old guy and blew her mind. Wow. Crazy!"

Jennifer sniffed. "The 'crazy' part I agree with. But he isn't some old guy. Your new grandfather is only five years older than your *young* mother."

"Wowww—"

The exclamation made Jennifer grimace. "For God's sake, is 'wow' the only word you kids know?"

Howie ignored her. "I'll bet he's after her dough, huh?"

Jennier tried unsuccessfully to stifle a smile. "You may have put your finger on a good reason, son. You just may have."

"Are we going back East to meet him?"

"No. They're coming here for Christmas."

Howie looked pleased. "Hey! Neat!"

Jennifer patted his knee. "Isn't that nice? You'll have someone your own age to play with."

Howie finished off the last of the soft drink and wiped his mouth on his forearm. "Forty isn't very young."

She glowered and shook a finger under his nose. "You just watch it, young man, or I'll cut you off without an acre." Then she gave him a playful swat. "Now go put your hair up and polish your beads. We're about ready to eat."

When Howie rose with a pained expression, she caught a glimpse of his soles. "And while you're at it, sterilize those feet and put on your shoes. I know they kill you natives, but you've got to learn our Christian ways." The boy gave his mother a withering look that translated "Square" and ambled out.

Howdy stifled a yawn and slid his legs out straight. "If I didn't know how good that kid is, I'd worry about him with that long hair and those goddamned beads."

She nodded toward the door. "Don't worry about him. He's just being fifteen. Worry about his new grandfather." Serious again, she set the brandy snifter aside. "Honey, there's no way Rob can get his hands on any part of the ranch, is there?"

Howdy looked up, amazed. "God, no! No way. Your mother can't lay a hand on anything but the income from her trust stock. The way your father set it up she's got to leave it to you and your offspring, except the percentage that goes to the foundation."

"Thank heaven for that. The worst he can do is spend her income. It's only money and if I thought this marriage was really going to make Mom happy I could bear it. But it's such a damned ungraceful situation. Sure, we can say, 'to hell with money,' but I can't say 'to hell with pride.' "

For all of his preconceptions, Howdy was not prepared for Robert Williamston III. As Chad Chadwick eased the Los Nidos chopper down onto the pad, Howdy could see Rob in the right-hand seat, apparently questioning the pilot about the operation of the ship. By the time Howdy and Jennifer were out of the car, the bride of three weeks was hurrying toward them with outstretched arms. The groom, a remarkably handsome man, was exacting a last-minute promise from Chad. "I'm going to hold you to that. I really want to try it. I got a little Benson up and down in one piece once, in Florida. But this is another bird." Howdy could see that Chad was pleased.

The feared introduction was made so effortless by Rob Williamston's easy graciousnes that Howdy was nonplused. Helpless to resist, he found himself being carried along by the force of the younger man's personality. After greeting Jennifer warmly, Rob turned back to Howdy.

"Catherine's eagerness to see you all is a good part of my enjoyment. But I'm going to be honest. I admit to a selfish desire to meet a living legend. Take my word for it, Howdy, you have no public relations officer like your mother-in-law." The man's handshake was good. And so was the face although it seemed older than Jen had led him to believe. But he looked right at you, and there was no discernible embarrassment at being married to a woman old enough to be his mother.

Howdy found himself thinking, "How in hell do you dig out of a snow job like this?" Uncomfortable, he excused himself and walked over to Chad, who was dragging luggage from the chopper.

The pilot greeted him with a perfunctory "Hi" and jerked his head in the direction of Santa Ana. "There's more at the airport. I couldn't handle it all this trip."

Howdy helped lower a wardrobe case: "What do you think?"

A warning look silenced him.

"Forgive me, fellows, I didn't mean to leave you with the baggage." Rob clamped a small case under each arm and grasped a larger one in each hand and headed toward the car. When he was beyond earshot, Howdy repeated the query. "Well, what's the verdict?"

"He's a bright son of a gun." The pilot studied the retreating figure. "I can't figure him out. But he looks to me like one of those characters who can steal a dame right out from under you."

Before a week had passed, Rob Williamston had made himself a welcome presence at Casa Grande. His ability to divert and amuse seemed endless. By the end of the third day he had won over young Howie. "Know what he did, Dad? He rode Bandido bareback and jumped him over the sawhorse and over the logs on Laberinta trail. He rides better than I do. He's like—wow!"

The boy's quick enthusiasm for the Easterner annoyed Howdy. Apparently in a matter of hours Rob had established a rapport that he had never quite managed himself.

Howdy felt certain that Howie respected him and admired his ability on the guitar and as a pilot. But his day-to-day relationship with young Howie was filled with too many long periods of detachment.

Howdy was the victim of a curious ambivalence; he welcomed and at the same time resented the presence of Robert Westbrook Williamston III.

It also annoyed Howdy that a time or two Jennifer had come close to defending Rob. But if Rob was attracted to Jen he concealed it well. A new brightness permeated the house and Jennifer was pleased to see Howdy responding. She wondered how much of his uncharacteristic animation stemmed from an unconscious need to compete, to keep his everlasting edge.

Late one night, after a stubborn session in the bedroom, Jennifer convinced Howdy that a cocktail party should be given during the Thanksgiving week. "Look, honey, we can't keep him in an isolation ward. All our friends know he's here. If we don't make some gesture they'll be completely convinced that the gossip is true, that we're embarrassed to present him. If we take the initiative he'll bedazzle them and they won't be so rough on Mother. The worst they can say is 'if she had to have a plaything at least she bought a delightful one.'"

Jennifer's prediction proved accurate. Some of the younger men, whose attractive, aggressive wives failed to conceal their admiration for Rob, left the party privately hating his guts. The more secure ones were unanimous in their acceptance. During the ensuing weeks the invitations to other parties reached such a peak that Jennifer was forced to plead prior family commitments.

They did accept a New Year's Eve party at the club. Rob had danced every other dance with Catherine until she herself had begged off. During his half dozen dances with Jennifer, Howdy had watched with transparent indifference.

Later, Howdy, half-joking, had accused her of encouraging Rob's attention. The subject would not have come up if both of them had not drunk full measures of champagne and brandy. But it had come up. And in a perverse way it pleased Jennifer. She would have liked Howdy to make love to her but he was either too far gone or too obstinate to respond to her tacit invitation.

534

Several days before the Williamstons' departure, Jennifer insisted that Howdy go over the M-Two plan with her mother. Another meeting would take place the following week.

After dinner, they drove down to the administration building, where the exhibits were still on display. For two hours Howdy went over the plan in some detail. Catherine said little but it was evident that she was impressed. Rob, who had followed the concept avidly, found it difficult to contain his enthusiasm. When Howdy finished, he bounced to his feet.

"Marvelous, Jennifer, Howdy, marvelous! The most exciting plan I've seen."

Howdy resisted the urge to ask how many such plans he'd been exposed to and contented himself with a noncommittal, "Good."

At Casa Grande, Rob paused at the front door to look back out over the broad lowlands. The fields were dark, but around their periphery the lights of the coastal communities and the newer, closer-lying suburban areas sparkled in the clear winter air. Rob indicated the dark panorama and said, "It must take real will-power to hold all those acres in agriculture when you could quadruple your worth by urbanizing the entire ranch."

Jennifer held her breath but Howdy's reply was deceptively mild. "Not if you're a country boy like me and want a little fresh air and elbow room as much as you want dollars."

An hour later, in bed, Catherine looked up from her book as Rob came out of the bathroom. He perched on the edge of the bed and kissed her temple lightly. "I can't help but think how fortunate you are, and Jennifer too, to have Howdy in the family. Apparently he's done wonders with the ranch. Certainly he's added vast amounts to the value of the stock."

"Indeed he has. I think that's why Steven was very happy to give him an interest when he married Jennifer and turn over most of the practical management to him."

Rob put his hand on hers. "It was a wise choice. But after looking at the potential in the MICROPOLIS plan, I wonder what Steven would have said about holding out the best subdivision acreage for bean and asparagus fields."

"I don't know, Rob. Generally he approved of Howdy's

535

decisions. Why do you ask? Do you question his judgment in this?"

Rob smiled deprecatingly and squeezed Catherine's hand. "I wouldn't say I disapprove. Good heavens, Catherine, I'm hardly qualified to criticize. Moreover, even if I were it would not really be my place to, would it?"

"I should think it would be your duty now, if you truly think you see a serious flaw in the plan."

Frowning, Rob rose from the bed. "I'm sure there's some explanation for it, Catherine. But I can't help wondering about two things. First, why doesn't Howdy consider planning the entire ranch into communites when urbanization is so much more profitable than farming? And second, why would he borrow millions and pay interest to build the shopping centers and recreation areas when the company could go public and raise money, interest-free, from the sale of stock?" He squinted quizzically. "I've had some experience in finance, just as Steven had. There'd be no trouble underwriting an issue. Heavens, love, with my, our connections in the East—" He broke off and shook his head. "More than that, there'd be no danger of your losing control of Los Nidos. You've said that between the three of you and the Vance Foundation, you control the company absolutely."

Rob turned to her with a disarming smile. "In any case, my love, I repeat, it's none of my business, really. And you'd be quite within your right to remind me that I'm being presumptuous." He slipped into the bed beside her. "Forgive me. Put it out of your mind. It was thoughtless of me to raise such a question when you're trying to woo Morpheus." He peered at the dust jacket of the book on the bed. "On the other hand, if you're reading *that* for entertainment, my lovely, I'm sure I can come up with at least one better suggestion."

Catherine allowed herself a small smile and inclined her head toward him playfully. "I don't think you're presumptuous, my sweet. But sometimes I think you're insatiable. Now go read until you're sleepy."

Grateful that she had not responded to his contrived overture, Rob laughed softly, kissed her again, and settled down with a copy of *Motor Age.*

In the master bedroom in the opposite wing of Casa

Grande, Howdy sprawled naked on top of the seven-foot-square bed and watched Jennifer undressing.

"I know we had to include your mother's little play-mate. But I can tell you one thing—I felt a hell of a lot easier before he knew so much about our plans."

"Relax, darling. That wasn't real interest he expressed. It was just lip service to make Mother happy. Actually, I think it may have been helpful."

Howdy snorted. "About as helpful as a skunk at a picnic." He raised his head to watch her before she spoke again. "You know something? I think the little boy in old Robbie appeals to your mother instinct, now, don't it?"

Jennifer stiffened and glared at him icily. "No. It *doesn't*, you bastard." A moment later she went into the bathroom nursing a feeling of righteous injury. But it was not unmixed with guilt.

The MICROPOLIS 2000 meetings lasted a week. Thirty-three million dollars in financing would be required to initiate the first phase that would include three complete communities. A San Francisco firm was employed to analyze the charters of each adjacent city. Ev Moses, knowing the startled sister cities would fight to keep their boundaries from being frozen by the new community that would dominate them, intended to incorporate in the M-Two Charter everything that was good in neighboring charters. It was one way to soften their opposition.

Both Ev Moses and Lloyd Wilson agreed that the beach cities in particular would be foolish to oppose MICROPOLIS 2000. They would be the ones to profit the most because they had a monopoly on shore-side recreation. There was no way for a developer to duplicate beaches for inland population.

The agruicultural land that would remain was the crucial bone of contention. Once those preserves were incorporated into the new city that would be beyond county control. The hostile communities could be expected to protest violently the moment they found out that might happen. The strategy the Los Nidos Ranch Company was using was precarious but it was the only way a sizeable portion of Southern California's best agricultural land could be kept out of the hands of the developers. It wouldn't work though, unless strong political power was applied at both state and national levels. Jennifer knew this and she knew that such strong pressure could be brought by only one man.

In mid-February they received a long-distance call from Catherine and Rob from their leased estate in Pound Ridge, New York. They had purchased a brownstone on East 71st Street in Manhattan. Rob's bachelor 'digs,' as he called them, had been in the building. They had also purchased the identical building next door. Both would be converted into a single three-story town house. Work would begin in early spring. Meanwhile, as soon as the plans were completed and the contract let, they would go to Palm Beach and hope to be in California again before the decorator began his work.

After one hour of conversation, Jennifer replaced the phone and retrieved the brandy snifter. Her face was a study of conflicting emotions. "Who says money can't buy happiness?"

Howdy looked up from the newspaper. "People who don't have money. Old Rob, for instance. He's parlayed a winning smile into a multimillion dollar purse, and on a slow track too."

Jennifer grimaced. "God Almighty! Isn't there any compassion in you at all? Is everyone wrong who doesn't play by your rules?"

Howdy smiled amiably. "Nope. But if they don't play by my rules, they don't play on my team. And I can't buy the notion that any able-bodied kept man has a right to play games with an old lady's misery and money. One day your mom will wake up and find out that the screwing she's getting isn't worth the screwing she's getting."

Jennifer studied her husband with icy detachment. "You know, darling, there are times when you can be a vulgar, dispicable, cob-wiping yokel."

Grinning broadly, Howdy rose. "That's not the latest news, is it?" Then his tone changed abruptly. "Look, I know what Catherine's income amounts to, after taxes. And I know pretty well what a double town house in Manhattan costs to buy and remodel. Little Robbie-boy is going to put your mom in hock. I like Catherine. And I feel sorry for her. I felt that way the day I first met her when you were a snot-nosed pigtailed kid showing off on a horse. I can see what's going to happen, and the mess is going to land on us. It sure as hell isn't hard to figure a he-whore like Williamston."

He crossed the room and looked at her hard. "So, I'll bet you a Rolls-Royce pickup truck that she'll be yelling for help before next Christmas. And six months after that, she'll be needing more income because Prince Charming will be pissing it down the drain faster than the treasury can print it." Howdy leveled a finger inches from her nose. "Mind my words. Everything I'm telling you is going to happen. It's not that I don't want her to be happy. I sure as hell do. But for God's sake, how much is a now-and-then piece of tail and a stream of charming horse shit worth?"

Jennifer eyed him coldly and deflected the offending finger. "I don't know about Mother, darling. But you ought to know what they're worth to me. And you're not even charming."

18 In March there were rumors in the press that the ranch was going to ask the county to place several thousand more acres of prime development land in the agricultural preserve. It was enough to make militant members of surrounding school boards bring great pressure on county supervisors to rescind the law that protected the preserves.

Howdy knew that some fears could be allayed by publicizing the fact that thirty million dollars would be spent in the county on labor and materials. But that was a drop in the bucket compared with the astronomical figures the aerospace industry tossed around. The county, in fact the entire state, was too dependent on Federal contracts for moon shots, satellites, and supersonic transports. California history might well be repeating a disastrous pattern. In the pastoral days, too much dependence on a single activity had cost Mexico all of Alta California.

Now, out of a total manufacturing labor force of one hundred and thirty thousand persons, fifty-seven percent of the workers were employed in aerospace or related industries. With more than fifty percent of the county's work force in one industry, Howdy had asked Ev Moses, "Who in hell can predict what will happen in a recession?" He knew it worried Ev, too, that savings and loan outfits were multiplying like rabbits.

Dr. Carl Werner of OMNISPACE had said, only half facetiously, "Don't worry too much about instability in the aerospace program, Mr. Goodwyn. We are the ultimate show business, the science that has made honest men out of Flash Gordon and Buck Rogers. We do not add to the gross national product in obvious ways; but we make our contribution in the one thing man cannot live without, high adventure and dreams of a great tomorrow. We will never be taken for granted."

Ev Moses, who had been present at the meeting, had scarcely waited for the outer door to close behind the brilliant scientist. "I'd say the good doctor knows more about elliptical orbits and propellants than human nature. There are only three things man does not take for granted—health, sex, and money."

Howdy recalled how he had started at the words. They were an almost exact paraphrase of Al Phelps' credo of thirty years earlier. The words had been worth remembering. In his own father's time it was taken for granted that the foundation of the nation's wealth was agriculture, the horse-sensical, grass roots society that set the political balance. And now, in his own time, he reflected unhappily, college boys only lately farm boys were banding together as a new generation of suburban householders to vote some of the nation's richest and most productive agricultural land out of existence to make room for what Lloyd Wilson called, "the Great Rubber-Stampede to Suburbia."

Perhaps rape was inevitable, Howdy conceded, but he'd be damned if he'd relax and enjoy it. He'd hold out at Los Nidos as long as possible, then turn pro and charge the bastards an arm and a leg for the privilege of overrunning the ranch's best land.

Alone in the Bell helicopter, Howdy cruised aimlessly over the ranch's vast acreage for the better part of an hour. Avoiding the subdivisions and schools, he dropped down to five hundred feet over the fields where men, recognizing the familiar red and white craft, signaled casual greetings.

Climbing, he inspected the firebreaks that the forestry crews had hacked out some years before. Lloyd Wilson hated those firebreaks. "They help," he had admitted, "but they're liabilities when we get flooding rains. They give up enough mud to start a small avalanche. When that's combined with the debris from the burned areas, you've got an incipient disaster. Fifty percent of the water we import to urban areas is returned as raw sewage and better than half of that can be processed. Billions of gallons a year. We should be pumping it up to irrigate new forests."

Lloyd had his chance to prove his theory now, with MICROPOLIS 2000. If it worked, even the Federal government might see that it was cheaper to prevent the fires than to fight them and lose thousands of acres of watershed each summer. Last summer, Southern California had been lucky. Only twenty-three thousand acres had been lost to fire in three counties. But this was a dry winter. The worst could still be in the offing.

On the way back to the hangar, Howdy dropped down again to inspect new acreage being set out in Valencia oranges. He spotted a parked bright green Jeepster. That would be his new superintendent, Carlos Morales.

Thinking about the progress Carlos had made gave Howdy a deep sense of satisfaction. The Mexican American was a third generation Los Nidos employee whose first language had been Spanish. He had gone to school and then on to the University of California at Davis. Later he had taken post-graduate work in viniculture and citrus growing at Redlands. There was no more promising young employee on the ranch. Howdy recalled that it had been Morales' suggestion to teach the ranch's Mexican-American workers English and to pay them a bonus for proficiency in the second language.

Quite logically, Morales had followed up with a suggestion that non-Mexican foremen and superintendents be taught Spanish and urged to learn the language with the same bonus incentive. As a result, communications had improved dramatically and with them had come a corresponding rise in productivity.

Howdy wondered if Cesar Chavez would do half as much for those workers who bought the crap being dished out by his United Farm Workers Organizing Committee. Howdy had been grimly amused by a quietly derisive remark Morales had made: "Those initials read backward spell COWFU. And that's what Chavez is peddling, all right!"

The thought of Chavez and the havoc his organizers could raise by making Los Nidos an undeserving example made Howdy curse aloud. "The blackmailing sons-of-bitches!" As he headed toward the hangar, he silently reaffirmed Lew Berwin's logic: The only solution would be a strong bi-partisan agricultural team in the senate. New laws were needed. Agriculture had no protection against labor.

It was bright twilight when Howdy returned to the house a few minutes past seven. Jennifer met him at the door with a drink. "How's the Sky Spy?"

He took the glass and gave her a peck on the nose. "I

wasn't snooping. I was trying to get far enough from the battle to see what I'm fighting."

Jennifer let him settle down before she spoke again. "I've got ginger-peachy news for you, darling."

"What's that?"

"Mother called today. When Rob finishes handling the remodeling of the town houses he wants to come out and help us with M-Two."

Howdy gave her a searching look. "He can help me by staying right the hell where he is, three thousand miles from here."

"He's serious."

"So am I."

"Mother said he wants to help arrange financing in New York. She says he has good contacts there."

"So do we." After a moment he looked up, questioning. "What did you tell her?"

"I said I'd talk to you and I said to tell Rob that you're grateful for the offer."

"I'm not. I want him to keep his effing nose out of M-Two. And I sure as hell don't want him yakking about it around Wall Street, or wherever his alleged connections are."

"Actually, Howdy, Mother says he's had as much finance background as Dad had. I didn't know that."

Thoroughly annoyed, Howdy arose abruptly. "I don't give a Goddamn if he was personal adviser to J. P. Morgan and Andrew Mellon. I don't want that fucking widow lover meddling in our business."

On the verge of anger, Jennifer got up to face him. "Really, Howdy. You don't have to like the man, but we can be civil to him for Mother's sake. That's all I'm thinking about, really. It's very important to her self-respect to feel that Rob is making some sort of a contribution."

"He is making a contribution by keeping Catherine happy, horizontally, vertically, any old way. That's all he's cut out for."

"Howdy! What went wrong today?"

Howdy swung the ice in the drink and took a swallow. "Nothing went wrong today, until now. In some areas I'll put up with him for your mother's sake. But you both better know that I'll go back to strumming a guitar and selling Peruny before I'll let him get mixed up in management or finance and I'm saying that knowing full well that you and your mother can outvote me and vote me out."

Suddenly very upset, Jennifer set her brandy glass down hard. "Shit, Howdy. Don't play showdown with me. I'm your loving wife, remember? I'm with you. And don't make the poor man into a monster. At least pretend to consider his offer, for Mom's sake. It'll make things a hell of a lot easier all around. She said Rob's been studying M-Two. He thinks it's the most exciting thing he's seen since—"

"Since your mother's checkbook?"

"Goddammit, Howdy, stop it. He thinks it's the most exciting new living concept he's ever heard of and he's been working on a financing plan that may save the company several millions in interest. He wants to talk to you about it."

For the first time in a long while, Jennifer saw the strange veil-like change in Howdy's eyes. Ignoring her words completely, he rose from the chair, set the unfinished bourbon on the side table, and looked off into the dining room where Rosita was setting the table for two. "Why only two? Where's the boy?"

Jennifer took her time replying. "He and Doug have something doing at school tonight. I told him he could have dinner at Doug's. Doug's father will drive him home about nine-thirty."

Dinner was eaten in uncharacteristic silence and Jennifer retired shortly after Howie came in. The boy sprawled with his father in the family room for a while watching a network special on the redwood forest controversy in northern California. When the commercials came on he excused himself and went off to his room. Neither father nor son was aware that the only exchange between them had been, "Hi, Dad."

"Hello, son!"

And, 'G'night, Dad."

"Good night, son."

It was enough for Howdy that his son was there with him for a while during the evening. Young Howie seemed to expect no more.

Early in May, Jennifer and Howdy received a letter from Catherine saying that she and Rob were flying out within the week. There had been a change in plans that they wished to discuss. Beyond that there was no hint. Speculation that had ranged from hopeful to the impossible ended at dinner on the night of their arrival, Catherine turned to Jennifer.

"I'm sure you will think that I've suddenly lost my mind, dear. But after Rob and I got into the bother of doing over those two brownstones it suddenly seemed like an unwise thing to do, particularly since Rob has really fallen in love with Southern California."

Jennifer shot an anxious glance at Howdy, whose impassive expression revealed nothing. "But Mother, I thought you had already bought the two buildings."

"When I wrote to you, dear, Rob planned to open the escrow the following week. There had been a very inexpensive option. But when we got the first estimates we felt it was the better part of wisdom to sacrifice the five thousand dollars rather than commit for a hundred times that. Actually, what we plan to do is keep the apartment at the hotel and look into building a little place out here. Both Rob and I love the solitude of Laberinta."

Jennifer looked at her mother in open disbelief. "But ever since I can remember, you have always said you could not abide canyon living. You said they made you feel penned in, that they were dark and dangerous."

Smiling tolerantly, Catherine placed her napkin beside her plate. "Dear, that was before I found out how dangerous the city has become. Rob and I are agreed on that."

Still unable to accept the change, Jennifer persisted. "Even so, mother, if you do want to live on the ranch again, even part of the year," she indicated the room, "this house is really yours. We should be the ones to find another place."

The thought seemed to horrify Catherine. "Indeed not. When you and Howard married I gave this place to you. There were no strings or reservations, Jennifer. If Rob and I decided this is a wise thing to do," she said as she turned to Howdy whose expression still revealed nothing, "after we've had everybody's counsel, then we shall do a modest place in the canyon. When Howie drove us up there last trip I was amazed at how beautiful it is. I'd forgotten, really. And we found an absolutely ideal place just below the old springs. Lovely old trees. Close to the stream." She turned to Howdy again. "Is there any reason why we should not do a little place up there, Howard?"

Howdy pushed back his chair and pondered briefly. "Nope. You can build there. If you're sure you want to. But I wouldn't put up anything too elaborate. And I sure as hell wouldn't pick a site too close to the creek."

Rob stirred uneasily. "Is there danger up there? From floods?"

Howdy nodded. "And fires. But you'd be all right with a little common-sense precaution. Since the burn-offs the stream gets pretty wild in the spring. Four cabins got washed away last year. They weren't ours. They were on the land Steve leased years ago. There are quite a few permanent people up in there now. If you and Catherine are really looking for solitude, you should know that the state stocks the stream and we allow fishermen in there from spring through the fall."

Sensing Rob's growing anxiety, Jennifer sought to reassure him. "Actually there are not all that many transients up where you two would be. And the regulars in the canyon love it and do a great deal to protect its natural beauty. They have their own private fire brigade and one of the men is a deputy fire warden for the county. I think there'd be little danger if you resist the temptation to build right on the stream like so many others do." Jennifer hoped she had sounded convincing and she silently upbraided Howdy for the subtle negativity that he had managed more by tone and manner than by words.

Later, in their bedroom, she chided him. "You were very clever, darling. You made Laberinta canyon sound like the setting for the apocalypse."

Howdy addressed the image of Jennifer reflected in the dressing table. "There are a lot of things I am. But there are a lot of things I am not and one of them is a hypocrite. I told you I don't want that son-of-a-bitch within three thousand miles of this ranch. And you'd better believe that I'm going to do everything I can to see that he's entertained elsewhere."

Jennifer turned on the flounced stool to face him. "Don't be a bastard. Mother has no family in the East anymore. Just a couple of distant cousins in Massachusetts. In spite of all of her talk I think she really feels this is home now. I mean California, the ranch." For a moment she studied him narrowly. "You know something? I'm beginning to think you're afraid of poor Rob."

Howdy came out of bed in one violent move. "You're

goddamned right I'm afraid of 'poor' Rob. I'm afraid of any poor blue blood with so little talent and pride that he'd rather play lapdog to a rich old lady than try for an honest living." He moved closer, shaking a finger in her face. "He may not be as bad as some. And that makes him even more dangerous to us. He may just have enough pride to feel that he's got to get involved in things here to justify the dough Catherine's lavishing on him. And all that can do is make my job twice as hard and cause a split in this family because sooner or later, if he starts fucking around with M-Two or anything else here, I'll kick his ass right off the place."

As angry as she was, the faint whiteness around Howdy's compressed lips warned Jennifer not to pursue the subject further for the time being. Cocking her head to one side, she eyed him critically. "Well, if that day ever comes, darling, I hope for Rob's sake that his 'ass' is better protected than yours is at the moment."

Suddenly aware that he was without pajamas, Howdy stalked back to the bed and pulled up the covers. Out of the corner of his eye, as he turned away from the light, he caught a glimpse of Jennifer back at the mirror again. He detected a touch of smugness in her amused smile. The picture of himself standing there shaking his finger under her nose in a towering bare-assed rage brought a reluctant smile to his face too. He'd handle Rob all right. And he'd do it without laying anything he valued on the line.

The site Catherine and Rob chose in Laberinta Canyon was in a clump of fine old sycamores well back from the stream. By early summer Lloyd Wilson Associates had completed preliminary plans for Casa Escondida, Hidden House, and the contracts for excavating and foundations had been let. In late September Catherine and Rob held a house warming. The cottage was large, rustic, made of stone and redwood and perfectly suited to its surroundings. Several days later young Howie remembered a number of ornate handcarved doors and panels that had been stored for years in one of the old adobe buildings near the ranch offices. When Rob and Catherine saw them they immediately arranged to have them cleaned up to replace the ones Wilson's architects had called for.

"Someone must have spent a fortune on these." Rob had been caressing the deeply stained oak *dibujos* the designs, primitive and unmistakably Mexican, that had been beautifully carved into the richly grained wood.

Catherine studied them, concentrating. "You know, I vaguely remember Steven's father referring to these once. But for the life of me I can't recall in what connection."

The architect's assistants, with some reluctance, had altered dimensions and two of the carved doors, used as a pair, were adapted for the front entrance. The entire job, not counting the token land lease, had cost seventy-eight thousand dollars.

Summer passed to fall. The days were occupied with furnishing, decorating, and landscaping. Several times Howie managed to coax Rob down to the beach for surfing lessons. But for the most part, he seemed intent on devoting as much time as possible to Catherine and Casa Escondida.

Howdy watched this devotion with distaste. "What a hell of a way for a guy to live. I'd rather haul garbage than be an old lady's kept man."

Jennifer winced but said nothing. One of the qualities that made Howard Goodwyn attractive was his independence, his insistence upon pulling more than his share of the load. He was rough, she admitted, often ruthless, frequently crude, and, lately, absorbed in ranch projects to the exclusion of all else, even politics. But for all of his neglect of family he was the most responsible man she had ever known.

Immediately after Labor Day, Catherine and Rob left for the East. After a look at the fall theater season, they would return to California for the holidays. Then they would go to Puerto Vallarta or Acapulco for a month or so. There had been some talk about possibly getting a place down there.

Lew and Myra Berwin flew down from San Francisco to spend New Year's Eve at Casa Grande. They drank, watched the New Year arrive in New York, danced to the Hi-Fi, toasted their own new year with champagne, finished off with stingers, and retired by one-thirty.

Jennifer had just gotten undressed when the silence was shattered by the flatulent flutter of a souped-up exhaust. A sports car skidded to a stop in the driveway, a door slammed, and a moment later she heard the car roar away down the hill. Howie let himself in the back door and went to the kitchen. Jennifer hesitated, then pulled on a robe and waited for him in the hallway. When he appeared, after several minutes, she could see that he was walking unsteadily. Her greeting startled him. A bit bleary, he stopped in his tracks and grinned at her stupidly.

"Hi, Mom. You still up?"

Jennifer folded her arms and inspected him deliberately.

"No. I'm sound asleep. And I'll give you three guesses. Where are you?"

Howie feigned injury. "What do you mean, 'where am I'?" He pointed to himself. "I'm home, before two o'clock, just like you and Dad said." He stood his ground defiantly as she came closer and sniffed.

"You smell funny. Have you had anything to drink?"

"Yeah, some milk." Jennifer reached out and unsnapped the formal tie that was dangling by one side of its clip.

"I can see that. It's dribbling down your chin. I mean did you kids fool around with any liquor?"

Howie pulled away and made an attempt at righteous indignation. "Wow! You're putting me on, Mom. I didn't drink a thing except punch at the club. They won't give us anything. You know that."

Jennifer frowned and sniffed again. "You smell funny just the same, kind of sicky sweet." Howie's face contorted with long-suffering innocence. "Well, cripes, Mom. We danced and ate a lot of stuff. I could smell like a lot of things."

"You do, baby." She turned him around and gave him an affectionate swat. "And you look plenty beat. Go shower and we'll talk in the morning." As he reached the bedroom door she called to him again. Howie stopped with an "Oh God, what now?" expression.

"Yeah, Mom?"

"Happy New Year, sweetie."

Lifting an arm wearily, he nodded. "Yeah, Happy New Year, Mom." In the doorway he paused again. "Mom."

"Yes?"

"Do grandma and Rob have anybody at the house?"

"No. Why?"

Howie shrugged. "I thought maybe Rob'd do something with me tomorrow. Like ride, maybe."

"Try him, darling. I'm sure he will. Good night, now."

In the master bedroom Jennifer climbed in beside

Howdy. "Your son came in looking a little goofy and smelling funny."

Howdy squinted at her sleepily. "When he stinks he's my son, huh?"

"I'm serious, Howdy. He's been drinking or something."

"Him and fifty million others." Grinning lasciviously, he moved his hand beneath the blanket until it came to rest on her bare stomach. Smoothing her skin lightly, he moved his nose inches from hers. "It's the 'or something' he's too young for." When Jennifer continued to regard him with a baleful stare his grin broadened. "Did anyone ever tell you you're beautiful?"

She shook her head. "Not when he's sober, no. And did anyone ever tell you that you get horny when you drink and you're a hell of a lot better when you don't?"

Howie appeared while they were having brunch in the patio beside the pool. He acknowledged the greetings perfunctorily and flopped down on a lounge chair. Jennifer turned to him, questioning.

"Didn't you see Rob, honey?"

"Yeah."

"Well?"

"He didn't want to do anything."

"Really? He should be feeling okay this morning. What's the trouble?"

Howie shrugged. "Don't know. He acted funny."

"You mean he wasn't his usual ebullient self?"

"He wasn't happy, if that's what you mean. He was down. Real down."

"Did you see your grandmother?"

"Yeah, for a second. She was down too. She didn't look very good."

"Oh?" Jennifer turned back to the chafing dish as Myra came up holding out Lew's plate for seconds.

"Trouble in paradise?"

A sharp look made Myra glance around furtively. "Sorry." She whispered the apology and continued in a barely audible voice. "I hope it had nothing to do with the way he was dancing with me last night. Your mother was watching him like a hawk."

Jennifer turned, perplexed. "For heaven's sake, what does that mean? I was there and reasonably alert, or so I thought."

550

"After the second dance your pretty blonde stepdaddy was 'ready Eddie.' "

Jennifer closed her eyes and groaned. "Oh, dear Jesus. Not *that* sick bit!"

Myra took the plate. "Pray for him, sweetie, not me. I didn't hang him up."

"I'm not inferring that you did. It's just beginning to happen, that's all. These March-November things never work out."

Myra arched a brow over a long green, knowing eye. "Especially not when March has a hard-on for somebody else. It's none of my business, but you and Howdy were batty to bring them out here."

After brunch Howdy turned to his son. "Your Uncle Lew and I are going to take the chopper and nose around. Care to come along?"

For a moment Howie thought it might be something to do. "No, Dad. I don't think so—I'll just goof off around here."

Howdy was visibly disappointed. "How about driving us down to the hangar?"

The boy brightened. "Hey! Cool! Call me on the short wave when you're coming back? I'll come get you, too."

Ten minutes later, at the hangar, Howdy repeated the usual caution. "Remember what I told you about driving?"

"Sure, stay on the ranch roads. Don't drive on the county roads until I get my learner's and be careful I don't flip it."

Howdy and Lew watched Howie wheel the jeep expertly around. Lew laughed sympathetically. "That's a horrible age to be. Remember?"

"I remember all right. I had to work my ass off. Back in Guymon in the late Twenties I didn't have time to wonder what I wanted to do. These kids have it too easy."

"Howdy, can I tell you something? It's the same with every generation. I remember Grandfather Sam giving me hell when I was Howie's age because I wanted to go out to Stinson Beach swimming on Sunday. He said Sunday was the start of the week and I should be learning the business."

Howdy smiled dryly. "The week never had a beginning or an end when I was a kid."

"For you, my friend, they still don't."

A half hour later Myra arrested a half-finished vodka and tonic inches from her lips and watched the helicopter rise from behind the trees and swing away to the west. "There go our men. Bless their throbbing middle-aged hearts."

Jennifer retrieved the brandy snifter. She and Myra had decided that what they needed was "a hair of the dog." "Howdy enjoys himself when Lew comes down."

Myra nodded. "Ditto for my guy. If you hadn't invited us, Lew would have dreamed up some excuse anyway. Those two have more fun than anybody with their grown-up games." She took a long swallow of her drink. "You know something, Jen? I think if I'd had my druthers I'd have asked God to fit me out with whiskers and a set of balls. How about you?"

Jennifer smiled pensively. "No. I like it this way."

"Sure you do. Why not? You're a part of the action around here. If I envy any female in the world, honey, I envy you."

"Why me?"

"Because you're on the inside." A note of sodden persistence had crept into Myra Berwin's voice. She regarded the empty glass petulantly and rose to refill it.

Jennifer took it from her. "Stay where you are, I'll fix it."

When Jennifer returned with the drink, Myra reached up eagerly. "Thanks, angel. You know something? I'm getting smashed again. Goody." She took a sip and approved it. "Now then, where the hell were we? Oh, yes. I remember. You're 'in' and I," she broke off and studied the glass, "and I'm nowhere."

Jennifer was in no mood for female confidences but Myra was determined. "It surprises you when I say I'm nowhere, doesn't it, Jen? I mean . . ." Myra gestured spastically and her cigarette flew from her fingers onto the glazed patio tile. She regarded it with unfocused eyes and shrugged. "To hell with it. Even if I am scared. Shitless."

"You? Scared? What on earth for?"

"Because Lew's reached the age where hard drivers like him begin to drop over."

Jennifer's first impulse was to reassure her, to say, "That's ridiculous. He's in wonderful shape." But she couldn't manage it.

Somehow it seemed to be tempting fate. A similar

552

vagrant worry had troubled her at times, usually after the death of one of Howdy's contemporaries. A distressing number of them were gone now. The most recent was Bronc Bronston, whom she had met while they were negotiating the sale of Rolling-O Productions to a television network. "But Myra, it could happen to any of us, an accident, anything." She pointed toward the lower fields. "Lately I worry about Howdy in the chopper."

Jennifer could see the glaze gathering in Myra's eyes, a moist alcoholic luminance not unlike the look of the imminent tears that had blurred her own vision in boarding-school days when her mother and father would come to say good-bye before they left for Europe There were times when Jennifer still could feel the tight lump of loneliness that had constricted her throat

The freshening breeze had begun to ruffle the surface of the pool. Myra shivered.

"How about going inside?" Jennifer asked.

Myra passed through the patio door a bit unsteadily. In the family room she perched precariously on a bar stool while Jennifer freshened their drinks. "Excuse me, doll. This isn't Mrs. Lewis Berwin's best day. As you can see. I am slightly fucked up on this first day of the new year of our Lord One Thousand Nine hundred and, screw it. I've had too many of them." She smirked at the glass. "Years. Not drinks."

Concerned, Jennifer suggested coffee. "No thanks, angel. I dont want the novacaine to wear off."

Usually Jennifer enjoyed her gabfests with Myra. Now she wished to God Howdy and Lew would come back.

Cautiously, Myra guided herself to Howdy's big chair at the side of the fireplace and collapsed into it. Several minutes passed in silence and then her mood seemed to change. "Baby, forgive me for crapping up the afternoon. Maybe I'd better go see a head-shrinker. I've made it all the way from Castoria to Serutan. I don't want to blow it now. I don't know what the hell's with me." She slumped cornerwise against the arm and the back of the chair. "Let's put it this way, if I don't have Lew, I don't have anything. His doctor told him to slow down and lose weight two years ago. He goes on a diet for two weeks. Then comes this bright idea that he can save California if he can promote Howdy. So now he's right back in the grind again, worse than ever. As sure as I'm here, I know

553

that he's not going to make it to the Social Security office. I just know it, honey." She lowered her head. "Up until a few years ago, we had a ball. Do you know when I started playing with colored crayons? When Lew began to speed up in the office and to slow down in the sack. We haven't had a real old-fashioned tooth-and-nail orgasm for two years. I used to love it when Lew would slide his 'Jolly Pink Giant' into me. I used to grab the hair on his shoulders, yell, 'Hallelujah,' and kick his galloping ass black and blue. For me, he was the greatest. And baby, I've known a few. Now, if we make it twice a month I have to work him like a Polak sausage stuffer. And half the time he leaves me hung higher than a hooker's douche bag." She broke off and raised both palms to her cheeks.

"Oh, Christ! There I go again. I'm sorry, Jen. I truly am. I had no intention of getting into this. I don't even know how it happened. It's just that I'm so—so—" She took her hands from her cheeks and held them out, appealing. "—so goddamned *lost*."

"Last night when Super-Jock tried to dry-fuck me on the dance floor, I almost got excited, for a second. Then I remembered what he is, a mother-grabbing he-whore. Is that what's going to happen to me when I'm a loaded widow? Next year? Five, ten years from now? All I know is, women who are over the hill have a lousy deal. Criminal."

Without warning, Myra leaped from the chair, drew her arm back and shattered her glass against the fireplace. Horrified at her own action, she stared open-mouthed at the debris, shot Jennifer a wild look, and fled from the room.

After dinner alone, Jennifer and Howdy retired to the family room. There Jennifer told Howdy about Myra's outburst. Slouched in his chair, Howdy listened with half-closed eyes. "Would you like to know what I think?"

Jennifer eyed him skeptically. "From the look on your face I'm not sure."

"I think she's setting up a real good alibi for a little screwing on the side."

Jennifer stared at him. "For God's sake, Howdy!"

"Don't brush it off too fast. Look at her track record. Do you think Myra trapped Lew with her beautiful brain?"

"Of course not. He wanted a stunning, sexy woman who wouldn't get under foot unless he asked her to. In return for that he's given her everything she ever wanted."

Howdy inclined his head in conditional agreement. "Could be. Except now that she's getting a little older maybe she feels she's not getting as many of Doctor Berwin's famous beef injections as she needs to convince herself that she's still a young swinger."

Jennifer concealed her surprise and her eyes narrowed to sapphire slits. "You're vicious, Howdy. Myra would rather cut off her head than cheat on Lew. She knows what she's got. And she truly loves him. She's told me so a dozen times. She'd do anything to make him happy."

Howdy's knowing grin was exasperating. "That's right. She'd do anything to make him happy and everything to convince herself she's not beginning to fall apart. Maybe I don't know much about women, but I know a hell of a lot about people. And the safest bet in the world is that under certain conditions they're going to behave mostly alike."

An outraged wail escaped Jennifer. "That is the vilest mess of mixed-up male reasoning I've ever heard. If you believe that crap then one of these days I expect you'll be having me trailed to make sure I'm not orgasming under some young stallion to prove I'm still good."

Howdy grinned broadly and deliberately lapsed into his old Southwestern drawl. "Not a chance. I figure to keep you squirming happily until I'm going on ninety. Then I'll just roll over with a smile on my face and check out. And since my last thoughts'll be about what a great lay you've been, I reckon the undertaker'll have a tough time getting the lid on the coffin."

"Oh God! How corny can you get?" But in spite of herself, Jennifer laughed and crossed to his chair, then slipped into his lap. For a time she wondered what he was thinking. After he had been a couple of hours with Lew, Jennifer felt pretty sure she'd be right on the first guess.

"Lew's hard to say 'no' to, isn't he?"

"Not really, if you want to."

"Oh? And here I've been feeling guilty about starting this idea." When Howdy did not respond she looked up at him curiously. "*I did* start it, you know."

"If it makes you feel guilty to believe that, go ahead."

She pushed away to look at him. "You always need that

555

damned 'edge' of yours, don't you? What are you so insecure about?"

"Nothing, if I don't make any stupid moves."

"You won't. You can't lose."

He eyed her sternly. "Don't *ever* say that! It's just plain inviting the stuff to hit the fan. Don't even think it."

"The power of positive thinking?"

"The weakness of being cocksure."

Jennifer nodded. "Where you're concerned, darling. I confess that's one of my weaknesses. I'm absolutely cocksure that if you really want to run for a Senate seat you'll make it. But even if you didn't win the primary, you couldn't lose."

"Why?"

"Because you'd have piled up enough support to make a deal for agriculture with the front runner."

Mildly surprised, Howdy studied Jennifer. "You've got things pretty well figured out, haven't you?"

"All but the most important thing."

"What's that?"

"Whether there'll be room for little old Jenny on the bandwagon."

During the long, deliberate silence Howdy watched Jennifer's uncertainty turn to hurt and then to defiance. His sudden laugh startled her and he reached out to draw her close again.

"Jen, I'm not going anywhere without you. You're my luck. Remember?"

Catherine and Rob returned from their Mexican vacation during the first week of February. The trip had been a huge success for Rob. Deeply tanned, he was filled with enthusiasm for the things his wife's money and his own vitality made possible. Catherine announced that they had put down an option on a house in the Mexican resort village. Howdy was barely able to conceal his disgust. Later he exploded to Jennifer.

"A twelve-hundred-a-month hotel apartment in New York, a seventy-thousand-plus house in the canyon, and now a sixty-five-thousand dollar shack in Acapulco. Christ on the cross! What next?"

"For heaven's sake, Howdy. What difference does it make? It's her money. She can afford it. And besides, you yourself said that you want him as far away from the ranch as possible."

Howdy turned on her and the flames crackling behind him in the huge family-room fireplace seemed to Jennifer to intensify his rage. "I do. God knows I do. But did you get a good look at your mother's face? Did you?"

"I hardly expect her to be a radiant bride at her age."

"Bride, hell. That's not what I'm talking about. I mean that look in her eyes that says she's just along for the ride, to pay the bills."

Jennifer gestured impatiently. "For God's sake, Howdy, who ever thought this was a love match? Least of all Mother. She's made a bargain she thinks she can live with, money for companionship. As long as she can live with it it's none of our business.

Howdy shook his head impatiently. "Look, Jen. It's not the dollars I'm thinking about. It's Catherine. The day is coming when she's going to be hurt a lot worse by the bargain she's made than by being lonely. Every time she writes a check she writes off some of her pride and self-respect. When that's all gone she'll still have money. Sure. But we're going to have a bitter old lady on our hands."

Suddenly grateful for a glimpse of an unexpected capacity for compassion in Howdy, Jennifer's eyes misted. "You're an incredible man. Just about the time I think I've got you all figured out at last, you take off the mask and show me still another man." Reaching up, she smoothed the graying hair at his left temple. "Gemini. I should have suspected that."

"You believe in that astrology junk if you want to. I'll just go along with human nature." He squeezed her shoulders. "Years ago, when you were a kid, I didn't understand Catherine. I thought she had all the warmth of a lemon popsicle. But after Steve was killed and I got to know her, I liked her a lot better. That's why I don't want to see her get kicked in the guts. For your sake, too."

Jennifer regarded him with wonder. "You're not twins. You're triplets!"

Howdy knew that when news of MICROPOLIS 2000 reached the labor union he could expect a strong reaction. He was not surprised when he learned that Luis Morales, chairman of the Regional Agricultural Workers Organizing Committee, appeared at the ranch. His cousin, Carlos

Morales, alerted Howdy. "Luis came by our house last night, Mr. Goodwyn. He was not at all subtle in his attempt to find out how much acreage would be taken out of agriculture production."

"What did you tell him?"

Carlos shrugged. "The truth, that I know nothing."

"Was there any union talk?" Howdy asked.

"Not in front of me. He knows how I feel about that for Los Nidos workers."

Howdy had never doubted that when the time came for a confrontation at Los Nidos it would be Luis Morales and his group who would make the first move, with Chavez backing. "Carlos, so you don't have to guess any more, no Class One land will be taken out of production for the M-Two Plan. Before your cousin gets our workers riled up and nervous, why don't you find a way for him to accidentally run into me?"

A knowing smile warmed Carlos' face. "I understand, Mr. Goodwyn."

Howdy left then for a leisurely walk through the packing house. Following the Valencias, Howdy watched the oranges drop through the rollers onto conveyors. There the ranch's force of Mexican-American women separated, graded, and boxed the fruit. They were a happy and contented lot. Most of them had husbands and children. Some had grown grandchildren who finished their schooling and were working on the ranch. Many of them were living rent-free in modern ranch cottages and receiving a good portion of their fresh food. They were good people making a good living under good conditions: the best in the country. But because human nature is so predictable, Howdy knew that many of them would listen to a Cesar Chavez and a Luis Morales and that a certain number would agree to go along with union demands. What they might get would actually amount to less than they were getting now, but there was no effective way to convince them of that.

Frustration and growing anger at what he conceived to be the injustice and plain stupidity of indiscriminate union demands filled Howdy as he drove through several miles of the ranch's citrus groves to the Casa Grande and lunch with Jennifer and Ev Moses.

Shortly before two o'clock the phone rang. Howdy took

the call in the family room. It was Carlos Morales, calling on the ranch's short-wave radiophone system.

"Mr. Goodwyn."

"Yes, Carlos?"

"I thought you'd like to know that the first two mobile home units have been trucked in for the new employee housing project. We'll be setting them on their pads this afternoon."

Howdy was mildly surprised that Carlos would trouble him at home about a fairly routine matter until he heard Carlos say, "I thought you'd be interested to know that my cousin is down here. I don't think he really believes this fancy housing is intended for field foremen and their families."

Howdy hesitated briefly. "I'll drop by. If Luis is still there maybe we can convince him. Thanks, Carlos." As he hung up Howdy smiled to himself and reaffirmed the wisdom of his choice for ranch superintendent. Behind the man's easy-going manner was a trained mind that missed nothing.

On the pretext of inspecting some experimental asparagus fields, Howdy circled around the housing to approach the project.

As he pulled into the area, he saw Carlos and his cousin standing by the excavation for one of the oversized septic tanks that would serve groups of four of the thousand-square-foot mobile homes. Carlos immediately excused himself and came over.

"I'm glad you happened by, Mr. Goodwyn." He indicated the first of the new units. "My wife got a look at the kitchens and bathrooms in these homes. She wants to know if we can trade the superintendent's house for one of them."

Silently Howdy blessed Carlos for scoring a telling point within earshot of his cousin.

"If we have any more trouble with the plumbing at Casa Grande, Carlos, we may put one of these up on the hill, too."

Turning to look over the area where twenty-five mobile homes would be installed in the first unit of the project, Howdy pretended to discover Luis Morales. Looking pleasantly surprised, he strode over and offered his hand. "Hello, Luis. I heard you were down visiting your family. Glad to see you." His arm swept the construction area, which included a community playground, a half-finished swimming pool, and two service buildings to house social rooms and laundromats. "Pretty fancy new housing, eh?"

Luis Morales smiled guardedly. "It will be a showplace all right."

The subtle inference that the ranch was constructing the model project as much for political advantage as for needed new housing was not lost on Howdy, but he betrayed none of the quick annoyance he felt. Instead, he smiled broadly. "I found out a long time ago in show business that the setting isn't the whole show. These houses are better, more livable, and about thirty percent cheaper than conventional construction of the same square footage." He pointed to a stack of components. "When they get the porches and lanais and carports hung on them, they'll equal any good tract house."

Luis Morales nodded. "At least they don't have the barracks look of a trailer park."

Howdy chuckled amiably. "They're for employees, not just ordinary people."

From Carlos, Luis Morales had already learned that there would be complete integration of Anglos and Mexican-Americans in the housing project. He had to conceal his overt approval of the plan, but privately he was delighted with it. He was seeing the sort of luxury quarters his own parents and grandparents dared not even dream about in their day. Howard Goodwyn was speaking the truth when he claimed that the housing represented an innovation, even for foremen. Nevertheless, he found it easy to convince himself that the ranch might have settled for inexpensive renovation of the present fifty-year-old cottages if the unions hadn't put increasing pressure on agribusiness. The pressure would be continued and increased.

Luis Morales was familiar with every detail of labor conditions on the ranch. Los Nidos would be the union's toughest organizing challenge. The old abuses were negligible. Living conditions, pay scales, and benefits were the best in the industry. This meant that excuses would have to be found, or situations created, that would justify organizing these workers. Los Nidos was the prime target in California's five-billion-dollar agribusiness. If it could be organized, all of the others would be forced to fall in line.

Luis' satisfaction at the progress he was seeing was lessened somewhat by the certain knowledge that when the confrontation came a lot of good workers on this ranch, including members of his own family, would be hurt. But that was part of the price. Time and time again he had told himself it had always been so in labor wars because it was the only way.

During the next week rumors about MICROPOLIS 2000 were so rampant that Howdy and Ev Moses were forced to hold a press conference. Lloyd Wilson and his associates gave the press the same exposure to the plans that he had given the Los Nidos owners. Afterwards, for a week, there was apparent press approval, even enthusiasm. Then the *La Playa Gazette* and the *Los Campos Journal,* the two widely read weeklies, published full-page editorials expressing grave concern. The changed point of view seemed inexplicable until Howdy learned that something called The Five Cities Committee had been formed to study the effect of MICROPOLIS 2000 on adjacent communities and take whatever legal action was indicated to avoid being "gobbled up by a new metropolitan monster."

Immediately, the local dailies and the regional editions of the Los Angeles papers began probing members of the Five Cities Committee. It didn't take long for the big papers and wire services to start interviewing local businessmen and city officials. Flattered and puffed with importance, some of them began issuing belligerent statements.

Howdy called a strategy meeting. Their PR men, Peter Daniels and Earl Hamlett, were there. He held up an advance copy of a statement by Mayor Howell for Ev, Jennifer, Lloyd Wilson, and others to see.

"I want you to listen to this. It'll give you a rough idea of what we're going to be up against."

GRAVE CONCERN EXPRESSED
OVER LOS NIDOS PROJECT

"Mayor Henry Howell of La Playa, recently elected chairman of the new Five Cities Committee, last night expressed fear over MICROPOLIS 2000, the huge city complex planned on more than fifty thousand of the Los Nidos Ranch Company's ninety thousand acres.

"Mayor Howell, said, 'As long as the friendly green giant in our backyards was content with his farming, we neighboring communities had little to fear from him and much to thank him for. But now that Howard Goodwyn seems determined to become the Howard Hughes of city building, we must reassess our positions.

"We do not quarrel with Mr. Goodwyn's contention that much good can come to our resorts from the influx of a half million people over the next two and a half decades. But we are disturbed by the very real possibility that many people attracted by the MICROPOLIS concept will come to look but will wish to settle in our long-established beach communities instead. The question arises—where will we put them within the confines of our present city limits? The answer is clear. We can't take many—unless we expand. The proposed boundaries of MICROPOLIS 2000 block inland annexation. That leaves only the coast, which is still in agriculture and grazing. Since it is potentially the most valuable commercial land they have they're not likely to let it go. It seems then that we may soon run the risk of becoming the fenced-in beach playground for a new city the size of Cincinnati or Denver or Atlanta."

Howdy flapped the clipping impatiently and tossed it aside. "Howell's just talking for the record. He's always been friendly. But he's going to start up some of the others."

Ev Moses smiled thinly. "I don't think we're going to have to play the card yet, but something tells me that open ocean-front acreage is going to come in very handy soon."

Jennifer, who had picked up the clipping, finished scanning it. "Oh, God, I suppose this means another battle with the Board of Supervisors?"

Howdy nodded. "And the County Planning Commission." He glanced over at Peter Daniels. "Two of the five supervisors are friendly but that fellow Evans was on the fence until the last minute with the preserve decision. Do we know where he stands now?"

The public-relations expert weighed his answer. "No. But we helped his campaign, quietly."

Howdy draped a leg over the chair arm. "Yeah, so quietly he might not've known who the money really came from."

Dousing his cigarette, Daniels looked around the table innocently. "If necessary we can find a way to whisper in his ear. But if we're going to have a fight the best thing to do is to start getting public opinion on our side."

It amused Howdy that the public relations and political patterns always seemed to be so similar. Daniels was suggesting the same strategy that Lew Berwin wanted to employ to fight agriculture's battle politically. "Okay. What I want one week from today is a preliminary plan of action on three fronts. I want an approach from Hamlett and Daniels on the best way to secure county planning approval, the best way to keep the Five Cities Committee from pushing the panic button, and the best way, on a long-term basis, to sell the taxpayers on the idea that M-Two will be good for their health and their pocketbooks."

Hamlett and Daniels struggled to conceal their chagrin. The problem Howard Goodwyn had just handed them was all but impossible to solve in so short a time. Hamlett, the elder of the partners, mentally canceled a long-planned weekend trip and resigned himself to a succession of eighteen-hour days.

The general discussion of alternatives continued for over an hour. No one present felt any real optimism. Jennifer and especially Ev Moses were aware of the flaws in the argument that new homes would provide more tax income for both county and state than the revenue received from agribusiness. Former governor Pat Brown had proved it simply was not true. But nobody had listened when he showed that taxes from farm income actually underwrote the cost of providing community services to lower-income housing. It cost an average of up to fifteen thousand dollars a family. Only homes at thirty-five thousand dollars and above paid their way. If urban sprawl overran the few remaining ranches in the county, the local government would go bankrupt trying to provide basic living amenities. The alternative would be to hike property taxes still more. The preserves had been a last ditch stand against the politicians who wanted to hold the line for urban home-owners by taxing the ranches out of existence. Supervisors who could get away with that could also be assured of a lot of sympathetic new voters in their districts. They won both ways, temporarily.

At the Casa Grande following the meeting, Howdy

paced the family room clutching a drink. Worried, Jennifer, perched uneasily on a bar stool, watching him. Seldom had she seen him so preoccupied.

"Howdy."

"What?"

"You always say 'fight the ones we can win and negotiate the ones we may lose.' It seems to me that's what we have to do."

"Yes, ma'am. But first we've got to figure out which ones we can win."

Disgustedly, Howdy switched on TV. NBC's meteorologist, Gordon Wier, appeared on the screen. Jennifer referred to him as "Weeping Wier, the Voice with a Tear." Wier announced that a new storm front was approaching from the Gulf of Alaska. Behind that was still another front that promised to supplement the rainfall that had begun shortly after the new year and had scarcely let up since. Howdy turned off the set and Jennifer grimaced. "If you don't like that forecast, darling, why don't you try Bill Keane on CBS? Maybe he's got better weather."

Howdy rebuked her with a glance. "Any weather's better than this. Dust clouds or rain clouds and nothing in between."

Jennifer did not discount the graveness of the problem. "Rita Morales came by today to show me that new Montel rug hooking needle she's been raving about. She said that Carlos is worried about the run-off from the national forest burn area above Laberinta."

"He should be. There's twenty-five thousand acres of ashes and not a damned stick of new growth."

"I know. Are the creeks up?"

"Some."

"What about Claro?"

"It's okay. But all the springs are running again for the first time in a couple of years. That means the moisture on top has gone in real fast, like a sponge."

"Were you up there before the meeting today?" Jennifer asked.

"Yeah."

"Did you stop at Mother's?"

"For a minute."

"Was everything all right?"

A humorless grin twisted Howdy's mouth. "Rob's pacing

around like a caged cat. He's a sun boy. He sure doesn't like this."

"Who does? Mother's got cabin fever, too. I called her to see what night they'd like to come down for dinner and she sounded as though she couldn't wait to take off."

"That's a hell of an idea. Why don't you talk them into trying Hawaii, too? We're going to start dozer crews clearing the flood channel. About the time they crank up under her window at seven in the morning, we'll all catch hell."

"When are they going to start?"

"Monday."

"That soon? We'd better have them down for dinner tomorrow night and sell them on an island trip. She hasn't been there and there's a lot more for her to do than at a ski lodge."

"You had enough of their glooms too?"

A bit stiff-necked, Jennifer paused midway to the bar. "You know damned well I'm not thinking of us. That marriage is only going to work as long as they keep up the happy playtime bit." She continued to the bar and leaned against it wearily. "I wish to God I'd talked Mom out of building the house. They should have taken a condominium down on the bay. If either of them ever really stops to think, the whole deal is going to fall apart." Howdy's mirthless chuckle deepened her frown. "What was that about?"

"That? That was about the truest thing you've ever said. Incidentally, where's Howie? Isn't he going to have dinner with us?"

"No. I told him he could stay out. They're having some kind of a special get-together tonight at the teacher's house."

"Oh? Where does this teacher live?"

The question reminded Jennifer that Howie had not said where. All he had volunteered was, "It's just a thing, Mom, at Mr. Smith's house."

She thought Alan Smith taught social science and knew that the kids thought he was groovy and that he lived at the beach. Beyond that she was hazy. The realization brought a twinge of guilt.

Before she could answer Howdy's first question, he interjected another. "I suppose Doug Connolly's with him?"

"Yes." Jennifer paused. She knew Howdy's chief concern was young Connolly's driving. "They're at the beach someplace. He promised to be home by midnight. Doug's got his license now and he'll drive Howie home. I said he could stay out on Fridays and Saturdays if his homework was done."

Howdy seemed satisfied. He set his glass aside as Rosita appeared to announce dinner.

Young Doug Connolly racked his MGB-GT into the yellow loading zone in front of the Beady Eye, the most garish of La Playa's several hippie shops. Howie swung the right-hand door open cautiously to clear the high curb. Huddled in the doorway were a half dozen soggy young people in the weird, improvised costumes that, with their long hair, beards and trappings, had become the *sine qua non* of their sub-society. Doug, who knew them all, scrunched down to greet God's Mother, a lummoxy, barefooted, immense-bosomed young woman of uncertain age. Her gross body was swathed in a triple sari of purple cotton. A nondescript undergarment was girdled by a tarnished golden drapery cord from whose ends dangled clusters of small brass elephant bells. Chicklet was there too, her stringy silver blonde hair hanging in tatters like the shredded remnants of a cheap bridal veil. She was sixteen, an Army brat whose tissue-thin blouse and plaster-snug Levis left no contour of her child-woman's body unrevealed. Her dead-white complexion had a bluish cast from the cold and from two bad trips on Syndicate acid. Doug had told Howie that the "bad shit" had nearly killed her the last time when God's Mother administered thorazine to bring her down. She had been strung out for two weeks. The dealer who had copped three grams in Tijuana and sold the caps all along the coast had managed a tengrand burn before the good people wised up. At the Beady Eye the word was around that some of the faithful had let a contract on him. But the narcos nailed him in San Diego and probably saved his skin.

Howie, not as fluent in hippie jargon as Doug, misunderstood. He thought "contract" referred to the Mafia. His apprehension had brought a derisive laugh.

"No, man! They wouldn't do anything merciful like shoot him. They'd just stash him in a pad and make him drop a dozen mikes of his own poison. That's enough to zonk him for six months. He'd come down a slobbering freak."

Doug had been smoking pot on weekends for over a year but had never dropped acid. "I would if I could be sure of the dealer. But Capso says there's not very much righteous stuff around anymore. I don't want to blow my mind so I don't drop. But I dig a good grass high. Like, wow! It's a groovy trip, especially with a chick. If I ever do get some good acid, like Big-O, I'm going to drop it with a chick who'll ball. I've listened to the guys rapping. They say it's freaky. You blow nothing but screamers."

Howie had been in the Beady Eye only once before and it had been fun, cool. Everybody had been friendly. Like Doug said, you could feel love. Even the Hairy Gross Dinger, in the greasy Tibetan yak jacket that made him look like a cross between Big Foot and a petroglyph from a French cave, had been real loving. His thing was scaring the dung out of tourists with an overwhelming brotherly love bit. "I'm a living lesson, Gold Kid," he had said to Howie. "I'm proof incarnate that horrible can be beautiful."

The hirsute monster had given Howie the name "Gold Kid." It had stuck. Howie was not certain that it had been intended as a compliment, but it made him feel he belonged. "Pot's all right, maybe better than liquor or beer," he had told Doug after the New Year's party. "But it doesn't stoke me like shooting a tube or body surfing at the wedge. Wow! That's something else! You can ride a big one clear out of yourself. You're unhitched!"

Doug had disagreed. "Man, that's a bad scene. Escape is not good. You got to get *into* yourself. Not out—that's what grass does and hash and acid. Speed too, if you geeze it right. You climb inside yourself and walk around in your own brains, like in *The Fantastic Voyage*."

Howie had scoffed at the idea. "How do you know all this? You talk like a real head, or whatever you call those freaky characters."

"Who said I knew it from doing it? Alan told us. We rapped all night Friday. Man, he's a brain. He'll shock you maybe. But he's turned on like a big light. That's why I want you to come."

"Be any chicks there?"

"Sure. But different ones. Nobody from school."

So, he was going to make that scene now. No passing

roaches around on back roads. Howie eased into the sports car with the roll of psychedelic posters Swazy had given him. Swazy ran the Beady Eye. His wife Newfy helped. Newfy had freaked out on magic mushrooms. They took her to the community hospital and when she was let loose the good ones at the Beady Eye passed a sack and paid the bill. The young doctor never sent his. Two months later he delivered the baby boy. They passed the bag again and made him take the money. Swazy had cracked up when the doctor was surprised that hippies had money. He didn't know that one gram of LSD would split into four thousand one-mike caps that retailed at from one to three bucks a dose. There was money all right. Doug's father was an officer in the bank where the Beady Eye kept its commercial account. It was always good for a solid five figures. Howie remembered that he himself had seen one hippie cash a seven-hundred-dollar postal money order from back home. The guy had said it was his monthly allowance. Lots of kids got money from home. Howie wondered aloud why kids from good homes wanted to do the Haight-Ashbury thing, flop in crash pads, and live worse than animals. Doug looked at him amazed.

"When you're turned on, man, you don't care about material comforts and stuff. Rapping and tripping and getting punked and making out—that's real. All the material stuff is for hang-ups. That's the matter with your folks and mine. Their values are unreal, man."

Alan Smith's canyon house was in La Playa set back from the highway by a hundred yards or so. It was an old bungalow with an air of shabby respectability. A cement-lined storm ditch ran in front of the house, necessitating access by a small bridge.

It was the first time Howie had been to the "Peda-gogues' Pad." Alan Smith, an academic type who affected owlish glasses, long hair, and wedged "chops" met them at the door with a great show of pleasure. Doug had been there several times but his allusions to the strange rites conducted in the pad struck Howie as being exaggerated, if not pure fiction. As soon as they were in the house, Doug made for a nearby staircase, leaving him alone with Alan.

"Take a look around, Howie. Then we'll go upstairs and meet the people. How do you like the vibes so far?"

Howie squinted to accommodate his eyes to the dim light. "Groovy! Real neat."

"It's a real super power house, a natural accumulator. Do you know about the orgone force, Howie?"

Howie looked at him blankly. "No."

Alan put an arm around his shoulders and laughed sympathetically. "Don't let that bother you, friend. If you dig what we do here, you'll learn. You'll learn fast. Doug says you're sharp, right on about most things that have to do with nature."

As he talked, Alan steered Howie inside. The transition was a shock. Howie could see into a forty-foot room with a fireplace that had been converted into a shrine. Above the mantel was a poster depicting the Hindu Trimutri of the Three-in-one God with Brahma, the Creator, as the central figure. Soft Indian music was coming from concealed speakers and the air was suffused with sandalwood incense.

Alan moved toward the stairs. "Come on up. I want you to meet some turned-on friends." He stopped at the top in front of a curtained doorway. "I don't think you'll know these friends, Howie. But they know you. Accept that. The fact that we're all here means that we have all known each other in other times, in other worlds."

The back of Howie's neck prickled and a strange excitement filled him. Alan reached to pull the drape aside. "Any light from the outside disturbs our meditation. It's part of our self-awareness discipline. So we've draped all of the windows with black sateen. We wish we could keep out all the noise too but the highway's too close."

The room, almost totally dark to unaccustomed eyes, was not much smaller than the one downstairs but Howie sensed the difference in feeling. The walls were completely covered with psychedelic posters, similar to the ones Doug had brought. Some were animated by special black lights with slowly revolving shutters. A low crescent-shaped table was in the center of the room, whose floor was entirely covered with thick black cotton shag. Howie could make out about a dozen persons seated around it on cushions. He saw Doug settling a cushion at the far end of the semicircle. No sound could be heard except the muted stereo, the gentle drubbing of rain, and the occasional frying of speeding tires on the wet canyon pavement.

As Alan Smith led Howie to the open end of the low table, the tiny lights dimmed out, leaving the room in total darkness. He felt the teacher move behind him.

"When the light comes on say, 'My name is Howie. I love you.' "

An instant later a small red spotlight illuminated his face and he found himself repeating the words. The spot snapped off and a flashlight beam shone on the face of a pretty Negro girl. She smiled, a wonderful, open smile.

"My name is Lorna. I love you, Howie."

The beam glided to the next face, a young man with a beard. "I'm Alex. I love you." Again and again the beam pinpointed the faces as each boy and girl said the words unself-consciously and with unaffected sincerity.

Finally, the spot snapped off and the tiny lights came up a bit. Alan was beside him, slipping a necklace of small beads over his head. He pointed to a vacant cushion between two girls and said, "Sit there, Howie, and know that I love you, too."

As he picked his way around the table, Howie wanted to ask how they could say they loved him when, aside from Doug Connolly and Alan, who knew him as a student, they didn't know a thing about him except his first name. He sat down and the girl on his right, Mala, took his hand in both of hers. They felt warm and strong.

"Slip off your shoes, Howie." She reached down to help. Cross-legged on the cushion, his Levi slims bound his knees. A girl named Jill on his other side, who sounded younger than Mala, leaned close and made a sympathetic little sound. "Next time wear something loose. You have to let your body be free. Do you surf?"

"Sure."

"Good. Then you know a lot about what we're learning already. You know about one kind of free." She reached up and pressed a cool palm to his cheek. "You have good vibes, Howie."

Mala heard and inclined her head toward him. "I could feel it when he came in." She let her temple rest against his. She smelled good. It was funny, he thought. She was warm and Jill was cool. But they both felt good, only in different ways. Around him the others were talking quietly while Alan arranged things on a taboret in the open end of the crescent-shaped table.

A match flared and Howie looked around. Alan Smith was applying the light to a squat brazier. Almost instantly, small varicolored flames leaped to life. Finger cymbals tinkled and Howie felt the girls reach for his hands. He clasped them and glanced around the semicircle. All were holding hands. Then the beginning of a strange chant, a *mantra*. Mala enunciated the unfamiliar words clearly in his ear, encouraging him to join in.

"*Hare Krishna, Hare Krishna, Krishna Krishna, Hare Hare, Hare Rama, Hare Rama, Rama Rama, Hare Hare* . . ." The words were half sung softly to a simple monotonous minor strain that quickly became hypnotic. Mala felt Howie relaxing and abandoning himself to the rhythm. She fondled his hand and moved closer.

". . . Hare Krishna Hare Krishna Krishna Krishna Hare Hare, Hare Rama, Hare Rama, Rama Rama, Hare Hare . . ."

After a quarter of an hour Howie was no longer aware of the beginning or ending of the *mantra*'s cycle. His sense of place had ceased to exist and in its place came an expanding sense of peace. He was no longer aware of Mala's hand or Jill's. They were part of a larger sensation. With eyes closed he seemed to be suspended in a velvety void. He was not even aware that the *mantra*'s rhythm had changed subtly when, by subjective assent, the group had begun to complete two full cycles in a single breath. Then the little cymbals were ringing again. The sound seemed to come from a great distance and the chant slowed down and began to fade.

He felt Mala's hand disengage and suddenly he realized that he was no longer holding Jill's. He could hear the rain again and, in the distance, tires were still frying on the wet pavement. Somewhere, down the canyon toward the beach, one siren was wailing and a second was sounding a steady "woop, woop, woop."

The flames were still flickering in the brazier and the air was heavy sweet with incense. The music had started again, louder, twangy, Oriental. Alan lifted his head and nodded. Zurin took an inlaid box from the table and passed it to Rick. It went along the line. When it got to Mala, Howie saw it was filled with joints of marijuana. She placed her lips against his ear in a half-caress that excited him and whispered, "Take one, love. It's Aggie." "Aggie," he knew, was Acaupulco Gold, the most righteous grass around. He took one and passed the box to Jill. A mo-

571

ment later a small aromatic candle was passed along. Aware that Mala was watching, he lit up casually.

Close beside him, Mala savored a long drag, exhaled with her eyes closed then lifted herself on her arms to free the cushion and reclined, facing Howie. He was surprised that she was such a large girl. And older, too.

He smothered a glowing cinder on his leg and resumed smoking. After several drags he began to feel it but it was different now. The first time it hadn't sent him any higher than a couple of beers would. The joint he'd smoked in Doug's car on New Year's Eve had done more. He'd gotten pretty zonked but not like now. This time he was going way out. He felt Mala snuggling her bare thighs against him. The feel of her made a freaky thing happen inside him. It went clear down to his crotch. Her voice jazzed him too.

"Alan told me how old you are, Howie. I still don't believe him. You're at least one thousand and sixteen, an old soul." She reached up and took his chin between long, warm fingers and turned his face toward hers. "I'm only one thousand and nineteen. At our age that's no difference at all." The way she looked at you was crazy, he thought. Real groovy.

"Even before I knew you I asked Alan to put us together."

The thing inside of him got worse, or better. When he squirmed uncomfortably, Mala smiled knowingly and pasted her body right up against him. She could turn you on by doing nothing. What a chick. She was not like some he had necked with until he had creamed his shorts from dry grinding. This chick was like the ones when he was dreaming. You felt them all over you until a come racked you numb and you didn't want it to quit. Mala was making him feel that way just being close and smiling and doing little things. And she was real, real, real.

Howie's body felt light. He tried to push himself upright, then dropped back giggling. Mala laughed softly and leaned over him. When she kissed his eyes he could feel the swell of her breasts on his neck and chin.

He had trouble with the joint. It was getting short. Mala had two roach clips fastened to the low neck of her shift. She took one and nipped it on, close to his lips, and asked for the shell ash tray. He reached out but stopped halfway. Jill was half on top of Doug rubbing his bare belly down under his belt. He straightened to look past Mala. He wanted to see the others. It was too dark but he knew everybody was flaked out.

He exhaled the last drag. Mala held out the shell while he worked the scorched paper free of the roach. "What are you going to be?"

He shrugged. "I don't know. I'm only a sophomore in High now." Then he felt like going goofy again. He was very funny, very funny. "I'm going to be a surfing major. I'm going to open my own college of surfing." The image of himself in a gown and mortarboard hanging ten at Doho and San Clemente gave him the dry hysterics. Then Mala—her face was beautiful so close—put him down flat with his head on the cushion and the mood passed. He started to ache inside and her face above his made him want to cry and tell her he loved her but it was all mixed up, like he wanted *her* to hold *him*, tight, against her big soft jugs that were hanging half out most of the time. Anyway, they made his mouth feel funny. He wanted to suck and kiss her all over, everywhere. Everything was all crazy, wanting to be mothered, wanting to get lost inside of her and come, so the ache would stop. But he couldn't do anything and she was bending over him, holding his face between big, warm hands and she sounded like his Mom . . .

"Are you all right, Howie?" Only it wasn't his mother's voice. It was Mala's, soft like her skin and smooth like the inside of her leg against the back of his hand. Thinking about that made it worse and he tried to hold off but it started and he couldn't do anything but let it go and when it did he didn't want it to stop and he didn't care because Mala was whispering and doing something and there were other sounds. Voices but no words; everything was changing, even the music. It had a beat now, like knocking, and there were more voices coming from somewhere down below. Mala had stopped rubbing him and she was sitting up. Alan was up too, moving toward the door. Then the strobe lights went out and there were scurrying sounds and nobody was close to him anymore. People were moving in the dark, quiet and quick, and the rain was louder, and there were heavy feet on the stairs, coming up, and men's voices, coming nearer and calling.

Howdy played the pick-up's spotlight over the basin

spillway at the mouth of Ciega Canyon. The powerful beam couldn't penetrate the sheeting downpour by more than fifty feet. It was enough to tell Howdy that the men had to get the portable clam dredge there immediately. Mud and debris from the saturated, burned-off slopes was beginning to clog the overflow channels. In the basin itself the water, three feet above any previous mark, was threatening to spill over an earthen barrier that was never intended to be a conventional dam. Temporary barriers farther up the canyon had been breached the previous day. Boulder-strewn slurry had slithered down the slopes and demolished the man-made obstacles as though they had been built of sand.

Carlos Morales stepped out for a closer look. In a moment he was back. "It's not going to hold much longer, Mr. Goodwyn. It's beginning to cut through this end already. If you'll take me back, I'll get the boys to run the dredge over here right away. If we can pick up enough to take the pressure off maybe we can work the rig out on the fill far enough to clear the south spillway."

Howdy played the spotlight on the flood again. "Okay, Carlos, try it. But don't take any chances. I'd rather dynamite a channel on this end and lose some fields than risk lives."

Twice on the way back to the ranch headquarters Howdy switched on the spotlight to examine water damage to new orange groves. The run-off had been too heavy for the culverts. In several places the water had boiled out of the drainage ditches paralleling the roads. One such overflow had cut a three-foot-deep channel at least fifty feet wide diagonally through a new grove. Carlos cursed quietly.

"That one's cost us a hundred trees already!"

The zero-graded, terraced strawberry fields, undamaged as yet, were rain-pocked lakes. Below them an experimental field of asparagus had been half destroyed and the water was still spreading. Howdy tried to alert equipment foreman Ruiz on the short-wave radio in the truck but the frequencies were jammed with cross talk. When they arrived at headquarters they found Ruiz in the service yard refueling the equipment.

"We could use six of these buckets tonight, Mr. Goodwyn. We can't get the blades close enough to the trouble anywhere." Howdy nodded and pointed toward the smaller of the two canyons.

"Get the mouth of Ciega clear first if you can. I'll see if we can rent anything from the construction companies."

The private line to Casa Grande was ringing insistently as Howdy entered his office. It was Jennifer. "God! I thought I'd never reach you. Hal Halstead wants you to call him at the La Playa police station as soon as you can. He called an hour ago, at least."

"What the hell for?"

"I'm not sure, Howdy." Her voice was close to breaking. "It's something about Howie. Some trouble. Hal won't tell me what it is. He wants to talk to you. Please call him right now, darling. I'll hold on this line."

Howdy punched in an outside line before Jennifer had quite finished. "This is an emergency, operator. Howard Goodwyn calling. I want Lieutenant Halstead at the La Playa station." After a brief delay the police operator came on. "The Lieutenant's on another line, Mr. Goodwyn."

"Well, tell him I'm waiting. He's been trying to get me."

"Yes, sir."

Howdy heard the line click on hold. He had just seated himself on the corner of the desk when the office lights blacked out. There had been annoying, but not serious power failures during the early part of the storm. Transformers had blown and the sub-stations had switched to alternate circuits. For some reason now it was taking longer, he thought. He peered through the second-story window but no lights were visible anywhere. The line clicked then and a heavy voice, flat with fatigue, grated in the earpiece.

"Halstead speaking."

"Hal. This is Howdy Goodwyn, Jen says you've been calling me."

"Yeah, I sure have. I've got some rough news for you. We've got your boy in custody."

"For Christ's sake what for?" The words were close to a shout.

"He was picked up in the canyon, sort of by accident. Two of my boys went in to help the county road crew warn the people to be ready to evacuate. They stumbled into a pot party, two teachers, some guys and girls from State College, and your kid and the Connolly kid."

"What the hell were they doing there?" Even as he asked it, Howdy knew it was a damn fool question.

"They were lying around on mats smoking marijuana and doing a lot of other stuff. We got Smith and a guy named Zurin charged with possession and contributing. We're holding the others in protective custody."

Howdy could think of nothing to say. Hung between shock and anger, he blurted the classic defense. "Shit, Hal. Howie doesn't know his ass from his elbow about dope and things. He's not even sixteen."

Although Los Nidos Ranch was out of the La Playa jurisdiction, Lieutenant Halstead and his men were often grateful recipients of unsolicited favors from the ranch. They liked Jennifer and Howdy and the boy had never been in any trouble more serious than surfing on a restricted city beach an hour too early, a misdemeanor that in the department's opinion should never have been made part of the local law. The lieutenant couldn't bring himself to say that the kid had been so stoned they had to pick him off the deck, that his shirt had been up around his ears, that his pants had been open and that he'd shot a juicy teenage wad as big as a Frisbee.

"He got into bad company, Howdy. We've been watching this Smith character for a couple of months. We're pretty certain he's got some connection with this New Left trouble on the State campus. And we know damn well now that we've got him cold on possession of narcotics. He had two kilos stashed in his place, plus about twenty made-up joints. Jack Connolly's over here now with his kid. I wish you'd get over here, too."

Jennifer was on the phone with her mother when Howdy pulled the pickup in close to the front of the blacked out Casa Grande and ducked inside. A flashlight lit the phone table. Relieved, she motioned to him to wait as she tried to hasten an end to the conversation. "Mother, Howdy's just come in. I've got to go out with him for a while. Tell him about it while I get into my things." She broke off then and held out the instrument.

Howdy grabbed it impatiently. "Yes?"

"Oh, thank heavens. I'm so glad you're there, Howdy. Rob's worried about our being up here in this storm. We have no lights. We're using candles."

"Don't worry about it. They'll get the power on soon. You'll be okay where you are."

"I've told him. But he says a couple of cottages below us are in danger. The Barker place is undercut. He says one whole corner of the house is hanging over the stream."

Howdy was not surprised. He had little sympathy for the canyonites who courted disaster by building right on the banks of the Rio Claro. Most of them had been in Laberinta long enough to know that a prolonged storm could swell the stream enough to endanger them. But even the old-timers who had lost their places years before went right on taking chances. Catherine and Rob would be safe because they were back fifty yards at least and twenty feet above the river road on the inside of a bend. The water could erode the opposite bank but it would never get to them.

Howdy glanced toward the door where Jennifer stood pulling on her rain gear. "Catherine, what transportation do you have up there?"

"Just the little open Jeep. The Mercedes is at the dealer's getting serviced and Rob's car is still in the shop being fixed."

"Why don't you two drive down here? Maybe he'll feel safer."

Jennifer was holding the door, beckoning impatiently.

"I've got to go now, Catherine. You have a key. Come on down. We'll be back in about an hour."

"Where on earth do you two have to go on a night like this?"

Howdy tried to keep the annoyance from his voice. "The boy is stuck down at the beach. Jen and I are going to get him. I don't want him driving through the canyon tonight."

"I don't blame you. Go along. We'll be all right. I'll tell Rob you said we're perfectly safe here."

In the car, Howdy repeated his conversation with Halstead. Jennifer just sat there beside him saying nothing. He suspected that she too was indulging in self-recrimination. Suddenly it occurred to him that all those "where did we go wrong?" jokes on TV weren't so damned funny any more. Something had gone wrong. But for Jesus Christ's sake, what? he asked himself. He'd never gotten into mess-es when he was a kid and most of the time, nobody was looking after him either. And for sure, nobody'd handed him things on a platter—motor scooters, hundred-and-fifty-dollar surf-boards, a quarter horse, two of them, or anything else. What he'd gotten he'd slugged for, and that included his guitar. Sure, he'd gotten his nuts popped a dozen times by the time he was sixteen. By now, Howie had probably managed a few pieces of tail, too. Who in hell cared as long as he didn't get a dose or some babe in trouble? But dope? Christ. Kids smoking that stuff. What the hell's the matter with them? But Howie, Holy Jesus, being held for—what the hell did Hal say? Just being in a place where marijuana was found? If that's the only charge it probably wouldn't be too bad. Hell. Most likely the kid didn't know what he was getting into. The Connolly kid probably did. He was older. A smart ass.

Howdy speeded up the wipers and leaned forward. The rain had been coming down for hours. The third storm in ten days had put so much water in the side ditches that it was hard to see the edge of the pavement. Half aloud, Howdy wished to God they'd get around to widening the canyon road.

His thoughts returned to the Connolly kid. At eighteen, he couldn't cop out by saying he didn't know what was going on. He'd hate like hell to be in Doug's father's place. Jack Connolly was a wheel in the Rotary and Chamber of Commerce besides being a bank official.

Jennifer remained huddled in the corner of the front seat. It was funny, Howdy thought, but she looked so small. He had never seen her look so defenseless.

"Don't get all hacked, honey, until we find out what's really playing. It's probably not as bad as it sounds."

Curling her legs up on the seat she angled toward him. "It's probably worse. Remember New Year's Eve when Howie came in acting strange and smelling funny? I told you about it."

"Yeah."

"I know now what he was doing. He smelled of mari-juana."

"You don't know that for sure."

"I do know it for sure. He was stoned, glassy-eyed. I thought he was just pooped from all that spastic dancing they do. But I know now. He was high. And that little son-of-a-bitch, Doug, is the one who put him up to it."

"How do you know it wasn't that Smith guy?"

"Maybe so, but I've never trusted that Connolly boy. Howie's big for his age. He's always wanting to be taken for eighteen. He could pass for it easy. He'd probably go along with anything the older boys were doing, just to be part of the gang."

"Sure. Up to a point. But I still don't think he'd walk into a thing like this with his eyes open."

Jennifer snorted. "We're about to find out, aren't we?" She uncurled her legs and turned front again. "Oh Lordy, this is going to look just peachy dandy in the papers." Another thought struck her and she moaned. "And what about Myra and Lew?" She imitated Myra's effusively sincere manner. "You two have been such *wonderful* parents. Howie's one of the dearest, nicest kids we know.' "

"For God's sake, stop it, Jen! The boy didn't kill anybody. He hasn't knocked up some girl. He hasn't stole anything. All that's happened is that he got picked up, accidentally, in a place where marijuana was being used. That doesn't prove anything so far as he's concerned. They can't give him life for that."

"Oh, God, Howdy! Quit trying to make it sound like a parking ticket. Don't you realize that he's being held in a jail? Behind bars? He's been arrested. That means he's got a record."

"It mean no such damned thing! Howie's got no record until he's been convicted. And they're not going to convict a kid of mine on a dope charge if I have to turn the whole fucking state upside down. Bet on it."

When Howie was brought into Lieutenant Halstead's office, Jennifer broke into silent tears. The boy's appearance shocked Howdy, too, but quickly the feeling turned to outrage. Obviously, the kid was still high. His eyes were glazed, unfocused, and his face, usually tanned, was pallid and twisted in a sickly grin. When Jennifer saw the semen stain, she closed her eyes and turned away. Howdy stared at it with disgust.

"Hi, Mom. Hi, Dad." The greeting was mumbled with eyes downcast.

Lieutenant Halstead dismissed the officer who had brought him in and led Howie to a chair. Steadying him, he looked from one parent to the other.

"I could tell you that I'm sorry we caught him up there.

But I'm not. He tells me he's never been with this bunch before. But how do we know that he wouldn't have been hooked if he'd gotten away with it a few times? Of his own accord, I don't think he would." He indicated another part of the building. "But he was in pretty fast company tonight. Except for young Connolly, most of them are confirmed 'heads.' "

Howdy rested a hand on his son's shoulder. "Let me take him home now, Hal, and I promise you, as God is my witness, you'll never see him here again, for any reason."

"I'm sorry, Howdy. He's been booked. He's got to stay here. But we'll try to set a hearing for the first thing Monday morning."

"Monday?" The question was a cry as Jennifer came to her feet. "Hal, this is Friday. Do you mean he has to stay in jail until Monday?"

"There's nothing I can do about it now, Jennifer. It's rotten luck that a kid like Howie had to get picked up and booked on a narcotics offense the first time. But it's rotten that any of them have to be brought here, even on traffic violations." He glanced at Howie and shook his head. "Most of these kids come from good homes. They're not bums. That's why we try to make it as light as we can." He indicated the boy. "We had no choice but to allege 'under the influence.' Look at his eyes." Halstead indicated the boy's dilated pupils.

"I can't brush that off. He was caught in a place where narcotics were being used. More than that, we're certain Smith's on an acid trip. He must have dropped earlier. He's worse now than when we booked him."

Jennifer moved in front of the officer, her eyes moist and appealing.

"There's nothing I can do, Jen. My boys didn't know who he was. But it wouldn't have made any difference. We'd have brought in the chief's kid if we'd caught him."

Howdy released his son and put an arm around Jennifer. "Hal, look. Who do I have to call to get the boy released into my custody? What's it take? Reagan? Who'll hear this thing on Monday?"

"It'll be heard in Juvenile Hall, Howdy. I don't know who's sitting Monday. But it doesn't matter. There's not a damn thing we can do anyway. The boy is booked, just like the others. They're all in the same boat. Jack Connolly's been trying, too."

Jennifer slipped free of Howdy's arm and moved to Howie, who had dropped heavily onto a straightbacked chair. His head fell against her waist. "I'm sorry, Mom, Dad." The words were thick, barely audible. Unblinking, his eyes remained fixed on the floor. Jennifer cradled his face against her coat and her own tears coursed, unashamed.

Howdy turned away, his face whitened with suppressed rage. There was no edge now and he knew it. This was one of the few times he couldn't handle a situation. It irked him all the more that his inability was apparent to both his wife and son. He needed to get out now, away someplace where he could think. There was always an angle. But who in hell could figure one with Halstead standing looking like an acid indigestion ad and Jen clutching Howie, fighting to control her sobs and the kid staring at the floor with his mouth hanging open like some kind of a drooling idiot.

A few minutes before 11:00 P.M. the weather instruments on top of the 6000-foot Diablo Peak recorded an unusual increase in temperature. Two feet of new snow had fallen during the past forty-eight hours. Most of the ski resorts had been isolated for more than a week. Road crews were fighting drifts thirty feet deep. Earlier, helicopters had been able to evacuate several ill persons and drop emergency supplies to stranded motorists. But for three full days now they had been grounded.

The snow turned from feathery flakes into heavy, wet blobs. By 11:15 P.M. it was mixed with rain and the marginal packs had begun to decay at the edges. By 11:30 P.M. slanting rain was slicing into the slopes turning the surface into an emulsion of mud, ash, shale, and small twigs. Soon the fluid mass began separating into sluggish streams. As they moved down the slopes above Laberinta Canyon they began to gather small boulders and burned chaparral. The heavier material gave way and added its weight to the force sluicing down the ridges.

The light rattle of rubble deepened as the larger debris was carried down. By the time the mass draining into the upper end of the canyon had reached the cliffs beneath the old caves, it had become a roiling torrent thundering downward toward the rising headwaters of the Rio Claro.

Rob Williamston turned from the front windows of Casa Escondida. "For God's sake, Catherine, I'll never understand you Californians. In the midst of the most disaster-prone area on earth you refuse to take even the most elementary precautions."

The toe of his rubber-soled shoe caught the edge of the throw rug by the front door. He kicked at it viciously. "Even at Fire Island we had sense enough to keep a Coleman lantern handy during the hurricane season. But here?" He pointed scornfully at the candles flickering on the mantel. "Here we have to ransack old storage boxes to find three stinking penny candles."

Catherine, curbing a growing annoyance at the harangue that had been increasing with the storm's intensity, turned back to the fireplace and poked at the last of the logs. Rob crossed the room and stood behind her. "You wouldn't get out of here earlier when the rain let up. So now we're both going to be drenched in the wretched rattletrap Jeep. That's if I'm lucky enough to get it started. I want to get you out of here, Catherine. That miserable creek is beginning to look like the Johnstown Flood."

Still outwardly calm, she turned to him. "I've told you, Rob, the lights will come on any minute now. We often lose them during storms, but not for long. And you do not have to worry about the creek. We are well out of its way, even if it does go rampaging a bit."

"Well out of its way, indeed." He strode to the door and opened it. "Listen. It sounds like Niagara. It's changed just in the last hour." He pointed toward the black upper reaches of the canyon. "And I don't like the sound of things up there. The water is moving boulders the size of Volkswagens." He closed the door and glanced at his watch. The radio was dead without power and the electric clock had stopped nearly a half hour earlier at three minutes to midnight.

"I want us out of here now, Catherine, while we can still get out. If you're going to be stubborn about it then by God you can stay here alone."

Patience and self-possession were two of Catherine's acknowledged virtues. She prided herself on them. One did not give in to adversity and fear. But another's poor deportment might be vexing enough to try one's patience.

"I am not being stubborn, my dear. I am simply telling you that we shall remain safe so long as we stay here. The site for this house was chosen with great forethought. I have no doubt that some of those cottages along the stream will be in danger if this keeps up. But we shall be perfectly safe here. I resent the inference that we Californians left our common sense in the East when we migrated." She turned away from the petulant face that anxiety had robbed of the quality she had mistaken for strength. "Although I must say that you're beginning to make me wonder whether or not I brought mine along this time."

Rob's reaction was instantaneous. "What does *that* mean, precisely?"

"It means, dear Robbie, that I'm having some second thoughts about you in this environment. Your behavior these past several hours has not exactly been reassuring." She started to move away but he reached out and turned her back roughly.

Repressed indignation strictured his throat. "If it's reassurance you want, I wonder if you know just how fortunate you are to have a husband who is willing to commit himself to solitary confinement in this backwoods prison? And as to my behavior, it is the result of your own. I have no doubt about my judgment. I am not worried about this house. But I am worried about that buckled asphalt goat trail out there that you call a road. I suspect Jennifer was worried too when she told us to come down to Casa Grande. Now get your things and let's get out of this dead end before we die in it."

Catherine regarded her husband with exasperating detachment. "All right, Robbie. We shall prepare for another soaking. But I think you should know that this melodramatic behavior of yours forces me to some odious comparisons."

Rob's retort died on his lips as the headlights of a car raked the room and a horn began blowing insistently. He got to the door as an older man in bright yellow rain wear was preparing to knock.

"Mr. Williamston?"

"Yes?"

"We need help down the road. Two houses have washed away. There was a grandmother and a small child in the Schmidt place. Could you get somebody from the ranch to

583

help us? We need trucks with work lights. We've got nothing but flashlights and some kerosene lamps. The phone lines are down too. We can't raise anybody." At the door Catherine recognized Ed Simmons, one of the old-time canyonites. "Come in. Let me try our phone."

She hurried to the end of the long breakfast bar and picked up the instrument. It was dead. Standing in the doorway to keep from dripping on the carpet, Simmons pointed to the Jeep in the carport. "You got a Citizens Band radio there. It's a slim chance here in the canyon, but maybe we can raise somebody outside."

Bareheaded and belted in an expensive trenchcoat, Rob stood with Simmons and alternated at the microphone. There was no response. All they could hear was unintelligible "hash" from emergency crews communicating on the same frequencies several miles beyond the effective range of their transmitter.

Catherine joined them. She had changed into slacks, black hooded rainwear, and boots. Somewhere she had found a large umbrella. The Jeep's engine, the wind gusting up the canyon, the rain pelting the carport roof, and the roar of the Rio Claro made it difficult to be heard. She leaned close to Simmons and shouted.

"Will this be any help?" She was pointing to the small accessory light clamped to the Jeep's windshield. The man flipped the switch and elevated the reflector. The beam penetrated a scant twenty yards through the sheeting downpour.

"It's a lot better than nothing, Mrs. Williamston."

"Good. Let's go down and see if we can help. You go on down in your car and show us the way. We'll be right behind you." After hasty thanks the man hunched and ran to his old sedan. Rob stared at her.

"For God's sake, Catherine, you're not serious? It's one thing to run for Jennifer's place." He pointed toward the river. "But to go out on a fool's errand? Those people are dead by now if they were washed away. Risking more lives doesn't make any sense."

She started to reply but Simmons was shouting from his car. "Don't try to cross the bridge. I just made it. The far side is undercutting. Pull up alongside me. I'll shine my lights where I think they need them."

Catherine turned to wave but Rob grasped her arm. "I

584

tell you, we are not going to get involved in any rescue operations. Those people don't mean a thing to us."

The last vestige of patience gone, Catherine wrenched her arm free. "Shut up and drive this car down there. Those people may not mean anything to you, but as the undisputed queen of over-age damned fools they mean something to me." She slid over to the passenger side. "Now drive it or I will."

The force of the storm stunned them as they pulled clear of the carport. Windshield wipers were useless. His face a mask of repressed rage, Rob leaned out the left side to follow the tail lights of Simmons' old sedan, frustrated and furious at the water streaming into his eyes.

For a half mile the two vehicles crept along the tortuous canyon road. On the right, dangerously close, they could make out the churning torrent. Here and there, huge sycamore trees had crashed into the stream, forming dam-like obstacles that caught and held small debris. Behind them the waters had risen to within inches of the right of way. Rob was badly shaken by the sight. "This is a fool's mission. Nobody could live in that." Catherine didn't bother to reply.

Ahead, Ed Simmons stopped the old sedan, flashing a warning with the brakes. Then he activated the left-turn blinker and angled to the opposite side of the road. Following cautiously, Rob probed the right edge with the spotlight. The narrow beam shone on angry back-pressure waves whose crests rose above the level of the road. Catherine could feel the rising panic in Rob as he dropped the Jeep into gear and gunned past the place, almost overrunning Simmons' car. It was a foolish thing to do in the short-coupled vehicle. They had been lucky. But she kept silent. Safely past the danger spot, he allowed the other car to pull ahead again. Twigs snapped off by the force of the wind whipped down on them. Another large tree crashed nearby on the opposite bank. Simmons' brake lights flickered again. On the far side of the stream, a flashlight winked on, made frantic circular signals directing their attention to the wooden bridge that provided sole access to the cottages strung along a quarter mile reach of river. It had collapsed at the far end.

An involuntary cry escaped Catherine. "They're stranded completely! We couldn't help them if we wanted to."

Rob cursed the blinding downpour. "Good! Then let's

get out of here while we're still able." He started to put the Jeep in gear again, but Catherine forced his hand away. Her strength surprised him.

"We stay right here. They need our lights. Pull up along side of Mr. Simmons and shine ours across with his."

"Catherine, so help me God . . ."

She whirled on him. "So help *me*, Robert Williamston, if you try to leave here without doing what you can to help, you will have forfeited the last shred of respect I have for you."

Before he could recover she was out of the Jeep. Standing in the headlight beams she directed him to turn right and pull up to the edge of the torrent. For an instant he considered leaving her with Simmons and making a run down the canyon for help but he couldn't bring himself to do it. Using extreme caution, he inched the vehicle into place. Simmons had tied an old cloth around his neck to keep the water from draining inside his collar. With one hand holding the cloth in place, he signaled with the other and shouted. "Try the spotlight, Mr. Williamston."

Rob switched it on but it was hardly more effective than the head-lamps, but car lights on the opposite side flared and a man stepped into their beam and waved frantically, pointing downstream. Simmons played the spot along the crumbling opposite bank. It rested on the grotesquely tilted ruins of a summer cabin. The sound of shattering lumber reached them. Rob swung the light upstream again in time to catch a section of screen porch breaking away. As they watched, it cartwheeled into the torrent and disappeared. Simmons turned to them in open-mouthed amazement. "I've never seen it like this, in twenty-five years."

Catherine called in an anxious tone. "Where are your people, Mr. Simmons?" He pointed directly across the torrent.

"In a woodshed on high ground. They'll be all right." His arm swung downstream toward the wreckage of the other cottage. "But if old lady Schmidt and the child didn't get out I don't think there's any hope for them."

Rob, indicating the torrent, pushed Catherine aside, saying, "There's no hope for any of us unless we get out of here and get some help. It's ridiculous to stand here shining lights. You can get in or stay here but I'm going to try to get down to the ranch."

Simmons peered across the bank. The figure in the headlights was still making futile attempts to communicate. "I think he's right, Mrs. Williamston. I don't know's anybody can do anything tonight. But it would be comforting if somebody outside knew the fix we're in."

Once again, above the din came the sound of heavy wood splintering and a tangle of gnarled sycamore limbs laced solid with debris swept through the corridor of light from the two vehicles. It pushed over the bank and Rob shouted and gunned the jeep in reverse. Catherine and Simmons cried out as the vehicle shot backward across the pavement, slammed tail first into the muddy bank, and stalled. Catherine got to him first.

"What an idiotic thing to do! What an absolutely idiotic thing. You might have killed both of us."

Grim-faced, Rob ignored her and restarted the engine. Catherine climbed in beside him, struggling to regain her composure. "All right! I'm satisfied there's nothing we can do here. We'll go to the ranch and see if we can get help there."

Drenched to the skin, Rob glowered at her, then bowed elaborately. "Very good, Madam, at your service."

About a mile above the Casa Grande, the canyon widened. When they rounded the last looming shoulder of high canyon wall they could hear the roar of the water again, very close to the road. Puzzled, Rob slowed to a crawl and repositioned the spotlight. Its beam, more effective now, swept across the torrent. The main channel, usually thirty yards or more west of the road, had cut in much closer. As they inched along in low gear, they could see great slices of undercut banks collapsing.

They were out of the canyon proper now, but the road stayed with the stream. They knew this area well. At the point where the pavement angled toward the center of the delta-like expanse of gravel and boulders, Rob stopped. His humiliation forgotten for the moment, he turned to Catherine, "I don't like this. The channel looks like it's moved quite close to the road up ahead." With his left hand he swept the beam slowly back and forth.

Catherine leaned out the other side. "It seems all right for the next few yards." Rob looked uncertain, then eased out the clutch; but after a minute, he stopped again.

"If you want to drive, Catherine, I'll walk ahead. This is

treacherous along here. I can't tell how close the water has cut to the road."

She shook her head. "No, let me get out. I'm more familiar with this road than you." He made no effort to dissuade her as she climbed out and hurried forward into the headlight beams.

Twice he came to a stop when Catherine signaled to him. The rain had lessened to a light drizzle and to the west he could see the diffused glow of a large subdivision. Behind him he could make out the mouth of Laberinta Canyon, a gaping, dead black maw. A chill shook him and for the first time he was aware of the cold.

Catherine was cautioning him to keep well to the left of center. He swung the spotlight more to the right and its beam revealed a fifty-foot-wide torrent. Startled, he tried to attract Catherine's attention by shining the light on her. She turned and for an instant looked full into it. He saw her squint and raise a hand to block out the glare. Then she waved and started to walk again. He directed the beam to the right briefly, then returned it to the road. Catherine had vanished. Puzzled, he jammed the brakes and swept the spotlight back and forth. He was certain that she could not have moved beyond its range. He probed the road again but there was only darkness. Panicked, Rob bore down on the horn. When Catherine did not appear he leaped out of the Jeep and ran forward, shouting. A few yards beyond he let out a cry and stopped inches short of the caved-in pavement. A large segment of undermined asphalt had broken off and dropped ten feet into the flood. Running wildly around the break, he shouted Catherine's name over and over. Continuing his search, he sucked in great sobbing breaths, screaming her name. Half-crazed, he raced back to the Jeep and gunned it recklessly around the cave-in. Sweeping the crumbling banks of the swollen stream he drove back and forth, searching, listening, until he had covered every foot of the quarter-mile reach where the waters had cut closest to the road. Then, abandoning the vehicle, he searched the edge of the torrent on foot.

The emergency crew found him an hour after daybreak slumped on the crumbled bank unconscious and chilled blue. Out of gas, the Jeep stood with its battery dead, within inches of the washed-out segment. They did not look for Catherine then because there was no one to tell them until later, when they notified Howdy, that Robert Williamston III had not been alone.

19 IN THE OLD HOLLYWOOD OFFICES of H.G. Enterprises, expanded and redone several times during the past two decades, Howard Goodwyn sat slumped in his comfortable old executive chair. It had been the first symbol of his new affluence as a radio star and it remained unchanged, a haven for concentrating on particularly sticky situations. Ev Moses sat nearby leafing through a stapled sheaf of legal papers. The intercom buzzed discreetly and Howdy lifted the key. "Yes?"

"It's Ward Roberts of the *Probe Show* again, Mr. Goodwyn."

Howdy was plainly annoyed. "Tell him I'm out, that I'll call him back."

"Yes, sir."

Ev Moses flipped over a page and glanced up. "Still after you to do an interview?" When Howdy grunted affirmatively, Moses smiled. "I suppose they want to probe your political future. Isn't that what Roberts said?"

"The hell they do." Howdy aimed a finger at the papers. "The son-of-a-bitch wants to probe into that, into the mess with Howie." His lips twisted. "And if they ever try to, they're going to get a public kick right in the ever-loving *cojones!*" Deliberatly, he had lapsed into his Western Movie Star drawl. Moses tapped the sheets.

"Considering the possible consequences of a narcotics charge, this isn't too bad, Howdy, if the boy keeps his nose clean."

"He will, Ev. Bet on that. I must have been blind. I didn't know what a great kid I had until I saw him in jail. In jail, for God's sake. And I'm the one that probably put him there, because I fluffed the kid, always too goddamned busy." He looked up and his eyes mirrored the first deep pain he had known in some time. "Now ain't that one hell of a speech for a father to make?"

Howdy had given Ev Moses the court papers decreeing

Howie a ward of the court. Ev agreed to look them over even though he knew it was pointless. The legal process was automatic and, as Howdy had discovered, not subject to influence or pressure. Ev Moses knew it had been a disquieting revelation to Howdy to discover that personal power couldn't always be relied upon. He knew, too, what it meant to his partner to lose an edge. Howdy had lost an important one with his own boy. As a friend and counselor, Ev knew there was little he could do but try to comfort Howdy.

He handed back the sheaf. "Personally I think the court showed excellent judgment. Howie could have drawn thirty days in Juvenile Hall. That could be rough. But as a ward, he's on formal probation until he's eighteen. At that time, if he doesn't violate, the probation will be terminated. If he stays clean until he's twenty-one, they'll seal his record."

Howdy straightened. "That means no criminal record, right?"

"Exactly. His record is sealed. Legally, it doesn't exist any more. It can't be brought up and used against him, ever."

Relieved, Howdy relaxed and redraped his leg over the chair arm. The typical mannerism made Ev smile inwardly. It was a good sign, that leg dangling. So was the grin.

"Ev, old pal, even if I am fifty-six years old, you'll see Reagan selling soap again before you see that record being used against my kid."

"Never say never. By the way, how did the boy take the downfall of—you should excuse the expression—his fair-haired hero?"

"Williamston?" Howdy smiled a bit sadly. "It's a funny thing, Ev. The kid seems to want to take part of the blame for his grandmother's death. He said if he hadn't gotten into trouble he'd have taken one of the ranch trucks and a portable generator into Laberinta as soon as the power went out. I guess we'll never know what really happened. Anyway, Howie's turned cold as a well-digger's butt where that prick is concerned. He won't even talk about him."

The attorney snorted. "I'm still not so sure a criminal charge wouldn't have been sustained."

Howdy's face darkened. "I know. I know. Something

591

could have been made out of Ed Simmons' testimony. It was no secret that Catherine and Rob were squabbling toward the end. But as far as I'm concerned we're best out of it this way. Lew Berwin agrees too, because of the possible political thing. A trial could have been messy. A two-hundred-thousand-buck settlement and the house in Acapulco in lieu of any claims on her estate was a hell of a bargain. So he'll piss it down the drain playing in the sun then look for another old broad. Let him. All I care is that we've heard the last of the sonuvabitch."

Ev nodded and rose to go. At the door he paused with his hand on the knob. "What are you going to do about this political talk?"

Howdy shrugged. "I don't know yet. Why?"

"If Lew talks you into running it might be smart to remember that the opposition has some strong ammunition now, with the circumstances surrounding Catherine's death and with the narcotics thing. It could get pretty rough."

Howdy regarded his friend with a humorless smile. "That's the wrong way to scare me, Ev. Rough I don't mind, as long as I've got the odds on my side."

Ev nodded obliquely. "You're not the first public figure whose kid has been busted on a narcotics charge. It hasn't seemed to hurt them—politically, at least." He shrugged again. "Who knows? Everybody's got a skeleton in the closet, I guess. As far as odds are concerned, gambling's not my long suit. Talk to Lew about that."

Howdy grinned. "You gambled on me."

Ev nodded vigorously. "A gamble you weren't, Mr. Goodwyn. You were a sure thing."

After Ev left, Howdy locked the probation papers in his personal file and placed a call to Lew Berwin in San Francisco. Lew brought up the subject on Howdy's mind first. "Believe it or not, Howdy, I was working for you. I had some of the valley growers in. I wanted to find out what they think of the picture so far."

"What picture?"

"The political picture. Your chances. The whole *schmiere*."

"That's what I called you about, Lew. Ever since the thing with Catherine, and then the rotten business with the kid, I'm not so damned pure any more. Better think about that before you talk it up too much."

Lew's laugh boomed through the earpiece. "We have." To Howdy his tone sounded a bit too reassuring. If a man had no alternatives he could bring a lot of rationalization to bear on his choice. Howdy suspected Lew Berwin was doing just that.

"Lew."

"Yeah? What?"

"I'm serious. That business cost me a lot of edge."

"I'm serious, too. By the time you file, it will be forgotten. It won't mean a thing." His manner changed. "Look, Howdy, you're the man the boys want. We've talked it over, upside down, ass-end to, every which way. Nothing's going to change that."

"Maybe you're right, Lew. But Ev says they'll dig all the way back to Angie."

"Let them, for Christ's sake! It wasn't you they caught fucking the major. You were the righteous, injured husband. The cuckold. Ev's off base on that. I think he's special pleading. He doesn't want you to leave the ranch and dump all of that responsibility on him."

Howdy's eyes grew troubled. "That's part of my concern too, to tell you the truth."

There was a charged silence at the other end of the line.

"Howdy. Let me tell you the truth. If you, or somebody who's as effective as you, doesn't get in and fight this thing from the inside a hell of a lot of ranches are going to be in bad trouble. I'm asking you to think about Los Nidos, sure. But we're asking you to think about the whole picture. You don't have to make up your mind now. You've got months yet. Just think it over some more."

Howdy was seriously concerned about his chances and the effect recent events might have on them. He understood well the fickleness of California's electorate. The "Capricious Million" could not be counted on by either party. Nobody could say that they might not take it into their heads to elect S. I. Hayakawa, John Wayne or Sam Yorty as United States Senator. The only predictable thing about California's politics was its utter unpredictability.

Nobody who really understood what westward migration was doing to California's agribusiness believed that the status quo could be maintained. Because Howdy knew this, he made an impulsive decision that could buy him some time.

"Lew, I'll tell you what. For a starter I'll agree to do *Probe*. But I'm going to take the questions cold. No set-ups. No bullshit. If I can handle them on that basis, and Ward Roberts is tough, then I'll make up my mind. How's that?"

Lew could not conceal his disappointment, but he understood. You let Howard Goodwyn do things his way. If he committed on his own terms you had a tiger by the tail. "Okay, Howdy. When you know the date send me a memo."

Howdy left the office early. Howie had made the La Playa swimming team and he had promised the boy that he would go to the first meet. He had also promised the boy that they would go down to the Hotel Cabo San Lucas in Baja California for some deep-sea fishing. Somehow he had to find ways to spend more time with Howie. The whole damned youth business was baffling. That morning Jen had read him a piece in the *Times* about a psychiatric association in New York that had been studying youth problems. The survey showed that most hippies came from well-educated, well-to-do families. The report said: "Many of them lack confidence in the structure of society." Most of the hippies described their parents as "non-authoritarian" and their main beef seemed to be that the establishment was hypocritical. He remembered bellowing at Jen, "Well, for Christ's sake, what's new about that? Don't they read history?"

On the TV screen the animated letters PROBE zoomed away from the viewer, formed an arrow and impaled themselves in the chest of the live silhouetted figure of Howard D. Goodwyn. Off camera, the announcer introduced the new show that "Probes to the heart of our most controversial issues."

The title dissolved to a close-up of Ward Roberts, an alert, attractive newsman in his late thirties, who began the introduction. Howdy moved to his chair and saw Camera 2 light up. A medium shot of them both appeared on the portable monitor. "Mr. Goodwyn, do you object if I report to our viewers the conversation we had when I contacted you about this appearance?"

Howdy smiled easily. "No. Go ahead."

Roberts looked earnestly into the lens. "Ladies and gentlemen, it is customary for *Probe*'s editorial staff to get together with our guests for a brief discussion of the subjects to be covered on the show.

"But Mr. Goodwyn insisted, as the condition of his appearance, that he be allowed to come on the air cold, without any knowledge of the direction or the the depths *Probe* would explore. We agreed to that gladly." He smiled across the desk at his guest. "So, Mr. Goodwyn, no holds barred, question one." Howdy saw Camera 3 zoom in for a tight close-up of his face. "It's been rumored around that you are considering a return to public life, this time in politics. Is that true?"

"It's true that it's been rumored around, all right."

Roberts was only mildly amused. "Let's put it this way, Mr. Goodwyn. Does the office of Governor of the State of California interest you?"

"Yes. Very much."

"In what respect, Mr. Goodwyn?"

Howdy frowned reflectively. "Well, three years ago I was one of two million seven hundred and forty-nine thousand voters who thought somebody else could do the job better."

Roberts ignored the stifled off-camera chortling and managed a grin.

In his penthouse condominium overlooking San Francisco Bay, Lew Berwin smiled conspiratorily at the half dozen leading growers from the Sacramento and San Joaquin valleys who were his guests. He turned back to the television set as the newsman prepared to pursue his point.

"Mr. Goodwyn, it is not *Probe*'s intention to turn this into a *de facto* impeachment proceeding but don't you think it's a trifle naïve not to take everything any candidate says with a grain of salt?"

"Generally, yes." Howdy looked into the lens and smiled engagingly. "Trouble is, so many of us got so used to believing our own soap commercials."

Again there were subdued snickers from the floor crew. In the control room overlooking the stage, the director turned to his technical director. "This guy's cool and slippery."

"There's twenty-five minutes yet, pal. Roberts'll skewer him," was the reply.

Roberts pressed ahead. "Mr. Goodwyn, you are operating head of one of California's largest and most successful ranches. Recently you announced a radical change in some of your plans, the incorporation of a new city of a half million people to be called Micropolis Two thousand.

"Mr. Goodwyn, the fact that the plans show that most of your ranch's prime agricultural land is protected in the heart of the over-all city suggests that you are building a sort of urban fortress around it. Have you done this because you feel a huge ranching operation such as yours is doomed to extinction and you are trying to save it?"

Smiling tolerantly, Howdy nodded. "That's partly right, Mr. Roberts. But I resent the inference that we are about to be put out of business. On the contrary." His manner turned serious. "Have you ever heard the expression, 'the highest and best use of land'?"

The question caught Roberts by surprise. "I have. Yes."

"Do you understand what that means in terms of land management?"

Roberts smiled smugly. "Suppose you tell our viewers, Mr. Goodwyn. I'm sure your explanation will be more expert than mine."

"The value of certain land changes as the economy changes, Mr. Roberts. In our case land that was once most valuable as hilly grazing land is now more valuable as residential subdivision land. As the people kept coming into the county we kept phasing out our cattle operation, moving to other states where land as cheap as this once was makes it more economical for us. Incidentally, that also helps keep beef prices at reasonable levels. So you can see that we are not building a fortress as you call it. On the contrary, we're actually making an economically sound move while opening up some beautiful land to a higher use. In order to make certain the people who will live there will live better than they can live elsewhere, we're spending millions to make certain we don't repeat the old mistakes that we see around us that have created urban sprawl and slums."

"On the face of it, Mr. Goodwyn, that sounds like a very benevolent attitude for a huge corporation. Los Nidos is to be congratulated."

"We're not a benevolent society. What we're doing is just good business."

Roberts smiled without humor. "In my business, Mr. Goodwyn, it's good business to keep probing until I get at the real truth of the matter." When he saw his guest's eyes narrow he broke into a broad smile. "I'm not suggesting that you are being evasive. But I'm betting that we're not going to get it all from you this afternoon. After all, this is not a court of law, Mr. Goodwyn, and it *is* your business. So let's get back to your political aspirations."

A resigned expression settled over Howdy's face. "I haven't admitted that I have any."

The director smiled at his technical director. "Okay, pal, who's doing the skewering now?" The response was a guttural obscenity.

On camera, Ward Roberts laughed self-consciously. "On the other hand, Mr. Goodwyn, you haven't denied that you have any either, and your presence on *Probe* suggests some sort of interest on your part, for the rumor is that you may enter politics in order to fight more effectively for agriculture or for agribusiness as it's called in this day when most small ranchers are being forced to quit." He emphasized the words to make clear the inference that big ranching was to blame and his guest was one of the principal defendants.

"Agriculture's my special interest politically speaking and every other way, Mr. Roberts. But let's get something straight first. What's driving small farmers and ranchers out of business in California is not competition from the large operators. It's rising taxes and rising labor costs and people pressure, urbanization of our best land. We big ranchers are just as worried as the small ones. We have close to a five-billion-dollar business to protect. That's not much compared to what the space boys will need this year to leave their footprints on the moon. But our billions put food on the table, here and around the world. Four counties in California grow more crops than forty-four other states put together. One of our counties, Kern, is the most productive farm county in the United States and acre for acre the most productive farm county in the world. Isn't that worth protecting? Doesn't that suggest that agriculture had better be my special interest and yours and every other Californian's?"

"Somehow, Mr. Goodwyn, I get the impression that *I'm* being interviewed, by an expert." Both men laughed. "But I'm going to keep trying, Mr. Goodwyn. Let's talk about labor. Cesar Chavez and his United Farm Workers Organizing Committee have forced some big agribusiness to sign—Di Giogio, Christian Brothers, Pirelli-Minetti, Almaden Vineyards, and others. Is this the beginning of a labor domino effect? And if so, what will it do to California Agriculture?"

Howdy pondered briefly. "I don't have a crystal ball, but unless we get some special protective legislation like the rest of industry has, or unless the unions make provisions for the small grower, it could mean increased costs, higher wholesale prices, and higher retail prices." He looked directly into the camera. "Anything Chavez does to us he'll do to you and every one of your viewers out there."

"What is the answer, Mr. Goodwyn?"

"Fair legislation to protect us, or mechanization, more machines, less labor, more efficient growing methods. The prices won't come down, of course. But perhaps we can hold them."

Roberts smiled shrewdly. "You wouldn't be overstating the case just a bit, for rather obvious reasons?"

"If we don't get some relief I'll invite you to ask that question again, in a couple of years."

Roberts laughed good-naturedly. "So, it boils down to more machines and fewer bodies?"

"It could. But some crops, like strawberries for instance, can't be machine-picked."

"What will happen with them?"

"We'll have to grow them in areas where climate and hand labor makes it economically possible. Probably in Mexico."

Roberts appeared genuinely interested. "Mr. Goodwyn, there are a great many things that you and I could probe if time permitted. For instance, pollution and its effect on crops, the hippies phenomenon, the whole tragic narcotics problem, but for now I'd like to move along to something all prospective candidates for any high office should give top priority to. Our minority groups. For instance, what do you think should be done about the demands of our black Americans and our Mexican Americans?"

In San Francisco, Lew Berwin threw up his hands. "It's anybody's ball game now. The bastard reminds everybody of the narcotics thing with the kid and then slips him this. Take it easy, Howdy."

For Jennifer, at Los Nidos, anxiety turned to dismay. She glanced uneasily at young Howie, who was watching with no apparent interest from his father's easy chair.

Resorting to his old Will Rogers "shy bit," Howdy lowered his head. His smile was deceptively uncertain. "Mr. Roberts, you're too smart to expect an off-the-cuff answer to such tough questions. An honest man wouldn't pretend to know the answers." He looked directly into the lens. "I sure don't. But let me say this, some of my best friends are Mexican Americans." Roberts' startled expression turned to relief when Howdy added, "My wife's grandmother, for instance.

"At Los Nidos, Mr. Roberts, about ninety-five percent of our help is Mexican American. I've gotten to know them well. Some of them are fourth generation. I even manage to speak a little Spanish, though I've got to admit they understand me better when I speak English.

"I think every franchised American citizen should be given an honest-to-God chance at the best education we can give him. And he should get an equal chance at any job he's qualified for and feels he wants to try."

Howdy paused for effect. "But if he gets that chance and doesn't take full advantage of it and still keeps crying about a lousy deal, then the taxpayers should say, 'Shut up, brother, and step down.'"

"What about those who for one reason or another simply can't bootstrap themselves up, even if they try?"

Howdy delayed his answer until the close-up was on him again. "We have to take care of them just as we care for any of our less fortunate people."

"Mr. Goodwyn, you have a reputation of putting your money where your mouth is. Would a man win or lose if he bet that Los Nidos did not always practice what its head man preaches?"

"The best way to answer that, Mr. Roberts, is to send you a half dozen of my Mexican American superintendents and foremen to be interviewed. Would you like that?"

Roberts matched Howdy's smile. "They'd be more than welcome. But wouldn't I find out that they have been coached and that they don't really have the same chance to work into the upper echelon of management that their non-minority opposite numbers have?"

Howdy answered with a flat, "You would not. As a matter of fact, you'd find out that my top ranch superintendent, a young man who graduated from the University of California's Agricultural College at Davis, is going to be made a vice president soon."

Roberts was genuinely surprised. "What's the man's name, if I may ask?"

"Carlos Morales."

"But Mr. Goodwyn, can you say in all honesty that promoting an exceptional minority member is not a form of tokenism?"

Howdy managed to conceal his anger. "I just wish I had twenty more like him."

Roberts eyed his guest a bit skeptically, then consulted his notes. "How many Mexican Americans do we have in California now?"

"About a million and a half."

"What's going to happen when this mechanization you predict begins to phase out their jobs?"

"We'll find other productive work for them. We already have a retraining program at Los Nidos—and not, by the way, at taxpayers' expense. At ours."

"What will they do?"

Howdy's concern was more than convincing. "It's hard to say, exactly, at this point in time. We are teaching some of them to operate the new machines. Others are learning maintenance. As the nature of our operation changes, there'll be plenty of chances for those who'll trouble to get an education. We're helping with that, too, by staggering work hours for those who want to attend schools."

"Do Mexican Americans have an equal opportunity at an education? Equal, for instance, to our black Americans?"

Howdy considered briefly. "No. I don't think so."

Roberts' eyebrows lifted. "Oh? Why?"

The furrows on Howdy's brow deepened and he explored his chin briefly. "Well—for one thing, the black American's first language is English. That's generally not true of the Mexican American kid. So the black kid and the brown kid don't start even on that score. The black kid has a definite edge." On the floor the black cameraman in the crew grinned and whispered over the intercom. "Man! I didn't know how lucky we is!" The director shushed the crew good-naturedly and called for a close-up on the newsman.

Unperturbed, Roberts smiled. "You've got ready answers, Mr. Goodwyn. Now let's talk some more about just how real this alleged threat to California agriculture is.

Are you saying that the time may come when there would no longer be any significant agriculture in the state?"

It was precisely the question Howdy had been waiting for. "California has roughy one hundred million acres. One half of the state is in National Parks and other public lands; one third is covered with forests; one fifth is desert and mountains. This year more than ten percent of our prime land is polluted. Subdividers are taking one hundred thousand acres a year out of production. Mr. Roberts, if the present rate of immigration holds, there will be no worthwhile agricultural land left in California by the year two thousand and thirty. In two thousand and fifty, all those people who haven't moved back to Iowa, Illinois, Nebraska, and Arkansas for their rich farm land will have to start digging for the most precious thing of all, good soil that'll grow cheap food."

Howdy leaned forward. "And do you know where they'll find it? Under the asphalt streets and deserted tract slums that were the biggest subdivisions of the Nineteen Sixties and Seventies."

Roberts eyed his guest a bit skeptically, then let an ingenuous smile spread over his face. "One can't help observing that you'd make a very persuasive man in politics, state or national . . . but then it's never *Probe*'s purpose to add fuel to rumors. So let me use the remaining time to cover a couple of highly sensitive areas.

"Mr. Goodwyn, what do you think is behind the growing use by young people of marijuana, LSD, amphetamines, and worse? Is it a rebellion similar in some respects to the one your generation staged when it drank illegal liquor in Prohibition days? Or is it something more serious?"

"Roberts," Howdy's voice was flat, "I had hoped you'd have the decency to avoid this subject under the circumstances. But if you have the poor taste to ask, I have the guts to answer. You know the answer to that question as well as I do. Did you ask it so your audience could watch a father who loves his son hurt a little in public, or do you really want a meaningful answer?"

Roberts was visibly flustered. "I know that we've been accused of deliberately staging Roman Holidays here, Mr. Goodwyn, but I assure you that was *not* my purpose in posing the question. What *Probe* is after is new insight

601

into problems. Our editorial staff felt you were uniquely qualified to shed some light on a very grave one."

Howdy allowed his manner to soften slightly. "Anybody who's thought twice about it knows that the violation of the Eighteenth Amendment was no kids' revolt. It was an adult rebellion against a stupid and unrealistic law. Today these kids are rebelling against lack of discipline. We haven't taught them who they are or given them a place of their own and made them stay in it until they earn their way out. So some of them take up causes—anti-war, conservation, brotherhood—to give them identity. The ones who take dope are retreating, copping out."

Eager to keep the exchange heated, Roberts broke in. "Agreed. But what about the adults who feel that the narcotics law is unrealistic in so far as marijuana is concerned? What about the ones who say it's no worse than liquor and should be legalized in compliance with the wishes of the majority? Do you agree?"

"I do not."

"Do you drink, Mr. Goodwyn? And do you smoke?"

"I take an occasional drink. I haven't smoked since I tried a five-cent cigar forty years ago."

"But if it was proved that marijuana is actually less harmful than tobacco and alcohol, would you condone its legal use?"

"I would not."

"Why?"

"Because there's no such thing as the unvarnished truth where billions of dollars in potential profit are concerned. The American Medical Association says it's proved that tobacco is the prime cause of lung cancer. The tobacco companies are spending millions to prove that it's not, that the real cause is air pollution. So the automobile companies and the power companies and oil companies spend more millions to prove that they're not to blame. Everybody's trying to blame everybody else in order to save their profits. I've been told, and I find it easy to believe, that an international syndicate is moving to control the principal marijuana-growing areas in the world, that they have an underground public relations campaign selling the idea that pot is easier on you than aspirin.

"And I've heard that the big tobacco companies are quietly making plans to get into the marijuana cigarette business the minute it's legalized and that they are quietly

602

helping to sell the notion of legalization. With that much money power behind an idea do you really think we'll ever hear the truth?"

Plainly apprehensive, Roberts sought refuge in professional righteousness. "Mr. Goodwyn, those are very serious allegations—like some that have been aimed at your interests."

Howdy laughed. "Those aren't allegations, Roberts. Those are rumors like the one you used to open this show."

Roberts managed a fleeting smile. "All right, Mr. Goodwyn, but I want to make it clear that, rumor or not, your point of view does not necessarily represent the point of view of this station or this commentator. Unfortunately, our time is up now. I want to thank you for appearing on *Probe* today, cold, the way you insisted, and submitting to some questions that were as difficult for us to ask as they must have been for you to answer. Thank you."

The director called for a close-up on Roberts and began pantomiming a flowing violin passage. The technical director began imitating him. A moment later a young assistant director followed suit. The sound man looked across at his companions. "What the fuck are you nuts doing?"

The director gave him a pitying look. "Are you deaf? We're playing the Establishment Waltz, you middle-aged peasant."

In San Francisco, Lew Berwin switched off the set. Myra, who had watched with him, stood up. "He was wonderful, Lew. Do you think he'll really buy the idea?"

"Who knows? But he's only got two choices, get into politics and try for protective legislation or resign himself to subdividing Los Nidos piecemeal. That's one more alternative than the rest of us have. That's why I've got two million in pledges if he'll enter the primary."

Myra thought about Jennifer. She also had two alternatives: lose her husband piecemeal to politics or lose the ranch the same way. "Does Howdy know about the pledges?"

Lew shook his head. "Nope. But he will next week."

At Casa Grande, Jennifer switched off the set and turned to Howie. "I thought your father was wonderful, didn't you?" The boy let his leg slip from the broad chair

603

arm in unconscious imitation of Howdy and got up heavily.

"Sure, Mom. Dad was neat."

In Los Angeles, at the public-relations offices of Hamlett and Daniels, Earl Hamlett turned to the staff assembled in the conference room.

"What do you think?"

A young political copywriter grinned smugly. "Wow! If that beautiful corn ball will just stick to the script we can get him elected God."

Jen's Jenny II, the new seven-passenger Aero Commander "Shrike," waited at the County Airport's private passenger ramp with its twin 290 horsepower, fuel-injected Lycoming engines idling while Howdy said his farewells to Jennifer and Howie.

In the pilot's seat Chad Chadwick was quietly explaining cockpit procedures to Howie—explaining what Howdy had promised his son he'd explain when the boy flew "co-pilot" with his father.

Howdy rested his hand on his son's shoulder and leaned in behind the front seat to speak with Jennifer. "I'm sorry as hell, honey. But I'll be down on Mexicana Friday noon. Ev and I have no choice. We've got to look into this new ag preserve hassle."

Jen nodded. "Do you believe Lew now, when he says the only way to fight is inside the political machine?"

"Not necessarily, hon. At least not nationally. Washington's not giving us trouble. It's the county and state level that's shooting us down. There's where the fight's going to be."

Jennifer tried to conceal her relief. At least they would not be uprooted and moved to Washington. "It would be a break if we could fight them on our own ground, wouldn't it?"

Howdy grinned at her reassuringly. "We'll fight on our ground. If we win—and by God we will—we'll still be 'millionaire ranchers.' He straightened and winked. "And if we lose, we'll just be *billionaire* subdividers!"

Chad Chadwick lifted an earphone and turned to address Howdy. "Which ain't exactly a fate worse than debt."

Jennifer grimaced and plugged her ears. "On that note, dear husband, we're off to Baja."

Howdy stepped back. "—noon, Friday—for sure!" Turning to Howie, he checked the boy's seatbelt and shoulder harness unnecessarily. "You and Chad charter a boat and get in a couple of days fishing. When I get down there we'll go out again and you two can lie about the big ones that got away. Okay?"

Howie ducked his head without turning away from the instrument panel. "Sure, Dad. See ya."

Over La Playa, the altimeter read fifty-five hundred feet. Chad was following the coast and still climbing, Jennifer could look down on the entire ranch. She had seen it many times from the air and always it had been beautiful.

The barren, corrugated slopes of the San Gabriel Mountains in the background, the velvety green foothills, in summer beige velvet, the corduroy rectangles of furrowed fields, all were contrasting but compatible elements in a panorama that never ceased to thrill her.

Scattered through the original boundaries she could see the troublesome "windows," small privately held farms that great-grandfather Steven Lewis had sold in fee simple during times of tight money. Some of them were still in citrus groves. The most troublesome ones were those closest to the encroaching urban sprawl on the north and west, well within the boundaries of MICROPOLIS 2000. Because they would be bidding against private subdividers, they would pay dearly to buy them back.

For years she had watched Howdy stave off the intruders seeking a foothold within the ranch itself. He had given those old-timers private loans, company loans, and often equipment and advice. But it was only a stop-gap measure. With MICROPOLIS 2000 announced publically, the day of reckoning was on them. Jennifer did not doubt at all that outside subdividers were behind attempts to nullify the ranch's agriculture preserves. She could still see Ward Roberts' incredulous expression when Howdy had said that if people kept coming into California at the present rate for the next fifty years there would be no more major agriculture left in the state.

Jennifer looked down at the freeway and the network of expressways crisscrossing the ranch. Each led to a creeping cross hatch of subdivision streets with their rubber-stamp tract houses, each rectangular backyard set with its own shimmering turquoise gem of a heated pool. The spectacle was breath-taking and ludicrous. Thousands of pools, including their own, were within minutes of the finest swimming beaches in the world. Enough was never enough for California!

In Steven Lewis' time they had dynamited their way three hundred miles northeastward across the mountains to the Owens Valley to drain off water for the first southern California developments. There had been a minor civil war over that.

In her father's time they had blasted and tunneled two hundred miles southeastward to the Colorado River to help slake southern California's insatiable thirst. There had been a major political war over that. But southern California had won again.

Now they were about to bring still more water from the north. For five hundred miles it would flow through the Feather River Project canals. Two and a half billion dollars would only be the beginning because another million people had come to live the good life in southern California since it had been planned. Like the freeways, it would be obsolete before it could be completed. And they were talking quietly about another huge project, the Dos Rios Dam on the middle fork of the Eel River in Mendicino County. Conservationists had pressured Reagan to stop it and, thank God, he had. That one would have turned Round Valley, the second largest level agricultural valley along the northern coast, into a reservoir. Covolo, a lovely little community that they had often visited, would have been inundated by three hundred feet of water that would flow to southern California to fill still more swimming pools and water still more lawns and private golf courses and irrigate fewer and fewer acres of the world's finest farmland.

The vision brought a contemptuous laugh from Jennifer. It was idiotic, immoral, the perverted act of a sick society. She glanced at young Howie, all concentration in the co-pilot's right-hand seat. Of his own volition, to please his father, he had been shorn of his long surfer's locks. Howie, their son, would be living in this world fifty years from now. And the odds were that he would be enormously wealthy. The subdividers were offering more per acre for land around Los Nidos than Howie's great-great-grandfather, Steven Lewis, had paid for the entire original *rancho.* Howard D. Goodwyn Junior and his family would be able to buy and sell Onassis.

If, at some time in the future, Howie did sell the remaining prime agricultural land, he would have traded for inflated dollars—Ev called them "phony mazuma—a place of beauty and a way of life that could never again be created in California. Jennifer closed her eyes and moaned inwardly. "Why does it always have to be the same?" she asked, not quite aloud. "Why don't people learn? We've made the mistake enough times here, going all the way back to my Mexican ancestors."

Rousing herself forcibly, she reached for the newspaper Howdy had tossed on the seat beside her. Idly, she glanced at the headlines and found in them little to cheer her up. She turned to the entertainment section and scanned Maggi Joyce's column. Hollywood society was still raving about the Jules Stein party. Lynn Carlin was starring opposite Jim Brown, whose handsome black face had unsettled Raquel Welch. Toward the bottom of the column a familiar name caught her eye and the single sentence made her gasp:

> *"The loneliest lady in Acapulco this season no longer is gilt-edged, double divorcee, Angela Goodwyn Layne—poor angel!"*

Something inside Jennifer's middle crumbled. She read the line again and again and the loneliness and rejection she had grown up with flooded back, making her vaguely sick at her stomach as a curious transmigration took place. It was her name she was reading and it was she sitting alone under the beach *ramada.* Sick and frightened, she pushed the paper aside violently enough to make Chad direct a quizzical glance over his shoulder. But the act had broken the fantasy pattern. And it was a pattern. The goddamned paper had not printed an item. It had reproduced a pattern, a too-familiar one whose beginning was lost in the miscellania of all of her yesterdays. Patterns were made for repeating.

Then, unaccountably, a voice that she scarcely remembered, that of her *abuelita,* her "little grandmother," Alicia, whispered and the voice was clearer than all the others:

> *"Donde una puerta se cierra, otra se abre—"*
> Whenever a door closes, another door opens.

20 HOWDY WATCHED UNTIL THE TWIN ENGINE Shrike was just a speck in the sky over Los Nidos. Then he crossed to the parking lot at the County Airport and headed for the southbound Interstate 5 freeway and the ranch.

From his study he called headquarters and asked the operator to contact Carlos Morales. He was told the young superintendent was in one of the fields supervising the installation of a new drip irrigation system. He left word to have Morales call him on the shortwave phone. Thirty minutes later the young Mexican-American was at the door of the Casa Grande.

Howdy ushered him into the study and indicated a chair.

"How about a cold beer?"

"Thanks, Mr. Goodwyn. I'm so dry I'm spitting cotton."

Howdy opened two bottles of Carta Blanca. After each man had drunk directly from the bottle, Howdy perched on the arm of his easy chair and pointed to the outside with his thumb.

"Carlos, Immigration is starting to make surprise field sweeps again. They haven't hit us yet, but they will when the new picking crews come on. Tell me—how do you see the illegal Mexican labor problem now—so far as Los Nidos is concerned?"

The superintendent's smooth brown brow furrowed thoughtfully.

"Not too bad, Mr. Goodwyn. It will get worse before it gets better though. We've had a few illegals in our picking crews—mostly in strawberries and some in asparagus. So far none in the citrus groves—or in avocados. I got rid of them. A lot of our green card workers are probably carrying fakes, but I can't prove it."

Howdy nodded. The counterfeit green cards and social security cards were almost impossible to detect. The ranch's position was that they were hired in good faith.

"What are we paying on straight time now, Carlos?"

"Two fifty—"

"And piece workers average about the same?" Howdy knew the

608

figures but he asked anyway. It was a part of his endless practice of double checking.

"The old timers average better than that, but on a per unit basis they are more cost-effective." Howdy knew that too, and once in a while it troubled his conscience a bit when he saw women in the fields bent over the rows driving themselves unmercifully.

"What about Caesar Chavez? Has he been checking us on hours—and illegals?"

"He's got some hired 'eyes' in our crews. I'm sure they keep him filled in."

Howdy took a long swig and blotted his mouth on the back of his hand.

"At what point do you think he'll begin pushing again?"

"I don't think he will —right now."

"Why not?"

"A lot of illegals are managing to stay because there's no practical way for the immigration people to get them out. The more who get away with it, the more potential members and muscle for his union. And that goes for the Teamsters too."

Carlos was confirming his own reasoning, Howdy thought, as he lowered himself into the chair.

"I smell a lot of trouble ahead," he said.

The young Mexican-American's grunt was noncommittal. After a brief lapse Howdy leaned forward.

"You know your Mexican history, Carlos. How up on the Mexican economy are you now? How do you see it?"

The superintendent nodded toward a stack of newspapers and magazines on a coffee table.

"I'm as up as they are. I see it pretty much like they do. It's not good. There's talk about devaluating the peso —fifty to the dollar some say."

Howdy shook his head sadly. "Mexican workers can't live on that. They'll start coming across the border like rats deserting a sinking ship."

Carlos Morales was tempted to say, "—or even like human beings —?" Instead, he said, "When California was made a state in 1850, the population of Mexico was seven and a half million.

"Sixty years later—in 1910, the year of the revolution —the population had only doubled. But in the thirty years from 1940 to 1970 the population has gone from nineteen million to over forty-eight million. And the way the mortality rate is declining and the birth rate is climbing there'll be a hundred million Mexicans by the turn of the century. Counting women, the work force is projected to be around twenty percent."

A mirthless laugh bounced Howdy's shoulders.

"A hundred million? But only, my friend, until fifty million of them pay coyotes to smuggle them across the border." He shook his head again. "Holy Jesus! They'll outnumber us!"

Carlos Morales managed a wry smile. "Yes sir—just like we outnumbered the *Californios* when we Yankees came pouring over the mountains from the east in 1849 looking for gold."

Howdy's smile was thin and his eyes narrowed as he looked across at his superintendent.

"We—?"

Carlos' smile was innocent. "After three generations in California, ten years of marriage to a redheaded Irish girl, and two kids, I think of my family as bona fide Yankee."

Howdy looked down and toyed with his beer bottle. He knew that young Morales had as much right to regard himself as a Yankee as any other third generation immigrant. The difference with the minority groups was in distance. Their original home boundaries were thousands of miles away, not just down the San Diego Freeway an hour's distance by car.

After a moment he looked up. Returning his superintendent's smile, he said,

"Carlos—give me your educated Yankee guess as to what we're going to be up against in the next ten years or so."

The Mexican-American brushed a strand of coarse, straight black hair from his forehead and gazed past Howdy to the big window that overlooked several hundred acres of the lower fields that were being readied for planting. The workers were all Mexican. At least half of them were Mexican nationals carrying work permits.

"There are no good figures on the ebb and flow of immigrants across our state borders from here to Texas," he said. "Some immigration people say it could be as high as a quarter of a million a year—estimating the illegals." He paused to recall some figures. "California's population is around twenty million now. It's coming up about eleven percent a year according to the last census. But there's no way to tell what it really is because of illegal immigration."

"The census figures say about four percent," Howdy interjected. Carlos seemed surprised. "I thought it would be higher."

"My guess is, it's twice that," Howdy said.

610

"Could be," Carlos conceded. "But we've got to study those figures. A lot of illegals stay here for less than a year. They earn enough money to buy some land of their own in Mexico and they go home. For the time being, the more cropland we lose to subdividers here, and the more acreage we have to lease south of the border, the fewer immigrants will come north."

He straightened and set his bottle aside.

"Unless I change my name to Smith or Jones, I'll be accused of special pleading, but I can see a time when we'll be damned glad to have a steady supply of Mexican pickers who are willing to do the field labor that machines can't do—and do it for what we can afford to pay."

Howdy gestured impatiently. "But for how long? Chavez is losing workers to the Teamsters because they promise to squeeze more out of the growers. Now Chavez is calling them and raising. Cheap field labor will be a thing of the past before we know it." Obviously growing more impatient at the prospect, he continued.

"When we get more mechanical pickers we'll have to use them down there too, to cut costs. So will the Mexican growers. The escalation is built in. When Mexican workers are displaced here—and in Mexico—they'll come back north looking for new kinds of work. Because our pay and living is better, and because they'll do work our own spoiled rotten domestic workers won't do, they'll stay in the States and be integrated in our population."

A thought passed through his mind—when rape is inevitable relax and enjoy it. The cynical aphorism twisted his mouth into a grim smile. But the word was not rape. It was change!

"It will only take two generations of little brown Mexican kids educated in our schools to do the trick!"

Carlos Morales laughed softly and regarded his boss. Howdy Goodwyn was not really a chauvinist—not at heart. There was no way he could be. At a time when most growers were exploiting Mexican and Mexican-American workers, he was helping them: Mexican blood flowed in Howdy Junior's veins. His Mexican roots ran back to the first Robles who came to Alta California with explorer Gaspar de Portolá in 1769.

"Those schools are important," he said softly. "That's how I made it—and how my father made it. My grandfather was a wetback."

Howdy nodded. "So—?" It was more a musing sound than a question.

"So—," Carlos Morales continued, "we'll have a bumper crop

of brown native sons and daughters whose surnames will sound as strange to you Anglos as Commodore Thomas ap-Catesby Jones' name sounded to my great, great grandfather in 1842 when that impatient navy officer embarrassed President Polk by sailing his warship into Monterey Bay and capturing California four years too early."

Howdy leaned back, smiling, and laced his fingers across his lean middle. "So," he said, "given a little more time, history is going to repeat itself. Is that it?"

Carlos Morales matched his smile and noted the resignation in his boss' tone. Both were reassuring as he replied,

"*Si, señor Goodwyn. El circulo estará completo—de neuvo.* The circle will be complete—again."